THE HEATH INTRODUCTION TO FICTION

The Heath Introduction to

Fiction

*with
a Preface
on Fiction and
Introductory Notes*

by John J. Clayton
University of Massachusetts, Amherst

D. C. Heath and Company
Lexington, Massachusetts   Toronto

International Standard Book Number: 0–669–99986–5

Library of Congress Catalog Card Number: 77–77435

CONTENTS

THE GREAT MODERNS

CONTEMPORARY FICTION

RECENT EXPERIMENTAL FICTION

FOREWORD

The *Preface—On Fiction,* the *Introductory Notes,* and the *Questions* are the work of John J. Clayton, University of Massachusetts, Amherst; the balance of the volume is our responsibility, though Professor Clayton also made valuable suggestions concerning the contents. We are grateful, in addition, to countless teachers of literature at colleges throughout the country for their recommendations. Their consensus is reflected in the majority of the fifty stories chosen for this anthology.

H. HOLTON JOHNSON, EDITOR

D. C. Heath and Company

PREFACE—ON FICTION

PREFACE–ON FICTION

By the time they get to college, most people have been dulled as readers. They have been taught to examine a story or a poem as if they were detectives, snooping for meaning, swooping down on innocent images—flowers, coffins, garbage pails—and turning them into symbols. The story contains a hidden meaning—I mean, Meaning—and "your mission, if you are willing to undertake it" is to decode that meaning.

Usually, after learning to misread, people stop reading. Or they forget what they've been taught and "just read for the story"—the excitement of a plot in which they can identify with the main character. Will he break out of his rotten marriage? Will she get away from the police? And that's a good beginning; it involves *caring*, feeling. But it is incomplete. In this Preface we hope to explore ways of reading fiction that make it powerful and beautiful.

Stories as Models of Reality

A model of reality: a creation that tells us what it's like to be alive in the writer's world; a creation that lets us put on the writer's lenses and see the world through them.

Such a model can look and sound like the world we usually inhabit, and we can apply our ordinary ways of thinking to become part of it. A photograph is usually this kind of model; so is a dollhouse; so is a miniature railroad. In fiction like this, which can be called "realistic" fiction, we hear voices like the voices we are used to, see images like the ones we know. The laws of nature inside the story correspond to the ones we already accept. In Tillie Olsen's beautiful short story "I Stand Here Ironing," the pressures of school,

1

of a family in poverty, are like the world we know. We ache for the girl, and we know, as her mother knows, that she is not going to become suddenly free and whole. She is not going to try on anyone's magic slipper. Whatever beauty she can salvage will come out of everyday pain and struggle.

But a model may look or sound unlike the world we know. Time might stand still, animals might talk, a person might fly. Death might appear as a character. Or the world in the story may be filled with grotesque figures out of somebody's nightmare. Still, fiction like this is *also* a model of reality. In Malamud's "Idiots First" another parent struggles to save a child. But, unlike Tillie Olsen, Malamud tells about a mysterious Mr. Death named Ginzburg, who can make time stand still for a person for one day.

A reader might shrug—this story isn't like "real life." Things don't happen that way. Well, it's true I've never seen a Ginzburg, but I feel that "Idiots First" is very "real," that its climax is a moment of wisdom and incredible beauty. It is not a reflection of our ordinary reality. It is a model of how one person, Bernard Malamud, sometimes *experiences* reality. It's as if a friend were to sit down with you and say, "You know how I see things? Let me tell you a story. Once there were three birds named Sam, Pedro, and Ivan, who lived in an evergreen forest." You probably wouldn't worry about your friend's sanity. You'd understand that the story was his way of tuning you in on his world—his *categories.* It's not that he believes in talking birds, any more than Doris Lessing, in "How I Finally Lost My Heart," believes that you can remove your physical heart and give it to someone in a subway car; but he has found an interesting and convenient means for getting you away from your usual ways of seeing. "Once upon a time there was an old couple, terribly poor, who had three sons." We know already, from our reading of fairy tales, that the first two sons will fail because of their lack of some important quality and that the youngest, who possesses this quality, will succeed. It's not at all "realistic," but it's very *real;* the model calls to mind the forces encountered in growing up, with life seen as a quest that rewards—rewards whatever: goodness, cleverness, courage, love.

Fiction as a model of the way writers sometimes experience their own world. This is most obvious as a story tends toward the *fable* or *parable.* Both are short narratives with very generalized characters, proving a point about human life. *Fables* often have supernatural elements—talking beasts, for instance; *parables,* like the ones told by Jesus, are constructed as exact analogies to human life. Usually, each part of the parable is equivalent to some aspect of the world.

Few stories in this collection are actual fables or parables. They are more complex than fables, richer in the texture of life than parables. But many approach parable or fable. In "Bontsha the Silent" a broken old Jew who suffered all his life in silence stands before the heavenly court. Appearing to be a celebration of patience, the story turns the tables on God—brilliantly—and expresses Peretz' complex vision of human suffering and divine response. Crane's "The Open Boat" has no angels and no heaven, but it approaches parable or fable nonetheless, projecting a stark model of the relation between human beings and the natural world. It's as if Crane were saying, "Sometimes I see human life as a struggle for survival in a lifeboat at sea." But the story is not just a statement about the indifference of nature. Crane has made us experience the life on that boat, made us experience the struggle to make sense of life. "The Open Boat" is a realistic story, but, like a parable, it communicates a vision of life.

Tolstoy's "The Death of Iván Ilých" is another story that is intensely realistic yet approaches parable. That is, it teaches us a lesson about human life, a lesson about how to live, and the characters and events stand for more than themselves. Tolstoy is writing a story about man in his relation to God and nature. How powerful is his vision of a world in which death forces us to choose an authentic life! But notice how different Tolstoy's creation is from the parables of the New Testament. Iván Ilých is one specific man, whose consciousness is stuffed with the paraphernalia of empty, upper-class life. In realistic style Tolstoy rubs our noses in that life, makes us long for pure air, for reality. False life, the longing for true life: these are the categories into which Tolstoy divides the world.

A farmer looks upon a wheatfield as a planting ground, a painter may see it as a landscape, a general as a battlefield, a lover as a retreat; in the same way, each writer sees in the world different aspects to focus on, different categories to comprehend. D. H. Lawrence creates in his fiction a model of a world divided into sensual impulses versus intellectual impulses, working-class life versus upper-class life, "dark" gods versus spirituality, body versus ego, feelings versus money, spontaneity versus artificiality. Lawrence sees and feels in those terms and he projects them into his fiction. The world we see in his "The Blind Man" or "The Rocking-Horse Winner" is not a replica of our world, not a photograph of it, but a highly organized, simplified structural model of Lawrence's world. And, for a time, it can become our world too; it can give us new eyes, it can deepen our perceptions.

In a sense, the world of a piece of fiction is a model in which life has been organized in a very special way. The point is not just to *assent* to the model, as to a formula in mathematics; we *live* it, it *lives in us*. And sometimes we are permanently changed—our lives are deeper, our ways of seeing the world more complete.

In class I sometimes ask students to write a page or so rendering what it was like to be sixteen years old. The papers turn out to be very different from one another. One focuses on a single "average" day, another on one significant moment, another on an analysis of his or her adolescence; one is a witty, self-ironic description of sexual confusion and a struggle to feel worthwhile. The point is not that each person had a different experience of being sixteen, but rather that we all could write many or all of these papers, depending on our mood and our audience (teacher? lover? public?) and on how we decide to look at the people we used to be. When students have finished the exercise, I ask, "How is what you just wrote a fiction?" A fiction—not a lie—a fiction like those in this anthology. We talk about *selection:* what did you decide to include? On what basis did you decide? What did you leave out because it didn't relate to the way you were seeing? (For instance, you might write about playing basketball with your friends and omit the times when you were alone and felt sad or scared.) I ask, "What did you leave out because it felt too threatening to include? What about your *tone* (your attitude toward your material and your audience, revealed by your style)? Were you being witty and charming so that what you originally experienced as pain now you tell us as comedy? Were you being tough? Why?" Clearly, the speaker in the narrative is not the whole of the writer, but one special part with one special voice, giving the reader one version of what it was like to be sixteen.

In other words, although the exercise called for *autobiography,* you created a *fiction!*

And there is no way *not* to.

I feel enormous excitement when I write these sentences: when I remember again that my own sense of my own life is fiction, a creation—even *which events* I choose to call "my life." Imagine that you are Catholic and ten years from now will become a Communist. Not only will your future change; *so will your past.* As a Catholic, you remember one set of events as significant; as a Communist, a whole other set becomes important. Suddenly your early volunteer work takes on new meaning; your relationship to parents and friends is seen as having been different from what you previously thought it. You reshuffle your life so that it flows "logically" to your new present.

Why does all this matter for the study of fiction? It means that there is no way you or any other writer can record or reflect reality. Even a "realist" must in fact create the world. Perception is creation; the world doesn't come to our senses "raw" but in predefined categories. As Robert Ornstein, in *The Psychology of Consciousness,* puts it, "as we mature, we attempt to make more and more consistent 'sense' out of the mass of information arriving at our receptors. We develop stereotyped systems, or *categories,* for sorting input. . . . Personal consciousness is a continual process of selection and construction." Just as fiction is! When we look at a work of fiction in this way, we think of it as expressing one coherent way of constructing reality, one way of being-in-the-world, one *model.* It is more like a jazz solo or a dance expressing a performer's sense of life than a duplication of "objective" reality. We are brought inside one person's vision of reality, and it doesn't matter whether, trying to make that vision clear and strong, the writer uses talking animals or silent policemen.

How do we experience the model? What elements should the reader grow aware of?

Angle of Vision (Point of View)

These terms refer to the vantage point from which the story is told. The usual term, *point of view,* often gets confused with *viewpoint* (attitude). Therefore, I will use *angle of vision* throughout this Preface.

Through whose eyes are we seeing the story? Is the author simply recounting events? Does the author know everything and tell it all to us? "Once upon a time in a far-off kingdom. . . ." Or "There was a man in the land of Uz whose name was Job; and that man was perfect and upright and one that feared God, and eschewed evil." Hearing this voice, we don't ask, "How do you know? Were you there?" The author *knows,* like a god, all-knowing, *omniscient.* The author can enter the mind of a character, evaluate a relationship, step back and tell us about the situation or about life.

This is the original mode of telling a story: a tale spun by a storyteller. It is not a natural mode; that is, it doesn't happen in everyday reality. If a friend tells us a story, we assume there is verification for it. If the story enters someone else's mind, we assume that our friend was told about it.

But we don't ask questions of the *storyteller,* who can summarize events, tell us what everyone is feeling, interpret, moralize. Wonderful freedom! And yet many authors, especially modern authors, avoid an omniscient angle of vision. Or they employ a *limited omniscient* angle of vision, in which they feel free to move from character to character, to skip from place to place, to generalize about the characters, but avoid explaining, interpreting, philosophizing. In the eighteenth century the voice behind the narrative was usually omniscient. Henry Fielding, the author of *Tom Jones,* felt comfortable in entering the mind of each character, evaluating actions, interpreting feelings, and stepping aside to comment on the state of the world. And in the nineteenth century Tolstoy can still step back from his character to say, "Iván Ilých's life had been most simple and most ordinary and therefore most terrible."

Why is omniscient narration less common in the twentieth century? First, the omniscient angle of vision assumes a model of reality that modern writers usually do not assume: a model in which there is a single, objective way of looking at reality. Many modern writers don't feel the security of a world that can be known like this; instead they are faced with the struggle of individual consciousness to understand reality. If the traditional view of God as all-knowing father has been questioned, so has the traditional view of the author as all-knowing portrayer of reality. Second, modern writers are fascinated by the alterations in reality created by a change in angle of vision. Let's come back for a moment to the exercise of rendering the experience of being sixteen. Think of the difference between (a) an account of a day from the angle of vision of an adult looking back at youthful experience and (b) a moment-by-moment exploration of the consciousness of the same sixteen-year-old. Now contrast both these angles of vision to (c) an account in first person by the sixteen-year-old.

> (a) The boy couldn't understand why she mattered so much to him, why he walked half a mile out of his way to stand in the shadow of a garage and look up at her window. He didn't understand that he felt he was nothing; that he had emptied himself of power and had given the power over to her, then longed for her as the possessor of that power.

> (b) Steamy night, so hot. He pressed against the garage wall for its coolness. His eyes, pressing to see through her curtains, to absorb her life into his, ached. "Oh, baby, baby. . . ." Pangs in the belly. Moaning, he laughed at himself for being so dumb.

> (c) Well, you should have seen me, standing in the dark mooning up at Sylvia's window. I'll bet you think I'm some peeping Tom, but I'm dumber than that, even. I just love her is all. And you think she'll look at me?

Or imagine a fourth angle oᵢ vision—Sylvia's. Or a fifth—the view of Sylvia's father when he sees someone lurking in the shadows across the street. Or a sixth—the view of a policeman called by Sylvia's father.

The decision over angle of vision is one of the most significant a writer makes. Let's outline the possibilities:

1. *Omniscient*.   As we have seen, the writer enters and leaves the minds of characters at will, explains and interprets at will. Of the examples above, (a) is told by an omniscient author. The writer choosing to take a position as omniscient author might now cross the

street and describe the girl in her bedroom, describe her fear and
excitement at seeing a strange figure across the street, describe her
quarreling with her father: "Don't call the police, Daddy. Suppose
it's someone we know. . . ."

2. Objective.   Here the writer limits omniscience—becomes a fly
on the wall, a camera eye, who sees, who hears. Action is reported,
dialogue is quoted, description is kept fairly free of metaphor:

> The boy held himself against the cool cement wall of the garage.
> A car with parking lights on turned the corner and rolled to a stop in
> front of her house. A cop stepped out, another from the passenger side.
> The boy held his breath. They started across the street; it was too late
> to slip away. He stood up straight and walked casually towards them.
> " 'Evening, officers."

An omniscient author speaking here might have described the boy's
feelings, might have compared his mind to swirling mud, might have
portrayed him as feeling choked, caged, scared as a rabbit. If all that
is lost, what does a writer gain by using an objective angle of vision?
First, the limitation can make a scene more dramatic, like a play or
film. The action tells the story without intrusion. Second, an objective angle of vision can be used effectively to make the reader fill in
what isn't said. Ernest Hemingway often creates a scene that is filled
with horror; by not commenting on the horror, he forces the reader
to experience it more deeply: the reader has to scream because the
writer does not. An example from "The Snows of Kilimanjaro":

> They shot the six cabinet ministers at half-past six in the morning
> against the wall of a hospital. There were pools of water in the court-
> yard. There were wet dead leaves on the paving of the courtyard. It
> rained hard. All the shutters of the hospital were nailed shut. One of the
> ministers was sick with typhoid. Two soldiers carried him downstairs
> and out into the rain. They tried to hold him up against the wall but
> he sat down in a puddle of water. The other five stood very quietly
> against the wall. Finally the officer told the soldiers it was no good trying
> to make him stand up. When they fired, he was sitting down in the
> water with his head on his knees.

In "The Lottery" Shirley Jackson doesn't limit herself as severely
as Hemingway, but she does refrain from entering the minds of
characters; basically, she describes and reports. Again it is largely the
unemotional report from an objective point of view that makes *us*
supply the shudder.

3. Over-the-shoulder.   This angle of vision is given to us in third
person (he, she), like omniscient and objective. But here the author
is "absent." What we see, as in (b) above, is limited to what one

character sees. What we gain is easy identification with a character; we experience his experience. For example:

> Suddenly he felt himself jerked off his feet, shoved against something hard. The garage wall. Then they were searching him. "Hey, listen—"
> "Okay, stand up. What were you doing—casing that house over there?"
> "Casing nothing. There's a girl—"
> "Some kind of nut, huh?"
> He was sweating and laughing and clearing his throat. He remembered when Mr. Creely had grabbed him for stealing comics and he figured he'd wind up in jail, and this time—oh, lord—maybe he would. And who'd believe him? And if they did, it would be worse. What would they say in school? Oh, lord, he'd have to split town.
> "Okay, let's go across the street and clean this thing up," one of the cops said. Oh, lord!

Often a writer is so sympathetic to the point-of-view character that it is easy to confuse the two. What does Chekhov, in the following passage from "The Name-Day Party," think about Olga's husband?

> Olga made up her mind to find her husband at once and to speak plainly and tell him what she thought: it was disgusting the way he appealed to women, seeking their admiration as if it were manna from heaven; it was unjust, dishonorable, that he should give to others what by right belonged to his wife, that he should hide his soul and conscience from her only to reveal them to the first pretty face that came along.

All we know for sure is what *Olga* feels. The moralizing is hers, the anger is hers. From the story as a whole we feel that Chekhov is sympathetic toward Olga. But he is *not* Olga; he isn't trapped in Olga's marriage. He uses Olga as the eyes through which the story is seen—because they are sensitive eyes and because it is Olga's consciousness that will be the stage for tragedy.

Sometimes, writers may use over-the-shoulder narration to describe the experience of characters they may personally detest. For example, in James Baldwin's "Going to Meet the Man" (not included in this anthology) we see racial struggle not from the angle of vision of the victim nor from an omniscient or objective position, but from the angle of vision of a brutal, warped policeman trying to get to sleep:

> This wasn't helping him to sleep. He turned again, toward Grace again, and moved close to her warm body. He felt something he had never felt before. He felt that he would like to hold her, hold her, hold her, and be buried in her like a child and never have to get up in the morning again and go downtown to face those faces, good Christ, they were ugly! and never have to enter that jail house again and smell that smell and hear that singing; never again feel that filthy, kinky, greasy hair under his hand, never again watch those black breasts leap against the leaping cattle prod, never hear those moans again or watch that

blood run down or the fat lips split or the sealed eyes struggle open. They were animals, they were no better than animals, what could be done with people like that? Here they had been in a civilized country for years and they still lived like animals.

If we didn't know James Baldwin to be black—and sane—how would we know that this isn't *his* picture of black people? In the context of the whole story, we would know by the intense distortions of perception, by the monomaniacal fascination of the character with black sexuality, by the tortured consciousness of the character, and by his terrible recollections of a lynching he saw when he was a child. We are made to experience the consciousness of a man whose sensuality has been alienated from him and who hates that sensuality and can experience it only in conjunction with cruelty.

If, in over-the-shoulder narration, we are limited to what a single character knows, we gain intense and direct experience of consciousness. It is a very different experience from listening to a story told in the first person ("I . . ."), for in that case the event is usually public, an experience for an audience, while in over-the-shoulder narration, we seem to be overhearing someone's ongoing experience.

4. First person. As in example (c) above, someone—an "I"—tells us a story, usually a story involving the speaker. As when a friend talks to us, we start by believing everything; we identify with the speaker and accept the story as told to us. And we probably assume that the *narrator* and the writer are one. But in fact the writer has created the narrator and may be very different from him. The reader has to attend not just to the *narrative* but also to the *narrator,* and look upon the narrator like a *character*.

Let us consider the extreme case first: sometimes the narrator is not only *different* from the writer but is crazy or confused—an *unreliable narrator;* we aren't meant to swallow what is said. In Chekhov's "Ninochka," for instance, we begin by identifying with the narrator. What a charming man! And we listen to his story about a poor, dull friend who had troubles with his wife. But soon we learn that our friendly narrator is the cause of some of those troubles—he's sleeping with his friend's wife. Now his pleasant narrative voice seems arrogant, full of false sympathy that disguises his contempt.

Charlotte Perkins Gilman has created, in "The Yellow Wall-Paper," a narrator who goes mad in the course of her story. We are meant to feel enormous sympathy for her position, but also to step outside her description of her condition. She blames herself and speaks of her husband as flawless, but we see her as a victim of nineteenth-century bourgeois marriage and her husband as her jailer. We are meant to see more than she sees—meant to understand her hallucinations as a strange form of wisdom.

Not all first person narrators are unreliable. But you should try to see even reliable narrators as dramatized characters, as part of the story. Baldwin's "Sonny's Blues," for instance, is told by the sympathetic brother of a black jazz musician who had been a heroin addict. The narrator is an ordinary, decent man; his brother Sonny has experienced a much deeper, more terrible level of life. It is as if we, like the narrator, are unable to experience that life directly. We see it dimly, through the narrator's eyes. As he learns to believe in Sonny, so do we.

Often, like Sonny's brother, the narrator is an ordinary person who tells us about an extraordinary person. Melville's "Bartleby the Scrivener" uses this form. A bland, conventional, humane lawyer tells us about a baffling, unconventional man. The lawyer's congenial perspective lets us get near Bartleby. The lawyer's concern becomes our concern. When a conventional narrator is used to look at an unconventional character, the fiction often centers around the conflict between society and the unique individual. "A Rose for Emily" is another story of this kind. The narrator is really not "I" but "We." He represents conventional society looking at a woman who fiercely refuses to accept the loss of an aristocratic, fantasized past. In these stories the narrator is a kind of *reader surrogate,* a substitute for the reader. We identify with the narrator's normal view and then are led into contact with the outsider, the madman, the genius.

But these are all fairly complicated uses of first person form. Sometimes, we are simply permitted to identify with the narrator. But even then, and even when the narrator's experiences are similar to the writer's, the narrator is different from the actual living author. Even autobiographical writing, as we have seen, tends to become a form of fiction. In the case of fiction per se, the writer is consciously creating a character to narrate, and that character is only one aspect of the writer. Isaac Babel, like his narrator, took part in the Russian Revolution and, like his narrator, struggled within himself to become a revolutionary. But in "My First Goose" the speaker has been simplified, the action tightly focused; all we see is the struggle of the narrator as a sensitive intellectual to take part in bloody revolutionary action. The reader's job is to feel this struggle, to listen to the voice of the speaker as if he were a dramatic character, not the author telling us what happened to him at the front.

5. Mixed. It is possible for the angle of vision to shift about in the middle of a story. An author may manipulate the angle of vision in much the same way that a filmmaker changes the position of a camera. The reader's job is to sense where the "camera" is and what it is doing there.

In "The Chrysanthemums" Steinbeck begins with a camera pulled back in an extreme long shot:

> The high gray-flannel fog of winter closed off the Salinas Valley from the sky and from all the rest of the world. On every side it sat like a lid on the mountains and made of the great valley a closed pot.

Later, the camera closes in on Elisa Allen. We see her in closeup:

> In the kitchen she reached behind the stove and felt the water tank. It was full of hot water from the noonday cooking. In the bathroom she tore off her soiled clothes and flung them into the corner. And then she scrubbed herself with a little block of pumice, legs and thighs, loins and chest and arms, until her skin was scratched and red.

Then we move over-the-shoulder to experience what she experiences:

> Before she was finished she heard the little thunder of hoofs and the shouts of Henry and his helper as they drove the red steers into the corral. She heard the gate bang shut and set herself for Henry's arrival.

What Steinbeck is doing is making us feel the life of this woman in relation to the larger world outside. He doesn't want us to be limited to what she knows. He wants us to feel how shut off from life she is, as if she were inside a pot under a heavy lid. To express his model of the relations between the longing individual and the confining environment, Steinbeck chooses to use a complex angle of vision.

Again, Tolstoy's "The Death of Iván Ilých" mixes points of view, angles of vision, to create meaning. The story begins in authorial detachment. But increasingly throughout the story the angle of vision moves closer to that of the character. Finally the camera is over the protagonist's shoulder: we are in touch with Iván Ilých's living spirit. This is the story of a man whose life has been a lie and of how, facing death, he learns to live in the truth—to go from being a *one* (one must do this, one certainly can't do that) to being an *I*. The shift in angle of vision is an expression of Tolstoy's way of seeing life, looking first at its external falsity, then at its internal truth.

Narrative Structure and Focus

As we have seen, *angle of vision* is not something given to a writer; it is chosen. The choice depends on the kind of story one wants to tell, on how one feels about the subject. The same is true of how a writer orders the events of a story and how the story is given focus. These are also tools, expressive of the writer's vision and of the need for specific dramatic effects.

Suppose you were telling a story of a young woman in a good marriage faced with a decision. Her husband is offered a job halfway across the country, but she has a fine position where she is, and she knows that she won't be able to find interesting work in the new city. The new job is important for her husband's career. She wonders whether to go or to stay.

Imagine your choices: first, consider *angle of vision:* Are you going to have the woman narrate her own story? Or should her husband tell it? Or will you tell it objectively, as if it were a case history? Or will you tell it in third person over-the-shoulder, following her consciousness? How do you decide? It depends on who you are and on what kind of story you want to tell. And now, another choice—*narrative structure:* Where do we come into the action? After the decision has been made? Then we can deal with its effects on the woman. Or during the making of the decision? Then we may be drawn into the woman's uncertainty and be led to question our own values. Or will the story broaden out to include a portrait of the marriage as well as the decision and its effects? It is even possible to flash back to relevant scenes from the woman's childhood, or to blur together ongoing events with vaguely remembered moments. And then—what about the simple ordering of events? Do we begin with the woman writing a letter to a friend, fighting with her husband, sitting at her desk at work?

So many choices! How does a writer decide?

In one sense, you don't have to decide; the story decides. You *discover,* after working on the story again and again and again, what it is that matters to you about the material: is it the effects, the decision, the pattern of behavior, the inner turmoil, etc., etc. . . . ? What *matters?* And so, my story and your story of more or less the same events will be quite different. Largely it depends on who we are, on the vision of the world we (half unconsciously) need to express. Then, too, it also depends on technical demands. For instance, since Melville wants us to look upon Bartleby with compassion, he begins his story not at the point that Bartleby refuses to perform work for other people but earlier, when he is a valuable clerk, a satisfactory "tool."

Olsen, in "I Stand Here Ironing," seems to have made some strange choices that break all the "rules" for a short story. The writer "should" focus on a short series of events in a limited time and space; Olsen creates a mother who remembers the entire growing up of her daughter. But that choice is determined by what really matters to Olsen: the struggle of the mother, as she irons and thinks—her guilt and pain about her daughter, her self-justification. We are there now with the mother, feeling her anguish and final affirmation. It's out of that core of concern that Olsen makes her choices. Joyce Carol Oates's brilliant "How I Contemplated the World from the Detroit House of Correction and Began My Life Over Again" focuses on the adolescent daughter. We see the girl trying to make sense out of her experience. The girl's mother would tell us a very different story. Think what a different story Faulkner would have written if, in "A Rose for Emily," he had dealt with the course of Emily's love affair while it was going on rather than after she was already dead.

How a Story Works

A young woman sits at a window, thinking. The thinking goes on—profoundly—for a couple of pages, then we hear about her childhood. Finally she walks out into the night. The end.

Why isn't this a story? What makes a story?

Conflict.   First, stories are built around a conflict, a conflict in which someone we care about is involved. Usually there's some hint of the conflict within the first paragraphs. The reader has to become concerned about the conflict, which may not be stated directly: what a character *wants* or *fears* or what *we see approaching* that the character does not see. Then, there must be an obstacle. Imagine this as a story: George wants someone to love. He walks into a room and finds Eloise. He loves her and is happy. Clearly, that's not a story. There's desire but no obstacle, and without an obstacle, there's no conflict. Of course, the obstacle doesn't have to be external—a bad guy, a hurricane. It can be internal—emotional or spiritual. Usually it is both internal and external.

We have seen how, in Steinbeck's "The Chrysanthemums," the description of the Salinas Valley expresses in the first few lines the conflict between the life in Elisa Allen and the deadening restrictions on that life. Elisa Allen does not understand, at the beginning of the story, that there *is* a conflict. The reader begins to feel it in the setting, in Elisa's isolation, in the contradiction between her energy and the life she has to live. Later, she feels it, too, but never with the clarity of the reader.

In Crane's "The Open Boat" we are drawn immediately into a pretty basic conflict: will the men in the boat survive? Here we find—and this is usually the case—that our first understanding of the conflict deepens, that what begins as a simple question of survival becomes the question of why men survive. Is nature arbitrary or meaningful? In Bellow's "Looking for Mr. Green," the initial conflict is obvious—the social worker is a kind of hunter; will he find Mr. Green so he can deliver the welfare check? But by the end of the story the conflict feels bigger than that. The search for Mr. Green expresses the search for human dignity, the worth of the ordinary human being—a question that is basic to all Bellow's fiction.

But before a story can work for you on that lofty level, you have to *care* on a much simpler level—care about the characters, care what happens. As a reader you have to identify with a character—or with the voice of the narrator (this remains even in experimental contemporary fiction that has discarded plot, character, coherent world). As a writer you have to create that identification. So *what* if a young woman is sitting by the window feeling lonely and afraid. Until she matters, until we feel connected to her and to her conflict, we're bored. The character is just a name. Her thoughts mean nothing.

And *action,* alone, is not *conflict,* though it can establish conflict. You can pour murder, mayhem, and sex into a story; unless we care about the characters and the meaning of the action to the characters, you have no conflict and no story. On the other hand, even the slightest action can be the focus of powerful conflict. And this makes sense. Think how, when you have been in love or have been fighting someone close to you, every moment is charged with energy; pouring a cup of coffee for the other person becomes a significant act. In Lawrence's "The Blind Man" the story turns on two men touching each other's faces: not a great deal of action—but the crisis of an intense conflict.

Dramatic form.   A story *grows* out of a conflict. *Grows.* Let's go back to the young woman at the window. Now imagine that her husband is packing to leave for a new job and that, having decided to stay where she is, the woman is torn, depressed, and scared. Now we have a conflict, and her thoughts about loneliness become interesting to us. Now something has to develop, to grow, out of that conflict. This is called the *rising action* or *complication*. In Poe's "Fall of the House of Usher," it includes the development of the narrator's terror, his learning about Roderick and his sister, whom Roderick entombs. In "The Rocking-Horse Winner" the rising action is built around the boy's increasing magical ability to make money by picking winners—and the increased tension in the house. And in the story of the young woman who decided to let her husband go off without her? There are many possibilities. It would be an interesting exercise to take the situation and plot out a number of different stories.

Climax.   The action rises to a *crisis* or *climax*. The climax should develop naturally out of the conflict and connect the threads of plot. At the same time, it should be meaningful—expressive of the writer's vision. Take "The Rocking-Horse Winner" again. Suppose that at the climax the boy makes a million pounds for his mother and becomes a famous racehorse tout; that would completely miss the point. Lawrence senses money hunger and the will to feed it as daemonic, destructive. The increasing "luck" of the boy *has to* move toward an ironic climax in which it is his "luck" that kills him. In the story about the woman choosing her career instead of going off with her husband, suppose that at the climax a telegram arrives offering her a position as good as his. That would solve her original problem, but the climax would come from the outside, not grown out of the story, and it would have nothing to do with the writer's concern for a woman struggling to face a decision.

Falling action and denouement (resolution). Picking up the pieces. Knots are unraveled, a new stability is reached. In "My First Goose" this section includes everything after the stabbing of the goose. Sometimes the falling action and resolution can be a few lines long, sometimes pages. The job of the denouement is to create a sense of the *wholeness* of the action, of its *necessity,* and to secure for the reader its vision.

Exposition. Sometimes the writer has to introduce information about events that took place before the story began, information *necessary to understand the story.* Generally, in a first draft a writer pours a generous amount of exposition into the beginning of a story, then realizes that most of it can be omitted or can be folded into the story so that it works but doesn't show. Sometimes an initial exposition can be omitted entirely. Malamud, for instance, in "Idiots First," starts with a *scene:*

> The thick ticking of the tin clock stopped. Mendel, dozing in the dark, awoke in fright. . . .

Why do modern writers often eliminate *exposition?* Because (1) it can be dull—we are told about events instead of experiencing them. (2) We lose a lot of energy by being spoon-fed information. It's more exciting to find yourself in the middle of a world and try to discover what it's like. (3) It's also closer to our experience of ordinary life. When we enter into an experience, we usually enter without a briefing.

There are times when exposition can be powerful. D. H. Lawrence gives us almost two pages of it at the beginning of "The Rocking-Horse Winner." And yet he doesn't have to; necessary information could have been folded into the initial dialogue between Paul and his mother, or the story could have begun with Paul already on the rocking horse and trying to explain things to the gardener. But listen to the effect of the first lines of exposition:

> There was a woman who was beautiful, who started with all the advantages, yet she had no luck. She married for love, and the love turned to dust. She had bonny children, yet she felt they had been thrust upon her, and she could not love them. . . .

In those lines Lawrence gives us something much more important than information. He gives us his voice—the voice of the *storyteller,* the one who knows. He gives us a *tone* (I'll talk about that in detail later) —the tone of a fairy tale in which there are moral certainties. He hypnotizes us with his repetition of parallelisms. We are not bored because we are attuned to the prophetic energy of the narrative voice.

Scene. When inexperienced writers attempt fiction, they usually tell a story by hopping from one event to the next until the story's done, presenting a series of expositions instead of creating a story we can live in. What an experienced writer learns is to hang the story on a small number of *scenes.* The scenes do most of the work: characterize, introduce the conflict, carry the significant action. As much as possible, the writer uses the scenes to tell what happens during the intervals between them. To get the pacing of the story right, a writer may choose to space out scenes with more leisurely narration, or may pile scene against scene for a more intense effect. Generally, over the past hundred years, the story has moved from a narrative voice that tells about events, interprets a great deal, generalizes a great deal, to an emphasis on *concreteness,* on *scene,* on *being there.*

A scene is not a report about an event—it is a *being-there.* An inexperienced writer may describe

a subway ride
a telephone call
a ride in the elevator
a conversation lasting six lines
a report of something happening

and then another narrative sequence. An experienced writer will begin, "Edward sat across from Laura on the windowseat he'd built for her last year, stroking the smooth pine as if it were a Siamese cat, giving himself comfort by the touch of the wood, the smell of the oils she used to polish it." What happened to the ride, the call, and so on? As William Burroughs says in *Naked Lunch,* "I am not American Express." In other words, I don't have to tell you the itineraries of my characters, to stay with them all the time. *I* may need to *feel* my character move across the city, but I don't have to write it.

The little scene between Edward and Laura begins in a terribly conventional way, but the conventions are just what I want you to see. To *be there,* to be in the scene rather than the reporter *of* a scene, the writer tries to make you smell and touch and see. Mathematical description doesn't do it very well: suppose I had written, ". . . stroking the smooth pine with a pressure of 23 grams in a tempo of one stroke every 1.37 seconds." The writer can more fully make you feel part of the scene by telling you that Edward stroked the wood as if it were a Siamese cat. Of course, *everything* in a scene can not and should not be treated in detail; if it were, the result would be a mess. There are things to emphasize in a scene and things to blur; a scene has to carry the conflict forward, not just be a place where characters talk.

Being there. Try this exercise: close your eyes and *be* in your childhood house, the one that comes most strongly to your memory. Imagine the kitchen, the living room, the bedrooms. Does the house have a cellar? An attic? Were those your secret places? Did you have a refuge in the back of a walk-in closet? What rooms in the house do you find yourself avoiding? What rooms are you drawn to? Now, see your mother or both your parents. Where are they? Can you hear a voice? Listen. Can you smell the house? Now, start to write a scene about your family—eating dinner or breakfast, getting ready for bed. As you write, try to make readers be there too. Let them smell the bacon, the sweat from an old T-shirt, the smell of planed wood in your father's shop. . . . Let them feel the spaces, the places of confinement. And let them feel your anxiety or pleasure or sadness. Can you compare your feelings to anything—to an animal, a prisoner?

If you try this exercise, you will *discover* what's important for you. And this is a crucial point: It is *not* true that a writer creating a scene has X effect in mind and manipulates *a, b,* and *c* to get it. Often there is an intuitive sense of what is wanted out of a scene, but in some ways, the writer has to discover (just as the reader does) what in the scene is important. The writer tries to *be there,* and if the effort truly succeeds, the reader will be too. "No surprise for the writer, no surprise for the reader," Robert Frost once said. And that is true. A writer may grow very conscious of process and effect, but there is always a time, writing narrative, writing a scene, when one is simply there, there for the language in which one's model of the world expresses itself.

Since the strong story usually hinges on a few scenes, most stories are limited in time, space, characters. A day, a week, an hour is typical. As we have seen, Tillie Olsen in "I Stand Here Ironing" captures a seventeen-year period by focusing on the narrative voice of the mother. It's really her story, *now.* McCullers' "A Tree, a Rock, a Cloud" gives us a capsule look at a man's adult life. But the story of that life is contained within an ongoing scene in a café, and the story is filtered through the awareness of a boy, learning about life. Often a first draft will cover many days, many scenes; then the writer will eliminate scenes and tighten the story down to a few scenes and a shorter time span.

As a reader, watch how a writer builds on scenes, puts you there in the scene, through imagery: *literal imagery*—the actual experience of the senses—and *figurative imagery*—imagery brought in from outside to convey experience, comparing an anxiety state to a flight of birds in the belly, a devotional love to a chalice borne through a throng of foes. Watch the way the writer gets you to care about a scene by how it carries forward the conflict in the story, and notice how dialogue and narrated action intensify that conflict.

Conflict, dramatic form, scene: these are not *rules* for fiction—they are elements which, over the years, have turned out to be useful—to hook us into a story and make it matter, make it work for us. But, as we will see, many experimental stories, especially contemporary stories, achieve their effects by assuming that the reader expects those elements, and then frustrating the expectations.

Everything in Fiction Is Expressive

Imagery. As soon as we get rid of the notion that a story is a record of some external reality, we see that *everything* in a story is expressive of the writer's vision of life, a subjective model of reality.

That doesn't mean you should go symbol hunting. It doesn't mean you should snoop through a story for the Meaning of each image. "There's a telephone in this story—aha!—a symbol of . . . communication!" I've seen professional critical essays—and student papers—like that—and that's foolish. Again, I don't believe that Steinbeck decided to be "symbolic" when he wrote the opening description of the Salinas Valley in "The Chrysanthemums." But when someone feels life in an intense way, then the external world becomes part of that vision—in this case, the vision of life cut off at the roots, cut off from a nourishing environment, life clamped down as if inside a *closed pot*. In those first lines we are hearing more than a setting described; we are hearing life described. The rest of the story will show us Elisa Allen as a woman of strength and energy whose life is sat on, shut away, just as the Salinas Valley is closed off; a woman who resists, but in a painfully inadequate way, the deadening of her powers.

Setting. The locale for a story is (consciously or unconsciously) chosen by a writer largely as a source of potential imagery. This imagery is often more than background. It can be, as in "The Chrysanthemums," one expression of the writer's vision. In Lawrence's "The Blind Man" the setting is divided between *house* and *farm*. They provide two opposed sets of images (light, polished furniture, servants, mirror; darkness, animals, odors, physical work) that reinforce the conflict of the story. We experience the conflict partly through these images.

The setting, and the pool of images it provides for the writer to draw from, establish the *atmosphere,* the mood of the setting. In Poe's "The Fall of the House of Usher" the atmosphere is tense with horror: Poe uses the crumbling stones and strange mists and dark donjons of the House of Usher as a state of being, a mode of consciousness. Bellow's drab, broken-down Chicago creates an atmosphere that acts almost as antagonist in "Looking for Mr. Green." It expresses a world in which individuals don't matter, an attitude Grebe, the leading character, must defeat.

Often the setting or imagery vibrates beyond its literal condition to become a metaphor for human life. The veil, in "The Minister's Black Veil," expresses Hawthorne's vision of people isolated from one another by their own sense of sin. Crane uses an open boat to express his sense of human beings as powerless against an irrational universe. These can be considered *central metaphors,* basic comparisons that run through a story and provide the substructure for its model of human experience.

In the section on scene we distinguished literal from figurative imagery. Again, *literal imagery* is the sensory world of the story— bedsheets, pots and pans, violins, the touch of a person's cold nose or sweaty fingers. *Figurative imagery* consists of comparisons to worlds outside: a vacuum cleaner like a hungry beetle, anger like a green flame, walking robotlike, kissing someone as if presenting a gift. These are *similes*—explicit comparisons introduced by "like" or "as." Here is a powerful simile from "My First Goose" by Isaac Babel: "His long legs were like girls sheathed to the neck in shining riding boots"—a simile that expresses a good deal about the story as a whole. Then, *metaphor*—an implicit comparison: a lover flies to his beloved, an angry man massacres the meat on his plate and executes the mushrooms with his fork. His eyes aim at the guests. At the close of "My First Goose," Babel's narrator says, "But my heart, stained with bloodshed, grated and brimmed over." The implicit comparisons plunge to the heart of the story. Then, *personification*—really a kind of buried metaphor: tired sofa, friendly lamp, a bathtub drain that groans and chokes, chokes and sputters. Babel's narrator says, "Evening wrapped about me the quickening moisture of its twilight sheets." Finally, there are *extended metaphors*, like this one from Baldwin's "Sonny's Blues":

> A great block of ice got settled in my belly and kept melting there slowly all day long, while I taught my classes algebra. It was a special kind of ice. It kept melting, sending trickles of ice water all up and down my veins, but it never got less. Sometimes it hardened and seemed

to expand until I felt my guts were going to come spilling out or that I was going to choke or scream.

While we have distinguished literal from figurative imagery, in another sense, *all* imagery is figurative. All imagery works on the level of metaphor because it creates the emotional-social-metaphysical world of the story. In Hemingway's "The Snows of Kilimanjaro," for instance, gangrene is not a comparison brought in from outside the story (as in, "Our relationship had died; gangrene had set in: it was time to amputate"); instead, it is the physical reality: the *protagonist* (the leading character, who makes the action or to whom the action happens) is dying of gangrene. But the image of painless atrophying is a powerful metaphor for the spiritual condition of the protagonist and for Hemingway's sense of life without grace.

We could speak of gangrene in "The Snows of Kilimanjaro" as a *symbol*, an image or action that represents, expresses, something larger than itself. In the same way, the black veil in "The Minister's Black Veil" or the open boat in Crane's "The Open Boat," which we have spoken of as images, we could describe as symbols. We could call the discarding of the chrysanthemum in the road in Steinbeck's "The Chrysanthemums" a symbolic action, and symbolic, too, the scrubbing that Elisa gives herself. We have avoided discussion of symbolism in this Preface not because it doesn't exist but because it may do more harm than good; some readers—including critics and teachers —hunt for symbols and when they capture them, feel that they know the story. A symbol is simply an expressive, meaningful image or action, and if we have preferred here to use the term *image,* it is because it is less likely to be perverted; it is less likely that a reader will try to turn a kiss into an equation for Love if we call it an image. Certainly it *is* necessary to stay aware of actions and images, literal and figurative. It *is* valuable to understand that an image or an act can express more than itself. But it is important not to think that the iron in Olsen's "I Stand Here Ironing" symbolizes (equals) the Pressure of the Environment, not to think that the ride on the rocking horse in Lawrence's "The Rocking-Horse Winner" symbolizes (equals) the Will. One danger is that the reader will oversimplify the story, either by finding symbols where they don't occur or by overemphasizing symbols to squeeze the whole story into a partial interpretation; another, greater danger is that the reader will substitute an abstract schematic meaning for the experience of life in the story.

It is true, however, that readers have to sensitize themselves to the imagery of a story and feel how it defines a world. To do this isn't easy; it takes practice, as listening to a symphony for the development of musical subjects takes practice. The first step in both cases is simply to *listen*—to read with the quiet around you that you would give to a painting or a piece of music. *Feel* the effect of the imagery on yourself; later you can go back and see how the images created that effect, what the effect *expresses*—what kind of world it helps create. As a writer, you need to let images—figurative and literal—*find you;* you need to come upon them half-unaware. In a sense you must do the same job as the reader: sensitize yourself, listen. Your rational mind is useful; it produces connections; it edits, revises, seizes a half-expressed feeling and expands it. But imagery comes from places in you that your conscious mind cannot get to; it knows more than "you" do, and you have to let it guide. Otherwise, your model of a world won't go beyond the superficial, secondhand models we all receive from the culture. Great fiction is subversive, liberating us from the world we are handed as children. That is perhaps its chief value for the writer and the reader.

Dialogue. Paddy Chayevsky, the dramatist and screen writer, was once accused of finding his brilliant dialogue with a tape recorder. Chayevsky retorted, "Tell me where I can buy a tape recorder that can write Chayevsky dialogue and I'll pay you $50,000." And of course there is no such tape recorder; one cannot record speech verbatim and come up with good dialogue. First, there's no way you can fully record speech in a narrative. For instance, speech overlaps; we talk at the same time. And we gesture and wrinkle up our noses and speak in *tones* that communicate as much as the words we use. None of this can be written down. And speech, when you make a *transcript* of it, is difficult to understand; syntax is confused, sentence emphasis is lost. Second, a recording of speech, even if it were possible, would be terribly boring and would lack focus.

In turning speech into dialogue, the writer has to convey the impression of recording living speech but actually has to *stylize* speech—select, omit, heighten—create a *quality that can substitute through style for the living experience*. That's not easy. And the quality is different for each writer.

Listen to the difference between two styles of writing dialogue. The first passage is from "The Snows of Kilimanjaro." A man and woman are on a safari in Africa: the man knows he is dying of gangrene; the woman is trying to help him recover.

> "Wouldn't you like me to read?" she asked. She was sitting on a canvas chair beside his cot. "There's a breeze coming up."
> "No thanks."
> "Maybe the truck will come."
> "I don't give a damn about the truck."
> "I do."
> "You give a damn about so many things that I don't."

> "Not so many, Harry."
> "What about a drink?"
> "It's supposed to be bad for you. It said in Black's to avoid all alcohol. You shouldn't drink."
> "Molo!" he shouted.
> "Yes, Bwana."
> "Bring whiskey-soda."
> "Yes, Bwana."
> "You shouldn't," she said. "That's what I mean by giving up. It says it's bad for you. I know it's bad for you."
> "No," he said. "It's good for me."

Do people talk in this way? Short sentences about trivia, repetition of sentence structure, repetition of phrases? Perhaps sometimes they do. But Hemingway has picked up this *sometimes* and exaggerated it into a style. Terse, bare, hard dialogue. And the narrator doesn't tell us much about how either of them are feeling; he's terse too. He reports the dialogue. There's a poetry in the simple sentences that echo one another, repeating words and rhythms and syntactical patterns. Notice that in the last exchange *she said* and *he said* are not necessary to identify the speakers. They are a rhythmic, repetitive element that increases the tension.

So much is unstated in this dialogue; there seems to be intense feeling crackling through the lines, but the feeling is not expressed. Hemingway is a master of the dialogue of the unstated, the dialogue of people holding back. Even when Harry expresses his rage further on in the story, he expresses it in vicious ironic comments. And this holding back is directly related to the conflict within Harry: he is a writer who has chosen an easy life rather than face the pain of writing about a world filled with suffering, a writer who is holding back his gift, letting it, like his leg, atrophy. And beyond this particular story, Hemingway's dialogue often expresses a vision of experience in which one learns to hold back—learns to repress feeling in order to survive.

The dialogue of Bernard Malamud is just as poetic, just as fiercely *styled* as that of Hemingway. In "The Magic Barrel" Leo is a young rabbinical student who turns to a marriage broker to find himself a wife. The broker lies and cajoles to make a match. Now, suddenly, Leo looks through the marriage broker's photos and comes upon one he loves:

> "Here is the one I want." Leo held forth the snapshot.
> Salzman slipped on his glasses and took the picture into his trembling hand. He turned ghastly and let out a groan.
> "What's the matter?" cried Leo.
> "Excuse me. Was an accident this picture. She isn't for you."
> Salzman frantically shoved the manila packet into his portfolio. He thrust the snapshot into his pocket and fled down the stairs.

Leo, after momentary paralysis, gave chase and cornered the marriage broker in the vestibule. The landlady made hysterical outcries but neither of them listened.

"Give me back the picture, Salzman."

"No." The pain in his eyes was terrible.

"Tell me who she is then."

"This I can't tell you. Excuse me."

He made to depart, but Leo, forgetting himself, seized the matchmaker by his tight coat and shook him frenziedly.

"Please," sighed Salzman. *"Please."*

Leo ashamedly let him go. "Tell me who she is," he begged. "It's very important for me to know."

"She is not for you. She is a wild one—wild, without shame. This is not a bride for a rabbi."

"What do you mean wild?"

"Like an animal. Like a dog. For her to be poor was a sin. This is why to me she is dead now."

"In God's name, what do you mean?"

"Her I can't introduce to you," Salzman cried.

"Why are you so excited?"

"Why, he asks," Salzman said, bursting into tears. "This is my baby, my Stella, she should burn in hell."

(1) How different the narrative voices are. Hemingway's voice is cold, terse, objective. It exudes tension. Malamud expresses feeling in intense language, nothing held back. His verbs "thrust," "shove," "seize," "beg." His adjectives are "ghastly," "trembling," "hysterical." Emotion is wild and terrible. Malamud doesn't use the language of trivia and the avoidance of statements of value. Things matter, matter intensely; powerful moral judgments are made.

(2) Something is unexpressed here, too—but the scene builds *toward* that expression, toward *opening*. In Hemingway the scene builds toward increasing, painful *tightness,* and it is the reader who has to supply the explosion latent in the dialogue.

(3) Malamud's marriage broker speaks in a dialect—the English has overtones of Yiddish in its inverted syntax. More—the Yiddish carries with it a set of cultural assumptions about human suffering that, if we understand them, turn Salzman's broken sentences into a kind of moaning cello. Malamud discovers in the Yiddish-English a powerful poetry, a poetry that intimates the reality of an everyday world in which spiritual dramas are enacted. Life is to be sought and perceived in its mystery—not deadened, avoided to stop pain.

But while Hemingway and Malamud give us in dialogue visions of two very different worlds, both ways of stylizing speech are wonderful. The dialogue is intense; it captures the beat of life as each experiences it.

Before dialogue can express a vision of life, it has to function in more basic ways. Notice in your reading how dialogue, while appearing "natural," actually conveys a good deal of exposition. Notice how, in contrast to real speech, the exchange of dialogue builds the drama of a scene, develops the conflict, moves the story forward. And notice, too, how in good dialogue irrelevancies are omitted, speech is selected to intensify the focus of the story, sentences are shaped to clarify what the writer wants to emphasize in the absence of tone, expression, gesture. In ordinary speech there is a great deal of repetition; in good dialogue the writer *uses* repetition to emphasize a quality of a character, a scene. That's very different from the repetition of ordinary speech.

In your reading, try to become aware both of how dialogue *works* in a story and of the ways in which writers use their particular style of making dialogue as one part of their expressive equipment, one element of their vision.

Tone.   If every element in fiction is expressive, every element helps establish the tone. *Tone* is the attitude that the author wants us to take toward the material, the way we are supposed to feel about character and situation. It refers especially to the quality of the narrative voice. Is the voice sneering at the characters? Building them up as noble creatures? Is the voice lyrical, asking us to experience the characters with a loving gentleness, or perhaps ironic, asking us to stand back and see contradictions between the way *characters* experience events and the way an *observer* does? Is the voice tough and terse? Or is it, as Hemingway's often is, hard-boiled but with an undercurrent of nostalgia or sentimentality?

For tone reflects a *choice*—a choice perhaps only half-conscious. It is *not* in the nature of the material. Here is the opening sentence of "A Rose for Emily." Let's quote it, then change its tone:

> When Miss Emily Grierson died, our whole town went to her funeral: the men through a sort of respectful affection for a fallen monument, the women mostly out of curiosity to see the inside of her house, which no one save an old manservant—a combined gardener and cook—had seen in at least ten years.

Now, let's rewrite that sentence without changing the "contents":

> Old Emily Grierson dropped dead at last, and the whole town invited themselves to her funeral. The men kind of liked the old lady—once she was really something! The women just wanted to snoop through her house—nobody but the guy who cooked for her and weeded her garden had been inside for maybe ten years.

What happened to poor William Faulkner between the two versions? Clearly, the second passage is no longer Faulkner. The attitude toward Miss Grierson is very different; the dignity of tone of Faulkner's narrator is replaced by a tough, vulgar, colloquial cynicism.

Readers must attune themselves to the voice—not lose touch with the attitude of the human speaker. This is especially important when the tone is *ironic*. *Irony* refers to some kind of contradiction—for example, between the story and the telling of the story or between the way we see a character and the character's own self-image. If we do not hear the ironic tone, we lose the story.

For instance, James Joyce begins "Clay" like this:

> The matron had given her leave to go out as soon as the women's tea was over and Maria looked forward to her evening out. The kitchen was spick and span: the cook said you could see yourself in the big copper boilers. The fire was nice and bright and on one of the side-tables were four very big barmbracks. These barmbracks seemed uncut; but if you went closer you would see that they had been cut into long thick even slices and were ready to be handed round at tea. Maria had cut them herself.

The tone of "Clay" is deeply connected to its point of view. Is the point of view, the angle of vision, that of the author, the sophisticated intellectual, James Joyce? *Spick and span, nice and bright.* No. We are looking over the shoulder of Maria herself, and the language is the language of Maria's consciousness. But underneath that consciousness, we already—in this first paragraph—begin to sense the presence of an ironic Joyce, smiling at this woman, so pleased at her own precision, order, cleanness.

In the next paragraph, the angle of vision shifts—we see Maria from outside:

> Maria was a very, very small person indeed but she had a very long nose and a very long chin. She talked a little through her nose, always soothingly: *Yes, my dear,* and *No, my dear.*

Joyce does not evaluate Maria for us, but he begins to point us toward an evaluation. A little person. A kind of witch? (We learn shortly that the story is taking place on Halloween!) But if she is a witch, she is a very mild and banal one—and very pleased with her own mildness:

> She was always sent for when the women quarrelled over their tubs and always succeeded in making peace. One day the matron had said to her:
> —Maria, you are a veritable peace-maker!
> And the sub-matron and two of the Board ladies had heard the compliment. And Ginger Mooney was always saying what she wouldn't do to the dummy who had charge of the irons if it wasn't for Maria. Everyone was so fond of Maria.

Listen to the banality of the observations; notice how the sentences often begin "And . . ."—creating a childlike quality. While we are, in this paragraph, seeing through the eyes of Maria, we have to be aware of the presence of someone who knows more than Maria, the presence of ironic laughter.

Tone is not easy to talk about with precision. It involves what the psychoanalyst Theodore Reik calls "listening with the third ear." Just as a psychoanalyst puts a good deal of attention on *how* the client speaks rather than on *what* is said, so when you read, you have to feel the *how*. You have to be sensitive to the quality of voice and to the way diction, syntax, rhythm, reverberation, and imagery create that quality.

Is the diction lofty, full of abstract words, or is it down-home, colloquial, rich in concrete images? Is the syntax (word order, sentence structure) complex or is it simple and compound? Rhythmically are the sentences crisp, hard, flat or are they long and lilting? Or, as in "Clay," are they in singsong? Are there reverberations in the style: do you hear the voice of a prophet? of the teller of a fairy tale? of the Old Wise Man? of a hipster? of a reporter? Does the voice change during the course of the story? Is it sometimes ironic, sometimes prophetic? Is the voice representative of the consciousness of the author—or, as in "Clay"—of a character? Do we have to sniff out the *real* tone beneath the surface tone of a character like Maria? It isn't easy to define the tone of a story properly—or even to be sure you're hearing it accurately. But at the same time, it's something we can do in an intuitive manner if we simply stay alive to the voice we hear.

After all, we do it every day. We listen to the voices of friends, colleagues, police officers, husbands, lovers, or children, and we love them, respect them, despise them, fear them, ignore them not so much on the basis of what they say as on the qualities of their voices, their gestures, their expression, their language. We may know someone who always speaks kindly, but at the end of every sentence the voice drops like a record slowing down, and we intuit that beneath the kindness lies a great deal of buried anger and bitterness. Or we hear a friend speaking at a meeting, and we can sense insecurity by the high-pitched monotone of the voice, the brief, abrupt sentences, the absoluteness of our friend's assertions. As best we can, we listen with the "third ear." In a piece of fiction, tone can't depend on gesture, physical qualities of voice, facial expression; we attune ourselves to language.

Imagine meeting a religious Catholic at a café. Perhaps he tells you a story, and the story is full of religious imagery. He isn't necessarily trying to be poetic; that is how his mind works. His comparisons may be to priests, chalices, crosses, churches. The narrator of "Araby" is a little like that; underlying his simple story of adolescent disillusionment is religious imagery that makes the reader feel in the boy's devotion and quest a kind of sacred mission. But the mission is a failure, and the narrator's voice is lyrical and sad as the boy's quest ends in an empty bazaar, where ordinary people gossip. If Christ drove the moneychangers out of the temple, the boy finds that the bazaar makes a poor temple and that the moneychangers get rid of him. It's the contradiction between religious idealism and lyricism and a dismal reality that creates the tone of irony in Joyce's story.

The tone of a writer is often consistent from story to story. There is a tone we recognize as Hemingway's, a tone we recognize as Hawthorne's. It is like brushstroke and color relationships in a painter's work. While the tone may change depending on the kind of story the writer is trying to write and on the narrator chosen to tell it, after reading a number of stories we become familiar with something consistent in their tone. We begin to feel we "know"—sense the basic values of—that author.

Theme, Model, Vision

To say it quickly and simply, *theme* is what controls all the expressive choices a writer makes in a story—what to put in, what to leave out, how to decide on the angle of vision, narrative structure, tone. But to say this is dangerous; it sounds as if a writer sits down with an abstract idea, for instance, The Destruction of the Authentic Self, and then writes "The Name-Day Party." It is true that a writer uses narrative to express an interpreted reality. But actually the theme is discovered in the course of writing, and usually it cannot be set down neatly without trivializing or oversimplifying. The theme should not be seen as "The Message." The real message is *the experience of the story and the model of life proposed by that experience. Theme* is an abstraction derived from that experience, useful for purposes of analysis but not to be treated as the goal of reading.

If in one sense theme is what controls every choice in a story, the theme itself responds to the writer's *vision of life,* and that vision is modeled forth in the story. I've already spoken about fiction as a model of the way the writer sometimes experiences life. A writer lives in a particular social group, a particular class, race, sex, society, species. Growing up in that world, one begins to see it in certain categories, begins to interpret it. Soon the interpretive schema becomes a filter for reality—a kind of computer program that only accepts certain kinds of data and accepts data into predefined categories; only reality that fits comes through, and so the schema is reinforced. In the process of living, the writer sees by means of the schema, by means of the "lens." But then comes the discovery that experiences bulge out beyond the confines of the schema, outside the program's categories, and there is new creative work to do in order to experience the world more fully. This process is a description not only of the artist growing up but of every one of us. We are all artists: not necessarily artists of literature, but artists in the way we create and re-create the world as we experience it. When we read fiction, we attune ourselves to another artist's vision of the world— and expand our own. We gain new awareness. We subtilize our categories or put them to question. We do that not by understanding the abstract statement of a theme but by living in the fiction, experiencing the world in the mode of the fiction.

A Dark Vision in Literature?

Why can't writers create happy stories? Why *can't* the boy in "The Rocking-Horse Winner" win money for his mother and become happy and famous? The problem is that, while fiction is not a literal reflection of reality, it is true to the writer's experience of reality. "The Rocking-Horse Winner" expresses Lawrence's vision of the destructiveness of human will in the service of materialism. The power of the story comes out of that vision, and to write a "happy ending" would be to falsify the vision.

More generally, how can anyone write honest, serious fiction and not include pain, suffering, and destruction? Even great comic fiction has to assert pleasure and joy in the face of darkness. One of the finest comic novels of this century is Joyce Cary's *The Horse's Mouth*. The hero, even while dying, celebrates the struggles he has had—sees those struggles as necessary to his creation and his happiness. What he does *not* do is to *deny* the reality of the struggle.

Fiction of any seriousness is responsive to the conditions of our lives. First, our lives as members of this society, this time: how it feels and what it means to work, to suffer, to struggle. Life is not a situation comedy on TV and it is the job of fiction to help us remember that. Second, fiction is responsive to our lives as human beings. It refuses to permit our lives to be cheapened by any superficial treatment. We are not the Pepsi Generation. We are more than that. Elisa, in "The Chrysanthemums," is not going to be saved by buying a new washing machine; the hard, hard years of growing up for Emily in "I Stand Here Ironing" cannot be erased by any number of visits to a psychiatrist.

Yet both stories assert that a kind of richness survives. And in their stories in this anthology, Tolstoy and Wright convince us, powerfully and against the force of reason, that the fact of dying is less significant than the assertion of authentic life. Something remains in most of the fiction in this anthology—remains for us if not for the

characters. Dokey's Sánchez doesn't live, but the values he represents live because of Dokey, and after reading him, they live in us.

Experimental Fiction

A story in which a poor man rides his coal bucket through the sky;
a story in which a writer parodies his own act of writing the story; a
story pretending to be notes for a high school essay; a story in which
the narrator creates an enormous balloon that covers half a city, then
dissolves it because "you" have come back!

What's going on?

What's *not* going on is more to the point. The writers are creating
models of experience in which the conventions of plot, rounded
character, realistic setting, consistent angle of vision—and all the
illusions of *realism*—are rejected. That doesn't mean they aren't
models of experience—they are. But the relation between experience
and these fictions is a lot harder to see.

To some people it seems like wasted effort. Why have writers gone
to the trouble of experimenting at all? Why have they bothered to
break from the conventions of realism?

There are different answers to this, depending on the nature of the
experiment.

**Breaking from the conventions of realism permits the use of
fantasy or magical elements.** A reader coming to Kafka's "Country
Doctor" after, say, "The Chrysanthemums" by Steinbeck, experiences
giddiness. A doctor who has to get into bed with his patient! Magical
horses that storm out of a pigsty! The reader is tempted to hunt for
an allegorical reading of each image: do the horses represent the will?
Do the pigsty and the wound represent repressed sexuality? What is
Kafka's hidden meaning? Is this a religious drama about salvation?
For years, critics have searched through Kafka for *allegorical interpretations*—consistent symbolic patterns—the secret meaning of the
works. On the other hand, many readers, fed up with hunting
symbols, treat the fictions as unintelligible dreams. Perhaps both
approaches are mistaken; perhaps the richest way to read Kafka is to
treat the landscape and character relationships in his fiction in the
same way we treat the world in Steinbeck's fiction: to accept his
world, to immerse ourselves in it, to see it as a model of experience.
Unlike Steinbeck's model, Kafka's is full of the illogical connections
of our dream lives, our hungers and terrors; it is a world—real
enough—in which commonsense expectations don't apply, in which
cause and effect feel right but are twisted in impossible ways. To find
in this world a rational, coded *Meaning* is to destroy our experience
of it.

Try to give yourself to Kafka. Let the elements reverberate for you. You might imagine every element of the story to be conflicting subpersonalities of one psyche. Every animal, every person—see them as aspects of a single self. Maybe of *your* self. Try on the experience.

The value of fantasy, then, of magical elements, of fairy tale, is to help you burrow beneath the norms of daytime reality into levels of experience just as real, though not as accessible. Fantasy can be a powerful tool for experiencing our lives. And it is also a tool of psychic liberation—often it is used to re-create in the reader (and in the writer, for that matter) the experience of freedom we are usually too locked into ordinary structures to feel. Brautigan is one writer who uses fantasy in just this way. He is a magician teaching us to re-experience our own freedom.

Breaking from the conventions of realism permits writers to examine the process of fictionalizing.   If you have some certainty about an objective reality, you can use the conventions of realistic fiction to represent that reality. But in this century reality is more and more written in quotes—"reality." We become aware that reality is not simply out there but equally a work of the imagination. We fictionalize continually in the process of perceiving—fictionalize in the way we select what is significant and make sense out of it. But if reality is not simply *given,* then how can we hope to record it? And, as we try, we become aware of how conventionalized our process of recording really is. We can hear the mechanism creak; we see the puppet master behind the stage.

And so the puppet master comes out into the light. We see him blow his nose, hitch up his pants, take up the strings. He talks about what he's doing—he doesn't let us forget that he's *doing* it, that this isn't reality: it's a puppet show. The unnerving suggestion behind that is your reality is just as fictional. It too is a puppet show. By focusing on the artifice of fictionalizing, the writer plays with the fictional aspect of all experience.

In the 1930's, Virginia Woolf was playing with this kind of fiction in stories like "An Unwritten Novel." The narrator, instead of telling a story, sees a woman on a train and begins to *imagine* the story of her life. But when the woman leaves the train, the narrator sees that the imaginings were false—reality resists the imagination. Still, the story we hear concerns the creative imagination, projecting itself onto the world.

John Barth, in "Lost in the Funhouse," written about thirty years later, goes much further. He tells the story, as if it is autobiographical but written from an over-the-shoulder angle of vision, of a boy who gets lost in the funhouse at Ocean City, Maryland. But from the very beginning, that conventional story is held up to a hall of mirrors—we see it *being made,* our noses are rubbed in the paraphernalia of the well-constructed story: Barth's narrator fights with himself to turn "Lost in the Funhouse" into that kind of story. But the story contradicts itself, loses direction, destroys its own plot, and looks at itself continually. Gradually we understand that this is not John Barth speaking. If the subject is a fourteen-year-old trying to find himself, the narrator is the same boy, older now, still trying to look and feel like everyone else. Trying to describe his experience within the conventions of realistic fiction, he is continually aware of the conventions *as* conventions. He is also aware that his literary self-consciousness serves the same function as his personal self-consciousness, his detachment from his own experience: it keeps him in some kind of control. This is a Portrait of the Artist as a Paranoid. At the same time, it is much more than a clever analysis of the relation between personal psychology and fictional form; it is a sad, tender, funny story about being lost in the larger funhouse called *the world.*

Breaking from the conventions of realism lets the writer emphasize the speaking voice. If, in modern expressionist or surrealist painting, we are forced to examine the texture of the surface, the brushwork, the *act of someone painting,* so in modern experimental fiction, we are forced to attend to the speaking voice. I've already spoken about "listening with the third ear." That's especially true for reading experimental fiction, in which characters may dissolve, in which plot may have no development, in which dialogue may sound as artificial as in a comic strip, in which the voice keeps reminding us that this is a fiction. We listen to that voice as we listen to the monologue of a stand-up comic. We hear a narrator create and struggle with his or her own creating. That narrator is not a typical first person narrator, as in Poe—a character talking to us. Neither is he or she the author. Often the narrator is simply a *voice*—a voice the author releases out of his or her bag of voices. But the voice is not the author as a whole. In Barthelme's "Balloon" the voice raps on and on about a fantastic balloon that fills the city. The voice creates the balloon, the reader imagines it and then—like a magician—the narrator lets the balloon dissolve. The fantasy here is not, as in Kafka, a technique for exploring our inner lives; the narrator is dancing, performing, playing with words.

Some readers feel that in fiction of this kind we are more directly in touch with a writer's vision than in traditional fiction, where plot and illusion may get in the way. I myself don't find very much difference: all writers create their fictional worlds; a writer may use traditional plot or no plot, rounded characterization or comic strip characterization—the choices still create the model of experience. The reader's job in any case is to walk around inside that model.

There Are Many Ways of Reading Fiction

There's no one "right" way to read a piece of fiction. There are many good ways. This does *not* mean that anyone's reading of a piece of fiction is equal to anyone else's. There are better and worse readings, depending on how well readers can attune themselves to the story, on how carefully they have looked at the language, become aware of the tone, understood the theme, noticed patterns of imagery, and in general, become quiet and really listened to a separate human being. But given equal attention and sensitivity to a story, there are many legitimate *approaches*.

As an example, let's look at "A Rose for Emily" (it would be a good idea to read the story before continuing) .

So far in this Preface a writer's reading of the story has been offered: one that emphasizes Faulkner's expressive choices. The story isn't something *given;* it is the result of conscious and unconscious choices: the choice of narrator—a first person narrator who represents the town; the choice of tone—dignified and quiet (in contrast to the tone of "The Fall of the House of Usher"); the choice of narrative order—notice how skillfully Faulkner lets his narrator avoid giving away Emily's secret. He jumbles the order of events and throws out false interpretations. Only reading the story for a second time do we realize the significance of Emily's refusal to acknowledge her father's death and let the town bury him; only in rereading do we understand the terrible smell from the house, the purchase of poison. Then there were the choice of rumor and surmise to heighten our expectations and to emphasize the contrast between the secret and public world, and the choices of ending the story with the discovery (no extended denouement) and the intense focus upon Emily's hair next to Homer's skeleton on the bed—a "long strand of iron-gray hair." *Iron-gray*—indicating that even as an old woman she slept with her dead lover, and indicating, too, the rigidity and power of Emily's character. Through his choices, Faulkner gets us into the experience of a legend, then of the terrible secret beneath the legend.

Or—you can read "A Rose for Emily" as a social critic, can talk about the way Emily Grierson represents, in extreme form, the traditional values of the townspeople, including the narrator. She is a fierce image of a mythologized aristocratic past, ennobled by a world caught up by change but hating change. Homer Barron—Emily's lover—is a construction foreman, a Yankee. He represents bourgeois "progress"—paving the sidewalks—and so his murder is not simply the act of a vengeful mad lover but the act of a world that refuses to change. In a reading like this you might talk in detail about the complicity of the town in Emily's madness, about the ways in which that madness is just an exaggeration of the madness of a dying, fixated South. You might go outside the text to discuss the deterioration of the landowning "aristocracy" in the South, the conflict between the values of this class and of the developing bourgeoisie.

Or you can see "A Rose for Emily" in psychological terms, as the story of a woman who could not give up her childhood, the world of her father. She refuses to let the town bury her father, refuses to acknowledge his death. Her rejection of progress—of street numbers, of taxes—shows her regression to a childhood in which her father was God-with-a-horsewhip, keeping her safe from her own adult sexuality. Her father dead, Emily explores her sexuality with Homer Barron, then visits upon him the judgment of the man with the horsewhip and isolates herself in a world of "flowing calligraphy in faded ink," an ancient house, a delusional system in which the past can be preserved.

In moral terms, it is the story of the seductiveness and destructiveness of fixation on an ideal world, the danger of living in a created, mythic past. This danger is just as real to a Russian Jew who hungers for the mythologized life of the *shtetl* (the tiny village communities of Jews in Eastern Europe) or to an American who longs for the "good old days." It is the story of the yearning to stop time, change, growth—to substitute for ongoing experience a past glory. To marry, instead of bury, the dead.

It's also possible to read "A Rose for Emily" with attention to its *thematic structure*. For example, consider the constrast between the public view and the private reality. That basic pattern infuses every part of the story. In public, there is the narrator, who represents the values of the townspeople; there is the gossip of the townspeople, serving as a kind of Greek chorus to the tragedy. In private, there is the secret life of Emily Grierson. In the same way, there is the public mythology versus the private horror; outside the house versus its terrible insides; the public image of a Southern lady versus the disgusting smell and hideous discovery; conventions versus desire; the idealized past versus the "gross, teeming world." These contrasts form the backbone of the story, the rationale behind Faulkner's expressive choices.

There are many other possible readings of "A Rose for Emily"— readings that concentrate on myth, that concentrate on the relations between men and women, that concentrate on the place of this story in the body of Faulkner's work as a whole. How can a reader choose which approach to take?

One answer is you don't have to choose. Many perspectives are valuable; use them as you need them—in the service of your experience of the story, in the service of what you want to *learn*. Another answer is that, in a sense, the reader doesn't have to choose an approach; it is the approach that chooses the reader! Just as you can see a work of fiction as expressing the writer's vision of the world, so you can see a critical approach as expressing the reader's vision of the world. Readers tend to be attracted to writers who are amenable to their way of looking. And they tend to see every writer through more or less the same set of lenses. If you look at the literary criticism of D. H. Lawrence, you find the same preoccupations you find in his fiction; every good critic has certain ways of seeing that are applied to writer after writer. In your reading, you have to truly listen to the writer, but you should listen in your own unique way. You have to read with your categories, your impulses, with what matters in your life. To do that does not mean to distort or disregard the fiction itself; it insures that your reading will deeply engage the work and make it live more fully in yourself and other people.

John J. Clayton

NINETEENTH-CENTURY FICTION

NATHANIEL HAWTHORNE

(1804-1864)

Hawthorne was born in Salem, Massachusetts, where, in the seventeenth century, one ancestor, Judge William Hathorne, had persecuted the Quakers and another, Judge John Hathorne, had presided at the infamous witch trials. Again and again Hawthorne turned back to this heavy past, not as history, certainly not out of nostalgia, but as a stage on which his deepest concerns about the inner life could be acted out sharply and intensely. He was fascinated by his Puritan ancestors, but really more concerned with his own tumultuous soul and the struggles in everyone over guilt and sin, isolation and alienation.

Hawthorne felt himself alienated from the America that was exploding around him; he longed to be a part of the common life and at the same time avoided it, a conflict that recurs in his fiction. Periods of work in the "world" alternated with years of isolation and literary production. He worked in the United States Customs House in Boston and for a short time belonged to the communal society of Brook Farm. He was married in 1842 and held the post of surveyor at the Salem Customs House from 1846 to 1849. During these years he published *Twice Told Tales* (1837) and *Mosses from an Old Manse* (1846) ; he was, however, not at all well known. Then, out of work in 1849–1850, he wrote *The Scarlet Letter* and became suddenly famous. *The House of the Seven Gables,* published a year later, was written at Lenox, Massachusetts, where he became a friend of Herman Melville's (who was about to publish *Moby Dick*) .

When an old friend from his days at Bowdoin College, Franklin Pierce, became President of the United States, Hawthorne was appointed consul at Liverpool. He lived abroad, in England and Italy, returning to Concord, Massachusetts, in 1860. Along with Pierce, he bitterly regretted the Civil War. Hawthorne died near the war's end, in 1864.

"The Minister's Black Veil" and "Young Goodman Brown" are both awesome stories about the results of self-determined isolation. In both, the protagonist is cut off from the community by his recognition of sin. If the stories make you look into your own heart at the secret places there, they also show the danger of such a look if it results in withdrawal rather than compassion.

[See Preface, p. 18 (imagery).]

The Minister's Black Veil

NATHANIEL HAWTHORNE

The sexton stood in the porch of Milford meeting-house, pulling busily at the bell-rope. The old people of the village came stooping along the street. Children, with bright faces, tripped merrily beside their parents, or mimicked a graver gait, in the conscious dignity of their Sunday clothes. Spruce bachelors looked sidelong at the pretty maidens, and fancied that the Sabbath sunshine made them prettier than on week days. When the throng had mostly streamed into the porch, the sexton began to toll the bell, keeping his eye on the Reverend Mr. Hooper's door. The first glimpse of the clergyman's figure was the signal for the bell to cease its summons.

"But what has good Parson Hooper got upon his face?" cried the sexton in astonishment.

All within hearing immediately turned about, and beheld the semblance of Mr. Hooper, pacing slowly his meditative way towards the meeting-house. With one accord they started, expressing more wonder than if some strange minister were coming to dust the cushions of Mr. Hooper's pulpit.

"Are you sure it is our parson?" inquired Goodman Gray of the sexton.

"Of a certainty it is good Mr. Hooper," replied the sexton. "He was to have exchanged pulpits with Parson Shute, of Westbury; but Parson Shute sent to excuse himself yesterday, being to preach a funeral sermon."

The cause of so much amazement may appear sufficiently slight. Mr. Hooper, a gentlemanly person, of about thirty, though still a bachelor, was dressed with due clerical neatness, as if a careful wife had starched his band, and brushed the weekly dust from his Sunday's garb. There was but one thing remarkable in his appearance. Swathed about his forehead, and hanging down over his face, so low as to be shaken by his breath, Mr. Hooper had on a black veil. On a nearer view it seemed to consist of two folds of crape, which entirely concealed his features, except the mouth and chin, but probably did not intercept his sight, further than to give a darkened aspect to all living and inanimate things. With this gloomy shade before him, good Mr. Hooper walked onward, at a slow and quiet pace, stooping somewhat, and looking on the ground, as is customary with abstracted men, yet nodding kindly to those of his parishioners who still waited on the meeting-house steps. But so wonder-struck were they that his greeting hardly met with a return.

"I can't really feel as if good Mr. Hooper's face was behind that piece of crape," said the sexton.

"I don't like it," muttered an old woman, as she hobbled into the meeting-house. "He has changed himself into something awful, only by hiding his face."

"Our parson has gone mad!" cried Goodman Gray, following him across the threshold.

A rumor of some unaccountable phenomenon had preceded Mr. Hooper into the meeting-house, and set all the congregation astir. Few could refrain from twisting their heads towards the door; many stood upright, and turned directly about; while several little boys clambered upon the seats, and came down again with a terrible racket. There was a general bustle, a rustling of the women's gowns and shuffling of the men's feet, greatly at variance with that hushed repose which should attend the entrance of the minister. But Mr. Hooper appeared not to notice the perturbation of his people. He entered with an almost noiseless step, bent his head mildly to the pews on each side, and bowed as he passed his oldest parishioner, a white-haired great-grandsire, who occupied an arm-chair in the centre of the aisle. It was strange to observe how slowly this venerable man became conscious of something singular in the appearance of his pastor. He seemed not fully to partake of the prevailing wonder, till Mr. Hooper had ascended the stairs, and showed himself in the pulpit, face to face with his congregation, except for the black veil. That mysterious emblem was never once withdrawn. It shook with his measured breath, as he gave out the psalm; it threw its obscurity between him and the holy page, as he read the Scriptures; and while he prayed, the veil lay heavily on his uplifted countenance. Did he seek to hide it from the dread Being whom he was addressing?

Such was the effect of this simple piece of crape, that more than one woman of delicate nerves was forced to leave the meeting-house. Yet perhaps the pale-faced congregation was almost as fearful a sight to the minister, as his black veil to them.

Mr. Hooper had the reputation of a good preacher, but not an energetic one: he strove to win his people heavenward by mild, persuasive influences, rather than to drive them thither by the thunders of the Word. The sermon which he now delivered was marked by the same characteristics of style and manner as the general series of his pulpit oratory. But there was something, either in the sentiment of the discourse itself, or in the imagination of the auditors, which made it greatly the most powerful effort that they had ever heard from their pastor's lips. It was tinged, rather more darkly than usual, with the gentle gloom of Mr. Hooper's temperament. The subject had reference to secret sin, and those sad mysteries which we hide from our nearest and dearest, and would fain conceal from our own consciousness, even forgetting that the Omniscient can detect them. A subtle power was breathed into his words. Each member of the congregation, the most innocent girl, and the man of hardened breast, felt as if the preacher had crept upon them, behind his awful veil, and discovered their hoarded iniquity of deed or thought. Many spread their clasped hands on their bosoms. There was nothing terrible in what Mr. Hooper said, at least, no violence; and yet, with every tremor of his melancholy voice, the hearers quaked. An unsought pathos came hand in hand with awe. So sensible were the audience of some unwonted attribute in their minister, that they longed for a breath of wind to blow aside the veil, almost believing that a stranger's visage would be discovered, though the form, gesture, and voice were those of Mr. Hooper.

At the close of the services, the people hurried out with indecorous confusion, eager to communicate their pent-up amazement, and conscious of lighter spirits the moment they lost sight of the black veil. Some gathered in little circles, huddled closely together, with their mouths all whispering in the centre; some went homeward alone, wrapt in silent meditation; some talked loudly, and profaned the Sabbath day with ostentatious laughter. A few shook their sagacious heads, intimating that they could penetrate the mystery; while one or two affirmed that there was no mystery at all, but only that Mr. Hooper's eyes were so weakened by the midnight lamp, as to require a shade. After a brief interval, forth came good Mr. Hooper also, in the rear of his flock. Turning his veiled face from one group to another, he paid due reverence to the hoary heads, saluted the middle aged with kind dignity as their friend and spiritual guide, greeted the young with mingled authority and love, and laid his hands on the little children's heads to bless them. Such was always his custom on the Sabbath day. Strange and bewildered looks repaid him for his courtesy. None, as on former occasions, aspired to the honor of walking by their pastor's side. Old Squire Saunders, doubtless by an accidental lapse of memory, neglected to invite Mr. Hooper to his table, where the good clergyman had been wont to bless the food, almost every Sunday since his settlement. He returned, therefore, to the parsonage, and, at the moment of closing the door, was observed to look back upon the people, all of whom had their eyes fixed upon the minister. A sad smile gleamed faintly from beneath the black veil, and flickered about his mouth, glimmering as he disappeared.

"How strange," said a lady, "that a simple black veil, such as any woman might wear on her bonnet, should become such a terrible thing on Mr. Hooper's face!"

"Something must surely be amiss with Mr. Hooper's intellects," observed her husband, the physician of the village. "But the strangest part of the affair is the effect of this vagary, even on a sober-minded man like myself. The black veil, though it covers only our pastor's face, throws its influence over his whole person, and makes him ghostlike from head to foot. Do you not feel it so?"

"Truly do I," replied the lady; "and I would not be alone with him for the world. I wonder he is not afraid to be alone with himself!"

"Men sometimes are so," said her husband.

The afternoon service was attended with similar circumstances. At its conclusion, the bell tolled for the funeral of a young lady. The relatives and friends were assembled in the house, and the more distant acquaintances stood about the door, speaking of the good qualities of the deceased, when their talk was interrupted by the appearance of Mr. Hooper, still covered with his black veil. It was now an appropriate emblem. The clergyman stepped into the room where the corpse was laid, and bent over the coffin, to take a last farewell of his deceased parishioner. As he stooped, the veil hung straight down from his forehead, so that, if her eyelids had not been closed forever, the dead maiden might have seen his face. Could Mr. Hooper be fearful of her glance, that he so hastily caught back the black veil? A person who watched the interview between the dead and living, scrupled not to affirm, that, at the instant when the clergyman's features were disclosed, the corpse had slightly shuddered, rustling the shroud and muslin cap, though the countenance retained the composure of death. A superstitious old woman was the only witness of this prodigy. From the coffin Mr. Hooper passed into the chamber of the mourners, and thence to the head of the staircase, to make the funeral prayer. It was a tender and heart-dissolving prayer, full of sorrow, yet so imbued with celestial hopes, that the music of a heavenly harp, swept by the fingers of the dead, seemed faintly to be heard among the saddest accents of the minister. The people trembled, though they but darkly understood him when he prayed that they, and himself, and all of mortal race, might be ready, as he trusted this young maiden had been, for the dreadful hour that should snatch the veil from their faces. The bearers went heavily forth, and the mourners followed, saddening all the street, with the dead before them, and Mr. Hooper in his black veil behind.

"Why do you look back?" said one in the procession to his partner.

"I had a fancy," replied she, "that the minister and the maiden's spirit were walking hand in hand."

"And so had I, at the same moment," said the other.

That night, the handsomest couple in Milford village were to be joined in wedlock. Though reckoned a melancholy man, Mr. Hooper had a placid cheerfulness for such occasions, which often excited a sympathetic smile where livelier merriment would have been thrown away. There was no quality of his disposition which made him more beloved than this. The company at the wedding awaited his arrival with impatience, trusting that the strange awe, which had gathered over him throughout the day, would now be dispelled. But such was not the result. When Mr. Hooper came, the first thing that their eyes rested on was the same horrible black veil, which had added deeper gloom to the funeral, and could portend nothing but evil to the wedding. Such was its immediate effect on the guests that a cloud seemed to have rolled duskily from beneath the black crape, and dimmed the light of the candles. The bridal pair stood up before the minister. But the bride's cold fingers quivered in the tremulous hand of the bridegroom, and her deathlike paleness caused a whisper that the maiden who had been buried a few hours before was come from her grave to be married. If ever another wedding were so dismal, it was that famous one where they tolled the wedding knell. After performing the ceremony, Mr. Hooper raised a glass of wine to his lips, wishing happiness to the new-married couple in a strain of mild pleasantry that ought to have brightened the features of the guests, like a cheerful gleam from the hearth. At that instant, catching a glimpse of his figure in the looking-glass, the black veil involved his own spirit in the horror with which it overwhelmed all others. His frame shuddered, his lips grew white, he spilt the untasted wine upon the carpet, and rushed forth into the darkness. For the Earth, too, had on her Black Veil.

The next day, the whole village of Milford talked of little else than Parson Hooper's black veil. That, and the mystery concealed behind it, supplied a topic for discussion between acquaintances meeting in the street, and good women gossiping at their open windows. It was the first item of news that the tavern-keeper told to his guests. The children babbled of it on their way to school. One imitative little imp covered his face with an old black handkerchief, thereby so affrighting his playmates that the panic seized himself, and he well-nigh lost his wits by his own waggery.

It was remarkable that of all the busybodies and impertinent people in the parish, not one ventured to put the plain question to Mr. Hooper, wherefore he did this thing. Hitherto, whenever there appeared the slightest call for such interference, he had never lacked advisers, nor shown himself averse to be guided by their judgment. If he erred at all, it was by so painful a degree of self-distrust, that even the mildest censure would lead him to consider an indifferent action as a crime. Yet, though so well acquainted with this amiable weakness, no individual among his parishioners chose to make the black veil a subject of friendly remonstrance. There was a feeling of dread, neither plainly confessed nor carefully concealed, which caused each to shift the responsibility upon another, till at length it was found expedient to send a deputation of the church, in order to deal with Mr. Hooper about the mystery, before it should grow into a scandal. Never did an embassy so ill discharge its duties. The minister received them with friendly courtesy, but became silent, after they were seated, leaving to his visitors the whole burden of introducing their important business. The topic, it might be supposed, was obvious enough. There was the black veil swathed round Mr. Hooper's forehead, and concealing every feature above his placid mouth, on which, at times, they could perceive the glimmering of a melancholy smile. But that piece of crape, to their imagination, seemed to hang down before his heart, the symbol of a fearful secret between him and them. Were the veil but cast aside, they might speak freely of it, but not till then. Thus they sat a considerable time, speechless, confused, and shrinking uneasily from Mr. Hooper's eye, which they felt to be fixed upon them with an invisible glance. Finally, the deputies returned abashed to their constituents, pronouncing the matter too weighty to be handled, except by a council of the churches, if, indeed, it might not require a general synod.

But there was one person in the village unappalled by the awe with which the black veil had impressed all beside herself. When the deputies returned without an explanation, or even venturing to demand one, she, with the calm energy of her character, determined to chase away the strange cloud that appeared to be settling round Mr. Hooper, every moment more darkly than before. As his plighted wife, it should be her privilege to know what the black veil concealed. At the minister's first visit, therefore, she entered upon the subject with a direct simplicity, which made the task easier both for him and her. After he had seated himself, she fixed her eyes steadfastly upon the veil, but could discern nothing of the dreadful gloom that had so overawed the multitude: it was but a double fold of crape, hanging down from his forehead to his mouth, and slightly stirring with his breath.

"No," said she aloud, and smiling, "there is nothing terrible in this piece of crape, except that it hides a face which I am always glad to look upon. Come, good sir, let the sun shine from behind the cloud. First lay aside your black veil: then tell me why you put it on."

Mr. Hooper's smile glimmered faintly.

"There is an hour to come," said he, "when all of us shall cast aside our veils. Take it not amiss, beloved friend, if I wear this piece of crape till then."

"Your words are a mystery, too," returned the young lady. "Take away the veil from them, at least."

"Elizabeth, I will," said he, "so far as my vow may suffer me. Know, then, this veil is a type and a symbol, and I am bound to wear it ever, both in light and darkness, in solitude and before the gaze of multitudes, and as with strangers, so with my familiar friends. No mortal eye will see it withdrawn. This dismal shade must separate me from the world: even you, Elizabeth, can never come behind it!"

"What grievous affliction hath befallen you," she earnestly inquired, "that you should thus darken your eyes forever?"

"If it be a sign of mourning," replied Mr. Hooper, "I, perhaps, like most other mortals, have sorrows dark enough to be typified by a black veil."

"But what if the world will not believe that it is the type of an innocent sorrow?" urged Elizabeth. "Beloved and respected as you are, there may be whispers that you hide your face under the consciousness of secret sin. For the sake of your holy office, do away this scandal!"

The color rose into her cheeks as she intimated the nature of the rumors that were already abroad in the village. But Mr. Hooper's mildness did not forsake him. He even smiled again—that same sad smile, which always appeared like a faint glimmering of light, proceeding from the obscurity beneath the veil.

"If I hide my face for sorrow, there is cause enough," he merely replied; "and if I cover it for secret sin, what mortal might not do the same?"

And with this gentle, but unconquerable obstinacy did he resist all her entreaties. At length Elizabeth sat silent. For a few moments she appeared lost in thought, considering, probably, what new methods might be tried to withdraw her lover from so dark a fantasy, which, if it had no other meaning, was perhaps a symptom of mental disease. Though of a firmer character than his own, the tears rolled down her cheeks. But, in an instant, as it were, a new feeling took the place of sorrow: her eyes were fixed insensibly on the black veil, when, like a sudden twilight in the air, its terrors fell around her. She arose, and stood trembling before him.

"And do you feel it then, at last?" said he mournfully.

She made no reply, but covered her eyes with her hand, and turned to leave the room. He rushed forward and caught her arm.

"Have patience with me, Elizabeth!" cried he, passionately. "Do not desert me, though this veil must be between us here on earth. Be mine, and hereafter there shall be no veil over my face, no darkness between our souls! It is but a mortal veil—it is not for eternity! O! you know not how lonely I am, and how frightened, to be alone behind my black veil. Do not leave me in this miserable obscurity forever!"

"Lift the veil but once, and look me in the face," said she.

"Never! It cannot be!" replied Mr. Hooper.

"Then farewell!" said Elizabeth.

She withdrew her arm from his grasp, and slowly departed, pausing at the door, to give one long shuddering gaze, that seemed almost to penetrate the mystery of the black veil. But, even amid his grief, Mr. Hooper smiled to think that only a material emblem had separated him from happiness, though the horrors, which it shadowed forth, must be drawn darkly between the fondest of lovers.

From that time no attempts were made to remove Mr. Hooper's black veil, or, by a direct appeal, to discover the secret which it was supposed to hide. By persons who claimed a superiority to popular prejudice, it was reckoned merely an eccentric whim, such as often mingles with the sober actions of men otherwise rational, and tinges them all with its own semblance of insanity. But with the multitude, good Mr. Hooper was irreparably a bugbear. He could not walk the street with any piece of mind, so conscious was he that the gentle and timid would turn aside to avoid him, and that others would make it a point of hardihood to throw themselves in his way. The impertinence of the latter class compelled him to give up his customary walk at sunset to the burial ground; for when he leaned pensively over the gate, there would always be faces behind the gravestones, peeping at his black veil. A fable went the rounds that the stare of the dead people drove him thence. It grieved him, to the very depth of his kind heart, to observe how the children fled from his approach, breaking up their merriest sports, while his melancholy figure was yet afar off. Their instinctive dread caused him to feel more strongly than aught else, that a preternatural horror was interwoven with the threads of the black crape. In truth, his own antipathy to the veil was known to be so great, that he never willingly passed before a mirror, nor stooped to drink at a still fountain, lest, in its peaceful bosom, he should be affrighted by himself. This was what gave plausibility to the whispers, that Mr. Hooper's conscience tortured him for some great crime too horrible to be entirely concealed, or otherwise than so obscurely intimated. Thus, from beneath the black veil, there rolled a cloud into the sunshine, an ambiguity of sin or sorrow, which enveloped the poor minister, so that love or sympathy could never reach him. It was said that ghost and fiend consorted with him there.

With self-shudderings and outward terrors, he walked continually in its shadow, groping darkly within his own soul, or gazing through a medium that saddened the whole world. Even the lawless wind, it was believed, respected his dreadful secret, and never blew aside the veil. But still good Mr. Hooper sadly smiled at the pale visages of the worldly throng as he passed by.

Among all its bad influences, the black veil had the one desirable effect, of making its wearer a very efficient clergyman. By the aid of his mysterious emblem—for there was no other apparent cause—he became a man of awful power over souls that were in agony for sin. His converts always regarded him with a dread peculiar to themselves, affirming, though but figuratively, that, before he brought them to celestial light, they had been with him behind the black veil. Its gloom, indeed, enabled him to sympathize with all dark affections. Dying sinners cried aloud for Mr. Hooper, and would not yield their breath till he appeared; though ever, as he stopped to whisper consolation, they shuddered at the veiled face so near their own. Such were the terrors of the black veil, even when Death had bared his visage! Strangers came long distances to attend service at his church, with the mere idle purpose of gazing at his figure, because it was forbidden them to behold his face. But many were made to quake ere they departed! Once, during Governor Belcher's administration, Mr. Hooper was appointed to preach the election sermon. Covered with his black veil, he stood before the chief magistrate, the council, and the representatives, and wrought so deep an impression, that the legislative measures of that year were characterized by all the gloom and piety of our earliest ancestral sway.

In this manner Mr. Hooper spent a long life, irreproachable in outward act, yet shrouded in dismal suspicions; kind and loving, though unloved, and dimly feared; a man apart from men, shunned in their health and joy, but ever summoned to their aid in mortal anguish. As years wore on, shedding their snows above his sable veil, he acquired a name throughout the New England churches, and they called him Father Hooper. Nearly all his parishioners, who were of mature age when he was settled, had been borne away by many a funeral: he had one congregation in the church, and a more crowded one in the churchyard; and having wrought so late into the evening, and done his work so well, it was now good Father Hooper's turn to rest.

Several persons were visible by the shaded candle-light, in the death chamber of the old clergyman. Natural connections he had none. But there was the decorously grave, though unmoved physician, seeking only to mitigate the last pangs of the patient whom he could not save. There were the deacons, and other eminently pious members of his church. There, also, was the Reverend Mr. Clark, of Westbury, a young and zealous divine, who had ridden in haste to pray by the bedside of the expiring minister. There was the nurse, no hired handmaiden of death, but one whose calm affection had endured thus long in secrecy, in solitude, amid the chill of age, and would not perish, even at the dying hour. Who, but Elizabeth! And there lay the hoary head of good Father Hooper upon the death pillow, with the black veil still swathed about his brow, and reaching down over his face, so that each more difficult gasp of his faint breath caused it to stir. All through life that piece of crape had hung between him and the world: it had separated him from cheerful brotherhood and woman's love, and kept him in that saddest of all prisons, his own heart; and still it lay upon his face, as if to deepen the gloom of his darksome chamber, and shade him from the sunshine of eternity.

For some time previous, his mind had been confused, wavering doubtfully between the past and the present, and hovering forward, as it were, at intervals, into the indistinctness of the world to come. There had been feverish turns, which tossed him from side to side, and wore away what little strength he had. But in his most convulsive struggles, and in the wildest vagaries of his intellect, when no other thought retained its sober influence, he still showed an awful solicitude lest the black veil should slip aside. Even if his bewildered soul could have forgotten, there was a faithful woman at his pillow, who, with averted eyes, would have covered that aged face, which she had last beheld in the comeliness of manhood. At length the death-stricken old man lay quietly in the torpor of mental and bodily exhaustion, with an imperceptible pulse, and breath that grew fainter and fainter, except when a long, deep, and irregular inspiration seemed to preclude the flight of his spirit.

The minister of Westbury approached the bedside.

"Venerable Father Hooper," said he, "the moment of your release is at hand. Are you ready for the lifting of the veil that shuts in time from eternity?"

Father Hooper at first replied merely by a feeble motion of his head; then, apprehensive, perhaps, that his meaning might be doubtful, he exerted himself to speak.

"Yea," said he, in faint accents, "my soul hath a patient weariness until that veil be lifted."

"And is it fitting," resumed the Reverend Mr. Clark, "that a man so given to prayer, of such a blameless example, holy in deed and thought, so far as mortal judgment may pronounce; is it fitting that a father in the church should leave a shadow on his memory, that may seem to blacken a life so pure? I pray you, my venerable brother, let not this thing be! Suffer us to be gladdened by your triumphant aspect as you go to your reward. Before the veil of eternity be lifted, let me cast aside this black veil from your face!"

And thus speaking, the Reverend Mr. Clark bent forward to reveal the mystery of so many years. But, exerting a sudden energy, that made all the beholders stand aghast, Father Hooper snatched both his hands from beneath the bedclothes, and pressed them strongly on the black veil, resolute to struggle, if the minister of Westbury would contend with a dying man.

"Never!" cried the veiled clergyman. "On earth, never!"

"Dark old man!" exclaimed the affrighted minister, "with what horrible crime upon your soul are you now passing to the judgment?"

Father Hooper's breath heaved; it rattled in his throat; but, with a mighty effort, grasping forward with his hands, he caught hold of life, and held it back till he should speak. He even raised himself in bed; and there he sat, shivering with the arms of death around him, while the black veil hung down, awful, at that last moment, in the gathered terrors of a lifetime. And yet the faint, sad smile, so often there, now seemed to glimmer from its obscurity, and linger on Father Hooper's lips.

"Why do you tremble at me alone?" cried he, turning his veiled face round the circle of pale spectators. "Tremble also at each other! Have men avoided me, and women shown no pity, and children screamed and fled, only for my black veil? What, but the mystery which it obscurely typifies, has made this piece of crape so awful? When the friend shows his inmost heart to his friend; the lover to his best beloved; when man does not vainly shrink from the eye of his Creator, loathsomely treasuring up the secret of his sin; then deem me a monster, for the symbol beneath which I have lived, and die! I look around me, and lo! on every visage a Black Veil!"

While his auditors shrank from one another, in mutual affright, Father Hooper fell back upon his pillow, a veiled corpse, with a faint smile lingering on the lips. Still veiled, they laid him in his coffin, and a veiled corpse they bore him to the grave. The grass of many years has sprung up and withered on that grave, the burial stone is moss-grown, and good Mr. Hooper's face is dust; but awful is still the thought that it mouldered beneath the Black Veil!

QUESTIONS

1. Why does a simple black veil so isolate Mr. Hooper? Why do his words become so potent?
2. The veil across the minister's eyes gives a "darkened aspect to all living and inanimate things." It is the opposite, then, of seeing the world

through rose-colored glasses. In what way does it intensify, in what ways distort, Mr. Hooper's vision?

3. "There is an hour to come . . . when all of us shall cast aside our veils," Mr. Hooper says to his fiancée. What veils does he mean? How are the veils we all wear like and unlike the one he wears?

4. The black veil is more than a prop in a story; it is a central image (see Preface, pp. 18–19) expressing a sense of life. *Whose* sense of life? Is Hawthorne trying to remind his reader of our secret sins or of our guilt and the isolation it creates? What do you think is the relation between Mr. Hooper and his author?

Young Goodman Brown

NATHANIEL HAWTHORNE

Young Goodman Brown came forth at sunset, into the street of Salem village, but put his head back, after crossing the threshold, to exchange a parting kiss with his young wife. And Faith, as the wife was aptly named, thrust her own pretty head into the street, letting the wind play with the pink ribbons of her cap, while she called to Goodman Brown.

"Dearest heart," whispered she, softly and rather sadly, when her lips were close to his ear, "prithee, put off your journey until sunrise, and sleep in your own bed to-night. A lone woman is troubled with such dreams and such thoughts, that she's afeard of herself, sometimes. Pray, tarry with me this night, dear husband, of all nights in the year!"

"My love and my Faith," replied young Goodman Brown, "of all nights in the year, this one night must I tarry away from thee. My journey, as thou callest it, forth and back again, must needs be done 'twixt now and sunrise. What, my sweet, pretty wife, dost thou doubt me already, and we but three months married!"

"Then God bless you!" said Faith with the pink ribbons, "and may you find all well, when you come back."

"Amen!" cried Goodman Brown. "Say thy prayers, dear Faith, and go to bed at dusk, and no harm will come to thee."

So they parted; and the young man pursued his way, until, being about to turn the corner by the meeting-house, he looked back and saw the head of Faith still peeping after him, with a melancholy air, in spite of her pink ribbons.

"Poor little Faith!" thought he, for his heart smote him. "What a wretch am I, to leave her on such an errand! She talks of dreams, too. Methought, as she spoke, there was trouble in her face, as if a dream had warned her what work is to be done to-night. But no, no! 't would kill her to think it. Well; she's a blessed angel on earth; and after this one night, I'll cling to her skirts and follow her to Heaven."

With this excellent resolve for the future, Goodman Brown felt himself justified in making more haste on his present evil purpose. He had taken a dreary road, darkened by all the gloomiest trees of the forest, which barely stood aside to let the narrow path creep through, and closed immediately behind. It was all as lonely as could be; and there is this peculiarity in such a solitude, that the traveller knows not who may be concealed by the innumerable trunks and the thick boughs overhead; so that, with lonely footsteps, he may yet be passing through an unseen multitude.

"There may be a devilish Indian behind every tree," said Goodman Brown to himself; and he glanced fearfully behind him, as he added, "What if the devil himself should be at my very elbow!"

His head being turned back, he passed a crook of the road, and looking forward again, beheld the figure of a man, in grave and decent attire, seated at the foot of an old tree. He arose at Goodman Brown's approach, and walked onward, side by side with him.

"You are late, Goodman Brown," said he. "The clock of the Old South was striking, as I came through Boston; and that is full fifteen minutes agone."

"Faith kept me back awhile," replied the young man, with a tremor in his voice, caused by the sudden appearance of his companion, though not wholly unexpected.

It was now deep dusk in the forest, and deepest in that part of it where these two were journeying. As nearly as could be discerned, the second traveller was about fifty years old, apparently in the same rank of life as Goodman Brown, and bearing a considerable resemblance to him, though perhaps more in expression than features. Still, they might have been taken for father and son. And yet, though the elder person was as simply clad as the younger, and as simple in manner too, he had an indescribable air of one who knew the world, and would not have felt abashed at the governor's dinner-table, or in King William's court, were it possible that his affairs should call him thither. But the only thing about him that could be fixed upon as remarkable, was his staff, which bore the likeness of a great black snake, so curiously wrought, that it might almost be seen to twist and wriggle itself like a living serpent. This, of course, must have been an ocular deception, assisted by the uncertain light.

"Come, Goodman Brown!" cried his fellow-traveller, "this is a dull pace for the beginning of a journey. Take my staff, if you are so soon weary."

"Friend," said the other, exchanging his slow pace for a full stop, "having kept covenant by meeting thee here, it is my purpose now to return whence I came. I have scruples, touching the matter thou wot'st of."

"Sayest thou so?" replied he of the serpent, smiling apart. "Let us walk on, nevertheless, reasoning as we go, and if I convince thee not, thou shalt turn back. We are but a little way in the forest, yet."

"Too far, too far!" exclaimed the goodman, unconsciously resuming his walk. "My father never went into the woods on such an errand, nor his father before him. We have been a race of honest men and good Christians, since the days of the martyrs. And shall I be the first of the name of Brown that ever took this path and kept—"

"Such company, thou wouldst say," observed the elder person, interrupting his pause. "Well said, Goodman Brown! I have been as well acquainted with your family as with ever a one among the Puritans; and that's no trifle to say. I helped your grandfather, the constable, when he lashed the Quaker woman so smartly through the streets of Salem. And it was I that brought your father a pitch-pine knot, kindled at my own hearth, to set fire to an Indian village, in King Philip's war. They were my good friends, both; and many a pleasant walk have we had along this path, and returned merrily after midnight. I would fain be friends with you, for their sake."

"If it be as thou sayest," replied Goodman Brown, "I marvel they never spoke of these matters. Or, verily, I marvel not, seeing that the least rumor of the sort would have driven them from New England. We are a people of prayer, and good works to boot, and abide no such wickedness."

"Wickedness or not," said the traveller with twisted staff, "I have a very general acquaintance here in New England. The deacons of many a church have drunk the communion wine with me; the selectmen, of divers towns, make me their chairman; and a majority of the Great and General Court are firm supporters of my interest. The governor and I, too—but these are state secrets."

"Can this be so!" cried Goodman Brown, with a stare of amazement at his undisturbed companion. "Howbeit, I have nothing to do with the governor and council; they have their own ways, and are no rule for a simple husbandman like me. But, were I to go on with thee, how should I meet the eye of that good old man, our minister, at Salem village? Oh, his voice would make me tremble, both Sabbath-day and lecture-day!"

Thus far, the elder traveller had listened with due gravity, but now burst into a fit of irrepressible mirth, shaking himself so violently, that his snakelike staff actually seemed to wriggle in sympathy.

"Ha! ha! ha!" shouted he, again and again; then composing himself, "Well, go on, Goodman Brown, go on; but, prithee, don't kill me with laughing!"

"Well, then, to end the matter at once," said Goodman Brown, considerably nettled, "there is my wife, Faith. It would break her dear little heart; and I'd rather break my own!"

"Nay, if that be the case," answered the other, "e'en go thy ways, Goodman Brown. I would not, for twenty old women like the one hobbling before us, that Faith should come to any harm."

As he spoke, he pointed his staff at a female figure on the path, in whom Goodman Brown recognized a very pious and exemplary dame, who had taught him his catechism in youth, and was still his moral and spiritual adviser, jointly with the minister and Deacon Gookin.

"A marvel, truly, that Goody Cloyse should be so far in the wilderness, at nightfall!" said he. "But, with your leave, friend, I shall take a cut through the woods, until we have left this Christian woman behind. Being a stranger to you, she might ask whom I was consorting with, and whither I was going."

"Be it so," said his fellow-traveller. "Betake you to the woods, and let me keep the path."

Accordingly, the young man turned aside, but took care to watch his companion, who advanced softly along the road, until he had come within a staff's length of the old dame. She, meanwhile, was making the best of her way, with singular speed for so aged a woman, and mumbling some indistinct words, a prayer, doubtless, as she went. The traveller put forth his staff, and touched her withered neck with what seemed the serpent's tail.

"The devil!" screamed the pious old lady.

"Then Goody Cloyse knows her old friend?" observed the traveller, confronting her, and leaning on his writhing stick.

"Ah, forsooth, and is it your worship, indeed?" cried the good dame. "Yea, truly is it, and in the very image of my old gossip, Goodman Brown, the grandfather of the silly fellow that now is. But, would your worship believe it? my broomstick hath strangely disappeared, stolen, as I suspect, by that unhanged witch, Goody Cory, and that, too, when I was all anointed with the juice of smallage and cinque-foil and wolf's-bane—"

"Mingled with fine wheat and the fat of a new-born babe," said the shape of old Goodman Brown.

"Ah, your worship knows the recipe," cried the old lady, cackling aloud. "So, as I was saying, being all ready for the meeting, and no horse to ride on, I made up my mind to foot it; for they tell me there is a nice young man to be taken into communion to-night. But now your good worship will lend me your arm, and we shall be there in a twinkling."

"That can hardly be," answered her friend. "I may not spare you my arm, Goody Cloyse, but here is my staff, if you will."

So saying, he threw it down at her feet, where, perhaps, it assumed life, being one of the rods which its owner had formerly lent to the Egyptian Magi. Of this fact, however, Goodman Brown could not take cognizance. He had cast up his eyes in astonishment, and looking down again, beheld neither Goody Cloyse nor the serpentine staff, but his fellow-traveller alone, who waited for him as calmly as if nothing had happened.

"That old woman taught me my catechism!" said the young man; and there was a world of meaning in this simple comment.

They continued to walk onward, while the elder traveller exhorted his companion to make good speed and persevere in the path, discoursing so aptly, that his arguments seemed rather to spring up in the bosom of his auditor, than to be suggested by himself. As they went he plucked a branch of maple, to serve for a walking-stick, and began to strip it of the twigs and little boughs, which were wet with evening dew. The moment his fingers touched them, they became strangely withered and dried up, as with a week's sunshine. Thus the pair proceeded, at a good free·pace, until suddenly, in a gloomy hollow of the road, Goodman Brown sat himself down on the stump of a tree, and refused to go any farther.

"Friend," said he, stubbornly, "my mind is made up. Not another step will I budge on this errand. What if a wretched old woman do choose to go to the devil, when I thought she was going to Heaven! Is that any reason why I should quit my dear Faith, and go after her?"

"You will think better of this by and by," said his acquaintance, composedly. "Sit here and rest yourself awhile; and when you feel like moving again, there is my staff to help you along."

Without more words, he threw his companion the maple stick, and was as speedily out of sight as if he had vanished into the deepening gloom. The young man sat a few moments by the roadside, applauding himself greatly, and thinking with how clear a conscience he should meet the minister, in his morning walk, nor shrink from the eye of good old Deacon Gookin. And what calm sleep would be his, that very night, which was to have been spent so wickedly, but purely and sweetly now, in the arms of Faith! Amidst these pleasant and praiseworthy meditations, Goodman Brown heard the tramp of horses along the road, and deemed it advisable to conceal himself within the verge of the forest, conscious of the guilty purpose that had brought him thither, though now so happily turned from it.

On came the hoof-tramps and the voices of the riders, two grave old voices, conversing soberly as they drew near. These mingled sounds appeared to pass along the road, within a few yards of the young man's hiding-place; but owing, doubtless, to the depth of the gloom, at that particular spot, neither the travellers nor their steeds were visible. Though their figures brushed the small boughs by the wayside, it could not be seen that they intercepted, even for a moment, the faint gleam from the strip of bright sky, athwart which they must have passed. Goodman Brown alternately crouched and stood on tiptoe, pulling aside the branches, and thrusting forth his head as far as he durst, without discerning so much as a shadow. It vexed him the more, because he could have sworn, were such a thing possible, that he recognized the voices of the minister and Deacon Gookin, jogging along quietly, as they were wont to do, when bound to some ordination or ecclesiastical council. While yet within hearing, one of the riders stopped to pluck a switch.

"Of the two, reverend Sir," said the voice like the deacon's, "I had rather miss an ordination dinner than to-night's meeting. They tell me that some of our community are to be here from Falmouth and beyond, and others from Connecticut and Rhode Island; besides several of the Indian powwows, who, after their fashion, know almost as much deviltry as the best of us. Moreover, there is a goodly young woman to be taken into communion."

"Mighty well, Deacon Gookin!" replied the solemn old tones of the minister. "Spur up, or we shall be late. Nothing can be done, you know, until I get on the ground."

The hoofs clattered again, and the voices, talking so strangely in the empty air, passed on through the forest, where no church had ever been gathered, nor solitary Christian prayed. Whither, then, could these holy men be journeying, so deep into the heathen wilderness? Young Goodman Brown caught hold of a tree, for support, being ready to sink down on the ground, faint and over-burthened with the heavy sickness of his heart. He looked up to the sky, doubting whether there really was a Heaven above him. Yet, there was the blue arch, and the stars brightening in it.

"With Heaven above, and Faith below, I will yet stand firm against the devil!" cried Goodman Brown.

While he still gazed upward, into the deep arch of the firmament, and had lifted his hands to pray, a cloud, though no wind was stirring, hurried across the zenith, and hid the brightening stars. The blue sky was still visible, except directly overhead, where this black mass of cloud was sweeping swiftly northward. Aloft in the air, as if from the depths of the cloud, came a confused and doubtful sound of voices. Once, the listener fancied that he could distinguish the accents of town's-people of his own, men and women, both pious and ungodly, many of whom he had met at the communion-table, and had seen others rioting at the tavern. The next moment, so indistinct were the sounds, he doubted whether he had heard aught but the murmur of the old forest, whispering without a wind. Then came a stronger swell of those familiar tones, heard daily in the sunshine, at Salem village, but never, until now, from a cloud at night. There was one voice, of a young woman, uttering lamentations, yet with an uncertain sorrow, and entreating for some favor, which, perhaps, it would grieve her to obtain. And all the unseen multitude, both saints and sinners, seemed to encourage her onward.

"Faith!" shouted Goodman Brown, in a voice of agony and desperation; and the echoes of the forest mocked him, crying—"Faith! Faith!" as if bewildered wretches were seeking her, all through the wilderness.

The cry of grief, rage, and terror was yet piercing the night, when the unhappy husband held his breath for a response. There was a scream, drowned immediately in a louder murmur of voices fading into far-off laughter, as the dark cloud swept away, leaving the clear and silent sky above Goodman Brown. But something fluttered lightly down through the air, and caught on the branch of a tree. The young man seized it and beheld a pink ribbon.

"My Faith is gone!" cried he, after one stupefied moment. "There is no good on earth, and sin is but a name. Come, devil! for to thee is this world given."

And maddened with despair, so that he laughed loud and long, did Goodman Brown grasp his staff and set forth again, at such a rate, that he seemed to fly along the forest path, rather than to walk or run. The road grew wilder and drearier, and more faintly traced, and vanished at length, leaving him in the heart of the dark wilderness, still rushing onward, with the instinct that guides mortal man to evil. The whole forest was peopled with frightful sounds; the creaking of the trees, the howling of wild beasts, and the yell of Indians; while, sometimes, the wind tolled like a distant church bell, and sometimes gave a broad roar around the traveller, as if all Nature were laughing him to scorn. But he was himself the chief horror of the scene, and shrank not from its other horrors.

"Ha! ha! ha!" roared Goodman Brown, when the wind laughed at him. "Let us hear which will laugh loudest! Think not to frighten me with your deviltry! Come witch, come wizard, come Indian powwow, come devil himself! and here comes Goodman Brown. You may as well fear him as he fear you!"

In truth, all through the haunted forest, there could be nothing more frightful than the figure of Goodman Brown. On he flew, among the black pines, brandishing his staff with frenzied gestures, now giving vent to an inspiration of horrid blasphemy, and now shouting forth such laughter, as set all the echoes of the forest laughing like demons around him. The fiend in his own shape is less hideous, than when he rages in the breast of man. Thus sped the demoniac on his course, until, quivering among the trees, he saw a red light before him, as when the felled trunks and branches of a clearing have been set on fire, and throw up their lurid blaze against the sky, at the hour of midnight. He paused, in a lull of the tempest that had driven him onward, and heard the swell of what seemed a hymn, rolling solemnly from a distance, with the weight of many voices. He knew the tune. It was a familiar one in the choir of the village meeting-house. The verse died heavily away, and was lengthened by a chorus, not of human voices, but of all the sounds of the benighted wilderness, pealing in awful harmony together. Goodman Brown cried out; and his cry was lost to his own ear, by its unison with the cry of the desert.

In the interval of silence, he stole forward, until the light glared full upon his eyes. At one extremity of an open space, hemmed in by the dark wall of the forest, arose a rock, bearing some rude, natural resemblance either to an altar or a pulpit, and surrounded by four blazing pines, their tops aflame, their stems untouched, like candles at an evening meeting. The mass of foliage, that had overgrown the summit of the rock, was all on fire, blazing high into the night, and fitfully illuminating the whole field. Each pendent twig and leafy festoon was in a blaze. As the red light arose and fell, a numerous congregation alternately shone forth, then disappeared in shadow, and again grew, as it were, out of the darkness, peopling the heart of the solitary woods at once.

"A grave and dark-clad company!" quoth Goodman Brown.

In truth, they were such. Among them, quivering to-and-fro, between gloom and splendor, appeared faces that would be seen, next day, at the council-board of the province, and others which, Sabbath after Sabbath, looked devoutly heavenward, and benignantly over the crowded pews, from the holiest pulpits in the land. Some affirm that the lady of the governor was there. At least, there were high dames well known to her, and wives of honored husbands, and widows a great multitude, and ancient maidens, all of excellent repute, and fair young girls, who trembled lest their mothers should espy them. Either the sudden gleams of light, flashing over the obscure field, bedazzled Goodman Brown, or he recognized a score of the church members of Salem village, famous for their especial sanctity. Good old Deacon Gookin had arrived, and waited at the skirts of that venerable saint, his reverend pastor. But, irreverently consorting with these grave, reputable, and pious people, these elders of the church, these chaste dames and dewy virgins, there were men of dissolute lives and women of spotted fame, wretches given over to all mean and filthy vice, and suspected even of horrid crimes. It was strange to see, that the good shrank not from the wicked, nor were the sinners abashed by the saints. Scattered, also, among their pale-faced enemies, were the Indian priests, or powwows, who had often scared their native forest with more hideous incantations than any known to English witchcraft.

"But, where is Faith?" thought Goodman Brown; and, as hope came into his heart, he trembled.

Another verse of the hymn arose, a slow and mournful strain, such as the pious love, but joined to words which expressed all that our nature can conceive of sin, and darkly hinted at far more. Unfathomable to mere mortals is the lore of fiends. Verse after verse was sung, and still the chorus of the desert swelled between, like the deepest tone of a mighty organ. And, with the final peal of that dreadful anthem, there came a sound, as if the roaring wind, the rushing streams, the howling beasts, and every other voice of the unconverted wilderness were mingling and according with the voice of guilty man, in homage to the prince of all. The four blazing pines threw up a loftier flame, and obscurely discovered shapes and visages of horror on the smoke-wreaths, above the impious assembly. At the same moment, the fire on the rock shot redly forth, and formed a glowing arch above its base, where now appeared a figure. With reverence be it spoken, the apparition bore no slight similitude, both in garb and manner, to some grave divine of the New England churches.

"Bring forth the converts!" cried a voice, that echoed through the field and rolled into the forest.

At the word, Goodman Brown stepped forth from the shadow of the trees, and approached the congregation, with whom he felt a loathful brotherhood, by the sympathy of all that was wicked in his heart. He could have well-nigh sworn, that the shape of his own dead father beckoned him to advance, looking downward from a smoke-wreath, while a woman, with dim features of despair, threw out her hand to warn him back. Was it his mother? But he had no power to retreat one step, nor to resist, even in thought, when the minister and good old Deacon Gookin seized his arms, and led him to the blazing rock. Thither came also the slender form of a veiled female, led between Goody Cloyse, that pious teacher of the catechism, and Martha Carrier, who had received the devil's promise to be queen of hell. A rampant hag was she! And there stood the proselytes, beneath the canopy of fire.

"Welcome, my children," said the dark figure, "to the communion of your race! Ye have found, thus young, your nature and your destiny. My children, look behind you!"

They turned; and flashing forth, as it were, in a sheet of flame, the fiend-worshippers were seen; the smile of welcome gleamed darkly on every visage.

"There," resumed the sable form, "are all whom ye have reverenced from youth. Ye deemed them holier than yourselves, and shrank from your own sin, contrasting it with their lives of righteousness and prayerful aspirations heavenward. Yet, here are they all, in my worshipping assembly! This night it shall be granted you to know their secret deeds; how hoary-bearded elders of the church have whispered wanton words to the young maids of their households; how many a woman, eager for widow's weeds, has given her husband a drink at bedtime, and let him sleep his last sleep in her bosom; how beardless youths have made haste to inherit their father's wealth; and how fair damsels—blush not, sweet ones!—have dug little graves in the garden, and bidden me, the sole guest, to an infant's funeral. By the sympathy of your human hearts for sin, ye shall scent out all the places—whether in church, bed-chamber, street, field, or forest— where crime has been committed, and shall exult to behold the whole earth one stain of guilt, one mighty blood-spot. Far more than this! It shall be yours to penetrate, in every bosom, the deep mystery of sin, the fountain of all wicked arts, and which inexhaustibly supplies more evil impulses than human power—than my power, at its utmost!—can make manifest in deeds. And now, my children, look upon each other."

They did so; and, by the blaze of the hell-kindled torches, the wretched man beheld his Faith, and the wife her husband, trembling before that unhallowed altar.

"Lo! there ye stand, my children," said the figure, in a deep and solemn tone, almost sad, with its despairing awfulness, as if his once angelic nature could yet mourn for our miserable race. "Depending upon one another's hearts, ye had still hoped that virtue were not all a dream! Now are ye undeceived!—Evil is the nature of mankind. Evil must be your only happiness. Welcome, again, my children, to the communion of your race!"

"Welcome!" repeated the fiend-worshippers, in one cry of despair and triumph.

And there they stood, the only pair, as it seemed, who were yet hesitating on the verge of wickedness, in this dark world. A basin was hollowed, naturally, in the rock. Did it contain water, reddened by the lurid light? or was it blood? or, perchance, a liquid flame? Herein did the Shape of Evil dip his hand, and prepare to lay the mark of baptism upon their foreheads, that they might be partakers of the mystery of sin, more conscious of the secret guilt of others, both in deed and thought, than they could now be of their own. The husband cast one look at his pale wife, and Faith at him. What polluted wretches would the next glance show them to each other, shuddering alike at what they disclosed and what they saw!

"Faith! Faith!" cried the husband. "Look up to Heaven, and resist the Wicked One!"

Whether Faith obeyed, he knew not. Hardly had he spoken, when he found himself amid calm night and solitude, listening to a roar of the wind, which died heavily away through the forest. He staggered against the rock, and felt it chill and damp, while a hanging twig, that had been all on fire, besprinkled his cheek with the coldest dew.

The next morning, young Goodman Brown came slowly into the street of Salem village staring around him like a bewildered man. The good old minister was taking a walk along the grave-yard, to get an appetite for breakfast and meditate his sermon, and bestowed a blessing, as he passed, on Goodman Brown. He shrank from the venerable saint, as if to avoid an anathema. Old Deacon Gookin was at domestic worship, and the holy words of his prayer were heard through the open window. "What God doth the wizard pray to?" quoth Goodman Brown. Goody Cloyse, that excellent old Christian, stood in the early sunshine, at her own lattice, catechising a little girl, who had brought her a pint of morning's milk. Goodman Brown snatched away the child, as from the grasp of the fiend himself. Turning the corner by the meeting-house, he spied the head of Faith, with the pink ribbons, gazing anxiously forth, and bursting into such joy at sight of him that she skipt along the street, and almost kissed her husband before the whole village. But Goodman Brown looked sternly and sadly into her face, and passed on without a greeting.

Had Goodman Brown fallen asleep in the forest, and only dreamed a wild dream of a witch-meeting?

Be it so, if you will. But, alas! it was a dream of evil omen for young Goodman Brown. A stern, a sad, a darkly meditative, a distrustful, if not a desperate man did he become, from the night of that fearful dream. On the Sabbath day, when the congregation were singing a holy psalm, he could not listen, because an anthem of sin rushed loudly upon his ear, and drowned all the blessed strain. When the minister spoke from the pulpit, with power and fervid eloquence, and with his hand on the open Bible, of the sacred truths of our religion, and of saint-like lives and triumphant deaths, and of future bliss or misery unutterable, then did Goodman Brown turn pale, dreading lest the roof should thunder down upon the gray blasphemer and his hearers. Often, awaking suddenly at midnight, he shrank from the bosom of Faith, and at morning or eventide, when the family knelt down at prayer, he scowled, and muttered to himself, and gazed sternly at his wife, and turned away. And when he had lived long, and was borne to his grave, a hoary corpse, followed by Faith, an aged woman, and children and grandchildren, a goodly procession, besides neighbors not a few, they carved no hopeful verse upon his tombstone; for his dying hour was gloom.

QUESTIONS

1. Like "The Minister's Black Veil," "Young Goodman Brown" concerns isolation from a community and secret sin. Unlike the minister, however, young Goodman Brown sees evil primarily in those around him—the respected, righteous citizens. Do you read the story as a satire on respectable society? Or do you see the journey as a fantasy of young Goodman Brown's, derived from his projected sense of evil? (*Projection:* the attribution to others of rejected parts of the self.)

2. As in a medieval morality play, the elements of the story are allegorical. *Allegory* is the dramatized interaction of personified abstractions (Justice, Truth, Faith) designed to teach a lesson. The characters mean more than themselves. Faith, clearly, is *faith*. The magical fellow-traveler is, of course, Satan himself. The journey through the forest may be representative of our journey through life and of our descent into dark areas of our souls. But the teaching is much less clear than in, say, *Pilgrim's Progress*, that famous seventeenth-century allegory. What *are* we to learn from the story? "His dying hour was gloom," Hawthorne writes. Does Hawthorne's story teach us of evil in the community, in our own hearts, in both? Or does he show the danger of perceiving evil and, on its account, separating yourself from the community?

3. The minister in "The Minister's Black Veil" is very much like Brown. Put them together to make a larger, combined story.

4. Why does the story begin where it does? (See Preface, pp. 11–13.)

EDGAR ALLAN POE

(1809-1849)

Born to a traveling theatrical family, Poe was orphaned at two and taken into the household of a wealthy Southern gentleman. Here he learned pride and an easy way of life but never felt part of the family. At the University of Virginia he fell into debt and, seen as a wastrel, was withdrawn by his foster father after a single term. A few years later, in 1831, he dropped out of West Point and in 1832 made a total break with his foster parents.

In their place he found a home with his impoverished cousins, and in 1835—Poe was twenty-six—he married his thirteen-year-old cousin, Virginia. Always sickly, she died a year before Poe, in 1848. Poe's personal life was painful, made worse by the drinking bouts that ruined his health. Professionally he was bitter; he believed himself brilliant, but while he did win recognition for stories and poems, he was ill paid as an editor and writer. He died in a Baltimore gutter in 1849. In a way Poe was the prototype of the American bohemian artist, the alienated writer, the dropout: Walt Whitman, Sherwood Anderson, Jack Kerouac. In a way he was also the prototype of the American writer who destroys himself with alcohol—like Fitzgerald and Kerouac.

Poe was a poet of disintegration, of the seduction of collapse, breakdown, dissolution of the psyche. The house of Usher is marked with a "barely perceptible fissure" that at the end of the story cracks open and destroys the house. Usher himself is attuned to death, and the final embrace with his dying sister is a kind of *liebestod,* a love-death, a love of and union with one's own soul in the state of death.

But Poe was also a careful, self-conscious craftsman in both poetry and fiction. He believed that it was the artist's job to know in advance the effect desired and then to design precisely the means of creating that effect—a strangely rationalistic theory for a writer so concerned with intense emotion. Watch how brilliantly he designs his imagery and builds his state of terror, until disintegration comes as a mad release of tension.

Later in the nineteenth century, writers, especially in France, turned to Poe as a great teacher both of poetry and of the short story—conceived as an aesthetic whole and plunging into the depths of the human mystery.

[See Preface, p. 14 (rising action).]

The Fall of the House of Usher

EDGAR ALLAN POE

> *Son coeur est un luth suspendu;*
> *Sitôt qu'on le touche il résonne.*
>
> DE BÉRANGER

During the whole of a dull, dark, and soundless day in the autumn of the year, when the clouds hung oppressively low in the heavens, I had been passing alone, on horseback, through a singularly dreary tract of country; and at length found myself, as the shades of the evening drew on, within view of the melancholy House of Usher. I knew not how it was—but, with the first glimpse of the building, a sense of insufferable gloom pervaded my spirit. I say insufferable; for the feeling was unrelieved by any of that half-pleasurable, because poetic, sentiment with which the mind usually receives even the sternest natural images of the desolate or terrible. I looked upon the scene before me—upon the mere house, and the simple landscape features of the domain, upon the bleak walls, upon the vacant eye-like windows, upon a few rank sedges, and upon a few white trunks of decayed trees—with an utter depression of soul which I can compare to no earthly sensation more properly than to the after-dream of the reveler upon opium; the bitter lapse into everyday life, the hideous dropping off of the veil. There was an iciness, a sinking, a sickening of the heart, an unredeemed dreariness of thought which no goading of the imagination could torture into aught of the sublime. What was it—I paused to think—what was it that so unnerved me in the contemplation of the House of Usher? It was a mystery all insoluble; nor could I grapple with the shadowy fancies that crowded upon me as I pondered. I was forced to fall back upon the unsatisfactory conclusion, that while, beyond doubt, there *are* combinations of very simple natural objects which have the power of thus affecting us, still the analysis of this power lies among considerations beyond our depth. It was possible, I reflected, that a mere different arrangement of the particulars of the scene, of the details of the picture, would be sufficient to modify, or perhaps to annihilate, its capacity for sorrowful impression; and, acting upon this idea, I reined my horse to the precipitous brink of a black and lurid tarn that lay in unruffled luster by the dwelling, and gazed down—but with a shudder even more thrilling than before—upon the re-modeled and inverted images of the gray sedge, and the ghastly tree stems, and the vacant and eye-like windows.

Nevertheless, in this mansion of gloom I now proposed to myself a sojourn of some weeks. Its proprietor, Roderick Usher, had been one of my boon companions in boyhood; but many years had elapsed since our last meeting. A letter, however, had lately reached me in a distant part of the country—a letter from him—which in its wildly importunate nature had admitted of no other than a personal reply. The MS. gave evidence of nervous agitation. The writer spoke of acute bodily illness, of a mental disorder which oppressed him, and of an earnest desire to see me, as his best and indeed his only personal friend, with a view of attempting, by the cheerfulness of my society, some alleviation of his malady. It was the manner in which all this, and much more, was said—it was the apparent *heart* that went with his request—which allowed me no room for hesitation; and I accordingly obeyed forthwith what I still considered a very singular summons.

Although as boys we had been even intimate associates, yet I really knew little of my friend. His reserve had been always excessive and habitual. I was aware, however, that his very ancient family had been noted, time out of mind, for a peculiar sensibility of temperament, displaying itself, through long ages, in many works of exalted art, and manifested of late in repeated deeds of munificent yet unobtrusive charity, as well as in a passionate devotion of the intricacies, perhaps even more than to the orthodox and easily recognizable beauties, of musical science. I had learned, too, the very remarkable fact that the stem of the Usher race, all time-honored as it was, had put forth at no period any enduring branch; in other words, that the entire family lay in the direct line of descent, and had always, with very trifling and very temporary variation, so lain. It was this deficiency, I considered, while running over in thought the perfect keeping of the character of the premises with the accredited character of the people, and while speculating upon the possible influence which the one, in the long lapse of centuries, might have exercised upon the other—it was this deficiency, perhaps, of collateral issue, and the consequent undeviating transmission from sire to son of the patrimony with the name, which had, at length, so identified the two as to merge the original title of the estate in the quaint and equivocal appellation of the "House of Usher"—an appellation which seemed to include, in the minds of the peasantry who used it, both the family and the family mansion.

I have said that the sole effect of my somewhat childish experiment, that of looking down within the tarn, had been to deepen the first singular impression. There can be no doubt that the consciousness of the rapid increase of my superstition—for why should I not so term it?—served mainly to accelerate the increase itself. Such, I have long known, is the paradoxical law of all sentiments having terror as a basis. And it might have been for this reason only, that, when I again uplifted my eyes to the house itself, from its image in the pool, there grew in my mind a strange fancy—a fancy so ridiculous, indeed, that I but mention it to show the vivid force of the sensations which oppressed me. I had so worked upon my imagination as really to believe that about the whole mansion and domain there hung an atmosphere peculiar to themselves and their immediate vicinity: an atmosphere which had no affinity with the air of heaven, but which had reeked up from the decayed trees, and the gray wall, and the silent tarn: a pestilent and mystic vapor, dull, sluggish, faintly discernible, and leaden-hued.

Shaking off from my spirit what *must* have been a dream, I scanned more narrowly the real aspect of the building. Its principal feature seemed to be that of an excessive antiquity. The discoloration of ages had been great. Minute fungi overspread the whole exterior, hanging in a fine tangled webwork from the eaves. Yet all this was apart from any extraordinary dilapidation. No portion of the masonry had fallen; and there appeared to be a wild inconsistency between its still perfect adaptation of parts and the crumbling condition of the individual stones. In this there was much that reminded me of the specious totality of old woodwork which has rotted for long years in some neglected vault, with no disturbance from the breath of the external air. Beyond this indication of excessive decay, however, the fabric gave little token of instability. Perhaps the eye of a scrutinizing observer might have discovered a barely perceptible fissure, which, extending from the roof of the building in front, made its way down the wall in a zigzag direction, until it became lost in the sullen waters of the tarn.

Noticing these things, I rode over a short causeway to the house. A servant in waiting took my horse, and I entered the Gothic archway of the hall. A valet, of stealthy step, thence conducted me, in silence, through many dark and intricate passages in my progress to the studio of his master. Much that I encountered on the way contributed, I know not how, to heighten the vague sentiments of which I have already spoken. While the objects around me—while the carvings of the ceilings, the somber tapestries of the walls, the ebon blackness of the floors, and the phantasmagoric armorial trophies which rattled as I strode, were but matters to which, or to such as which, I had been accustomed from my infancy—while I hesitated not to acknowledge how familiar was all this—I still wondered to find how unfamiliar were the fancies which ordinary images were stirring up. On one of the staircases, I met the physician of the family. His countenance, I thought, wore a mingled expression of low cunning and perplexity. He accosted me with trepidation and passed on. The valet now threw open a door and ushered me into the presence of his master.

The room in which I found myself was very large and lofty. The windows were long, narrow, and pointed, and at so vast a distance from the black oaken floor as to be altogether inaccessible from within. Feeble gleams of encrimsoned light made their way through the trellised panes, and served to render sufficiently distinct the more prominent objects around; the eye, however, struggled in vain to reach the remoter angles of the chamber, or the recesses of the vaulted and fretted ceiling. Dark draperies hung upon the walls. The general furniture was profuse, comfortless, antique, and tattered. Many books and musical instruments lay scattered about, but failed to give any vitality to the scene. I felt that I breathed an atmosphere of sorrow. An air of stern, deep, and irredeemable gloom hung over and pervaded all.

Upon my entrance, Usher arose from a sofa on which he had been lying at full length, and greeted me with a vivacious warmth which had much in it, I at first thought, of an overdone cordiality—of the constrained effort of the *ennuyé* man of the world. A glance, however, at his countenance, convinced me of his perfect sincerity. We sat down; and for some moments, while he spoke not, I gazed upon him with a feeling half of pity, half of awe. Surely man had never before so terribly altered in so brief a period as had Roderick Usher! It was with difficulty that I could bring myself to admit the identity of the wan being before me with the companion of my boyhood. Yet the character of his face had been at all times remarkable. A cadaverousness of complexion; an eye large, liquid, and luminous beyond comparison; lips somewhat thin and very pallid, but of a surpassingly beautiful curve; a nose of a delicate Hebrew model, but with a breadth of nostril unusual in similar formations; a finely molded chin, speaking, in its want of prominence, of a want of moral energy; hair of a more than weblike softness and tenuity; these features, with an inordinate expansion above the regions of the temple, made up altogether a countenance not easily to be forgotten. And now in the mere exaggeration of the prevailing character of these features, and of the expression they were wont to convey, lay so much of change that I doubted to whom I spoke. The now ghostly pallor of the skin, and the now miraculous luster of the eye, above all things startled and even awed me. The silken hair, too, had been suffered to grow all unheeded, and as, in its wild gossamer texture, it floated rather than fell about the face, I could not, even with effort, connect its arabesque expression with any idea of simple humanity.

In the manner of my friend I was at once struck with an incoherence, an inconsistency; and I soon found this to arise from a series of feeble and futile struggles to overcome an habitual trepidancy, an excessive nervous agitation. For something of this nature I had indeed been prepared, no less by his letter than by reminiscences of certain boyish traits, and by conclusions deduced from his peculiar physical conformation and temperament. His action was alternatively vivacious and sullen. His voice varied rapidly from a tremulous indecision (when the animal spirits seemed utterly in abeyance) to that species of energetic concision—that abrupt, weighty, unhurried, and hollow-sounding enunciation—that leaden, self-balanced and perfectly modulated guttural utterance—which may be observed in the lost drunkard, or the irreclaimable eater of opium, during the periods of his most intense excitement.

It was thus that he spoke of the object of my visit, of his earnest desire to see me, and of the solace he expected me to afford him. He entered, at some length, into what he conceived to be the nature of his malady. It was, he said, a constitutional and a family evil, and one for which he despaired to find a remedy—a mere nervous affection, he immediately added, which would undoubtedly soon pass off. It displayed itself in a host of unnatural sensations. Some of these, as he detailed them, interested and bewildered me: although, perhaps, the terms and the general manner of the narration had their weight. He suffered much from a morbid acuteness of the senses; the most insipid food was alone endurable; he could wear only garments of a certain texture; the odors of all flowers were oppressive; his eyes were tortured by even a faint light; and there were but peculiar sounds, and these from stringed instruments, which did not inspire him with horror.

To an anomalous species of terror I found him a bounden slave. "I shall perish," said he, "I *must* perish in this deplorable folly. Thus, thus, and not otherwise, shall I be lost. I dread the events of the future, not in themselves, but in their results. I shudder at the thought of any, even the most trivial, incident, which may operate upon this intolerable agitation of soul. I have, indeed, no abhorrence of danger, except in its absolute effect—in terror. In this unnerved—in this pitiable condition—I feel that the period will sooner or later arrive when I must abandon life and reason together, in some struggle with the grim phantasm, FEAR."

I learned moreover at intervals, and through broken and equivocal hints, another singular feature of his mental condition. He was enchained by certain superstitious impressions in regard to the dwelling which he tenanted, and whence, for many years, he had never ventured forth—in regard to an influence whose supposititious force was conveyed in terms too shadowy here to be restated—an influence which some peculiarities in the mere form and substance of his family mansion, had, by dint of long sufferance, he said, obtained over his spirit—an effect which the physique of the gray walls and turrets, and of the dim tarn into which they all looked down, had, at length, brought about upon the morale of his existence.

He admitted, however, although with hesitation, that much of the peculiar gloom which thus afflicted him could be traced to a more natural and far more palpable origin—to the severe and long-continued illness, indeed to the evidently approaching dissolution, of a tenderly beloved sister—his sole companion for long years, his last and only relative on earth. "Her decease," he said, with a bitterness which I can never forget, "would leave him (him the hopeless and the frail) the last of the ancient race of the Ushers." While he spoke, the lady Madeline (for so was she called) passed slowly through a remote portion of the apartment, and, without having noticed my presence, disappeared. I regarded her with an utter astonishment not unmingled with dread, and yet I found it impossible to account for such feelings. A sensation of stupor oppressed me, as my eyes followed her retreating steps. When a door, at length, closed upon her, my glance sought instinctively and eagerly the countenance of the brother, but he had buried his face in his hands, and I could only perceive that a far more than ordinary wanness had overspread the emaciated fingers through which trickled many passionate tears.

The disease of the lady Madeline had long baffled the skill of her physicians. A settled apathy, a gradual wasting away of the person, and frequent although transient affections of a partially cataleptical character, were the unusual diagnosis. Hitherto she had steadily borne up against the pressure of her malady, and had not betaken herself finally to bed; but, on the closing in of the evening of my arrival at the house, she succumbed (as her brother told me at night with inexpressible agitation) to the prostrating power of the destroyer; and I learned that the glimpse I had obtained of her person would thus probably be the last I should obtain—that the lady, at least while living, would be seen by me no more.

For several days ensuing, her name was unmentioned by either Usher or myself; and during this period I was busied in earnest endeavors to alleviate the melancholy of my friend. We painted and read together; or I listened, as if in a dream, to the wild improvisation of his speaking guitar. And thus, as a closer and still closer intimacy admitted me more unreservedly into the recesses of his spirit, the more bitterly did I perceive the futility of all attempt at cheering a mind from which darkness, as if an inherent positive quality, poured forth upon all objects of the moral and physical universe, in one unceasing radiation of gloom.

I shall ever bear about me a memory of the many solemn hours I thus spent alone with the master of the House of Usher. Yet I should fail in any attempt to convey an idea of the exact character of the studies, or of the occupations, in which he involved me, or led me the way. An excited and highly distempered ideality threw a sulphurous luster over all. His long improvised dirges will ring forever in my ears. Among other things, I hold painfully in mind a certain singular perversion and amplification of the wild air of the last waltz of Von Weber. From the paintings over which his elaborate fancy brooded, and which grew, touch by touch, into vagueness at which I shuddered the more thrillingly because I shuddered knowing not why;—from these paintings (vivid as their images now are before me) I would in vain endeavor to educe more than a small portion which should lie within the compass of merely written words. By the utter simplicity, by the nakedness of his designs, he arrested and overawed attention. If ever mortal painted an idea, that mortal was Roderick Usher. For me at least, in the circumstances then surrounding me, there arose, out of the pure abstractions which the hypochondriac contrived to throw upon his canvas, an intensity of intolerable awe, no shadow of which felt I ever yet in the contemplation of the certainly glowing yet too concrete reveries of Fuseli.

One of the phantasmagoric conceptions of my friend, partaking not so rigidly of the spirit of abstraction, may be shadowed forth, although feebly, in words. A small picture presented the interior of an immensely long and rectangular vault or tunnel, with low walls, smooth, white, and without interruption or device. Certain accessory points of the design served well to convey the idea that this excavation lay at an exceeding depth below the surface of the earth. No outlet was observed in any portion of its vast extent, and no torch or other artificial source of light was discernible; yet a flood of intense rays rolled throughout, and bathed the whole in a ghastly and inappropriate splendor.

I have just spoken of that morbid condition of the auditory nerve which rendered all music intolerable to the sufferer, with the exception of certain effects of stringed instruments. It was, perhaps, the narrow limits to which he thus confined himself upon the guitar, which gave birth, in great measure, to the fantastic character of his performances. But the fervid *facility* of his *impromptus* could not be so accounted for. They must have been, and were, in the notes, as well as in the words of his wild fantasias (for he not unfrequently accompanied himself with rhymed verbal improvisations), the result of that intense mental collectedness and concentration to which I have previously alluded as observable only in particular moments of the highest artificial excitement. The words of one of these rhapsodies I have easily remembered. I was, perhaps, the more forcibly impressed with it, as he gave it, because, in the under or mystic current of its meaning, I fancied that I perceived, and for the first time, a full consciousness, on the part of Usher, of the tottering of his lofty reason upon her throne. The verses, which were entitled "The Haunted Palace," ran very nearly, if not accurately, thus:

I

In the greenest of our valleys,
    By good angels tenanted,
Once a fair and stately palace—
    Radiant palace—reared its head.
In the monarch Thought's dominion,
    It stood there!
Never seraph spread a pinion
    Over fabric half so fair.

II

Banners yellow, glorious, golden,
    On its roof did float and flow,
(This—all this—was in the olden
    Time long ago)
And every gentle air that dallied,
    In that sweet day,
Along the ramparts plumed and pallid,
    A wingèd odor went away.

III

Wanderers in that happy valley
    Through two luminous windows saw
Spirits moving musically
    To a lute's well-tunèd law,
Round about a throne where, sitting,
    (Porphyrogene!)
In state his glory well befitting,
    The ruler of the realm was seen.

IV

And all with pearl and ruby glowing
    Was the fair palace door,
Through which came flowing, flowing, flowing,
    And sparkling evermore,
A troop of Echoes whose sweet duty
    Was but to sing,
In voices of surpassing beauty,
    The wit and wisdom of their king.

V

But evil things, in robes of sorrow,
　　Assailed the monarch's high estate;
(Ah, let us mourn, for never morrow
　　Shall dawn upon him, desolate!)
And round about his home the glory
　　That blushed and bloomed
Is but a dim-remembered story
　　Of the old time entombed.

VI

And travellers now within that valley
　　Through the red-litten windows see
Vast forms that move fantastically
　　To a discordant melody;
While, like a rapid ghastly river,
　　Through the pale door,
A hideous throng rush out forever,
　　And laugh—but smile no more.

I well remember that suggestions arising from this ballad led us into a train of thought, wherein there became manifest an opinion of Usher's which I mention not so much on account of its novelty (for other men have thought thus) as on account of the pertinacity with which he maintained it. This opinion, in its general form, was that of the sentience of all vegetable things. But in his disordered fancy the idea had assumed a more daring character, and trespassed, under certain conditions, upon the kingdom of inorganization. I lack words to express the full extent, or the earnest *abandon* of his persuasion. The belief, however, was connected (as I have previously hinted) with the gray stones of the home of his forefathers. The conditions of the sentience had been here, he imagined, fulfilled in the method of collocation of these stones—in the order of their arrangement, as well as in that of the many fungi which overspread them, and of the decayed trees which stood around—above all, in the long undisturbed endurance of this arrangement, and in its reduplication in the still waters of the tarn. Its evidence—the evidence of the sentience—was to be seen, he said (and I here started as he spoke), in the gradual yet certain condensation of an atmosphere of their own about the waters and the walls. The result was discoverable, he added, in that silent, yet importunate and terrible influence which for centuries had molded the destinies of his family, and which made *him* what I now saw him—what he was. Such opinions need no comment, and I will make none.

Our books—the books which, for years, had formed no small portion of the mental existence of the invalid—were, as might be supposed, in strict keeping with this character of phantasm. We pored together over such works as the Ververt and Chartreuse of

Gresset; the Belphegor of Machiavelli; the Heaven and Hell of Swedenborg; the Subterranean Voyage of Nicholas Klimm by Holberg; the Chiromancy of Robert Flud, of Jean D'Indaginé, and of De la Chambre; the Journey into the Blue Distance of Tieck; and the City of the Sun of Campanella. One favorite volume was a small octavo edition of the *Directorium Inquisitorium,* by the Dominican Eymeric de Gironne; and there were passages in Pomponius Mela, about the old African Satyrs and Ægipans, over which Usher would sit dreaming for hours. His chief delight, however, was found in the perusal of an exceedingly rare and curious book in quarto Gothic—the manual of a forgotten church—the *Vigiliæ Mortuorum Secundum Chorum Ecclesiæ Maguntinæ.*

I could not help thinking of the wild ritual of this work, and of its probable influence upon the hypochondriac, when one evening, having informed me abruptly that the lady Madeline was no more, he stated his intention of preserving her corpse for a fortnight (previously to its final interment) in one of the numerous vaults within the main walls of the building. The worldly reason, however, assigned for this singular proceeding was one which I did not feel at liberty to dispute. The brother had been led to his resolution (so he told me) by consideration of the unusual character of the malady of the deceased, of certain obtrusive and eager inquiries on the part of her medical men, and of the remote and exposed situation of the burial-ground of the family. I will not deny that when I called to mind the sinister countenance of the person whom I met upon the staircase, on the day of my arrival at the house, I had no desire to oppose what I regarded as at best but a harmless, and by no means an unnatural, precaution.

At the request of Usher, I personally aided him in the arrangements for the temporary entombment. The body having been encoffined, we two alone bore it to its rest. The vault in which we placed it (and which had been so long unopened that our torches, half smothered in its oppressive atmoshpere, gave us little opportunity for investigation) was small, damp, and entirely without means of admission for light; lying, at great depth, immediately beneath that portion of the building in which was my own sleeping apartment. It had been used, apparently, in remote feudal times, for the worst purposes of a donjon-keep, and in later days as a place of deposit for powder, or some other highly combustible substance, as a portion of its floor, and the whole interior of a long archway through which we reached it, were carefully sheathed with copper. The door, of massive iron, had been also similarly protected. Its immense weight caused an unusually sharp grating sound, as it moved upon its hinges.

Having deposited our mournful burden upon trestles within this region of horror, we partially turned aside the yet unscrewed lid of the coffin, and looked upon the face of the tenant. A striking similitude between the brother and sister now first arrested my attention; and Usher divining, perhaps, my thoughts, murmured out some few words from which I learned that the deceased and himself had been twins, and that sympathies of a scarcely intelligible nature had always existed between them. Our glances, however, rested not long upon the dead—for we could not regard her unawed. The disease which had thus entombed the lady in the maturity of youth, had left, as usual in all maladies of a strictly cataleptical character, the mockery of a faint blush upon the bosom and the face, and that suspiciously lingering smile upon the lip which is so terrible in death. We replaced and screwed down the lid, and, having secured the door of iron, made our way, with toil, into the scarcely less gloomy apartments of the upper portion of the house.

And now, some days of bitter grief having elapsed, an observable change came over the features of the mental disorder of my friend. His ordinary manner had vanished. His ordinary occupations were neglected or forgotten. He roamed from chamber to chamber with hurried, unequal, and objectless step. The pallor of his countenance had assumed, if possible, a more ghastly hue—but the luminousness of his eye had utterly gone out. The once occasional huskiness of his tone was heard no more; and a tremulous quaver, as if of extreme terror, habitually characterized his utterance. There were times, indeed, when I thought his unceasingly agitated mind was laboring with some oppressive secret, to divulge which he struggled for the necessary courage. At times, again, I was obliged to resolve all into the mere inexplicable vagaries of madness, for I beheld him gazing upon vacancy for long hours, in an attitude of the profoundest attention, as if listening to some imaginary sound. It was no wonder that his condition terrified—that it infected me. I felt creeping upon me, by slow yet certain degrees, the wild influences of his own fantastic yet impressive superstitions.

It was, especially, upon retiring to bed late in the night of the seventh or eighth day after the placing of the lady Madeline within the donjon, that I experienced the full power of such feelings. Sleep came not near my couch, while the hours waned and waned away. I struggled to reason off the nervousness which had dominion over me. I endeavored to believe that much, if not all, of what I felt was due to the bewildering influence of the gloomy furniture of the room—of the dark and tattered draperies which, tortured into motion by the breath of a rising tempest, swayed fitfully to and fro upon the walls, and rustled uneasily about the decorations of the bed. But my efforts were fruitless. An irrepressible tremor gradually pervaded my frame; and at length there sat upon my very heart an incubus of utterly causeless alarm. Shaking this off with a gasp and a struggle, I uplifted myself upon the pillows, and, peering earnestly within the intense darkness of the chamber, hearkened—I know not why, except that an instinctive spirit prompted me—to certain low and indefinite sounds which came, through the pauses of the storm, at long intervals, I knew not whence. Overpowered by an intense sentiment of horror, unaccountable yet unendurable, I threw on my clothes with haste (for I felt that I should sleep no more during the night) and endeavored to arouse myself from the pitiable condition into which I had fallen, by pacing rapidly to and fro through the apartment.

I had taken but few turns in this manner, when a light step on an adjoining staircase arrested my attention. I presently recognized it as that of Usher. In an instant afterward he rapped with a gentle touch at my door, and entered, bearing a lamp. His countenance was, as usual, cadaverously wan—but, moreover, there was a species of mad hilarity in his eyes—an evidently restrained *hysteria* in his whole demeanor. His air appalled me—but anything was preferable to the solitude which I had so long endured, and I even welcomed his presence as a relief.

"And you have not seen it?" he said abruptly, after having stared about him for some moments in silence—"you have not then seen it?—but, stay! you shall." Thus speaking, and having carefully shaded his lamp, he hurried to one of the casements, and threw it freely open to the storm.

The impetuous fury of the entering gust nearly lifted us from our feet. It was, indeed, a tempestuous yet sternly beautiful night, and one wildly singular in its terror and its beauty. A whirlwind had apparently collected its force in our vicinity; for there were frequent and violent alterations in the direction of the wind; and the exceeding density of the clouds (which hung so low as to press upon the turrets of the house) did not prevent our perceiving the lifelike velocity with which they flew careening from all points against each other, without passing away into the distance. I say that even their exceeding density did not prevent our perceiving this; yet we had no glimpse of the moon or stars, nor was there any flashing forth of the lightning. But the under surfaces of the huge masses of agitated vapor, as well as all terrestrial objects immediately around us, were glowing in the unnatural light of a faintly luminous and distinctly visible gaseous exhalation which hung about and enshrouded the mansion.

"You must not—you shall not behold this!" said I, shudderingly, to Usher, as I led him with a gentle violence from the window to a seat. "These appearances, which bewilder you, are merely electrical phenomena not uncommon—or it may be that they have their ghastly origin in the rank miasma of the tarn. Let us close this casement; the air is chilling and dangerous to your frame. Here is one of your favorite romances. I will read, and you shall listen;—and so we will pass away this terrible night together."

The antique volume which I had taken up was the *Mad Trist* of Sir Launcelot Canning; but I had called it a favorite of Usher's more in sad jest than in earnest; for, in truth, there is little in its uncouth and unimaginative prolixity which could have had interest for the lofty and spiritual ideality of my friend. It was, however, the only book immediately at hand; and I indulged a vague hope that the excitement which now agitated the hypochondriac might find relief (for the history of mental disorder is full of similar anomalies) even in the extremeness of the folly which I should read. Could I have judged, indeed, by the wild overstrained air of vivacity with which he hearkened, or apparently hearkened, to the words of the tale, I might well have congratulated myself upon the success of my design.

I had arrived at that well-known portion of the story where Ethelred, the hero of the Trist, having sought in vain for peaceable admission into the dwelling of the hermit, proceeds to make good an entrance by force. Here, it will be remembered, the words of the narrative run thus:

> "And Ethelred, who was by nature of a doughty heart, and who was now mighty withal, on account of the powerfulness of the wine which he had drunken, waited no longer to hold parley with the hermit, who, in sooth, was of an obstinate and maliceful turn, but, feeling the rain upon his shoulders, and fearing the rising of the tempest, uplifted his mace outright, and, with blows, made quickly room in the plankings of the door for his gauntleted hand; and now pulling therewith sturdily, he so cracked, and ripped, and tore all asunder, that the noise of the dry and hollow-sounding wood alarummed and reverberated throughout the forest."

At the termination of this sentence I started, and for a moment paused; for it appeared to me (although I at once concluded that my excited fancy had deceived me) —it appeared to me that from some very remote portion of the mansion there came, indistinctly, to my ears, what might have been, in its exact similarity of character, the echo (but a stifled and dull one certainly) of the very cracking and ripping sound which Sir Launcelot had so particularly described. It was, beyond doubt, the coincidence alone which had arrested my attention; for, amid the rattling of the sashes of the casements, and the ordinary commingled noises of the still increasing storm, the sound, in itself, had nothing, surely, which should have interested or disturbed me. I continued the story:

> "But the good champion Ethelred, now entering within the door, was sore enraged and amazed to perceive no signal of the maliceful hermit; but, in the stead thereof, a dragon of a scaly and prodigious demeanor,

and of a fiery tongue, which sate in guard before a palace of gold, with a floor of silver; and upon the wall there hung a shield of shining brass with this legend enwritten—
       Who entereth herein, a conqueror hath bin;
       Who slayeth the dragon, the shield he shall win
And Ethelred uplifted his mace, and struck upon the head of the dragon, which fell before him, and gave up his pesty breath, with a shriek so horrid and harsh, and withal so piercing, that Ethelred had fain to close his ears with his hands against the dreadful noise of it, the like whereof was never before heard."

Here again I paused abruptly, and now with a feeling of wild amazement; for there could be no doubt whatever that, in this instance, I did actually hear (although from what direction it proceeded I found it impossible to say) a low and apparently distant, but harsh, protracted, and most unusual screaming or grating sound —the exact counterpart of what my fancy had already conjured up for the dragon's unnatural shriek as described by the romancer.

Oppressed, as I certainly was, upon the occurrence of this second and most extraordinary coincidence, by a thousand conflicting sensations, in which wonder and extreme terror were predominant, I still retained sufficient presence of mind to avoid exciting, by any observation, the sensitive nervousness of my companion. I was by no means certain that he had noticed the sounds in question; although, assuredly, a strange alteration had during the last few minutes taken place in his demeanor. From a position fronting my own, he had gradually brought round his chair, so as to sit with his face to the door of the chamber; and thus I could but partially perceive his features, although I saw that his lips trembled as if he were murmuring inaudibly. His head had dropped upon his breast—yet I knew that he was not asleep, from the wide and rigid opening of the eye as I caught a glance of it in profile. The motion of his body, too, was at variance with this idea—for he rocked from side to side with a gentle yet constant and uniform sway. Having rapidly taken notice of all this, I resumed the narrative of Sir Launcelot, which thus proceeded:

"And now, the champion having escaped from the terrible fury of the dragon, bethinking himself of the brazen shield, and of the breaking up of the enchantment which was upon it, removed the carcass from out of the way before him, and approached valorously over the silver pavement of the castle to where the shield was upon the wall; which in sooth tarried not for his full coming, but fell down at his feet upon the silver floor, with a mighty great and terrible ringing sound."

No sooner had these syllables passed my lips, than—as if a shield of brass had indeed, at the moment, fallen heavily upon a floor of silver—I became aware of a distinct, hollow, metallic and clangorous, yet apparently muffled reverberation. Completely unnerved, I leaped to my feet; but the measured rocking movement of Usher was undisturbed. I rushed to the chair in which he sat. His eyes were bent fixedly before him, and throughout his whole countenance there reigned a stony rigidity. But, as I placed my hand upon his shoulder, there came a strong shudder over his whole person; a sickly smile quivered about his lips; and I saw that he spoke in a low, hurried, and gibbering murmur, as if unconscious of my presence. Bending closely over him, I at length drank in the hideous import of his words.

"Not hear it?—yes, I hear it, and *have* heard it. Long—long—long—many minutes, many hours, many days, have I heard it—yet I dared not—oh, pity me, miserable wretch that I am!—I dared not—*I dared not speak! We have put her living in the tomb!* Said I not that my senses were acute? I *now* tell you that I heard her first feeble movements in the hollow coffin. I heard them—many, many days ago—yet I dared not—*I dared not speak!* And now—tonight—Ethelred—ha! ha!—the breaking of the hermit's door, and the death-cry of the dragon, and the clangor of the shield!—say, rather, the rending of her coffin, and the grating of the iron hinges of her prison, and her struggles within the coppered archway of the vault! Oh, whither shall I fly? Will she not be here anon? Is she not hurrying to upbraid me for my haste? Have I not heard her footsteps on the stair? Do I not distinguish that heavy and horrible beating of her heart? Madman!"—here he sprang furiously to his feet, and shrieked out his syllables, as if in the effort he were giving up his soul—*"Madman! I tell you that she now stands without the door!"*

As if in the superhuman energy of his utterance there had been found the potency of a spell, the huge antique panels to which the speaker pointed drew slowly back, upon the instant, their ponderous and ebony jaws. It was the work of the rushing gust—but then without the doors there *did* stand the lofty and enshrouded figure of the lady Madeline of Usher. There was blood upon her white robes, and the evidence of some bitter struggle upon every portion of her emaciated frame. For a moment she remained trembling and reeling to and fro upon the threshold—then, with a low moaning cry, fell heavily inward upon the person of her brother, and, in her violent and now final death-agonies, bore him to the floor a corpse, and a victim to the terrors he had anticipated.

From that chamber, and from that mansion, I fled aghast. The storm was still abroad in all its wrath as I found myself crossing the old causeway. Suddenly there shot along the path a wild light, and I turned to see whence a gleam so unusual could have issued; for the vast house and its shadows were alone behind me. The radiance was that of the full, setting, and blood-red moon, which now shone vividly through that once barely discernible fissure, of which I have before spoken as extending from the roof of the building, in a zigzag direction, to the base. While I gazed, this fissure rapidly widened— there came a fierce breath of the whirlwind—the entire orb of the satellite burst at once upon my sight—my brain reeled as I saw the mighty walls rushing asunder—there was a long tumultuous shouting sound like the voice of a thousand waters—and the deep and dank tarn at my feet closed sullenly and silently over the fragments of the House of Usher.

QUESTIONS

1. Discuss the angle of vision in "The Fall of the House of Usher." (See Preface, pp. 5–11.) Who, if not Poe himself, is telling the story? Why has Poe chosen this narrator? How would the story change if told by an omniscient author?

2. How does the *atmosphere* (the quality of the setting, the mood deriving from the setting) function? (See Preface, pp. 19–21, imagery.) To what extent does it describe qualities of the psyche?

3. The plot of the story is improbable; the atmosphere of horror exaggerated; the character of Usher melodramatic. Does Poe, in spite of these qualities, move the reader? What in the reader is he able to touch? (See Preface, pp. 1–5.)

4. Roderick Usher is said to bury emotion as well as his sister. Discuss the analogy.

5. There is an intensely involuted quality to the Ushers; there is no "collateral line"—only one son produces one son. Now, his sister dead, Roderick Usher says that the family will end. Is this a hint of a history of incestuous marriage in the Ushers? Even if incest is implied, clearly this is not a "realistic" story, and we are not meant to examine Usher as if he were the object of a case study. Then what is the significance of the intimacy between Usher and his sister?

6. Discuss the analogy between the story of the Ushers and the romance about the knight and the dragon.

HERMAN MELVILLE

(1819-1891)

"Bartleby the Scrivener" was written by a man who, like Bartleby himself, rejected and felt rejected by the commercial world of the 1850's. Bartleby "preferred not to": not to be a scrivener (a clerk-copyist), not to engage in alienated labor, work that means nothing except a paycheck to the worker. Melville also *preferred not to:* successful at first as a writer of South Sea adventures and shipboard tales roughly based on his years at sea (aged twenty-two to twenty-five), he balked at continuing to write simple narratives, refusing to be a hack writer. "Dollars damn me," he wrote. "What I feel most moved to write, that is banned—it will not pay. Yet, altogether write the *other* way I cannot." Unlike Bartleby, however, he did not break down into near catatonic withdrawal. And in the story, Melville seems at least as sympathetic to the wealthy narrator as to Bartleby himself.

Early success followed by failure, bitterness, withdrawal: this had been the pattern of Melville's father as well. Dying when Melville was twelve, his father left the family impoverished. Melville was not able to attend college. After teaching elementary school and casting about for work, he went to sea, first in a merchant ship (the basis of *Redburn*), then on a whaler bound for Cape Horn and the Pacific. Jumping ship in the South Seas, he lived with natives, sailed to Tahiti and was imprisoned, but escaped and signed onto a Nantucket whaler. In Honolulu he joined the navy and sailed on the U.S.S. *United States* for a year (the basis of *White Jacket*). Home again, he began to read furiously—Shakespeare, the Bible, Carlyle—and to produce an amazing outpouring of books: *Typee* (1846), *Omoo* (1847), *Mardi* (1849), *Redburn* (1849), *White Jacket* (1850), *Moby Dick* (1851), and *Pierre* (1852). After this, attacked by critics, he wrote less and grew increasingly bitter. To a large extent he was dependent on the support of his wife's family and of her inheritance. In 1866 he was appointed deputy inspector of customs in New York City. He still wrote—mostly poetry—but he was forgotten as a writer. His powerful story "Billy Budd," written the year of his death (1891), was not published until 1924. It was only in the 1920's that Melville was recognized as a great American writer. Since then his reputation has steadily risen.

"Bartleby" is a key work in understanding Melville and a study of the outsider comparable to Dostoyevsky's "Notes from Underground." It is also, simply, a brilliant narrative.

[See Preface, p. 10 (first person narrator) and p. 12 (narrative structure).]

Bartleby the Scrivener

HERMAN MELVILLE

I am a rather elderly man. The nature of my avocations, for the last thirty years, has brought me into more than ordinary contact with what would seem an interesting and somewhat singular set of men, of whom, as yet, nothing, that I know of, has ever been written—I mean, the law-copyists, or scriveners. I have known very many of them, professionally and privately, and, if I pleased, could relate divers histories, at which good-natured gentlemen might smile, and sentimental souls might weep. But I waive the biographies of all other scriveners, for a few passages in the life of Bartleby, who was a scrivener, the strangest I ever saw, or heard of. While, of other law-copyists, I might write the complete life, of Bartleby nothing of that sort can be done. I believe that no materials exist, for a full and satisfactory biography of this man. It is an irreparable loss to literature. Bartleby was one of those beings of whom nothing is ascertainable, except from the original sources, and, in his case, those are very small. What my own astonished eyes saw of Bartleby, *that* is all I know of him, except, indeed, one vague report, which will appear in the sequel.

Ere introducing the scrivener, as he first appeared to me, it is fit I make some mention of myself, my *employés,* my business, my chambers, and general surroundings; because some such description is indispensable to an adequate understanding of the chief character about to be presented. Imprimis: I am a man who, from his youth upwards, has been filled with a profound conviction that the easiest

way of life is the best. Hence, though I belong to a profession proverbially energetic and nervous, even to turbulence, at times, yet nothing of that sort have I ever suffered to invade my peace. I am one of
those unambitious lawyers who never addresses a jury, or in any way
draws down public applause; but, in the cool tranquillity of a snug
retreat, do a snug business among rich men's bonds, and mortgages,
and title-deeds. All who know me, consider me an eminently *safe*
man. The late John Jacob Astor,[1] a personage little given to poetic
enthusiasm, had no hesitation in pronouncing my first grand point to
be prudence; my next, method. I do not speak it in vanity, but
simply record the fact, that I was not unemployed in my profession
by the late John Jacob Astor, a name which, I admit, I love to
repeat; for it hath a rounded and orbicular sound to it, and rings
like unto bullion. I will freely add, that I was not insensible to the
late John Jacob Astor's good opinion.

. Some time prior to the period at which this little history begins, my
avocations had been largely increased. The good old office, now
extinct in the State of New York, of a Master in Chancery, had been
conferred upon me. It was not a very arduous office, but very pleasantly remunerative. I seldom lose my temper; much more seldom
indulge in dangerous indignation at wrongs and outrages; but, I
must be permitted to be rash here, and declare, that I consider the
sudden and violent abrogation of the office of Master in Chancery, by
the new Constitution, as a ——— premature act; inasmuch as I had
counted upon a life-lease of the profits, whereas I only received those
of a few short years. But this is by the way.

My chambers were up stairs, at No. — Wall Street. At one end,
they looked upon the white wall of the interior of a spacious sky-light
shaft, penetrating the building from top to bottom.

This view might have been considered rather tame than otherwise,
deficient in what landscape painters call "life." But, if so, the view
from the other end of my chambers offered, at least, a contrast, if
nothing more. In that direction, my windows commanded an unobstructed view of a lofty brick wall, black by age and everlasting
shade; which wall required no spy-glass to bring out its lurking
beauties, but, for the benefit of all near-sighted spectators, was
pushed up to within ten feet of my window panes. Owing to the great
height of the surrounding buildings, and my chambers being on the
second floor, the interval between this wall and mine not a little
resembled a huge square cistern.

At the period just preceding the advent of Bartleby, I had two
persons as copyists in my employment, and a promising lad as an

---

[1] *John Jacob Astor:* (1763–1848) an American fur trader and financier.

office-boy. First, Turkey; second, Nippers; third, Ginger Nut. These
may seem names, the like of which are not usually found in the
Directory. In truth, they were nicknames, mutually conferred upon
each other by my three clerks, and were deemed expressive of their
respective persons or characters. Turkey was a short, pursy Englishman, of about my own age—that is, somewhere not far from sixty. In
the morning, one might say, his face was of a fine florid hue, but after
twelve o'clock, meridian—his dinner hour—it blazed like a grate full
of Christmas coals; and continued blazing—but, as it were, with a
gradual wane—till six o'clock, P.M., or thereabouts; after which, I saw
no more of the proprietor of the face, which, gaining its meridian
with the sun, seemed to set with it, to rise, culminate, and decline the
following day, with the like regularity and undiminished glory.
There are many singular coincidences I have known in the course of
my life, not the least among which was the fact, that, exactly when
Turkey displayed his fullest beams from his red and radiant countenance, just then, too, at that critical moment, began the daily period
when I considered his business capacities as seriously disturbed for
the remainder of the twenty-four hours. Not that he was absolutely
idle, or averse to business, then; far from it. The difficulty was, he
was apt to be altogether too energetic. There was a strange, inflamed,
flurried, flighty recklessness of activity about him. He would be
incautious in dipping his pen into his inkstand. All his blots upon
my documents were dropped there after twelve o'clock, meridian.
Indeed, not only would he be reckless, and sadly given to making
blots in the afternoon, but, some days, he went further, and was
rather noisy. At such times, too, his face flamed with augmented
blazonry, as if cannel coal had been heaped on anthracite. He made
an unpleasant racket with his chair; spilled his sand-box; in mending
his pens, impatiently split them all to pieces, and threw them on the
floor in a sudden passion; stood up, and leaned over his table, boxing
his papers about in a most indecorous manner, very sad to behold in
an elderly man like him. Nevertheless, as he was in many ways a most
valuable person to me, and all the time before twelve o'clock, meridian, was the quickest, steadiest creature, too, accomplishing a great
deal of work in a style not easily to be matched—for these reasons, I
was willing to overlook his eccentricities, though, indeed, occasionally, I remonstrated with him. I did this very gently, however, because, though the civilest, nay, the blandest and most reverential of
men in the morning, yet, in the afternoon, he was disposed, upon
provocation, to be slightly rash with his tongue—in fact, insolent.
Now, valuing his morning services as I did, and resolved not to lose
them—yet, at the same time, made uncomfortable by his inflamed
ways after twelve o'clock—and being a man of peace, unwilling by
my admonitions to call forth unseemly retorts from him, I took upon

me, one Saturday noon (he was always worse on Saturdays) to hint to him, very kindly, that, perhaps, now that he was growing old, it might be well to abridge his labors; in short, he need not come to my chambers after twelve o'clock, but, dinner over, had best go home to his lodgings, and rest himself till tea-time. But no; he insisted upon his afternoon devotions. His countenance became intolerably fervid, as he oratorically assured me—gesticulating with a long ruler at the other end of the room—that if his services in the morning were useful, how indispensable, then, in the afternoon?

"With submission, sir," said Turkey, on this occasion, "I consider myself your right-hand man. In the morning I but marshal and deploy my columns; but in the afternoon I put myself at their head, and gallantly charge the foe, thus"—and he made a violent thrust with the ruler.

"But the blots, Turkey," intimated I.

"True; but, with submission, sir, behold these hairs! I am getting old. Surely, sir, a blot or two of a warm afternoon is not to be severely urged against gray hairs. Old age—even if it blot the page— is honorable. With submission, sir, we *both* are getting old."

This appeal to my fellow-feeling was hardly to be resisted. At all events, I saw that go he would not. So, I made up my mind to let him stay, resolving, nevertheless, to see to it that, during the afternoon, he had to do with my less important papers.

Nippers, the second on my list, was a whiskered, sallow, and, upon the whole, rather piratical-looking young man, of about five and twenty. I always deemed him the victim of two evil powers—ambition and indigestion. The ambition was evinced by a certain impatience of the duties of a mere copyist, an unwarrantable usurpation of strictly professional affairs, such as the original drawing up of legal documents. The indigestion seemed betokened in an occasional nervous testiness and grinning irritability, causing the teeth to audibly grind together over mistakes committed in copying; unnecessary maledictions, hissed, rather than spoken, in the heat of business; and especially by a continual discontent with the height of the table where he worked. Though of a very ingenious mechanical turn, Nippers could never get this table to suit him. He put chips under it, blocks of various sorts, bits of pasteboard, and at last went so far as to attempt an exquisite adjustment, by final pieces of folded blotting-paper. But no invention would answer. If, for the sake of easing his back, he brought the table lid at a sharp angle well up towards his chin, and wrote there like a man using the steep roof of a Dutch house for his desk, then he declared that it stopped the circulation in his arms. If now he lowered the table to his waistbands, and stooped over it in writing, then there was a sore aching in his back. In short, the truth of the matter was, Nippers knew not what he wanted. Or, if he wanted anything, it was to be rid of a scrivener's table altogether. Among the manifestations of his diseased ambition was a fondness he had for receiving visits from certain ambiguous-looking fellows in seedy coats, whom he called his clients. Indeed, I was aware that not only was he, at times, considerable of a ward-politician, but he occasionally did a little business at the Justices' courts, and was not unknown on the steps of the Tombs. I have good reason to believe, however, that one individual who called upon him at my chambers, and who, with a grand air, he insisted was his client, was no other than a dun, and the alleged title-deed, a bill. But, with all his failings, and the annoyances he caused me, Nippers, like his compatriot Turkey, was a very useful man to me; wrote a neat, swift hand; and, when he chose, was not deficient in a gentlemanly sort of deportment. Added to this, he always dressed in a gentlemanly sort of way; and so, incidentally, reflected credit upon my chambers. Whereas, with respect to Turkey, I had much ado to keep him from being a reproach to me. His clothes were apt to look oily, and smell of eating-houses. He wore his pantaloons very loose and baggy in summer. His coats were execrable; his hat not to be handled. But while the hat was a thing of indifference to me, inasmuch as his natural civility and deference, as a dependent Englishman, always led him to doff it the moment he entered the room, yet his coat was another matter. Concerning his coats, I reasoned with him; but with no effect. The truth was, I suppose, that a man with so small an income could not afford to sport such a lustrous face and a lustrous coat at one and the same time. As Nippers once observed, Turkey's money went chiefly for red ink. One winter day, I presented Turkey with a highly respectable-looking coat of my own—a padded gray coat, of a most comfortable warmth, and which buttoned straight up from the knee to the neck. I thought Turkey would appreciate the favor, and abate his rashness and obstreperousness of afternoons. But no; I verily believe that buttoning himself up in so downy and blanket-like a coat had a pernicious effect upon him—upon the same principle that too much oats are bad for horses. In fact, precisely as a rash, restive horse is said to feel his oats, so Turkey felt his coat. It made him insolent. He was a man whom prosperity harmed.

Though, concerning the self-indulgent habits of Turkey, I had my own private surmises, yet, touching Nippers, I was well persuaded that, whatever might be his faults in other respects, he was, at least, a temperate young man. But, indeed, nature herself seemed to have been his vintner, and, at his birth, charged him so thoroughly with an irritable, brandy-like disposition, that all subsequent potations were needless. When I consider how, amid the stillness of my chambers, Nippers would sometimes impatiently rise from his seat, and stooping over his table, spread his arms wide apart, seize the whole desk, and move it, and jerk it, with a grim, grinding motion on the floor, as if the table were a perverse voluntary agent, intent on thwarting and vexing him, I plainly perceive that, for Nippers, brandy-and-water were altogether superfluous.

It was fortunate for me that, owing to its peculiar cause—indigestion—the iritability and consequent nervousness of Nippers were mainly observable in the morning, while in the afternoon he was comparatively mild. So that, Turkey's paroxysms only coming on about twelve o'clock, I never had to do with their eccentricities at one time. Their fits relieved each other, like guards. When Nippers' was on, Turkey's was off; and *vice versa*. This was a good natural arrangement, under the circumstances.

Ginger Nut, the third on my list, was a lad, some twelve years old. His father was a car-man, ambitious of seeing his son on the bench instead of a cart, before he died. So he sent him to my office, as student at law, errand-boy, cleaner and sweeper, at the rate of one dollar a week. He had a little desk to himself, but he did not use it much. Upon inspection, the drawer exhibited a great array of the shells of various sorts of nuts. Indeed, to this quick-witted youth, the whole noble science of the law was contained in a nut-shell. Not the least among the employments of Ginger Nut, as well as one which he discharged with the most alacrity, was his duty as cake and apple purveyor for Turkey and Nippers. Copying law-papers being proverbially a dry, husky sort of business, my two scriveners were fain to moisten their mouths very often with Spitzenbergs, to be had at the numerous stalls nigh the Custom House and Post Office. Also, they sent Ginger Nut very frequently for that peculiar cake—small, flat, round, and very spicy—after which he had been named by them. Of a cold morning, when business was but dull, Turkey would gobble up scores of these cakes, as if they were mere wafers—indeed, they sell them at the rate of six or eight for a penny—the scrape of his pen blending with the crunching of the crisp particles in his mouth. Of all the fiery afternoon blunders and flurried rashnesses of Turkey, was his once moistening a ginger-cake between his lips, and clapping it on to a mortgage, for a seal. I came within an ace of dismissing him then. But he mollified me by making an oriental bow, and saying—

"With submission, sir, it was generous of me to find you in stationery on my own account."

Now my original business—that of a conveyancer and title hunter, and drawer-up of recondite documents of all sorts—was considerably increased by receiving the master's office. There was now great work for scriveners. Not only must I push the clerks already with me, but I must have additional help.

In answer to my advertisement, a motionless young man one morning stood upon my office threshold, the door being open, for it was summer. I can see that figure now—pallidly neat, pitiably respectable, incurably forlorn! It was Bartleby.

After a few words touching his qualifications, I engaged him, glad to have among my corps of copyists a man of so singularly sedate an aspect, which I thought might operate beneficially upon the flighty temper of Turkey, and the fiery one of Nippers.

I should have stated before that ground glass folding-doors divided my premises into two parts, one of which was occupied by my scriveners, the other by myself. According to my humor, I threw open these doors, or closed them. I resolved to assign Bartleby a corner by the folding-doors, but on my side of them, so as to have this quiet man within easy call, in case any trifling thing was to be done. I placed his desk close up to a small side-window in that part of the room, a window which originally had afforded a lateral view of certain grimy backyards and bricks, but which, owing to subsequent erections, commanded at present no view at all, though it gave some light. Within three feet of the panes was a wall, and the light came down from far above, between two lofty buildings, as from a very small opening in a dome. Still further to a satisfactory arrangement, I procured a high green folding screen, which might entirely isolate Bartleby from my sight, though not remove him from my voice. And thus, in a manner, privacy and society were conjoined.

At first, Bartleby did an extraordinary quantity of writing. As if long famishing for something to copy, he seemed to gorge himself on my documents. There was no pause for digestion. He ran a day and night line, copying by sun-light and by candle-light. I should have been quite delighted with his application, had he been cheerfully industrious. But he wrote on silently, palely, mechanically.

It is, of course, an indispensable part of a scrivener's business to verify the accuracy of his copy, word by word. Where there are two or more scriveners in an office, they assist each other in this examination, one reading from the copy, the other holding the original. It is a very dull, wearisome, and lethargic affair. I can readily imagine that, to some sanguine temperaments, it would be altogether intolerable. For example, I cannot credit that the mettlesome poet, Byron, would have contentedly sat down with Bartleby to examine a law document of, say five hundred pages, closely written in a crimpy hand.

Now and then, in the haste of business, it had been my habit to assist in comparing some brief document myself, calling Turkey or Nippers for this purpose. One object I had, in placing Bartleby so handy to me behind the screen, was, to avail myself of his services on such trivial occasions. It was on the third day, I think, of his being with me, and before any necessity had arisen for having his own writing examined, that, being much hurried to complete a small affair I had in hand, I abruptly called to Bartleby. In my haste and natural expectancy of instant compliance, I sat with my head bent over the original on my desk, and my right hand sideways, and somewhat nervously extended with the copy, so that, immediately upon emerging from his retreat, Bartleby might snatch it and proceed to business without the least delay.

In this very attitude did I sit when I called to him, rapidly stating what it was I wanted him to do—namely, to examine a small paper with me. Imagine my surprise, nay, my consternation, when, without moving from his privacy, Bartleby, in a singularly mild, firm voice, replied, "I would prefer not to."

I sat awhile in perfect silence, rallying my stunned faculties. Immediately it occurred to me that my ears had deceived me, or Bartleby had entirely misunderstood my meaning. I repeated my request in the clearest tone I could assume; but in quite as clear a one came the previous reply, "I would prefer not to."

"Prefer not to," echoed I, rising in high excitement, and crossing the room with a stride. "What do you mean? Are you moon-struck? I want you to help me compare this sheet here—take it," and I thrust it towards him.

"I would prefer not to," said he.

I looked at him steadfastly. His face was leanly composed; his gray eye dimly calm. Not a wrinkle of agitation rippled him. Had there been the least uneasiness, anger, impatience or impertinence in his manner; in other words, had there been any thing ordinarily human about him, doubtless I should have violently dismissed him from the premises. But as it was, I should have as soon thought of turning my pale plaster-of-paris bust of Cicero out of doors. I stood gazing at him awhile, as he went on with his own writing, and then reseated myself at my desk. This is very strange, thought I. What had one best do? But my business hurried me. I concluded to forget the matter for the present, reserving it for my future leisure. So calling Nippers from the other room, the paper was speedily examined.

A few days after this, Bartleby concluded four lengthy documents, being quadruplicates of a week's testimony taken before me in my High Court of Chancery. It became necessary to examine them. It was an important suit, and great accuracy was imperative. Having all things arranged, I called Turkey, Nippers, and Ginger Nut, from the next room, meaning to place the four copies in the hands of my four clerks, while I should read from the original. Accordingly, Turkey, Nippers, and Ginger Nut had taken their seats in a row, each with his document in his hand, when I called to Bartleby to join this interesting group.

"Bartleby! quick, I am waiting."

I heard a slow scrape of his chair legs on the uncarpeted floor, and soon he appeared standing at the entrance of his hermitage.

"What is wanted?" said he, mildly.

"The copies, the copies," said I, hurriedly. "We are going to examine them. There"—and I held towards him the fourth quadruplicate.

"I would prefer not to," he said, and gently disappeared behind the screen.

For a few moments I was turned into a pillar of salt, standing at the head of my seated column of clerks. Recovering myself, I advanced towards the screen, and demanded the reason for such extraordinary conduct.

"*Why* do you refuse?"

"I would prefer not to."

With any other man I should have flown outright into a dreadful passion, scorned all further words, and thrust him ignominiously from my presence. But there was something about Bartleby that not only strangely disarmed me, but, in a wonderful manner, touched and disconcerted me. I began to reason with him.

"These are your own copies we are about to examine. It is labor saving to you, because one examination will answer for your four papers. It is common usage. Every copyist is bound to help examine his copy. Is it not so? Will you not speak? Answer!"

"I prefer not to," he replied in a flutelike tone. It seemed to me that, while I had been addressing him, he carefully revolved every statement that I made; fully comprehended the meaning; could not gainsay the irresistible conclusion; but, at the same time, some paramount consideration prevailed with him to reply as he did.

"You are decided, then, not to comply with my request—a request made according to common usage and common sense?"

He briefly gave me to understand, that on that point my judgment was sound. Yes: his decision was irreversible.

It is not seldom the case that, when a man is browbeaten in some unprecedented and violently unreasonable way, he begins to stagger in his own plainest faith. He begins, as it were, vaguely to surmise that, wonderful as it may be, all the justice and all the reason is on the other side. Accordingly, if any disinterested persons are present, he turns to them for some reinforcement of his own faltering mind.

"Turkey," said I, "what do you think of this? Am I not right?"

"With submission, sir," said Turkey, in his blandest tone, "I think that you are."

"Nippers," said I, "what do *you* think of it?"

"I think I should kick him out of the office."

(The reader, of nice perceptions, will here perceive that, it being morning, Turkey's answer is couched in polite and tranquil terms, but Nippers' replies in ill-tempered ones. Or, to repeat a previous sentence, Nippers' ugly mood was on duty, and Turkey's off.)

"Ginger Nut," said I, willing to enlist the smallest suffrage in my behalf, "what do *you* think of it?"

"I think, sir, he's a little *luny*," replied Ginger Nut, with a grin.

"You hear what they say," said I, turning towards the screen, "come forth and do your duty."

But he vouchsafed no reply. I pondered a moment in sore perplexity. But once more business hurried me. I determined again to postpone the consideration of this dilemma to my future leisure. With a little trouble we made out to examine the papers without Bartleby, though at every page or two Turkey deferentially dropped his opinion, that this proceeding was quite out of the common; while Nippers, twitching in his chair with a dyspeptic nervousness, ground out, between his set teeth, occasional hissing maledictions against the stubborn oaf behind the screen. And for his (Nippers') part, this was the first and the last time he would do another man's business without pay.

Meanwhile Bartleby sat in his hermitage, oblivious to everything but his own peculiar business there.

Some days passed, the scrivener being employed upon another lengthy work. His late remarkable conduct led me to regard his ways narrowly. I observed that he never went to dinner; indeed, that he never went anywhere. As yet I had never, of my personal knowledge, known him to be outside of my office. He was a perpetual sentry in the corner. At about eleven o'clock though, in the morning, I noticed that Ginger Nut would advance toward the opening in Bartleby's screen, as if silently beckoned thither by a gesture invisible to me where I sat. The boy would then leave the office, jingling a few pence, and reappear with a handful of ginger-nuts, which he delivered in the hermitage, receiving two of the cakes for his trouble.

He lives, then, on ginger-nuts, thought I; never eats a dinner, properly speaking; he must be a vegetarian, then; but no; he never eats even vegetables, he eats nothing but ginger-nuts. My mind then ran on in reveries concerning the probable effects upon the human constitution of living entirely on ginger-nuts. Ginger-nuts are so called, because they contain ginger as one of their peculiar constituents, and the final flavoring one. Now, what was ginger? A hot, spicy thing. Was Bartleby hot and spicy? Not at all. Ginger, then, had no effect upon Bartleby. Probably he preferred it should have none.

Nothing so aggravates an earnest person as a passive resistance. If the individual so resisted be of a not inhumane temper, and the resisting one perfectly harmless in his passivity, then, in the better moods of the former, he will endeavor charitably to construe to his imagination what proves impossible to be solved by his judgment. Even so, for the most part, I regarded Bartleby and his ways. Poor fellow! thought I, he means no mischief; it is plain he intends no insolence; his aspect sufficiently evinces that his eccentricities are involuntary. He is useful to me. I can get along with him. If I turn him away, the chances are he will fall in with some less-indulgent employer, and then he will be rudely treated, and perhaps driven forth miserably to starve. Yes. Here I can cheaply purchase a delicious self-approval. To befriend Bartleby; to humor him in his strange willfulness, will cost me little or nothing, while I lay up in my soul what will eventually prove a sweet morsel for my conscience. But this mood was not invariable with me. The passiveness of Bartleby sometimes irritated me. I felt strangely goaded on to encounter him in new opposition—to elicit some angry spark from him answerable to my own. But, indeed, I might as well have essayed to strike fire with my knuckles against a bit of Windsor soap. But one afternoon the evil impulse in me mastered me, and the following little scene ensued:

"Bartleby," said I, "when those papers are all copied, I will compare them with you."

"I would prefer not to."

"How? Surely you do not mean to persist in that mulish vagary?" No answer.

I threw open the folding-doors near by, and, turning upon Turkey and Nippers, exclaimed:

"Bartleby a second time says, he won't examine his papers. What do you think of it, Turkey?"

It was afternoon, be it remembered. Turkey sat glowing like a brass boiler; his bald head steaming; his hands reeling among his blotted papers.

"Think of it?" roared Turkey; "I think I'll just step behind his screen, and black his eyes for him!"

So saying, Turkey rose to his feet and threw his arms into a pugilistic position. He was hurrying away to make good his promise, when I detained him, alarmed at the effect of incautiously rousing Turkey's combativeness after dinner.

"Sit down, Turkey," said I, "and hear what Nippers has to say. What do you think of it, Nippers? Would I not be justified in immediately dismissing Bartleby?"

"Excuse me, that is for you to decide, sir. I think his conduct quite unusual, and, indeed, unjust, as regards Turkey and myself. But it may only be a passing whim."

"Ah," exclaimed I, "you have strangely changed your mind, then—you speak very gently of him now."

"All beer," cried Turkey; "gentleness is effects of beer—Nippers and I dined together to-day. You see how gentle *I* am, sir. Shall I go and black his eyes?"

"You refer to Bartleby, I suppose. No, not to-day, Turkey," I replied; "pray, put up your fists."

I closed the doors, and again advanced towards Bartleby. I felt additional incentives tempting me to my fate. I burned to be rebelled against again. I remember that Bartleby never left the office.

"Bartleby," said I, "Ginger Nut is away; just step around to the Post Office, won't you? (it was but a three minutes' walk), and see if there is anything for me."

"I would prefer not to."

"You *will* not?"

"I *prefer* not."

I staggered to my desk, and sat there in a deep study. My blind inveteracy returned. Was there any other thing in which I could procure myself to be ignominiously repulsed by this lean, penniless wight?—my hired clerk? What added thing is there, prefectly reasonable, that he will be sure to refuse to do?

"Bartleby!"

No answer.

"Bartleby," in a louder tone.

No answer.

"Bartleby," I roared.

Like a very ghost, agreeably to the laws of magical invocation, at the third summons, he appeared at the entrance of his hermitage.

"Go to the next room, and tell Nippers to come to me."

"I prefer not to," he respectfully and slowly said, and mildly disappeared.

"Very good, Bartleby," said I, in a quiet sort of serenely-severe self-possessed tone, intimating the unalterable purpose of some terrible retribution very close at hand. But upon the whole, as it was drawing towards my dinner-hour, I thought it best to put on my hat and walk home for the day, suffering much from perplexity and distress of mind.

Shall I acknowledge it? The conclusion of this whole business was, that it soon became a fixed fact of my chambers, that a pale young scrivener, by the name of Bartleby, had a desk there; that he copied for me at the usual rate of four cents a folio (one hundred words); but he was permanently exempt from examining the work done by him, that duty being transferred to Turkey and Nippers, out of compliment, doubtless, to their superior acuteness; moreover, said Bartleby was never, on any account, to be dispatched on the most trivial errand of any sort; and that even if entreated to take upon him such a matter, it was generally understood that he would "prefer not to"—in other words, that he would refuse point-blank.

As days passed on, I became considerably reconciled to Bartleby. His steadiness, his freedom from all dissipation, his incessant industry (except when he chose to throw himself into a standing revery behind his screen), his great stillness, his unalterableness of demeanor under all circumstances, made him a valuable acquisition. One prime thing was this—*he was always there*—first in the morning, continually through the day, and the last at night. I had a singular confidence in his honesty. I felt my most precious papers perfectly safe in his hands. Sometimes, to be sure, I could not, for the very soul of me, avoid falling into sudden spasmodic passions with him. For it was exceeding difficult to bear in mind all the time those strange peculiarities, privileges, and unheard of exemptions, forming the tacit stipulations on Bartleby's part under which he remained in my office. Now and then, in the eagerness of dispatching pressing business, I would inadvertently summon Bartleby, in a short, rapid tone, to put his finger, say, on the incipient tie of a bit of red tape with which I was about compressing some papers. Of course, from behind the screen the usual answer, "I prefer not to," was sure to come; and then, how could a human creature, with the common infirmities of our nature, refrain from bitterly exclaiming upon such perverseness—such unreasonableness. However, every added repulse of this sort which I received only tended to lessen the probability of my repeating the inadvertence.

Here it must be said, that according to the custom of most legal gentlemen occupying chambers in densely-populated law buildings, there were several keys to my door. One was kept by a woman residing in the attic, which person weekly scrubbed and daily swept and dusted my apartments. Another was kept by Turkey for convenience sake. The third I sometimes carried in my own pocket. The fourth I knew not who had.

Now, one Sunday morning I happened to go to Trinity Church, to hear a celebrated preacher, and finding myself rather early on the ground I thought I would walk around to my chambers for a while. Luckily I had my key with me; but upon applying it to the lock, I found it resisted by something inserted from the inside. Quite surprised, I called out; when to my consternation a key was turned from within; and thrusting his lean visage at me, and holding the door ajar, the apparition of Bartleby appeared, in his shirt sleeves, and otherwise in a strangely tattered deshabille, saying quietly that he was sorry, but he was deeply engaged just then, and—preferred not admitting me at present. In a brief word or two, he moreover added, that perhaps I had better walk around the block two or three times, and by that time he would probably have concluded his affairs.

Now, the utterly unsurmised appearance of Bartleby, tenanting my law-chambers of a Sunday morning, with his cadaverously gentlemanly *nonchalance,* yet withal firm and self-possessed, had such a strange effect upon me, that incontinently I slunk away from my own door, and did as desired. But not without sundry twinges of impotent rebellion against the mild effrontery of this unaccountable scrivener. Indeed, it was his wonderful mildness chiefly, which not only disarmed me, but unmanned me as it were. For I consider that one, for the time, is somehow unmanned when he tranquilly permits his hired clerk to dictate to him, and order him away from his own premises. Furthermore, I was full of uneasiness as to what Bartleby could possibly be doing in my office in his shirt sleeves, and in an otherwise dismantled condition of a Sunday morning. Was anything amiss going on? Nay, that was out of the question. It was not to be thought of for a moment that Bartleby was an immoral person. But what could he be doing there?—copying? Nay again, whatever might be his eccentricities, Bartleby was an eminently decorous person. He would be the last man to sit down to his desk in any state approaching to nudity. Besides, it was Sunday; and there was something about Bartleby that forbade the supposition that he would by any secular occupation violate the proprieties of the day.

Nevertheless, my mind was not pacified; and full of a restless curiosity, at last I returned to the door. Without hindrance I inserted my key, opened it, and entered. Bartleby was not to be seen. I looked round anxiously, peeped behind his screen; but it was very plain that he was gone. Upon more closely examining the place, I surmised that for an indefinite period Bartleby must have ate, dressed, and slept in my office, and that, too, without plate, mirror, or bed. The cushioned seat of a rickety old sofa in one corner bore the faint impression of a lean, reclining form. Rolled away under his desk, I found a blanket; on a chair, a tin basin, with soap and a ragged towel; in a newspaper a few crumbs of ginger-nuts and a morsel of cheese. Yes, thought I, it is evident enough that Bartleby has been making his home here, keeping bachelor's hall all by himself. Immediately then the thought came sweeping across me, what miserable friendlessness and loneliness are here revealed! His poverty is great; but his solitude, how horrible! Think of it. Of a Sunday, Wall Street is deserted as Petra;[2] and every night of every day it is an emptiness. This building, too, which of week-days hums with industry and life, at nightfall echoes with sheer vacancy, and all through Sunday is forlorn. And here Bartleby makes his home; sole spectator of a solitude which he has seen all populous—a sort of innocent and transformed Marius brooding among the ruins of Carthage!

For the first time in my life a feeling of over-powering stinging

---

[2] *Petra:* ancient city in Syria.

melancholy seized me. Before, I had never experienced aught but a not unpleasing sadness. The bond of a common humanity now drew me irresistibly to gloom. A fraternal melancholy! For both I and Bartleby were sons of Adam. I remembered the bright silks and sparkling faces I had seen that day, in gala trim, swan-like sailing down the Mississippi of Broadway; and I contrasted them with the pallid copyist, and thought to myself, Ah, happiness courts the light, so we deem the world is gay; but misery hides aloof, so we deem that misery there is none. These sad fancyings—chimeras, doubtless, of a sick and silly brain—led on to other and more special thoughts, concerning the eccentricities of Bartleby. Presentiments of strange discoveries hovered round me. The scrivener's pale form appeared to me laid out, among uncaring strangers, in its shivering winding sheet.

Suddenly I was attracted by Bartleby's closed desk, the key in open sight left in the lock.

I mean no mischief, seek the gratification of no heartless curiosity, thought I; besides, the desk is mine, and its contents, too, so I will make bold to look within. Everything was methodically arranged, the papers smoothly placed. The pigeon holes were deep, and removing the files of documents, I groped into their recesses. Presently I felt something there, and dragged it out. It was an old bandanna handkerchief, heavy and knotted. I opened it, and saw it was a saving's bank.

I now recalled all the quiet mysteries which I had noted in the man. I remembered that he never spoke but to answer; that, though at intervals he had considerable time to himself, yet I had never seen him reading—no, not even a newspaper; that for long periods he would stand looking out, at his pale window behind the screen, upon the dead brick wall; I was quite sure he never visited any refectory or eating house; while his pale face clearly indicated that he never drank beer like Turkey, or tea and coffee even, like other men; that he never went anywhere in particular that I could learn; never went out for a walk, unless, indeed, that was the case at present; that he had declined telling who he was, or whence he came, or whether he had any relatives in the world; that though so thin and pale, he never complained of ill health. And more than all, I remembered a certain unconscious air of pallid—how shall I call it?—of pallid haughtiness, say, or rather an austere reserve about him, which had positively awed me into my tame compliance with his eccentricities, when I had feared to ask him to do the slightest incidental thing for me, even though I might know, from his long-continued motionlessness, that behind his screen he must be standing in one of those dead-wall reveries of his.

Revolving all these things, and coupling them with the recently discovered fact, that he made my office his constant abiding place and home, and not forgetful of his morbid moodiness; revolving all these things, a prudential feeling began to steal over me. My first emotions had been those of pure melancholy and sincerest pity; but just in proportion as the forlornness of Bartleby grew and grew to my imagination, did that same melancholy merge into fear, that pity into repulsion. So true it is, and so terrible, too, that up to a certain point the thought or sight of misery enlists our best affections; but, in certain special cases, beyond that point it does not. They err who would assert that invariably this is owing to the inherent selfishness of the human heart. It rather proceeds from a certain hopelessness of remedying excessive and organic ill. To a sensitive being, pity is not seldom pain. And when at last it is perceived that such pity cannot lead to effectual succor, common sense bids the soul be rid of it. What I saw that morning persuaded me that the scrivener was the victim of inate and incurable disorder. I might give alms to his body; but his body did not pain him; it was his soul that suffered, and his soul I could not reach.

I did not accomplish the purpose of going to Trinity Church that morning. Somehow, the things I had seen disqualified me for the time from church-going. I walked homeward, thinking what I would do with Bartleby. Finally, I resolved upon this—I would put certain calm questions to him the next morning, touching his history, etc., and if he declined to answer them openly and unreservedly (and I supposed he would prefer not), then to give him a twenty dollar bill over and above whatever I might owe him, and tell him his services were no longer required; but that if in any other way I could assist him, I would be happy to do so, especially if he desired to return to his native place, wherever that might be, I would willingly help to defray the expenses. Moreover, if, after reaching home, he found himself at any time in want of aid, a letter from him would be sure of a reply.

The next morning came.

"Bartleby," said I, gently calling to him behind his screen.

No reply.

"Bartleby," said I, in a still gentler tone, "come here; I am not going to ask you to do anything you would prefer not to do—I simply wish to speak to you."

Upon this he noiselessly slid into view.

"Will you tell me, Bartleby, where you were born?"

"I would prefer not to."

"Will you tell me *anything* about yourself?"

"I would prefer not to."

"But what reasonable objection can you have to speak to me? I feel friendly towards you."

He did not look at me while I spoke, but kept his glance fixed upon my bust of Cicero, which, as I then sat, was directly behind me, some six inches above my head.

"What is your answer, Bartleby," said I, after waiting a considerable time for a reply, during which his countenance remained immovable, only there was the faintest conceivable tremor of the white attenuated mouth.

"At present I prefer to give no answer," he said, and retired into his hermitage.

It was rather weak in me I confess, but his manner, on this occasion, nettled me. Not only did there seem to lurk in it a certain calm disdain, but his perverseness seemed ungrateful, considering the undeniable good usage and indulgence he had received from me.

Again I sat ruminating what I should do. Mortified as I was at his behavior, and resolved as I had been to dismiss him when I entered my office, nevertheless I strangely felt something superstitious knocking at my heart, and forbidding me to carry out my purpose, and denouncing me for a villain if I dared to breathe one bitter word against this forlornest of mankind. At last, familiarly drawing my chair behind his screen, I sat down and said: "Bartleby, never mind, then, about revealing your history; but let me entreat you, as a friend, to comply as far as may be with the usages of this office. Say now, you will help to examine papers to-morrow or next day: in short, say now, that in a day or two you will begin to be a little reasonable:—say so, Bartleby."

"At present I would prefer not to be a little reasonable," was his mildly cadaverous reply.

Just then the folding-doors opened, and Nippers approached. He seemed suffering from an unusually bad night's rest, induced by severer indigestion than common. He overheard those final words of Bartleby.

"*Prefer not,* eh?" gritted Nippers—"I'd *prefer* him, if I were you, sir," addressing me—"I'd *prefer* him; I'd give him preferences, the stubborn mule! What is it, sir, pray, that he *prefers* not to do now?"

Bartleby moved not a limb.

"Mr. Nippers," said I, "I'd prefer that you would withdraw for the present."

Somehow, of late, I had got into the way of involuntarily using this word "prefer" upon all sorts of not exactly suitable occasions. And I trembled to think that my contact with the scrivener had already and seriously affected me in a mental way. And what further and deeper aberration might it not yet produce? This apprehension had not been without efficacy in determining me to summary measures.

As Nippers, looking very sour and sulky, was departing, Turkey blandly and deferentially approached.

"With submission, sir," said he, "yesterday I was thinking abut Bartleby here, and I think that if he would but prefer to take a quart of good ale every day, it would do much towards mending him, and enabling him to assist in examining his papers."

"So you have got the word, too," said I, slightly excited.

"With submission, what word, sir," asked Turkey, respectfully crowding himself into the contracted space behind the screen, and by so doing, making me jostle the scrivener. "What word, sir?"

"I would prefer to be left alone here," said Bartleby, as if offended at being mobbed in his privacy.

"*That's* the word, Turkey," said I—"*that's* it."

"Oh, *prefer?* oh yes—queer word. I never use it myself. But, sir, as I was saying, if he would but prefer—"

"Turkey," interrupted I, "you will please withdraw."

"Oh, certainly, sir, if you prefer that I should."

As he opened the folding-door to retire, Nippers at his desk caught a glimpse of me, and asked whether I would prefer to have a certain paper copied on blue paper or white. He did not in the least roguishly accent the word prefer. It was plain that it involuntarily rolled from his tongue. I thought to myself, surely I must get rid of a demented man, who already has in some degree turned the tongues, if not the heads of myself and clerks. But I thought it prudent not to break the dismission at once.

The next day I noticed that Bartleby did nothing but stand at his window in his dead-wall revery. Upon asking him why he did not write, he said that he had decided upon doing no more writing.

"Why, how now? what next?" exclaimed I, "do no more writing?"

"No more."

"And what is the reason?"

"Do you not see the reason for yourself," he indifferently replied.

I looked steadfastly at thim, and perceived that his eyes looked dull and glazed. Instantly it occurred to me, that his unexampled diligence in copying by his dim window for the first few weeks of his stay with me might have temporarily impaired his vision.

I was touched. I said something in condolence with him. I hinted that of course he did wisely in abstaining from writing for a while; and urged him to embrace that opportunity of taking wholesome exercise in the open air. This, however, he did not do. A few days after this, my other clerks being absent, and being in a great hurry to dispatch certain letters by the mail, I thought that, having nothing else earthly to do, Bartleby would surely be less inflexible than usual, and carry these letters to the post-office. But he blankly declined. So, much to my inconvenience, I went myself.

Still added days went by. Whether Bartleby's eyes improved or not, I could not say. To all appearance, I thought they did. But when I asked him if they did, he vouchsafed no answer. At all events, he would do no copying. At last, in reply to my urgings, he informed me that he had permanently given up copying.

"What!" exclaimed I; "suppose your eyes should get entirely well—better than ever before—would you not copy then?"

"I have given up copying," he answered, and slid aside.

He remained as ever, a fixture in my chamber. Nay—if that were possible—he became still more of a fixture than before. What was to be done? He would do nothing in the office; why should he stay there? In plain fact, he had now become a millstone to me, not only useless as a necklace, but afflictive to bear. Yet I was sorry for him. I speak less than truth when I say that, on his own account, he occasioned me uneasiness. If he would but have named a single relative or friend, I would instantly have written, and urged their taking the poor fellow away to some convenient retreat. But he seemed alone, absolutely alone in the universe. A bit of wreck in the mid Atlantic. At length, necessities connected with my business tyrannized over all other considerations. Decently as I could, I told Bartleby that in six days time he must unconditionally leave the office. I warned him to take measures, in the interval, for procuring some other abode. I offered to assist him in this endeavor, if he himself would but take the first step towards a removal. "And when you finally quit me, Bartleby," added I, "I shall see that you go not away entirely unprovided. Six days from this hour, remember."

At the expiration of that period, I peeped behind the screen, and lo! Bartleby was there.

I buttoned up my coat, balanced myself; advanced slowly towards him, touched his shoulder, and said, "The time has come; you must quit this place; I am sorry for you; here is money; but you must go."

"I would prefer not," he replied, with his back still towards me.

"You *must*."

He remained silent.

Now I had an unbounded confidence in this man's common honesty. He had frequently restored to me sixpences and shillings carelessly dropped upon the floor, for I am apt to be very reckless in such shirt-button affairs. The proceeding, then, which followed will not be deemed extraordinary.

"Bartleby," said I, "I owe you twelve dollars on account; here are thirty-two; the odd twenty are yours—Will you take it?" and I handed the bills towards him.

But he made no motion.

"I will leave them here, then," putting them under a weight on the table. Then taking my hat and cane and going to the door, I tranquilly turned and added—"After you have removed your things from these offices, Bartleby, you will of course lock the door—since every one is now gone for the day but you—and if you please, slip your key underneath the mat, so that I may have it in the morning. I shall not see you again; so good-by to you. If, hereafter, in your new place of abode, I can be of any service to you, do not fail to advise me by letter. Good-by, Bartleby, and fare you well."

But he answered not a word; like the last column of some ruined temple, he remained standing mute and solitary in the middle of the otherwise deserted room.

As I walked home in a pensive mood, my vanity got the better of my pity. I could not but highly plume myself on my masterly management in getting rid of Bartleby. Masterly I call it, and such it must appear to any dispassionate thinker. The beauty of my procedure seemed to consist in its perfect quietness. There was no vulgar bullying, no bravado of any sort, no choleric hectoring, and striding to and fro across the apartment, jerking out vehement commands for Bartleby to bundle himself off with his beggarly traps. Nothing of the kind. Without loudly bidding Bartleby depart—as an inferior genius might have done—I *assumed* the ground that depart he must; and upon that assumption built all I had to say. The more I thought over my procedure, the more I was charmed with it. Nevertheless, next morning, upon awakening, I had my doubts—I had somehow slept off the fumes of vanity. One of the coolest and wisest hours a man has, is just after he awakes in the morning. My procedure seemed as sagacious as ever—but only in theory. How it would prove in practice—there was the rub. It was truly a beautiful thought to have assumed Bartleby's departure; but, after all, that assumption was simply my own, and none of Bartleby's. The great point was, not whether I had assumed that he would quit me, but whether he would prefer so to do. He was more a man of preferences than assumptions.

After breakfast, I walked down town, arguing the probabilities *pro* and *con*. One moment I thought it would prove a miserable failure, and Bartleby would be found all alive at my office as usual; the next moment it seemed certain that I should find his chair empty. And so I kept veering about. At the corner of Broadway and Canal Street, I saw quite an excited group of people standing in earnest conversation.

"I'll take odds he doesn't," said a voice as I passed.

"Doesn't go?—done!" said I, "put up your money."

I was instinctively putting my hand in my pocket to produce my own, when I remembered that this was an election day. The words I had overheard bore no reference to Bartleby, but to the success or nonsuccess of some candidate for the mayoralty. In my intent frame of mind, I had, as it were, imagined that all Broadway shared in my excitement, and were debating the same question with me. I passed on, very thankful that the uproar of the street screened my momentary absent-mindedness.

As I had intended, I was earlier than usual at my office door. I stood listening for a moment. All was still. He must be gone. I tried the knob. The door was locked. Yes, my procedure had worked to a charm; he indeed must be vanished. Yet a certain melancholy mixed with this: I was almost sorry for my brilliant success. I was fumbling under the door mat for the key, which Bartleby was to have left there for me, when accidentally my knee knocked against a panel, producing a summoning sound, and in response a voice came to me from within—"Not yet; I am occupied."

It was Bartleby.

I was thunderstruck. For an instant I stood like the man who, pipe in mouth, was killed one cloudless afternoon long ago in Virginia, by summer lightning; at his own warm open window he was killed, and remained leaning out there upon the dreamy afternoon, till some one touched him, when he fell.

"Not gone!" I murmured at last. But again obeying that wondrous ascendancy which the inscrutable scrivener had over me, and from which ascendancy, for all my chafing, I could not completely escape, I slowly went down stairs and out into the street, and while walking round the block, considered what I should next do in this unheard-of perplexity. Turn the man out by an actual thrusting I could not; to drive him away by calling him hard names would not do; calling in the police was an unpleasant idea; and yet, permit him to enjoy his cadaverous triumph over me—this, too, I could not think of. What was to be done? or, if nothing could be done, was there anything further that I could *assume* in the matter? Yes, as before I had prospectively assumed that Bartleby would depart, so now I might retrospectively assume that departed he was. In the legitimate carrying out of this assumption, I might enter my office in a great hurry, and pretending not to see Bartleby at all, walk straight against him as if he were air. Such a proceeding would in a singular degree have the appearance of a home-thrust. It was hardly possible that Bartleby could withstand such an application of the doctrine of assumptions. But upon second thoughts the success of the plan seemed rather dubious. I resolved to argue the matter over with him again.

"Bartleby," said I, entering the office, with a quietly severe expression, "I am seriously displeased. I am pained, Bartleby. I had thought better of you. I had imagined you of such a gentlemanly organization, that in any delicate dilemma a slight hint would suffice—in short, an assumption. But it appears I am deceived. Why," I added, unaffectedly starting, "you have not even touched that money yet," pointing to it, just where I had left it the evening previous.

He answered nothing.

"Will you, or will you not, quit me?" I now demanded in a sudden passion, advancing close to him.

"I would prefer *not* to quit you," he replied, gently emphasizing the *not*.

"What earthly right have you to stay here? Do you pay any rent? Do you pay my taxes? Or is this property yours?"

He answered nothing.

"Are you ready to go on and write now? Are your eyes recovered? Could you copy a small paper for me this morning? or help examine a few lines? or step round to the post-office? In a word, will you do anything at all, to give a coloring to your refusal to depart the premises?"

He silently retired into his hermitage.

I was now in such a state of nervous resentment that I thought it but prudent to check myself at present from further demonstrations. Bartleby and I were alone. I remembered the tragedy of the unfortunate Adams and the still more unfortunate Colt in the solitary office of the latter; and how poor Colt, being dreadfully incensed by Adams, and imprudently permitting himself to get wildly excited, was at unawares hurried into his fatal act—an act which certainly no man could possibly deplore more than the actor himself. Often it had occurred to me in my ponderings upon the subject, that had that altercation taken place in the public street, or at a private residence, it would not have terminated as it did. It was the circumstance of being alone in a solitary office, up stairs, of a building entirely unhallowed by humanizing domestic associations—an uncarpeted office, doubtless, of a dusty, haggard sort of appearance—this it must have been, which greatly helped to enhance the irritable desperation of the hapless Colt.[3]

But when this old Adam of resentment rose in me and tempted me concerning Bartleby, I grappled him and threw him. How? Why, simply by recalling the divine injunction: "A new commandment give I unto you, that ye love one another." Yes, this it was that saved me. Aside from higher considerations, charity often operates as a vastly wise and prudent principle—a great safeguard to its possessor. Men have committed murder for jealousy's sake, and anger's sake, and hatred's sake, and selfishness' sake, and spiritual pride's sake; but no man, that ever I heard of, ever committed a diabolical murder for

---

[3] *Adams . . . Colt:* a widely publicized murder-case in which John C. Colt killed Samuel Adams, in New York City, in January, 1842.

sweet charity's sake. Mere self-interest, then, if no better motive can be enlisted, should, especially with high-tempered men, prompt all beings to charity and philanthropy. At any rate, upon the occasion in question, I strove to drown my exasperated feelings towards the scrivener by benevolently construing his conduct. Poor fellow, poor fellow! thought I, he don't mean anything; and besides, he has seen hard times, and ought to be indulged.

I endeavored, also, immediately to occupy myself, and at the same time to comfort my despondency. I tried to fancy, that in the course of the morning, at such time as might prove agreeable to him, Bartleby, of his own free accord, would emerge from his hermitage and take up some decided line of march in the direction of the door. But no. Half-past twelve o'clock came; Turkey began to glow in the face, overturn his inkstand, and become generally obstreperous; Nippers abated down into quietude and courtesy; Ginger Nut munched his noon apple; and Bartleby remained standing at his window in one of his profoundest dead-wall reveries. Will it be credited? Ought I to acknowledge it? That afternoon I left the office without saying one further word to him.

Some days now passed, during which, at leisure intervals I looked a little into "Edwards on the Will," and "Priestly on Necessity." Under the circumstances, those books induced a salutary feeling. Gradually I slid into the persuasion that these troubles of mine, touching the scrivener, had been all predestinated from eternity, and Bartleby was billeted upon me for some mysterious purpose of an allwise Providence, which it was not for a mere mortal like me to fathom. Yes, Bartleby, stay there behind your screen, thought I; I shall persecute you no more; you are harmless and noiseless as any of these old chairs; in short, I never feel so private as when I know you are here. At last I see it, I feel it; I penetrate to the predestinated purpose of my life. I am content. Others may have loftier parts to enact; but my mission in this world, Bartleby, is to furnish you with office-room for such period as you may see fit to remain.

I believe that this wise and blessed frame of mind would have continued with me, had it not been for the unsolicited and uncharitable remarks obtruded upon me by my professional friends who visited the rooms. But thus it often is, that the constant friction of illiberal minds wears out at last the best resolves of the more generous. Though to be sure, when I reflected upon it, it was not strange that people entering my office should be struck by the peculiar aspect of the unaccountable Bartleby, and so be tempted to throw out some sinister observations concerning him. Sometimes an attorney, having business with me, and calling at my office, and finding no one but the scrivener there, would undertake to obtain some sort of precise information from him touching my whereabouts;

but without heeding his idle talk, Bartleby would remain standing immovable in the middle of the room. So after contemplating him in that position for a time, the attorney would depart, no wiser than he came.

Also, when a reference was going on, and the room full of lawyers and witnesses, and business driving fast, some deeply-occupied legal gentleman present, seeing Bartleby wholly unemployed, would request him to run round to his (the legal gentleman's) office and fetch some papers for him. Thereupon, Bartleby would tranquilly decline, and yet remain idle as before. Then the lawyer would give a great stare, and turn to me. And what could I say? At last I was made aware that all through the circle of my professional acquaintance, a whisper of wonder was running round, having reference to the strange creature I kept at my office. This worried me very much. And as the idea came upon me of his possibly turning out a long-lived man, and keep occupying my chambers, and denying my authority; and perplexing my visitors; and scandalizing my professional reputation; and casting a general gloom over the premises; keeping soul and body together to the last upon his savings (for doubtless he spent but half a dime a day), and in the end perhaps outlive me, and claim possession of my office by right of his perpetual occupancy: as all these dark anticipations crowded upon me more and more, and my friends continually intruded their relentless remarks upon the apparition in my room; a great change was wrought in me. I resolved to gather all my faculties together, and forever rid me of this intolerable incubus.

Ere revolving any complicated project, however, adapted to this end, I first simply suggested to Bartleby the propriety of his permanent departure. In a calm and serious tone, I commended the idea to his careful and mature consideration. But, having taken three days to meditate upon it, he apprised me, that his original determination remained the same; in short, that he still preferred to abide with me.

What shall I do? I now said to myself, buttoning up my coat to the last button. What shall I do? what ought I to do? what does conscience say I *should* do with this man, or, rather, ghost. Rid myself of him, I must; go, he shall. But how? You will not thrust him, the poor, pale, passive mortal—you will not thrust such a helpless creature out of your door? you will not dishonor yourself by such cruelty? No, I will not, I cannot do that. Rather would I let him live and die here, and then mason up his remains in the wall. What, then, will you do? For all your coaxing, he will not budge. Bribes he leaves under your own paper-weight on your table; in short, it is quite plain that he prefers to cling to you.

Then something severe, something unusual must be done. What! surely you will not have him collared by a constable, and commit his innocent pallor to the common jail? And upon what ground could you procure such a thing to be done?—a vagrant, is he? What! he a vagrant, a wanderer, who refuses to budge? It is because he will *not* be a vagrant, then, that you seek to count him *as* a vagrant. That is too absurd. No visible means of support: there I have him. Wrong again: for indubitably he *does* support himself, and that is the only unanswerable proof that any man can show of his possessing the means so to do. No more, then. Since he will not quit me, I must quit him. I will change my offices; I will move elsewhere, and give him fair notice, that if I find him on my new premises I will then proceed against him as a common trespasser.

Acting accordingly, next day I thus addressed him: "I find these chambers too far from the City Hall; the air is unwholesome. In a word, I propose to remove my offices next week, and shall no longer require your services. I tell you this now, in order that you may seek another place."

He made no reply, and nothing more was said.

On the appointed day I engaged carts and men, proceeded to my chambers, and, having but little furniture, everything was removed in a few hours. Throughout, the scrivener remained standing behind the screen, which I directed to be removed the last thing. It was withdrawn; and, being folded up like a huge folio, left him the motionless occupant of a naked room. I stood in the entry watching him a moment, while something from within me upbraided me.

I re-entered, with my hand in my pocket—and—and my heart in my mouth.

"Good-by, Bartleby; I am going—good-by, and God some way bless you; and take that," slipping something in his hand. But it dropped upon the floor, and then—strange to say—I tore myself from him whom I had so longed to be rid of.

Established in my new quarters, for a day or two I kept the door locked, and started at every footfall in the passages. When I returned to my rooms, after any little absence, I would pause at the threshold for an instant, and attentively listen, ere applying my key. But these fears were needless. Bartleby never came nigh me.

I thought all was going well, when a perturbed-looking stranger visited me, inquiring whether I was the person who had recently occupied rooms at No. — Wall Street.

Full of forebodings, I replied that I was.

"Then, sir," said the stranger, who proved a lawyer, "you are responsible for the man you left there. He refuses to do any copying; he refuses to do anything; he says he prefers not to; and he refuses to quit the premises."

"I am very sorry, sir," said I, with assumed tranquillity, but an inward tremor, "but, really, the man you allude to is nothing to me—he is no relation or apprentice of mine, that you should hold me responsible for him."

"In mercy's name, who is he?"

"I certainly cannot inform you. I know nothing about him. Formerly I employed him as a copyist; but he has done nothing for me now for some time past."

"I shall settle him, then—good morning, sir."

Several days passed, and I heard nothing more; and, though I often felt a charitable prompting to call at the place and see poor Bartleby, yet a certain squeamishness, of I know not what, withheld me.

All is over with him, by this time, thought I, at last, when, through another week, no further intelligence reached me. But, coming to my room the day after, I found several persons waiting at my door in a high state of nervous excitement.

"That's the man—here he comes," cried the foremost one, whom I recognized as the lawyer who had previously called upon me alone.

"You must take him away, sir, at once," cried a portly person among them, advancing upon me, and whom I knew to be the landlord of No. — Wall Street. "These gentlemen, my tenants, cannot stand it any longer; Mr. B——," pointing to the lawyer, "has turned him out of his room, and he now persists in haunting the building generally, sitting upon the banisters of the stairs by day, and sleeping in the entry by night. Everybody is concerned; clients are leaving the offices; some fears are entertained of a mob; something you must do, and that without delay."

Aghast at this torrent, I fell back before it, and would fain have locked myself in my new quarters. In vain I persisted that Bartleby was nothing to me—no more than to any one else. In vain—I was the last person known to have anything to do with him, and they held me to the terrible account. Fearful, then, of being exposed in the papers (as one person present obscurely threatened), I considered the matter, and, at length, said, that if the lawyer would give me a confidential interview with the scrivener, in his (the lawyer's) own room, I would, that afternoon, strive my best to rid them of the nuisance they complained of.

Going up stairs to my old haunt, there was Bartleby silently sitting upon the banister at the landing.

"What are you doing here, Bartleby?" said I.

"Sitting upon the banister," he mildly replied.

I motioned him into the lawyer's room, who then left us.

"Bartleby," said I, "are you aware that you are the cause of great tribulation to me, by persisting in occupying entry after being dismissed from the office?"

No answer.

"Now one of two things must take place. Either you must do something, or something must be done to you. Now what sort of business would you like to engage in? Would you like to re-engage in copying for some one?"

"No; I would prefer not to make any change."

"Would you like a clerkship in a dry-goods store?"

"There is too much confinement about that. No, I would not like a clerkship; but I am not particular."

"Too much confinement," I cried, "why you keep yourself confined all the time!"

"I would prefer not to take a clerkship," he rejoined, as if to settle that little item at once.

"How would a bar-tender's business suit you? There is no trying of the eye-sight in that."

"I would not like it at all; though, as I said before, I am not particular."

His unwonted wordiness inspirited me. I returned to the charge.

"Well, then, would you like to travel through the country collecting bills for the merchants? That would improve your health."

"No, I would prefer to be doing something else."

"How, then, would going as a companion to Europe, to entertain some young gentleman with your conversation—how would that suit you?"

"Not at all. It does not strike me that there is anything definite about that. I like to be stationary. But I am not particular."

"Stationary you shall be, then," I cried, now losing all patience, and, for the first time in all my exasperating connection with him, fairly flying into a passion. "If you do not go away from these premises before night, I shall feel bound—indeed, I *am* bound—to—to—to quit the premises myself!" I rather absurdly concluded, knowing not with what possible threat to try to frighten his immobility into compliance. Despairing of all further efforts, I was precipitately leaving him, when a final thought occurred to me—one which had not been wholly unindulged before.

"Bartleby," said I, in the kindest tone I could assume under such exciting circumstances, "will you go home with me now—not to my office, but my dwelling—and remain there till we can conclude upon some convenient arrangement for you at our leisure? Come, let us start now, right away."

"No: at present I would prefer not to make any change at all."

I answered nothing; but, effectually dodging every one by the suddenness and rapidity of my flight, rushed from the building, ran up Wall Street towards Broadway, and, jumping into the first omnibus, was soon removed from pursuit. As soon as tranquillity returned, I distinctly perceived that I had now done all that I possibly could, both in respect to the demands of the landlord and his tenants, and with regard to my own desire and sense of duty, to benefit Bartleby, and shield him from rude persecution. I now strove to be entirely care-free and quiescent; and my conscience justified me in the attempt; though, indeed, it was not so successful as I could have wished. So fearful was I of being again hunted out by the incensed landlord and his exasperated tenants, that, surrendering my business to Nippers, for a few days, I drove about the upper part of the town and through the suburbs, in my rockaway; crossed over to Jersey City and Hoboken, and paid fugitive visits to Manhattanville and Astoria. In fact, I almost lived in my rockaway for the time.

When again I entered my office, lo, a note from the landlord lay upon the desk. I opened it with trembling hands. It informed me that the writer had sent to the police, and had Bartleby removed to the Tombs as a vagrant. Moreover, since I knew more about him than any one else, he wished me to appear at that place, and make a suitable statement of the facts. These tidings had a conflicting effect upon me. At first I was indignant; but, at last, almost approved. The landlord's energetic, summary disposition, had led him to adopt a procedure which I do not think I would have decided upon myself; and yet, as a last resort, under such peculiar circumstances, it seemed the only plan.

As I afterwards learned, the poor scrivener, when told that he must be conducted to the Tombs, offered not the slightest obstacle, but, in his pale, unmoving way, silently acquiesced.

Some of the compassionate and curious bystanders joined the party; and headed by one of the constables arm in arm with Bartleby, the silent procession filed its way through all the noise, and heat, and joy of the roaring thoroughfares at noon.

The same day I received the note, I went to the Tombs, or, to speak more properly, the Halls of Justice. Seeking the right officer, I stated the purpose of my call, and was informed that the individual I described was, indeed, within. I then assured the functionary that Bartleby was a perfectly honest man, and greatly to be compassionated, however unaccountably eccentric. I narrated all I knew, and closed by suggesting the idea of letting him remain in as indulgent confinement as possible, till something less harsh might be done— though, indeed, I hardly knew what. At all events, if nothing else could be decided upon, the almshouse must receive him. I then begged to have an interview.

Being under no disgraceful charge, and quite serene and harmless in all his ways, they had permitted him freely to wander about the prison, and, especially, in the inclosed grass-platted yards thereof. And so I found him there, standing all alone in the quietest of the yards, his face towards a high wall, while all around, from the narrow slits of the jail windows, I thought I saw peering out upon him the eyes of murderers and thieves.

"Bartleby!"

"I know you," he said without looking round—"and I want nothing to say to you."

"It was not I that brought you here, Bartleby," said I, keenly pained at his implied suspicion. "And to you, this should not be so vile a place. Nothing reproachful attaches to you by being here. And see, it is not so sad a place as one might think. Look, there is the sky, and here is the grass."

"I know where I am," he replied, but would say nothing more, and so I left him.

As I entered the corridor again, a broad meat-like man, in an apron, accosted me, and, jerking his thumb over his shoulder, said—"Is that your friend?"

"Yes."

"Does he want to starve? If he does, let him live on the prison fare, that's all."

"Who are you?" asked I, not knowing what to make of such an unofficially speaking person in such a place.

"I am the grub-man. Such gentlemen as have friends here, hire me to provide them with something good to eat."

"Is this so?" said I, turning to the turnkey.

He said it was.

"Well, then," said I, slipping some silver into the grub-man's hands (for so they called him), "I want you to give particular attention to my friend there; let him have the best dinner you can get. And you must be as polite to him as possible."

"Introduce me, will you?" said the grub-man, looking at me with an expression which seemed to say he was all impatience for an opportunity to give a specimen of his breeding.

Thinking it would prove of benefit to the scrivener, I acquiesced; and, asking the grub-man his name, went up with him to Bartleby.

"Bartleby, this is a friend; you will find him very useful to you."

"Your sarvant, sir, your sarvant," said the grub-man, making a low salutation behind his apron. "Hope you find it pleasant here, sir; nice grounds—cool apartments—hope you'll stay with us sometime—try to make it agreeable. What will you have for dinner to-day?"

"I prefer not to dine to-day," said Bartleby, turning away. "It would disagree with me; I am unused to dinners." So saying, he slowly moved to the other side of the inclosure, and took up a position fronting the dead-wall.

"How's this?" said the grub-man, addressing me with a stare of astonishment, "He's odd, ain't he?"

"I think he is a little deranged," said I, sadly.

"Deranged? deranged is it? Well, now, upon my word, I thought that friend of yourn was a gentleman forger; they are always pale and genteel-like, them forgers. I can't help pity 'em—can't help it, sir. Did you know Monroe Edwards?" he added, touchingly, and paused. Then, laying his hand piteously on my shoulder, sighed, "he died of consumption at Sing-Sing. So you weren't acquainted with Monroe?"

"No, I was never socially acquainted with any forgers. But I cannot stop longer. Look to my friend yonder. You will not lose by it. I will see you again."

Some few days after this, I again obtained admission to the Tombs, and went through the corridors in quest of Bartleby; but without finding him.

"I saw him coming from his cell not long ago," said a turnkey, "may be he's gone to loiter in the yards."

So I went in that direction.

"Are you looking for the silent man?" said another turnkey, passing me. "Yonder he lies—sleeping in the yard there. 'Tis not twenty minutes since I saw him lie down."

The yard was entirely quiet. It was not accessible to the common prisoners. The surrounding walls, of amazing thickness, kept off all sounds behind them. The Egyptian character of the masonry weighed upon me with its gloom. But a soft imprisoned turf grew under foot. The heart of the eternal pyramids, it seemed, wherein, by some strange magic, through the clefts, grass-seed, dropped by birds, had sprung.

Strangely huddled at the base of the wall, his knees drawn up, and lying on his side, his head touching the cold stones, I saw the wasted Bartleby. But nothing stirred. I paused; then went close up to him; stooped over, and saw that his dim eyes were open; otherwise he seemed profoundly sleeping. Something prompted me to touch him. I felt his hand, when a tingling shiver ran up my arm and down my spine to my feet.

The round face of the grub-man peered upon me now. "His dinner is ready. Won't he dine to-day, either? Or does he live without dining?"

"Lives without dining," said I, and closed the eyes.

"Eh!—He's asleep, ain't he?"

"With kings and counselors," murmured I.

※

There would seem little need for proceeding further in this history. Imagination will readily supply the meagre recital of poor Bartleby's interment. But, ere parting with the reader, let me say, that if this little narrative has sufficiently interested him, to awaken curiosity as to who Bartleby was, and what manner of life he led prior to the present narrator's making his acquaintance, I can only reply, that in such curiosity I fully share, but am wholly unable to gratify it. Yet here I hardly know whether I should divulge one little item of rumor, which came to my ear a few months after the scrivener's decease. Upon what basis it rested, I could never ascertain; and hence, how true it is I cannot now tell. But, inasmuch as this vague report has not been without a certain suggestive interest to me, however sad, it may prove the same with some others; and so I will briefly mention it. The report was this: that Bartleby had been a subordinate clerk in the Dead Letter Office at Washington, from which he had been suddenly removed by a change in the administration. When I think over this rumor, hardly can I express the emotions which seize me. Dead letters! does it not sound like dead men? Conceive a man by nature and misfortune prone to a pallid hopelessness, can any business seem more fitted to heighten it than that of continually handling these dead letters, and assorting them for the flames? For by the cartload they are annually burned. Sometimes from out the folded paper the pale clerk takes a ring—the finger it was meant for, perhaps, moulders in the grave; a bank-note sent in swiftest charity—he whom it would relieve, nor eats nor hungers any more; pardon for those who died despairing; hope for those who died unhoping; good tidings for those who died stifled by unrelieved calamities. On errands of life, these letters speed to death.

Ah, Bartleby! Ah, humanity!

QUESTIONS

1. Imagine the story told by someone else—one of the other clerks, Bartleby himself. Why has Melville chosen the angle of vision of the lawyer? (See Preface, pp. 5–11.)
2. Describe the narrator. Consider his actions and his voice (see Preface, p. 10, pp. 24–27). How does his voice function in the story?
3. Notice all the *walls* in the story: the view from the office windows, the walls within the office, the walls of the prison, Wall Street. What is the effect of this pattern of imagery (see Preface, pp. 19–21)? What social and psychological significance does it have?
4. What is the power of Bartleby? Why isn't he seen simply as a madman? Why does he affect the narrator so strongly?
5. Describe the moral struggle of the narrator. What is the meaning of his final cry, "Ah, Bartleby! Ah, humanity!"
6. Consider "Bartleby" as a tragi-*comedy*. What comic elements do you see? What could Melville have done to turn the story totally comic? Why didn't he do so?

LEO TOLSTOY

(1828-1910)

Born in Russia, Tolstoy grew up as an aristocrat, and as an aristocrat entered the casual, luxurious life of a wealthy young man in Moscow and St. Petersburg. Beginning to write fiction as an artillery officer, he was encouraged by Turgenev. In 1869, he published *War and Peace,* a magnificent, massive historical novel of Russia at the time of Napoleon's invasion. In 1877 came *Anna Karenina,* a story of a woman who, stifled by a tedious marriage, takes a lover; beyond that, it is a powerful novel about love, about religious faith, about the peasants and their values, about the way to live one's life. Tolstoy was always deeply concerned with the spiritual life. He rejected the conventional social world and, as he grew older, became transformed; he renounced any art that did not serve man's soul, and wrote deeply spiritual works like *The Resurrection.*

"The Death of Iván Ilých" is not a dogmatic Christian story, but it makes one confront the shallow, conventional self one usually lives within. Iván Ilých is not unusually stupid and shallow, not unusually hypocritical. He is an ordinary successful man, a judge of high standing with a charming family and lovely home. But Tolstoy sees this life as misleading, empty: "Iván Ilých's life had been most simple and most ordinary and therefore most terrible"—*terrible* because, like the lives of most of us, it sheltered him from himself as a human being, from his condition as a creature who would die. He was allowed to waste his life. In a sense his life folds into meaning only at its end, when, comforted by his schoolboy son, he sees a kind of light and for the first time feels free.

Toward the end of his life, Tolstoy became a religious teacher, a *guru;* he fathered a Christian sect and influenced millions of believers.

[See Preface, p. 2 (parable), p. 10 (mixed angle of vision).]

The Death of Iván Ilých

LEO TOLSTOY

I

During an interval in the Melvínski trial in the large building of the Law Courts the members and public prosecutor met in Iván Egórobich Shébek's private room, where the conversation turned on the celebrated Krasóvski case. Fëdor Vasílievich warmly maintained that it was not subject to their jurisdiction, Iván Egórovich maintained the contrary, while Peter Ivánovich, not having entered into the discussion at the start, took no part in it but looked through the *Gazette* which had just been handed in.

"Gentlemen," he said, "Iván Ilých has died!"

"You don't say so!"

"Here, read it yourself," replied Peter Ivánovich, handing Fëdor Vasílievich the paper still damp from the press. Surrounded by a black border were the words: "Praskóvya Fëdorovna Goloviná, with profound sorrow, informs relatives and friends of the demise of her beloved husband Iván Ilých Golovín, Member of the Court of Justice, which occurred on February the 4th of this year 1882. The funeral will take place on Friday at one o'clock in the afternoon."

Iván Ilých had been a colleague of the gentlemen present and was liked by them all. He had been ill for some weeks with an illness said to be incurable. His post had been kept open for him, but there had been conjectures that in case of his death Alexéev might receive his appointment, and that either Vínnikov or Shtábel would succeed Alexéev. So on receiving the news of Iván Ilých's death the first thought of each of the gentlemen in that private room was of the changes and promotions it might occasion among themselves or their acquaintances.

"I shall be sure to get Shtábel's place or Vínnikov's," thought Fëdor Vasílievich. "I was promised that long ago, and the promotion means an extra eight hundred rubles a year for me besides the allowance."

"Now I must apply for my brother-in-law's transfer from Kalúga," thought Peter Ivánovich. "My wife will be very glad, and then she won't be able to say that I never do anything for her relations."

"I thought he would never leave his bed again," said Peter Ivánovich aloud. "It's very sad."

From *The Death of Iván Ilých and Other Stories* by Leo Tolstoy, translated by Louise and Aylmer Maude and published by Oxford University Press. Reprinted by permission of the publisher.

"But what really was the matter with him?"

"The doctors couldn't say—at least they could, but each of them said something different. When last I saw him I thought he was getting better."

"And I haven't been to see him since the holidays. I always meant to go."

"Had he any property?"

"I think his wife had a little—but something quite trifling."

"We shall have to go to see her, but they live so terribly far away."

"Far away from you, you mean. Everything's far away from your place."

"You see, he never can forgive my living on the other side of the river," said Peter Ivánovich, smiling at Shébek. Then, still talking of the distances between different parts of the city, they returned to the Court.

Besides considerations as to the possible transfers and promotions likely to result from Iván Ilých's death, the mere fact of the death of a near acquaintance aroused, as usual, in all who heard of it the complacent feeling that, "it is he who is dead and not I."

Each one thought or felt, "Well, he's dead but I'm alive!" But the more intimate of Iván Ilých's acquaintances, his so-called friends, could not help thinking also that they would now have to fulfill the very tiresome demands of propriety by attending the funeral service and paying a visit of condolence to the widow.

Fëdor Vasílievich and Peter Ivánovich had been his nearest acquaintances. Peter Ivánovich had studied law with Iván Ilých and had considered himself to be under obligations to him.

Having told his wife at dinner-time of Iván Ilých's death, and of his conjecture that it might be possible to get her brother transferred to their circuit, Peter Ivánovich sacrificed his usual nap, put on his evening clothes, and drove to Iván Ilých's house.

At the entrance stood a carriage and two cabs. Leaning against the wall in the hall downstairs near the cloak-stand was a coffin-lid covered with cloth of gold, ornamented with gold cord and tassels, that had been polished up with metal powder. Two ladies in black were taking off their fur cloaks. Peter Ivánovich recognized one of them as Iván Ilých's sister, but the other was a stranger to him. His colleague Schwartz was just coming downstairs, but on seeing Peter Ivánovich enter he stopped and winked at him, as if to say: "Iván Ilých has made a mess of things—not like you and me."

Schwartz's face with his Piccadilly whiskers, and his slim figure in evening dress, had as usual an air of elegant solemnity which contrasted with the playfulness of his character and had a special piquancy here, or so it seemed to Peter Ivánovich.

Peter Ivánovich allowed the ladies to precede him and slowly followed them upstairs. Schwartz did not come down but remained where he was, and Peter Ivánovich understood that he wanted to arrange where they should play bridge that evening. The ladies went upstairs to the widow's room, and Schwartz with seriously compressed lips but a playful look in his eyes, indicated by a twist of his eyebrows the room to the right where the body lay.

Peter Ivánovich, like everyone else on such occasions, entered feeling uncertain what he would have to do. All he knew was that at such times it is always safe to cross oneself. But he was not quite sure whether one should make obeisances while doing so. He therefore adopted a middle course. On entering the room he began crossing himself and made a slight movement resembling a bow. At the same time, as far as the motion of his head and arm allowed, he surveyed the room. Two young men—apparently nephews, one of whom was a high-school pupil—were leaving the room, crossing themselves as they did so. An old woman was standing motionless, and a lady with strangely arched eyebrows was saying something to her in a whisper. A vigorous, resolute Church Reader, in a frock-coat, was reading something in a loud voice with an expression that precluded any contradiction. The butler's assistant, Gerásim, stepping lightly in front of Peter Ivánovich, was strewing something on the floor. Noticing this, Peter Ivánovich was immediately aware of a faint odour of a decomposing body.

The last time he had called on Iván Ilých, Peter Ivánovich had seen Gerásim in the study. Iván Ilých had been particularly fond of him and he was performing the duty of a sick-nurse.

Peter Ivánovich continued to make the sign of the cross slightly inclining his head in an intermediate direction between the coffin, the Reader, and the icons on the table in a corner of the room. Afterwards, when it seemed to him that this movement of his arm in crossing himself had gone on too long, he stopped and began to look at the corpse.

The dead man lay, as dead men always lie, in a specially heavy way, his rigid limbs sunk in the soft cushions of the coffin, with the head forever bowed on the pillow. His yellow waxen brow with bald patches over his sunken temples was thrust up in the way peculiar to the dead, the protruding nose seeming to press on the upper lip. He was much changed and had grown even thinner since Peter Ivánovich had last seen him, but, as is always the case with the dead, his face was handsomer and above all more dignified than when he was alive. The expression on the face said that what was necessary had been accomplished, and accomplished rightly. Besides this there was in that expression a reproach and a warning to the living. This warning seemed to Peter Ivánovich out of place, or at least not applicable to him. He felt a certain discomfort and so he hurriedly crossed himself once more and turned and went out of the door—too hurriedly and too regardless of propriety, as he himself was aware.

Schwartz was waiting for him in the adjoining room with legs spread wide apart and both hands toying with his top-hat behind his back. The mere sight of that playful, well-groomed, and elegant figure refreshed Peter Ivánovich. He felt that Schwartz was above all these happenings and would not surrender to any depressing influences. His very look said that this incident of a church service for Iván Ilých could not be a sufficient reason for infringing the order of the session—in other words, that it would certainly not prevent his unwrapping a new pack of cards and shuffling them that evening while a footman placed four fresh candles on the table: in fact, there was no reason for supposing that this incident would hinder their spending the evening agreeably. Indeed he said this in a whisper as Peter Ivánovich passed him, proposing that they should meet for a game at Fëdor Vasílievich's. But apparently Peter Ivánovich was not destined to play bridge that evening. Praskóvya Fëdorovna (a short, fat woman who despite all efforts to the contrary had continued to broaden steadily from her shoulders downwards and who had the same extraordinarily arched eyebrows as the lady who had been standing by the coffin), dressed all in black, her head covered with lace, came out of her own room with some other ladies, conducted them to the room where the dead body lay, and said: "The service will begin immediately. Please go in."

Schwartz, making an indefinite bow, stood still, evidently neither accepting nor declining this invitation. Praskóvya Fëdorovna recognizing Peter Ivánovich, sighed, went close up to him, took his hand, and said: "I know you were a true friend to Iván Ilých . . ." and looked at him awaiting some suitable response. And Peter Ivánovich knew that, just as it had been the right thing to cross himself in that room, so what he had to do here was to press her hand, sigh, and say, "Believe me . . ." So he did all this and as he did it felt that the desired result had been achieved: that both he and she were touched.

"Come with me. I want to speak to you before it begins," said the widow. "Give me your arm."

Peter Ivánovich gave her his arm and they went to the inner rooms, passing Schwartz who winked at Peter Ivánovich compassionately.

"That does for our bridge! Don't object if we find another player. Perhaps you can cut in when you do escape," said his playful look.

Peter Ivánovich sighed still more deeply and despondently, and Praskóvya Fëdorovna pressed his arm gratefully. When they reached the drawing-room, upholstered in pink cretonne and lighted by a dim lamp, they sat down at the table—she on a sofa and Peter

Ivánovich on a low pouffe, the springs of which yielded spasmodically under his weight. Praskóvya Fëdorovna had been on the point of warning him to take another seat, but felt that such a warning was out of keeping with her present condition and so changed her mind. As he sat down on the pouffe Peter Ivánovich recalled how Iván Ilých had arranged this room and had consulted him regarding this pink cretonne with green leaves. The whole room was full of furniture and knick-knacks, and on her way to the sofa the lace of the widow's black shawl caught on the carved edge of the table. Peter Ivánovich rose to detach it, and the springs of the pouffe, relieved of his weight, rose also and gave him a push. The widow began detaching her shawl herself, and Peter Ivánovich again sat down, suppressing the rebellious springs of the pouffe under him. But the widow had not quite freed herself and Peter Ivánovich got up again, and again the pouffe rebelled and even creaked. When this was all over she took out a clean cambric handkerchief and began to weep. The episode with the shawl and the struggle with the pouffe had cooled Peter Ivánovich's emotions and he sat there with a sullen look on his face. This awkward situation was interrupted by Sokolóv, Iván Ilých's butler, who came to report that the plot in the cemetery that Praskóvya Fëdorovna had chosen would cost two hundred rubles. She stopped weeping and, looking at Peter Ivánovich with the air of a victim, remarked in French that it was very hard for her. Peter Ivánovich made a silent gesture signifying his full conviction that it must indeed be so.

"Please smoke," she said in a magnanimous yet crushed voice, and turned to discuss with Sokolóv the price of the plot for the grave.

Peter Ivánovich while lighting his cigarette heard her inquiring very circumstantially into the price of different plots in the cemetery and finally decide which she would take. When that was done she gave instructions about engaging the choir. Sokolóv then left the room.

"I look after everything myself," she told Peter Ivánovich, shifting the albums that lay on the table; and noticing that the table was endangered by his cigarette-ash, she immediately passed him an ashtray, saying as she did so: "I consider it an affectation to say that my grief prevents my attending to practical affairs. On the contrary, if anything can—I won't say console me, but—distract me, it is seeing to everything concerning him." She again took out her handkerchief as if preparing to cry, but suddenly, as if mastering her feeling, she shook herself and began to speak calmly. "But there is something I want to talk to you about."

Peter Ivánovich bowed, keeping control of the springs of the pouffe, which immediately began quivering under him.

"He suffered terribly the last few days."

"Did he?" said Peter Ivánovich.

"Oh, terribly! He screamed unceasingly, not for minutes but for hours. For the last three days he screamed incessantly. It was unendurable. I cannot understand how I bore it; you could hear him three rooms off. Oh, what I have suffered!"

"Is it possible that he was conscious all that time?" asked Peter Ivánovich.

"Yes," she whispered. "To the last moment. He took leave of us a quarter of an hour before he died, and asked us to take Volódya away."

The thought of the sufferings of this man he had known so intimately, first as a merry little boy, then as a school-mate, and later as a grown-up colleague, suddenly struck Peter Ivánovich with horror, despite an unpleasant consciousness of his own and this woman's dissimulation. He again saw that brow, and that nose pressing down on the lip, and felt afraid for himself.

"Three days of frightful suffering and then death! Why, that might suddenly, at any time, happen to me," he thought, and for a moment felt terrified. But—he did not himself know how—the customary reflection at once occurred to him that this had happened to Iván Ilých and not to him, and that it should not and could not happen to him, and that to think that it could would be yielding to depression which he ought not to do, as Schwartz's expression plainly showed. After which reflection Peter Ivánovich felt reassured, and began to ask with interest about the details of Iván Ilých's death, as though death was an accident natural to Iván Ilých but certainly not to himself.

After many details of the really dreadful physical sufferings Iván Ilých had endured (which details he learnt only from the effect those sufferings had produced on Praskóvya Fëdorovna's nerves) the widow apparently found it necessary to get to business.

"Oh, Peter Ivánovich, how hard it is! How terribly, terribly hard!" and she again began to weep.

Peter Ivánovich sighed and waited for her to finish blowing her nose. When she had done so he said, "Believe me . . ." and she again began talking and brought out what was evidently her chief concern with him—namely, to question him as to how she could obtain a grant of money from the government on the occasion of her husband's death. She made it appear that she was asking Peter Ivánovich's advice about her pension, but he soon saw that she already knew about that to the minutest detail, more even than he did himself. She knew how much could be got out of the government in consequence of her husband's death, but wanted to find out whether she could not possibly extract something more. Peter Ivánovich tried to think of some means of doing so, but after reflecting for a while and, out of propriety, condemning the government for its niggardliness, he said he thought that nothing more could be got. Then she sighed and evidently began to devise means of getting rid of her visitor. Noticing this, he put out his cigarette, rose, pressed her hand, and went out into the anteroom.

In the dining-room where the clock stood that Iván Ilých had liked so much and had bought at an antique shop, Peter Ivánovich met a priest and a few acquaintances who had come to attend the service, and he recognized Iván Ilých's daughter, a handsome young woman. She was in black and her slim figure appeared slimmer than ever. She had a gloomy, determined, almost angry expression, and bowed to Peter Ivánovich as though he were in some way to blame. Behind her, with the same offended look, stood a wealthy young man, an examining magistrate, whom Peter Ivánovich also knew and who was her fiancé, as he had heard. He bowed mournfully to them and was about to pass into the death-chamber, when from under the stairs appeared the figure of Iván Ilých's schoolboy son, who was extremely like his father. He seemed a little Iván Ilých, such as Peter Ivánovich remembered when they studied law together. His tear-stained eyes had in them the look that is seen in the eyes of boys of thirteen or fourteen who are not pure-minded. When he saw Peter Ivánovich he scowled morosely and shamefacedly. Peter Ivánovich nodded to him and entered the death-chamber. The service began: candles, groans, incense, tears, and sobs. Peter Ivánovich stood looking gloomily down at his feet. He did not look once at the dead man, did not yield to any depressing influence, and was one of the first to leave the room. There was no one in the anteroom, but Gerásim darted out of the dead man's room, rummaged with his strong hands among the fur coats to find Peter Ivánovich's and helped him on with it.

"Well, friend Gerásim," said Peter Ivánovich, so as to say something. "It's a sad affair, isn't it?"

"It's God's will. We shall all come to it some day," said Gerásim, displaying his teeth—the even, white teeth of a healthy peasant—and, like a man in the thick of urgent work, he briskly opened the front door, called the coachman, helped Peter Ivánovich into the sledge, and sprang back to the porch as if in readiness for what he had to do next.

Peter Ivánovich found the fresh air particularly pleasant after the smell of incense, the dead body, and carbolic acid.

"Where to, sir?" asked the coachman.

"It's not too late even now. . . . I'll call round on Fëdor Vasílievich."

He accordingly drove there and found them just finishing the first rubber, so that it was quite convenient for him to cut in.

II

Iván Ilých's life had been most simple and most ordinary and therefore most terrible.

He had been a member of the Court of Justice, and died at the age of forty-five. His father had been an official who after serving in various ministries and departments in Petersburg had made the sort of career which brings men to positions from which by reason of their long service they cannot be dismissed, though they are obviously unfit to hold any responsible position, and for whom therefore posts are specially created, which though fictitious carry salaries of from six to ten thousand rubles that are not fictitious, and in receipt of which they live on to a great age.

Such was the Privy Councillor and superfluous member of various superfluous institutions, Ilýa Epímovich Golovín.

He had three sons, of whom Iván Ilých was the second. The eldest son was following in his father's footsteps only in another department, and was already approaching that stage in the service at which a similar sinecure would be reached. The third son was a failure. He had ruined his prospects in a number of positions and was now serving in the railway department. His father and brothers, and still more their wives, not merely disliked meeting him, but avoided remembering his existence unless compelled to do so. His sister had married Baron Greff, a Petersburg official of her father's type. Iván Ilých was *le phénix de la famille* as people said. He was neither as cold and formal as his elder brother nor as wild as the younger, but was a happy mean between them—an intelligent, polished, lively and agreeable man. He had studied with his younger brother at the School of Law, but the latter had failed to complete the course and was expelled when he was in the fifth class. Iván Ilých finished the course well. Even when he was at the School of Law he was just what he remained for the rest of his life: a capable, cheerful, good-natured, and sociable man, though strict in the fulfilment of what he considered to be his duty: and he considered his duty to be what was so considered by those in authority. Neither as a boy nor as a man was he a toady, but from early youth was by nature attracted to people of high station as a fly is drawn to the light, assimilating their ways and views of life and establishing friendly relations with them. All the enthusiasms of childhood and youth passed without leaving much trace on him; he succumbed to sensuality, to vanity, and latterly among the highest classes to liberalism, but always within limits which his instinct unfailingly indicated to him as correct.

At school he had done things which had formerly seemed to him very horrid and made him feel disgusted with himself when he did them; but when later on he saw that such actions were done by people of good position and that they did not regard them as wrong, he was able not exactly to regard them as right, but to forget about them entirely or not be at all troubled at remembering them.

Having graduated from the School of Law and qualified for the tenth rank of the civil service, and having received money from his father for his equipment, Iván Ilých ordered himself clothes at Scharmer's, the fashionable tailor, hung a medallion inscribed *respice finem* on his watch-chain, took leave of his professor and the prince who was patron of the school, had a farewell dinner with his comrades at Donon's first-class restaurant, and with his new and fashionable portmanteau, linen, clothes, shaving and other toilet appliances, and a travelling rug, all purchased at the best shops, he set off for one of the provinces where, through his father's influence, he had been attached to the Governor as an official for special service.

In the province Iván Ilých soon arranged as easy and agreeable a position for himself as he had had at the School of Law. He performed his official tasks, made his career, and at the same time amused himself pleasantly and decorously. Occasionally he paid official visits to country districts, where he behaved with dignity both to his superiors and inferiors, and performed the duties entrusted to him, which related chiefly to the sectarians, with an exactness and incorruptible honesty of which he could not but feel proud.

In official matters, despite his youth and taste for frivolous gaiety, he was exceedingly reserved, punctilious, and even severe; but in society he was often amusing and witty, and always good-natured, correct in his manner, and *bon enfant*, as the governor and his wife—with whom he was like one of the family—used to say of him.

In the provinces he had an affair with a lady who made advances to the elegant young lawyer, and there was also a milliner; and there were carousals with aides-de-camp who visited the district, and after-supper visits to a certain outlying street of doubtful reputation; and there was too some obsequiousness to his chief and even to his chief's wife, but all this was done with such a tone of good breeding that no hard names could be applied to it. It all came under the heading of the French saying: *"Il faut que jeunesse se passe."* It was all done with clean hands, in clean linen, with French phrases, and above all among people of the best society and consequently with the approval of people of rank.

So Iván Ilých served for five years and then came a change in his official life. The new and reformed judicial institutions were introduced, and new men were needed. Iván Ilých became such a new man. He was offered the post of Examining Magistrate, and he accepted it though the post was in another province and obliged him to give up the connexions he had formed and to make new ones. His friends met to give him a send-off; they had a group-photograph taken and presented him with a silver cigarette-case, and he set off to his new post.

As examining magistrate Iván Ilých was just as *comme il faut* and decorous a man, inspiring general respect and capable of separating his official duties from his private life, as he had been when acting as an official on special service. His duties now as examining magistrate were far more interesting and attractive than before. In his former position it had been pleasant to wear an undress uniform made by Scharmer, and to pass through the crowd of petitioners and officials who were timorously awaiting an audience with the governor, and who envied him as with free and easy gait he went straight into his chief's private room to have a cup of tea and a cigarette with him. But not many people had then been directly dependent on him— only police officials and the sectarians when he went on special missions—and he liked to treat them politely, almost as comrades, as if he were letting them feel that he who had the power to crush them was treating them in this simple, friendly way. There were then but few such people. But now, as an examining magistrate, Iván Ilých felt that everyone without exception, even the most important and self-satisfied, was in his power, and that he need only write a few words on a sheet of paper with a certain heading, and this or that important, self-satisfied person would be brought before him in the role of an accused person or a witness, and if he did not choose to allow him to sit down, would have to stand before him and answer his questions. Iván Ilých never abused his power; he tried on the contrary to soften its expression, but the consciousness of it and of the possibility of softening its effect, supplied the chief interest and attraction of his office. In his work itself, especially in his examinations, he very soon acquired a method of eliminating all considerations irrelevant to the legal aspect of the case, and reducing even the most complicated case to a form in which it would be presented on paper only in its externals, completely excluding his personal opinion of the matter, while above all observing every prescribed formality. The work was new and Iván Ilých was one of the first men to apply the new Code of 1864.[1]

On taking up the post of examining magistrate in a new town, he made new acquaintances and connexions, placed himself on a new footing, and assumed a somewhat different tone. He took up an attitude of rather dignified aloofness towards the provincial authorities, but picked out the best circle of legal gentlemen and wealthy

---

[1] The emancipation of the serfs in 1861 was followed by a thorough all-round reform of judicial proceedings.—Aylmer Maud [translator].

gentry living in the town and assumed a tone of slight dissatisfaction with the government, of moderate liberalism, and of enlightened citizenship. At the same time, without at all altering the elegance of his toilet, he ceased shaving his chin and allowed his beard to grow as it pleased.

Iván Ilých settled down very pleasantly in this new town. The society there, which inclined towards opposition to the Governor, was friendly, his salary was larger, and he began to play *vint* [a form of bridge], which he found added not a little to the pleasure of life, for he had a capacity for cards, played good-humouredly, and calculated rapidly and astutely, so that he usually won.

After living there for two years he met his future wife, Praskóvya Fëdorovna Míkhel, who was the most attractive, clever, and brilliant girl of the set in which he moved, and among other amusements and relaxation from his labours as examining magistrate, Iván Ilých established light and playful relations with her.

While he had been an official on special service he had been accustomed to dance, but now as an examining magistrate it was exceptional for him to do so. If he danced now, he did it as if to show that though he served under the reformed order of things, and had reached the fifth official rank, yet when it came to dancing he could do it better than most people. So at the end of an evening he sometimes danced with Praskóvya Fëdorovna, and it was chiefly during these dances that he captivated her. She fell in love with him. Iván Ilých had at first no definite intention of marrying, but when the girl fell in love with him he said to himself: "Really, why shouldn't I marry?"

Praskóvya Fëdorovna came of a good family, was not bad looking, and had some little property. Iván Ilých might have aspired to a more brilliant match, but even this was good. He had his salary, and she, he hoped, would have an equal income. She was well connected, and was a sweet, pretty, and thoroughly correct young woman. To say that Iván Ilých married because he fell in love with Praskóvya Fëdorovna and found that she sympathized with his views of life would be as incorrect as to say that he married because his social circle approved of the match. He was swayed by both these considerations: the marriage gave him personal satisfaction, and at the same time it was considered the right thing by the most highly placed of his associates.

So Iván Ilých got married.

The preparations for marriage and the beginning of married life, with its conjugal caresses, the new furniture, new crockery, and new linen, were very pleasant until his wife became pregnant—so that Iván Ilých had begun to think that marriage would not impair the easy, agreeable, gay and always decorous character of his life, approved of by society and regarded by himself as natural, but would even improve it. But from the first months of his wife's pregnancy, something new, unpleasant, depressing, and unseemly, and from which there was no way of escape, unexpectedly showed itself.

His wife, without any reason—*de gaieté de coeur* as Iván Ilých expressed it to himself—began to disturb the pleasure and propriety of their life. She began to be jealous without any cause, expected him to devote his whole attention to her, found fault with everything, and made coarse and ill-mannered scenes.

At first Iván Ilých hoped to escape from the unpleasantness of this state of affairs by the same easy and decorous relation to life that had served him heretofore: he tried to ignore his wife's disagreeable moods, continued to live in his usual easy and pleasant way, invited friends to his house for a game of cards, and also tried going out to his club or spending his evenings with friends. But one day his wife began upbraiding him so vigorously, using such coarse words, and continued to abuse him every time he did not fulfil her demands, so resolutely and with such evident determination not to give way till he submitted—that is, till he stayed at home and was bored just as she was—that he became alarmed. He now realized that matrimony— at any rate with Praskóvya Fëdorovna—was not always conducive to the pleasures and amenities of life but on the contrary often infringed both comfort and propriety, and that he must therefore entrench himself against such infringement. And Iván Ilých began to seek for means of doing so. His official duties were the one thing that imposed upon Praskóvya Fëdorovna, and by means of his official work and the duties attached to it he began struggling with his wife to secure his own independence.

With the birth of their child, the attempts to feed it and the various failures in doing so, and with the real and imaginary illnesses of mother and child, in which Iván Ilých's sympathy was demanded but about which he understood nothing, the need of securing for himself an existence outside his family life became still more imperative.

As his wife grew more irritable and exacting and Iván Ilých transferred the centre of gravity of his life more and more to his official work, so did he grow to like his work better and became more ambitious than before.

Very soon, within a year of his wedding, Iván Ilých had realized that marriage, though it may add some comforts to life, is in fact a very intricate and difficult affair towards which in order to perform one's duty, that is, to lead a decorous life approved of by society, one must adopt a definite attitude just as towards one's official duties.

And Iván Ilých evolved such an attitude towards married life. He only required of it those conveniences—dinner at home, housewife, and bed—which it could give him, and above all that propriety of external forms required by public opinion. For the rest he looked for light-hearted pleasure and propriety, and was very thankful when he found them, but if he met with antagonism and querulousness he at once retired into his separate fenced-off world of official duties, where he found satisfaction.

Iván Ilých was esteemed a good official, and after three years was made Assistant Public Prosecutor. His new duties, their importance, the possibility of indicting and imprisoning anyone he chose, the publicity his speeches received, and the success he had in all these things, made his work still more attractive.

More children came. His wife became more and more querulous and ill-tempered, but the attitude Iván Ilých had adopted towards his home life rendered him almost impervious to her grumbling.

After seven years' service in that town he was transferred to another province as Public Prosecutor. They moved, but were short of money and his wife did not like the place they moved to. Though the salary was higher the cost of living was greater, besides which two of their children died and family life became still more unpleasant for him.

Praskóvya Fëdorovna blamed her husband for every inconvenience they encountered in their new home. Most of the conversations between husband and wife, especially as to the children's education, led to topics which recalled former disputes, and those disputes were apt to flare up at any moment. There remained only those rare periods of amorousness which still came to them at times but did not last long. These were islets at which they anchored for a while and then again set out upon that ocean of veiled hostility which showed itself in their aloofness from one another. This aloofness might have grieved Iván Ilých had he considered that it ought not to exist, but he now regarded the position as normal, and even made it the goal at which he aimed in family life. His aim was to free himself more and more from those unpleasantnesses and to give them a semblance of harmlessness and propriety. He attained this by spending less and less time with his family, and when obliged to be at home he tried to safeguard his position by the presence of outsiders. The chief thing however was that he had his official duties. The whole interest of his life now centred in the official world and that interest absorbed him. The consciousness of his power, being able to ruin anybody he wished to ruin, the importance, even the external dignity of his entry into court, or meetings with his subordinates, his success with superiors and inferiors, and above all his masterly handling of cases, of which he was conscious—all this gave him pleasure and filled his life, together with chats with his colleagues, dinners, and bridge. So that on the whole Iván Ilých's life continued to flow as he considered it should do—pleasantly and properly.

So things continued for another seven years. His eldest daughter was already sixteen, another child had died, and only one son was left, a schoolboy and a subject of dissension. Iván Ilých wanted to put him in the School of Law, but to spite him Praskóvya Fëdorovna entered him at the High School. The daughter had been educated at home and had turned out well: the boy did not learn badly either.

III

So Iván Ilých lived for seventeen years after his marriage. He was already a Public Prosecutor of long standing, and had declined several proposed transfers while awaiting a more desirable post, when an unanticipated occurrence quite upset the peaceful course of his life. He was expecting to be offered the post of presiding judge in a University town, but Happe somehow came to the front and obtained the appointment instead. Iván Ilých became irritable, reproached Happe, and quarrelled both with him and with his immediate superiors—who became colder to him and again passed him over when other appointments were made.

This was in 1880, the hardest year of Iván Ilých's life. It was then that it became evident on the one hand that his salary was insufficient for them to live on, and on the other that he had been forgotten, and not only this, but that what was for him the greatest and most cruel injustice appeared to others a quite ordinary occurrence. Even his father did not consider it his duty to help him. Iván Ilých felt himself abandoned by everyone, and that they regarded his position with a salary of 3,500 rubles as quite normal and even fortunate. He also knew that with the consciousness of the injustices done him, with his wife's incessant nagging, and with the debts he had contracted by living beyond his means, his position was far from normal.

In order to save money that summer he obtained leave of absence and went with his wife to live in the country at her brother's place.

In the country, without his work, he experienced *ennui* for the first time in his life, and not only *ennui* but intolerable depression, and he decided that it was impossible to go on living like that, and that it was necessary to take energetic measures.

Having passed a sleepless night pacing up and down the veranda, he decided to go to Petersburg and bestir himself, in order to punish those who had failed to appreciate him and to get transferred to another ministry.

Next day, despite many protests from his wife and her brother, he started for Petersburg with the sole object of obtaining a post with a salary of five thousand rubles a year. He was no longer bent on any particular department, or tendency, or kind of activity. All he now wanted was an appointment to another post with a salary of five thousand rubles, either in the administration, in the banks, with the railways, in one of the Empress Márya's Institutions, or even in the customs—but it had to carry with it a salary of five thousand rubles and be in a ministry other than that in which they had failed to appreciate him.

And this quest of Iván Ilých's was crowned with remarkable and unexpected success. At Kursk an acquaintance of his, F. I. Ilyín, got into the first-class carriage, sat down beside Iván Ilých, and told him of a telegram just received by the Governor of Kursk announcing that a change was about to take place in the ministry: Peter Ivánovich was to be superseded by Iván Semënovich.

The proposed change, apart from its significance for Russia, had a special significance for Iván Ilých, because by bringing forward a new man, Peter Petróvich, and consequently his friend Zachár Ivánovich, it was highly favourable for Iván Ilých, since Zachár Ivánovich was a friend and colleague of his.

In Moscow this news was confirmed, and on reaching Petersburg Iván Ilých found Zachár Ivánovich and received a definite promise of an appointment in his former Department of Justice.

A week later he telegraphed to his wife: "Zachár in Miller's place. I shall receive appointment on presentation of report."

Thanks to this change of personnel, Iván Ilých had unexpectedly obtained an appointment in his former ministry which placed him two stages above his former colleagues besides giving him five thousand rubles salary and three thousand five hundred rubles for expenses connected with his removal. All his ill humour towards his former enemies and the whole department vanished, and Iván Ilých was completely happy.

He returned to the country more cheerful and contented than he had been for a long time. Praskóvya Fëdorovna also cheered up and a truce was arranged between them. Iván Ilých told of how he had been fêted by everybody in Petersburg, how all those who had been his enemies were put to shame and now fawned on him, how envious they were of his appointment, and how much everybody in Petersburg had liked him.

Praskóvya Fëdorovna listened to all this and appeared to believe it. She did not contradict anything, but only made plans for their life in the town to which they were going. Iván Ilých saw with delight that these plans were his plans, that he and his wife agreed, and that, after a stumble, his life was regaining its due and natural character of pleasant lightheartedness and decorum.

Iván Ilých had come back for a short time only, for he had to take up his new duties on the 10th of September. Moreover, he needed time to settle into the new place, to move all his belongings from the province, and to buy and order many additional things: in a word, to make such arrangements as he had resolved on, which were almost exactly what Praskóvya Fëdorovna too had decided on.

Now that everything had happened so fortunately, and that he and his wife were at one in their aims and moreover saw so little of one another, they got on together better than they had done since the first years of marriage. Iván Ilých had thought of taking his family away with him at once, but the insistence of his wife's brother and her sister-in-law, who had suddenly become particularly amiable and friendly to him and his family, induced him to depart alone.

So he departed, and the cheerful state of mind induced by his success and by the harmony between his wife and himself, the one intensifying the other, did not leave him. He found a delightful house, just the thing both he and his wife had dreamt of. Spacious, lofty reception rooms in the old style, a convenient and dignified study, rooms for his wife and daughter, a study for his son—it might have been specially built for them. Iván Ilých himself superintended the arrangements, chose the wall-papers, supplemented the furniture (preferably with antiques which he considered particularly *comme il faut*), and supervised the upholstering. Everything progressed and progressed and approached the ideal he had set for himself: even when things were only half completed they exceeded his expectations. He saw what a refined and elegant character, free from vulgarity, it would all have when it was ready. On falling asleep he pictured to himself how the reception-room would look. Looking at the yet unfinished drawing-room he could see the fireplace, the screen, the what-not, the little chairs dotted here and there, the dishes and plates on the walls, and the bronzes, as they would be when everything was in place. He was pleased by the thought of how his wife and daughter, who shared his taste in this matter, would be impressed by it. They were certainly not expecting as much. He had been particularly successful in finding, and buying cheaply, antiques which gave a particularly aristocratic character to the whole place. But in his letters he intentionally understated everything in order to be able to surprise them. All this so absorbed him that his new duties—though he liked his official work—interested him less than he had expected. Sometimes he even had moments of absent-mindedness during the Court Sessions, and would consider whether he should have straight or curved cornices for his curtains. He was so interested in it all that he often did things himself, rearranging the furniture, or rehanging the curtains. Once when mounting a step-ladder to show the upholsterer, who did not understand, how he wanted the hangings draped, he made a false step and slipped, but being a strong and agile man he clung on and only knocked his side against the knob of the window frame. The bruised place was painful but the pain soon passed, and he felt particularly bright and well just then. He wrote: "I feel fifteen years younger." He thought he would have everything ready by September, but it dragged on till mid-October. But the result was charming not only in his eyes but to everyone who saw it.

In reality it was just what is usually seen in the houses of people of moderate means who want to appear rich, and therefore succeed only in resembling others like themselves: there were damasks, dark wood, plants, rugs, and dull and polished bronzes—all the things people of a certain class have in order to resemble other people of that class. His house was so like the others that it would never have been noticed, but to him it all seemed to be quite exceptional. He was very happy when he met his family at the station and brought them to the newly furnished house all lit up, where a footman in a white tie opened the door into the hall decorated with plants, and when they went on into the drawing-room and the study uttering exclamations of delight. He conducted them everywhere, drank in their praises eagerly, and beamed with pleasure. At tea that evening, when Praskóvya Fëdorovna among other things asked him about his fall, he laughed, and showed them how he had gone flying and had frightened the upholsterer.

"It's a good thing I'm a bit of an athlete. Another man might have been killed, but I merely knocked myself, just here; it hurts when it's touched, but it's passing off already—it's only a bruise."

So they began living in their new home—in which, as always happens, when they got thoroughly settled in they found they were just one room short—and with the increased income, which as always was just a little (some five hundred rubles) too little, but it was all very nice.

Things went particularly well at first, before everything was finally arranged and while something had still to be done: this thing bought, that thing ordered, another thing moved, and something else adjusted. Though there were some disputes between husband and wife, they were both so well satisfied and had so much to do that it all passed off without any serious quarrels. When nothing was left to arrange it became rather dull and something seemed to be lacking, but they were then making acquaintances, forming habits, and life was growing fuller.

Iván Ilých spent his mornings at the law court and came home to dinner, and at first he was generally in a good humour, though he occasionally became irritable just on account of his house. (Every spot on the tablecloth or the upholstery, and every broken window-blind string, irritated him. He had devoted so much trouble to arranging it all that every disturbance of it distressed him.) But on the whole his life ran its course as he believed life should do: easily, pleasantly, and decorously.

He got up at nine, drank his coffee, read the paper, and then put on his undress uniform and went to the law courts. There the harness in which he worked had already been stretched to fit him and he donned it without a hitch: petitioners, inquiries at the chancery, the chancery itself, and the sittings public and administrative. In all this the thing was to exclude everything fresh and vital, which always disturbs the regular course of official business, and to admit only official relations with people, and then only on official grounds. A man would come, for instance, wanting some information. Iván Ilých, as one in whose sphere the matter did not lie, would have nothing to do with him: but if the man had some business with him in his official capacity, something that could be expressed on officially stamped paper, he would do everything, positively everything he could within the limits of such relations, and in doing so would maintain the semblance of friendly human relations, that is, would observe the courtesies of life. As soon as the official relations ended, so did everything else. Iván Ilých possessed this capacity to separate his real life from the official side of affairs and not mix the two, in the highest degree, and by long practice and natural aptitude had brought it to such a pitch that sometimes, in the manner of a virtuoso, he would even allow himself to let the human and official relations mingle. He let himself do this just because he felt that he could at any time he chose resume the strictly official attitude again and drop the human relation. And he did it all easily, pleasantly, correctly, and even artistically. In the intervals between the sessions he smoked, drank tea, chatted a little about politics, a little about general topics, a little about cards, but most of all about official appointments. Tired, but with the feelings of a virtuoso—one of the first violins who has played his part in an orchestra with precision—he would return home to find that his wife and daughter had been out paying calls, or had a visitor, and that his son had been to school, had done his homework with his tutor, and was duly learning what is taught at High Schools. Everything was as it should be. After dinner, if they had no visitors, Iván Ilých sometimes read a book that was being much discussed at the time, and in the evening settled down to work, that is, read official papers, compared the depositions of witnesses, and noted paragraphs of the Code applying to them. This was neither dull nor amusing. It was dull when he might have been playing bridge, but if no bridge was available it was at any rate better than doing nothing or sitting with his wife. Iván Ilých's chief pleasure was giving little dinners to which he invited men and women of good social position, and just as his drawing-room resembled all other drawing-rooms so did his enjoyable little parties resemble all other such parties.

Once they even gave a dance. Iván Ilých enjoyed it and everything went off well, except that it led to a violent quarrel with his wife about the cakes and sweets. Praskóvya Fëdorovna had made her own plans, but Iván Ilých insisted on getting everything from an expensive confectioner and ordered too many cakes, and the quarrel occurred because some of those cakes were left over and the confectioner's bill came to forty-five rubles. It was a great and disagreeable quarrel. Praskóvya Fëdorovna called him "a fool and an imbecile," and he clutched at his head and made angry allusions to divorce.

But the dance itself had been enjoyable. The best people were there, and Iván Ilých had danced with Princess Trúfonova, a sister of the distinguished founder of the Society "Bear by Burden."

The pleasures connected with his work were pleasure of ambition; his social pleasures were those of vanity; but Iván Ilých's greatest pleasure was playing bridge. He acknowledged that whatever disagreeable incident happened in his life, the pleasure that beamed like a ray of light above everything else was to sit down to bridge with good players, not noisy partners, and of course to four-handed bridge (with five players it was annoying to have to stand out, though one pretended not to mind), to play a clever and serious game (when the cards allowed it) and then to have supper and drink a glass of wine. After a game of bridge, especially if he had won a little (to win a large sum was unpleasant), Iván Ilých went to bed in specially good humour.

So they lived. They formed a circle of acquaintances among the best people and were visited by people of importance and by young folk. In their views as to their acquaintances, husband, wife and daughter were entirely agreed, and tacitly and unanimously kept at arm's length and shook off the various shabby friends and relations who, with much show of affection, gushed into the drawing-room with its Japanese plates on the walls. Soon these shabby friends ceased to obtrude themselves and only the best people remained in the Golovíns' set.

Young men made up to Lisa, and Petríshchev, an examining magistrate and Dmítri Ivánovich Petríshchev's son and sole heir, began to be so attentive to her that Iván Ilých had already spoken to Praskóvya Fëdorovna about it, and considered whether they should not arrange a party for them, or get up some private theatricals.

So they lived, and all went well, without change, and life flowed pleasantly.

IV

They were all in good health. It could not be called ill health if Iván Ilých sometimes said that he had a queer taste in his mouth and felt some discomfort in his left side.

But this discomfort increased and, though not exactly painful, grew into a sense of pressure in his side accompanied by ill humor. And his irritability became worse and worse and began to mar the agreeable, easy, and correct life that had established itself in the Golovín family. Quarrels between husband and wife became more and more frequent, and soon the ease and amenity disappeared and even the decorum was rarely maintained. Scenes again became frequent, and very few of those islets remained on which husband and wife could meet without an explosion. Praskóvya Fëdorovna now had good reason to say that her husband's temper was trying. With characteristic exaggeration she said he had always had a dreadful temper, and that it had needed all her good nature to put up with it for twenty years. It was true that now the quarrels were started by him. His bursts of temper always came just before dinner, often just as he began to eat his soup. Sometimes he noticed that a plate or dish was chipped, or the food was not right, or his son put his elbow on the table, or his daughter's hair was not done as he liked it, and for all this he blamed Praskóvya Fëdorovna. At first she retorted and said disagreeable things to him, but once or twice he fell into such a rage at the beginning of dinner that she realized it was due to some physical derangement brought on by taking food, and so she restrained herself and did not answer, but only hurried to get the dinner over. She regarded this self-restraint as highly praiseworthy. Having come to the conclusion that her husband had a dreadful temper and made her life miserable, she began to feel sorry for herself, and the more she pitied herself the more she hated her husband. She began to wish he would die; yet she did not want him to die because then his salary would cease. And this irritated her against him still more. She considered herself dreadfully unhappy just because not even his death could save her, and though she concealed her exasperation, that hidden exasperation of hers increased his irritation also.

After one scene in which Iván Ilých had been particularly unfair and after which he had said in explanation that he certainly was irritable but that it was due to his not being well, she said that if he was ill it should be attended to, and insisted on his going to see a celebrated doctor.

He went. Everything took place as he had expected and as it always does. There was the usual waiting and the important air assumed by the doctor, with which he was so familiar (resembling that which he himself assumed in court), and the sounding and listening, and the questions which called for answers that were foregone conclusions and were evidently unnecessary, and the look of importance which implied that "if only you put yourself in our hands we will arrange everything—we know indubitably how it has to be done, always in the same way for everybody alike." It was all just as it was in the law courts. The doctor put on just the same air towards him as he himself put on towards an accused person.

The doctor said that so-and-so indicated that there was so-and-so inside the patient, but if the investigation of so-and-so did not confirm this, then he must assume that and that. If he assumed that and that, then . . . and so on. To Iván Ilých only one question was important: was his case serious or not? But the doctor ignored that inappropriate question. From his point of view it was not the one under consideration, the real question was to decide between a floating kidney, chronic catarrh, or appendicitis. It was not a question of Iván Ilých's life or death, but one between a floating kidney and appendicitis. And that question the doctor solved brilliantly, as it seemed to Iván Ilých, in favour of the appendix, with the reservation that should an examination of the urine give fresh indications the matter would be reconsidered. All this was just what Iván Ilých had himself brilliantly accomplished a thousand times in dealing with men on trial. The doctor summed up just as brilliantly, looking over his spectacles triumphantly and even gaily at the accused. From the doctor's summing up Iván Ilých concluded that things were bad, but that for the doctor, and perhaps for everybody else, it was a matter of indifference, though for him it was bad. And this conclusion struck him painfully, arousing in him a great feeling of pity for himself and of bitterness towards the doctor's indifference to a matter of such importance.

He said nothing of this, but rose, placed the doctor's fee on the table, and remarked with a sigh: "We sick people probably often put inappropriate questions. But tell me, in general, is this complaint dangerous, or not? . . ."

The doctor looked at him sternly over his spectacles with one eye, as if to say: "Prisoner, if you will not keep to the questions put to you, I shall be obliged to have you removed from the court."

"I have already told you what I consider necessary and proper. The analysis may show something more." And the doctor bowed.

Iván Ilých went out slowly, seated himself disconsolately in his sledge, and drove home. All the way home he was going over what the doctor had said, trying to translate those complicated, obscure, scientific phrases into plain language and find in them an answer to the question: "Is my condition bad? Is it very bad? Or is there as yet nothing much wrong?" And it seemed to him that the meaning of what the doctor had said was that it was very bad. Everything in the streets seemed depressing. The cabmen, the houses, the passers-by, and the shops, were dismal. His ache, this dull gnawing ache that never ceased for a moment, seemed to have acquired a new and more serious significance from the doctor's dubious remarks. Iván Ilých now watched it with a new and oppressive feeling.

He reached home and began to tell his wife about it. She listened, but in the middle of his account his daughter came in with her hat on, ready to go out with her mother. She sat down reluctantly to listen to this tedious story, but could not stand it long, and her mother too did not hear him to the end.

"Well, I am very glad," she said. "Mind now to take your medicine regularly. Give me the prescription and I'll send Gerásim to the chemist's." And she went to get ready to go out.

While she was in the room Iván Ilých had hardly taken time to breathe, but he sighed deeply when she left it.

"Well," he thought, "perhaps it isn't so bad after all."

He began taking his medicine and following the doctor's directions, which had been altered after the examination of the urine. But then it happened that there was a contradiction between the indications drawn from the examination of the urine and the symptoms that showed themselves. It turned out that what was happening differed from what the doctor had told him, and that he had either forgotten, or blundered, or hidden something from him. He could not, however, be blamed for that, and Iván Ilých still obeyed his orders implicitly and at first derived some comfort from doing so.

From the time of his visit to the doctor, Iván Ilých's chief occupation was the exact fulfilment of the doctor's instructions regarding hygiene and the taking of medicine, and the observation of his pain and his excretions. His chief interests came to be people's ailments and people's health. When sickness, deaths, or recoveries, were mentioned in his presence, especially when the illness resembled his own, he listened with agitation which he tried to hide, asked questions, and applied what he heard to his own case.

The pain did not grow less, but Iván Ilých made efforts to force himself to think that he was better. And he could do this so long as nothing agitated him. But as soon as he had any unpleasantness with his wife, any lack of success in his official work, or held bad cards at bridge, he was at once acutely sensible of his disease. He had formerly borne such mischances, hoping soon to adjust what was wrong, to master it and attain success, or make a grand slam. But now every mischance upset him and plunged him into despair. He would say to himself: "There now, just as I was beginning to get better and the medicine had begun to take effect, comes this accursed misfortune, or unpleasantness. . . ." And he was furious with the mishap, or with the people who were causing the unpleasantness and killing him, for he felt that his fury was killing him but could not restrain it. One would have thought that it should have been clear to him that this exasperation with circumstances and people aggravated his illness, and that he ought therefore to ignore unpleasant occurrences. But he drew the very opposite conclusion: he said that he needed peace, and he watched for everything that might disturb it and became irritable at the slightest infringement of it. His condition was rendered worse by the fact that he read medical books and consulted doctors. The progress of his disease was so gradual that he could deceive himself when comparing one day with another—the difference was so slight. But when he consulted the doctors it seemed to him that he was getting worse, and even very rapidly. Yet despite this he was continually consulting them.

That month he went to see another celebrity, who told him almost the same as the first had done but put his questions rather differently, and the interview with this celebrity only increased Iván Ilých's doubts and fears. A friend of a friend of his, a very good doctor, diagnosed his illness again quite differently from the others, and though he predicted recovery, his questions and suppositions bewildered Iván Ilých still more and increased his doubts. A homeopathist diagnosed the disease in yet another way, and prescribed medicine which Iván Ilých took secretly for a week. But after a week, not feeling any improvement and having lost confidence both in the former doctor's treatment and in this one's, he became still more despondent. One day a lady acquaintance mentioned a cure effected by a wonder-working icon. Iván Ilých caught himself listening attentively and beginning to believe that it had occurred. This incident alarmed him. "Has my mind really weakened to such an extent?" he asked himself. "Nonsense! It's all rubbish. I mustn't give way to nervous fears but having chosen a doctor must keep strictly to his treatment. That is what I will do. Now it's all settled. I won't think about it, but will follow the treatment seriously till summer, and then we shall see. From now there must be no more of this wavering!" This was easy to say but impossible to carry out. The pain in his side oppressed him and seemed to grow worse and more incessant, while the taste in his mouth grew stranger and stranger. It seemed to him that his breath had a disgusting smell, and he was conscious of a loss of appetite and strength. There was no deceiving himself: something terrible, new, and more important than anything before in his life, was taking place within him of which he alone was aware. Those about him did not understand or would not understand it, but thought everything in the world was going on as usual. That tormented Iván Ilých more than anything. He saw that his household, especially his wife and daughter who were in a perfect whirl of visiting, did not understand anything of it and were annoyed that he was so depressed and so exacting, as if he were to blame for it. Though they tried to disguise it he saw that he was an obstacle in their path, and that his wife had adopted a definite line in regard to his illness and kept to it regardless of anything he said or did. Her attitude was this: "You know," she would say to her friends, "Iván Ilých can't do as other people do, and keep to the treatment prescribed for him. One day he'll take his drops and keep strictly to his diet and go to bed in good time, but the next day unless I watch him he'll suddenly forget his medicine, eat sturgeon—which is forbidden—and sit up playing cards till one o'clock in the morning."

"Oh, come, when was that?" Iván Ilých would ask in vexation. "Only once at Peter Ivánovich's."

"And yesterday with Shébek."

"Well, even if I hadn't stayed up, this pain would have kept me awake."

"Be that as it may you'll never get well like that, but will always make us wretched."

Praskóvya Fëdorovna's attitude to Iván Ilých's illness, as she expressed it both to others and to him, was that it was his own fault and was another of the annoyances he caused her. Iván Ilých felt that this opinion escaped her involuntarily—but that did not make it easier for him.

At the law courts too, Iván Ilých noticed, or thought he noticed, a strange attitude towards himself. It sometimes seemed to him that people were watching him inquisitively as a man whose place might soon be vacant. Then again, his friends would suddenly begin to chaff him in a friendly way about his low spirits, as if the awful, horrible, and unheard-of thing that was going on within him, incessantly gnawing at him and irresistibly drawing him away, was a very agreeable subject for jests. Schwartz in particular irritated him by his jocularity, vivacity, and *savoir-faire,* which reminded him of what he himself had been ten years ago.

Friends came to make up a set and they sat down to cards. They dealt, bending the new cards to soften them, and he sorted the diamonds in his hand and found he had seven. His partner said "No trumps" and supported him with two diamonds. What more could be wished for? It ought to be jolly and lively. They would make a grand slam. But suddenly Iván Ilých was conscious of that gnawing pain, that taste in his mouth, and it seemed ridiculous that in such circumstances he should be pleased to make a grand slam.

He looked at his partner Mikháil Mikháylovich, who rapped the table with his strong hand and instead of snatching up the tricks pushed the cards courteously and indulgently towards Iván Ilých that he might have the pleasure of gathering them up without the trouble of stretching out his hand for them. "Does he think I am too weak to stretch out my arm?" thought Iván Ilých, and forgetting what he was doing he overtrumped his partner, missing the grand slam by three tricks. And what was most awful of all was that he saw how upset Mikháil Mikháylovich was about it but did not himself care. And it was dreadful to realize why he did not care.

They all saw that he was suffering, and said: "We can stop if you are tired. Take a rest." Lie down? No, he was not at all tired, and he finished the rubber. All were gloomy and silent. Iván Ilých felt that he had diffused this gloom over them and could not dispel it. They had supper and went away, and Iván Ilých was left alone with the consciousness that his life was poisoned and was poisoning the lives of others, and that this poison did not weaken but penetrated more and more deeply into his whole being.

With this consciousness, and with physical pain besides the terror, he must go to bed, often to lie awake the greater part of the night. Next morning he had to get up again, dress, go to the law courts, speak, and write; or if he did not go out, spend at home those twenty-four hours a day each of which was a torture. And he had to live thus all alone on the brink of an abyss, with no one who understood or pitied him.

V

So one month passed and then another. Just before the New Year his brother-in-law came to town and stayed at their house. Iván Ilých was at the law courts and Praskóvya Fëdorovna had gone shopping. When Iván Ilých came home and entered his study he found his brother-in-law there—a healthy, florid man—unpacking his portmanteau himself. He raised his head on hearing Iván Ilých's footsteps and looked up at him for a moment without a word. That stare told Iván Ilých everything. His brother-in-law opened his mouth to utter an exclamation of surprise but checked himself, and that action confirmed it all.

"I have changed, eh?"

"Yes, there is a change."

And after that, try as he would to get his brother-in-law to return to the subject of his looks, the latter would say nothing about it. Praskóvya Fëdorovna came home and her brother went out to her. Iván Ilých locked the door and began to examine himself in the glass, first full face, then in profile. He took up a portrait of himself taken with his wife, and compared it with what he saw in the glass. The change in him was immense. Then he bared his arms to the elbow, looked at them, drew the sleeves down again, sat down on an ottoman, and grew blacker than night.

"No, no, this won't do!" he said to himself, and jumped up, went to the table, took up some law papers and began to read them, but could not continue. He unlocked the door and went into the reception-room. The door leading to the drawing-room was shut. He approached it on tiptoe and listened.

"No, you are exaggerating!" Praskóvya Fëdorovna was saying.

"Exaggerating! Don't you see it? Why, he's a dead man! Look at his eyes—there's no light in them. But what is it that is wrong with him?"

"No one knows. Nikoláevich [that was another doctor] said something, but I don't know what. And Leshchetítsky [this was the celebrated specialist] said quite the contrary. . . ."

Iván Ilých walked away, went to his own room, lay down, and began musing: "The kidney, a floating kidney." He recalled all the doctors had told him of how it detached itself and swayed about. And by an effort of imagination he tried to catch that kidney and arrest it and support it. So little was needed for this, it seemed to him. "No, I'll go to see Peter Ivánovich again." [That was the friend whose friend was a doctor.] He rang, ordered the carriage, and got ready to go.

"Where are you going, Jean?" asked his wife, with a specially sad and exceptionally kind look.

This exceptionally kind look irritated him. He looked morosely at her.

"I must go to see Peter Ivánovich."

He went to see Peter Ivánovich, and together they went to see his friend, the doctor. He was in, and Iván Ilých had a long talk with him.

Reviewing the anatomical and physiological details of what in the doctor's opinion was going on inside him, he understood it all.

There was something, a small thing, in the vermiform appendix. It might all come right. Only stimulate the energy of one organ and check the activity of another, then absorption would take place and everything would come right. He got home rather late for dinner, ate his dinner, and conversed cheerfully, but could not for a long time bring himself to go back to work in his room. At last, however, he went to his study and did what was necessary, but the consciousness that he had put something aside—an important, intimate matter which he would revert to when his work was done—never left him. When he had finished his work he remembered that this intimate matter was the thought of his vermiform appendix. But he did not give himself up to it, and went to the drawing-room for tea. There were callers there, including the examining magistrate who was a desirable match for his daughter, and they were conversing, playing the piano and singing. Iván Ilých, as Praskóvya Fëdorovna remarked, spent that evening more cheerfully than usual, but he never for a moment forgot that he had postponed the important matter of the appendix. At eleven o'clock he said good-night and went to his bedroom. Since his illness he had slept alone in a small room next to his study. He undressed and took up a novel by Zola, but instead of reading it he fell into thought, and in his imagination that desired improvement in the vermiform appendix occurred. There was the absorption and evacuation and the re-establishment of normal activity. "Yes, that's it!" he said to himself. "One need only assist nature, that's all." He remembered his medicine, rose, took it, and lay down on his back watching for the beneficent action of the medicine and for it to lessen the pain. "I need only take it regularly and avoid all injurious influences. I am already feeling better, much better." He began touching his side: it was not painful to the touch. "There, I really don't feel it. It's much better already." He put out the light and turned on his side . . . "The appendix is getting better, absorption is occurring." Suddenly he felt the old familiar, dull, gnawing pain, stubborn and serious. There was the same familiar loathsome taste in his mouth. His heart sank and he felt dazed. "My God! My God!" he muttered. "Again, again; And it will never cease." And suddenly the matter presented itself in a quite different aspect. "Vermiform appendix; Kidney!" he said to himself. "It's not a question of appendix or kidney, but of life . . . and death. Yes, life was there and now it is going, going and I cannot stop it. Yes. Why deceive myself? Isn't it obvious to everyone but me that I'm dying, and that it's only a question of weeks, days . . . it may happen this moment. There was light and now there is darkness. I was here and now I'm going there! Where?" A chill came over him, his breathing ceased, and he felt only the throbbing of his heart.

"When I am not, what will there be? There will be nothing. Then where shall I be when I am no more? Can this be dying? No, I don't want to!" He jumped up and tried to light the candle, felt for it with trembling hands, dropped candle and candlestick on the floor, and fell back on his pillow.

"What's the use? It makes no difference," he said to himself, staring with wide-open eyes into the darkness. "Death. Yes, death. And none of them know or wish to know it, and they have no pity for me. Now they are playing." (He heard through the door the distant sound of a song and its accompaniment.) "It's all the same to them, but they will die too! Fools! I first, and they later, but it will be the same for them. And now they are merry . . . the beasts!"

Anger choked him and he was agonizingly, unbearably miserable. "It is impossible that all men have been doomed to suffer this awful horror!" He raised himself.

"Something must be wrong. I must calm myself—must think it all over from the beginning." And he again began thinking. "Yes, the beginning of my illness: I knocked my side, but I was still quite well that day and the next. It hurt a little, then rather more. I saw the doctors, then followed despondency and anguish, more doctors, and I drew nearer to the abyss. My strength grew less and I kept coming nearer and nearer, and now I have wasted away and there is no light in my eyes. I think of the appendix—but this is death! I think of mending the appendix, and all the while here is death! Can it really be death?" Again terror seized him and he gasped for breath. He leant down and began feeling for the matches, pressing with his elbow on the stand beside the bed. It was in his way and hurt him, he grew furious with it, pressed on it still harder, and upset it. Breathless and in despair he fell on his back, expecting death to come immediately.

Meanwhile the visitors were leaving. Praskóvya Fëdorovna was seeing them off. She heard something fall and came in.

"What has happened?"

"Nothing. I knocked it over accidentally."

She went out and returned with a candle. He lay there panting heavily, like a man who has run a thousand yards, and stared upwards at her with a fixed look.

"What is it, Jean?"

"No . . . o . . . thing. I upset it." ("Why speak of it? She won't understand," he thought.)

And in truth she did not understand. She picked up the stand, lit his candle, and hurried away to see another visitor off. When she came back he still lay on his back, looking upwards.

"What is it? Do you feel worse?"

"Yes."

She shook her head and sat down.

"Do you know, Jean, I think we must ask Leshchetítsky to come and see you here."

This meant calling in the famous specialist, regardless of expense. He smiled malignantly and said "No." She remained a little longer and then went up to him and kissed his forehead.

While she was kissing him he hated her from the bottom of his soul and with difficulty refrained from pushing her away.

"Good-night. Please God you'll sleep."

"Yes."

VI

Iván Ilých saw that he was dying, and he was in continual despair.

In the depth of his heart he knew he was dying, but not only was he not accustomed to the thought, he simply did not and could not grasp it.

The syllogism he had learnt from Kiezewetter's Logic: "Caius is a man, men are mortal, therefore Caius is mortal," had always seemed to him correct as applied to Caius, but certainly not as applied to himself. That Caius—man in the abstract—was mortal, was perfectly correct, but he was not Caius, not an abstract man, but a creature quite, quite separate from all others. He had been little Ványa, with a mamma and a papa, with Mítya and Volódya, with the toys, a coachman and a nurse, afterwards with Kátenka and with all the joys, griefs, and delights of childhood, boyhood, and youth. What did Caius know of the smell of that striped leather ball Ványa had been so fond of? Had Caius kissed his mother's hand like that, and did the silk of her dress rustle so for Caius? Had he rioted like that at school when the pastry was bad? Had Caius been in love like that? Could Caius preside at a session as he did? "Caius really was mortal, and it was right for him to die; but for me, little Ványa, Iván Ilých, with all my thoughts and emotions, it's altogether a different matter. It cannot be that I ought to die. That would be too terrible."

Such was his feeling.

"If I had to die like Caius I should have known it was so. An inner voice would have told me so, but there was nothing of the sort in me and I and all my friends felt that our case was quite different from that of Caius. And now here it is!" he said to himself. "It can't be. It's impossible! But here it is. How is this? How is one to understand it?"

He could not understand it, and tried to drive this false, incorrect, morbid thought away and to replace it by other proper and healthy thoughts. But that thought, and not the thought only but the reality itself, seemed to come and confront him.

And to replace that thought he called up a succession of others, hoping to find in them some support. He tried to get back into the former current of thoughts that had once screened the thought of death from him. But strange to say, all that had formerly shut off, hidden, and destroyed, his consciousness of death, no longer had that effect. Iván Ilých now spent most of his time in attempting to re-establish that old current. He would say to himself: "I will take up my duties again—after all I used to live by them." And banishing all doubts he would go to the law courts, enter into conversation with his colleagues, and sit carelessly as was his wont, scanning the crowd with a thoughtful look and leaning both his emaciated arms on the arms of his oak chair; bending over as usual to a colleague and drawing his papers nearer he would interchange whispers with him, and then suddenly raising his eyes and sitting erect would pronounce certain words and open the proceedings. But suddenly in the midst of those proceedings the pain in his side, regardless of the stage the proceedings had reached, would begin its own gnawing work. Iván Ilých would turn his attention to it and try to drive the thought of it away, but without success. *It* would come and stand before him and look at him, and he would be petrified and the light would die out of his eyes, and he would again begin asking himself whether *It* alone was true. And his colleagues and subordinates would see with surprise and distress that he, the brilliant and subtle judge, was becoming confused and making mistakes. He would shake himself, try to pull himself together, manage somehow to bring the sitting to a close, and return home with the sorrowful consciousness that his judicial labours could not as formerly hide from him what he wanted them to hide, and could not deliver him from *It*. And what was worst of all was that *It* drew his attention to itself not in order to make him take some action but only that he should look at *It*, look it straight in the face: look at it and without doing anything, suffer inexpressibly.

And to save himself from this condition Iván Ilých looked for consolations—new screens—and new screens were found and for a while seemed to save him, but then they immediately fell to pieces or rather became transparent, as if *It* penetrated them and nothing could veil *It*.

In these latter days he would go into the drawing-room he had arranged—that drawing-room where he had fallen and for the sake of which (how bitterly ridiculous it seemed) he had sacrificed his life—for he knew that his illness originated with that knock. He would enter and see that something had scratched the polished table. He would look for the cause of this and find that it was the bronze ornamentation of an album, that had got bent. He would take up the expensive album which he had lovingly arranged, and feel vexed with his daughter and her friends for their untidiness—for the album was torn here and there and some of the photographs turned upside down. He would put it carefully in order and bend the ornamentation back into position. Then it would occur to him to place all those things in another corner of the room, near the plants. He would call the footman, but his daughter or wife would come to help him. They would not agree, and his wife would contradict him, and he would dispute and grow angry. But that was all right, for then he did not think about *It*. *It* was invisible.

But then, when he was moving something himself, his wife would say: "Let the servants do it. You will hurt yourself again." And suddenly *It* would flash through the screen and he would see it. *It* was just a flash, and he hoped it would disappear, but he would involuntarily pay attention to his side. "It sits there as before, gnawing just the same!" And he could no longer forget *It*, but could distinctly see it looking at him from behind the flowers. "What is it all for?"

"It really is so! I lost my life over that curtain as I might have done when storming a fort. Is that possible? How terrible and how stupid. It can't be true! It can't, but it is."

He would go to his study, lie down, and again be alone with *It:* face to face with *It*. And nothing could be done with *It* except to look at it and shudder.

VII

How it happened it is impossible to say because it came about step by step, unnoticed, but in the third month of Iván Ilých's illness, his wife, his daughter, his son, his acquaintances, the doctors, the servants, and above all he himself, were aware that the whole interest he had for other people was whether he would soon vacate his place, and at last release the living from the discomfort caused by his presence and be himself released from his sufferings.

He slept less and less. He was given opium and hypodermic injections of morphine, but this did not relieve him. The dull depression he experienced in a somnolent condition at first gave him a little relief, but only as something new, afterwards it became as distressing as the pain itself or even more so.

Special foods were prepared for him by the doctors' orders, but all those foods became increasingly distasteful and disgusting to him.

For his excretions also special arrangements had to be made, and this was a torment to him every time—a torment from the uncleanliness, the unseemliness, and the smell, and from knowing that another person had to take part in it.

But just through this most unpleasant matter Iván Ilých obtained comfort. Gerásim, the butler's young assistant, always came in to carry the things out. Gerásim was a clean, fresh peasant lad, grown stout on town food and always cheerful and bright. At first the sight of him, in his clean Russian peasant costume, engaged on that disgusting task embarrassed Iván Ilých.

Once when he got up from the commode too weak to draw up his trousers, he dropped into a soft armchair and looked with horror at his bare, enfeebled thighs with the muscles so sharply marked on them.

Gerásim with a firm light tread, his heavy boots emitting a pleasant smell of tar and fresh winter air, came in wearing a clean Hessian apron, the sleeves of his print shirt tucked up over his strong bare young arms; and refraining from looking at his sick master out of consideration for his feelings, and restraining the joy of life that beamed from his face, went up to the commode.

"Gerásim!" said Iván Ilých in a weak voice.

Gerásim started, evidently afraid he might have committed some blunder, and with a rapid movement turned his fresh, kind, simple young face which just showed the first downy signs of a beard.

"Yes, sir?"

"That must be very unpleasant for you. You must forgive me. I am helpless."

"Oh, why, sir," and Gerásim's eyes beamed and he showed his glistening white teeth, "what's a little trouble? It's a case of illness with you, sir."

And his deft strong hands did their accustomed task, and he went out of the room stepping lightly. Five minutes later he as lightly returned.

Iván Ilých was still sitting in the same position in the armchair.

"Gerásim," he said when the latter had replaced the freshly-washed utensil. "Please come here and help me." Gerásim went up to him. "Lift me up. It is hard for me to get up, and I have sent Dmítri away."

Gerásim went up to him, grasped his master with his strong arms deftly but gently, in the same way that he stepped—lifted him, supported him with one hand, and with the other drew up his trousers and would have set him down again, but Iván Ilých asked to be led to the sofa. Gerásim, without an effort and without apparent pressure, led him, almost lifting him, to the sofa and placed him on it.

"Thank you. How easily and well you do it all!"

Gerásim smiled again and turned to leave the room. But Iván Ilých felt his presence such a comfort that he did not want to let him go.

"One thing more, please move up that chair. No, the other one—under my feet. It is easier for me when my feet are raised."

Gerásim brought the chair, set it down gently in place, and raised Iván Ilých's legs on to it. It seemed to Iván Ilých that he felt better while Gerásim was holding up his legs.

"It's better when my legs are higher," he said. "Place that cushion under them."

Gerásim did so. He again lifted the legs and placed them, and again Iván Ilých felt better while Gerásim held his legs. When he set them down Iván Ilých fancied he felt worse.

"Gerásim," he said. "Are you busy now?"

"Not at all, sir," said Gerásim, who had learnt from the townsfolk how to speak to gentlefolk.

"What have you still to do?"

"What have I to do? I've done everything except chopping the logs for to-morrow."

"Then hold my legs up a bit higher, can you?"

"Of course I can. Why not?" And Gerásim raised his master's legs higher and Iván Ilých thought that in that position he did not feel any pain at all.

"And how about the logs?"

"Don't trouble about that, sir. There's plenty of time."

Iván Ilých told Gerásim to sit down and hold his legs, and began to talk to him. And strange to say it seemed to him that he felt better while Gerásim held his legs up.

After that Iván Ilých would sometimes call Gerásim and get him to hold his legs on his shoulders, and he liked talking to him. Gerásim did it all easily, willingly, simply, and with a good nature that touched Iván Ilých. Health, strength, and vitality in other people were offensive to him, but Gerásim's strength and vitality did not mortify but soothed him.

What tormented Iván Ilých most was the deception, the lie, which for some reason they all accepted, that he was not dying but was simply ill, and that he only need keep quiet and undergo a treatment and then something very good would result. He however knew that do what they would nothing would come of it, only still more agonizing suffering and death. This deception tortured him—their not wishing to admit what they all knew and what he knew, but wanting to lie to him concerning his terrible condition, and wishing and forcing him to participate in that lie. Those lies—lies enacted over him on the eve of his death and destined to degrade this awful, solemn act to the level of their visitings, their curtains, their sturgeon for dinner—were a terrible agony for Iván Ilých. And strangely enough, many times when they were going through their antics over him he had been within a hairbreadth of calling out to them: "Stop lying! You know and I know that I am dying. Then at least stop lying about it!" But he had never had the spirit to do it. The awful, terrible act of his dying was, he could see, reduced by those about him to the level of a casual, unpleasant, and almost indecorous incident (as if someone entered a drawing-room diffusing an unpleasant odour) and this was done by that very decorum which he had served all his life long. He saw that no one felt for him, because no one even wished to grasp his position. Only Gerásim recognized it and pitied him. And so Iván Ilých felt at ease only with him. He felt comforted when Gerásim supported his legs (sometimes all night long) and refused to go to bed, saying: "Don't you worry, Iván Ilých. I'll get sleep enough later on," or when he suddenly became familiar and exclaimed: "If you weren't sick it would be another matter, but as it is, why should I grudge a little trouble?" Gerásim alone did not lie; everything showed that he alone understood the facts of the case and did not consider it necessary to disguise them, but simply felt sorry for his emaciated and enfeebled master. Once when Iván Ilých was sending him away he even said straight out: "We shall all of us

die, so why should I grudge a little trouble?"—expressing the fact
that he did not think his work burdensome, because he was doing it
for a dying man and hoped someone would do the same for him
when his time came.

Apart from this lying, or because of it, what most tormented Iván
Ilých was that no one pitied him as he wished to be pitied. At certain
moments after prolonged suffering he wished most of all (though he
would have been ashamed to confess it) for someone to pity him as a
sick child is pitied. He longed to be petted and comforted. He knew
he was an important functionary, that he had a beard turning grey,
and that therefore what he longed for was impossible, but still he
longed for it. And in Gerásim's attitude towards him there was
something akin to what he wished for, and so that attitude comforted
him. Iván Ilých wanted to weep, wanted to be petted and cried over,
and then his colleague Shébek would come, and instead of weeping
and being petted, Iván Ilých would assume a serious, severe, and
profound air, and by force of habit would express his opinion on a
decision of the Court of Cassation and would stubbornly insist on
that view. This falsity around him and within him did more than
anything else to poison his last days.

VIII

It was morning. He knew it was morning because Gerásim had
gone, and Peter the footman had come and put out the candles,
drawn back one of the curtains, and begun quietly to tidy up.
Whether it was morning or evening, Friday or Sunday, made no
difference, it was all just the same: the gnawing, unmitigated,
agonizing pain, never ceasing for an instant, the consciousness of life
inexorably waning but not yet extinguished, that approach of that
ever dreaded and hateful Death which was the only reality, and
always the same falsity. What were days, weeks, hours, in such a
case?

"Will you have some tea, sir?"

"He wants things to be regular, and wishes the gentlefolk to drink
tea in the morning," thought Iván Ilých, and only said "No."

"Wouldn't you like to move onto the sofa, sir?"

"He wants to tidy up the room, and I'm in the way. I am uncleanliness and disorder," he thought, and said only:

"No, leave me alone."

The man went on bustling about. Iván Ilých stretched out his
hand. Peter came up, ready to help.

"What is it, sir?"

"My watch."

Peter took the watch which was close at hand and gave it to his master.

"Half-past eight. Are they up?"

"No sir, except Vladímir Ivánich" (the son) "who has gone to school. Praskóvya Fëdorovna ordered me to wake her if you asked for her. Shall I do so?"

"No, there's no need to." "Perhaps I'd better have some tea," he thought, and added aloud: "Yes, bring me some tea."

Peter went to the door but Iván Ilých dreaded being left alone. "How can I keep him here? Oh yes, my medicine." "Peter, give me my medicine." "Why not? Perhaps it may still do me some good." He took a spoonful and swallowed it. "No, it won't help. It's all tom-foolery, all deception," he decided as soon as he became aware of the familiar, sickly, hopeless taste. "No, I can't believe in it any longer. But the pain, why this pain? If it would only cease just for a moment!" And he moaned. Peter turned towards him. "It's all right. Go and fetch me some tea."

Peter went out. Left alone Iván Ilých groaned not so much with pain, terrible though that was, as from mental anguish. Always and for ever the same, always these endless days and nights. If only it would come quicker! If only *what* would come quicker? Death, darkness? . . . No, no! Anything rather than death!

When Peter returned with the tea on a tray, Iván Ilých stared at him for a time in perplexity, not realizing who and what he was. Peter was disconcerted by that look and his embarrassment brought Iván Ilých to himself.

"Oh, tea! All right, put it down. Only help me to wash and put on a clean shirt."

And Iván Ilých began to wash. With pauses for rest, he washed his hands and then his face, cleaned his teeth, brushed his hair, and looked in the glass. He was terrified by what he saw, especially by the limp way in which his hair clung to his pallid forehead.

While his shirt was being changed he knew that he would be still more frightened at the sight of his body, so he avoided looking at it. Finally he was ready. He drew on a dressing-gown, wrapped himself in a plaid, and sat down in the armchair to take his tea. For a moment he felt refreshed, but as soon as he began to drink the tea he was again aware of the same taste, and the pain also returned. He finished it with an effort, and then lay down stretching out his legs, and dismissed Peter.

Always the same. Now a spark of hope flashes up, then a sea of despair rages, and always pain; always pain, always despair, and always the same. When alone he had a dreadful and distressing desire to call someone, but he knew beforehand that with others present it

would be still worse. "Another dose of morphine—to lose consciousness. I will tell him, the doctor, that he must think of something else.
It's impossible, impossible, to go on like this."

An hour and another pass like that. But now there is a ring at the
door bell. Perhaps it's the doctor? It is. He comes in fresh, hearty,
plump, and cheerful, with that look on his face that seems to say:
"There now, you're in a panic about something, but we'll arrange it
all for you directly!" The doctor knows this expression is out of place
here, but he has put it on once for all and can't take it off—like a
man who has put on a frock-coat in the morning to pay a round of
calls.

The doctor rubs his hands vigorously and reassuringly.

"Brr! How cold it is! There's such a sharp frost; just let me warm
myself!" he says, as if it were only a matter of waiting till he was
warm, and then he would put everything right.

"Well now, how are you?"

Iván Ilých feels that the doctor would like to say: "Well, how are
our affairs?" but that even he feels that this would not do, and says
instead: "What sort of a night have you had?"

Iván Ilých looks at him as much as to say: "Are you really never
ashamed of lying?" But the doctor does not wish to understand this
question, and Iván Ilých says: "Just as terrible as ever. The pain
never leaves me and never subsides. If only something. . . ."

"Yes, you sick people are always like that. . . . There, now I think
I am warm enough. Even Praskóvya Fëdorovna, who is so particular,
could find no fault with my temperature. Well, now I can say good-
morning," and the doctor presses his patient's hand.

Then, dropping his former playfulness, he begins with a most
serious face to examine the patient, feeling his pulse and taking his
temperature, and then begins the sounding and auscultation.

Iván Ilých knows quite well and definitely that all this is nonsense
and pure deception, but when the doctor, getting down on his knee,
leans over him, putting his ear first higher then lower, and performs
various gymnastic movements over him with a significant expression
on his face, Iván Ilých submits to it all as he used to submit to the
speeches of the lawyers, though he knew very well that they were all
lying and why they were lying.

The doctor, kneeling on the sofa, is still sounding him when
Praskóvya Fëdorovna's silk dress rustles at the door and she is heard
scolding Peter for not having let her know of the doctor's arrival.

She comes in, kisses her husband, and at once proceeds to prove
that she has been up a long time already, and only owing to a
misunderstanding failed to be there when the doctor arrived.

Iván Ilých looks at her, scans her all over, sets against her the
whiteness and plumpness and cleanness of her hands and neck, the

gloss of her hair, and the sparkle of her vivacious eyes. He hates her with his whole soul. And the thrill of hatred he feels for her makes him suffer from her touch.

Her attitude towards him and his disease is still the same. Just as the doctor had adopted a certain relation to his patient which he could not abandon, so had she formed one towards him—that he was not doing something he ought to do and was himself to blame, and that she reproached him lovingly for this—and she could not now change that attitude.

"You see he doesn't listen to me and doesn't take his medicine at the proper time. And above all he lies in a position that is no doubt bad for him—with his legs up."

She described how he made Gerásim hold his legs up.

The doctor smiled with a contemptuous affability that said: "What's to be done? These sick people do have foolish fancies of that kind, but we must forgive them."

When the examination was over the doctor looked at his watch, and then Praskóvya Fëdorovna announced to Iván Ilých that it was of course as he pleased, but she had sent to-day for a celebrated specialist who would examine him and have a consultation with Michael Danílovich (their regular doctor).

"Please don't raise any objections. I am doing this for my own sake," she said ironically, letting it be felt that she was doing it all for his sake and only said this to leave him no right to refuse. He remained silent, knitting his brows. He felt that he was so surrounded and involved in a mesh of falsity that it was hard to unravel anything.

Everything she did for him was entirely for her own sake, and she told him she was doing for herself what she actually was doing for herself, as if that was so incredible that he must understand the opposite.

At half-past eleven the celebrated specialist arrived. Again the sounding began and the significant conversations in his presence and in another room, about the kidneys and the appendix, and the questions and answers, with such an air of importance that again, instead of the real question of life and death which now alone confronted him, the question arose of the kidney and appendix which were not behaving as they ought to and would now be attacked by Michael Danílovich and the specialist and forced to amend their ways.

The celebrated specialist took leave of him with a serious though not hopeless look, and in reply to the timid question Iván Ilých, with eyes glistening with fear and hope, put to him as to whether there was a chance of recovery, said that he could not vouch for it but there was a possibility. The look of hope with which Iván Ilých watched the doctor out was so pathetic that Praskóvya Fëdorovna, seeing it, even wept as she left the room to hand the doctor his fee.

The gleam of hope kindled by the doctor's encouragement did not last long. The same room, the same pictures, curtains, wall-paper, medicine bottles, were all there, and the same aching suffering body, and Iván Ilých began to moan. They gave him a subcutaneous injection and he sank into oblivion.

It was twilight when he came to. They brought him his dinner and he swallowed some beef tea with difficulty, and then everything was the same again and night was coming on.

After dinner, at seven o'clock, Praskóvya Fëdorovna came into the room in evening dress, her full bosom pushed up by her corset, and with traces of powder on her face. She had reminded him in the morning that they were going to the theatre. Sarah Bernhardt was visiting the town and they had a box, which he had insisted on their taking. Now he had forgotten about it and her toilet offended him, but he concealed his vexation when he remembered that he had himself insisted on their securing a box and going because it would be an instructive and aesthetic pleasure for the children.

Praskóvya Fëdorovna came in, self-satisfied but yet with a rather guilty air. She sat down and asked how he was but, as he saw, only for the sake of asking and not in order to learn about it, knowing that there was nothing to learn—and then went on to what she really wanted to say: that she would not on any account have gone but that the box had been taken and Helen and their daughter were going, as well as Petríshchev (the examining magistrate, their daughter's fiancé) and that it was out of the question to let them go alone; but that she would have much preferred to sit with him for a while; and he must be sure to follow the doctor's orders while she was away.

"Oh, and Fëdor Petróvich" (the fiancé) "would like to come in. May he? And Lisa?"

"All right."

Their daughter came in in full evening dress, her fresh young flesh exposed (making a show of that very flesh which in his own case caused so much suffering), strong, healthy, evidently in love, and impatient with illness, suffering, and death, because they interfered with her happiness.

Fëdor Petróvich came in too, in evening dress, his hair curled *à la Capoul,* a tight still collar round his long sinewy neck, an enormous white shirt-front and narrow black trousers tightly stretched over his strong thighs. He had one white glove tightly drawn on, and was holding his opera hat in his hand.

Following him the schoolboy crept in unnoticed, in a new uniform, poor little fellow, and wearing gloves. Terribly dark shadows showed under his eyes, the meaning of which Iván Ilých knew well.

His son had always seemed pathetic to him, and now it was dreadful to see the boy's frightened look of pity. It seemed to Iván Ilých that Vásya was the only one besides Gerásim who understood and pitied him.

They all sat down and again asked how he was. A silence followed. Lisa asked her mother about the opera-glasses, and there was an altercation between mother and daughter as to who had taken them and where they had been put. This occasioned some unpleasantness.

Fëdor Petróvich inquired of Iván Ilých whether he had ever seen Sarah Bernhardt. Iván Ilých did not at first catch the question, but then replied: "No, have you seen her before?"

"Yes, in *Adrienne Lecouvreur.*"

Praskóvya Fëdorovna mentioned some rôles in which Sarah Bernhardt was particularly good. Her daughter disagreed. Conversation sprang up as to the elegance and realism of her acting—the sort of conversation that is always repeated and is always the same.

In the midst of the conversation Fëdor Petróvich glanced at Iván Ilých and became silent. The others also looked at him and grew silent. Iván Ilých was staring with glittering eyes straight before him, evidently indignant with them. This had to be rectified, but it was impossible to do so. The silence had to be broken, but for a time no one dared to break it and they all became afraid that the conventional deception would suddenly become obvious and the truth become plain to all. Lisa was the first to pluck up courage and break that silence, but by trying to hide what everybody was feeling, she betrayed it.

"Well, if we are going it's time to start," she said, looking at her watch, a present from her father, and with a faint and significant smile at Fëdor Petróvich relating to something known only to them. She got up with a rustle of her dress.

They all rose, said good-night, and went away.

When they had gone it seemed to Iván Ilých that he felt better; the falsity had gone with them. But the pain remained—that same pain and that same fear that made everything monotonously alike, nothing harder and nothing easier. Everything was worse.

Again minute followed minute and hour followed hour. Everything remained the same and there was no cessation. And the inevitable end of it all became more and more terrible.

"Yes, send Gerásim here," he replied to a question Peter asked.

IX

His wife returned late at night. She came in on tiptoe, but he heard her, opened his eyes, and made haste to close them again. She wished to send Gerásim away and to sit with him herself, but he opened his eyes and said: "No, go away."

"Are you in great pain?"

"Always the same."

"Take some opium."

He agreed and took some. She went away.

Till about three in the morning he was in a state of stupefied misery. It seemed to him that he and his pain were being thrust into a narrow, deep black sack, but though they were pushed further and further in they could not be pushed to the bottom. And this, terrible enough in itself, was accompanied by suffering. He was frightened yet wanted to fall through the sack, he struggled but yet co-operated. And suddenly he broke through, fell, and regained consciousness. Gerásim was sitting at the foot of the bed dozing quietly and patiently, while he himself lay with his emaciated stockinged legs resting on Gerásim's shoulders; the same shaded candle was there and the same unceasing pain.

"Go away, Gerásim," he whispered.

"It's all right, sir. I'll stay a while."

"No. Go away."

He removed his legs from Gerásim's shoulders, turned sideways onto his arm, and felt sorry for himself. He only waited till Gerásim had gone into the next room and then restrained himself no longer but wept like a child. He wept on account of his helplessness, his terrible loneliness, the cruelty of man, the cruelty of God, and the absence of God.

"Why hast Thou done all this? Why hast Thou brought me here? Why, why dost Thou torment me so terribly?"

He did not expect an answer and yet wept because there was no answer and could be none. The pain again grew more acute, but he did not stir and did not call. He said to himself: "Go on! Strike me! But what is it for? What have I done to Thee? What is it for?"

Then he grew quiet and not only ceased weeping but even held his breath and became all attention. It was as though he were listening not to an audible voice but to the voice of his soul, to the current of thoughts arising within him.

"What is it you want?" was the first clear conception capable of expression in words, that he heard.

"What do you want? What do you want?" he repeated to himself.

"What do I want? To live and not to suffer," he answered.

And again he listened with such concentrated attention that even his pain did not distract him.

"To live? How?" asked his inner voice.

"Why, to live as I used to—well and pleasantly."

"As you lived before, well and pleasantly?" the voice repeated.

And in imagination he began to recall the best moments of his pleasant life. But strange to say none of these best moments of his pleasant life now seemed at all what they had then seemed—none of them except the first recollections of childhood. There, in childhood, there had been something really pleasant with which it would be possible to live if it could return. But the child who had experienced that happiness existed no longer, it was like a reminiscence of somebody else.

As soon as the period began which had produced the present Iván Ilých, all that had then seemed joys now melted before his sight and turned into something trivial and often nasty.

And the further he departed from childhood and the nearer he came to the present the more worthless and doubtful were the joys. This began with the School of Law. A little that was really good was still found there—there was lightheartedness, friendship, and hope. But in the upper classes there had already been fewer of such good moments. Then during the first years of his official career, when he was in the service of the Governor, some pleasant moments again occurred: they were the memories of love for a woman. Then all became confused and there was still less of what was good; later on again there was still less that was good, and the further he went the less there was. His marriage, a mere accident, then the disenchantment that followed it, his wife's bad breath and the sensuality and hypocrisy: then that deadly official life and those preoccupations about money, a year of it, and two, and ten, and twenty, and always the same thing. And the longer it lasted the more deadly it became. "It is as if I had been going downhill while I imagined I was going up. And that is really what it was. I was going up in public opinion, but to the same extent life was ebbing away from me. And now it is all done and there is only death."

"Then what does it mean? Why? It can't be that life is so senseless and horrible. But if it really has been so horrible and senseless, why must I die in agony? There is something wrong!"

"Maybe I did not live as I ought to have done," it suddenly occurred to him. "But how could that be, when I did everything properly?" he replied, and immediately dismissed from his mind this, the sole solution of all the riddles of life and death, as something quite impossible.

"Then what do you want now? To live: Live how? Live as you lived in the law courts when the usher proclaimed 'The judge is coming!' The judge is coming, the judge!" he repeated to himself. "Here he is, the judge. But I am not guilty!" he exclaimed angrily. "What is it for?" And he ceased crying, but turning his face to the wall continued to ponder on the same question: Why, and for what purpose, is there all this horror? But however much he pondered he found no answer. And whenever the thought occurred to him, as it often did, that it all resulted from his not having lived as he ought to have done, he at once recalled the correctness of his whole life and dismissed so strange an idea.

X

Another fortnight passed. Iván Ilých now no longer left his sofa. He would not lie in bed but lay on the sofa, facing the wall nearly all the time. He suffered ever the same unceasing agonies and in his loneliness pondered always on the same insoluble question: "What is this? Can it be that it is Death?" And the inner voice answered: "Yes, it is Death."

"Why these sufferings?" And the voice answered, "For no reason— they just are so." Beyond and besides this there was nothing.

From the very beginning of his illness, ever since he had first been to see the doctor, Iván Ilých's life had been divided between two contrary and alternating moods: now it was despair and the expectation of this uncomprehended and terrible death, and now hope and an intently interested observation of the functioning of his organs. Now before his eyes there was only a kidney or an intestine that temporarily evaded its duty, and now only that incomprehensible and dreadful death from which it was impossible to escape.

These two states of mind had alternated from the very beginning of his illness, but the further it progressed the more doubtful and fantastic became the conception of the kidney, and the more real the sense of impending death.

He had but to call to mind what he had been three months before and what he was now, to call to mind with what regularity he had been going downhill, for every possibility of hope to be shattered.

Latterly during that loneliness in which he found himself as he lay facing the back of the sofa, a loneliness in the midst of a populous town and surrounded by numerous acquaintances and relations but that yet could not have been more complete anywhere—either at the bottom of the sea or under the earth—during that terrible loneliness Iván Ilých had lived only in memories of the past. Pictures of his past rose before him one after another. They always began with what was nearest in time and then went back to what was most remote—to his childhood—and rested there. If he thought of the stewed prunes that had been offered him that day, his mind went back to the raw shrivelled French plums of his childhood, their peculiar flavour and the flow of saliva when he sucked their stones, and along with the memory of that taste came a whole series of memories of those days: his nurse, his brother, and their toys. "No, I mustn't think of that.

. . . It is too painful," Iván Ilých said to himself, and brought himself back to the present—to the button on the back of the sofa and the creases in its morocco. "Morocco is expensive, but it does not wear well: there had been a quarrel about it. It was a different kind of quarrel and a different kind of morocco that time when we tore father's portfolio and were punished, and mamma brought us some tarts. . . ." And again his thoughts dwelt on his childhood, and again it was painful and he tried to banish them and fix his mind on something else.

Then again together with that chain of memories another series passed through his mind—of how his illness had progressed and grown worse. There also the further back he looked the more life there had been. There had been more of what was good in life and more of life itself. The two merged together. "Just as the pain went on getting worse and worse so my life grew worse and worse," he thought. "There is one bright spot there at the back, at the beginning of life, and afterwards all becomes blacker and blacker and proceeds more and more rapidly—in inverse ratio to the square of the distance from death," thought Iván Ilých. And the example of a stone falling downwards with increasing velocity entered his mind. Life, a series of increasing sufferings, flies further and further towards its end—the most terrible suffering. "I am flying. . . ." He shuddered, shifted himself, and tried to resist, but was already aware that resistance was impossible, and again with eyes weary of gazing but unable to cease seeing what was before them, he stared at the back of the sofa and waited—awaiting that dreadful fall and shock and destruction.

"Resistance is impossible!" he said to himself. "If I could only understand what it is all for! But that too is impossible. An explanation would be possible if it could be said that I have not lived as I ought to. But it is impossible to say that," and he remembered all the legality, correctitude, and propriety of his life. "That at any rate can certainly not be admitted," he thought, and his lips smiled ironically as if someone could see that smile and be taken in by it. "There is no explanation! Agony, death. . . . What for?"

XI

Another two weeks went by in this way and during that fortnight an event occurred that Iván Ilých and his wife had desired. Petríschev formally proposed. It happened in the evening. The next day Praskóvya Fëdorovna came into her husband's room considering how best to inform him of it, but that very night there had been a fresh change for the worse in his condition. She found him still lying on the sofa but in a different position. He lay on his back, groaning and staring fixedly straight in front of him.

She began to remind him of his medicines, but he turned his eyes towards her with such a look that she did not finish what she was saying; so great an animosity, to her in particular, did that look express.

"For Christ's sake, let me die in peace!" he said.

She would have gone away, but just then their daughter came in and went up to say good morning. He looked at her as he had done at his wife, and in reply to her inquiry about his health said dryly that he would soon free them all of himself. They were both silent and after sitting with him for a while went away.

"Is it our fault?" Lisa said to her mother. "It's as if we were to blame! I am sorry for papa, but why should we be tortured?"

The doctor came at his usual time. Iván Ilých answered "Yes" and "No," never taking his angry eyes from him, and at last said: "You know you can do nothing for me, so leave me alone."

"We can ease your sufferings."

"You can't even do that. Let me be."

The doctor went into the drawing-room and told Praskóvya Fëdorovna that the case was very serious and that the only resource left was opium to allay her husband's sufferings, which must be terrible.

It was true, as the doctor said, that Iván Ilých's physical sufferings were terrible, but worse than the physical sufferings were his mental sufferings, which were his chief torture.

His mental sufferings were due to the fact that that night, as he looked at Gerásim's sleepy, good-natured face with its prominent cheekbones, the question suddenly occurred to him: "What if my whole life has really been wrong?"

It occurred to him that what appeared perfectly impossible before, namely that he had not spent his life as he should have done, might after all be true. It occurred to him that his scarcely perceptible attempts to struggle against what was considered good by the most highly placed people, those scarcely noticeable impulses which he had immediately suppressed, might have been the real thing, and all the rest false. And his professional duties and the whole arrangement of his life and of his family, and all his social and official interests, might all have been false. He tried to defend all those things to himself and suddenly felt the weakness of what he was defending. There was nothing to defend.

"But if that is so," he said to himself, "and I am leaving this life with the consciousness that I have lost all that was given me and it is impossible to rectify it—what then?"

He lay on his back and began to pass his life in review in quite a new way. In the morning when he saw first his footman, then his wife, then his daughter, and then the doctor, their every word and movement confirmed to him the awful truth that had been revealed to him during the night. In them he saw himself—all that for which he had lived—and saw clearly that it was not real at all, but a terrible and huge deception which had hidden both life and death. This consciousness intensified his physical suffering tenfold. He groaned and tossed about, and pulled at his clothing which choked and stifled him. And he hated them on that account.

He was given a large dose of opium and became unconscious, but at noon his sufferings began again. He drove everybody away and tossed from side to side.

His wife came to him and said:

"Jean, my dear, do this for me. It can't do any harm and often helps. Healthy people often do it."

He opened his eyes wide.

"What? Take communion? Why? It's unnecessary! However. . . ." She began to cry.

"Yes, do, my dear. I'll send for our priest. He is such a nice man."

"All right. Very well," he muttered.

Then the priest came and heard his confession. Iván Ilých was softened and seemed to feel a relief from his doubts and consequently from his sufferings, and for a moment there came a ray of hope. He again began to think of the vermiform appendix and the possibility of correcting it. He received the sacrament with tears in his eyes.

When they laid him down again afterwards he felt a moment's ease, and the hope that he might live awoke in him again. He began to think of the operation that had been suggested to him. "To live! I want to live!" he said to himself.

His wife came in to congratulate him after his communion, and when uttering the usual conventional words she added:

"You feel better, don't you?"

Without looking at her he said "Yes."

Her dress, her figure, the expression of her face, the tone of her voice, all revealed the same thing. "This is wrong, it is not as it should be. All you have lived for and still live for is falsehood and deception, hiding life and death from you." And as soon as he admitted that thought, his hatred and his agonizing physical suffering again sprang up, and with that suffering a consciousness of the unavoidable, approaching end. And to this was added a new sensation of grinding shooting pain and a feeling of suffocation.

The expression of his face when he uttered that "yes" was dreadful. Having uttered it, he looked her straight in the eyes, turned on his face with a rapidity extraordinary in his weak state and shouted:

"Go away! Go away and leave me alone!"

XII

From that moment the screaming began that continued for three days, and was so terrible that one could not hear it through two closed doors without horror. At the moment he answered his wife he realized that he was lost, that there was no return, that the end had come, the very end, and his doubts were still unsolved and remained doubts.

"Oh! Oh! Oh!" he cried in various intonations. He had begun by screaming "I won't!" and continued screaming on the letter "o."

For three whole days, during which time did not exist for him, he struggled in that black sack into which he was being thrust by an invisible, resistless force. He struggled as a man condemned to death struggles in the hands of the executioner, knowing that he cannot save himself. And every moment he felt that despite all his efforts he was drawing nearer and nearer to what terrified him. He felt that his agony was due to his being thrust into that black hole and still more to his not being able to get right into it. He was hindered from getting into it by his conviction that his life had been a good one. That very justification of his life held him fast and prevented his moving forward, and it caused him most torment of all.

Suddenly some force struck him in the chest and side, making it still harder to breathe, and he fell through the hole and there at the bottom was a light. What had happened to him was like the sensation one sometimes experiences in a railway carriage when one thinks one is going backwards while one is really going forwards and suddenly becomes aware of the real direction.

"Yes, it was all not the right thing," he said to himself, "but that's no matter. It can be done. But what *is* the right thing?" he asked himself, and suddenly grew quiet.

This occurred at the end of the third day, two hours before his death. Just then his schoolboy son had crept softly in and gone up to the bedside. The dying man was still screaming desperately and waving his arms. His hand fell on the boy's head, and the boy caught it, pressed it to his lips, and began to cry.

At that very moment Iván Ilých fell through and caught sight of the light, and it was revealed to him that though his life had not been what it should have been, this could still be rectified. He asked himself, "What *is* the right thing?" and grew still, listening. Then he felt that someone was kissing his hand. He opened his eyes, looked at his son, and felt sorry for him. His wife came up to him and he glanced at her. She was gazing at him open-mouthed, with undried tears on her nose and cheek and a despairing look on her face. He felt sorry for her too.

"Yes, I am making them wretched," he thought. "They are sorry, but it will be better for them when I die." He wished to say this but had not the strength to utter it. "Besides, why speak? I must act," he thought. With a look at his wife he indicated his son and said: "Take him away . . . sorry for him . . . sorry for you too. . . ." He tried to add, "forgive me," but said "forego" and waved his hand, knowing that He whose understanding mattered would understand.

And suddenly it grew clear to him that what had been oppressing him and would not leave him was all dropping away at once from two sides, from ten sides, and from all sides. He was sorry for them, he must act so as not to hurt them: release them and free himself from these sufferings. "How good and how simple!" he thought. "And the pain?" he asked himself. "What has become of it? Where are you, pain?"

He turned his attention to it.

"Yes, here it is. Well, what of it? Let the pain be."

"And death . . . where is it?"

He sought his former accustomed fear of death and did not find it. "Where is it? What death?" There was no fear because there was no death.

In place of death there was light.

"So that's what it is!" he suddenly exclaimed aloud. "What joy!"

To him all this happened in a single instant, and the meaning of that instant did not change. For those present his agony continued for another two hours. Something rattled in his throat, his emaciated body twitched, then the gasping and rattle became less and less frequent.

"It is finished!" said someone near him.

He heard these words and repeated them in his soul.

"Death is finished," he said to himself. "It is no more!"

He drew in a breath, stopped in the midst of a sigh, stretched out, and died.

QUESTIONS

1. What is the effect of beginning with Iván Ilých's death, then describing his career, and finally getting to his dying? (See Preface, p. 11.)
2. To what extent are you or the people around you living in a way comparable to Iván Ilých? To what extent are you living very differently?
3. What is the attitude of the survivors to death? What is the significance of this attitude in the story? What is the significance of *death* in the story?
4. Contrast the treatment of death here and in Poe's "The Fall of the House of Usher."

5. Tolstoy describes a "good" conventional marriage. What is wrong with it? Why do the partners stay in it? How does it function in Iván Ilých's system of defenses?

6. "Maybe I did not live as I ought to have done. . . . But how could that be, when I did everything properly?" Answer Iván Ilých.

7. Tolstoy tells us that two hours before his death Iván Ilých understands that "though his life had not been what it should have been, this could still be rectified." Discuss.

8. Discuss the flexible angle of vision in the story. (See Preface, pp. 5–11.)

9. Compare and contrast Tolstoy's story with Chekhov's "The Name-Day Party" (p. 175). Pay attention to *theme* (see Preface, p. 27).

I. L. PERETZ

(1851-1915)

A Polish Jew, Peretz involved himself in community activities. His work as a lawyer, teacher, and businessman was complemented by his lively efforts as a liberal reformer; he wrote these tales in Yiddish, at a time when to write in Yiddish rather than Hebrew represented a radical break with the past. The tales come from folk tradition but have been subtly reworked by a cosmopolitan intellectual at home in many languages, many literatures.

There is a tension in Peretz' work between the intellectual enlightenment that was available to Jews in the nineteenth century for the first time, and the traditions and religious devotion of the Jewish people. And so these are religious stories from a skeptical perspective. Peretz' attitude to suffering is not that of the humble worshipper who accepts God's will; both stories stand in ironic relation to that kind of devotion. But they are religious stories nonetheless and are deeply connected to Peretz' roots in Judaism and the Jewish people.

Bontsha the Silent

I. L. PERETZ

Here on earth the death of Bontsha the Silent made no impression at all. Ask anyone: Who was Bontsha, how did he live, and how did he die? Did his strength slowly fade, did his heart slowly give out—or did the very marrow of his bones melt under the weight of his burdens? Who knows? Perhaps he just died from not eating—starvation, it's called.

If a horse, dragging a cart through the streets, should fall, people would run from blocks around to stare, newspapers would write about this fascinating event, a monument would be put up to mark the very spot where the horse had fallen. Had the horse belonged to a race as numerous as that of human beings, he wouldn't have been paid this honor. How many horses are there, after all? But human beings—there must be a thousand million of them!

Bontsha was a human being; he lived unknown, in silence, and in silence he died. He passed through our world like a shadow. When Bontsha was born no one took a drink of wine; there was no sound of glasses clinking. When he was confirmed he made no speech of celebration. He existed like a grain of sand at the rim of a vast ocean, amid millions of other grains of sand exactly similar, and when the wind at last lifted him up and carried him across to the other shore of that ocean, no one noticed, no one at all.

During his lifetime his feet left no mark upon the dust of the streets; after his death the wind blew away the board that marked his grave. The wife of the gravedigger came upon that bit of wood, lying far off from the grave, and she picked it up and used it to make a fire under the potatoes she was cooking; it was just right. Three days after Bontsha's death no one knew where he lay, neither the gravedigger nor anyone else. If Bontsha had had a headstone, someone, even after a hundred years, might have come across it, might still have been able to read the carved words, and his name, Bontsha the Silent, might not have vanished from this earth.

His likeness remained in no one's memory, in no one's heart. A shadow! Nothing! Finished!

In loneliness he lived, and in loneliness he died. Had it not been for the infernal human racket someone or other might have heard the sound of Bontsha's bones cracking under the weight of his burdens; someone might have glanced around and seen that Bontsha was also a human being, that he had two frightened eyes and a silent trembling mouth; someone might have noticed how, even when he bore no actual load upon his back, he still walked with his head bowed down to earth, as though while living he was already searching for his grave.

When Bontsha was brought to the hospital ten people were waiting for him to die and leave them his narrow little cot; when he was brought from the hospital to the morgue twenty were waiting to occupy his pall; when he was taken out of the morgue forty were waiting to lie where he would lie forever. Who knows how many are now waiting to snatch from him that bit of earth?

In silence he was born, in silence he lived, in silence he died—and in an even vaster silence he was put into the ground.

Ah, but in the other world it was not so! No! In Paradise the death of Bontsha was an overwhelming event. The great trumpet of the Messiah announced through the seven heavens: Bontsha the Silent is dead! The most exalted angels, with the most imposing wings, hurried, flew, to tell one another, "Do you know who has died? Bontsha! Bontsha the Silent!"

And the new, the young little angels with brilliant eyes, with golden wings and silver shoes, ran to greet Bontsha, laughing in their joy. The sound of their wings, the sound of their silver shoes, as they ran to meet him, and the bubbling of their laughter, filled all Paradise with jubilation, and God Himself knew that Bontsha the Silent was at last here.

In the great gateway to heaven Abraham, our father, stretched out his arms in welcome and benediction. "Peace be with you!" And on his old face a deep sweet smile appeared.

What, exactly, was going on up there in Paradise?

There, in Paradise, two angels came bearing a golden throne for Bontsha to sit upon, and for his head a golden crown with glittering jewels.

"But why the throne, the crown, already?" two important saints asked. "He hasn't even been tried before the heavenly court of justice to which each new arrival must submit." Their voices were touched with envy. "What's going on here, anyway?"

And the angels answered the two important saints that, yes, Bontsha's trial hadn't started yet, but it would only be a formality, even the prosecutor wouldn't dare open his mouth. Why, the whole thing wouldn't take five minutes!

"What's the matter with you?" the angels asked. "Don't you know whom you're dealing with? You're dealing with Bontsha, Bontsha the Silent!"

When the young, the singing angels encircled Bontsha in love, when Abraham, our father, embraced him again and again, as a very old friend, when Bontsha heard that a throne waited for him, and for his head a crown, and that when he would stand trial in the court of heaven no one would say a word against him—when he heard all this, Bontsha, exactly as in the other world, was silent. He was silent with fear. His heart shook, in his veins ran ice, and he knew this must all be a dream or simply a mistake.

He was used to both, to dreams and mistakes. How often, in that other world, had he not dreamed that he was wildly shoveling up money from the street, that whole fortunes lay there on the street beneath his hands—and then he would wake and find himself a beggar again, more miserable than before the dream.

How often in that other world had someone smiled at him, said a pleasant word—and then, passing and turning back for another look, had seen his mistake and spat at Bontsha.

Wouldn't that be just my luck, he thought now, and he was afraid to lift his eyes, lest the dream end, lest he awake and find himself again on earth, lying somewhere in a pit of snakes and loathesome vipers, and he was afraid to make the smallest sound, to move so much as an eyelash; he trembled and he could not hear the paeans of the angels; he could not see them as they danced in stately celebration about him; he could not answer the loving greeting of Abraham, our father, "Peace be with you!" And when at last he was led into the great court of justice in Paradise he couldn't even say "Good morning." He was paralyzed with fear.

And when his shrinking eyes beheld the floor of the courtroom of justice, his fear, if possible, increased. The floor was of purest alabaster, embedded with glittering diamonds. On such a floor stand my feet, thought Bontsha. My feet! He was beside himself with fear. Who knows, he thought, for what very rich man, or great learned rabbi, or even saint, this whole thing's meant? The rich man will arrive, and then it will all be over. He lowered his eyes; he closed them.

In his fear he did not hear when his name was called out in the pure angelic voice: "Bontsha the Silent!" Through the ringing in his ears he could make out no words, only the sound of that voice like the sound of music, of a violin.

Yet did he, perhaps, after all, catch the sound of his own name, "Bontsha the Silent?" And then the voice added, "To him that name is as becoming as a frock coat to a rich man."

What's that? What's he saying? Bontsha wondered, and then he heard an impatient voice interrupting the speech of his defending angel. "Rich man! Frock coat! No metaphors, please! And no sarcasm!"

"He never," began the defending angel again, "complained, not against God, not against man; his eye never grew red with hatred, he never raised a protest against heaven."

Bontsha couldn't understand a word, and the harsh voice of the prosecuting angel broke in once more. "Never mind the rhetoric, please!"

"His sufferings were unspeakable. Here, look upon a man who was more tormented than Job!"

Who? Bontsha wondered. Who is this man?

"Facts! Facts! Never mind the flowery business and stick to the facts, please!" the judge called out.

"When he was eight days old he was circumcised—"

"Such realistic details are unnecessary—"

"The knife slipped, and he did not even try to staunch the flow of blood—"

"—are distasteful. Simply give us the important facts."

"Even then, an infant, he was silent, he did not cry out his pain," Bontsha's defender continued. "He kept his silence, even when his mother died, and he was handed over, a boy of thirteen, to a snake, a viper—a stepmother!"

Hm, Bontsha thought, could they mean me?

"She begrudged him every bite of food, even the moldy rotten bread and the gristle of meat that she threw at him, while she herself drank coffee with cream."

"Irrelevant and immaterial," said the judge.

"For all that, she didn't begrudge him her pointed nails in his flesh—flesh that showed black and blue through the rags he wore. In winter, in the bitterest cold, she made him chop wood in the yard, barefoot! More than once were his feet frozen, and his hands, that were too young, too tender, to lift the heavy logs and chop them. But he was always silent, he never complained, not even to his father—"

"Complain! To that drunkard!" The voice of the prosecuting angel rose derisively, and Bontsha's body grew cold with the memory of fear.

"He never complained," the defender continued, "and he was always lonely. He never had a friend, never was sent to school, never was given a new suit of clothes, never knew one moment of freedom."

"Objection! Objection!" the prosecutor cried out angrily. "He's only trying to appeal to the emotions with these flights of rhetoric!"

"He was silent even when his father, raving drunk, dragged him out of the house by the hair and flung him into the winter night, into the snowy, frozen night. He picked himself up quietly from the snow and wandered into the distance where his eyes led him.

"During his wanderings he was always silent; during his agony of hunger he begged only with his eyes. And at last, on a damp spring night, he drifted to a great city, drifted there like a leaf before the wind, and on his very first night, scarcely seen, scarcely heard, he was thrown into jail. He remained silent, he never protested, he never asked, Why, what for? The doors of the jail were opened again, and, free, he looked for the most lowly filthy work, and still he remained silent.

"More terrible even than the work itself was the search for work. Tormented and ground down by pain, by the cramp of pain in an empty stomach, he never protested, he always kept silent.

"Soiled by the filth of a strange city, spat upon by unknown mouths, driven from the streets, into the roadways, where, a human beast of burden, he pursued his work, a porter, carrying the heaviest loads upon his back, scurrying between carriages, carts, and horses, staring death in the eyes every moment, he still kept silent.

"He never reckoned up how many pounds he must haul to earn a penny; how many times, with each step, he stumbled and fell for that penny. He never reckoned up how many times he almost vomited out his very soul, begging for his earnings. He never reckoned up his bad luck, the other's good luck. No, never. He remained silent. He never even demanded his own earnings; like a beggar, he waited at the door for what was rightfully his, and only in the depths of his eyes was there an unspoken longing. 'Come back later!' they'd order him; and, like a shadow, he would vanish, and then, like a shadow, would return and stand waiting, his eyes begging, imploring, for what was his. He remained silent even when they cheated him, keeping back, with one excuse or another, most of his earnings, or giving him bad money. Yes, he never protested, he always remained silent.

"Once," the defending angel went on, "Bontsha crossed the road-way to the fountain for drink, and in that moment his whole life was miraculously changed. What miracle happened to change his whole life? A splendid coach, with tires of rubber, plunged past, dragged by runaway horses; the coachman, fallen, lay in the street, his head split open. From the mouths of the frightened horses spilled foam, and in their wild eyes sparks struck like fire in a dark night, and inside the carriage sat a man, half alive, half dead, and Bontsha caught at the reins and held the horses. The man who sat inside and whose life was saved, a Jew, a philanthropist, never forgot what Bontsha had done for him. He handed him the whip of the dead driver, and Bontsha, then and there, became a coachman—no longer a common porter! And what's more, his great benefactor married him off, and what's still more, this great philanthropist himself provided a child for Bontsha to look after.

"And still Bontsha never said a word, never protested."

They mean me, I really do believe they mean me, Bontsha encouraged himself, but still he didn't have the gall to open his eyes, to look up at his judge.

"He never protested. He remained silent even when that great philanthropist shortly thereafter went into bankruptcy without even having paid Bontsha one cent of his wages.

"He was silent even when his wife ran off and left him with her helpless infant. He was silent when, fifteen years later, that same helpless infant had grown up and become strong enough to throw Bontsha out of the house."

They mean me, Bontsha rejoiced, they really mean me.

"He even remained silent," continued the defending angel, "when that same benefactor and philanthropist went out of bankruptcy, as suddenly as he'd gone into it, and still didn't pay Bontsha one cent of what he owed him. No, more than that. This person, as befits a fine gentleman who has gone through bankruptcy, again went driving the great coach with the tires of rubber, and now, now he had a new coachman, and Bontsha, again a porter in the roadway, was run over by coachman, carriage, horses. And still, in his agony, Bontsha did not cry out; he remained silent. He did not even tell the police who had done this to him. Even in the hospital, where everyone is allowed to scream, he remained silent. He lay in utter loneliness on his cot, abandoned by the doctor, by the nurse; he had not the few pennies to pay them—and he made no murmur. He was silent in that awful moment just before he was about to die, and he was silent in that very moment when he did die. And never one murmur of protest against man, never one murmur of protest against God!"

Now Bontsha begins to tremble again. He senses that after his defender has finished, his prosecutor will rise to state the case against him. Who knows of what he will be accused? Bontsha, in that other world on earth, forgot each present moment as it slipped behind him to become the past. Now the defending angel has brought everything back to his mind again—but who knows what forgotten sins the prosecutor will bring to mind?

The prosecutor rises. "Gentlemen!" he begins in a harsh and bitter voice, and then he stops. "Gentlemen—" he begins again, and now his voice is less harsh, and again he stops. And finally, in a very soft voice, the same prosecutor says, "Gentlemen, he was always silent— and now I too will be silent."

The great court of justice grows very still, and at last from the judge's chair a new voice rises, loving, tender. "Bontsha my child, Bontsha"—the voice swells like a great harp—"my heart's child . . ."

Within Bontsha his very soul begins to weep. He would like to open his eyes, to raise them, but they are darkened with tears. It is so sweet to cry. Never until now has it been sweet to cry.

"My child, my Bontsha . . ."

Not since his mother died has he heard such words, and spoken in such a voice.

"My child," the judge begins again, "you have always suffered, and you have always kept silent. There isn't one secret place in your body without its bleeding wound; there isn't one secret place in your soul without its wound and blood. And you never protested. You always were silent.

"There, in that other world, no one understood you. You never understood yourself. You never understood that you need not have been silent, that you could have cried out and that your outcries would have brought down the world itself and ended it. You never understood your sleeping strength. There in that other world, that world of lies, your silence was never rewarded, but here in Paradise is the world of truth, here in Paradise you will be rewarded. You, the judge can neither condemn nor pass sentence upon. For you there is not only one portion of Paradise, one little share. No, for you there is everything! Whatever you want! Everything is yours!"

Now for the first time Bontsha lifts his eyes. He is blinded by light. The splendor of light lies everywhere, upon the walls, upon the vast ceiling, the angels blaze with light, the judge. He drops his weary eyes.

"Really?" he asks, doubtful, and a little embarrassed.

"Really!" the judge answers. "Really! I tell you, everything is yours. Everything in Paradise is yours. Choose! Take! Whatever you want! You will only take what is yours!"

"Really?" Bontsha asks again, and now his voice is stronger, more assured.

And the judge and all the heavenly host answer, "Really! Really! Really!"

"Well then"—and Bontsha smiles for the first time—"well then, what I would like, Your Excellency, is to have, every morning for breakfast, a hot roll with fresh butter."

A silence falls upon the great hall, and it is more terrible than Bontsha's has ever been, and slowly the judge and the angels bend their heads in shame at this unending meekness they have created on earth.

Then the silence is shattered. The prosecutor laughs aloud, a bitter laugh.

If Not Higher

I. L. PERETZ

Early every Friday morning, at the time of the Penitential Prayers, the Rabbi of Nemirov would vanish.

He was nowhere to be seen—neither in the synagogue nor in the two Houses of Study nor at a *minyan*. And he was certainly not at home. His door stood open; whoever wished could go in and out; no one would steal from the rabbi. But not a living creature was within.

Where could the rabbi be? Where should he be? In heaven, no doubt. A rabbi has plenty of business to take care of just before the Days of Awe. Jews, God bless them, need livelihood, peace, health, and good matches. They want to be pious and good, but our sins are so great, and Satan of the thousand eyes watches the whole earth from one end to the other. What he sees he reports; he denounces, informs. Who can help us if not the rabbi!

That's what the people thought.

But once a Litvak came, and he laughed. You know the Litvaks. They think little of the Holy Books but stuff themselves with Talmud and law. So this Litvak points to a passage in the *Gemarah* —it sticks in your eyes—where it is written that even Moses, our Teacher, did not ascend to heaven during his lifetime but remained suspended two and a half feet below. Go argue with a Litvak!

So where can the rabbi be?

"That's not my business," said the Litvak, shrugging. Yet all the while—what a Litvak can do!—he is scheming to find out.

That same night, right after the evening prayers, the Litvak steals into the rabbi's room, slides under the rabbi's bed, and waits. He'll watch all night and discover where the rabbi vanishes and what he does during the Pentitential Prayers.

Someone else might have got drowsy and fallen asleep, but a Litvak is never at a loss; he recites a whole tractate of the Talmud by heart.

At dawn he hears the call to prayers.

The rabbi has already been awake for a long time. The Litvak has heard him groaning for a whole hour.

Whoever has heard the Rabbi of Nemirov groan knows how much

From *A Treasury of Yiddish Stories* edited by Irving Howe and Eliezer Greenberg. Copyright 1953, 1954 by The Viking Press, Inc. Reprinted by permission of The Viking Press. Translated by Marie Syrkin.

sorrow for all Israel, how much suffering, lies in each groan. A man's heart might break, hearing it. But a Litvak is made of iron; he listens and remains where he is. The rabbi, long life to him, lies on the bed, and the Litvak under the bed.

Then the Litvak hears the beds in the house begin to creak; he hears people jumping out of their beds, mumbling a few Jewish words, pouring water on their fingernails, banging doors. Everyone has left. It is again quiet and dark; a bit of light from the moon shines through the shutters.

(Afterward the Litvak admitted that when he found himself alone with the rabbi a great fear took hold of him. Goose pimples spread across his skin, and the roots of his earlocks pricked him like needles. A trifle: to be alone with the rabbi at the time of the Penitential Prayers! But a Litvak is stubborn. So he quivered like a fish in water and remained where he was.)

Finally the rabbi, long life to him, arises. First he does what befits a Jew. Then he goes to the clothes closet and takes out a bundle of peasant clothes: linen trousers, high boots, a coat, a big felt hat, and a long wide leather belt studded with brass nails. The rabbi gets dressed. From his coat pocket dangles the end of a heavy peasant rope.

The rabbi goes out, and the Litvak follows him.

On the way the rabbi stops in the kitchen, bends down, takes an ax from under the bed, puts it in his belt, and leaves the house. The Litvak trembles but continues to follow.

The hushed dread of the Days of Awe hangs over the dark streets. Every once in a while a cry rises from some *minyan* reciting the Penitential Prayers, or from a sickbed. The rabbi hugs the sides of the streets, keeping to the shade of the houses. He glides from house to house, and the Litvak after him. The Litvak hears the sound of his heartbeats mingling with the sound of the rabbi's heavy steps. But he keeps on going and follows the rabbi to the outskirts of the town.

A small wood stands behind the town.

The rabbi, long life to him, enters the wood. He takes thirty or forty steps and stops by a small tree. The Litvak, overcome with amazement, watches the rabbi take the ax out of his belt and strike the tree. He hears the tree creak and fall. The rabbi chops the tree into logs and the logs into sticks. Then he makes a bundle of the wood and ties it with the rope in his pocket. He puts the bundle of wood on his back, shoves the ax back into his belt, and returns to the town.

He stops at a back street beside a small broken-down shack and knocks at the window.

"Who is there?" asks a frightened voice. The Litvak recognizes it as the voice of a sick Jewish woman.

"I," answers the rabbi in the accent of a peasant.

"Who is I?"

Again the rabbi answers in Russian. "Vassil."

"Who is Vassil, and what do you want?"

"I have wood to sell, very cheap." And, not waiting for the woman's reply, he goes into the house.

The Litvak steals in after him. In the gray light of early morning he sees a poor room with broken, miserable furnishings. A sick woman, wrapped in rags, lies on the bed. She complains bitterly, "Buy? How can I buy? Where will a poor widow get money?"

"I'll lend it to you," answers the supposed Vassil. "It's only six cents."

"And how will I ever pay you back?" said the poor woman, groaning.

"Foolish one," says the rabbi reproachfully. "See, you are a poor sick Jew, and I am ready to trust you with a little wood. I am sure you'll pay. While you, you have such a great and mighty God and you don't trust him for six cents."

"And who will kindle the fire?" said the widow. "Have I the strength to get up? My son is at work."

"I'll kindle the fire," answers the rabbi.

As the rabbi put the wood into the oven he recited, in a groan, the first portion of the Penitential Prayers.

As he kindled the fire and the wood burned brightly, he recited, a bit more joyously, the second portion of the Penitential Prayers. When the fire was set he recited the third portion, and then he shut the stove.

The Litvak who saw all this became a disciple of the rabbi.

And ever after, when another disciple tells how the Rabbi of Nemirov ascends to heaven at the time of the Penitential Prayers, the Litvak does not laugh. He only adds quietly, "If not higher."

ANTON CHEKHOV

(1860-1904)

Chekhov had to write in order to help pay for his medical studies in Moscow. But, by the time he became a doctor, he found he was more interested in writing than in medicine. Paid badly and forced to limit his stories to 100 newspaper lines, he nonetheless turned out hundreds of stories and learned his craft. After he was awarded the Pushkin Prize for a collection of stories, in 1888, he began to write longer fiction—like "The Name-Day Party"—and magnificent plays like *The Sea Gull, Uncle Vanya, The Three Sisters,* and *The Cherry Orchard.* Chekhov died at age forty-four of tuberculosis.

If Chekhov paid for his medical studies by writing, often in his stories we are aware of a doctor examining society and the heart. He stands back from his characters and lets them present themselves to us by what they say and do.

"Ninochka" is an interesting first person study, a story in which the hypocritical victimizer tells the tale and we learn more than he tells. In "The Name-Day Party" Chekhov shows us people struggling to live an authentic life. It is perhaps one of the most painful and powerful stories in this anthology.

Ninochka: A Love Story

ANTON CHEKHOV

The door opened quietly and my good friend Pavel Sergeyevich Vikhlyenev entered. Although a young man, he was sickly, old-looking, and, in general—with his round shoulders, long nose, and gaunt features—unattractive. But, on the other hand, his face was so bland, soft, and undefined that every time you looked at it you experienced a strange desire to get hold of it with your five fingers and to feel, as it were, the doughy soft-heartedness and warmth of my friend. Like all bookish people, he was quiet, diffident, and shy; besides which, at this time he was paler than usual, and for some reason violently agitated.

"What's the matter with you?" I asked, glancing at his white face and faintly trembling lips. "Are you sick, or has there been another misunderstanding with your wife? You don't look yourself."

After hesitating for a moment Vikhlyenev coughed slightly, then with a gesture of despair said "Yes . . . with Ninochka again. I've been so miserable I couldn't sleep all night, and, as you see, I'm barely alive. Damn it all! Other people don't let things get them down; they take injury, loss, or pain lightly. But it requires a mere trifle to depress and upset me."

"But what happened?"

"A trifle—a little domestic drama. But I'll tell you the whole story, if you like. Yesterday my Ninochka did not go out. She took it into her head to spend an evening with me and stayed at home. I was, of course, overjoyed. She usually goes out to a meeting somewhere at night, and since that's the only time I'm at home, you can imagine how I was . . . well . . . I was overjoyed. But then, you have never been married, so you don't know how cozy and warm it feels when you come home from work to find the woman you live for. . . . Ah!"

Vikhlyenev made an inventory of the charms of married life. Then he wiped the perspiration from his forehead, and continued. "Ninochka thought she'd like to spend an evening with me. Well, you know how I am—dull, heavy, and far from clever. It's not much fun to be with me; I'm forever at my drafting board or my soil filters; I never play, or dance, or joke. And you must admit that Ninochka is pleasure-loving. Youth has its rights, don't you think so? Well, I began by showing her various little things, photographs and one thing and another, told her some stories, and then I suddenly remembered that I had some old letters in my desk, among them some that were very funny. In my student days I had friends who wrote devilishly clever letters: you read them and you split your guts laughing! I pulled the letters out of the desk and commenced reading them to Ninochka. I read her one, then another, then a third, and suddenly—the whole thing broke down! In one letter she came across the phrase: 'Katya sends her regards.' To a jealous wife such a phrase is like a sharp knife, and my Ninochka—an Othello in petticoats! The questions rained down on my unfortunate head: Who is this Katya? And how? And why? I explained to her that she was in some way a kind of first love, something out of my young student life, my salad days, to which it was impossible to attach any significance whatsoever. Every youth, I told her, has his Katya; it would be impossible not to—but my Ninochka wouldn't listen. She imagined—God knows what!—and started to cry. After the tears, hysterics. 'You're vile, filthy,' she screamed. 'You hid your past from me! You probably have some kind of a Katya even now, and you're hiding it from me!' I tried and I tried to reassure her, but to no avail. Masculine logic never convinced a woman. In the end I begged her forgiveness—on my knees. I crawled, and where did it get me? She went to bed in hysterics—she in the bedroom and I on the sofa in my study. This morning she was pouting, wouldn't look at me, and spoke to me as though I were a stranger. She threatens to move to her mother's, and she probably will—I know her!"

"Hm-m. Not a very pleasant story."

"Women are incomprehensible to me! Granting that Ninochka is young, pure, fastidious, and can't help being shocked by something so earthy—is that so hard to forgive? I may be guilty, but I begged her forgiveness—I crawled on my knees! I even, if you must know, wept!"

"Yes, women are a great riddle."

"My dear friend, you have a strong influence over Ninochka. She respects you; she sees in you an authority. Please, go and see her. Exert your influence, and make her understand how wrong she is. I am suffering, my friend. If this goes on one more day I won't be able to endure it. Go—be a friend!"

"But do you think that would be . . . proper?"

"Why not? You and she have been friends almost since childhood. She trusts you. As a friend, please go!"

Vikhlyenev's tearful pleading touched me. I dressed and went to see his wife. I found Ninochka engaged in her favorite occupation: she was sitting on the sofa, one leg crossed over the other, blinking her beautiful eyes and doing nothing. When I came in she jumped up and ran to me; then she glanced round, quietly closed the door, and, with the lightness of a feather, clung to my neck. (You must not think, dear reader, that this is a misprint. For a year now, I had been sharing with Vikhlyenev his conjugal obligations.)

"What deviltry have you thought up now?" I asked Ninochka, seating her beside me.

"What do you mean?"

"Again you have managed to torment your better half. He came to see me today and told me all about it."

"Oh—that! So he found someone to complain to!"

"What actually happened?"

"Oh, not much. I was bored last night . . . and got angry because I had no place to go, so, out of spite, I started nagging him about his Katya. I cried simply from boredom—and how can I explain that to him?"

"But you know, my darling, that's cruel and inhuman. He's so nervous, and yet you plague him with your scenes."

"Oh, that's nothing. He loves it when I act jealous. And there's no better blind than fictitious jealousy. But let's drop it. I don't like it when you start talking about my milksop; I'm fed up with him! Let's have tea."

"Well, in any case, stop tormenting him. You know, he's pathetic: he describes his happiness and his faith in your love so frankly and sincerely that it makes one uncomfortable. Do control yourself somehow; show him some affection; lie! One word from you and he's in seventh heaven."

Ninochka frowned and pouted, but a little later when Vikhlyenev came in and timidly looked into my face, she gaily and affectionately smiled at him.

"You're just in time for tea!" she said to him. "How clever of you, my pet, never to be late. Lemon or cream for you?"

Vikhlyenev, not expecting such a welcome, was moved; he kissed his wife's hand warmly, and embraced me. This embrace was so absurd and so untimely that both Ninochka and I blushed.

"Blessed are the peacemakers!" clucked the happy husband. "You've made her listen to reason; and why? Because you're a man of the world; you mingle in society, and you know all the fine points of a woman's heart! Ha! Ha! Ha! I'm a clumsy ox; when one word is needed, I say ten; when I should kiss her hand or something, I start to find fault! Ha! Ha!"

After tea Vikhlyenev led me into his study, buttonholed me, and mumbled, "I don't know how to thank you, my dear friend. Believe me, I suffered; I was tortured; and now I am so happy—I'm simply overwhelmed! And this isn't the first time that you've pulled me out of a terrible situation. My dear friend—now, don't refuse me—I have here a little something. . . . It's just a little model locomotive that I made myself; I got a medal for it at the exposition. Take it as a token of my gratitude . . . my friendship. Do me this favor!"

Naturally, I refused in every possible way, but Vikhlyenev was insistent and, like it or not, I had to accept his precious gift.

Days, weeks, months passed. Sooner or later the ugly truth was bound to be revealed to him in all its enormity. When, by accident, he did find out, he turned frightfully pale, sat down on the sofa, and stared dully at the ceiling without saying a word. A heartache has to express itself in some kind of movement, and he began to turn from side to side on the sofa in an agonizing way. Even these movements were circumscribed by his milksop nature.

A week later, somewhat recovered from the shock of this news, he came to see me. We were both embarrassed and avoided looking at each other. I began to spout some sort of nonsense about free love, marital selfishness, submission to fate.

"It wasn't about that—" he interrupted meekly, "all that I understand perfectly. In matters of the heart, no one is guilty. What concerns me is the other side of the business . . . the purely practical. You see, I don't know life at all, and where the actual arrangements . . . the social conventions are concerned, I'm a real greenhorn. So, help me, my friend! Tell me, what is Ninochka supposed to do now? Should she go on living with me, or do you think it would be better if she moved in with you?"

Having deliberated briefly, we left it at this: Ninochka would continue to live at Vikhlyenev's; I would go to see her whenever I liked, and he would take the corner room, which formerly had been the storeroom, for himself. This room was rather dark and damp, and the entrance to it was through the kitchen, but, on the other hand, he could perfectly well shut himself up in it and not be a nuisance to anyone.

The Name-Day Party

ANTON CHEKHOV

I

After dinner, with its eight courses and endless conversation, Olga Mikhailovna, whose husband's name day was being celebrated, went out into the garden. The obligation to smile and talk continuously, the stupidity of the servants, the clatter of dishes, the long intervals between courses, and the corset she had put' on to conceal her pregnancy from her guests, had wearied her to the point of exhaustion. She longed to get away from the house, to sit in the shade and rest in thoughts of the child that was to be born to her in two months. She was accustomed to these thoughts coming to her as she turned to her left from the big avenue into a narrow path; here, in the deep shade of plum and cherry trees, where dry branches scratched her neck and shoulders and spiderwebs lighted on her face, when the image of a little person of indeterminate sex and obscure features would rise in her mind, it seemed to her that it was not a spiderweb caressingly tickling her face and neck, but this little creature, and when, at the end of the path, the sparse wattle hedge came into view, and beyond it paunchy beehives with tiled roofs, when the still stagnant air began to smell of hay and honey and the urgent buzzing of bees could be heard, then the little person took complete possession of Olga Mikhailovna. She would sit down on the bench near a hut of woven branches and sink into a reverie.

This time too she went as far as the bench, sat down, and commenced thinking, but instead of the little person, it was the big persons she had just left who came to her mind. She was deeply perturbed that she, the hostess, had deserted her guests, and she recalled how her husband, Pyotr Dmitrich, and her uncle, Nikolai Nikolaich, had argued at dinner about trial by jury, the press, and education for women—her husband, as usual, arguing partly to flaunt his conservatism before his guests, but chiefly for the sake of disagreeing with her uncle, whom he disliked, while her uncle contradicted him and caviled at every word he uttered so that the company should see that he, in spite of his fifty-nine years, had retained his youthful freshness of spirit and freedom of thought. And toward the end of dinner Olga Mikhailovna could no longer contain herself and she too began making an awkward defense of university education for women—not that higher education was in need of her support, but she wanted to annoy her husband, who, to her mind, was unfair. The guests grew tired of the dispute, but that did not prevent them from intervening and talking a great deal, although none of them had the slightest interest in either trial by jury or the education of women. . . .

Olga Mikhailovna was sitting on the hither side of the wattle hedge near the hut. The sun was hidden behind clouds and the atmosphere and trees lowered as before rain; nevertheless it was hot and sultry. The hay, which had been cut under the trees on St. Peter's Eve, lay ungathered, looking sadly wilted and discolored, and giving off a heavy cloying smell. It was still. From behind the hedge came the monotonous buzzing of bees. . . .

Suddenly there was the sound of voices and footsteps. Someone was coming along the path toward the apiary.

"It's sultry!" said a feminine voice. "What do you think—will it rain or not?"

"It will rain, my charmer, but not before evening," a very familiar male voice answered languidly. "And it will be a good rain."

Olga Mikhailovna decided that if she quickly hid in the hut, they would pass by without seeing her, and she would not have to talk and force herself to smile. She picked up her skirts and bent down to enter the little hut. Instantly she felt a wave of hot steamy air on her face, neck, and arms. Had it not been for the closeness, the suffocating smell of rye bread, fennel, and brushwood, this would have been the perfect place to hide from her visitors, here under a thatched roof in the dusk, and to think about the little person. It was quiet and cozy.

"What a charming spot!" said the feminine voice. "Let's sit down here, Pyotr Dmitrich."

Olga Mikhailovna peeped through a crack between two branches. She saw her husband, Pyotr Dmitrich, and Lyubochka Sheller, a seventeen-year-old girl not long out of boarding school. Pyotr Dmitrich, with his hat on the back of his head, indolent and sluggish from having drunk too much at dinner, shambled along by the hedge, then stopped and raked some hay into a heap with his foot; Lyubochka, rosy from the heat, and extremely pretty as always, stood with her hands behind her back watching the languid movements of his big handsome body.

Olga Mikhailovna knew that her husband was attractive to women and she did not enjoy seeing him with them. There was nothing out of the way in Pyotr Dmitrich's raking the hay together so he could sit there and chat about trivialities with Lyubochka, nor was there anything out of the way in pretty little Lyubochka's sweetly gazing at him, and yet Olga Mikhailovna felt annoyed with her husband, and both frightened and pleased that she could listen to them.

"Sit down, enchantress," said Pyotr Dmitrich, sinking down onto the hay and stretching. "That's right. . . . Well, tell me something."

"Oh, yes! As soon as I start telling you anything, you'll fall asleep!"

"I? . . . Fall asleep? Allah forbid! How could I fall asleep with eyes like yours looking at me?"

And there was nothing out of the way in what her husband said or the fact that he was lolling with his hat on the back of his head in the presence of a lady. He was spoiled by women, knew that they found him attractive, and always adopted a special tone with them that everyone said was becoming to him. He was behaving with Lyubochka exactly as he did with all women. Nevertheless, Olga Mikhailovna was jealous.

"Tell me, please," Lyubochka began, after a brief silence, "is it true that you are being prosecuted?"

"I? Yes, it's true. . . . I am now ranked with the villains, my charmer."

"But what for?"

"For nothing . . . just . . . oh, it's chiefly because of politics," yawned Pyotr Dmitrich. "The struggle between the Right and Left. I, an obscurantist, a reactionary, made so bold as to use an expression in an official paper that is offensive to such impeccable Gladstones as Vladimir Pavlovich Vladimirov and our district justice of the peace, Kuzma Grigorevich Vostryakov."

Pyotr Dmitrich again yawned and continued:

"We have a system in which you can speak disparagingly of the sun, the moon, of anything you please, but Heaven preserve you from touching the Liberals! Heaven preserve you! A Liberal is exactly like one of those nasty dried toadstools that sprays you with a cloud of dust if you accidentally touch it with your finger."

"But what happened to you?"

"Nothing much. The whole thing was a case of much ado about nothing. A certain schoolteacher, a detestable individual of parochial background, presents Vostryakov with a petition against a tavernkeeper, accusing him of contumely and assault and battery in a public place. Everything points to the fact that both the schoolteacher and the tavernkeeper were drunk as shoemakers and that they behaved equally abominably. If there was any offensive behavior, it undoubtedly was mutual. Vostryakov ought to have fined them both for disturbing the peace and thrown them out of court—and that would have been that! But instead what do we do? As usual, what's always in the foreground with us is never the individual, never the facts, but the trademark, the label. A teacher, no matter how great a scoundrel he may be, is always right just because he's a teacher; and a tavernkeeper is always guilty because he's a tavern-keeper and a kulak. Vostryakov gave him a jail sentence, and he appealed to the circuit court. The circuit court triumphantly upheld Vostryakov's decision. Well, I stuck to my opinion. . . . Got a little hot, that's all."

Pyotr Dmitrich spoke calmly, with nonchalant irony. In reality the impending trial worried him intensely. Olga Mikhailovna remembered how on his return from the unfortunate session he had tried to conceal from the entire household how troubled he was and how dissatisfied with himself. As an intelligent man he could not help feeling that he had gone too far in expressing his personal opinion. And how many lies had been required to conceal this feeling from others and himself! How many futile conversations, how much grumbling and insincere laughter at what was not in the least laughable! On learning that he was going to be prosecuted, he immediately felt harassed and depressed; he began to sleep badly, and more and more often stood at a window drumming on the pane with his fingers. And he was ashamed to admit to his wife that he was worried, and this vexed her. . . .

"I heard that you were in the province of Poltava," said Lyu-bochka.

"Yes, I was," replied Pyotr Dmitrich. "I just got back the day before yesterday."

"It must be nice there."

"It is. Really very nice. I arrived just in time for haymaking, and, I can tell you, haymaking in the Ukraine is the most poetic time of year. Here we have a big house, a big garden, a lot of servants and commotion, and you don't see the mowing; it all passes unnoticed here. But there at the farm I have a level meadow of forty-five acres spread out before me: you can see the mowers from any window. They are mowing in the meadow, mowing in the garden—no visitors, no fuss, nothing to prevent your seeing, hearing, and feeling only the haymaking. Outdoors and indoors there's the smell of hay. From sunrise to sunset the clang of scythes. Altogether my dear Little Russia is a lovely country. Would you believe it, when I was drinking water at old wells with shadoofs, or filthy vodka in those Jewish taverns, when, on quiet evenings, I could hear the sound of Ukrainian fiddles and tambourines, I was tempted by a fascinating idea—to settle down on my farm and live there the rest of my life, far from these circuit courts, clever conversations, philosophizing women, and lengthy dinners. . . ."

Pyotr Dmitrich was not lying. He felt oppressed and really longed to rest. And he had gone to Poltava simply to avoid looking at his study, his servants, his acquaintances, and everything that could remind him of his wounded pride and his mistakes.

Lyubochka suddenly jumped up, waving her arms about in fright. "Oh, a bee, a bee!" she screamed. "It will sting!"

"Nonsense, it won't sting," said Pyotr Dmitrich. "What a coward you are!"

"No, no, no!" cried Lyubochka, looking back at the bee as she hurried off.

Pyotr Dmitrich followed her with a tender melancholy gaze. He was probably thinking of his farm as he looked at her, of solitude, and (who knows?) perhaps even of how warm and cozy life on his farm would be if this girl were his wife—young, pure, fresh, uncorrupted by higher education, and not pregnant. . . .

When their voices and footsteps had died away, Olga Mikhailovna came out of the hut and walked toward the house. She felt like crying. By now she was terribly jealous. She could understand that her husband was exhausted, dissatisfied with himself, and ashamed; that people are aloof when they feel ashamed, especially from those nearest to them, and confide in strangers; she also realized that she had nothing to fear from Lyubochka or from any of those women who were drinking coffee in the house. But it all seemed so inconceivable, so dreadful, and Olga Mikhailovna almost felt that Pyotr Dmitrich only half belonged to her.

"He has no right!" she muttered, trying to comprehend her jealousy and vexation. "He has absolutely no right! And I'm going to tell him so right now!"

She made up her mind to find her husband at once and to speak plainly and tell him what she thought: it was disgusting the way he appealed to women, seeking their admiration as if it were manna from heaven; it was unjust, dishonorable, that he should give to others what by right belonged to his wife, that he should hide his soul and conscience from her only to reveal them to the first pretty face that came along. What harm had his wife done him? What was she guilty of? After all, she was fed up with his lying; he was constantly showing off, flirting, saying things he didn't mean, trying to appear different from what he was and what he ought to be. Why this deceit? Was it becoming in a decent man? When he lied he was dishonoring himself and those to whom he lied, and showing disrespect for what he lied about. Didn't he understand that if he gave himself airs and was captious at the judicial table, or held forth at the dinner table on the prerogatives of the authorities merely to provoke her uncle, didn't he realize that this showed he hadn't the least respect for the court, for himself, for those who were listening to him and watching him?

As she turned into the big avenue, Olga Mikhailovna tried to look as if she had just gone off to attend to some household matter. On the veranda the gentlemen were drinking liqueur and eating berries.

One of them, the examining magistrate, a stout elderly man, a humorist and wit, must have been telling a vulgar story, for, seeing his hostess, he suddenly clapped his hand over his fat lips, goggled his eyes, and sat down. Olga Mikhailovna did not like the local officials. Nor did she care for their awkward ceremonious wives, their back-biting, their frequent visits, and their flattery of her husband, whom they all hated. And now, after having eaten their fill, as they sat drinking and showing no sign of leaving, their presence was acutely irksome to her, but not wishing to appear impolite, she smiled cordially at the examining magistrate and shook a finger at him. She crossed the hall and drawing room, smiling and looking as if she had gone to give an order or to make some arrangement. "God grant no one stops me!" she thought, but then forced herself to pause in the drawing room and listen politely to a young man who was playing the piano; after a moment she cried: "Bravo! Bravo, Monsieur Georges!" and, clapping her hands twice, went on.

She found her husband in his study. He was sitting at the table lost in thought. His expression was austere, preoccupied, guilty. This was not the Pyotr Dmitrich who had been arguing at dinner and whom his guests knew, but a different man—exhausted, guilty, dissatisfied with himself, whom no one but his wife knew. He must have come to his study for cigarettes. Before him lay an open cigarette case full of cigarettes, and his hand was still in the drawer of the table. As he was taking out the cigarettes he had become absorbed in his thoughts.

Olga Mikhailovna felt sorry for him. It was as clear as day that the man was tormented and could find no peace, and was, perhaps, undergoing a struggle with himself. Olga Mikhailovna went up to the table without a word; in a desire to show her husband that she had forgotten the argument at dinner and was no longer angry with him, she shut the cigarette case and put it in his side pocket.

"What shall I say to him?" she wondered. "I'll say that lying is like a forest—the farther one goes into it the more difficult it is to get out. I'll say: you were carried away by the fictitious role you were playing and went too far; you have offended people who were attached to you and who have done you no harm. Go now and apologize to them, laugh at yourself, and you will feel better. And if you want peace and solitude, we will go away together."

Meeting his wife's eyes, Pyotr Dmitrich's face instantly assumed the expression it had worn at dinner and in the garden—indifferent and slightly ironical; he yawned and stood up.

"It's after five," he said, looking at his watch. "If our guests mercifully leave us by eleven, that still leaves another six hours. A cheerful prospect, I must say!"

And, whistling, he unhurriedly walked out of the study with his usual self-assured gait. She heard him cross the hall and drawing room with a sedate step, heard his sedate laugh as he called: "Bra-a-o! Bra-a-o!" to the young man at the piano. Then the footsteps died away; he must have gone into the garden.

And now it was not jealousy, not vexation, but genuine hatred of his walk, his insincere voice and laugh, that took possession of Olga Mikhailovna. She went to the window and looked out into the garden. Pyotr Dmitrich was walking along the avenue with one hand in his pocket, snapping the fingers of his other hand; he swung along, head thrown back, looking as if he were well satisfied with himself, his dinner, his digestion, and with nature. . . .

Two little schoolboys, the sons of Madam Chizhevskaya, having just arrived, now appeared in the avenue; they were accompanied by their tutor, a student wearing a white tunic and very narrow trousers. When they reached Pyotr Dmitrich, they stopped, probably to congratulate him on his name day. With a graceful movement of his shoulders, he patted the children on their cheeks and negligently offered his hand to the student without looking at him. The student must have commended the weather and compared it to the climate of St. Petersburg, for Pyotr Dmitrich said in a loud voice—not as if he were speaking to a guest but in a tone he might have taken with a court bailiff or a witness:

"How's that, sir? Cold in Petersburg? And here, my dear sir, we have the most salubrious air and fruits of the earth in abundance. Eh? What?"

And thrusting one hand into his pocket and snapping the fingers of his other hand, he walked on. Olga Mikhailovna continued to gaze at the back of his head in perplexity till he disappeared behind the nut grove. How had a man of thirty-four come by that sedate military bearing? Where had he acquired that ponderous, elegant manner, the authoritative resonance in his voice, all those *How's that, sir*'s, *To be sure*'s, and *My dear sir*'s?

Olga Mikhailovna recalled how in the first months of her marriage, to relieve the boredom of staying home alone, she had driven to town, to the circuit court where Pyotr Dmitrich sometimes presided in place of her godfather, Count Aleksei Petrovich. In the presidential chair, wearing his uniform and a chain on his breast, he was completely changed. Imposing gestures, a thunderous voice, *How's that, sir? To be sure,* the patronizing tone. . . . All that was ordinary, human, and characteristic of him, everything, in fact, that Olga Mikhailovna was accustomed to seeing in him at home, had vanished in grandeur, and there in the presidential chair sat, not Pyotr Dmitrich, but some other man whom everyone called Mr. President. His consciousness of being a power made it impossible for him to sit still, and he seized every opportunity to ring his bell, look sternly at the public, and shout. . . . Where had he acquired that short-sightedness and deafness, when all at once he would find it difficult to see and hear, and, frowning majestically, would demand that people speak louder, and come closer to the table? From the height of his grandeur he had trouble distinguishing faces and sounds, so that if Olga Mikhailovna herself had approached him, he no doubt would have shouted: "What's your name?" He addressed peasant witnesses familiarly, roared at the public in a voice that could be heard in the street, and was absolutely impossible in his treatment of lawyers. If an attorney addressed him, Pyotr Dmitrich sat half turned away, squinting at the ceiling, hoping by this to show that an attorney was utterly superfluous here, that he neither acknowledged him nor listened to him; but when a poorly dressed local lawyer spoke to him, then Pyotr Dmitrich was all ears and measured the man with a derisive, withering glance, as if to say: "You see what we have for lawyers these days!"

"Just what are you trying to say?" he would interrupt.

If an oratorical attorney tried to use some foreign word and said "factitious" instead of "fictitious" Pyotr Dmitrich instantly became very animated: "How's that, sir? Eh? Factitious? What does that mean?" And then he remarked admonishingly: "Don't use words you can't understand." And when the attorney had finished his speech, he would walk away from the table red and perspiring, while Pyotr Dmitrich, with a self-satisfied smile, leaned back in his chair exulting over his victory. In his treatment of lawyers he was to some extent imitating Count Aleksei Petrovich, but when, for instance, the Count would say: "Counsel for the defense, keep quiet for a while!" it sounded paternally good-natured and natural, while when Pyotr Dmitrich said it, it was rude and forced.

II

The sound of applause reached her. The young man had finished playing. Olga Mikhailovna was reminded of her guests and hurried to the drawing room.

"I have so enjoyed your playing," she said, going up to the piano. "I was listening to you with delight. You have a remarkable talent! But don't you think our piano is out of tune?"

At that moment the two schoolboys came into the room with the student.

"Good heavens! Mitya and Kolya?" Olga Mikhailovna drawled joyously as she went to meet them. "How you have grown! I hardly recognized you! Where is your mama?"

"I congratulate you on the name day," the student began, rather unceremoniously. "I wish you all the best. Yekaterina Andreyevna sends her congratulations and begs you to excuse her. She's not feeling very well."

"How unkind of her! I've been looking forward to seeing her all day. How long is it since you left Petersburg? What's the weather like there now?" And without waiting for an answer, she looked tenderly at the little boys and again said: "How they have grown! It wasn't so long ago that they were coming here with their nurse, and now they are in school! The old grow older and the young grow up. . . . Have you had dinner?"

"Oh, please don't trouble!" said the student.

"Then you haven't had dinner?"

"For heaven's sake, don't trouble!"

"But you are hungry, aren't you?" Olga Mikhailovna asked in a rude harsh tone, fraught with impatience and annoyance; the words had slipped out unintentionally, and she instantly blushed and commenced coughing and smiling. "How they have grown!" she said softly.

"Please don't trouble," said the student once more.

The student begged her not to trouble and the children remained silent; obviously all three were hungry. Olga Mikhailovna led them into the dining room and ordered Vasily to set the table.

"Your mama is unkind!" she said, seating them at the table. "She has quite forgotten me. Unkind, unkind, unkind. . . . You must tell her so. And what are you studying?" she asked the student.

"Medicine."

"Oh, I'm very partial to doctors. I'm sorry my husband isn't a doctor. What courage it must take to perform operations and dissect corpses! Dreadful! Aren't you afraid? I think I should die of fear! You'll have vodka, of course?"

"Please don't trouble."

"You must have something to drink after your journey. I'm a woman, but even I drink sometimes. And Mitya and Kolya will drink Malaga. Don't worry, it's not a strong wine. What fine young men they are, really! They'll soon be thinking of getting married."

Olga Mikhailovna talked without a pause. She knew from experience that it is far easier and less tiring to talk than to listen. When you talk you don't have to strain your attention, try to think of answers, or even change your facial expression. But she inadvertently asked the student a serious question, to which he was answering at great length, and she was obliged to listen. The student knew that she had gone to the university and made an effort to appear earnest as he talked to her.

"And what are you studying?" she asked, forgetting that she had already put the question to him.

"Medicine."

Olga Mikhailovna remembered that she had been away from the ladies for a long time.

"Really? So you are going to be a doctor?" she said, getting up. "That's splendid. I regret that I didn't take up medicine. Now, you have your dinner, gentlemen, and then come out to the garden. I'll introduce you to the young ladies."

She glanced at her watch as she went out; it was five minutes to six. She was amazed that the time passed so slowly and thought with dread that there were still six hours until midnight, when her guests would leave. How would she get through those six hours? What could she think of to say? How should she behave toward her husband?

There was not a soul in the drawing room or on the veranda. The guests had all wandered off into the garden.

"I shall have to suggest a walk to the birch grove before tea, or else boating," thought Olga Mikhailovna, hurrying to the croquet lawn where she heard laughter and talking. "And the old people can play vint. . . ."

On her way she met Grigory the footman coming back with empty bottles.

"Where are the ladies?" she asked.

"They have gone to the raspberry patch. The master is there too."

"Oh, good Lord!" someone on the croquet lawn shouted in exasperation. "But I've told you the same thing a thousand times already! You have to see Bulgarians to understand them! You can't go by the papers!"

Either because of this outburst or for some other reason, Olga Mikhailovna suddenly felt terribly weak all over, especially in her legs and shoulders. All at once she felt she did not want to speak, to listen, or to move.

"Grigory," she said listlessly, and with an effort, "when you serve tea or anything, please don't look to me, don't ask me anything, don't even speak to me about it. . . . See to everything yourself and . . . and don't make a clatter with your feet. I implore you . . . I can't, because . . ."

She continued on her way to the croquet lawn without finishing what she was saying, then, remembering the ladies, she turned toward the raspberry patch. The sky, the air, and trees, still sullen, promised rain; it was hot and sultry; a great flock of crows, anticipating the storm, flew over the garden cawing. The closer the paths came to the kitchen gardens the more narrow, dark, and overgrown they were; on one of them, hidden in a thicket of wild pears, sorrel, young oaks and hops, clouds of tiny black flies enveloped her. She covered her face with her hands and forced herself to think of the little person. . . .

Through her imagination coursed the figures of Grigory, Mitya, Kolya, and the faces of the peasants who had come with their congratulations in the morning. . . .

Hearing footsteps, she opened her eyes. Her uncle, Nikolai Nikolaich, was coming rapidly toward her.

"It's you, dear! I'm glad . . ." he began, out of breath, "a word with you. . . ." He mopped his red, clean-shaven chin with his handkerchief and, stepping back abruptly, clasped his hands and opened his eyes wide. "My dear, how long can this go on?" he spluttered. "I ask you: is there no limit? Not to speak of the demoralizing effect of his martinet views, and the fact that he offends all that is sacred, all that is best in me and in every honest, thinking man—I say nothing of that, but he could at least behave decently! What is all this, anyhow? He shouts, snarls, gives himself airs, acts like some sort of Bonaparte, never lets anyone else say a word. . . . What the devil's the matter with him? Those lordly gestures, laughing like a general, that patronizing tone! And permit me to ask you: who is he? I am asking you: just who is he? His wife's husband, that's who he is; a titular councilor with a small estate who has had the good luck to marry wealth! An upstart and a *Junker,* like so many others! A character out of Shchedrin! I swear to God, either he is suffering from megalomania, or that senile old rat Count Aleksei Petrovich is right when he says that children and young people today develop late and go on playing at being cab drivers and generals till they're forty!"

"It's true, true," agreed Olga Mikhailovna. "Please let me go. . . ."

"Now just think: what is all this leading to?" continued her uncle, barring her way. "How will this playing at being a conservative and a general end? He's already being prosecuted! Prosecuted! And I'm very glad! All his bluster and hullabaloo has landed him right in the prisoners' dock. And it's not as if it were in the circuit court or anything like that—it's in a higher court! I can't conceive of anything worse! And furthermore he has quarreled with everyone! Today is his name day and, look, Vostryakov's not here, nor Vladimirov, nor Shevud, nor the Count. . . . There's no one more conservative than Count Aleksei Petrovich, but even he hasn't come. And he'll never come again! You'll see, he won't come!"

"Oh, good Lord! But what has all this to do with me?" asked Olga Mikhailovna.

"What has it to do with you? You're his wife! You are a clever woman, you've had a university education, and it is in your power to make an honest worker of him!"

"The courses I took didn't teach me how to influence difficult people. It seems I ought to apologize to everyone for having gone to the university," said Olga Mikhailovna sharply. "You know, Uncle, if you had to listen to the same tune over and over again all day long you wouldn't be able to sit still, you'd get up and run away. I hear the same thing day in and day out the whole year. It's time you took pity on me!"

Her uncle made a very solemn face, gave her a quizzical look, and curled his lip in a mocking smile.

"So that's how it is!" he crooned like an old woman. "Excuse me!" he said with a courtly bow. "If you yourself have fallen under his influence and have betrayed your convictions, you should have said so before. I beg your pardon!"

"Yes, I have betrayed my convictions!" she cried. "Now crow over that!"

"I beg your pardon!" he made a final ceremonious bow, turning a little to one side and shrinking into himself, then with a click of his heels, went on his way.

"Idiot!" thought Olga Mikhailovna. "I hope he goes home."

She found the ladies and young people in the kitchen gardens among the raspberry bushes. Some were eating raspberries, others, who had had their fill, were sauntering through the strawberry beds or rifling the sugar peas. A little to one side of the raspberry patch, near a spreading apple tree propped up by stakes pulled out of an old fence, Pyotr Dmitrich was mowing grass. His hair hung over his forehead, his necktie was untied, and his watch chain dangled from his buttonhole. In every step and swing of the scythe one sensed his skill and an enormous physical strength. Near him stood Lyubochka and Natalya and Valentina, or Nata and Vata, as they were called, two anemic, unhealthily stout blond girls of sixteen or seventeen, the daughters of Colonel Bukreyev, a neighbor, both in white dresses and looking amazingly alike. Pyotr Dmitrich was teaching them to mow.

"It's very simple," he said. "You have only to know how to hold the scythe and not get too hot about it; that is, don't use any more force than necessary. Like this. . . . Would you like to try now?" He offered the scythe to Lyubochka. "Here you are!"

Blushing and laughing, Lyubochka awkwardly took hold of the scythe.

"Don't be afraid, Lyubov Aleksandrovna!" called Olga Mikhailovna in a voice loud enough for all the ladies to hear that she was among them. "Don't be afraid! You'd better learn! If you marry a Tolstoyan he will make you mow."

Lyubochka lifted the scythe, but again burst into laughter and helplessly let it fall. She felt ashamed, yet pleased at being talked to as if she were grown-up. Nata, neither shy nor smiling, but with a cold serious expression, took up the scythe and with one sweep got it tangled in the grass; Vata, also unsmiling, as cool and solemn as her sister, without a word took the scythe and plunged it into the earth. This accomplished, they linked arms and walked off to the raspberry bushes without a word.

Pyotr Dmitrich laughed and capered about like a boy, and this childishly frolicsome mood, in which he became extravagantly good-natured, was far more becoming to him than any other. Olga Mikhailovna loved him when he was in such a mood. But this boyishness generally did not last long. And now, having diverted himself with the scythe, he found it necessary to introduce a note of seriousness.

"You know, when I'm mowing, I feel healthier and more normal," he said. "If I were forced to limit myself to only an intellectual life, I believe I'd go out of my mind. I feel that I wasn't born to be a man of culture! I ought to mow, plow, sow, drive the horses. . . ."

And Pyotr Dmitrich and the ladies began to discuss culture, the advantages of physical labor, and the evils of money and property. Listening to her husband, for some reason Olga Mikhailovna thought of her dowry.

"The time will come, I suppose, when he won't forgive me for being richer than he," she thought. "He is proud and vain. He will probably conceive a hatred for me because of all he owes me."

She stopped near Colonel Bukreyev, who was eating raspberries and also taking part in the conversation.

"Come," he said, making room for her. "The ripest ones are here. . . . And, of course, according to Proudhon," he raised his voice and went on, "property is theft. But, I must confess, I don't consider him a philosopher. For me, the French are not authorities—I've washed my hands of them!"

"Well, as far as your Proudhons and Buckles and all the rest of them are concerned—I'm not up on them," said Pyotr Dmitrich. "When it comes to philosophy, you'll have to deal with my wife. She took courses in all your Schopenhauers and Proudhons, and knows them inside out."

Olga Mikhailovna began to feel weary again. She walked back through the garden, along the narrow path by the apple and pear trees, looking once more as if she had something very important to do. She came to the gardener's cottage. . . . Varvara, the gardener's wife, was sitting in the doorway with her four little children, all with large shaven heads. She too was pregnant and expected to be confined by St. Elijah's Day. After greeting her, Olga Mikhailovna stood silently gazing at her and the children, then asked:

"Well, how do you feel?"

"Oh, all right. . . ."

A silence fell. The two women seemed to understand each other without words.

"It's terrifying to give birth for the first time," said Olga Mikhailovna after a moment's thought. "I keep feeling I won't get through it, that I shall die."

"That's how I felt, but here I am, alive. . . . You imagine all sorts of things. . . ."

Varvara, now about to have her fifth child and feeling slightly superior because of her experience, took a somewhat didactic tone with her mistress, and Olga Mikhailovna could not help feeling her authority; she would have liked to talk to her of the child, of her fears and sensations, but she was afraid it might seem trivial and naive to Varvara. She waited in silence for her to say something.

"Olga, we're going back to the house!" Pyotr Dmitrich called to her from the raspberry patch.

Olga Mikhailovna enjoyed being silent, watching Varvara and waiting for her to speak. She would have been willing to stand there till nightfall, without speech or obligation. But she had to go. She had hardly left the cottage when Lyubochka, Vata, and Nata came running to catch up with her. All at once the sisters stood rooted to the spot a couple of yards from her, while Lyubochka ran up and flung herself on her neck.

"Darling! Beautiful! Precious!" she babbled. "Do let us have tea on the island!"

"On the island! The island!" chorused the doubles Vata and Nata unsmilingly.

"But it's going to rain, my dears."

"It isn't, it isn't!" cried Lyubochka with a rueful expression. "They've all agreed to go! Dearest! Darling!"

"They've all decided to go to the island for tea," Pyotr Dmitrich said as he joined them. "You arrange things. . . . We'll all go in the boats and the samovars and the rest of it must be sent by carriage with the servants."

He walked beside his wife, slipping his arm through hers.

Olga Mikhailovna had a desire to say something disagreeable to her husband, something caustic, even to mention her dowry perhaps—the crueler the better, she felt. After thinking for a moment, she said:

"Why is it Count Aleksei Petrovich hasn't come? What a pity!"

"I'm very glad he hasn't come," lied Pyotr Dmitrich. "I'm fed up with that old idiot, sick to death of him."

"And yet before dinner you couldn't wait to see him!"

III

Half an hour later the guests were crowded together on the bank near a piling to which the boats were tied. There was a great deal of talking and laughing, and so much unnecessary bustling about that they were unable to get settled in the boats. Three of the boats were overflowing with passengers, and two stood empty. The keys for these boats were nowhere to be found and people kept running back and forth from the river to the house looking for them. Some said that Grigory had the keys, others that the steward had them, while a third group advised sending for the blacksmith to break the locks. They all talked at once, interrupting and shouting one another down. Pyotr Dmitrich impatiently strode up and down the bank shouting:

"What's the meaning of this? The keys are supposed to be left in the hall window! Who has dared to take them from there? The steward can get a boat of his own if he wants one!"

At last the keys were found. Then it turned out that two sculls were missing. Again there was a great hubbub. Pyotr Dmitrich, having grown tired of striding up and down, jumped into a long narrow skiff hollowed out of a poplar, rocking it so that he almost fell into the water, and pushed off. One after another the boats followed him, amid loud laughter and the squeals of the ladies.

The white cloudy sky, the trees on the riverside, the reeds, and the boats with their passengers and sculls, were all reflected in the water as in a mirror; under the boats, far below the bottomless depths, was another sky with birds flying across it. The bank on which the house stood was high, steep, and covered with trees; the other bank was sloping and green with broad water-meadows and shimmering coves. The boats had gone a hundred yards when from behind a melancholy, drooping willow on the slope of the bank some huts and a herd of cows came into sight; singing, drunken shouts, and the strains of a concertina were heard.

Fishing boats darted here and there on the river as the men cast their nets for the night. In one boat sat a group of music lovers drunkenly playing homemade violins and cellos.

Olga Mikhailovna sat at the tiller. She smiled affably and talked a great deal to entertain her guests, all the while looking askance at her husband. He was standing up in the first boat, sculling. The light sharp-prowed skiff, which his guests called the *Corsair* and Pyotr Dmitrich for some reason of his own called the *Penderaklia,* sped along; it had an agile, crafty look, as if it resented the burdensome Pyotr Dmitrich and was just waiting for the right moment to slip out from under him. Olga Mikhailovna kept glancing at her husband; she loathed his good looks, loathed the back of his neck, his posture, his familiar manner with women; she hated all those women sitting in his boat, was jealous of them, and at the same time was constantly trembling with fear that the unsteady craft might overturn and cause some mishap.

"Careful, Pyotr!" she called, her heart sinking with fear. "Sit down in the boat! We are convinced of your valor without that!"

She was also disturbed by the people who were in her boat. They were all perfectly nice ordinary people, like so many others, but now they seemed to her extraordinary and evil. She saw nothing but falsity in every one of them. "That young man with the brown hair, handsome beard, and gold spectacles, who is rowing," she thought, "is nothing but a very fortunate, rich, well-fed, mother's darling, whom everyone considers an honest, freethinking, progressive man. It's hardly a year since he graduated from the university and took up life here in the district, but he already speaks of himself as 'we zemstvo workers.' In another year he will be bored, like so many others, and go off to Petersburg, and to justify his desertion, he will tell everyone that the zemstvo is absolutely useless, that it was a disappointment to him. And from the other boat his young wife doesn't take her eyes off him; she believes that he is a 'zemstvo worker,' just as next year she will believe that the zemstvo is useless. And then there is that stout carefully shaven gentleman in the straw hat with a wide ribbon and an expensive cigar in his mouth. One who likes to say: 'Time to drop the fantasy and get to work!' He has Yorkshire pigs, Butler hives, pineapples, rapeseed oil, an oil press, a cheese dairy, and Italian double-entry bookkeeping. But every summer he sells his timber and mortgages part of his land in order to spend the autumn with his mistress in the Crimea. And there's Uncle Nikolai Nikolaich, who is furious with Pyotr Dmitrich and yet, for some reason, doesn't go home."

Olga Mikhailovna glanced at the other boats and saw in them only odd, uninteresting people who were either pretentious or not very intelligent. She thought of all the people she knew in the district and was unable to recall a single one of whom she could say or think anything good. They all seemed to her untalented, insipid, stupid, narrow, false, and hardhearted; they all said what they did not think, and did what they did not want to do. Boredom and despair were stifling her; she wanted to stop smiling at once, to spring up and shout: "I am sick of you!" and then jump out of the boat and swim to shore.

"Friends, let's take Pyotr Dmitrich in tow!" someone shouted.

"Tow him! Tow him!" the others chimed in. "Olga Mikhailovna, take your husband in tow."

In order to do this, Olga Mikhailovna, who was at the tiller, had to seize the right moment and deftly catch hold of the *Penderaklia* by the chain in the prow of the boat. When she leaned over to reach for it, Pyotr Dmitrich frowned and looked at her in alarm.

"I hope you won't catch cold out here!" he said.

"If you're so worried about me and the child," she thought, "why do you torment me?"

Pyotr Dmitrich acknowledged his defeat, and, not wanting to be towed, jumped from the *Penderaklia* into the boat that was already overcrowded, and so recklessly that it careened violently and everyone screamed in terror.

"Now he has jumped to please the ladies," thought Olga Mikhailovna. "He knows how splendid it looks. . . ."

Her hands and feet began to tremble, from ill humor and vexation as she thought, from the strain of smiling and the discomfort she felt all through her body. To conceal the trembling from her guests, she tried to talk louder, to laugh and keep moving. . . .

"If I should suddenly burst into tears," she thought, "I'll say I have a toothache. . . ."

But at last the boats reached the "Isle of Good Hope," as they called the peninsula formed by the river bending at an acute angle; it was covered with a grove of old birch trees, oaks, willows, and poplars. Tables had already been set under the trees, smoke rose from the samovars, and Vasily and Grigory, in dress coats and white knitted gloves, were busy with the tea things. On the other bank, opposite the "Isle of Good Hope," stood the carriages that had brought the provisions. The baskets and parcels had been ferried to the island in a little boat very much like the *Penderaklia*. The footmen, the coachmen, and the peasant who was sitting in the boat had the festive, holiday expression seen only in children and servants.

While Olga Mikhailovna was brewing the tea and filling the first glasses, the guests were busy with liqueurs and sweetmeats. Then began the customary commotion of drinking tea at picnics, which is so tiresome and exhausting for hostesses. Grigory and Vasily hardly had time to carry the glasses around before empty glasses were being held out to Olga Mikhailovna. One asked for it without sugar, another wanted it stronger, another weak, a fourth declined. Olga Mikhailovna had to remember, then to call: "Ivan Petrovich, is it without sugar for you?" or "Gentlemen, which of you wanted it weak?" But whoever had asked for it weak or without sugar had forgotten about it by then, and, carried away by a pleasant conversation, took the first glass that came to hand. Disconsolate figures wandered like shadows off to one side of the table, pretending to look for mushrooms in the grass, or reading the labels on boxes—they were the ones for whom there were no glassses. "Have you had tea?"

Olga Mikhailovna kept asking. And whoever she asked would beg her not to trouble, adding: "I'll wait," though it would have suited her better if her guests had not waited but made haste.

Some, engrossed in conversation, drank their tea slowly, keeping their glasses for half an hour, while others, especially those who had drunk a great deal at dinner, did not leave the table, and drank glass after glass, so that Olga Mikhailovna scarcely had time to keep them filled. One young wag sipped his tea through a piece of sugar and kept saying: "Sinner that I am, I love to indulge myself in the Chinese herb!" From time to time, sighing deeply, he would ask: "One more tiny little dish of tea, if you please!" He drank continually, bit noisily into pieces of sugar, and thought it all very amusing and original and that he was giving a perfect imitation of a merchant. No one realized how agonizing all these trifles were to the hostess, and, indeed, it would have been hard to tell, as Olga Mikhailovna went on smiling amiably and talking nonsense.

She began to feel ill. . . . She was irritated by the crowd, the laughter, the questions, the jocular young man, the stupefied footmen who had run their legs off, the children hanging around the table; irritated by Vata looking like Nata, and Kolya like Mitya, so that it was impossible to tell which of them had had tea and which had not. She felt that her forced smile of cordiality was turning into an angry expression, and that she would burst into tears at any minute.

"Rain, my friends!" someone cried.

Everyone looked at the sky.

"Yes, it really is rain," Pyotr Dmitrich affirmed, and wiped his cheek.

The sky let fall only a few drops; the real rain had not begun, but everyone forsook his tea and made haste to leave. At first they all wanted to drive back in the carriages, but then changed their minds and made for the boats. On the pretext that she had to get home as soon as possible to make arrangements for supper, Olga Mikhailovna asked to be excused for leaving the company and went home in a carriage.

The first thing she did when she was seated in the carriage was to let her face rest from smiling. With an angry expression she drove through the village, with an angry expression acknowledged the bows of the peasants she passed. When she got home she went by the back way to the bedroom and lay down on her husband's bed.

"Merciful God!" she whispered. "What is all this drudgery for? Why do all those people crowd in here and pretend they are enjoying themselves? Why do I smile and lie? I don't understand, I don't understand!"

She heard footsteps and voices. Her guests had come back.

"Let them come," she thought, "I shall go on lying here."

A maidservant came in and said:

"Madam, Marya Grigoryevna is leaving."

Olga Mikhailovna jumped up, tidied her hair, and hurried out of the room.

"Marya Grigoryevna, what is the meaning of this?" she began in a hurt tone as she went to meet her. "Where are you off to in such a hurry?"

"I must go, darling, I really must! I've stayed too long as it is. My children are expecting me home."

"What a shame! Why didn't you bring the children with you?"

"If you will let me, dear, I'll bring them on an ordinary day, but today—"

"Oh, please do," Olga Mikhailovna interrupted. "I'll be delighted! Your children are such darlings! Kiss them all for me. . . . But really, I'm hurt! I don't understand why you are in such a hurry!"

"I must go, I really must. . . . Good-bye, dear. Take care of yourself. In your condition, you know . . ."

They kissed each other. After seeing her to her carriage, Olga Mikhailovna went to the ladies in the drawing room. The lamps were lighted and the gentlemen were sitting down to cards.

IV

After supper, at a quarter past twelve, everyone began to leave. Seeing her guests off, Olga Mikhailovna stood on the porch saying:

"You really ought to take a shawl. . . . It's getting a little cool. I hope you won't catch cold!"

"Don't worry, Olga Mikhailovna," someone called back, getting into a carriage. "Well, good-bye! Don't forget, we are expecting you! Don't disappoint us!"

"Who-a!" a coachman cried, curbing his horses.

"Go ahead, Denis! Good-bye, Olga Mikhailovna!"

"Kiss the children for me!"

The carriage set off and instantly disappeared into the darkness. In the red circle of light cast by a lamp on the road, another pair or trio of impatient horses would appear and the silhouette of a coachman with his arms stretched out before him. And once more there were kisses, reproaches, entreaties to come again, or to take a shawl. Pyotr Dmitrich kept running out and helping the ladies into their carriages.

"Now you go by Yefremovshchina," he directed the coachman. "It's shorter by way of Mankino, but the road is worse. If you don't watch out you might overturn. . . . Good-bye, my charmer! *Milles compliments* to your artist!"

"Good-bye, darling Olga Mikhailovna! Go into the house, or you'll catch cold! It's damp."

"Whoa! You're a frisky one!"

"Where did you get these horses?" asked Pyotr Dmitrich.

"They were bought from Khaidarov in Lent," replied the coachman.

"Splendid horses. . . ."

And Pyotr Dmitrich clapped the trace horse on the haunch.

"Well, go ahead! God give you luck!"

At last everyone had gone. The red circle of light on the road wavered, floated off to the side, diminished, and went out, as Vasily carried away the lamp from the entrance. Generally after seeing their visitors off Pyotr Dmitrich and Olga Mikhailovna would dance about the drawing room, face to face and clapping their hands as they sang: "They've gone! They've gone!" But this time Olga Mikhailovna was not equal to it. She went to the bedroom, undressed, and got into bed.

She felt as if she would fall asleep instantly and sleep soundly. Her legs and shoulders ached painfully, her head felt leaden from so much talk, and, as before, she had a sensation of discomfort all through her body. She covered her head and lay still for a few minutes, then peeped out from under the blanket at the icon lamp, and, listening to the silence, smiled.

"Lovely, lovely . . ." she whispered, curling up her legs, which felt as if they had grown longer from so much walking. "Sleep, sleep. . . ."

Her legs would not stay still, and she turned over on her other side. A huge fly darted about the room, buzzing and thumping against the ceiling. She also heard Grigory and Vasily in the drawing room, stepping cautiously as they cleared the tables; it seemed to her that she could not be at ease and fall asleep till these sounds had ceased. And again she impatiently turned over. She heard her husband's voice in the drawing room. Someone must be staying the night, for Pyotr Dmitrich was addressing whoever it was in a loud voice, saying:

"I don't say that Count Aleksei Petrovich is a hypocrite. But he necessarily appears to be one because all of you gentlemen attempt to see in him something other than what he actually is. His madness is regarded as originality, his condescension as kindheartedness, his complete lack of convictions as conservatism. Let us suppose that he is, in fact, a conservative of the stamp of '84. But what, essentially, is conservatism?"

Pyotr Dmitrich, angry at Count Aleksei Petrovich, at his guests, and at himself, was unburdening his mind. He abused the Count and his visitors, and in his vexation with himself was ready to hold forth and say what he thought. After seeing his visitor to his room, he paced the drawing room, walked through the dining room, down the corridor, into his study, back to the drawing room, and into the bedroom. Olga Mikhailovna lay on her back with the blanket only up to her waist (by now she felt hot), and with an infuriated expression watched the fly thumping against the ceiling.

"Is someone staying overnight?" she asked.

"Yegorov."

Pyotr Dmitrich undressed and got into his bed. Without speaking, he lit a cigarette, and he too fell to watching the fly. His face looked troubled and austere. Olga Mikhailovna gazed at his handsome profile for five minutes in silence. It seemed to her that if her husband were to turn to her suddenly and say: "Olya, I'm so miserable!" she would burst into tears or laugh, and she would feel better. She thought that the aching of her legs and the discomfort of her whole body was a result of the tension in her soul.

"Pyotr, what are you thinking about?" she asked.

"Oh, nothing . . ." replied her husband.

"You've been having secrets from me lately. It's not right."

"Why isn't it right? We all have our own personal life, and consequently are bound to have our secrets."

"Personal life . . . our secrets. . . . Those are just words! Can't you understand that you are hurting me?" said Olga Mikhailovna, sitting up in bed. "If you are troubled, why do you conceal it from me? Why is it you find it more convenient to confide in other women instead of your wife? I heard you today at the apiary, opening your heart to Lyubochka!"

"Well, I congratulate you. I'm very glad you heard me."

This meant: leave me alone, don't bother me when I'm thinking! Olga Mikhailovna was outraged. The irritation, hatred, and anger that had been accumulating in her during the whole day suddenly boiled over; she felt impelled to speak her mind to her husband at once instead of waiting till the next day; she wanted to wound him, to have her revenge. . . . With an effort to control herself, to keep from screaming, she said:

"You may as well know that all this is revolting—revolting—revolting! I've hated you all day—you see what you've done!"

Pyotr Dmitrich sat up in bed.

"Revolting, revolting, revolting!" Olga Mikhailovna went on, trembling all over. "Don't congratulate me! You'd better congratulate yourself! It's shameful, a disgrace! You've lied so much you're ashamed to be alone in a room with your wife! You're a deceitful man! I see through you—I understand every step you take!"

"Olya, I wish you would give me warning when you're out of sorts so I can sleep in my study."

And Pyotr Dmitrich picked up his pillow and walked out of the room. Olga Mikhailovna had not forseen this. For several minutes she sat in silence, open-mouthed, trembling, staring at the door through which her husband had escaped, trying to understand what it meant. Was this one of the devices used by deceitful people when they are in the wrong, or was it an insult deliberately aimed at her pride? How was she to take it? She recalled her cousin, a jolly young officer, who had often told her that when "my spouse starts picking on me" at night, he generally took his pillow and went whistling into his study, leaving his wife in a foolish, ludicrous position. This officer was married to a rich, capricious, silly woman whom he did not respect but merely put up with.

Olga Mikhailovna jumped out of bed. To her mind there was only one thing left for her to do: to dress as quickly as possible and leave the house forever. The house belonged to her, but so much the worse for Pyotr Dmitrich. Without considering whether it was necessary or not, she rushed to the study to inform her husband of her decision (Feminine logic!" flashed through her mind), and, in farewell, to say something biting and wounding. . . .

Pyotr Dmitrich was lying on the sofa, pretending to read a newspaper. Near him stood a lighted candle on a chair. His face was hidden behind the newspaper.

"Will you kindly tell me the meaning of this? I'm asking you!"

"I'm asking you . . ." Pyotr Dmitrich mimicked her, not showing his face. "It's sickening, Olya. I give you my word, I'm exhausted, I'm not up to this now. . . . We can do our quarreling tomorrow."

"No. I understand you perfectly," she went on. "You hate me. Yes—yes! You hate me for being richer than you! You will never forgive me for it, and you will always lie to me!" ("Feminine logic!" again flashed through her mind.) "I know you're laughing at me right now. . . . I'm absolutely convinced that you married me so you would have property rights . . . and those wretched horses. . . . Oh, I'm so miserable!"

Pyotr Dmitrich dropped his newspaper and sat up. The unexpected insult had stunned him. He looked at his wife in confusion, a childishly helpless smile on his face, his hands outstretched as if to ward off a blow.

"Olya!" he cried beseechingly.

And expecting her to say something more that was awful, he shrank against the back of the sofa, his huge figure looking as childishly helpless as his smile.

"Olya, how could you say it?" he whispered.

Olga Mikhailovna came to herself. She was suddenly conscious of her passionate love for this man, and realized that this was her husband, Pyotr Dmitrich, without whom she could not live for one day, and who passionately loved her too. She sobbed loudly in an unnatural voice, and putting her hands to her head, ran back to the bedroom.

She threw herself onto the bed and the room resounded with her spasmodic, hysterical sobbing; it choked her and caused her arms and legs to contract. Remembering the guest who was sleeping three or four rooms away, she buried her head under the pillow, and tried to stifle her sobs, but the pillow slipped to the floor, and she herself all but fell in her effort to retrieve it. She reached for the blanket to pull it up to her face, but her hands refused to obey her and tore convulsively at everything she touched.

She felt that all was lost, that the lie she had spoken to wound her husband had shattered her life into a thousand pieces. He would never forgive her. The insult she had hurled at him was not the sort that could be smoothed over with caresses, with vows. . . . How could she convince her husband that she herself did not believe what she had said?

"It's all over! All over!" she cried, not noticing that the pillow had slipped to the floor again. "For God's sake, for God's sake!"

Her cries, no doubt, had by now roused the guest and the servants, and tomorrow the whole district would know that she had had hysterics, and everyone would blame Pyotr Dmitrich. She made an effort to restrain herself, but her sobs grew louder and louder every minute.

"For God's sake!" she cried in a strange voice, not knowing why she kept repeating this. "For God's sake!"

It seemed to her that the bed was heaving under her, that her legs were entangled in the blanket. Pyotr Dmitrich came into the room in his dressing gown carrying a candle.

"Olya, hush!" he said.

She raised herself to her knees in bed, and squinting at the light said through her sobs:

"Try to understand . . . understand . . ."

She wanted to tell him that she had been worn out by their visitors, by his lying and her own, that it was seething inside her, but all she could say was:

"Understand . . . understand . . ."

"Here, drink this," he said, giving her some water.

She took the glass obediently and began drinking, but the water splashed and spilled over her hands, her breast, her knees. . . .

"I must look hideous," she thought.

Pyotr Dmitrich put her back into bed without a word, covered her with the blanket, took the candle, and went out.

"For God's sake!" Olga Mikhailovna cried. "Pyotr, understand . . . understand . . ."

All at once something gripped her below the stomach and in the lower part of the back with such violence that it silenced her wailing and made her bite the pillow in agony. But the pain abated and she commenced sobbing again.

The maid came in, arranged the blanket over her, and anxiously asked:

"Mistress, darling, what is the matter?"

"Get out of here!" said Pyotr Dmitrich sternly, as he went up to the bed.

"Understand . . . understand . . ." Olga Mikhailovna kept saying.

"Olya, I beg you to calm yourself!" he said. "I didn't mean to hurt you. I wouldn't have left the room if I had known it would affect you in this way. I was simply depressed. I tell you, in all honesty . . ."

"Understand. . . . You were lying. . . . I was lying. . . ."

"I understand. . . . Come now, that's enough. I understand . . ." he said tenderly, and sat down on the bed beside her. "You spoke in anger, it's natural. . . . I swear to God, I love you more than anything on earth, and when I married you I never once thought of your being rich. I loved you infinitely, and that was all. . . . Believe me. I have never been in need of money or known the value of it, consequently I've never been conscious of the difference between your means and mine. It has always seemed to me that we were equally well off. As for my being deceitful in little things . . . it's true, of course. Till now my life has not been arranged in a very serious way, and it somehow seemed impossible to avoid lying. I feel depressed by it now myself. Let's not talk about it any more, for heaven's sake! . . ."

Olga Mikhailovna again felt a sharp pain, and clutched at her husband's sleeve.

"I am in such pain, pain, pain!" she said rapidly. "Oh, such pain!"

"Damn all those visitors!" muttered Pyotr Dmitrich, getting up. "You ought not to have gone to the island today!" he cried. "What an idiot I am—why didn't I stop you? Oh, good Lord!"

He scratched his head in exasperation, threw up his hands, and left the room.

After that he kept coming back, sitting on the bed beside her, and talking a great deal, now tenderly, now angrily; but she hardly heard him. Her sobs alternated with terrible pains, each more violent and prolonged than the last. At first she held her breath and bit the pillow when the pains gripped her, but later she uttered shameless, harrowing screams. At one moment, seeing her husband near her, she remembered that she had insulted him, and without quite knowing whether she was delirious or whether it really was Pyotr Dmitrich, she seized his hand in both of hers and began kissing it.

"You were lying . . . I was lying . . ." she wanted to justify herself. "Understand . . . understand. . . . They have worn me out . . . driven me out of my wits. . . ."

"Olya, we are not alone," said Pyotr Dmitrich.

Olga Mikhailovna raised her head and saw Varvara on her knees before a chest, opening the bottom drawer. The top drawers were already open. Then she stood up, flushed from her exertions, and with a cold, solemn expression, tried to unlock a little chest.

"Marya, I can't unlock it!" she said in a whisper. "Unlock it, will you?"

Marya, the maid, was digging a candle end out of the candlestick in order to put a fresh one in. She went to Varvara and helped her to unlock the chest.

"There should be nothing locked," whispered Varvara. "Open this basket, my dear. . . . Master," she turned to Pyotr Dmitrich, "you should send to Father Mikhail to unlock the holy gates. You must!"

"Do whatever you like," said Pyotr Dmitrich, breathing heavily, "only, for God's sake, hurry—get the doctor or the midwife! Has Vasily gone? Send someone else as well. Send your husband!"

"I am giving birth . . ." thought Olga Mikhailovna. "Varvara," she moaned, "but he won't be born alive!"

"It's going to be all right, all right, mistress," whispered Varvara. "God willing, he'll be alive! He'll be alive!"

When Olga Mikhailovna came to herself after a pain, she was no longer sobbing or tossing from side to side, but was moaning. She could not help moaning, even in the intervals between pains. The candles were still burning, but daylight was coming in through the blinds. It was probably about five o'clock in the morning. A modest-looking woman in a white apron, someone she did not know, was sitting at a little round table in the bedroom. From the way she sat, it appeared that she had been sitting there for some time. Olga Mikhailovna surmised that this was the midwife.

"Will it be over soon?" she asked, and detected an odd, unfamiliar note, never before heard in her voice. "I must be dying in childbirth," she thought.

Pyotr Dmitrich came cautiously into the bedroom, dressed for the day, and stood at the window with his back to his wife. He raised the blind and looked out the window.

"What rain!" he said.

"What time is it?" asked Olga Mikhailovna, in order to hear her own unfamiliar voice once more.

"A quarter to six," answered the midwife.

"And what if I really am dying?" thought Olga Mikhailovna, looking at her husband's head and at the windowpanes on which the rain was beating. "How will he live without me? With whom will he have tea and dinner . . . talk to in the evening . . . sleep?"

And he seemed to her like a little orphaned child; she felt sorry for him and wanted to say something nice, something loving and consoling. She remembered how in the spring he had wanted to buy himself hounds, but because she found hunting a cruel and dangerous sport, she had prevented him from buying them.

"Pyotr, buy yourself hounds . . ." she moaned.

He lowered the blind and went to the bed; he was about to say something to her when there was another pain and she uttered a piercing, heart-rending scream.

The pains, the repeated screaming and moaning, had stupefied her. She heard, saw, and sometimes spoke, but she understood very little and was conscious only of the pain, or that she was going to be in pain again. It seemed to her that the name-day party had taken place, not the day before, but a long long time ago, a year perhaps; and that her new, agonizing life had gone on longer than her childhood, her schooldays at the institute, her university years, her married life . . . and would go on and on, endlessly. She saw them bring tea to the midwife, summon her to the midday meal, and later to dinner; she saw Pyotr Dmitrich grow accustomed to coming in, standing at the window for some time, and going out again; saw strange men, the maid, Varvara . . . Varvara saying nothing but: "He will be, he will," and looking angry when anyone closed the drawers of the chest. Olga Mikhailovna watched the light change in the windows and in the room: at one time it was twilight, then it turned murky, like fog, then bright daylight, as it had been the day before at dinner, and again twilight. . . . And each of these changes lasted as long as her childhood, her schooldays at the institute, her years at the university. . . .

In the evening two doctors—one bald and bony with a broad red beard, the other with a swarthy Jewish face and cheap spectacles—performed some sort of operation on her. She was completely indifferent to these strange men handling her body. By now she had no shame, no will, and anyone might do with her as he pleased. If someone had rushed at her with a knife, had insulted Pyotr Dmitrich, or had deprived her of her right to the little person, she would not have said a word.

She was given chloroform for the operation. When she came to the pain was still there and unbearable. It was night. And Olga Mikhailovna remembered another such night—the same stillness, the icon lamp, the midwife sitting motionless near the bed, the drawers of the chest pulled out, and Pyotr Dmitrich standing at the window—but that was a long long time ago. . . .

V

"I am not dead . . ." thought Olga Mikhailovna when the pain was over and she began to be aware of her surroundings.

A bright summer day looked in at both wide-open windows; outside in the garden the sparrows and magpies kept up an incessant chatter.

The drawers of the chest were shut now, and her husband's bed had been made. The midwife, the maid, and Varvara were no longer in the bedroom; only Pyotr Dmitrich, as before, stood motionless at the window, looking into the garden. But there was no sound of an infant's cry, no congratulations and rejoicing; it was evident that the little person had not been born alive.

"Pyotr!" Olga Mikhailovna called to her husband.

Pyotr Dmitrich turned to her. A great deal of time must have passed since the last guest had departed and Olga Mikhailovna had insulted her husband, for Pyotr Dmitrich was perceptibly thinner and looked very drawn.

"What is it?" he asked, going to her.

He looked away; his lips twitched and his face wore a childishly helpless smile.

"Is it all over?" she asked.

Pyotr Dmitrich tried to answer her, but his lips began to quiver, and his mouth twisted into a grimace, like an old man, like her toothless old uncle Nikolai Nikolaich.

"Olya!" he said, wringing his hands, and great tears suddenly fell from his eyes. "Olya! I don't care about property qualifications, or circuit courts" (he sobbed) "or about any particular views, or those guests, or your dowry. . . . I don't care about anything! Why didn't we take care of our child? Oh, what's the use of talking!"

And with a gesture of despair, he went out of the room.

But nothing mattered to Olga Mikhailovna now. Her mind was hazy from the chloroform, her soul was empty. . . . The dull indifference to life that she felt when the two doctors performed the operation had not yet left her.

CHARLOTTE PERKINS GILMAN

(1860-1935)

"The Yellow Wall-Paper" has been published in a collection of ghost stories, but the real horror in the story is in the effects of conventional nineteenth-century marriage on a sensitive woman.

Gilman, born in New England in 1860, was brought up by her mother after her father deserted the family. Even as an adolescent she was aware of the "injustices under which women suffered." For Gilman the suffrage movement did not go deep enough into the problems of the relations of men and women; she grew increasingly radical and committed. Married to a gentle, undomineering artist, she was still oppressed by her role as wife, oppressed to the point of nervous breakdown. She divorced her husband, gave up her child, and began her career in earnest as lecturer and writer on feminism, a career that lasted well into the 1920's. A significant scholar, she wrote *Women and Economics,* which, like "The Yellow Wall-Paper," has recently been revived.

She wrote "The Yellow Wall-Paper" in 1890 and published it only after difficulty. Generally, it has been published as a ghost story or a study of insanity. Only recently has its real horror been understood. Notice that the husband in the story is not seen as villainous and domineering; rather he is paternal, treating his wife like a little girl. His kind treatment is, of course, part of the disease. By the end of the story the narrator has become the woman behind the wallpaper; she has gone mad. But Gilman wants us to see that in her madness she expresses something real about the relations between men and women.

The Yellow Wall-Paper

CHARLOTTE PERKINS GILMAN

It is very seldom that mere ordinary people like John and myself secure ancestral halls for the summer.

A colonial mansion, a hereditary estate, I would say a haunted house, and reach the height of romantic felicity—but that would be asking too much of fate!

Still I will proudly declare that there is something queer about it.

Else, why should it be let so cheaply? And why have stood so long untenanted?

John laughs at me, of course, but one expects that in marriage.

John is practical in the extreme. He has no patience with faith, an intense horror of superstition, and he scoffs openly at any talk of things not to be felt and seen and put down in figures.

John is a physician, and *perhaps*— (I would not say it to a living soul, of course, but this is dead paper and a great relief to my mind) —*perhaps* that is one reason I do not get well faster.

You see he does not believe I am sick!

And what can one do?

If a physician of high standing, and one's own husband, assures friends and relatives that there is really nothing the matter with one but temporary nervous depression—a slight hysterical tendency—what is one to do?

My brother is also a physician, and also of high standing, and he says the same thing.

So I take phosphates or phospites—whichever it is, and tonics, and journeys, and air, and exercise, and am absolutely forbidden to "work" until I am well again.

Personally, I disagree with their ideas.

Personally, I believe that congenial work, with excitement and change, would do me good.

But what is one to do?

I did write for a while in spite of them; but it *does* exhaust me a good deal—having to be so sly about it, or else meet with heavy opposition.

I sometimes fancy that in my condition if I had less opposition and more society and stimulus—but John says the very worst thing I can do is to think about my condition, and I confess it always makes me feel bad.

So I will let it alone and talk about the house.

The most beautiful place! It is quite alone, standing well back from the road, quite three miles from the village. It makes me think of English places that you read about, for there are hedges and walls and gates that lock, and lots of separate little houses for the gardeners and people.

There is a *delicious* garden! I never saw such a garden—large and shady, full of box-bordered paths, and lined with long grape-covered arbors with seats under them.

There were greenhouses, too, but they are all broken now.

There was some legal trouble, I believe, something about the heirs and coheirs; anyhow, the place has been empty for years.

That spoils my ghostliness, I am afraid, but I don't care—there is something strange about the house—I can feel it.

I even said so to John one moonlight evening, but he said what I felt was a *draught*, and shut the window.

I get unreasonably angry with John sometimes. I'm sure I never used to be so sensitive. I think it is due to this nervous condition.

But John says if I feel so, I shall neglect proper self-control; so I take pains to control myself—before him, at least, and that makes me very tired.

I don't like our room a bit. I wanted one downstairs that opened on the piazza and had roses all over the window, and such pretty old-fashioned chintz hangings! but John would not hear of it.

He said there was only one window and not room for two beds, and no near room for him if he took another.

He is very careful and loving, and hardly lets me stir without special direction.

I have a schedule prescription for each hour in the day; he takes all care from me, and so I feel basely ungrateful not to value it more.

He said we came here solely on my account, that I was to have perfect rest and all the air I could get. "Your exercise depends on your strength, my dear," said he, "and your food somewhat on your appetite; but air you can absorb all the time." So we took the nursery at the top of the house.

It is a big, airy room, the whole floor nearly, with windows that look all ways, and air and sunshine galore. It was nursery first and then playroom and gymnasium, I should judge; for the windows are barred for little children, and there are rings and things in the walls.

The paint and paper look as if a boys' school had used it. It is stripped off—the paper—in great patches all around the head of my bed, about as far as I can reach, and in a great place on the other side of the room low down. I never saw a worse paper in my life.

One of those sprawling flamboyant patterns committing every artistic sin.

It is dull enough to confuse the eye in following, pronounced enough to constantly irritate and provoke study, and when you follow the lame uncertain curves for a little distance they suddenly commit suicide—plunge off at outrageous angles, destroy themselves in unheard of contradictions.

The color is repellent, almost revolting; a smouldering unclean yellow, strangely faded by the slow-turning sunlight.

It is a dull yet lurid orange in some places, a sickly sulphur tint in others.

No wonder the children hated it! I should hate it myself if I had to live in this room long.

There comes John, and I must put this away,—he hates to have me write a word.

We have been here two weeks, and I haven't felt like writing before, since that first day.

I am sitting by the window now, up in this atrocious nursery, and there is nothing to hinder my writing as much as I please, save lack of strength.

John is away all day, and even some nights when his cases are serious.

I am glad my case is not serious!

But these nervous troubles are dreadfully depressing.

John does not know how much I really suffer. He knows there is no *reason* to suffer, and that satisfies him.

Of course it is only nervousness. It does weigh on me so not to do my duty in any way!

I meant to be such a help to John, such a real rest and comfort, and here I am a comparative burden already!

Nobody would believe what an effort it is to do what little I am able,—to dress and entertain, and order things.

It is fortunate Mary is so good with the baby. Such a dear baby!

And yet I *cannot* be with him, it makes me so nervous.

I suppose John never was nervous in his life. He laughs at me so about this wall-paper!

At first he meant to repaper the room, but afterwards he said that I was letting it get the better of me, and that nothing was worse for a nervous patient than to give way to such fancies.

He said that after the wall-paper was changed it would be the heavy bedstead, and then the barred windows, and then that gate at the head of the stairs, and so on.

"You know the place is doing you good," he said, "and really, dear, I don't care to renovate the house just for a three months' rental."

"Then do let us go downstairs," I said, "there are such pretty rooms there."

Then he took me in his arms and called me a blessed little goose, and said he would go down to the cellar, if I wished, and have it whitewashed into the bargain.

But he is right enough about the beds and windows and things.

It is an airy and comfortable room as any one need wish, and, of course, I would not be so silly as to make him uncomfortable just for a whim.

I'm really getting quite fond of the big room, all but that horrid paper.

Out of one window I can see the garden, those mysterious deep-shaded arbors, the riotous old-fashioned flowers, and bushes and gnarly trees.

Out of another I get a lovely view of the bay and a little private wharf belonging to the estate. There is a beautiful shaded lane that runs down there from the house. I always fancy I see people walking in these numerous paths and arbors, but John has cautioned me not to give way to fancy in the least. He says that with my imaginative power and habit of story-making, a nervous weakness like mine is sure to lead to all manner of excited fancies, and that I ought to use my will and good sense to check the tendency. So I try.

I think sometimes that if I were only well enough to write a little it would relieve the press of ideas and rest me.

But I find I get pretty tired when I try.

It is so discouraging not to have any advice and companionship about my work. When I get really well, John says we will ask Cousin Henry and Julia down for a long visit; but he says he would as soon put fireworks in my pillow-case as to let me have those stimulating people about now.

I wish I could get well faster.

But I must not think about that. This paper looks to me as if it *knew* what a vicious influence it had!

There is a recurrent spot where the pattern lolls like a broken neck and two bulbous eyes stare at you upside down.

I get positively angry with the impertinence of it and the everlastingness. Up and down and sideways they crawl, and those absurd, unblinking eyes are everywhere. There is one place where two breadths didn't match, and the eyes go all up and down the line, one a little higher than the other.

I never saw so much expression in an inanimate thing before, and we all know how much expression they have! I used to lie awake as a child and get more entertainment and terror out of blank walls and plain furniture than most children could find in a toy-store.

I remember what a kindly wink the knobs of our big, old bureau used to have, and there was one chair that always seemed like a strong friend.

I used to feel that if any of the other things looked too fierce I could always hop into that chair and be safe.

The furniture in this room is no worse than inharmonious, however, for we had to bring it all from downstairs. I suppose when this was used as a playroom they had to take the nursery things out, and no wonder! I never saw such ravages as the children have made here.

The wall-paper, as I said before, is torn off in spots, and it sticketh closer than a brother—they must have had perseverance as well as hatred.

Then the floor is scratched and gouged and splintered, the plaster itself is dug out here and there, and this great heavy bed which is all we found in the room, looks as if it had been through the wars.

But I don't mind it a bit—only the paper.

There comes John's sister. Such a dear girl as she is, and so careful of me! I must not let her find me writing.

She is a perfect and enthusiastic housekeeper, and hopes for no better profession. I verily believe she thinks it is the writing which made me sick!

But I can write when she is out, and see her a long way off from these windows.

There is one that commands the road, a lovely shaded winding road, and one that just looks off over the country. A lovely country, too, full of great elms and velvet meadows.

This wall-paper has a kind of sub-pattern in a different shade, a particularly irritating one, for you can only see it in certain lights, and not clearly then.

But in the places where it isn't faded and where the sun is just so—I can see a strange, provoking, formless sort of figure, that seems to skulk about behind that silly and conspicuous front design.

There's sister on the stairs!

Well, the Fourth of July is over! The people are all gone and I am tired out. John thought it might do me good to see a little company, so we just had mother and Nellie and the children down for a week.

Of course I didn't do a thing. Jennie sees to everything now.

But it tired me all the same.

John says if I don't pick up faster he shall send me to Weir Mitchell in the fall.

But I don't want to go there at all. I had a friend who was in his hands once, and she says he is just like John and my brother, only more so!

Besides, it is such an undertaking to go so far.

I don't feel as if it was worth while to turn my hand over for anything, and I'm getting dreadfully fretful and querulous.

I cry at nothing, and cry most of the time.

Of course I don't when John is here, or anybody else, but when I am alone.

And I am alone a good deal just now. John is kept in town very often by serious cases, and Jennie is good and lets me alone when I want her to.

So I walk a little in the garden or down that lovely lane, sit on the porch under the roses, and lie down up here a good deal.

I'm getting really fond of the room in spite of the wall-paper. Perhaps *because* of the wall-paper.

It dwells in my mind so!

I lie here on this great immovable bed—it is nailed down, I believe—and follow that pattern about by the hour. It is as good as gymnastics, I assure you. I start, we'll say, at the bottom, down in the corner over there where it has not been touched, and I determine for the thousandth time that I *will* follow that pointless pattern to some sort of a conclusion.

I know a little of the principle of design, and I know this thing was not arranged on any laws of radiation, or alternation, or repetition, or symmetry, or anything else that I ever heard of.

It is repeated, of course, by the breadths, but not otherwise.

Looked at in one way each breadth stands alone, the bloated curves and flourishes—a kind of "debased Romanesque" with *delirium tremens*—go waddling up and down in isolated columns of fatuity.

But, on the other hand, they connect diagonally, and the sprawling outlines run off in great slanting waves of optic horror, like a lot of wallowing seaweeds in full chase.

The whole thing goes horizontally, too, at least it seems so, and I exhaust myself in trying to distinguish the order of its going in that direction.

They have used a horizontal breadth for a frieze, and that adds wonderfully to the confusion.

There is one end of the room where it is almost intact, and there, when the crosslights fade and the low sun shines directly upon it, I can almost fancy radiation after all,—the interminable grotesques seem to form around a common centre and rush off in headlong plunges of equal distraction.

It makes me tired to follow it. I will take a nap I guess.

I don't know why I should write this.

I don't want to.

I don't feel able.

And I know John would think it absurd. But I *must* say what I feel and think in some way—it is such a relief!

But the effort is getting to be greater than the relief.

Half the time now I am awfully lazy, and lie down ever so much.

John says I mustn't lose my strength, and has me take cod liver oil and lots of tonics and things, to say nothing of ale and wine and rare meat.

Dear John! He loves me very dearly, and hates to have me sick. I tried to have a real earnest reasonable talk with him the other day, and tell him how I wish he would let me go and make a visit to Cousin Henry and Julia.

But he said I wasn't able to go, nor able to stand it after I got there; and I did not make out a very good case for myself, for I was crying before I had finished.

It is getting to be a great effort for me to think straight. Just this nervous weakness I suppose.

And dear John gathered me up in his arms, and just carried me upstairs and laid me on the bed, and sat by me and read to me till it tired my head.

He said I was his darling and his comfort and all he had, and that I must take care of myself for his sake, and keep well.

He says no one but myself can help me out of it, that I must use my will and self-control and not let any silly fancies run away with me.

There's one comfort, the baby is well and happy, and does not have to occupy this nursery with the horrid wall-paper.

If we had not used it, that blessed child would have! What a fortunate escape! Why, I wouldn't have a child of mine, an impressionable little thing, live in such a room for worlds.

I never thought of it before, but it is lucky that John kept me here after all, I can stand it so much easier than a baby, you see.

Of course I never mention it to them any more—I am too wise,—but I keep watch of it all the same.

There are things in that paper that nobody knows but me, or ever will.

Behind that outside pattern the dim shapes get clearer every day.

It is always the same shape, only very numerous.

And it is like a woman stooping down and creeping about behind that pattern. I don't like it a bit. I wonder—I begin to think—I wish John would take me away from here!

It is so hard to talk with John about my case, because he is so wise, and because he loves me so.

But I tried it last night.

It was moonlight. The moon shines in all around just as the sun does.

I hate to see it sometimes, it creeps so slowly, and always comes in by one window or another.

John was asleep and I hated to waken him, so I kept still and watched the moonlight on that undulating wall-paper till I felt creepy.

The faint figure behind seemed to shake the pattern, just as if she wanted to get out.

I got up softly and went to feel and see if the paper *did* move, and when I came back John was awake.

"What is it, little girl?" he said. "Don't go walking about like that—you'll get cold."

I thought it was a good time to talk, so I told him that I really was not gaining here, and that I wished he would take me away.

"Why darling!" said he, "our lease will be up in three weeks, and I can't see how to leave before.

"The repairs are not done at home, and I cannot possibly leave town just now. Of course if you were in any danger, I could and would, but you really are better, dear, whether you can see it or not. I am a doctor, dear, and I know. You are gaining flesh and color, your appetite is better, I feel really much easier about you."

"I don't weigh a bit more," said I, "nor as much; and my appetite may be better in the evening when you are here, but it is worse in the morning when you are away!"

"Bless her little heart!" said he with a big hug, "she shall be as sick as she pleases! But now let's improve the shining hours by going to sleep, and talk about it in the morning!"

"And you won't go away?" I asked gloomily.

"Why, how can I, dear? It is only three weeks more and then we will take a nice little trip of a few days while Jennie is getting the house ready. Really dear you are better!"

"Better in body perhaps—" I began, and stopped short, for he sat up straight and looked at me with such a stern, reproachful look that I could not say another word.

"My darling," said he, "I beg of you, for my sake and for our child's sake, as well as for your own, that you will never for one instant let that idea enter your mind! There is nothing so dangerous, so fascinating, to a temperament like yours. It is a false and foolish fancy. Can you not trust me as a physician when I tell you so?"

So of course I said no more on that score, and we went to sleep before long. He thought I was asleep first, but I wasn't, and lay there for hours trying to decide whether that front pattern and the back pattern really did move together or separately.

On a pattern like this, by daylight, there is a lack of sequence, a defiance of law, that is a constant irritant to a normal mind.

The color is hideous enough, and unreliable enough, and infuriating enough, but the pattern is torturing.

You think you have mastered it, but just as you get well underway in following, it turns a back-somersault and there you are. It slaps you in the face, knocks you down, and tramples upon you. It is like a bad dream.

The outside pattern is a florid arabesque, reminding one of a fungus. If you can imagine a toadstool in joints, an interminable string of toadstools, budding and sprouting in endless convolutions—why, that is something like it.

That is, sometimes!

There is one marked peculiarity about this paper, a thing nobody seems to notice but myself, and that is that it changes as the light changes.

When the sun shoots in through the east window—I always watch for that first long, straight ray—it changes so quickly that I never can quite believe it.

That is why I watch it always.

By moonlight—the moon shines in all night when there is a moon—I wouldn't know it was the same paper.

At night in any kind of light, in twilight, candle light, lamplight, and worst of all by moonlight, it becomes bars! The outside pattern I mean, and the woman behind it is as plain as can be.

I didn't realize for a long time what the thing was that showed behind, that dim sub-pattern, but now I am quite sure it is a woman.

By daylight she is subdued, quiet. I fancy it is the pattern that keeps her so still. It is so puzzling. It keeps me quiet by the hour.

I lie down ever so much now. John says it is good for me, and to sleep all I can.

Indeed he started the habit by making me lie down for an hour after each meal.

It is a very bad habit I am convinced, for you see I don't sleep.

And that cultivates deceit, for I don't tell them I'm awake—O no!

The fact is I am getting a little afraid of John.

He seems very queer sometimes, and even Jennie has an inexplicable look.

It strikes me occasionally, just as a scientific hypothesis,—that perhaps it is the paper!

I have watched John when he did not know I was looking, and come into the room suddenly on the most innocent excuses, and I've caught him several times *looking at the paper!* And Jennie too. I caught Jennie with her hand on it once.

She didn't know I was in the room, and when I asked her in a quiet, a very quiet voice, with the most restrained manner possible, what she was doing with the paper—she turned around as if she had been caught stealing, and looked quite angry—asked me why I should frighten her so!

Then she said that the paper stained everything it touched, that she had found yellow smooches on all my clothes and John's, and she wished we would be more careful!

Did not that sound innocent? But I know she was studying that pattern, and I am determined that nobody shall find it out but myself!

Life is very much more exciting now than it used to be. You see I have something more to expect, to look forward to, to watch. I really do eat better, and am more quiet than I was.

John is so pleased to see me improve! He laughed a little the other day, and said I seemed to be flourishing in spite of my wall-paper.

I turned it off with a laugh. I had no intention of telling him it was *because* of the wall-paper—he would make fun of me. He might even want to take me away.

I don't want to leave now until I have found it out. There is a week more, and I think that will be enough.

I'm feeling ever so much better! I don't sleep much at night, for it is so interesting to watch developments; but I sleep a good deal in the daytime.

In the daytime it is tiresome and perplexing.

There are always new shoots on the fungus, and new shades of yellow all over it. I cannot keep count of them, though I have tried conscientiously.

It is the strangest yellow, that wall-paper! It makes me think of all the yellow things I ever saw—not beautiful ones like buttercups, but old foul, bad yellow things.

But there is something else about that paper—the smell! I noticed it the moment we came into the room, but with so much air and sun it was not bad. Now we have had a week of fog and rain, and whether the windows are open or not, the smell is here.

It creeps all over the house.

I find it hovering in the dining-room, skulking in the parlor, hiding in the hall, lying in wait for me on the stairs.

It gets into my hair.

Even when I go to ride, if I turn my head suddenly and surprise it—there is that smell!

Such a peculiar odor, too! I have spent hours in trying to analyze it, to find what it smelled like.

It is not bad—at first, and very gentle, but quite the subtlest, most enduring odor I ever met.

In this damp weather it is awful, I wake up in the night and find it hanging over me.

It used to disturb me at first. I thought seriously of burning the house—to reach the smell.

But now I am used to it. The only thing I can think of that it is like is the *color* of the paper! A yellow smell.

There is a very funny mark on this wall, low down, near the mopboard. A streak that runs round the room. It goes behind every piece of furniture, except the bed, a long, straight, even *smooch,* as if it had been rubbed over and over.

I wonder how it was done and who did it, and what they did it for. Round and round and round—round and round and round—it makes me dizzy!

I really have discovered something at last.

Through watching so much at night, when it changes so, I have finally found out.

The front pattern *does* move—and no wonder! The woman behind shakes it!

Sometimes I think there are a great many women behind, and sometimes only one, and she crawls around fast, and her crawling shakes it all over.

Then in the very bright spots she keeps still, and in the very shady spots she just takes hold of the bars and shakes them hard.

And she is all the time trying to climb through. But nobody could climb through that pattern—it strangles so; I think that is why it has so many heads.

They get through, and then the pattern strangles them off and turns them upside down, and makes their eyes white!

If those heads were covered or taken off it would not be half so bad.

I think that woman gets out in the daytime!

And I'll tell you why—privately—I've seen her!

I can see her out of every one of my windows!

It is the same woman, I know, for she is always creeping, and most women do not creep by daylight.

I see her on that long road under the trees, creeping along, and when a carriage comes she hides under the blackberry vines.

I don't blame her a bit. It must be very humiliating to be caught creeping by daylight!

I always lock the door when I creep by daylight. I can't do it at night, for I know John would suspect something at once.

And John is so queer now, that I don't want to irritate him. I wish he would take another room! Besides, I don't want anybody to get that woman out at night but myself.

I often wonder if I could see her out of all the windows at once.

But, turn as fast as I can, I can only see out of one at one time.

And though I always see her, she *may* be able to creep faster than I can turn!

I have watched her sometimes away off in the open country, creeping as fast as a cloud shadow in a high wind.

If only that top pattern could be gotten off from the under one! I mean to try it, little by little.

I have found out another funny thing, but I shan't tell it this time! It does not do to trust people too much.

There are only two more days to get this paper off, and I believe John is beginning to notice. I don't like the look in his eyes.

And I heard him ask Jennie a lot of professional questions about me. She had a very good report to give.

She said I slept a good deal in the daytime.

John knows I don't sleep very well at night, for all I'm so quiet!

He asked me all sorts of questions, too, and pretended to be very loving and kind.

As if I couldn't see through him!

Still, I don't wonder he acts so, sleeping under this paper for three months.

It only interests me, but I feel sure John and Jennie are secretly affected by it.

Hurrah! This is the last day, but it is enough. John to stay in town over night, and won't be out until this evening.

Jennie wanted to sleep with me—the sly thing! but I told her I should undoubtedly rest better for a night all alone.

That was clever, for really I wasn't alone a bit! As soon as it was moonlight and that poor thing began to crawl and shake the pattern, I got up and ran to help her.

I pulled and she shook, I shook and she pulled, and before morning we had peeled off yards of that paper.

A strip about as high as my head and half around the room.

And then when the sun came and that awful pattern began to laugh at me, I declared I would finish it to-day!

We go away to-morrow, and they are moving all my furniture down again to leave things as they were before.

Jennie looked at the wall in amazement, but I told her merrily that I did it out of pure spite at the vicious thing.

She laughed and said she wouldn't mind doing it herself, but I must not get tired.

How she betrayed herself that time!

But I am here, and no person touches this paper but me,—not *alive!*

She tried to get me out of the room—it was too patent! But I said it was so quiet and empty and clean now that I believed I would lie down again and sleep all I could; and not to wake me even for dinner—I would call when I woke.

So now she is gone, and the servants are gone, and the things are gone, and there is nothing left but that great bedstead nailed down, with the canvas mattress we found on it.

We shall sleep downstairs to-night, and take the boat home to-morrow.

I quite enjoy the room, now it is bare again.

How those children did tear about here!

This bedstead is fairly gnawed!

But I must get to work.

I have locked the door and thrown the key down into the front path.

I don't want to go out, and I don't want to have anybody come in, till John comes.

I want to astonish him.

I've got a rope up here that even Jennie did not find. If that woman does get out, and tries to get away, I can tie her!

But I forgot I could not reach far without anything to stand on!

This bed will *not* move!

I tried to lift and push it until I was lame, and then I got so angry I bit off a little piece at one corner—but it hurt my teeth.

Then I peeled off all the paper I could reach standing on the floor. It sticks horribly and the pattern just enjoys it! All those strangled heads and bulbous eyes and waddling fungus growths just shriek with derision!

I am getting angry enough to do something desperate. To jump out of the window would be admirable exercise, but the bars are too strong even to try.

Besides I wouldn't do it. Of course not. I know well enough that a step like that is improper and might be misconstrued.

I don't like to *look* out of the windows even—there are so many of those creeping women, and they creep so fast.

I wonder if they all come out of that wall-paper as I did?

But I am securely fastened now by my well-hidden rope—you don't get *me* out in the road there!

I suppose I shall have to get back behind the pattern when it comes night, and that is hard!

It is so pleasant to be out in this great room and creep around as I please!

I don't want to go outside. I won't, even if Jennie asks me to.

For outside you have to creep on the ground, and everything is green instead of yellow.

But here I can creep smoothly on the floor, and my shoulder just fits in that long smooch around the wall, so I cannot lose my way.

Why there's John at the door!

It is no use, young man, you can't open it!

How he does call and pound!

Now he's crying for an axe.

It would be a shame to break down that beautiful door!

"John dear!" said I in the gentlest voice, "the key is down by the front steps, under a plantain leaf!"

That silenced him for a few moments.

Then he said—very quietly indeed, "Open the door, my darling!"

"I can't," said I. "The key is down by the front door under a plantain leaf!"

And then I said it again, several times, very gently and slowly, and said it so often that he had to go and see, and he got it of course, and came in. He stopped short by the door.

"What is the matter?" he cried. "For God's sake, what are you doing!"

I kept on creeping just the same, but I looked at him over my shoulder.

"I've got out at last," said I, "in spite of you and Jennie. And I've pulled off most of the paper, so you can't put me back!"

Now why should that man have fainted? But he did, and right across my path by the wall, so that I had to creep over him every time!

STEPHEN CRANE

(1871-1900)

Crane died of tuberculosis when he was twenty-nine, before most careers begin. Yet by then he had written a good deal of important fiction. *Maggie,* the first naturalistic novel in America, about a woman who is forced by her environment to turn to prostitution, shocked Victorian America, but *The Red Badge of Courage* (1895), about a young man initiated into battle in the Civil War, made him a huge success, especially in England. As a correspondent he saw actual battle—the Spanish-American War and the Greek-Turkish War—only after he had written *The Red Badge of Courage.* Afterwards, he felt that his intuitions had been right.

Returning from Cuba, he suffered the shipwreck that serves as the basis for "The Open Boat." But, as critic after critic has pointed out, the story is far more than a simple narrative of survival. It is also the story of exposure to an indifferent universe, a universe which, by the end of the story, the survivors felt able to "interpret." This story is that interpretation.

[See Preface, p. 2 (parable), p. 13 (conflict), p. 18 (imagery).]

The Open Boat

A Tale intended to be after the fact. Being the Experience of Four Men from the Sunk Steamer "Commodore"

STEPHEN CRANE

I

None of them knew the color of the sky. Their eyes glanced level, and were fastened upon the waves that swept toward them. These waves were of the hue of slate, save for the tops, which were of foaming white, and all of the men knew the colors of the sea. The horizon narrowed and widened, and dipped and rose, and at all times its edge was jagged with waves that seemed thrust up in points like rocks.

Many a man ought to have a bath-tub larger than the boat which here rode upon the sea. These waves were most wrongfully and barbarously abrupt and tall, and each froth-top was a problem in small boat navigation.

The cook squatted in the bottom and looked with both eyes at the six inches of gunwale which separated him from the ocean. His sleeves were rolled over his fat forearms, and the two flaps of his unbuttoned vest dangled as he bent to bail out the boat. Often he said: "Gawd! That was a narrow clip." As he remarked it he invariably gazed eastward over the broken sea.

The oiler, steering with one of the two oars in the boat, sometimes raised himself suddenly to keep clear of water that swirled in over the stern. It was a thin little oar and it seemed often ready to snap.

The correspondent, pulling at the other oar, watched the waves and wondered why he was there.

The injured captain, lying in the bow, was at this time buried in that profound dejection and indifference which comes, temporarily at least, to even the bravest and most enduring when, willy nilly, the firm fails, the army loses, the ship goes down. The mind of the master of a vessel is rooted deep in the timbers of her, though he command for a day or a decade, and this captain had on him the stern impression of a scene in the grays of dawn of seven turned faces, and later a stump of a top-mast with a white ball on it that slashed to and fro at the waves, went low and lower, and down. Thereafter there was something strange in his voice. Although steady, it was deep with mourning, and of a quality beyond oration or tears.

"Keep 'er a little more south, Billie," said he.

" 'A little more south,' sir," said the oiler in the stern.

A seat in this boat was not unlike a seat upon a bucking broncho, and, by the same token, a broncho is not much smaller. The craft pranced and reared, and plunged like an animal. As each wave came, and she rose for it, she seemed like a horse making at a fence outrageously high. The manner of her scramble over these walls of water is a mystic thing, and, moreover, at the top of them were ordinarily these problems in white water, the foam racing down from the summit of each wave, requiring a new leap, and a leap from the air. Then, after scornfully bumping a crest, she would slide, and race, and splash down a long incline, and arrive bobbing and nodding in front of the next menace.

A singular disadvantage of the sea lies in the fact that after successfully surmounting one wave you discover that there is another behind it just as important and just as nervously anxious to do something effective in the way of swamping boats. In a ten-foot dingey one can get an idea of the resources of the sea in the line of waves that is not probable to the average experience which is never at sea in a dingey. As each slaty wall of water approached, it shut all else from the view of the men in the boat, and it was not difficult to imagine that this particular wave was the final outburst of the ocean, the last effort of the grim water. There was a terrible grace in the move of the waves, and they came in silence, save for the snarling of the crests.

In the wan light, the faces of the men must have been gray. Their eyes must have glinted in strange ways as they gazed steadily astern. Viewed from a balcony, the whole thing would doubtless have been weirdly picturesque. But the men in the boat had no time to see it, and if they had had leisure there were other things to occupy their minds. The sun swung steadily up the sky, and they knew it was broad day because the color of the sea changed from slate to emerald-green, streaked with amber lights, and the foam was like tumbling snow. The process of the breaking day was unknown to them. They were aware only of this effect upon the color of the waves that rolled toward them.

In disjointed sentences the cook and the correspondent argued as to the difference between a life-saving station and a house of refuge. The cook had said: "There's a house of refuge just north of the Mosquito Inlet Light, and as soon as they see us, they'll come off in their boat and pick us up."

"As soon as who see us?" said the correspondent.

"The crew," said the cook.

"Houses of refuge don't have crews," said the correspondent. "As I understand them, they are only places where clothes and grub are stored for the benefit of shipwrecked people. They don't carry crews."

"Oh, yes, they do," said the cook.

"No, they don't," said the correspondent.

"Well, we're not there yet, anyhow," said the oiler, in the stern.

"Well," said the cook, "perhaps it's not a house of refuge that I'm thinking of as being near Mosquito Inlet Light. Perhaps it's a life-saving station."

"We're not there yet," said the oiler, in the stern.

II

As the boat bounced from the top of each wave, the wind tore through the hair of the hatless men, and as the craft plopped her stern down again the spray slashed past them. The crest of each of these waves was a hill, from the top of which the men surveyed, for a moment, a broad tumultuous expanse, shining and wind-riven. It was probably splendid. It was probably glorious, this play of the free sea, wild with lights of emerald and white and amber.

"Bully good thing it's an on-shore wind," said the cook. "If not, where would we be? Wouldn't have a show."

"That's right," said the correspondent.

The busy oiler nodded his assent.

Then the captain, in the bow, chuckled in a way that expressed humor, contempt, tragedy, all in one. "Do you think we've got much of a show now, boys?" said he.

Whereupon the three were silent, save for a trifle of hemming and hawing. To express any particular optimism at this time they felt to be childish and stupid, but they all doubtless possessed this sense of the situation in their mind. A young man thinks doggedly at such times. On the other hand, the ethics of their condition was decidedly against any open suggestion of hopelessness. So they were silent.

"Oh, well," said the captain, soothing his children, "we'll get ashore all right."

But there was that in his tone which made them think, so the oiler quoth: "Yes! If this wind holds!"

The cook was bailing: "Yes! If we don't catch hell in the surf."

Canton flannel gulls flew near and far. Sometimes they sat down on the sea, near patches of brown seaweed that rolled over the waves with a movement like carpets on a line in a gale. The birds sat comfortably in groups, and they were envied by some in the dingey, for the wrath of the sea was no more to them than it was to a covey of prairie chickens a thousand miles inland. Often they came very close and stared at the men with black bead-like eyes. At these times they were uncanny and sinister in their unblinking scrutiny, and the men hooted angrily at them, telling them to be gone. One came, and evidently decided to alight on the top of the captain's head. The bird flew parallel to the boat and did not circle, but made short sidelong jumps in the air in chicken-fashion. His black eyes were wistfully fixed upon the captain's head. "Ugly brute," said the oiler to the bird. "You look as if you were made with a jack-knife." The cook and the correspondent swore darkly at the creature. The captain naturally wished to knock it away with the end of the heavy painter; but he did not dare do it, because anything resembling an emphatic gesture would have capsized this freighted boat, and so with his open hand, the captain gently and carefully waved the gull away. After it had been discouraged from the pursuit the captain breathed easier on account of his hair, and others breathed easier because the bird struck their minds at this time as being somehow gruesome and ominous.

In the meantime the oiler and the correspondent rowed. And also they rowed.

They sat together in the same seat, and each rowed an oar. Then the oiler took both oars; then the correspondent took both oars; then the oiler; then the correspondent. They rowed and they rowed. The very ticklish part of the business was when the time came for the reclining one in the stern to take his turn at the oars. By the very last star of truth, it is easier to steal eggs from under a hen than it was to change seats in the dingey. First the man in the stern slid his hand along the thwart and moved with care, as if he were of Sèvres. Then the man in the rowing seat slid his hand along the other thwart. It was all done with the most extraordinary care. As the two sidled past each other, the whole party kept watchful eyes on the coming wave, and the captain cried: "Look out now! Steady there!"

The brown mats of seaweed that appeared from time to time were like islands, bits of earth. They were travelling, apparently, neither one way nor the other. They were, to all intents, stationary. They informed the men in the boat that it was making progress slowly toward the land.

The captain, rearing cautiously in the bow, after the dingey soared on a great swell, said that he had seen the lighthouse at Mosquito Inlet. Presently the cook remarked that he had seen it. The correspondent was at the oars then, and for some reason he too wished to look at the lighthouse, but his back was toward the far shore and the waves were important, and for some time he could not seize an opportunity to turn his head. But at last there came a wave more gentle than the others, and when at the crest of it he swiftly scoured the western horizon.

"See it?" said the captain.

"No," said the correspondent slowly. "I didn't see anything."

"Look again," said the captain. He pointed. "It's exactly in that direction."

At the top of another wave, the correspondent did as he was bid, and this time his eyes chanced on a small still thing on the edge of the swaying horizon. It was precisely like the point of a pin. It took an anxious eye to find a lighthouse so tiny.

"Think we'll make it, captain?"

"If this wind holds and the boat don't swamp, we can't do much else," said the captain.

The little boat, lifted by each towering sea, and splashed viciously by the crests, made progress that in the absence of seaweed was not apparent to those in her. She seemed just a wee thing wallowing, miraculously top up, at the mercy of five oceans. Occasionally, a great spread of water, like white flames, swarmed into her.

"Bail her, cook," said the captain serenely.

"All right, captain," said the cheerful cook.

III

It would be difficult to describe the subtle brotherhood of men that was here established on the seas. No one said that it was so. No one mentioned it. But it dwelt in the boat, and each man felt it warm him. They were a captain, an oiler, a cook, and a correspondent, and they were friends, friends in a more curiously iron-bound degree than may be common. The hurt captain, lying against the water-jar in the bow, spoke always in a low voice and calmly, but he could never command a more ready and swiftly obedient crew than the motley three of the dingey. It was more than a mere recognition of what was best for the common safety. There was surely in it a quality that was personal and heartfelt. And after this devotion to the commander of the boat there was this comradeship that the correspondent, for instance, who had been taught to be cynical of men, knew even at the time was the best experience of his life. But no one said that it was so. No one mentioned it.

"I wish we had a sail," remarked the captain. "We might try my overcoat on the end of an oar and give you two boys a chance to rest." So the cook and the correspondent held the mast and spread wide the overcoat. The oiler steered, and the little boat made good way with her new rig. Sometimes the oiler had to scull sharply to keep a sea from breaking into the boat, but otherwise sailing was a success.

Meanwhile the lighthouse had been growing slowly larger. It had now almost assumed color, and appeared like a little gray shadow on the sky. The man at the oars could not be prevented from turning his head rather often to try for a glimpse of this little gray shadow.

At last, from the top of each wave the men in the tossing boat could see land. Even as the lighthouse was an upright shadow on the sky, this land seemed but a long black shadow on the sea. It certainly was thinner than paper. "We must be about opposite New Smyrna," said the cook, who had coasted this shore often in schooners. "Captain, by the way, I believe they abandoned that life-saving station there about a year ago."

"Did they?" said the captain.

The wind slowly died away. The cook and the correspondent were not now obliged to slave in order to hold high the oar. But the waves continued their old impetuous swooping at the dingey, and the little craft, no longer under way, struggled woundily over them. The oiler or the correspondent took the oars again.

Shipwrecks are apropos of nothing. If men could only train for them and have them occur when the men had reached pink condition, there would be less drowning at sea. Of the four in the dingey none had slept any time worth mentioning for two days and two nights previous to embarking in the dingey, and in the excitement of clambering about the deck of a foundering ship they had also forgotten to eat heartily.

For these reasons, and for others, neither the oiler nor the correspondent was fond of rowing at this time. The correspondent wondered ingenuously how in the name of all that was sane could there be people who thought it amusing to row a boat. It was not an amusement; it was a diabolical punishment, and even a genius of mental aberrations could never conclude that it was anything but a horror to the muscles and a crime against the back. He mentioned to the boat in general how the amusement of rowing struck him, and the weary-faced oiler smiled in full sympathy. Previously to the foundering, by the way, the oiler had worked double-watch in the engine-room of the ship.

"Take her easy, now, boys," said the captain. "Don't spend yourselves. If we have to run a surf you'll need all your strength, because we'll sure have to swim for it. Take your time."

Slowly the land arose from the sea. From a black line it became a line of black and a line of white, trees and sand. Finally, the captain said that he could make out a house on the shore. "That's the house of refuge, sure," said the cook. "They'll see us before long, and come out after us."

The distant lighthouse reared high. "The keeper ought to be able to make us out now, if he's looking through a glass," said the captain. "He'll notify the life-saving people."

"None of those other boats could have got ashore to give word of the wreck," said the oiler, in a low voice. "Else the life-boat would be out hunting us."

Slowly and beautifully the land loomed out of the sea. The wind came again. It had veered from the north-east to the south-east. Finally, a new sound struck the ears of the men in the boat. It was the low thunder of the surf on the shore. "We'll never be able to make the lighthouse now," said the captain. "Swing her head a little more north, Billie."

" 'A little more north,' sir," said the oiler.

Whereupon the little boat turned her nose once more down the wind, and all but the oarsman watched the shore grow. Under the influence of this expansion doubt and direful apprehension was leaving the minds of the men. The management of the boat was still most absorbing, but it could not prevent a quiet cheerfulness. In an hour, perhaps, they would be ashore.

Their backbones had become thoroughly used to balancing in the boat, and they now rode this wild colt of a dingey like circus men. The correspondent thought that he had been drenched to the skin, but happening to feel in the top pocket of his coat, he found therein eight cigars. Four of them were soaked with sea-water; four were perfectly scatheless. After a search, somebody produced three dry matches, and thereupon the four waifs rode in their little boat, and with an assurance of an impending rescue shining in their eyes, puffed at the big cigars and judged well and ill of all men. Everybody took a drink of water.

IV

"Cook," remarked the captain, "there don't seem to be any signs of life about your house of refuge."

"No," replied the cook. "Funny they don't see us!"

A broad stretch of lowly coast lay before the eyes of the men. It was of low dunes topped with dark vegetation. The roar of the surf was plain, and sometimes they could see the white lip of a wave as it spun up the beach. A tiny house was blocked out black upon the sky. Southward, the slim lighthouse lifted its little gray length.

Tide, wind, and waves were swinging the dingey northward. "Funny they don't see us," said the men.

The surf's roar was here dulled, but its tone was, nevertheless, thunderous and mighty. As the boat swam over the great rollers, the men sat listening to this roar. "We'll swamp sure," said everybody.

It is fair to say here that there was not a life-saving station within twenty miles in either direction, but the men did not know this fact, and in consequence they made dark and opprobrious remarks concerning the eyesight of the nation's life-savers. Four scowling men sat in the dingey and surpassed records in the invention of epithets.

"Funny they don't see us."

The light-heartedness of a former time had completely faded. To their sharpened minds it was easy to conjure pictures of all kinds of incompetency and blindness and, indeed, cowardice. There was the shore of the populous land, and it was bitter and bitter to them that from it came no sign.

"Well," said the captain, ultimately, "I suppose we'll have to make a try for ourselves. If we stay out here too long, we'll none of us have strength left to swim after the boat swamps."

And so the oiler, who was at the oars, turned the boat straight for the shore. There was a sudden tightening of muscles. There was some thinking.

"If we don't all get ashore—" said the captain. "If we don't all get ashore, I suppose you fellows know where to send news of my finish?"

They then briefly exchanged some addresses and admonitions. As for the reflections of the men, there was a great deal of rage in them. Perchance they might be formulated thus: "If I am going to be drowned—if I am going to be drowned—if I am going to be drowned, why, in the name of the seven mad gods who rule the sea, was I allowed to come thus far and contemplate sand and trees? Was I brought here merely to have my nose dragged away as I was about to nibble the sacred cheese of life? It is preposterous. If this old ninny-woman, Fate, cannot do better than this, she should be deprived of the management of men's fortunes. She is an old hen who knows not her intention. If she has decided to drown me, why did she not do it in the beginning and save me all this trouble? The whole affair is absurd. . . . But no, she cannot mean to drown me. She dare not drown me. She cannot drown me. Not after all this work." Afterward the man might have had an impulse to shake his fist at the clouds: "Just you drown me, now, and then hear what I call you!"

The billows that came at this time were more formidable. They seemed always just about to break and roll over the little boat in a turmoil of foam. There was a preparatory and long growl in the speech of them. No mind unused to the sea would have concluded that the dingey could ascend these sheer heights in time. The shore was still afar. The oiler was a wily surfman. "Boys," he said swiftly, "she won't live three minutes more, and we're too far out to swim. Shall I take her to sea again, captain?"

"Yes! Go ahead!" said the captain.

This oiler, by a series of quick miracles, and fast and steady oarsmanship, turned the boat in the middle of the surf and took her safely to sea again.

There was a considerable silence as the boat bumped over the furrowed sea to deeper water. Then somebody in gloom spoke. "Well, anyhow, they must have seen us from the shore by now."

The gulls went in slanting flight up the wind toward the gray desolate east. A squall, marked by dingy clouds, and clouds brick-red, like smoke from a burning building, appeared from the south-east.

"What do you think of those life-saving people? Ain't they peaches?"

"Funny they haven't seen us."

"Maybe they think we're out here for sport! Maybe they think we're fishin'. Maybe they think we're damned fools."

It was a long afternoon. A changed tide tried to force them southward, but wind and wave said northward. Far ahead, where coastline, sea, and sky formed their mighty angle, there were little dots which seemed to indicate a city on the shore.

"St. Augustine?"

The captain shook his head. "Too near Mosquito Inlet."

And the oiler rowed, and then the correspondent rowed. Then the oiler rowed. It was a weary business. The human back can become the seat of more aches and pains than are registered in books for the composite anatomy of a regiment. It is a limited area, but it can become the theater of innumerable muscular conflicts, tangles, wrenches, knots, and other comforts.

"Did you ever like to row, Billie?" asked the correspondent.

"No," said the oiler. "Hang it!"

When one exchanged the rowing-seat for a place in the bottom of the boat, he suffered a bodily depression that caused him to be careless of everything save an obligation to wiggle one finger. There was cold sea-water swashing to and fro in the boat, and he lay in it. His head, pillowed on a thwart, was within an inch of the swirl of a wave crest, and sometimes a particularly obstreperous sea came inboard and drenched him once more. But these matters did not annoy him. It is almost certain that if the boat had capsized he would have tumbled comfortably out upon the ocean as if he felt sure that it was a great soft mattress.

"Look! There's a man on the shore!"

"Where?"

"There! See 'im? See 'im?"

"Yes, sure! He's walking along."

"Now he's stopped. Look! He's facing us!"

"He's waving at us!"

"So he is! By thunder!"

"Ah, now we're all right! Now we're all right! There'll be a boat out here for us in half an hour."

"He's going on. He's running. He's going up to that house there."

The remote beach seemed lower than the sea, and it required a searching glance to discern the little black figure. The captain saw a floating stick and they rowed to it. A bath-towel was by some weird chance in the boat, and tying this on the stick, the captain waved it. The oarsman did not dare turn his head, so he was obliged to ask questions.

"What's he doing now?"

"He's standing still again. He's looking. I think. . . . There he goes again. Toward the house. . . . Now he's stopped again."

"Is he waving at us?"

"No, not now! he was, though."

"Look! There comes another man!"

"He's running."

"Look at him go, would you."

"Why, he's on a bicycle. Now he's met the other man. They're both waving at us. Look!"

"There comes something up the beach."

"What the devil is that thing?"

"Why, it looks like a boat."

"Why, certainly it's a boat."

"No, it's on wheels."

"Yes, so it is. Well, that must be the life-boat. They drag them along shore on a wagon."

"That's the life-boat, sure."

"No, by—, it's—it's an omnibus."

"I tell you it's a life-boat."

"It is not! It's an omnibus. I can see it plain. See? One of these big hotel omnibuses."

"By thunder, you're right. It's an omnibus, sure as fate. What do you suppose they are doing with an omnibus? Maybe they are going around collecting the life-crew, hey?"

"That's it, likely. Look! There's a fellow waving a little black flag. He's standing on the steps of the omnibus. There come those other two fellows. Now they're all talking together. Look at the fellow with the flag. Maybe he ain't waving it."

"That ain't a flag, is it? That's his coat. Why, certainly, that's his coat."

"So it is. It's his coat. He's taken it off and is waving it around his head. But would you look at him swing it."

"Oh, say, there isn't any life-saving station there. That's just a winter resort hotel omnibus that has brought over some of the boarders to see us drown."

"What's that idiot with the coat mean? What's he signaling, any-how?"

"It looks as if he were trying to tell us to go north. There must be a life-saving station up there."

"No! He thinks we're fishing. Just giving us a merry hand. See? Ah, there, Willie."

"Well, I wish I could make something out of those signals. What do you suppose he means?"

"He don't mean anything. He's just playing."

"Well, if he'd just signal us to try the surf again, or to go to sea and wait, or go north, or go south, or go to hell—there would be some reason in it. But look at him. He just stands there and keeps his coat revolving like a wheel. The ass!"

"There come more people."

"Now there's quite a mob. Look! Isn't that a boat."

"Where? Oh, I see where you mean. No, that's no boat."

"That fellow is still waving his coat."

"He must think we like to see him do that. Why don't he quit it? It don't mean anything."

"I don't know. I think he is trying to make us go north. It must be that there's a life-saving station there somewhere."

"Say, he ain't tired yet. Look at 'im wave."

"Wonder how long he can keep that up. He's been revolving his coat ever since he caught sight of us. He's an idiot. Why aren't they getting men to bring a boat out? A fishing boat—one of those big yawls—could come out here all right. Why don't he do something?"

"Oh, it's all right, now."

"They'll have a boat out here for us in less than no time, now that they've seen us."

A faint yellow tone came into the sky over the low land. The shadows on the sea slowly deepened. The wind bore coldness with it, and the men began to shiver.

"Holy smoke!" said one, allowing his voice to express his impious mood, "if we keep on monkeying out here! If we've got to flounder out here all night!"

"Oh, we'll never have to stay here all night! Don't you worry. They've seen us now, and it won't be long before they'll come chasing out after us."

The shore grew dusky. The man waving a coat blended gradually into this gloom, and it swallowed in the same manner the omnibus and the group of people. The spray, when it dashed uproariously over the side, made the voyagers shrink and swear like men who were being branded.

"I'd like to catch the chump who waved the coat. I feel like soaking him one, just for luck."

"Why? What did he do?"

"Oh, nothing, but then he seemed so damned cheerful."

In the meantime the oiler rowed, and then the correspondent rowed, and then the oiler rowed. Gray-faced and bowed forward, they mechanically, turn by turn, plied the leaden oars. The form of the lighthouse had vanished from the southern horizon, but finally a pale star appeared, just lifting from the sea. The streaked saffron in the west passed before the all-merging darkness, and the sea to the

east was black. The land had vanished, and was expressed only by
the low and drear thunder of the surf.

"If I am going to be drowned—if I am going to be drowned—if I
am going to be drowned, why, in the name of the seven mad gods
who rule the sea, was I allowed to come thus far and contemplate
sand and trees? Was I brought here merely to have my nose dragged
away as I was about to nibble the sacred cheese of life?"

The patient captain, drooped over the water-jar, was sometimes
obliged to speak to the oarsman.

"Keep her head up! Keep her head up!"

" 'Keep her head up,' sir." The voices were weary and low.

This was surely a quiet evening. All save the oarsman lay heavily
and listlessly in the boat's bottom. As for him, his eyes were just
capable of noting the tall black waves that swept forward in a most
sinister silence, save for an occasional subdued growl of a crest.

The cook's head was on a thwart, and he looked without interest at
the water under his nose. He was deep in other scenes. Finally he
spoke. "Billie," he murmured, dreamfully, "what kind of pie do you
like best?"

V

"Pie," said the oiler and the correspondent, agitatedly. "Don't talk
about those things, blast you!"

"Well," said the cook, "I was just thinking about ham sandwiches,
and—"

A night on the sea in an open boat is a long night. As darkness
settled finally, the shine of the light, lifting from the sea in the south,
changed to full gold. On the northern horizon a new light appeared,
a small bluish gleam on the edge of the waters. These two lights were
the furniture of the world. Otherwise there was nothing but waves.

Two men huddled in the stern, and distances were so magnificent
in the dingey that the rower was enabled to keep his feet partly
warmed by thrusting them under his companions. Their legs indeed
extended far under the rowing-seat until they touched the feet of the
captain forward. Sometimes, despite the efforts of the tired oarsman,
a wave came piling into the boat, an icy wave of the night, and the
chilling water soaked them anew. They would twist their bodies for a
moment and groan, and sleep the dead sleep once more, while the
water in the boat gurgled about them as the craft rocked.

The plan of the oiler and the correspondent was for one to row
until he lost the ability, and then arouse the other from his sea-water
couch in the bottom of the boat.

The oiler plied the oars until his head drooped forward, and the overpowering sleep blinded him. And he rowed yet afterward. Then he touched a man in the bottom of the boat, and called his name. "Will you spell me for a little while?" he said, meekly.

"Sure, Billie," said the correspondent, awakening and dragging himself to a sitting position. They exchanged places carefully, and the oiler, cuddling down in the sea-water at the cook's side, seemed to go to sleep instantly.

The particular violence of the sea had ceased. The waves came without snarling. The obligation of the man at the oars was to keep the boat headed so that the tilt of the rollers would not capsize her, and to preserve her from filling when the crests rushed past. The black waves were silent and hard to be seen in the darkness. Often one was almost upon the boat before the oarsman was aware.

In a low voice the correspondent addressed the captain. He was not sure that the captain was awake, although this iron man seemed to be always awake. "Captain, shall I keep her making for that light north, sir?"

The same steady voice answered him. "Yes. Keep it about two points off the port bow."

The cook had tied a life-belt around himself in order to get even the warmth which this clumsy cork contrivance could donate, and he seemed almost stove-like when a rower, whose teeth invariably chattered wildly as soon as he ceased his labor, dropped down to sleep.

The correspondent, as he rowed, looked down at the two men sleeping underfoot. The cook's arm was around the oiler's shoulders, and, with their fragmentary clothing and haggard faces, they were the babes of the sea, a grotesque rendering of the old babes in the wood.

Later he must have grown stupid at his work, for suddenly there was a growling of water, and a crest came with a roar and a swash into the boat, and it was a wonder that it did not set the cook afloat in his life-belt. The cook continued to sleep, but the oiler sat up, blinking his eyes and shaking with the new cold.

"Oh, I'm awful sorry, Billie," said the correspondent, contritely.

"That's all right, old boy," said the oiler, and lay down again and was asleep.

Presently it seemed that even the captain dozed, and the correspondent thought that he was the one man afloat on all the oceans. The wind had a voice as it came over the waves, and it was sadder than the end.

There was a long, loud swishing astern of the boat, and a gleaming trail of phosphorescence, like blue flame, was furrowed on the black waters. It might have been made by a monstrous knife.

Then there came a stillness, while the correspondent breathed with the open mouth and looked at the sea.

Suddenly there was another swish and another long flash of bluish light, and this time it was alongside the boat, and might almost have been reached with an oar. The correspondent saw an enormous fin speed like a shadow through the water, hurling the crystalline spray and leaving the long glowing trail.

The correspondent looked over his shoulder at the captain. His face was hidden, and he seemed to be asleep. He looked at the babes of the sea. They certainly were asleep. So, being bereft of sympathy, he leaned a little way to one side and swore softly into the sea.

But the thing did not then leave the vicinity of the boat. Ahead or astern, on one side or the other, at intervals long or short, fled the long sparkling streak, and there was to be heard the whiroo of the dark fin. The speed and power of the thing was greatly to be admired. It cut the water like a gigantic and keen projectile.

The presence of this biding thing did not affect the man with the same horror that it would if he had been a picnicker. He simply looked at the sea dully and swore in an undertone.

Nevertheless, it is true that he did not wish to be alone. He wished one of his companions to awaken by chance and keep him company with it. But the captain hung motionless over the water-jar, and the oiler and the cook in the bottom of the boat were plunged in slumber.

VI

"If I am going to be drowned—if I am going to be drowned—if I am going to be drowned, why, in the name of the seven mad gods who rule the sea, was I allowed to come thus far and contemplate sand and trees?"

During this dismal night, it may be remarked that a man would conclude that it was really the intention of the seven mad gods to drown him, despite the abominable injustice of it. For it was certainly an abominable injustice to drown a man who had worked so hard, so hard. The man felt it would be a crime most unnatural. Other people had drowned at sea since galleys swarmed with painted sails, but still—

When it occurs to a man that nature does not regard him as important, and that she feels she would not maim the universe by disposing of him, he at first wishes to throw bricks at the temple, and he hates deeply the fact that there are no bricks and no temples. Any visible expression of nature would surely be pelleted with his jeers.

Then, if there be no tangible thing to hoot he feels, perhaps, the desire to confront a personification and indulge in pleas, bowed to one knee, and with hands supplicant, saying: "Yes, but I love myself."

A high cold star on a winter's night is the word he feels that she says to him. Thereafter he knows the pathos of his situation.

The men in the dingey had not discussed these matters, but each had, no doubt, reflected upon them in silence and according to his mind. There was seldom any expression upon their faces save the general one of complete weariness. Speech was devoted to the business of the boat.

To chime the notes of his emotion, a verse mysteriously entered the correspondent's head. He had even forgotten that he had forgotten this verse, but it suddenly was in his mind.

"A soldier of the Legion lay dying in Algiers,
There was lack of woman's nursing, there was dearth of woman's tears;
But a comrade stood beside him, and he took that comrade's hand,
And he said: 'I shall never see my own, my native land.' "

In his childhood, the correspondent had been made acquainted with the fact that a soldier of the Legion lay dying in Algiers, but he had never regarded the fact as important. Myriads of his schoolfellows had informed him of the soldier's plight, but the dinning had naturally ended by making him perfectly indifferent. He had never considered it his affair that a soldier of the Legion lay dying in Algiers, nor had it appeared to him as a matter for sorrow. It was less to him than the breaking of a pencil's point.

Now, however, it quaintly came to him as a human, living thing. It was no longer merely a picture of a few throes in the breast of a poet, meanwhile drinking tea and warming his feet at the grate; it was an actuality—stern, mournful, and fine.

The correspondent plainly saw the soldier. He lay on the sand with his feet out straight and still. While his pale left hand was upon his chest in an attempt to thwart the going of his life, the blood came between his fingers. In the far Algerian distance, a city of low square forms was set against a sky that was faint with the last sunset hues. The correspondent, plying the oars and dreaming of the slow and slower movements of the lips of the soldier, was moved by a profound and perfectly impersonal comprehension. He was sorry for the soldier of the Legion who lay dying in Algiers.

The thing which had followed the boat and waited had evidently grown bored at the delay. There was no longer to be heard the slash of the cut water, and there was no longer the flame of the long trail. The light in the north still glimmered, but it was apparently no nearer to the boat. Sometimes the boom of the surf rang in the correspondent's ears, and he turned the craft seaward then and rowed harder. Southward, someone had evidently built a watch-fire on the beach. It was too low and too far to be seen, but it made a shimmering, roseate reflection upon the bluff back of it, and this could be discerned from the boat. The wind came stronger, and sometimes a wave suddenly raged out like a mountain-cat, and there was to be seen the sheen and sparkle of a broken crest.

The captain, in the bow, moved on his water-jar and sat erect. "Pretty long night," he observed to the correspondent. He looked at the shore. "Those life-saving people take their time."

"Did you see that shark playing around?"

"Yes, I saw him. He was a big fellow, all right."

"Wish I had known you were awake."

Later the correspondent spoke into the bottom of the boat.

"Billie!" There was a slow and gradual disentanglement. "Billie, will you spell me?"

"Sure," said the oiler.

As soon as the correspondent touched the cold comfortable sea-water in the bottom of the boat, and had huddled close to the cook's life-belt he was deep in sleep, despite the fact that his teeth played all the popular airs. This sleep was so good to him that it was but a moment before he heard a voice call his name in a tone that demonstrated the last stages of exhaustion. "Will you spell me?"

"Sure, Billie."

The light in the north had mysteriously vanished, but the correspondent took his course from the wide-awake captain.

Later in the night they took the boat farther out to sea, and the captain directed the cook to take one oar at the stern and keep the boat facing the seas. He was to call out if he should hear the thunder of the surf. This plan enabled the oiler and the correspondent to get respite together. "We'll give those boys a chance to get into shape again," said the captain. They curled down and, after a few preliminary chatterings and trembles, slept once more the dead sleep. Neither knew they had bequeathed to the cook the company of another shark, or perhaps the same shark.

As the boat caroused on the waves, spray occasionally bumped over the side and gave them a fresh soaking, but this had no power to break their repose. The ominous slash of the wind and the water affected them as it would have affected mummies.

"Boys," said the cook, with the notes of every reluctance in his voice, "she's drifted in pretty close. I guess one of you had better take her to sea again." The correspondent, aroused, heard the crash of the toppled crests.

As he was rowing, the captain gave him some whiskey-and-water, and this steadied the chills out of him. "If I ever get ashore and anybody shows me even a photograph of an oar—"

At last there was a short conversation.
"Billie . . . Billie, will you spell me?"
"Sure," said the oiler.

VII

When the correspondent again opened his eyes, the sea and the sky were each of the gray hue of the dawning. Later, carmine and gold was painted upon the waters. The morning appeared finally, in its splendor, with a sky of pure blue, and the sunlight flamed on the tips of the waves.

On the distant dunes were set many little black cottages, and a tall white windmill reared above them. No man, nor dog, nor bicycle appeared on the beach. The cottages might have formed a deserted village.

The voyagers scanned the shore. A conference was held in the boat. "Well," said the captain, "if no help is coming, we might better try a run through the surf right away. If we stay out here much longer we will be too weak to do anything for ourselves at all." The others silently acquiesced in this reasoning. The boat was headed for the beach. The correspondent wondered if none ever ascended the tall wind-tower, and if then they never looked seaward. This tower was a giant, standing with its back to the plight of the ants. It represented in a degree, to the correspondent, the serenity of nature amid the struggles of the individual—nature in the wind, and nature in the vision of men. She did not seem cruel to him then, nor beneficent, nor treacherous, nor wise. But she was indifferent, flatly indifferent. It is, perhaps, plausible that a man in this situation, impressed with the unconcern of the universe, should see the innumerable flaws of his life, and have them taste wickedly in his mind and wish for another chance. A distinction between right and wrong seems absurdly clear to him, then, in this new ignorance of the grave-edge, and he understands that if he were given another opportunity he would mend his conduct and his words, and be better and brighter during an introduction or at a tea.

"Now, boys," said the captain, "she is going to swamp sure. All we can do is to work her in as far as possible, and then when she swamps, pile out and scramble for the beach. Keep cool now, and don't jump until she swamps sure."

The oiler took the oars. Over his shoulders he scanned the surf. "Captain," he said, "I think I'd better bring her about, and keep her head-on to the seas and back her in."

"All right, Billie," said the captain. "Back her in." The oiler swung the boat then and, seated in the stern, the cook and the correspondent were obliged to look over their shoulders to contemplate the lonely and indifferent shore.

The monstrous in-shore rollers heaved the boat high until the men were again enabled to see the white sheets of water scudding up the slanted beach. "We won't get in very close," said the captain. Each time a man could wrest his attention from the rollers, he turned his glance toward the shore, and in the expression of the eyes during this contemplation there was a singular quality. The correspondent, observing the others, knew that they were not afraid, but the full meaning of their glances was shrouded.

As for himself, he was too tired to grapple fundamentally with the fact. He tried to coerce his mind into thinking of it, but the mind was dominated at this time by the muscles, and the muscles said they did not care. It merely occurred to him that if he should drown it would be a shame.

There were no hurried words, no pallor, no plain agitation. The men simply looked at the shore. "Now, remember to get well clear of the boat when you jump," said the captain.

Seaward the crest of a roller suddenly fell with a thunderous crash, and the long white comber came roaring down upon the boat.

"Steady now," said the captain. The men were silent. They turned their eyes from the shore to the comber and waited. The boat slid up the incline, leaped at the furious top, bounced over it, and swung down the long back of the waves. Some water had been shipped and the cook bailed it out.

But the next crest crashed also. The tumbling, boiling flood of white water caught the boat and whirled it almost perpendicular. Water swarmed in from all sides. The correspondent had his hands on the gunwale at this time, and when the water entered at that place he swiftly withdrew his fingers, as if he objected to wetting them.

The little boat, drunken with this weight of water, reeled and snuggled deeper into the sea.

"Bail her out, cook! Bail her out," said the captain.

"All right, captain," said the cook.

"Now, boys, the next one will do for us, sure," said the oiler. "Mind to jump clear of the boat."

The third wave moved forward, huge, furious, implacable. It fairly swallowed the dingey, and almost simultaneously the men tumbled into the sea. A piece of life-belt had lain in the bottom of the boat, and as the correspondent went overboard he held this to his chest with his left hand.

The January water was icy, and he reflected immediately that it was colder than he had expected to find it off the coast of Florida.

This appeared to his dazed mind as a fact important enough to be noted at the time. The coldness of the water was sad; it was tragic. This fact was somehow so mixed and confused with his opinion of his own situation that it seemed almost a proper reason for tears. The water was cold.

When he came to the surface he was conscious of little but the noisy water. Afterward he saw his companions in the sea. The oiler was ahead in the race. He was swimming strongly and rapidly. Off to the correspondent's left, the cook's great white and corked back bulged out of the water, and in the rear the captain was hanging with his one good hand to the keel of the overturned dingey.

There is a certain immovable quality to a shore, and the correspondent wondered at it amid the confusion of the sea.

It seemed also very attractive, but the correspondent knew that it was a long journey, and he paddled leisurely. The piece of life-preserver lay under him, and sometimes he whirled down the incline of a wave as if he were on a hand-sled.

But finally he arrived at a place in the sea where travel was beset with difficulty. He did not pause swimming to inquire what manner of current had caught him, but there his progress ceased. The shore was set before him like a bit of scenery on a stage, and he looked at it and understood with his eyes each detail of it.

As the cook passed, much farther to the left, the captain was calling to him, "Turn over on your back, cook! Turn over on your back and use the oar."

"All right, sir." The cook turned on his back, and, paddling with an oar, went ahead as if he were a canoe.

Presently the boat also passed to the left of the correspondent with the captain clinging with one hand to the keel. He would have appeared like a man raising himself to look over a board fence, if it were not for the extraordinary gymnastics of the boat. The correspondent marvelled that the captain could still hold to it.

They passed on, nearer to shore—the oiler, the cook, the captain—and following them went the water-jar, bouncing gaily over the seas.

The correspondent remained in the grip of this strange new enemy—a current. The shore, with its white slope of sand and its green bluff, topped with little silent cottages, was spread like a picture before him. It was very near to him then, but he was impressed as one who in a gallery looks at a scene from Brittany or Algiers.

He thought: "I am going to drown? Can it be possible? Can it be possible? Can it be possible?" Perhaps an individual must consider his own death to be the final phenomenon of nature.

But later a wave perhaps whirled him out of this small deadly current, for he found suddenly that he could again make progress toward the shore. Later still, he was aware that the captain, clinging with one hand to the keel of the dingey, had his face turned away from the shore and toward him, and was calling his name. "Come to the boat! Come to the boat!"

In his struggle to reach the captain and the boat, he reflected that when one gets properly wearied, drowning must really be a comfortable arrangement, a cessation of hostilities accompanied by a large degree of relief, and he was glad of it, for the main thing in his mind for some moments had been horror of the temporary agony. He did not wish to be hurt.

Presently he saw a man running along the shore. He was undressing with most remarkable speed. Coat, trousers, shirt, everything flew magically off him.

"Come to the boat," called the captain.

"All right, captain." As the correspondent paddled, he saw the captain let himself down to bottom and leave the boat. Then the correspondent performed his one little marvel of the voyage. A large wave caught him and flung him with ease and supreme speed completely over the boat and far beyond it. It struck him even then as an event in gymnastics, and a true miracle of the sea. An overturned boat in the surf is not a plaything to a swimming man.

The correspondent arrived in water that reached only to his waist, but his condition did not enable him to stand for more than a moment. Each wave knocked him into a heap, and the under-tow pulled at him.

Then he saw the man who had been running and undressing, and undressing and running, come bounding into the water. He dragged ashore the cook, and then waded toward the captain, but the captain waved him away, and sent him to the correspondent. He was naked, naked as a tree in winter, but a halo was about his head, and he shone like a saint. He gave a strong pull, and a long drag, and a bully heave at the correspondent's hand. The correspondent, schooled in the minor formulae, said: "Thanks, old man." But suddenly the man cried: "What's that?" He pointed a swift finger. The correspondent said: "Go."

In the shallows, face downward, lay the oiler. His forehead touched sand that was periodically, between each wave, clear of the sea.

The correspondent did not know all that transpired afterward. When he achieved safe ground he fell, striking the sand with each particular part of his body. It was as if he had dropped from a roof, but the thud was grateful to him.

It seems that instantly the beach was populated with men, with blankets, clothes, and flasks, and women with coffee-pots and all the remedies sacred to their minds. The welcome of the land to the men from the sea was warm and generous, but a still and dripping shape was carried slowly up the beach, and the land's welcome for it could only be the different and sinister hospitality of the grave.

When it came night, the white waves paced to and fro in the moonlight, and the wind brought the sound of the great sea's voice to the men on shore, and they felt that they could then be interpreters.

THE GREAT MODERNS

HENRY JAMES

(1843-1916)

James was born in New York City into an American intellectual aristocracy: his grandfather's fortune had allowed his father to devote himself to theological and philosophical studies and to the education of his children. Henry James, Sr. was a friend of Emerson, Carlyle, Hawthorne, Thackeray, and Thoreau; Henry, Jr. and his brothers and sisters were permitted to join in the conversations that took place in their home. During the Civil War a back injury made it impossible for James to enlist; in 1862 he went to Harvard, already sure of his vocation as a writer.

After the war James spent a year in Europe. When he was there he discovered that the woman he loved, Minny Temple, had died. James was to remain a bachelor and a celibate the rest of his life. But in Europe, too, he stretched his wings and felt that for the first time he was fully alive.

During the next years James wrote travel pieces, critical pieces, short stories. In 1875 he published *Roderick Hudson,* his first significant novel, and in the same year he went to live in Europe permanently, except for brief visits to the United States. He settled in London, moved in fashionable and literary society, and wrote a number of novels about innocence and experience, about Americans in Europe, including *The Americans, Daisy Miller,* and *The Portrait of a Lady.* In 1881 James's mother died and he returned home; his father died the same year and, a few months later, his brother Wilky. He returned to London in 1883.

James was strongly influenced at this time by the scandalous new French writers, among them Flaubert and Zola. They brought to the novel a critical self-consciousness he shared—their sense of dedication to craft—though he did not share their interest in "seamy" material.

Out of that common commitment came important new critical writings that tried to establish the novel as an art form. In 1886 James published the novels *The Bostonians* and *The Princess Casamassima*. His lack of popular success led him to write shorter works, including drama; but he was not a success as a dramatist, and in the mid-1890's he began writing novels and stories once again.

Now he was settled happily in a house on the Sussex coast, where he lived until old age made it necessary for him to move to London. Here he wrote his most important novels, *The Wings of the Dove, The Ambassadors,* and *The Golden Bowl,* all from 1902 to 1905. Still not a popular novelist, he was a writer's writer, an artistic guide to a number of young aspirants. Collected editions of his work, to each volume of which James wrote lengthy critical introductions, were published. He was awarded honorary degrees by Harvard and Oxford both, and critical books about his work had already appeared by the time of his death.

In 1914, out of sympathy with the British cause in the First World War, he took British citizenship; in 1915, he was granted the Order of Merit. He died in the middle of the war, in 1916. Never popular, after his death James was recognized as one of the masters of modern fiction, a powerful influence on writers and on critics.

"The Beast in the Jungle" is one of James's greatest stories. It deals with a theme common to him: the person afraid of experience, withdrawn from the world, and so losing the chance to love and to live. It may seem strange that a writer who insisted on *dramatizing* narrative, on *showing* rather than *telling,* should speak so abstractly. But if James was a realist, he did not, like Steinbeck, say, dwell on an environment that shapes character and defines action; rather he was realistic about perception, about psychology, about the nuances of the mind. This makes him difficult to read; he requires patience. But when he communicates the truth about those nuances, he is stunning, exciting, dramatic, though in a quiet way.

The Beast in the Jungle

HENRY JAMES

I

What determined the speech that startled him in the course of their encounter scarcely matters, being probably but some words spoken by himself quite without intention—spoken as they lingered and slowly moved together after their renewal of acquaintance. He had been conveyed by friends an hour or two before to the house at which she was staying; the party of visitors at the other house, of whom he was one, and thanks to whom it was his theory, as always, that he was lost in the crowd, had been invited over to luncheon. There had been after luncheon much dispersal, all in the interest of the original motive, a view of Weatherend itself and the fine things, intrinsic features, pictures, heirlooms, treasures of all the arts, that made the place almost famous; and the great rooms were so numerous that guests could wander at their will, hang back from the principal group and in cases where they took such matters with the last seriousness give themselves up to mysterious appreciations and measurements. There were persons to be observed, singly or in couples, bending toward objects in out-of-the-way corners with their hands on their knees and their heads nodding quite as with the emphasis of an excited sense of smell. When they were two they either mingled their sounds of ecstasy or melted into silences of even deeper import, so that there were aspects of the occasion that gave it for Marcher much the air of the "look round," previous to a sale highly advertised, that excites or quenches, as may be, the dream of acquisition. The dream of acquisition at Weatherend would have had to be wild indeed, and John Marcher found himself, among such suggestions, disconcerted almost equally by the presence of those who knew too much and by that of those who knew nothing. But great rooms caused so much poetry and history to press upon him that he needed some straying apart to feel in a proper relation with them, though this impulse was not, as happened, like the gloating of some of his companions, to be compared to the movements of a dog sniffing a cupboard. It had an issue promptly enough in a direction that was not to have been calculated.

It led, briefly, in the course of the October afternoon, to his closer meeting with May Bartram, whose face, a reminder, yet not quite a remembrance, as they sat much separated at a very long table, had begun merely by troubling him rather pleasantly. It affected him as the sequel of something of which he had lost the beginning. He knew it, and for the time quite welcomed it, as a continuation, but didn't know what it continued, which was an interest or an amusement the greater as he was also somehow aware—yet without a direct sign from her—that the young woman herself hadn't lost the thread. She hadn't lost it, but she wouldn't give it back to him, he saw, without some putting forth of his hand for it; and he not only saw that, but saw several things more, things odd enough in the light of the fact that at the moment some accident of grouping brought them face to face he was still merely fumbling with the idea that any contact between them in the past would have had no importance. If it had had no importance he scarcely knew why his actual impression of her should so seem to have so much; the answer to which, however, was that in such a life as they all appeared to be leading for the moment one could but take things as they came. He was satisfied, without in the least being able to say why, that this young lady might roughly have ranked in the house as a poor relation; satisfied also that she was not there on a brief visit, but was more or less a part of the establishment—almost a working, a remunerated part. Didn't she enjoy at periods a protection that she paid for by helping, among other services, to show the place and explain it, deal with the tiresome people, answer questions about the dates of the building, the styles of the furniture, the authorship of the pictures, the favourite haunts of the ghost? It wasn't that she looked as if you could have given her shillings—it was impossible to look less so. Yet when she finally drifted toward him, distinctly handsome, though ever so much older—older than when he had seen her before—it might have been as an effect of her guessing that he had, within the couple of hours, devoted more imagination to her than to all the others put together, and had thereby penetrated to a kind of truth that the others were too stupid for. She *was* there on harder terms than any one; she was there as a consequence of things suffered, one way and another, in the interval of years; and she remembered him very much as she was remembered—only a good deal better.

By the time they at last thus came to speech they were alone in one of the rooms—remarkable for a fine portrait over the chimney-place —out of which their friends had passed, and the charm of it was that even before they had spoken they had practically arranged with each other to stay behind for talk. The charm, happily, was in other things too—partly in there being scarce a spot at Weatherend without something to stay behind for. It was in the way the autumn day looked into the high windows as it waned; the way the red light, breaking at the close from under a low sombre sky, reached out in a long shaft and played over old wainscots, old tapestry, old gold, old colour. It was most of all perhaps in the way she came to him as if, since she had been turned on to deal with the simpler sort, he might, should he choose to keep the whole thing down, just take her mild attention for a part of her general business. As soon as he heard her voice, however, the gap was filled up and the missing link supplied; the slight irony he divined in her attitude lost its advantage. He almost jumped at it to get there before her. "I met you years and years ago in Rome. I remember all about it." She confessed to disappointment—she had been so sure he didn't; and to prove how well he did he began to pour forth the particular recollections that popped up as he called for them. Her face and her voice, all at his service now, worked the miracle—the impression operating like the torch of a lamplighter who touches into flame, one by one, a long row of gas-jets. Marcher flattered himself the illumination was brilliant, yet he was really still more pleased on her showing him, with amusement, that in his haste to make everything right he had got most things rather wrong. It hadn't been at Rome—it had been at Naples; and it hadn't been eight years before—it had been more nearly ten. She hadn't been, either, with her uncle and aunt, but with her mother and her brother; in addition to which it was not with the Pembles *he* had been, but with the Boyers, coming down in their company from Rome—a point on which she insisted, a little to his confusion, and as to which she had her evidence in hand. The Boyers she had known, but didn't know the Pembles, though she had heard of them, and it was the people he was with who had made them acquainted. The incident of the thunderstorm that had raged round them with such violence as to drive them for refuge into an excavation—this incident had not occurred at the Palace of the Cæsars, but at Pompeii, on an occasion when they had been present there at an important find.

He accepted her amendments, he enjoyed her corrections, though the moral of them was, she pointed out, that he *really* didn't remember the least thing about her; and he only felt it as a drawback that when all was made strictly historic there didn't appear much of anything left. They lingered together still, she neglecting her office—for from the moment he was so clever she had no proper right to him—and both neglecting the house, just waiting as to see if a memory or two more wouldn't again breathe on them. It hadn't taken them many minutes, after all, to put down on the table, like the cards of a pack, those that constituted their respective hands; only what came out was that the pack was unfortunately not perfect—that the past, invoked, invited, encouraged, could give them, naturally, no more than it had. It had made them anciently meet—her at twenty, him at twenty-five, but nothing was so strange, they seemed to say to each other, as that, while so occupied, it hadn't done a little more for them. They looked at each other as with the feeling of an occasion missed; the present would have been so much better if the other, in the far distance, in the foreign land, hadn't been so stupidly meagre. There weren't apparently, all counted, more than a dozen little old things that had succeeded in coming to pass between them; trivialities of youth, simplicities of freshness, stupidities of ignorance, small possible germs, but too deeply buried—too deeply (didn't it seem?) to sprout after so many years. Marcher could only feel he ought to have rendered her some service—saved her from a capsized boat in the Bay or at least recovered her dressing-bag, filched from her cab in the streets of Naples by a lazzarone with a stiletto. Or it would have been nice if he could have been taken with fever all alone at his hotel, and she could have come to look after him, to write to his people, to drive him out in convalescence. *Then* they would be in possession of the something or other that their actual show seemed to lack. It yet somehow presented itself, this show, as too good to be spoiled; so that they were reduced for a few minutes more to wondering a little helplessly why—since they seemed to know a certain number of the same people—their reunion had been so long averted. They didn't use that name for it, but their delay from minute to minute to join the others was a kind of confession that they didn't quite want it to be a failure. Their attempted supposition of reasons for their not having met but showed how little they knew of each other. There came in fact a moment when Marcher felt a positive pang. It was vain to pretend she was an old friend, for all the communities were wanting, in spite of which it was an old friend that he saw she would have suited him. He had new ones enough—was surrounded with them for instance on the stage of the other house; as a new one he probably wouldn't have so much as noticed her. He would have liked to invent something, get her to make-believe with him that some passage of a romantic or critical kind *had* originally occurred. He was really almost reaching out in imagination—as against time—for something that would do, and saying to himself that if it didn't come this sketch of a fresh start would show for quite awkwardly bungled. They would separate, and now for no second or third chance. They would have tried and not succeeded. Then it was, just at the turn, as he afterwards made it out to himself, that, everything else failing, she herself decided to take up the case and, as it were, save the situation. He felt as soon as she spoke that she had been consciously keeping back what she said and hoping to get on without it; a scruple in her that immensely touched him when, by the end of three or four minutes more, he was able to measure it. What she brought out, at any rate, quite cleared the air and supplied the link—the link it was so odd he should frivolously have managed to lose.

"You know you told me something I've never forgotten and that again and again has made me think of you since; it was that tremendously hot day when we went to Sorrento, across the bay, for the breeze. What I allude to was what you said to me, on the way back, as we sat under the awning of the boat enjoying the cool. Have you forgotten?"

He had forgotten and was even more surprised than ashamed. But the great thing was that he saw in this no vulgar reminder of any "sweet" speech. The vanity of women had long memories, but she was making no claim on him of a compliment or a mistake. With another woman, a totally different one, he might have feared the recall possibly even some imbecile "offer." So, in having to say that he had indeed forgotten, he was conscious rather of a loss than of a gain; he already saw an interest in the matter of her mention. "I try to think—but I give it up. Yet I remember the Sorrento day."

"I'm not very sure you do," May Bartram after a moment said; "and I'm not very sure I ought to want you to. It's dreadful to bring a person back at any time to what he was ten years before. If you've lived away from it," she smiled, "so much the better."

"Ah if *you* haven't why should I?" he asked.

"Lived away, you mean, from what I myself was?"

"From what *I* was. I was of course an ass," Marcher went on; "but I would rather know from you just the sort of ass I was than—from the moment you have something in your mind—not know anything."

Still, however, she hesitated. "But if you've completely ceased to be that sort—?"

"Why I can then all the more bear to know. Besides, perhaps I haven't."

"Perhaps. Yet if you haven't," she added, "I should suppose you'd remember. Not indeed that *I* in the least connect with my impression the invidious name you use. If I had only thought you foolish," she explained, "the thing I speak of wouldn't so have remained with me. It was about yourself." She waited as if it might come to him; but as, only meeting her eyes in wonder, he gave no sign, she burnt her ships. "Has it ever happened?"

Then it was that, while he continued to stare, a light broke for him and the blood slowly came to his face, which began to burn with recognition. "Do you mean I told you—?" But he faltered, lest what came to him shouldn't be right, lest he should only give himself away.

"It was something about yourself that it was natural one shouldn't forget—that is if one remembered you at all. That's why I ask you," she smiled, "if the thing you then spoke of has ever come to pass?"

Oh then he saw, but he was lost in wonder and found himself embarrassed. This, he also saw, made her sorry for him, as if her allusion had been a mistake. It took him but a moment, however, to feel it hadn't been, much as it had been a surprise. After the first little shock of it her knowledge on the contrary began, even if rather strangely, to taste sweet to him. She was the only other person in the world then who would have it, and she had had it all these years, while the fact of his having so breathed his secret had unaccountably faded from him. No wonder they couldn't have met as if nothing had happened. "I judge," he finally said, "that I know what you mean. Only I had strangely enough lost any sense of having taken you so far into my confidence."

"Is it because you've taken so many others as well?"

"I've taken nobody. Not a creature since then."

"So that I'm the only person who knows?"

"The only person in the world."

"Well," she quickly replied, "I myself have never spoken. I've never, never repeated of you what you told me." She looked at him so that he perfectly believed her. Their eyes met over it in such a way that he was without a doubt. "And I never will."

She spoke with an earnestness that, as if almost excessive, put him at ease about her possible derision. Somehow the whole question was a new luxury to him—that is from the moment she was in possession. If she didn't take the sarcastic view she clearly took the sympathetic, and that was what he had had, in all the long time, from no one whomsoever. What he felt was that he couldn't at present have begun to tell her, and yet could profit perhaps exquisitely by the accident of having done so of old. "Please don't then. We're just right as it is."

"Oh I am," she laughed, "if you are!" To which she added: "Then you do still feel in the same way?"

It was impossible he shouldn't take to himself that she was really interested, though it all kept coming as perfect surprise. He had thought of himself so long as abominably alone, and lo he wasn't alone a bit. He hadn't been, it appeared, for an hour—since those moments on the Sorrento boat. It was *she* who had been, he seemed to see as he looked at her—she who had been made so by the graceless fact of his lapse of fidelity. To tell her what he had told her—what had it been but to ask something of her? something that she had given, in her charity, without his having, by a remembrance, by a return of the spirit, failing another encounter, so much as thanked her. What he had asked of her had been simply at first not to laugh at him. She had beautifully not done so for ten years, and she was not doing so now. So he had endless gratitude to make up. Only for that he must see just how he had figured to her. "What, exactly, was the account I gave—?"

"Of the way you did feel? Well, it was very simple. You said you had had from your earliest time, as the deepest thing within you, the sense of being kept for something rare and strange, possibly prodigious and terrible, that was sooner or later to happen to you, that you had in your bones the foreboding and the conviction of, and that would perhaps overwhelm you."

"Do you call that very simple?" John Marcher asked.

She thought a moment. "It was perhaps because I seemed, as you spoke, to understand it."

"You do understand it?" he eagerly asked.

Again she kept her kind eyes on him. "You still have the belief?"

"Oh!" he exclaimed helplessly. There was too much to say.

"Whatever it's to be," she clearly made out, "it hasn't yet come."

He shook his head in complete surrender now. "It hasn't yet come. Only, you know, it isn't anything I'm to *do*, achieve in the world, to be distinguished or admired for. I'm not such an ass as *that*. It would be much better, no doubt, if I were."

"It's to be something you're merely to suffer?"

"Well, say to wait for—to have to meet, to face, to see suddenly break out in my life; possibly destroying all further consciousness, possibly annihilating me; possibly, on the other hand, only altering everything, striking at the root of all my world and leaving me to the consequences, however they shape themselves."

She took this in, but the light in her eyes continued for him not to be that of mockery. "Isn't what you describe perhaps but the expectation—or at any rate the sense of danger, familiar to so many people—of falling in love?"

John Marcher wondered. "Did you ask me that before?"

"No—I wasn't so free-and-easy then. But it's what strikes me now."

"Of course," he said after a moment, "it strikes you. Of course it strikes *me*. Of course what's in store for me may be no more than that. The only thing is," he went on, "that I think if it had been that I should by this time know."

"Do you mean because you've *been* in love?" And then as he but looked at her in silence: "You've been in love, and it hasn't meant such a cataclysm, hasn't proved the great affair?"

"Here I am, you see. It hasn't been overwhelming."

"Then it hasn't been love," said May Bartram.

"Well, I at least thought it was. I took for that—I've taken it till now. It was agreeable, it was delightful, it was miserable," he explained. "But it wasn't strange. It wasn't what *my* affair's to be."

"You want something all to yourself—something that nobody else knows or *has* known?"

"It isn't a question of what I 'want'—God knows I don't want anything. It's only a question of the apprehension that haunts me— that I live with day by day."

He said this so lucidly and consistently that he could see it further impose itself. If she hadn't been interested before she'd have been interested now. "Is it a sense of coming violence?"

Evidently now too again he liked to talk of it. "I don't think of it as—when it does come—necessarily violent. I only think of it as natural and as of course above all unmistakeable. I think of it simply as *the* thing. *The* thing will of itself appear natural."

"Then how will it appear strange?"

Marcher bethought himself. "It won't—to *me*."

"To whom then?"

"Well," he replied, smiling at last, "say to you."

"Oh then I'm to be present?"

"Why you *are* present—since you know."

"I see." She turned it over. "But I mean at the catastrophe."

At this their lightness gave way to their gravity; it was as if the long look they exchanged held them together.

"It will only depend on yourself—if you'll watch with me."

"Are you afraid?" she asked.

"Don't leave me *now*," he went on.

"Are you afraid?" she repeated.

"Do you think me simply out of my mind?" he pursued instead of answering. "Do I merely strike you as a harmless lunatic?"

"No," said May Bartram. "I understand you. I believe you."

"You mean you feel how my obsession—poor old thing!—may correspond to some possible reality?"

"To some possible reality."

"Then you *will* watch with me?"

She hesitated, then for the third time put her question. "Are you afraid?"

"Did I tell you I was—at Naples?"

"No, you said nothing about it."

"Then I don't know. And I should *like* to know," said John Marcher. "You'll tell me yourself whether you think so. If you'll watch with me you'll see."

"Very good then." They had been moving by this time across the room, and at the door, before passing out, they paused as for the full wind-up of their understanding. "I'll watch with you," said May Bartram.

II

The fact that she "knew"—knew and yet neither chaffed him nor betrayed him—had in a short time begun to constitute between them a goodly bond, which became more marked when, within the year that followed their afternoon at Weatherend, the opportunities for meeting multiplied. The event that thus promoted these occasions was the death of the ancient lady her great-aunt, under whose wing, since losing her mother, she had to such an extent found shelter, and who, though but the widowed mother of the new successor to the property, had succeeded—thanks to a high tone and a high temper— in not forfeiting the supreme position at the great house. The deposition of this personage arrived but with her death, which, followed by many changes, made in particular a difference for the young woman in whom Marcher's expert attention had recognised from the first a dependent with a pride that might ache though it didn't bristle. Nothing for a long time had made him easier than the thought that the aching must have been soothed by Miss Bartram's now finding herself able to set up a small home in London. She had acquired property, to an amount that made that luxury just possible, under her aunt's extremely complicated will, and when the whole matter began to be straightened out, which indeed took time, she let him know the happy issue was at last in view. He had seen her again before that day, both because she had more than once accompanied the ancient lady to town and because he had paid another visit to the friends who so conveniently made of Weatherend one of the charms of their own hospitality. These friends had taken him back there; he had achieved there again with Miss Bartram some quiet detachment; and he had in London succeeded in persuading her to more than one brief absence from her aunt. They went together, on these latter occasions, to the National Gallery and the South Kensington Museum, where, among vivid reminders, they talked of Italy at large—not now attempting to recover, as at first, the taste of their youth and their ignorance. That recovery, the first day at Weatherend, had served its purpose well, had given them quite enough; so that they were, to Marcher's sense, no longer hovering about the head-waters of their stream, but had felt their boat pushed sharply off and down the current.

They were literally afloat together; for our gentleman this was marked, quite as marked as that the fortunate cause of it was just the buried treasure of her knowledge. He had with his own hands dug up this little hoard, brought to light—that is to within reach of the dim day constituted by their discretions and privacies—the objects of value the hiding-place of which he had, after putting it into the ground himself, so strangely, so long forgotten. The rare luck of his having again just stumbled on the spot made him indifferent to any other question; he would doubtless have devoted more time to the odd accident of his lapse of memory if he hadn't been moved to devote so much to the sweetness, the comfort, as he felt, for the future, that this accident itself had helped to keep fresh. It had never entered into his plan that any one should "know," and mainly for the reason that it wasn't in him to tell any one. That would have been impossible, for nothing but the amusement of a cold world would have waited on it. Since, however, a mysterious fate had opened his mouth betimes, in spite of him, he would count that a compensation and profit by it to the utmost. That the right person *should* know tempered the asperity of his secret more even than his shyness had permitted him to imagine; and May Bartram was clearly right, because—well, because there she was. Her knowledge simply settled it; he would have been sure enough by this time had she been wrong. There was that in his situation, no doubt, that disposed him too much to see her as a mere confidant, taking all her light for him from the fact—the fact only—of interest in his predicament; from her mercy, sympathy, seriousness, her consent not to regard him as the funniest of the funny. Aware, in fine, that her price for him was just in her giving him this constant sense of his being admirably spared, he was careful to remember that she had also a life of her own, with things that might happen to *her*, things that in friendship one should likewise take account of. Something fairly remarkable came to pass with him, for that matter, in this connexion—something represented by a certain passage of his consciousness, in the suddenest way, from one extreme to the other.

He had thought himself, so long as nobody knew, the most disinterested person in the world, carrying his concentrated burden, his perpetual suspense, ever so quietly, holding his tongue about it, giving others no glimpse of it nor of its effect upon his life, asking of them no allowance and only making on his side all those that were asked. He hadn't disturbed people with the queerness of their having to know a haunted man, though he had had moments of rather special temptation on hearing them say they were forsooth "unsettled." If they were as unsettled as he was—he who had never been settled for an hour in his life—they would know what it meant. Yet it wasn't, all the same, for him to make them, and he listened to them civilly enough. This was why he had such good—though possibly such rather colourless—manners; this was why, above all, he could regard himself, in a greedy world, as decently—as in fact perhaps even a little sublimely—unselfish. Our point is accordingly that he valued this character quite sufficiently to measure his present danger of letting it lapse, against which he promised himself to be much on his guard. He was quite ready, none the less, to be selfish just a little, since surely no more charming occasion for it had come to him. "Just a little," in a word, was just as much as Miss Bartram, taking one day with another, would let him. He never would be in the least coercive, and would keep well before him the lines on which consideration for her—the very highest—ought to proceed. He would thoroughly establish the heads under which her affairs, her requirements, her peculiarities—he went so far as to give them the latitude of that name—would come into their intercourse. All this naturally was a sign of how much he took the intercourse itself for granted. There was nothing more to be done about *that*. It simply existed; had sprung into being with her first penetrating question to him in the autumn light there at Weatherend. The real form it should have taken on the basis that stood out large was the form of their marrying. But the devil in this was that the very basis itself put marrying out of the question. His conviction, his apprehension, his obsession, in short, wasn't a privilege he could invite a woman to share; and that consequence of it was precisely what was the matter with him. Something or other lay in wait for him, amid the twists and the turns of the months and the years, like a crouching beast in the jungle. It signified little whether the crouching beast were destined to slay him or to be slain. The definite point was the inevitable spring of the creature; and the definite lesson from that was that a man of feeling didn't cause himself to be accompanied by a lady on a tiger-hunt. Such was the image under which he had ended by figuring his life.

They had at first, none the less, in the scattered hours spent together, made no allusion to that view of it; which was a sign he was handsomely alert to give that he didn't expect, that he in fact didn't care, always to be talking about it. Such a feature in one's outlook was really like a hump on one's back. The difference it made every minute of the day existed quite independently of discussion. One discussed of course *like* a hunchback, for there was always, if nothing else, the hunchback face. That remained, and she was watching him; but people watched best, as a general thing, in silence, so that such would be predominantly the manner of their vigil. Yet he didn't want, at the same time, to be tense and solemn; tense and solemn was what he imagined he too much showed for with other people. The thing to be, with the one person who knew, was easy and natural—to make the reference rather than be seeming to avoid it, to avoid it rather than be seeming to make it, and to keep it, in any case, familiar, facetious even, rather than pedantic and portentous. Some such consideration as the latter was doubtless in his mind for instance when he wrote pleasantly to Miss Bartram that perhaps the great thing he had so long felt as in the lap of the gods was no more than this circumstance, which touched him so nearly, of her acquiring a house in London. It was the first allusion they had yet again made, needing any other hitherto so little; but when she replied, after having given him the news, that she was by no means satisfied with such a trifle as the climax to so special a suspense, she almost set him wondering if she hadn't even a larger conception of singularity for him than he had for himself. He was at all events destined to become aware little by little, as time went by, that she was all the while looking at his life, judging it, measuring it, in the light of the thing she knew, which grew to be at last, with the consecration of the years, never mentioned between them save as "the real truth" about him. That had always been his own form of reference to it, but she adopted the form so quietly that, looking back at the end of a period, he knew there was no moment at which it was traceable that she had, as he might say, got inside his idea, or exchanged the attitude of beautifully indulging for that of still more beautifully believing him.

It was always open to him to accuse her of seeing him but as the most harmless of maniacs, and this, in the long run—since it covered so much ground—was his easiest description of their friendship. He had a screw loose for her, but she liked him in spite of it and was practically, against the rest of the world, his kind wise keeper, unremunerated but fairly amused and, in the absence of other near ties, not disreputably occupied. The rest of the world of course thought him queer, but she, she only, knew how, and above all why, queer; which was precisely what enabled her to dispose the concealing veil in the right folds. She took his gaiety from him—since it had to pass with them for gaiety—as she took everything else; but she certainly so far justified by her unerring touch his finer sense of the degree to which he had ended by convincing her. *She* at least never spoke of the secret of his life except as "the real truth about you," and she had in fact a wonderful way of making it seem, as such, the secret of her own life too. That was in fine how he so constantly felt her as allowing for him; he couldn't on the whole call it anything else. He allowed for himself, but she, exactly, allowed still more; partly because, better placed for a sight of the matter, she traced his unhappy perversion through reaches of its course into which he could scarce follow it. He knew how he felt, but, besides knowing that, she knew how he *looked* as well; he knew each of the things of importance he was insidiously kept from doing, but she could add up the amount they made, understand how much, with a lighter weight on his spirit, he might have done, and thereby establish how, clever as he was, he fell short. Above all she was in the secret of the difference between the forms he went through—those of his little office under Government, those of caring for his modest patrimony, for his library, for his garden in the country, for the people in London whose invitations he accepted and repaid—and the detachment that reigned beneath them and that made of all behaviour, all that could in the least be called behaviour, a long act of dissimulation. What it had come to was that he wore a mask painted with the social simper, out of the eye-holes of which there looked eyes of an expression not in the least matching the other features. This the stupid world, even after years, had never more than half-discovered. It was only May Bartram who had, and she achieved, by an art indescribable, the feat of at once—or perhaps it was only alternately—meeting the eyes from in front and mingling her own vision, as from over his shoulder, with their peep through the apertures.

So while they grew older together she did watch with him, and so she let this association give shape and colour to her own existence. Beneath *her* forms as well detachment had learned to sit, and behaviour had become for her, in the social sense, a false account of herself. There was but one account of her that would have been true all the while and that she could give straight to nobody, least of all to John Marcher. Her whole attitude was a virtual statement, but the perception of that only seemed called to take its place for him as one of the many things necessarily crowded out of his consciousness. If she had moreover, like himself, to make sacrifices to their real truth, it was to be granted that her compensation might have affected her as more prompt and more natural. They had long periods, in this London time, during which, when they were together, a stranger might have listened to them without in the least pricking up his ears; on the other hand the real truth was equally liable at any moment to rise to the surface, and the auditor would then have wondered indeed what they were talking about. They had from an early hour made up their mind that society was, luckily, unintelligent, and the margin allowed them by this had fairly become one of their commonplaces. Yet there were still moments when the situation turned almost fresh—usually under the effect of some expression drawn from herself. Her expressions doubtless repeated themselves, but her intervals were generous. "What saves us, you know, is that we answer so completely to so usual an appearance: that of the man and woman whose friendship has become such a daily habit—or almost—as to be at last indispensable." That for instance was a remark she had frequently enough had occasion to make, though she had given it at different times different developments. What we are especially concerned with is the turn it happened to take from her one afternoon when he had come to see her in honour of her birthday. This anniversary had fallen on a Sunday, at a season of thick fog and general outward gloom; but he had brought her his customary offering, having known her now long enough to have established a hundred small traditions. It was one of his proofs to himself, the present he made her on her birthday, that he hadn't sunk into real selfishness. It was mostly nothing more than a small trinket, but it was always fine of its kind, and he was regularly careful to pay for it more than he thought he could afford. "Our habit saves you at least, don't you see? because it makes you, after all, for the vulgar, indistinguishable from other men. What's the most inveterate mark of men in general? Why the capacity to spend endless time with dull women—to spend it I won't say without being bored, but without minding that they are, without being driven off at a tangent by it; which comes to the same thing. I'm your dull woman, a part of the daily bread for which you pray at church. That covers your tracks more than anything."

"And what covers yours?" asked Marcher, whom his dull woman could mostly to this extent amuse. "I see of course what you mean by your saving me, in this way and that, so far as other people are concerned—I've seen it all along. Only what is it that saves *you?* I often think, you know, of that."

She looked as if she sometimes thought of that too, but rather in a different way. "Where other people, you mean, are concerned?"

"Well, you're really so in with me, you know—as a sort of result of my being so in with yourself. I mean of my having such an immense regard for you, being so tremendously mindful of all you've done for me. I sometimes ask myself if it's quite fair. Fair I mean to have so involved and—since one may say it—interested you. I almost feel as if you hadn't really had time to do anything else."

"Anything else but be interested?" she asked. "Ah what else does one ever want to be? If I've been 'watching' with you, as we long ago agreed I was to do, watching's always in itself an absorption."

"Oh certainly," John Marcher said, "if you hadn't had your curiosity—! Only doesn't it sometimes come to you as time goes on that your curiosity isn't being particularly repaid?"

May Bartram had a pause. "Do you ask that, by any chance, because you feel at all that yours isn't? I mean because you have to wait so long."

Oh he understood what she meant! "For the thing to happen that never does happen? For the beast to jump out? No, I'm just where I was about it. It isn't a matter as to which I can *choose,* I can decide for a change. It isn't one as to which there *can* be a change. It's in the lap of the gods. One's in the hands of one's law—there one is. As to the form the law will take, the way it will operate, that's its own affair."

"Yes," Miss Bartram replied; "of course one's fate's coming, of course it *has* come in its own form and its own way, all the while. Only, you know, the form and the way in your case were to have been—well, something so exceptional and, as one may say, so particularly *your* own."

Something in this made him look at her with suspicion. "You say 'were to *have* been,' as if in your heart you had begun to doubt."

"Oh!" she vaguely protested.

"As if you believed," he went on, "that nothing will now take place."

She shook her head slowly but rather inscrutably. "You're far from my thought."

He continued to look at her. "What then is the matter with you?"

"Well," she said after another wait, "the matter with me is simply that I'm more sure than ever my curiosity, as you call it, will be but too well repaid."

They were frankly grave now; he had got up from his seat, had turned once more about the little drawing-room to which, year after year, he brought his inevitable topic; in which he had, as he might have said, tasted their intimate community with every sauce, where every object was as familiar to him as the things of his own house and the very carpets were worn with his fitful walk very much as the desks in old counting-houses are worn by the elbows of generations of clerks. The generations of his nervous moods had been at work there, and the place was the written history of his whole middle life. Under the impression of what his friend had just said he knew himself, for some reason, more aware of these things; which made him, after a moment, stop again before her. "Is it possibly that you've grown afraid?"

"Afraid?" He thought, as she repeated the word, that his question had made her, a little, change colour; so that, lest he should have touched on a truth, he explained very kindly: "You remember that that was what you asked *me* long ago—that first day at Weatherend."

"Oh yes, and you told me you didn't know—that I was to see for myself. We've said little about it since, even in so long a time."

"Precisely," Marcher interposed—"quite as if it were too delicate a matter for us to make free with. Quite as if we might find, on pressure, that I *am* afraid. For then," he said, "we shouldn't, should we? quite know what to do."

She had for the time no answer to this question. "There have been days when I thought you were. Only, of course," she added, "there have been days when we have thought almost anything."

"Everything. Oh!" Marcher softly groaned as with a gasp, half-spent, at the face, more uncovered just then than it had been for a long while, of the imagination always with them. It had always had its incalculable moments of glaring out, quite as with the very eyes of the very Beast, and, used as he was to them, they could still draw from him the tribute of a sigh that rose from the depths of his being. All they had thought, first and last, rolled over him; the past seemed to have been reduced to mere barren speculation. This in fact was what the place had just struck him as so full of—the simplification of everything but the state of suspense. That remained only by seeming to hang in the void surrounding it. Even his original fear, if fear it had been, had lost itself in the desert. "I judge, however," he continued, "that you see I'm not afraid now."

"What I see, as I make it out, is that you've achieved something almost unprecedented in the way of getting used to danger. Living with it so long and so closely you've lost your sense of it; you know it's there, but you're indifferent, and you cease even, as of old, to have to whistle in the dark. Considering what the danger is," May Bartram wound up, "I'm bound to say I don't think your attitude could well be surpassed."

John Marcher faintly smiled. "It's heroic?"

"Certainly—call it that."

It was what he would have liked indeed to call it. "I *am* then a man of courage?"

"That's what you were to show me."

He still, however, wondered. "But doesn't the man of courage know what he's afraid of—or *not* afraid of? I don't know *that,* you see. I don't focus it. I can't name it. I only know I'm exposed."

"Yes, but exposed—how shall I say?—so directly. So intimately. That's surely enough."

"Enough to make you feel then—as what we may call the end and the upshot of our watch—that I'm not afraid?"

"You're not afraid. But it isn't," she said, "the end of our watch. That is it isn't the end of yours. You've everything still to see."

"Then why haven't *you?*" he asked. He had had, all along, to-day, the sense of her keeping something back, and he still had it. As this was his first impression of that it quite made a date. The case was the more marked as she didn't at first answer; which in turn made him go on. "You know something I don't." Then his voice, for that of a man of courage, trembled a little. "You know what's to happen." Her silence, with the face she showed, was almost a confession—it made him sure. "You know, and you're afraid to tell me. It's so bad that you're afraid I'll find out."

All this might be true, for she did look as if, unexpectedly to her, he had crossed some mystic line that she had secretly drawn round her. Yet she might, after all, not have worried; and the real climax was that he himself, at all events, needn't. "You'll never find out."

III

It was all to have made, none the less, as I have said, a date; which came out in the fact that again and again, even after long intervals, other things that passed between them wore in relation to this hour but the character of recalls and results. Its immediate effect had been indeed rather to lighten insistence—almost to provoke a reaction; as if their topic had dropped by its own weight and as if moreover, for that matter, Marcher had been visited by one of his occasional warnings against egotism. He had kept up, he felt, and very decently on the whole, his consciousness of the importance of not being selfish, and it was true that he had never sinned in that direction without promptly enough trying to press the scales the other way. He often repaired his fault, the season permitting, by inviting his friend to accompany him to the opera; and it not infrequently thus happened that, to show he didn't wish her to have but one sort of food for her mind, he was the cause of her appearing there with him a dozen nights in the month. It even happened that, seeing her home at such times, he occasionally went in with her to finish, as he called it, the evening, and, the better to make his point, sat down to the frugal but always careful little supper that awaited his pleasure. His point was made, he thought, by his not eternally insisting with her on himself; made for instance, at such hours, when it befell that, her piano at hand and each of them familiar with it, they went over passages of the opera together. It chanced to be on one of these occasions, however, that he reminded her of her not having answered a certain question he had put to her during the talk that had taken place between them on her last birthday. "What is it that saves *you?*"— saved her, he meant, from that appearance of variation from the usual human type. If he had practically escaped remark, as she pretended, by doing, in the most important particular, what most men do—find the answer to life in patching up an alliance of a sort with a woman no better than himself—how had she escaped it, and how could the alliance, such as it was, since they must suppose it had been more or less noticed, have failed to make her rather positively talked about?

"I never said," May Bartram replied, "that it hadn't made me a good deal talked about."

"Ah well then you're not 'saved.' "

"It hasn't been a question for me. If you've had your woman I've had," she said, "my man."

"And you mean that makes you all right?"

Oh it was always as if there were so much to say! "I don't know why it shouldn't make me—humanly, which is what we're speaking of—as right as it makes you."

"I see," Marcher returned. " 'Humanly,' no doubt, as showing that you're living for something. Not, that is, just for me and my secret."

May Bartram smiled. "I don't pretend it exactly shows that I'm not living for you. It's my intimacy with you that's in question."

He laughed as he saw what she meant. "Yes, but since, as you say, I'm only, so far as people make out, ordinary, you're—aren't you?— no more than ordinary either. You help me to pass for a man like another. So if I *am,* as I understand you, you're not compromised. Is that it?"

She had another of her waits, but she spoke clearly enough. "That's it. It's all that concerns me—to help you to pass for a man like another."

He was careful to acknowledge the remark handsomely. "How kind, how beautiful, you are to me! How shall I ever repay you?"

She had her last grave pause, as if there might be a choice of ways. But she chose. "By going on as you are."

It was into this going on as he was that they relapsed, and really for so long a time that the day inevitably came for a further sounding of their depths. These depths, constantly bridged over by a structure firm enough in spite of its lightness and of its occasional oscillation in the somewhat vertiginous air, invited on occasion, in the interest of their nerves, a dropping of the plummet and a measurement of the abyss. A difference had been made moreover, once for all, by the fact that she had all the while not appeared to feel the need of rebutting his charge of an idea within her that she didn't dare to express—a charge uttered just before one of the fullest of their later discussions ended. It had come up for him then that she "knew" something and that what she knew was bad—too bad to tell him. When he had spoken of it as visibly so bad that she was afraid he might find it out, her reply had left the matter too equivocal to be let alone and yet, for Marcher's special sensibility, almost too formidable again to touch. He circled about it at a distance that alternately narrowed and widened and that still wasn't much affected by the consciousness in him that there was nothing she could "know," after all, any better than he did. She had no source of knowledge he hadn't equally—except of course that she might have finer nerves. That was what women had where they were interested; they made out things, where people were concerned, that the people often couldn't have made out for themselves. Their nerves, their sensibility, their imagination, were conductors and revealers, and the beauty of May Bartram was in particular that she had given herself so to his case. He felt in these days what, oddly enough, he had never felt before, the growth of a dread of losing her by some catastrophe—some catastrophe that yet wouldn't at all be *the* catastrophe: partly because she had almost of a sudden begun to strike him as more useful to him than ever yet, and partly by reason of an appearance of uncertainty in her health, coincident and equally new. It was characteristic of the inner detachment he had hitherto so successfully cultivated and to which our whole account of him is a reference, it was characteristic that his complications, such as they were, had never yet seemed so as at this crisis to thicken about him, even to the point of making him ask himself if he were, by any chance, of a truth, within sight or sound, within touch or reach, within the immediate jurisdiction, of the thing that waited.

When the day came, as come it had to, that his friend confessed to him her fear of a deep disorder in her blood, he felt somehow the shadow of a change and the chill of a shock. He immediately began to imagine aggravations and disasters, and above all to think of her peril as the direct menace for himself of personal privation. This indeed gave him one of those partial recoveries of equanimity that were agreeable to him—it showed him that what was still first in his mind was the loss she herself might suffer. "What if she should have to die before knowing, before seeing—?" It would have been brutal, in the early stages of her trouble, to put that question to her; but it had immediately sounded for him to his own concern, and the possibility was what most made him sorry for her. If she did "know," moreover, in the sense of her having had some—what should he think?—mystical irresistible light, this would make the matter not better, but worse, inasmuch as her original adoption of his own curiosity had quite become the basis of her life. She had been living to see what would *be* to be seen, and it would quite lacerate her to have to give up before the accomplishment of the vision. These reflexions, as I say, quickened his generosity; yet, make them as he might, he saw himself, with the lapse of the period, more and more disconcerted. It lapsed for him with a strange steady sweep, and the oddest oddity was that it gave him, independently of the threat of much inconvenience, almost the only positive surprise his career, if career it could be called, had yet offered him. She kept the house as she had never done; he had to go to her to see her—she could meet him nowhere now, though there was scarce a corner of their loved old London in which she hadn't in the past, at one time or another, done so; and he found her always seated by her fire in the deep old-fashioned chair she was less and less able to leave. He had been struck one day, after an absence exceeding his usual measure, with her suddenly looking much older to him than he had ever thought of her being; then he recognised that the suddenness was all on his side—he had just simply and suddenly noticed. She looked older because inevitably, after so many years, she *was* old, or almost; which was of course true in still greater measure of her companion. If she was old, or almost, John Marcher assuredly was, and yet it was her showing of the lesson, not his own, that brought the truth home to him. His surprises began here; when once they had begun they multiplied; they came rather with a rush: it was as if, in the oddest way in the world, they had all been kept back, sown in a thick cluster, for the late afternoon of life, the time at which for people in general the unexpected has died out.

One of them was that he should have caught himself—for he *had* so done—*really* wondering if the great accident would take form now as nothing more than his being condemned to see this charming

woman, this admirable friend, pass away from him. He had never so
unreservedly qualified her as while confronted in thought with such a
possibility; in spite of which there was small doubt for him that as an
answer to his long riddle the mere effacement of even so fine a feature
of his situation would be an abject anticlimax. It would represent, as
connected with his past attitude, a drop of dignity under the shadow
of which his existence could only become the most grotesque of
failures. He had been far from holding it a failure—long as he had
waited for the appearance that was to make it a success. He had
waited for quite another thing, not for such a thing as that. The
breath of his good faith came short, however, as he recognised how
long he had waited, or how long at least his companion had. That
she, at all events, might be recorded as having waited in vain—this
affected him sharply, and all the more because of his at first having
done little more than amuse himself with the idea. It grew more
grave as the gravity of her condition grew, and the state of mind it
produced in him, which he himself ended by watching as if it had
been some definite disfigurement of his outer person, may pass for
another of his surprises. This conjoined itself still with another, the
really stupefying consciousness of a question that he would have
allowed to shape itself had he dared. What did everything mean—
what, that is, did *she* mean, she and her vain waiting and her
probable death and the soundless admonition of it all—unless that,
at this time of day, it was simply, it was overwhelmingly too late? He
had never at any stage of his queer consciousness admitted the
whisper of such a correction; he had never till within these last few
months been so false to his conviction as not to hold that what was to
come to him had time, whether *he* struck himself as having it or not.
That at last, at last, he certainly hadn't it, to speak of, or had it but
in the scantiest measure—such, soon enough, as things went with
him, became the inference with which his old obsession had to
reckon: and this it was not helped to do by the more and more
confirmed appearance that the great vagueness casting the long
shadow in which he had lived had, to attest itself, almost no margin
left. Since it was in Time that he was to have met his fate, so it was in
Time that his fate was to have acted; and as he waked up to the sense
of no longer being young, which was exactly the sense of being stale,
just as that, in turn, was the sense of being weak, he waked up to
another matter beside. It all hung together; they were subject, he and
the great vagueness, to an equal and indivisible law. When the
possibilities themselves had accordingly turned stale, when the secret
of the gods had grown faint, had perhaps even quite evaporated,
that, and that only, was failure. It wouldn't have been failure to be
bankrupt, dishonoured, pilloried, hanged; it was failure not to be
anything. And so, in the dark valley into which his path had taken

its unlooked-for twist, he wondered not a little as he groped. He didn't care what awful crash might overtake him, with what ignominy or what monstrosity he might yet be associated—since he wasn't after all too utterly old to suffer—if it would only be decently proportionate to the posture he had kept, all his life, in the threatened presence of it. He had but one desire left—that he shouldn't have been "sold."

IV

Then it was that, one afternoon, while the spring of the year was young and new she met all in her own way his frankest betrayal of these alarms. He had gone in late to see her, but evening hadn't settled and she was presented to him in that long fresh light of waning April days which affects us often with a sadness sharper than the greyest hours of autumn. The week had been warm, the spring was supposed to have begun early, and May Bartram sat, for the first time in the year, without a fire; a fact that, to Marcher's sense, gave the scene of which she formed part a smooth and ultimate look, an air of knowing, in its immaculate order and cold meaningless cheer, that it would never see a fire again. Her own aspect—he could scarce have said why—intensified this note. Almost as white as wax, with the marks and signs in her face as numerous and as fine as if they had been etched by a needle, with soft white draperies relieved by a faded green scarf on the delicate tone of which the years had further refined, she was the picture of a serene and exquisite but impenetrable sphinx, whose head, or indeed all whose person, might have been powdered with silver. She was a sphinx, yet with her white petals and green fronds she might have been a lily too—only an artificial lily, wonderfully imitated and constantly kept, without dust or stain, though not exempt from a slight droop and a complexity of faint creases, under some clear glass bell. The perfection of household care, of high polish and finish, always reigned in her rooms, but they now looked most as if everything had been wound up, tucked in, put away, so that she might sit with folded hands and with nothing more to do. She was "out of it," to Marcher's vision; her work was over; she communicated with him as across some gulf or from some island of rest that she had already reached, and it made him feel strangely abandoned. Was it—or rather wasn't it—that if for so long she had been watching with him the answer to their question must have swum into her ken and taken on its name, so that her occupation was verily gone? He had as much as charged her with this in saying to her, many months before, that she even then knew something she was keeping from him. It was a point he had never since ventured to press, vaguely fearing as he did that it might become a difference, perhaps a disagreement, between them. He had in this later time turned nervous, which was what he in all the other years had never been; and the oddity was that his nervousness should have waited till he had begun to doubt, should have held off so long as he was sure. There was something, it seemed to him, that the wrong word would bring down on his head, something that would so at least ease off his tension. But he wanted not to speak the wrong word; that would make everything ugly. He wanted the knowledge he lacked to drop on him, if drop it could, by its own august weight. If she was to forsake him it was surely for her to take leave. This was why he didn't directly ask her again what she knew; but it was also why, approaching the matter from another side, he said to her in the course of his visit: "What do you regard as the very worst that at this time of day *can* happen to me?"

He had asked her that in the past often enough; they had, with the odd irregular rhythm of their intensities and avoidances, exchanged ideas about it and then had seen the ideas washed away by cool intervals, washed like figures traced in sea-sand. It had ever been the mark of their talk that the oldest allusions in it required but a little dismissal and reaction to come out again, sounding for the hour as new. She could thus at present meet his enquiry quite freshly and patiently. "Oh yes, I've repeatedly thought, only it always seemed to me of old that I couldn't quite make up my mind. I thought of dreadful things, between which it was difficult to choose; and so must you have done."

"Rather! I feel now as if I had scarce done anything else. I appear to myself to have spent my life in thinking of nothing *but* dreadful things. A great many of them I've at different times named to you, but there were others I couldn't name."

"They were too, too dreadful?"

"Too, too dreadful—some of them."

She looked at him a minute, and there came to him as he met it an inconsequent sense that her eyes, when one got their full clearness, were still as beautiful as they had been in youth, only beautiful with a strange cold light—a light that somehow was a part of the effect, if it wasn't rather a part of the cause, of the pale hard sweetness of the season and the hour. "And yet," she said at last, "there are horrors we've mentioned."

It deepened the strangeness to see her, as such a figure in such a picture, talk of "horrors," but she was to do in a few minutes something stranger yet—though even of this he was to take the full measure but afterwards—and the note of it already trembled. It was, for the matter of that, one of the signs that her eyes were having again the higher flicker of their prime. He had to admit, however, what she said. "Oh yes, there were times when we did go far." He caught himself in the act of speaking as if it all were over. Well, he wished it were; and the consummation depended for him clearly more and more on his friend.

But she had now a soft smile. "Oh far—!"

It was oddly ironic. "Do you mean you're prepared to go further?"

She was frail and ancient and charming as she continued to look at him, yet it was rather as if she had lost the thread. "Do you consider that we went far?"

"Why I thought it the point you were just making—that we *had* looked most things in the face."

"Including each other?" She still smiled. "But you're quite right. We've had together great imaginations, often great fears; but some of them have been unspoken."

"Then the worst—we haven't faced that. I *could* face it, I believe, if I knew what you think it. I feel," he explained, "as if I had lost my power to conceive such things." And he wondered if he looked as blank as he sounded. "It's spent."

"Then why do you assume," she asked, "that mine isn't?"

"Because you've given me signs to the contrary. It isn't a question for you of conceiving, imagining, comparing. It isn't a question now of choosing." At last he came out with it. "You know something I don't. You've shown me that before."

These last words had affected her, he made out in a moment, exceedingly, and she spoke with firmness. "I've shown you, my dear, nothing."

He shook his head. "You can't hide it."

"Oh, oh!" May Bartram sounded over what she couldn't hide. It was almost a smothered groan.

"You admitted it months ago, when I spoke of it to you as of something you were afraid I should find out. Your answer was that I couldn't, that I wouldn't, and I don't pretend I have. But you had something therefore in mind, and I now see how it must have been, how it still is, the possibility that, of all possibilities, has settled itself for you as the worst. This," he went on, "is why I appeal to you. I'm only afraid of ignorance to-day—I'm not afraid of knowledge." And then as for a while she said nothing: "What makes me sure is that I see in your face and feel here, in this air and amid these appearances, that you're out of it. You've done. You've had your experience. You leave me to my fate."

Well, she listened, motionless and white in her chair, as on a decision to be made, so that her manner was fairly an avowal, though still, with a small fine inner stiffness, an imperfect surrender. "It *would* be the worst," she finally let herself say. "I mean the thing I've never said."

It hushed him a moment. "More monstrous than all the monstrosities we've named?"

"More monstrous. Isn't that what you sufficiently express," she asked, "in calling it the worst?"

Marcher thought. "Assuredly—if you mean, as I do, something that includes all the loss and all the shame that are thinkable."

"It would if it *should* happen," said May Bartram. "What we're speaking of, remember, is only my idea."

"It's your belief," Marcher returned. "That's enough for me. I feel your beliefs are right. Therefore if, having this one, you give me no more light on it, you abandon me."

"No, no!" she repeated. "I'm with you—don't you see?—still." And as to make it more vivid to him she rose from her chair—a movement she seldom risked in these days—and showed herself, all draped and all soft, in her fairness and slimness. "I haven't forsaken you."

It was really, in its effort against weakness, a generous assurance, and had the success of the impulse not, happily, been great, it would have touched him to pain more than to pleasure. But the cold charm in her eyes had spread, as she hovered before him, to all the rest of her person, so that it was for the minute almost a recovery of youth. He couldn't pity her for that; he could only take her as she showed— as capable even yet of helping him. It was as if, at the same time, her light might at any instant go out; wherefore he must make the most of it. There passed before him with intensity the three or four things he wanted most to know; but the question that came of itself to his lips really covered the others. "Then tell me if I shall consciously suffer."

She promptly shook her head. "Never!"

It confirmed the authority he imputed to her, and it produced on him an extraordinary effect. "Well, what's better than that? Do you call that the worst?"

"You think nothing is better?" she asked.

She seemed to mean something so special that he again sharply wondered, though still with the dawn of a prospect of relief. "Why not, if one doesn't *know?*" After which, as their eyes, over his question, met in a silence, the dawn deepened and something to his purpose came prodigiously out of her very face. His own, as he took it in, suddenly flushed to the forehead, and he gasped with the force of a perception to which, on the instant, everything fitted. The sound of his gasp filled the air; then he became articulate. "I see—if I don't suffer!"

In her own look, however, was doubt. "You see what?"

"Why what you mean—what you've always meant."

She again shook her head. "What I mean isn't what I've always meant. It's different."

"It's something new?"

She hung back from it a little. "Something new. It's not what you think. I see what you think."

His divination drew breath then; only her correction might be wrong. "It isn't that I *am* a blockhead?" he asked between faintness and grimness. "It isn't that it's all a mistake?"

"A mistake?" she pityingly echoed. *That* possibility, for her, he saw, would be monstrous; and if she guaranteed him the immunity from pain it would accordingly not be what she had in mind. "Oh no," she declared; "it's nothing of that sort. You've been right."

Yet he couldn't help asking himself if she weren't, thus pressed, speaking but to save him. It seemed to him he should be most in a hole if his history should prove all a platitude. "Are you telling me the truth, so that I shan't have been a bigger idiot than I can bear to know? I *haven't* lived with a vain imagination, in the most besotted illusion? I haven't waited but to see the door shut in my face?"

She shook her head again. "However the case stands *that* isn't the truth. Whatever the reality, it *is* a reality. The door isn't shut. The door's open," said May Bartram.

"Then something's to come?"

She waited once again, always with her cold sweet eyes on him. "It's never too late." She had, with her gliding step, diminished the distance between them, and she stood nearer to him, close to him, a minute, as if still charged with the unspoken. Her movement might have been for some finer emphasis of what she was at once hesitating and deciding to say. He had been standing by the chimney-piece, fireless and sparely adorned, a small perfect old French clock and two morsels of rosy Dresden constituting all its furniture; and her hand grasped the shelf while she kept him waiting, grasped it a little as for support and encouragement. She only kept him waiting, however; that is he only waited. It had become suddenly, from her movement and attitude, beautiful and vivid to him that she had something more to give him; her wasted face delicately shone with it—it glittered almost as with the white lustre of silver in her expression. She was right, incontestably, for what he saw in her face was the truth, and strangely, without consequence, while their talk of it as dreadful was still in the air, she appeared to present it as inordinately soft. This, prompting bewilderment, made him but gape the more gratefully for her revelation, so that they continued for some minutes silent, her face shining at him, her contact imponderably pressing, and his stare all kind but all expectant. The end, none the less, was that what he had expected failed to come to him. Something else took place instead, which seemed to consist at first in the mere closing of her eyes. She gave way at the same instant to a slow fine shudder, and though he remained staring—though he stared in fact but the harder

—turned off and regained her chair. It was the end of what she had been intending, but it left him thinking only of that.

"Well, you don't say—?"

She had touched in her passage a bell near the chimney and had sunk back strangely pale. "I'm afraid I'm too ill."

"Too ill to tell me?" It sprang up sharp to him, and almost to his lips, the fear she might die without giving him light. He checked himself in time from so expressing his question, but she answered as if she had heard the words.

"Don't you know—now?"

" 'Now'—?" She had spoken as if some difference had been made within the moment. But her maid, quickly obedient to her bell, was already with them. "I know nothing." And he was afterwards to say to himself that he must have spoken with odious impatience, such an impatience as to show that, supremely disconcerted, he washed his hands of the whole question.

"Oh!" said May Bartram.

"Are you in pain?" he asked as the woman went to her.

"No," said May Bartram.

Her maid, who had put an arm round her as if to take her to her room, fixed on him eyes that appealingly contradicted her; in spite of which, however, he showed once more his mystification, "What then has happened?"

She was once more, with her companion's help, on her feet, and feeling withdrawal imposed on him, he had blankly found his hat and gloves and had reached the door. Yet he waited for her answer. "What *was* to," she said.

V

He came back the next day, but she was then unable to see him, and as it was literally the first time this had occurred in the long stretch of their acquaintance he turned away, defeated and sore, almost angry—or feeling at least that such a break in their custom was really the beginning of the end—and wandered alone with his thoughts, especially with the one he was least able to keep down. She was dying and he would lose her; she was dying and life would end. He stopped in the Park, into which he had passed, and stared before him at his recurrent doubt. Away from her the doubt pressed again; in her presence he had believed her, but as he felt his forlornness he threw himself into the explanation that, nearest at hand, had most of a miserable warmth for him and least of a cold torment. She had deceived him to save him—to put him off with something in which he should be able to rest. What could the thing that was to happen to him be, after all, but just this thing that had begun to happen? Her dying, her death, his consequent solitude—*that* was what he had figured as the Beast in the Jungle, that was what had been in the lap of the gods. He had had her word for it as he left her—what else on earth could she have meant? It wasn't a thing of a monstrous order; not a fate rare and distinguished; not a stroke of fortune that overwhelmed and immortalised; it had only the stamp of the common doom. But poor Marcher at this hour judged the common doom sufficient. It would serve his turn, and even as the connsummation of infinite waiting he would bend his pride to accept it. He sat down on a bench in the twilight. He hadn't been a fool. Something had *been*, as she had said, to come. Before he rose indeed it had quite struck him that the final fact really matched with the long avenue through which he had to reach it. As sharing his suspense and as giving herself all, giving her life, to bring it to an end, she had come with him every step of the way. He had lived by her aid, and to leave her behind would be cruelly, damnably to miss her. What could be more overwhelming than that?

Well, he was to know within the week, for though she kept him a while at bay, left him restless and wretched during a series of days on each of which he asked about her only again to have to turn away, she ended his trial by receiving him where she had always received him. Yet she had been brought out at some hazard into the presence of so many of the things that were, consciously, vainly, half their past, and there was scant service left in the gentleness of her mere desire, all too visible, to check his obsession and wind up his long trouble. That was clearly what she wanted, the one thing more for her own peace while she could still put out her hand. He was so affected by her state that, once seated by her chair, he was moved to let everything go; it was she herself therefore who brought him back, took up again, before she dismissed him, her last word of the other time. She showed how she wished to leave their business in order. "I'm not sure you understood. You've nothing to wait for more. It *has* come."

Oh how he looked at her! "Really?"

"Really."

"The thing that, as you said, *was* to?"

"The thing that we began in our youth to watch for."

Face to face with her once more he believed her; it was a claim to which he had so abjectly little to oppose. "You mean that it has come as a positive definite occurrence, with a name and a date?"

"Positive. Definite. I don't know about the 'name,' but oh with a date!"

He found himself again too helplessly at sea. "But come in the night—come and passed me by?"

May Bartram had her strange faint smile. "Oh no, it hasn't passed you by!"

"But if I haven't been aware of it and it hasn't touched me—?"

"Ah your not being aware of it"—and she seemed to hesitate an instant to deal with this—"your not being aware of it is the strangeness *in* the strangeness. It's the wonder *of* the wonder." She spoke as with the softness almost of a sick child, yet now at last, at the end of all, with the perfect straightness of a sibyl. She visibly knew that she knew, and the effect on him was of something co-ordinate, in its high character, with the law that had ruled him. It was the true voice of the law; so on her lips would the law itself have sounded. "It *has* touched you," she went on. "It has done its office. It has made you all its own."

"So utterly without my knowing it?"

"So utterly without your knowing it." His hand, as he leaned to her, was on the arm of her chair, and, dimly smiling always now, she placed her own on it. "It's enough if *I* know it."

"Oh!" he confusedly breathed, as she herself of late so often had done.

"What I long ago said is true. You'll never know now, and I think you ought to be content. You've *had* it," said May Bartram.

"But had what?"

"Why what was to have marked you out. The proof of your law. It has acted. I'm too glad," she then bravely added, "to have been able to see what it's *not*."

He continued to attach his eyes to her, and with the sense that it was all beyond him, and that *she* was too, he would still have sharply challenged her hadn't he so felt it an abuse of her weakness to do more than take devoutly what she gave him, take it hushed as to a revelation. If he did speak, it was out of the foreknowledge of his loneliness to come. "If you're glad of what it's 'not' it might then have been worse?"

She turned her eyes away, she looked straight before her; with which after a moment: "Well, you know our fears."

He wondered. "It's something then we never feared?"

On this slowly she turned to him. "Did we ever dream, with all our dreams, that we should sit and talk of it thus?"

He tried for a little to make out that they had; but it was as if their dreams, numberless enough, were in solution in some thick cold mist through which thought lost itself. "It might have been that we couldn't talk?"

"Well"—she did her best for him—"not from this side. This, you see," she said, "is the *other* side."

"I think," poor Marcher returned, "that all sides are the same to me." Then, however, as she gently shook her head in correction: "We mightn't, as it were, have got across—?"

"To where we are—no. We're *here*"—she made her weak emphasis.

"And much good does it do us!" was her friend's frank comment.

"It does us the good it can. It does us the good that *it* isn't here. It's past. It's behind," said May Bartram. "Before—" but her voice dropped.

He had got up, not to tire her, but it was hard to combat his yearning. She after all told him nothing but that his light had failed—which he knew well enough without her. "Before—?" he blankly echoed.

"Before, you see, it was always to *come*. That kept it present."

"Oh I don't care what comes now! Besides," Marcher added, "it seems to me I liked it better present, as you say, than I can like it absent with *your* absence."

"Oh mine!"—and her pale hands made light of it.

"With the absence of everything." He had a dreadful sense of standing there before her for—so far as anything but this proved, this bottomless drop was concerned—the last time of their life. It rested on him with a weight he felt he could scarce bear, and this weight it apparently was that still pressed out what remained in him of speakable protest. "I believe you; but I can't begin to pretend I understand. *Nothing*, for me, is past; nothing *will* pass till I pass myself, which I pray my stars may be as soon as possible. Say, however," he added, "that I've eaten my cake, as you contend, to the last crumb—how can the thing I've never felt at all be the thing I was marked out to feel?"

She met him perhaps less directly, but she met him unperturbed. "You take your 'feelings' for granted. You were to suffer your fate. That was not necessarily to know it."

"How in the world—when what is such knowledge but suffering?"

She looked up at him a while in silence. "No—you don't understand."

"I suffer," said John Marcher.

"Don't, don't!"

"How can I help at least *that*?"

"*Don't!*" May Bartram repeated.

She spoke it in a tone so special, in spite of her weakness, that he stared an instant—stared as if some light, hitherto hidden, had shimmered across his vision. Darkness again closed over it, but the gleam had already become for him an idea. "Because I haven't the right—?"

"Don't *know*—when you needn't," she mercifully urged. "You needn't—for we shouldn't."

"Shouldn't?" If he could but know what she meant!

"No—it's too much."

"Too much?" he still asked but, with a mystification that was the next moment of a sudden to give way. Her words, if they meant something, affected him in this light—the light also of her wasted face—as meaning *all,* and the sense of what knowledge had been for herself came over him with a rush which broke through into a question. "Is it of that then you're dying?"

She but watched him, gravely at first, as to see, with this, where he was, and she might have seen something or feared something that moved her sympathy. "I would live for you still—if I could." Her eyes closed for a little, as if, withdrawn into herself, she were for a last time trying. "But I can't!" she said as she raised them again to take leave of him.

She couldn't indeed, as but too promptly and sharply appeared, and he had no vision of her after this that was anything but darkness and doom. They had parted for ever in that strange talk; access to her chamber of pain, rigidly guarded, was almost wholly forbidden him; he was feeling now moreover, in the face of doctors, nurses, the two or three relatives attracted doubtless by the presumption of what she had to "leave," how few were the rights, as they were called in such cases, that he had to put forward, and how odd it might even seem that their intimacy shouldn't have given him more of them. The stupidest fourth cousin had more, even though she had been nothing in such a person's life. She had been a feature of features in *his,* for what else was it to have been so indispensable? Strange beyond saying were the ways of existence, baffling for him the anomaly of his lack, as he felt it to be, of producible claim. A woman might have been, as it were, everything to him, and it might yet present him in no connexion that any one seemed held to recognise. If this was the case in these closing weeks it was the case more sharply on the occasion of the last offices rendered, in the great grey London cemetery, to what had been mortal, to what had been precious, in his friend. The concourse at her grave was not numerous, but he saw himself treated as scarce more nearly concerned with it than if there had been a thousand others. He was in short from this moment face to face with the fact that he was to profit extra-ordinarily little by the interest May Bartram had taken in him. He couldn't quite have said what he expected, but he hadn't surely expected this approach to a double privation. Not only had her interest failed him, but he seemed to feel himself unattended—and for a reason he couldn't seize—by the distinction, the dignity, the propriety, if nothing else, of the man markedly bereaved. It was as if in the view of society he had not *been* markedly bereaved, as if there still failed some sign or proof of it, and as if none the less his character could never be affirmed nor the deficiency ever made up. There were moments as the weeks went by when he would have liked, by some almost aggressive act, to take his stand on the intimacy of his loss, in order that it *might* be questioned and his retort, to the relief of his spirit, so recorded; but the moments of an irritation more helpless followed fast on these, the moments during which, turning things over with a good conscience but with a bare horizon, he found himself wondering if he oughtn't to have begun, so to speak, further back.

He found himself wondering indeed at many things, and this last speculation had others to keep it company. What could he have done, after all, in her lifetime, without giving them both, as it were, away? He couldn't have made known she was watching him, for that would have published the superstition of the Beast. This was what closed his mouth now—now that the Jungle had been threshed to vacancy and that the Beast had stolen away. It sounded too foolish and too flat; the difference for him in this particular, the extinction in his life of the element of suspense, was such as in fact to surprise him. He could scarce have said what the effect resembled; the abrupt cessation, the positive prohibition, of music perhaps, more than anything else, in some place all adjusted and all accustomed to sonority and to attention. If he could at any rate have conceived lifting the veil from his image at some moment of the past (what had he done, after all, if not lift it to *her?*) so to do this to-day, to talk to people at large of the Jungle cleared and confide to them that he now felt it as safe, would have been not only to see them listen as to a goodwife's tale, but really to hear himself tell one. What it presently came to in truth was that poor Marcher waded through his beaten grass, where no life stirred, where no breath sounded, where no evil eye seemed to gleam from a possible lair, very much as if vaguely looking for the Beast, and still more as if acutely missing it. He walked about in an existence that had grown strangely more spacious, and, stopping fitfully in places where the undergrowth of life struck him as closer, asked himself yearningly, wondered secretly and sorely, if it would have lurked here or there. It would have at all events *sprung;* what was at least complete was his belief in the truth itself of the assurance given him. The change from his old sense to his new was absolute and final: what was to happen *had* so absolutely and finally happened that he was as little able to know a fear for his future as to know a hope; so absent in short was any question of anything still to come. He was to live entirely with the other question, that of his unidentified past, that of his having to see his fortune impenetrably muffled and masked.

The torment of this vision became then his occupation; he couldn't perhaps have consented to live but for the possibility of guessing. She had told him, his friend, not to guess; she had forbidden him, so far as he might, to know, and she had even in a sort denied the power in him to learn: which were so many things, precisely, to deprive him of rest. It wasn't that he wanted, he argued for fairness, that anything past and done should repeat itself; it was only that he shouldn't, as an anticlimax, have been taken sleeping so sound as not to be able to win back by an effort of thought the lost stuff of consciousness. He declared to himself at moments that he would either win it back or have done with consciousness for ever; he made this idea his one motive in fine, made it so much his passion that none other, to compare with it, seemed ever to have touched him. The lost stuff of consciousness became thus for him as a strayed or stolen child to an unappeasable father; he hunted it up and down very much as if he were knocking at doors and enquiring of the police. This was the spirit in which, inevitably, he set himself to travel; he started on a journey that was to be as long as he could make it; it danced before him that, as the other side of the globe couldn't possibly have less to say to him, it might, by a possibility of suggestion, have more. Before he quitted London, however, he made a pilgrimage to May Bartram's grave, took his way to it through the endless avenues of the grim suburban metropolis, sought it out in the wilderness of tombs, and, though he had come but for the renewal of the act of farewell, found himself, when he had at last stood by it, beguiled into long intensities. He stood for an hour, powerless to turn away and yet powerless to penetrate the darkness of death; fixing with his eyes her inscribed name and date, beating his forehead against the fact of the secret they kept, drawing his breath, while he waited, as if some sense would in pity of him rise from the stones. He kneeled on the stones, however, in vain; they kept what they concealed; and if the face of the tomb did become a face for him it was because her two names became a pair of eyes that didn't know him. He gave them a last long look, but no palest light broke.

VI

He stayed away, after this, for a year; he visited the depths of Asia, spending himself on scenes of romantic interest, of superlative sanctity; but what was present to him everywhere was that for a man who had known what *he* had known the world was vulgar and vain. The state of mind in which he had lived for so many years shone out to him, in reflexion, as a light that coloured and refined, a light beside which the glow of the East was garish cheap and thin. The terrible truth was that he had lost—with everything else—a distinction as well; the things he saw couldn't help being common when he had become common to look at them. He was simply now one of them himself—he was in the dust, without a peg for the sense of difference; and there were hours when, before the temples of gods and the sepulchres of kings, his spirit turned for nobleness of association to the barely discriminated slab in the London suburb. That had become for him, and more intensely with time and distance, his one witness of a past glory. It was all that was left to him for proof or pride, yet the past glories of Pharaohs were nothing to him as he thought of it. Small wonder then that he came back to it on the morrow of his return. He was drawn there this time as irresistibly as the other, yet with a confidence, almost, that was doubtless the effect of the many months that had elapsed. He had lived, in spite of himself, into his change of feeling, and in wandering over the earth had wandered, as might be said, from the circumference to the centre of his desert. He had settled to his safety and accepted perforce his extinction; figuring to himself, with some colour, in the likeness of certain little old men he remembered to have seen, of whom, all meagre and wizened as they might look, it was related that they had in their time fought twenty duels or been loved by ten princesses. They indeed had been wondrous for others while he was but wondrous for himself; which, however, was exactly the cause of his haste to renew the wonder by getting back, as he might put it, into his own presence. That had quickened his steps and checked his delay. If his visit was prompt it was because he had been separated so long from the part of himself that alone he now valued.

It's accordingly not false to say that he reached his goal with a certain elation and stood there again with a certain assurance. The creature beneath the sod *knew* of his rare experience, so that, strangely now, the place had lost for him its mere blankness of expression. It met him in mildness—not, as before, in mockery; it wore for him the air of conscious greeting that we find, after absence, in things that have closely belonged to us and which seem to confess of themselves to the connexion. The plot of ground, the graven tablet, the tended flowers affected him so as belonging to him that he resembled for the hour a contented landlord reviewing a piece of property. Whatever had happened—well, had happened. He had not come back this time with the vanity of that question, his former worrying "What, *what?*" now practically so spent. Yet he would none the less never again so cut himself off from the spot; he would come back to it every month, for if he did nothing else by its aid he at least held up his head. It thus grew for him, in the oddest way, a positive resource; he carried out his idea of periodical returns, which took their place at last among the most inveterate of his habits. What it all amounted to, oddly enough, was that in his finally so simplified world this garden of death gave him the few square feet of earth on which he could still most live. It was as if, being nothing anywhere else for any one, nothing even for himself, he were just everything here, and if not for a crowd of witnesses or indeed for any witness but John Marcher, then by clear right of the register that he could scan like an open page. The open page was the tomb of his friend, and *there* were the facts of the past, there the truth of his life, there the backward reaches in which he could lose himself. He did this from time to time with such effect that he seemed to wander through the old years with his hand in the arm of a companion who was, in the most extraordinary manner, his other, his younger self; and to wander, which was more extraordinary yet, round and round a third presence—not wandering she, but stationary, still, whose eyes, turning with his revolution, never ceased to follow him, and whose seat was his point, so to speak, of orientation. Thus in short he settled to live—feeding all on the sense that he once *had* lived, and dependent on it not alone for a support but for an identity.

It sufficed him in its way for months and the year elapsed; it would doubtless even have carried him further but for an accident, superficially slight, which moved him, quite in another direction, with a force beyond any of his impressions of Egypt or of India. It was a thing of the merest chance—the turn, as he afterwards felt, of a hair, though he was indeed to live to believe that if light hadn't come to him in this particular fashion it would still have come in another. He was to live to believe this, I say, though he was not to live, I may not less definitely mention, to do much else. We allow him at any rate the benefit of the conviction, struggling up for him at the end, that, whatever might have happened or not happened, he would have come round of himself to the light. The incident of an autumn day had put the match to the train laid from of old by his misery. With the light before him he knew that even of late his ache had only been smothered. It was strangely drugged, but it throbbed; at the touch it began to bleed. And the touch, in the event, was the face of a fellow mortal. This face, one grey afternoon when the leaves were thick in the alleys, looked into Marcher's own, at the cemetery, with an expression like the cut of a blade. He felt it, that is, so deep down that he winced at the steady thrust. The person who so mutely assaulted him was a figure he had noticed, on reaching his own goal, absorbed by a grave a short distance away, a grave apparently fresh, so that the emotion of the visitor would probably match it for frankness. This fact alone forbade further attention, though during the time he stayed he remained vaguely conscious of his neighbour, a middle-aged man apparently, in mourning, whose bowed back, among the clustered monuments and mortuary yews, was constantly presented. Marcher's theory that these were elements in contact with which he himself revived, had suffered, on this occasion, it may be granted, a marked, an excessive check. The autumn day was dire for him as none had recently been, and he rested with a heaviness he had not yet known on the low stone table that bore May Bartram's name. He rested without power to move, as if some spring in him, some spell vouchsafed, had suddenly been broken for ever. If he could have done that moment as he wanted he would simply have stretched himself on the slab that was ready to take him, treating it as a place prepared to receive his last sleep. What in all the wide world had he now to keep awake for? He stared before him with the question, and it was then that, as one of the cemetery walks passed near him, he caught the shock of the face.

His neighbour at the other grave had withdrawn, as he himself, with force enough in him, would have done by now, and was advancing along the path on his way to one of the gates. This brought him close, and his pace was slow, so that—and all the more as there was a kind of hunger in his look—the two men were for a minute directly confronted. Marcher knew him at once for one of the deeply stricken—a perception so sharp that nothing else in the picture comparatively lived, neither his dress, his age, nor his presumable character and class; nothing lived but the deep ravage of the features he showed. He *showed* them—that was the point; he was moved, as he passed, by some impulse that was either a signal for sympathy or, more possibly, a challenge to an opposed sorrow. He might already have been aware of our friend, might at some previous hour have noticed in him the smooth habit of the scene, with which the state of his own senses so scantly consorted, and might thereby have been stirred as by an overt discord. What Marcher was at all events conscious of was in the first place that the image of scarred passion presented to him was conscious too—of something that profaned the air; and in the second that, roused, startled, shocked, he was yet the next moment looking after it, as it went, with envy. The most extraordinary thing that had happened to him—though he had given that name to other matters as well—took place, after his immediate vague stare, as a consequence of this impression. The stranger passed, but the raw glare of his grief remained, making our friend wonder in pity what wrong, what wound it expressed, what injury not to be healed. What had the man *had,* to make him by the loss of it so bleed and yet live?

Something—and this reached him with a pang—that *he,* John Marcher, hadn't; the proof of which was precisely John Marcher's arid end. No passion had ever touched him, for this was what passion meant; he had survived and maundered and pined, but where had been *his* deep ravage? The extraordinary thing we speak of was the sudden rush of the result of this question. The sight that had just met his eyes named to him, as in letters of quick flame, something he had utterly, insanely missed, and what he had missed made these things a train of fire, made them mark themselves in an anguish of inward throbs. He had seen *outside* of his life, not learned it within, the way a woman was mourned when she had been loved for herself: such was the force of his conviction of the meaning of the stranger's face, which still flared for him as a smoky torch. It hadn't come to him, the knowledge, on the wings of experience; it had brushed him, jostled him, upset him, with the disrespect of chance, the insolence of accident. Now that the illumination had begun, however, it blazed to the zenith, and what he presently stood there gazing at was the rounded void of his life. He gazed, he drew breath, in vain; he turned in his dismay, and, turning, he had before him in sharper incision than ever the open page of his story. The name on the tablet smote him as the passage of his neighbour had done, and what it said to him, full in the face, was that *she* was what he had missed. This was the awful thought, the answer to all the past, the vision at the dread clearness of which he grew as cold as the stone beneath him. Everything fell together, confessed, explained, overwhelmed; leaving him most of all stupefied at the blindness he had cherished. The fate he had been marked for he had met with a vengeance—he had emptied the cup to the lees; he had been the man of his time, *the* man, to whom nothing on earth was to have happened. That was the rare stroke—that was his visitation. So he saw it, as we say, in pale horror, while the pieces fitted and fitted. So *she* had seen it while he didn't, and so she served at this hour to drive the truth home. It was the truth, vivid and monstrous, that all the while he had waited the wait was itself his portion. This the companion of his vigil had at a given moment made out, and she had then offered him the chance to baffle his doom. One's doom, however, was never baffled, and on the day she told him his own had come down she had seen him but stupidly stare at the escape she offered him.

The escape would have been to love her; then, *then* he would have lived. *She* had lived—who could say now with what passion?—since she had loved him for himself; whereas he had never thought of her (ah how it hugely glared at him!) but in the chill of his egotism and the light of her use. Her spoken words came back to him—the chain stretched and stretched. The Beast had lurked indeed, and the Beast, at its hour, had sprung; it had sprung in that twilight of the cold April when, pale, ill, wasted, but all beautiful, and perhaps even then recoverable, she had risen from her chair to stand before him and let him imaginably guess. It had sprung as he didn't guess; it had sprung as she hopelessly turned from him, and the mark, by the time he left her, had fallen where it *was* to fall. He had justified his fear and achieved his fate; he had failed, with the last exactitude, of all he was to fail of; and a moan now rose to his lips as he remembered she had prayed he mightn't know. This horror of waking—*this* was knowledge, knowledge under the breath of which the very tears in his eyes seemed to freeze. Through them, none the less, he tried to fix it and hold it; he kept it there before him so that he might feel the pain. That at least, belated and bitter, had something of the taste of life. But the bitterness suddenly sickened him, and it was as if, horribly, he saw, in the truth, in the cruelty of his image, what had been appointed and done. He saw the Jungle of his life and saw the lurking Beast; then, while he looked, perceived it, as by a stir of the air, rise, huge and hideous, for the leap that was to settle him. His eyes darkened—it was close; and, instinctively turning, in his hallucination, to avoid it, he flung himself, face down, on the tomb.

JOSEPH CONRAD

(1857-1924)

Conrad, one of the masters of modern British fiction, grew up without a word of English. He was born Josef Teodor Konrad Nalecz Korzeniowski, the son of a Polish patriot, who was sent by the Russians, the masters of Poland, into bitter exile north of Moscow. There, Conrad's mother died; then, when the boy was eleven, his father died as well. Brought up largely by a strict, aristocratic maternal uncle, he left home for adventure when he was seventeen. He found it: as a sailor in Marseilles, France, he was involved in revolution and gun running; at times he fell into despair (it seems likely he attempted suicide, though he claimed to have been wounded in a duel); he alternated between empty inactivity and passionate energy. When he was twenty-two, he joined the British navy and in eight years had his master's papers, in ten his first command as a merchant seaman.

Unable to obtain a second command, Conrad accepted a post as steamboat captain on the Congo River, a place that had haunted his imagination since he was a boy. He returned to England broken in health and spirit, nauseated by the government-sanctioned murder and theft that he had seen in Africa. Later he described the Congo adventures in *The Heart of Darkness*.

At sea he began to write: stories of adventure, stories of challenge. He used the experiences of his life as a seaman to understand the human heart in conflict with itself, to understand the longing of human beings to match up to the demands of their own dreams. After his trip to the Congo, he wrote intensely, and, in 1892, showed the manuscript of *Almayer's Folly* to a passenger aboard the *Torrens*, of which he was first mate. The passenger was John Galsworthy, well-known English novelist, who encouraged him. In 1893 he settled in

England, married soon after, and became a professional writer. In 1898 he met Ford Madox Ford, novelist and man of letters, who collaborated with Conrad, taught him much about his craft, and became his close friend. During the next few years Conrad wrote *The Heart of Darkness, Lord Jim, Nostromo, The Secret Sharer*—most of his best work, though it was not until after Ford and Conrad had quarreled and grown apart that *Chance* brought fame to Conrad in 1913. By the time of the First World War Conrad was no longer producing important fiction, but he had become a significant figure in modern literature. He died in 1924.

Youth

JOSEPH CONRAD

This could have occurred nowhere but in England, where men and sea interpenetrate, so to speak—the sea entering into the life of most men, and the men knowing something or everything about the sea, in the way of amusement, of travel, or of bread-winning.

We were sitting round a mahogany table that reflected the bottle, the claret glasses, and our faces as we leaned on our elbows. There was a director of companies, an accountant, a lawyer, Marlow, and myself. The director had been a *Conway* boy, the accountant had served four years at sea, the lawyer—a fine crusted Tory, High Churchman, the best of old fellows, the soul of honor—had been chief officer in the P. & O. service in the good old days when mail-boats were square-rigged at least on two masts, and used to come down the China Sea before a fair monsoon with stun'-sails set alow and aloft. We all began life in the merchant service. Between the five of us there was the strong bond of the sea, and also the fellowship of the craft, which no amount of enthusiasm for yachting, cruising, and so on can give, since one is only the amusement of life and the other is life itself.

Marlow (at least I think that is how he spelt his name) told the story, or rather the chronicle, of a voyage:

"Yes, I have seen a little of the Eastern seas; but what I remember best is my first voyage there. You fellows know there are those voyages that seem ordered for the illustration of life, that might stand for a symbol of existence. You fight, work, sweat, nearly kill yourself, sometimes do kill yourself, trying to accomplish something—and you can't. Not from any fault of yours. You simply can do nothing, neither great nor little—not a thing in the world—not even marry an old maid, or get a wretched 600-ton cargo of coal to its port of destination.

"It was altogether a memorable affair. It was my first voyage to the East, and my first voyage as second mate; it was also my skipper's first command. You'll admit it was time. He was sixty if a day; a little man, with a broad, not very straight back, with bowed shoulders and one leg more bandy than the other, he had that queer twisted-about appearance you see so often in men who work in the fields. He had a nutcracker face—chin and nose trying to come together over a sunken mouth—and it was framed in iron-gray fluffy hair, that looked like a chin strap of cotton-wool sprinkled with coal dust. And he had blue eyes in that old face of his, which were amazingly like a boy's, with that candid expression some quite common men preserve to the end of their days by a rare internal gift of simplicity of heart and rectitude of soul. What induced him to accept me was a wonder. I had come out of a crack Australian clipper, where I had been third officer, and he seemed to have a prejudice against crack clippers as aristocratic and high-toned. He said to me, 'You know, in this ship you will have to work.' I said I had to work in every ship I had ever been in. 'Ah, but this is different, and you gentlemen out of them big ships; . . . but there! I dare say you will do. Join tomorrow.'

"I joined tomorrow. It was twenty-two years ago; and I was just twenty. How time passes! It was one of the happiest days of my life. Fancy! Second mate for the first time—a really responsible officer! I wouldn't have thrown up my new billet for a fortune. The mate looked me over carefully. He was also an old chap, but of another stamp. He had a Roman nose, a snow-white, long beard, and his name was Mahon, but he insisted that it should be pronounced Mann. He was well connected; yet there was something wrong with his luck, and he had never got on.

"As to the captain, he had been for years in coasters, then in the Mediterranean, and last in the West Indian trade. He had never been round the Capes. He could just write a kind of sketchy hand, and didn't care for writing at all. Both were thorough good seamen of course, and between those two old chaps I felt like a small boy between two grandfathers.

"The ship also was old. Her name was the *Judea*. Queer name, isn't it? She belonged to a man Wilmer, Wilcox—some name like that; but he has been bankrupt and dead these twenty years or more, and his name don't matter. She had been laid up in Shadwell basin for ever so long. You can imagine her state. She was all rust, dust, grime—soot aloft, dirt on deck. To me it was like coming out of a palace into a ruined cottage. She was about 400 tons, had a primitive windlass, wooden latches on the doors, not a bit of brass about her, and a big square stern. There was on it, below her name in big letters, a lot of scroll work, with the gilt off, and some sort of a coat of arms, with the motto 'Do or Die' underneath. I remember it took my fancy immensely. There was a touch of romance in it, something that made me love the old thing—something that appealed to my youth!

"We left London in ballast—sand ballast—to load a cargo of coal in a northern port for Bankok. Bankok! I thrilled. I had been six years at sea, but had only seen Melbourne and Sydney, very good places, charming places in their way—but Bankok!

"We worked out of the Thames under canvas, with a North Sea pilot on board. His name was Jermyn, and he dodged all day long about the galley drying his handkerchief before the stove. Apparently he never slept. He was a dismal man, with a perpetual tear sparkling at the end of his nose, who either had been in trouble, or was in trouble, or expected to be in trouble—couldn't be happy unless something went wrong. He mistrusted my youth, my common sense, and my seamanship, and made a point of showing it in a hundred little ways. I dare say he was right. It seems to me I knew very little then, and I know not much more now; but I cherish a hate for that Jermyn to this day.

"We were a week working up as far as Yarmouth Roads, and then we got into a gale—the famous October gale of twenty-two years ago. It was wind, lightning, sleet, snow, and a terrific sea. We were flying light, and you may imagine how bad it was when I tell you we had smashed bulwarks and a flooded deck. On the second night she shifted her ballast into the lee bow, and by that time we had been blown off somewhere on the Dogger Bank. There was nothing for it but go below with shovels and try to right her, and there we were in that vast hold, gloomy like a cavern, the tallow dips stuck and flickering on the beams, the gale howling above, the ship tossing about like mad on her side; there we all were, Jermyn, the captain, everyone, hardly able to keep our feet, engaged on that gravedigger's work, and trying to toss shovelfuls of wet sand up to windward. At every tumble of the ship you could see vaguely in the dim light men falling down with a great flourish of shovels. One of the ship's boys (we had two), impressed by the weirdness of the scene, wept as if his heart would break. We could hear him blubbering somewhere in the shadows.

"On the third day the gale died out, and by-and-by a north-country tug picked us up. We took sixteen days in all to get from London to the Tyne! When we got into dock we had lost our turn for loading, and they hauled us off to a tier where we remained for a month. Mrs. Beard (the captain's name was Beard) came from Colchester to see the old man. She lived on board. The crew of runners had left, and there remained only the officers, one boy, and the steward, a mulatto who answered to the name of Abraham. Mrs. Beard was an old woman, with a face all wrinkled and ruddy like a winter apple, and the figure of a young girl. She caught sight of me once, sewing on a button, and insisted on having my shirts to repair. This was something different from the captains' wives I had known on board crack clippers. When I brought her the shirts, she said: 'And the socks? They want mending, I am sure, and John's—Captain Beard's— things are all in order now. I would be glad of something to do.' Bless the old woman. She overhauled my outfit for me, and meantime I read for the first time 'Sartor Resartus' and Burnaby's 'Ride to Khiva.' I didn't understand much of the first then; but I remember I preferred the soldier to the philosopher at the time; a preference which life has only confirmed. One was a man, and the other was either more—or less. However, they are both dead, and Mrs. Beard is dead, and youth, strength, genius, thoughts, achievements, simple hearts—all die . . . No matter.

"They loaded us at last. We shipped a crew. Eight able seamen and two boys. We hauled off one evening to the buoys at the dock-gates, ready to go out, and with a fair prospect of beginning the voyage next day. Mrs. Beard was to start for home by a late train. When the ship was fast we went to tea. We sat rather silent through the meal—Mahon, the old couple, and I. I finished first, and slipped away for a smoke, my cabin being in a deckhouse just against the poop. It was high water, blowing fresh with a drizzle; the double dock-gates were opened, and the steam colliers were going in and out in the darkness with their lights burning bright, a great plashing of propellers, rattling of winches, and a lot of hailing on the pier-heads. I watched the procession of headlights gliding high and of green lights gliding low in the night, when suddenly a red gleam flashed at me, vanished, came into view again, and remained. The fore-end of a steamer loomed up close. I shouted down the cabin, 'Come up, quick!' and then heard a startled voice saying afar in the dark, 'Stop her, sir.' A bell jingled. Another voice cried warningly, 'We are going right into that bark, sir.' The answer to this was a gruff 'All right,' and the next thing was a heavy crash as the steamer struck a glancing blow with the bluff of her bow about our fore-rigging. There was a moment of confusion, yelling, and running about. Steam roared. Then somebody was heard saying, 'All clear, sir.' . . . 'Are you all right?' asked the gruff voice. I had jumped forward to see the damage, and hailed back, 'I think so.' 'Easy astern,' said the gruff voice. A bell jingled. 'What steamer is that?' screamed Mahon. By that time she was no more to us than a bulky shadow maneuvering a little way off. They shouted at us some name—a woman's name, Miranda or Melissa—or some such thing. 'This means another month in this beastly hole,' said Mahon to me, as we peered with lamps about the splintered bulwarks and broken braces. 'But where's the captain?'

"We had not heard or seen anything of him all that time. We went aft to look. A doleful voice arose hailing somewhere in the middle of the dock, '*Judea* ahoy!' . . . How the devil did he get there? . . . 'Hallo!' we shouted. 'I am adrift in our boat without oars,' he cried. A belated waterman offered his services, and Mahon struck a bargain with him for half-a-crown to tow our skipper alongside; but it was Mrs. Beard that came up the ladder first. They had been floating about the dock in that mizzly cold rain for nearly an hour. I was never so surprised in my life.

"It appears that when he heard my shout 'Come up,' he understood at once what was the matter, caught up his wife, ran on deck, and across, and down into our boat, which was fast to the ladder. Not bad for a sixty-year-old. Just imagine that old fellow saving heroically in his arms that old woman—the woman of his life. He set her down on a thwart, and was ready to climb back on board when the painter came adrift somehow, and away they went together. Of course in the confusion we did not hear him shouting. He looked abashed. She said cheerfully, 'I suppose it does not matter my losing the train now?' 'No, Jenny—you go below and get warm,' he growled. Then to us: 'A sailor has no business with a wife—I say. There I was, out of the ship. Well, no harm done this time. Let's go and look at what that fool of a steamer smashed.'

"It wasn't much, but it delayed us three weeks. At the end of that time, the captain being engaged with his agents, I carried Mrs. Beard's bag to the railway station and put her all comfy into a third-class carriage. She lowered the window to say, 'You are a good young man. If you see John—Captain Beard—without his muffler at night, just remind him from me to keep his throat well wrapped up.' 'Certainly, Mrs. Beard,' I said. 'You are a good young man; I noticed how attentive you are to John—to Captain—' The train pulled out suddenly; I took my cap off to the old woman: I never saw her again . . . Pass the bottle.

"We went to sea next day. When we made that start for Bankok we had been already three months out of London. We had expected to be a fortnight or so—at the outside.

"It was January, and the weather was beautiful—the beautiful sunny winter weather that has more charm than in the summertime, because it is unexpected, and crisp, and you know it won't, it can't, last long. It's like a windfall, like a godsend, like an unexpected piece of luck.

"It lasted all down the North Sea, all down Channel; and it lasted till we were three hundred miles or so to the westward of the Lizards: then the wind went round to the sou'west and began to pipe up. In two days it blew a gale. The *Judea,* hove to, wallowed on the

Atlantic like an old candlebox. It blew day after day: it blew with spite, without interval, without mercy, without rest. The world was nothing but an immensity of great foaming waves rushing at us, under a sky low enough to touch with the hand and dirty like a smoked ceiling. In the stormy space surrounding us there was as much flying spray as air. Day after day and night after night there was nothing round the ship but the howl of the wind, the tumult of the sea, the noise of water pouring over her deck. There was no rest for her and no rest for us. She tossed, she pitched, she stood on her head, she sat on her tail, she rollled, she groaned, and we had to hold on while on deck and cling to our bunks when below, in a constant effort of body and worry of mind.

"One night Mahon spoke through the small window of my berth. It opened right into my very bed, and I was lying there sleepless, in my boots, feeling as though I had not slept for years, and could not if I tried. He said excitedly—

" 'You got the sounding-rod in here, Marlow? I can't get the pumps to suck. By God! it's no child's play.'

"I gave him the sounding-rod and lay down again, trying to think of various things—but I thought only of the pumps. When I came on deck they were still at it, and my watch relieved at the pumps. By the light of the lantern brought on deck to examine the sounding-rod I caught a glimpse of their weary, serious faces. We pumped all the four hours. We pumped all night, all day, all the week,—watch and watch. She was working herself loose, and leaked badly—not enough to drown us at once, but enough to kill us with the work at the pumps. And while we pumped the ship was going from us piecemeal: the bulwarks went, the stanchions were torn out, the ventilators smashed, the cabin door burst in. There was not a dry spot in the ship. She was being gutted bit by bit. The longboat changed, as if by magic, into matchwood where she stood in her gripes. I had lashed her myself, and was rather proud of my handiwork, which had withstood so long the malice of the sea. And we pumped. And there was no break in the weather. The sea was white like a sheet of foam, like a caldron of boiling milk; there was not a break in the clouds, no—not the size of a man's hand—no, not for so much as ten seconds. There was for us no sky, there were for us no stars, no sun, no universe—nothing but angry clouds and an infuriated sea. We pumped watch and watch, for dear life; and it seemed to last for months, for years, for all eternity, as though we had been dead and gone to a hell for sailors. We forgot the day of the week, the name of the month, what year it was, and whether we had ever been ashore. The sails blew away, she lay broadside on under a weather-cloth, the ocean poured over her, and we did not care. We turned those handles, and had the eyes of idiots. As soon as we had crawled on deck I used to take a round turn with a rope about the men, the pumps, and the mainmast, and we turned, we turned incessantly, with the water to our waists, to our necks, over our heads. It was all one. We had forgotten how it felt to be dry.

"And there was somewhere in me the thought: By Jove! this is the deuce of an adventure—something you read about; and it is my first voyage as second mate—and I am only twenty—and here I am lasting it out as well as any of these men, and keeping my chaps up to the mark. I was pleased. I would not have given up the experience for worlds. I had moments of exultation. Whenever the old dismantled craft pitched heavily with her counter high in the air, she seemed to me to throw up, like an appeal, like a defiance, like a cry to the clouds without mercy, the words written on her stern: '*Judea,* London. Do or Die.'

"O youth! The strength of it, the faith of it, the imagination of it! To me she was not an old rattletrap carting about the world a lot of coal for a freight—to me she was the endeavor, the test, the trial of life. I think of her with pleasure, with affection, with regret—as you would think of someone dead you have loved. I shall never forget her . . . Pass the bottle.

"One night when, tied to the mast, as I explained, we were pumping on, deafened with the wind, and without spirit enough in us to wish ourselves dead, a heavy sea crashed aboard and swept clean over us. As soon as I got my breath I shouted, as in duty bound, 'Keep on, boys!' when suddenly I felt something hard floating on deck strike the calf of my leg. I made a grab at it and missed. It was so dark we could not see each other's faces within a foot—you understand.

"After that thump the ship kept quiet for a while, and the thing, whatever it was, struck my leg again. This time I caught it—and it was a saucepan. At first, being stupid with fatigue and thinking of nothing but the pumps, I did not understand what I had in my hand. Suddenly it dawned upon me, and I shouted, 'Boys, the house on deck is gone. Leave this, and let's look for the cook.'

"There was a deckhouse forward, which contained the galley, the cook's berth, and the quarters of the crew. As we had expected for days to see it swept away, the hands had been ordered to sleep in the cabin—the only safe place in the ship. The steward, Abraham, however, persisted in clinging to his berth, stupidly, like a mule—from sheer fright I believe, like an animal that won't leave a stable falling in an earthquake. So we went to look for him. It was chancing death, since once out of our lashings we were as exposed as if on a raft. But we went. The house was shattered as if a shell had exploded inside. Most of it had gone overboard—stove, men's quarters, and their property, all was gone; but two posts, holding a portion of the bulkhead to which Abraham's bunk was attached, remained as if by a miracle. We groped in the ruins and came upon this, and there he was, sitting in 'his bunk, surrounded by foam and wreckage, jabbering cheerfully to himself. He was out of his mind; completely and for ever mad, with this sudden shock coming upon the fag-end of his endurance. We snatched him up, lugged him aft, and pitched him head-first down the cabin companion. You understand there was no time to carry him down with infinite precautions and wait to see how he got on. Those below would pick him up at the bottom of the stairs all right. We were in a hurry to go back to the pumps. That business could not wait. A bad leak is an inhuman thing.

"One would think that the sole purpose of that fiendish gale had been to make a lunatic of that poor devil of a mulatto. It eased before morning, and next day the sky cleared, and as the sea went down the leak took up. When it came to bending a fresh set of sails the crew demanded to put back—and really there was nothing else to do. Boats gone, decks swept clean, cabin gutted, men without a stitch but what they stood in, stores spoiled, ship strained. We put her head for home, and—would you believe it? The wind came east right in our teeth. It blew fresh, it blew continuously. We had to beat up every inch of the way, but she did not leak so badly, the water keeping comparatively smooth. Two hours' pumping in every four is no joke—but it kept her afloat as far as Falmouth.

"The good people there live on casualties of the sea, and no doubt were glad to see us. A hungry crowd of shipwrights sharpened their chisels at the sight of that carcass of a ship. And, by Jove! they had pretty pickings off us before they were done. I fancy the owner was already in a tight place. There were delays. Then it was decided to take part of the cargo out and calk her topsides. This was done, the repairs finished, cargo reshipped; a new crew came on board, and we went out—for Bankok. At the end of a week we were back again. The crew said they weren't going to Bankok—a hundred and fifty days' passage—in a something hooker that wanted pumping eight hours out of the twenty-four; and the nautical papers inserted again the little paragraph: '*Judea*. Bark. Tyne to Bankok; coals; put back to Falmouth leaky and with crew refusing duty.'

"There were more delays—more tinkering. The owner came down for a day, and said she was as right as a little fiddle. Poor old Captain Beard looked like the ghost of a Geordie skipper—through the worry and humiliation of it. Remember he was sixty, and it was his first command. Mahon said it was a foolish business, and would end badly. I loved the ship more than ever, and wanted awfully to get to Bankok. To Bankok! Magic name, blessed name. Mesopotamia wasn't a patch on it. Remember I was twenty, and it was my first second mate's billet, and the East was waiting for me.

"We went out and anchored in the outer roads with a fresh

crew—the third. She leaked worse than ever. It was as if those confounded shipwrights had actually made a hole in her. This time we did not even go outside. The crew simply refused to man the windlass.

"They towed us back to the inner harbor, and we became a fixture, a feature, an institution of the place. People pointed us out to visitors as 'That 'ere bark that's going to Bankok—has been here six months—put back three times.' On holidays the small boys pulling about in boats would hail, '*Judea*, ahoy!' and if a head showed above the rail shouted, 'Where you bound to?—Bankok?' and jeered. We were only three on board. The poor old skipper mooned in the cabin. Mahon undertook the cooking, and unexpectedly developed all a Frenchman's genius for preparing nice little messes. I looked languidly after the rigging. We became citizens of Falmouth. Every shopkeeper knew us. At the barber's or tobacconist's they asked familiarly, 'Do you think you will ever get to Bankok?' Meantime the owner, the underwriters, and the charterers squabbled amongst themselves in London, and our pay went on . . . Pass the bottle.

"It was horrid. Morally it was worse than pumping for life. It seemed as though we had been forgotten by the world, belonged to nobody, would get nowhere; it seeemed that, as if bewitched, we would have to live for ever and ever in that inner harbor, a derision and a byword to generations of longshore loafers and dishonest boatmen. I obtained three months' pay and a five days' leave, and made a rush for London. It took me a day to get there and pretty well another to come back—but three months' pay went all the same. I don't know what I did with it. I went to a music hall, I believe, lunched, dined, and supped in a swell place in Regent Street, and was back to time, with nothing but a complete set of Byron's works and a new railway rug to show for three months' work. The boatman who pulled me off to the ship said: 'Hallo! I thought you had left the old thing. *She* will never get to Bankok.' 'That's all *you* know about it,' I said scornfully—but I didn't like that prophecy at all.

"Suddenly a man, some kind of agent to somebody, appeared with full powers. He had grog blossoms all over his face, an indomitable energy, and was a jolly soul. We leaped into life again. A hulk came alongside, took our cargo, and then we went into dry dock to get our copper stripped. No wonder she leaked. The poor thing, strained beyond endurance by the gale, had, as if in disgust, spat out all the oakum of her lower seams. She was recalked, new coppered, and made as tight as a bottle. We went back to the hulk and reshipped our cargo.

"Then on a fine moonlight night, all the rats left the ship.

"We had been infested with them. They had destroyed our sails, consumed more stores than the crew, affably shared our beds and our dangers, and now, when the ship was made seaworthy, concluded to clear out. I called Mahon to enjoy the spectacle. Rat after rat appeared on our rail, took a last look over his shoulder, and leaped with a hollow thud into the empty hulk. We tried to count them, but soon lost the tale. Mahon said: 'Well, well! don't talk to me about the intelligence of rats. They ought to have left before, when we had that narrow squeak from foundering. There you have the proof how silly is the superstition about them. They leave a good ship for an old rotten hulk, where there is nothing to eat, too, the fools! . . . I don't believe they know what is safe or what is good for them, any more than you or I.'

"And after some more talk we agreed that the wisdom of rats had been grossly overrated, being in fact no greater than that of men.

"The story of the ship was known, by this, all up the Channel from Land's End to the Forelands, and we could get no crew on the south coast. They sent us one all complete from Liverpool, and we left once more—for Bankok.

"We had fair breezes, smooth water right into the tropics, and the old *Judea* lumbered along in the sunshine. When she went eight knots everything cracked aloft, and we tied our caps to our heads; but mostly she strolled on at the rate of three miles an hour. What could you expect? She was tired—that old ship. Her youth was where mine is—where yours is—you fellows who listen to this yarn; and what friend would throw your years and your weariness in your face? We didn't grumble at her. To us aft, at least, it seemed as though we had been born in her, reared in her, had lived in her for ages, had never known any other ship. I would just as soon have abused the old village church at home for not being a cathedral.

"And for me there was also my youth to make me patient. There was all the East before me, and all life, and the thought that I had been tried in that ship and had come out pretty well. And I thought of men of old who, centuries ago, went that road in ships that sailed no better, to the land of palms, and spices, and yellow sands, and of brown nations ruled by kings more cruel than Nero the Roman and more splendid than Solomon the Jew. The old bark lumbered on, heavy with her age and the burden of her cargo, while I lived the life of youth in ignorance and hope. She lumbered on through an interminable procession of days; and the fresh gilding flashed back at the setting sun, seemed to cry out over the darkening sea the words painted on her stern, '*Judea*, London. Do or Die.'

"Then we entered the Indian Ocean and steered northerly for Java Head. The winds were light. Weeks slipped by. She crawled on, do or die, and people at home began to think of posting us as overdue.

"One Saturday evening, I being off duty, the men asked me to give them an extra bucket of water or so—for washing clothes. As I did not wish to screw on the fresh-water pump so late, I went forward whistling, and with a key in my hand to unlock the forepeak scuttle, intending to serve the water out of a spare tank we kept there.

"The smell down below was as unexpected as it was frightful. One would have thought hundreds of paraffin lamps had been flaring and smoking in that hole for days. I was glad to get out. The man with me coughed and said, 'Funny smell, sir.' I answered negligently, 'It's good for the health, they say,' and walked aft.

"The first thing I did was to put my head down the square of the midship ventilator. As I lifted the lid a visible breath, something like a thin fog, a puff of faint haze, rose from the opening. The ascending air was hot, and had a heavy, sooty, paraffiny smell. I gave one sniff, and put down the lid gently. It was no use choking myself. The cargo was on fire.

"Next day she began to smoke in earnest. You see it was to be expected, for though the coal was of a safe kind, that cargo had been so handled, so broken up with handling, that it looked more like smithy coal than anything else. Then it had been wetted—more than once. It rained all the time we were taking it back from the hulk, and now with this long passage it got heated, and there was another case of spontaneous combustion.

"The captain called us into the cabin. He had a chart spread on the table, and looked unhappy. He said, 'The coast of West Australia is near, but I mean to proceed to our destination. It is the hurricane month too; but we will just keep her head for Bankok, and fight the fire. No more putting back anywhere, if we all get roasted. We will try first to stifle this 'ere damned combustion by want of air.'

"We tried. We battened down everything, and still she smoked. The smoke kept coming out through imperceptible crevices; it forced itself through bulkheads and covers; it oozed here and there and everywhere in slender threads, in an invisible film, in an incomprehensible manner. It made its way into the cabin, into the forecastle; it poisoned the sheltered places on the deck; it could be sniffed as high as the mainyard. It was clear that if the smoke came out the air came in. This was disheartening. This combustion refused to be stifled.

"We resolved to try water, and took the hatches off. Enormous volumes of smoke, whitish, yellowish, thick, greasy, misty, choking, ascended as high as the trucks. All hands cleared out aft. Then the poisonous cloud blew away, and we went back to work in a smoke that was no thicker now than that of an ordinary factory chimney.

"We rigged the force pump, got the hose along, and by-and-by it burst. Well, it was as old as the ship—a prehistoric hose, and past repair. Then we pumped with the feeble head-pump, drew water with buckets, and in this way managed in time to pour lots of Indian

Ocean into the main hatch. The bright stream flashed in sunshine, fell into a layer of white crawling smoke, and vanished on the black surface of coal. Steam ascended mingling with the smoke. We poured salt water as into a barrel without a bottom. It was our fate to pump in that ship, to pump out of her, to pump into her; and after keeping water out of her to save ourselves from being drowned, we frantically poured water into her to save ourselves from being burnt.

"And she crawled on, do or die, in the serene weather. The sky was a miracle of purity, a miracle of azure. The sea was polished, was blue, was pellucid, was sparkling like a precious stone, extending on all sides, all round to the horizon—as if the whole terrestrial globe had been one jewel, one colossal sapphire, a single gem fashioned into a planet. And on the luster of the great calm waters the *Judea* glided imperceptibly, enveloped in languid and unclean vapors, in a lazy cloud that drifted to leeward, light and slow: a pestiferous cloud defiling the splendor of sea and sky.

"All this time of course we saw no fire. The cargo smoldered at the bottom somewhere. Once Mahon, as we were working side by side, said to me with a queer smile: 'Now, if she only would spring a tidy leak—like that time when we first left the Channel—it would put a stopper on this fire. Wouldn't it?' I remarked irrelevantly, 'Do you remember the rats?'

"We fought the fire and sailed the ship too as carefully as though nothing had been the matter. The steward cooked and attended on us. Of the other twelve men, eight worked while four rested. Everyone took his turn, captain included. There was equality, and if not exactly fraternity, then a deal of good feeling. Sometimes a man, as he dashed a bucketful of water down the hatchway, would yell out, 'Hurrah for Bankok!' and the rest laughed. But generally we were taciturn and serious—and thirsty. Oh! how thirsty! And we had to be careful with the water. Strict allowance. The ship smoked, the sun blazed . . . Pass the bottle.

"We tried everything. We even made an attempt to dig down to the fire. No good, of course. No man could remain more than a minute below. Mahon, who went first, fainted there, and the man who went to fetch him out did likewise. We lugged them out on deck. Then I leaped down to show how easily it could be done. They had learned wisdom by that time, and contented themselves by fishing for me with a chain-hook tied to a broom handle, I believe. I did not offer to go and fetch up my shovel, which was left down below.

"Things began to look bad. We put the longboat into the water. The second boat was ready to swing out. We had also another, a fourteen-foot thing, on davits aft, where it was quite safe.

"Then behold, the smoke suddenly decreased. We redoubled our efforts to flood the bottom of the ship. In two days there was no smoke at all. Everybody was on the broad grin. This was on a Friday. On Saturday no work, but sailing the ship of course was done. The men washed their clothes and their faces for the first time in a fortnight, and had a special dinner given them. They spoke of spontaneous combustion with contempt, and implied *they* were the boys to put out combustions. Somehow we all felt as though we each had inherited a large fortune. But a beastly smell of burning hung about the ship. Captain Beard had hollow eyes and sunken cheeks. I had never noticed so much before how twisted and bowed he was. He and Mahon prowled soberly about hatches and ventilators, sniffing. It struck me suddenly poor Mahon was a very, very old chap. As to me, I was as pleased and proud as though I had helped to win a great naval battle. O! Youth!

"The night was fine. In the morning a homeward-bound ship passed us hull down—the first we had seen for months; but we were nearing the land at last, Java Head being about 190 miles off, and nearly due north.

"Next day it was my watch on deck from eight to twelve. At breakfast the captain observed, 'It's wonderful how that smell hangs about the cabin.' About ten, the mate being on the poop, I stepped down on the main deck for a moment. The carpenter's bench stood abaft the mainmast: I leaned against it sucking at my pipe, and the carpenter, a young chap, came to talk to me. He remarked, 'I think we have done very well, haven't we?' and then I perceived with annoyance the fool was trying to tilt the bench. I said curtly, 'Don't, Chips,' and immediately became aware of a queer sensation, of an absurd delusion—I seemed somehow to be in the air. I heard all round me like a pent-up breath released—as if a thousand giants simultaneously had said Phoo!—and felt a dull concussion which made my ribs ache suddenly. No doubt about it—I was in the air, and my body was describing a short parabola. But short as it was, I had the time to think several thoughts in, as far as I can remember, the following order: 'This can't be the carpenter—What is it?—Some accident—Submarine volcano?—Coals, gas!—By Jove! we are being blown up—Everybody's dead—I am falling into the afterhatch—I see fire in it.'

"The coal dust suspended in the air of the hold had glowed dull red at the moment of the explosion. In the twinkling of an eye, in an infinitesimal fraction of a second since the first tilt of the bench, I was sprawling full length on the cargo. I picked myself up and scrambled out. It was quick like a rebound. The deck was a wilderness of smashed timber, lying crosswise like trees in a wood after a hurricane; an immense curtain of soiled rags waved gently before me—it was the mainsail blown to strips. I thought, The masts will be toppling over directly; and to get out of the way bolted on all fours towards the poop-ladder. The first person I saw was Mahon, with eyes like saucers, his mouth open, and the long white hair standing straight on end round his head like a silver halo. He was just about to go down when the sight of the main deck stirring, heaving up, and changing into splinters before his eyes, petrified him on the top step. I stared at him in unbelief, and he stared at me with a queer kind of shocked curiosity. I did not know that I had no hair, no eyebrows, no eyelashes, that my young mustache was burnt off, that my face was black, one cheek laid open, my nose cut, and my chin bleeding. I had lost my cap, one of my slippers, and my shirt was torn to rags. Of all this I was not aware. I was amazed to see the ship still afloat, the poop-deck whole—and, most of all, to see anybody alive. Also the peace of the sky and the serenity of the sea were distinctly surprising. I suppose I expected to see them convulsed with horror . . . Pass the bottle.

"There was a voice hailing the ship from somewhere—in the air, in the sky—I couldn't tell. Presently I saw the captain—and he was mad. He asked me eagerly, 'Where's the cabin-table?' and to hear such a question was a frightful shock. I had just been blown up, you understand, and vibrated with that experience—I wasn't quite sure whether I was alive. Mahon began to stamp with both feet and yelled at him, 'Good God! don't you see the deck's blown out of her?' I found my voice, and stammered out as if conscious of some gross neglect of duty, 'I don't know where the cabin-table is.' It was like an absurd dream.

"Do you know what he wanted next? Well, he wanted to trim the yards. Very placidly, and as if lost in thought, he insisted on having the foreyard squared. 'I don't know if there's anybody alive,' said Mahon, almost tearfully. 'Surely,' he said, gently, 'there will be enough left to square the foreyard.'

"The old chap, it seems, was in his own berth, winding up the chronometers, when the shock sent him spinning. Immediately it occurred to him—as he said afterwards—that the ship had struck something, and he ran out into the cabin. There, he saw, the cabin-table had vanished somewhere. The deck being blown up, it had fallen down into the lazarette of course. Where we had our breakfast that morning he saw only a great hole in the floor. This appeared to him so awfully mysterious, and impressed him so immensely, that what he saw and heard after he got on deck were mere trifles in comparison. And, mark, he noticed directly the wheel deserted and his bark off her course—and his only thought was to get that miserable, stripped, undecked, smoldering shell of a ship back again with her head pointing at her port of destination. Bankok! That's what he was after. I tell you this quiet, bowed, bandy-legged, almost deformed little man was immense in the singleness of his idea and in his placid ignorance of our agitation. He motioned us forward with a commanding gesture, and went to take the wheel himself.

"Yes: that was the first thing we did—trim the yards of that wreck! No one was killed, or even disabled, but everyone was more or less hurt. You should have seen them! Some were in rags, with black faces, like coal-heavers, like sweeps, and had bullet heads that seemed closely cropped, but were in fact singed to the skin. Others, of the watch below, awakened by being shot out from their collapsing bunks, shivered incessantly, and kept on groaning even as we went about our work. But they all worked. That crew of Liverpool hard cases had in them the right stuff. It's my experience they always have. It is the sea that gives it—the vastness, the loneliness surrounding their dark stolid souls. Ah! Well! we stumbled, we crept, we fell, we barked our shins on the wreckage, we hauled. The masts stood, but we did not know how much they might be charred down below. It was nearly calm, but a long swell ran from the west and made her roll. They might go at any moment. We looked at them with apprehension. One could not foresee which way they would fall.

"Then we retreated aft and looked about us. The deck was a tangle of planks on edge, of planks on end, of splinters, of ruined woodwork. The masts rose from that chaos like big trees above a matted undergrowth. The interstices of that mass of wreckage were full of something whitish, sluggish, stirring—of something that was like a greasy fog. The smoke of the invisible fire was coming up again, was trailing, like a poisonous thick mist in some valley choked with dead wood. Already lazy wisps were beginning to curl upwards amongst the mass of splinters. Here and there a piece of timber, stuck upright, resembled a post. Half of a fife-rail had been shot through the foresail, and the sky made a patch of glorious blue in the ignobly soiled canvas. A portion of several boards holding together had fallen across the rail, and one end protruded overboard, like a gangway leading upon nothing, like a gangway leading over the deep sea, leading to death—as if inviting us to walk the plank at once and be done with our ridiculous troubles. And still the air, the sky—a ghost, something invisible was hailing the ship.

"Someone had the sense to look over, and there was the helmsman, who had impulsively jumped overboard, anxious to come back. He yelled and swam lustily like a merman, keeping up with the ship. We threw him a rope, and presently he stood amongst us streaming with water and very crestfallen. The captain had surrendered the wheel, and apart, elbow on rail and chin in hand, gazed at the sea wistfully. We asked ourselves, What next? I thought, Now, this is something like. This is great. I wonder what will happen. O youth!

"Suddenly Mahon sighted a steamer far astern. Captain Beard

said, 'We may do something with her yet.' We hoisted two flags, which said in the international language of the sea, 'On fire. Want immediate assistance.' The steamer grew bigger rapidly, and by-and-by spoke with two flags on her foremast, 'I am coming to your assistance.'

"In half an hour she was abreast, to windward, within hail, and rolling slightly, with her engines stopped. We lost our composure, and yelled all together with excitement, 'We've been blown up.' A man in a white helmet, on the bridge, cried, 'Yes! All right! all right! and he nodded his head, and smiled, and made soothing motions with his hand as though at a lot of frightened children. One of the boats dropped in the water, and walked towards us upon the sea with her long oars. Four Calashes pulled a swinging stroke. This was my first sight of Malay seamen. I've known them since, but what struck me then was their unconcern: they came alongside, and even the bowman standing up and holding to our main-chains with the boat-hook did not deign to lift his head for a glance. I thought people who had been blown up deserved more attention.

"A little man, dry like a chip and agile like a monkey, clambered up. It was the mate of the steamer. He gave one look, and cried, 'O boys—you had better quit.'

"We were silent. He talked apart with the captain for a time—seemed to argue with him. Then they went away together to the steamer.

"When our skipper came back we learned that the steamer was the *Sommerville,* Captain Nash, from West Australia to Singapore via Batavia with mails, and that the agreement was she should tow us to Anjer or Batavia, if possible, where we could extinguish the fire by scuttling, and then proceed on our voyage—to Bankok! The old man seemed excited. 'We will do it yet,' he said to Mahon, fiercely. He shook his fist at the sky. Nobody else said a word.

"At noon the steamer began to tow. She went ahead slim and high, and what was left of the *Judea* followed at the end of seventy fathom of tow-rope—followed her swiftly like a cloud of smoke with mastheads protruding above. We went aloft to furl the sails. We coughed on the yards, and were careful about the bunts. Do you see the lot of us there, putting a neat furl on the sails of that ship doomed to arrive nowhere? There was not a man who didn't think that at any moment the masts would topple over. From aloft we could not see the ship for smoke, and they worked carefully, passing the gaskets with even turns. 'Harbor furl—aloft there!' cried Mahon from below.

"You understand this? I don't think one of those chaps expected to get down in the usual way. When we did I heard them saying to each other, 'Well, I thought we would come down overboard, in a lump—

sticks and all—blame me if I didn't.' 'That's what I was thinking to myself,' would answer wearily another battered and bandaged scarecrow. And, mind, these were men without the drilled-in habit of obedience. To an onlooker they would be a lot of profane scallywags without a redeeming point. What made them do it—what made them obey me when I, thinking consciously how fine it was, made them drop the bunt of the foresail twice to try and do it better? What? They had no professional reputation—no examples, no praise. It wasn't a sense of duty; they all knew well enough how to shirk, and laze, and dodge—when they had a mind to it—and mostly they had. Was it the two pounds ten a month that sent them there? They didn't think their pay half good enough. No; it was something in them, something inborn and subtle and everlasting. I don't say positively that the crew of a French or German merchantman wouldn't have done it, but I doubt whether it would have been done in the same way. There was a completeness in it, something solid like a principle, and masterful like an instinct—a disclosure of something secret—of that hidden something, that gift, of good or evil that makes racial difference, that shapes the fate of nations.

"It was that night at ten that, for the first time since we had been fighting it, we saw the fire. The speed of the towing had fanned the smoldering destruction. A blue gleam appeared forward, shining below the wreck of the deck. It wavered in patches, it seemed to stir and creep like the light of a glowworm. I saw it first, and told Mahon. 'Then the game's up,' he said. 'We had better stop this towing, or she will burst out suddenly fore and aft before we can clear out.' We set up a yell; rang bells to attract their attention; they towed on. At last Mahon and I had to crawl forward and cut the rope with an ax. There was no time to cast off the lashings. Red tongues could be seen licking the wilderness of splinters under our feet as we made our way back to the poop.

"Of course they very soon found out in the steamer that the rope was gone. She gave a loud blast of her whistle, her lights were seen sweeping in a wide circle, she came up ranging close alongside, and stopped. We were all in a tight group on the poop looking at her. Every man had saved a little bundle or a bag. Suddenly a conical flame with a twisted top shot up forward and threw upon the black sea a circle of light, with the two vessels side by side and heaving gently in its center. Captain Beard had been sitting on the gratings still and mute for hours, but now he rose slowly and advanced in front of us, to the mizzen-shrouds. Captain Nash hailed: 'Come along! Look sharp. I have mail bags on board. I will take you and your boats to Singapore.'

"'Thank you! No!' said our skipper. 'We must see the last of the ship.'

"'I can't stand by any longer,' shouted the other. 'Mails—you know.'

"'Ay! ay! We are all right.'

"'Very well! I'll report you in Singapore . . . Good-by!'"

"He waved his hand. Our men dropped their bundles quietly. The steamer moved ahead, and passing out of the circle of light, vanished at once from our sight, dazzled by the fire which burned fiercely. And then I knew that I would see the East first as commander of a small boat. I thought it fine; and the fidelity to the old ship was fine. We should see the last of her. Oh the glamour of youth! Oh the fire of it, more dazzling than the flames of the burning ship, throwing a magic light on the wide earth, leaping audaciously to the sky, presently to be quenched by time, more cruel, more pitiless, more bitter than the sea—and like the flames of the burning ship surrounded by an impenetrable night.

"The old man warned us in his gentle and inflexible way that it was part of our duty to save for the underwriters as much as we could of the ship's gear. Accordingly we went to work aft, while she blazed forward to give us plenty of light. We lugged out a lot of rubbish. What didn't we save? An old barometer fixed with an absurd quantity of screws nearly cost me my life: a sudden rush of smoke came upon me, and I just got away in time. There were various stores, bolts of canvas, coils of rope; the poop looked like a marine bazaar, and the boats were lumbered to the gunwales. One would have thought the old man wanted to take as much as he could of his first command with him. He was very, very quiet, but off his balance evidently. Would you believe it? He wanted to take a length of old streamcable and a kedge-anchor with him in the longboat. We said, 'Ay, ay, sir,' deferentially, and on the quiet let the thing slip overboard. The heavy medicine chest went that way, two bags of green coffee, tins of paint—fancy, paint!—a whole lot of things. Then I was ordered with two hands into the boats to make a stowage and get them ready against the time it would be proper for us to leave the ship.

"We put everything straight, stepped the longboat's mast for our skipper, who was to take charge of her, and I was not sorry to sit down for a moment. My face felt raw, every limb ached as if broken, I was aware of all my ribs, and would have sworn to a twist in the backbone. The boats, fast astern, lay in a deep shadow, and all around I could see the circle of the sea lighted by the fire. A gigantic flame arose forward straight and clear. It flared fierce, with noises like the whir of wings, with rumbles as of thunder. There were cracks, detonations, and from the cone of flame the sparks flew upwards, as man is born to trouble, to leaky ships, and to ships that burn.

"What bothered me was that the ship, lying broadside to the swell and to such wind as there was—a mere breath—the boats would not keep astern where they were safe, but persisted, in a pig-headed way boats have, in getting under the counter and then swinging alongside. They were knocking about dangerously and coming near the flame, while the ship rolled on them, and, of course, there was always the danger of the masts going over the side at any moment. I and my two boat-keepers kept them off as best we could with oars and boat-hooks; but to be constantly at it became exasperating, since there was no reason why we should not leave at once. We could not see those on board, nor could we imagine what caused the delay. The boat-keepers were swearing feebly, and I had not only my share of the work, but also had to keep at it two men who showed a constant inclination to lay themselves down and let things slide.

"At last I hailed 'On deck there,' and someone looked over. 'We're ready here,' I said. The head disappeared, and very soon popped up again. 'The captain says, All right, sir, and to keep the boats well clear of the ship.'

"Half an hour passed. Suddenly there was a frightful racket, rattle, clanking of chain, hiss of water, and millions of sparks flew up into the shivering column of smoke that stood leaning slightly above the ship. The catheads had burned away, and the two red-hot anchors had gone to the bottom, tearing out after them two hundred fathom of red-hot chain. The ship trembled, the mass of flame swayed as if ready to collapse, and the fore top-gallant-mast fell. It darted down like an arrow of fire, shot under, and instantly leaping up within an oar's-length of the boats, floated quietly, very black on the luminous sea. I hailed the deck again. After some time a man in an unexpectedly cheerful but also muffled tone, as though he had been trying to speak with his mouth shut, informed me, 'Coming directly, sir,' and vanished. For a long time I heard nothing but the whir and roar of the fire. There were also whistling sounds. The boats jumped, tugged at the painters, ran at each other playfully, knocked their sides together, or, do what we would, swung in a bunch against the ship's side. I couldn't stand it any longer, and swarming up a rope, clambered aboard over the stern.

"It was as bright as day. Coming up like this, the sheet of fire facing me was a terrifying sight, and the heat seemed hardly bearable at first. On a settee cushion dragged out of the cabin, Captain Beard, with his legs drawn up and one arm under his head, slept with the light playing on him. Do you know what the rest were busy about? They were sitting on deck right aft, round an open case, eating bread and cheese and drinking bottled stout.

"On the background of flames twisting in fierce tongues above their heads they seemed at home like salamanders, and looked like a band of desperate pirates. The fire sparkled in the whites of their eyes, gleamed on patches of white skin seen through the torn shirts. Each had the marks as of a battle about him—bandaged heads, tied-up arms, a strip of dirty rag round a knee—and each man had a bottle between his legs and a chunk of cheese in his hand. Mahon got up. With his handsome and disreputable head, his hooked profile, his long white beard, and with an uncorked bottle in his hand, he resembled one of those reckless sea-robbers of old making merry amidst violence and disaster. 'The last meal on board,' he explained solemnly. 'We had nothing to eat all day, and it was no use leaving all this.' He flourished the bottle and indicated the sleeping skipper. 'He said he couldn't swallow anything, so I got him to lie down,' he went on; and as I stared, 'I don't know whether you are aware, young fellow, the man had no sleep to speak of for days—and there will be dam' little sleep in the boats.' 'There will be no boats by-and-by if you fool about much longer,' I said, indignantly. I walked up to the skipper and shook him by the shoulder. At last he opened his eyes, but did not move. 'Time to leave her, sir,' I said, quietly.

"He got up painfully, looked at the flames, at the sea sparkling round the ship, and black, black as ink farther away; he looked at the stars shining dim through a thin veil of smoke in a sky black, black as Erebus.

" 'Youngest first,' he said.

"And the ordinary seaman, wiping his mouth with the back of his hand, got up, clambered over the taffrail, and vanished. Others followed. One, on the point of going over, stopped short to drain his bottle, and with a great swing of his arm flung it at the fire. 'Take this!' he cried.

"The skipper lingered disconsolately, and we left him to commune alone for awhile with his first command. Then I went up again and brought him away at last. It was time. The ironwork on the poop was hot to the touch.

"Then the painter of the longboat was cut, and the three boats, tied together, drifted clear of the ship. It was just sixteen hours after the explosion when we abandoned her. Mahon had charge of the second boat, and I had the smallest—the 14-foot thing. The longboat would have taken the lot of us; but the skipper said we must save as much property as we could—for the underwriters—and so I got my first command. I had two men with me, a bag of biscuits, a few tins of meat, and a beaker of water. I was ordered to keep close to the longboat, that in case of bad weather we might be taken into her.

"And do you know what I thought? I thought I would part company as soon as I could. I wanted to have my first command all to myself. I wasn't going to sail in a squadron if there were a chance for independent cruising. I would make land by myself. I would beat the other boats. Youth! All youth! The silly, charming, beautiful youth.

"But we did not make a start at once. We must see the last of the ship. And so the boats drifted about that night, heaving and setting on the swell. The men dozed, waked, sighed, groaned. I looked at the burning ship.

"Between the darkness of earth and heaven she was burning fiercely upon a disc of purple sea shot by the blood-red play of gleams; upon a disc of water glittering and sinister. A high, clear flame, an immense and lonely flame, ascended from the ocean, and from its summit the black smoke poured continuously at the sky. She burned furiously, mournful and imposing like a funeral pile kindled in the night, surrounded by the sea, watched over by the stars. A magnificent death had come like a grace, like a gift, like a reward to that old ship at the end of her laborious days. The surrender of her weary ghost to the keeping of stars and sea was stirring like the sight of a glorious triumph. The masts fell just before daybreak, and for a moment there was a burst and turmoil of sparks that seemed to fill with flying fire the night patient and watchful, the vast night lying silent upon the sea. At daylight she was only a charred shell, floating still under a cloud of smoke and bearing a glowing mass of coal within.

"Then the oars were got out, and the boats forming in a line moved round her remains as if in procession—the longboat leading. As we pulled across her stern a slim dart of fire shot out viciously at us, and suddenly she went down, head first, in a great hiss of steam. The unconsumed stern was the last to sink; but the paint had gone, had cracked, had peeled off, and there were no letters, there was no word, no stubborn device that was like her soul, to flash at the rising sun her creed and her name.

"We made our way north. A breeze sprang up, and about noon all the boats came together for the last time. I had no mast or sail in mine, but I made a mast out of a spare oar and hoisted a boat-awning for a sail, with a boat-hook for a yard. She was certainly overmasted, but I had the satisfaction of knowing that with the wind aft I could beat the other two. I had to wait for them. Then we all had a look at the captain's chart, and, after a sociable meal of hard bread and water, got our last instructions. These were simple: steer north, and keep together as much as possible. 'Be careful with that jury rig, Marlow,' said the captain; and Mahon, as I sailed proudly past his boat, wrinkled his curved nose and hailed, 'You will sail that ship of yours under water if you don't look out, young fellow.' He was a malicious old man—and may the deep sea where he sleeps now rock him gently, rock him tenderly to the end of time!

"Before sunset a thick rain-squall passed over the two boats, which were far astern, and that was the last I saw of them for a time. Next day I sat steering my cockle-shell—my first command—with nothing

but water and sky around me. I did sight in the afternoon the upper
sails of a ship far away, but said nothing, and my men did not notice
her. You see I was afraid she might be homeward bound, and I had
no mind to turn back from the portals of the East. I was steering for
Java—another blessed name—like Bankok, you know. I steered many
days.

"I need not tell you what it is to be knocking about in an open
boat. I remember nights and days of calm when we pulled, we
pulled, and the boat seemed to stand still, as if bewitched within the
circle of the sea horizon. I remember the heat, the deluge of rain-
squalls that kept us bailing for dear life (but filled our water cask),
and I remember sixteen hours on end with a mouth dry as a cinder
and a steering-oar over the stern to keep my first command head on
to a breaking sea. I did not know how good a man I was till then. I
remember the drawn faces, the dejected figures of my two men, and I
remember my youth and the feeling that will never come back any
more—the feeling that I could last for ever, outlast the sea, the earth,
and all men; the deceitful feeling that lures us on to joys, to perils, to
love, to vain effort—to death; the triumphant conviction of strength,
the heat of life in the handful of dust, the glow in the heart that with
every year grows dim, grows cold, grows small, and expires—and
expires, too soon, too soon—before life itself.

"And this is how I see the East. I have seen its secret places and
have looked into its very soul; but now I see it always from a small
boat, a high outline of mountains, blue and afar in the morning; like
faint mist at noon; a jagged wall of purple at sunset. I have the feel
of the oar in my hand, the vision of a scorching blue sea in my eyes.
And I see a bay, a wide bay, smooth as glass and polished like ice,
shimmering in the dark. A red light burns far off upon the gloom of
the land, and the night is soft and warm. We drag at the oars with
aching arms, and suddenly a puff of wind, a puff faint and tepid and
laden with strange odors of blossoms, of aromatic wood, comes out of
the still night—the first sigh of the East on my face. That I can never
forget. It was impalpable and enslaving, like a charm, like a whispered promise of mysterious delight.

"We had been pulling this finishing spell for eleven hours. Two
pulled, and he whose turn it was to rest sat at the tiller. We had
made out the red light in that bay and steered for it, guessing it must
mark some small coasting port. We passed two vessels, outlandish and
high-sterned, sleeping at anchor, and, approaching the light, now
very dim, ran the boat's nose against the end of a jutting wharf. We
were blind with fatigue. My men dropped the oars and fell off the
thwarts as if dead. I made fast to a pile. A current rippled softly. The
scented obscurity of the shore was grouped into vast masses, a density
of colossal clumps of vegetation, probably—mute and fantastic

shapes. And at their foot the semicircle of a beach gleamed faintly, like an illusion. There was not a light, not a stir, not a sound. The mysterious East faced me, perfumed like a flower, silent like death, dark like a grave.

"And I sat weary beyond expression, exulting like a conqueror, sleepless and entranced as if before a profound, a fateful enigma.

"A splashing of oars, a measured dip reverberating on the level of water, intensified by the silence of the shore into loud claps, made me jump up. A boat, a European boat, was coming in. I invoked the name of the dead; I hailed: *Judea* ahoy! A thin shout answered.

"It was the captain. I had beaten the flagship by three hours, and I was glad to hear the old man's voice again, tremulous and tired. 'Is it you, Marlow?' 'Mind the end of that jetty, sir,' I cried.

"He approached cautiously, and brought up with the deep-sea lead-line which we had saved—for the underwriters. I eased my painter and fell alongside. He sat, a broken figure at the stern, wet with dew, his hands clasped in his lap. His men were asleep already. 'I had a terrible time of it,' he murmured. 'Mahon is behind—not very far.' We conversed in whispers, in low whispers, as if afraid to wake up the land. Guns, thunder, earthquakes would not have awakened the men just then.

"Looking around as we talked, I saw away at sea a bright light traveling in the night. 'There's a steamer passing the bay,' I said. She was not passing, she was entering, and she even came close and anchored. 'I wish,' said the old man, 'you would find out whether she is English. Perhaps they could give us a passage somewhere.' He seemed nervously anxious. So by dint of punching and kicking I started one of my men into a state of somnambulism, and giving him an oar, took another and pulled towards the lights of the steamer.

"There was a murmur of voices in her, metallic hollow clangs of the engine room, footsteps on the deck. Her ports shone, round like dilated eyes. Shapes moved about, and there was a shadowy man high up on the bridge. He heard my oars.

"And then, before I could open my lips, the East spoke to me, but it was in a Western voice. A torrent of words was poured into the enigmatical, the fateful silence; outlandish, angry words, mixed with words and even whole sentences of good English, less strange but even more surprising. The voice swore and cursed violently; it riddled the solemn peace of the bay by a volley of abuse. It began by calling me Pig, and from that went crescendo into unmentionable adjectives—in English. The man up there raged aloud in two languages, and with a sincerity in his fury that almost convinced me I had, in some way, sinned against the harmony of the universe. I could hardly see him, but began to think he would work himself into a fit.

"Suddenly he ceased, and I could hear him snorting and blowing like a porpoise. I said—

" 'What steamer is this, pray?'

" 'Eh? What's this? And who are you?'

" 'Castaway crew of an English bark burnt at sea. We came here tonight. I am the second mate. The captain is in the longboat, and wishes to know if you would give us a passage somewhere.'

" 'Oh, my goodness! I say . . . This is the *Celestial* from Singapore on her return trip. I'll arrange with your captain in the morning . . . and . . . I say . . . did you hear me just now?'

" 'I should think the whole bay heard you.'

" 'I thought you were a shore boat. Now, look here—this infernal lazy scoundrel of a caretaker has gone to sleep again—curse him. The light is out, and I nearly ran foul of the end of this damned jetty. This is the third time he plays me this trick. Now, I ask you, can anybody stand this kind of thing? It's enough to drive a man out of his mind. I'll report him . . . I'll get the Assistant Resident to give him the sack, by . . . See—there's no light. It's out, isn't it? I take you to witness the light's out. There should be a light, you know. A red light on the—'

" 'There was a light,' I said, mildly.

" 'But it's out, man! What's the use of talking like this? You can see for yourself it's out—don't you? If you had to take a valuable steamer along this God-forsaken coast you would want a light too. I'll kick him from end to end of his miserable wharf. You'll see if I don't. I will—'

" 'So I may tell my captain you'll take us?' I broke in.

" 'Yes, I'll take you. Good night,' he said, brusquely.

"I pulled back, made fast again to the jetty, and then went to sleep at last. I had faced the silence of the East. I had heard some of its languages. But when I opened my eyes again the silence was as complete as though it had never been broken. I was lying in a flood of light, and the sky had never looked so far, so high, before. I opened my eyes and lay without moving.

"And then I saw the men of the East—they were looking at me. The whole length of the jetty was full of people. I saw brown, bronze, yellow faces, the black eyes, the glitter, the color of an Eastern crowd. And all these beings stared without a murmur, without a sigh, without a movement. They stared down at the boats, at the sleeping men who at night had come to them from the sea. Nothing moved. The fronds of palms stood still against the sky. Not a branch stirred along the shore, and the brown roofs of hidden houses peeped through the green foliage, through the big leaves that hung shining and still like leaves forged of heavy metal. This was the East of the ancient navigators, so old, so mysterious, resplendent and somber, living and unchanged, full of danger and promise. And these were the men. I sat up suddenly. A wave of movement passed through the crowd from end to end, passed along the heads, swayed the bodies, ran along the jetty like a ripple on the water, like a breath of wind on a field—and all was still again. I see it now—the wide sweep of the bay, the glittering sands, the wealth of green infinite and varied, the sea blue like the sea of a dream, the crowd of attentive faces, the blaze of vivid color—the water reflecting it all, the curve of the shore, the jetty, the high-sterned outlandish craft floating still, and the three boats with tired men from the West sleeping unconscious of the land and the people and of the violence of sunshine. They slept thrown across the thwarts, curled on bottom-boards, in the careless attitudes of death. The head of the old skipper, leaning back in the stern of the longboat, had fallen on his breast, and he looked as though he would never wake. Farther out old Mahon's face was upturned to the sky, with the long white beard spread out on his breast, as though he had been shot where he sat at the tiller; and a man, all in a heap in the bow of the boat, slept with both arms embracing the stem-head and with his cheek laid on the gunwale. The East looked at them without a sound.

"I have known its fascinations since: I have seen the mysterious shores, the still water, the lands of brown nations, where a stealthy Nemesis lies in wait, pursues, overtakes so many of the conquering race, who are proud of their wisdom, of their knowledge, of their strength. But for me all the East is contained in that vision of my youth. It is all in that moment when I opened my young eyes on it. I came upon it from a tussle with the sea—and I was young—and I saw it looking at me. And this is all that is left of it! Only a moment; a moment of strength, of romance, of glamour—of youth! . . . A flick of sunshine upon a strange shore, the time to remember, the time for a sigh, and—good-by!—Night—Good-by . . . !"

He drank.

"Ah! The good old time—the good old time. Youth and the sea. Glamour and the sea! The good, strong sea, the salt, bitter sea, that could whisper to you and roar at you and knock your breath out of you."

He drank again.

"By all that's wonderful, it is the sea, I believe, the sea itself—or is it youth alone? Who can tell? But you here—you all had something out of life: money, love—whatever one gets on shore—and, tell me, wasn't that the best time, that time when we were young at sea; young and had nothing, on the sea that gives nothing, except hard knocks—and sometimes a chance to feel your strength—that only—that you all regret?"

And we all nodded at him: the man of finance, the man of accounts, the man of law, we all nodded at him over the polished table that like a still sheet of brown water reflected our faces, lined, wrinkled; our faces marked by toil, by deceptions, by success, by love; our weary eyes looking still, looking always, looking anxiously for something out of life, that while it is expected is already gone—has passed unseen, in a sigh, in a flash—together with the youth, with the strength, with the romance of illusions.

VIRGINIA WOOLF

(1878-1941)

Virginia Woolf, represented here by only one short story, is one of the major figures in modern fiction; but it is as a novelist, not short story writer, that she is known. The daughter of the respected British scholar, critic, and biographer Leslie Stephen, she was self-educated by access to his library rather than by study in a university. After her father's death she took up residence in Bloomsbury, an unfashionable section of London, where she hosted a brilliant circle of friends, including Clive Bell, Lytton Strachey, and E. M. Forster. In 1907 she married Leonard Woolf, an enormously compassionate and understanding man, who helped nurse her through the emotional breakdowns that usually followed publication of a serious work. Together they founded Hogarth Press to print her work and the work of writers they respected. Her novels include *The Voyage Out, Jacob's Room, Mrs. Dalloway, To the Lighthouse,* and *The Waves.* She wrote volumes of critical essays and brilliant works of feminist polemic, including *A Room of One's Own.*

Woolf experimented in capturing moments of consciousness and weaving them into a pattern. Told in the abstract, her novels have little plot: A society lady plans and carries out a party while across town a man she doesn't know kills himself (*Mrs. Dalloway*). A family of children grow up, age, gather together at a party (*The Years*). Two trips to a lighthouse are planned ten years apart; between the first, which never comes off, and the second, which does, ten years pass and the novel's central character dies (*To the Lighthouse*). The essence of such works cannot be summarized; everything depends on significant moments of consciousness. In "An Unwritten Novel" we are in touch with the consciousness of the narrator, turning what she sees into fiction, yet loving the reality she can't know. You may want to consider this story about the creative process in connection with Barth's "Lost in the Funhouse," Barthelme's "The Balloon," Roth's "Looking at Kafka," Fort's "The Coal Shoveller," Brautigan's "Sea, Sea Rider," and Oates's "How I Contemplated . . ." (pp. 719 ff.) .

[See Preface, p. 30 (fiction about the process of fictionalizing).]

An Unwritten Novel

VIRGINIA WOLF

Such an expression of unhappiness was enough by itself to make one's eyes slide above the paper's edge to the poor woman's face—insignificant without that look, almost a symbol of human destiny with it. Life's what you see in people's eyes; life's what they learn, and, having learnt it, never, though they seek to hide it, cease to be aware of—what? That life's like that, it seems. Five faces opposite—five mature faces—and the knowledge in each face. Strange, though, how people want to conceal it! Marks of reticence are on all those faces: lips shut, eyes shaded, each one of the five doing something to hide or stultify his knowledge. One smokes; another reads; a third checks entries in a pocket book; a fourth stares at the map of the line framed opposite; and the fifth—the terrible thing about the fifth is that she does nothing at all. She looks at life. Ah, but my poor, unfortunate woman, do play the game—do, for all our sakes, conceal it!

As if she heard me, she looked up, shifted slightly in her seat and sighed. She seemed to apologize and at the same time to say to me, "If only you knew!" Then she looked at life again. "But I do know," I answered silently, glancing at the *Times* for manners' sake. "I know the whole business. 'Peace between Germany and the Allied Powers was yesterday officially ushered in at Paris—Signor Nitti, the Italian Prime Minister—a passenger train at Doncaster was in collision with a goods train . . .' We all know—the *Times* knows—but we pretend we don't." My eyes had once more crept over the paper's rim. She shuddered, twitched her arm queerly to the middle of her back and

From *A Haunted House and Other Stories* by Virginia Woolf; copyright, 1944, 1972, by Harcourt Brace Jovanovich, Inc. and reprinted with their permission and that of the Author's Literary Estate & The Hogarth Press.

shook her head. Again I dipped into my great reservoir of life. "Take what you like," I continued, "births, deaths, marriages, Court Circular, the habits of birds, Leonardo da Vinci, the Sandhills murder, high wages and the cost of living—oh, take what you like," I repeated, "it's all in the *Times!*" Again with infinite weariness she moved her head from side to side until, like a top exhausted with spinning, it settled on her neck.

The *Times* was no protection against such sorrow as hers. But other human beings forbade intercourse. The best thing to do against life was to fold the paper so that it made a perfect square, crisp, thick, impervious even to life. This done, I glanced up quickly, armed with a shield of my own. She pierced through my shield; she gazed into my eyes as if searching any sediment of courage at the depths of them and damping it to clay. Her twitch alone denied all hope, discounted all illusion.

So we rattled through Surrey and across the border into Sussex. But with my eyes upon life I did not see that the other travellers had left, one by one, till, save for the man who read, we were alone together. Here was Three Bridges station. We drew slowly down the platform and stopped. Was he going to leave us? I prayed both ways—I prayed last that he might stay. At that instant he roused himself, crumpled his paper contemptuously, like a thing done with, burst open the door, and left us alone.

The unhappy woman, leaning a little forward, palely and colourlessly addressed me—talked of stations and holidays, of brothers at Eastbourne, and the time of year, which was, I forget now, early or late. But at last looking from the window and seeing, I knew, only life, she breathed, "Staying away—that's the drawback of it—" Ah, now we approached the catastrophe. "My sister-in-law"—the bitterness of her tone was like lemon on cold steel, and speaking, not to me, but to herself, she muttered, "nonsense, she would say—that's what they all say," and while she spoke she fidgeted as though the skin on her back were as a plucked fowl's in a poulterer's shop-window.

"Oh, that cow!" she broke off nervously, as though the great wooden cow in the meadow had shocked her and saved her from some indiscretion. Then she shuddered, and then she made the awkward angular movement that I had seen before, as if, after the spasm, some spot between the shoulders burnt or itched. Then again she looked the most unhappy woman in the world, and I once more reproached her, though not with the same conviction, for if there were a reason, and if I knew the reason, the stigma was removed from life.

"Sisters-in-law," I said—

Her lips pursed as if to spit venom at the word; pursed they remained. All she did was to take her glove and rub hard at a spot on the window-pane. She rubbed as if she would rub something out for ever—some stain, some indelible contamination. Indeed, the spot remained for all her rubbing, and back she sank with the shudder and the clutch of the arm I had come to expect. Something impelled me to take my glove and rub my window. There, too, was a little speck on the glass. For all my rubbing it remained. And then the spasm went through me; I crooked my arm and plucked at the middle of my back. My skin, too, felt like the damp chicken's skin in the poulterer's shop-window; one spot between the shoulders itched and irritated, felt clammy, felt raw. Could I reach it? Surreptitiously I tried. She saw me. A smile of infinite irony, infinite sorrow, flitted and faded from her face. But she had communicated, shared her secret, passed her poison; she would speak no more. Leaning back in my corner, shielding my eyes from her eyes, seeing only the slopes and hollows, greys and purples, of the winter's landscape. I read her message, deciphered her secret, reading it beneath her gaze.

Hilda's the sister-in-law. Hilda? Hilda? Hilda Marsh—Hilda the blooming, the full bosomed, the matronly. Hilda stands at the door as the cab draws up, holding a coin. "Poor Minnie, more of a grasshopper than ever—old cloak she had last year. Well, well, with two children these days one can't do more. No, Minnie, I've got it; here you are, cabby—none of your ways with me. Come in, Minnie. Oh, I could carry *you,* let alone your basket!" So they go into the dining-room. "Aunt Minnie, children."

Slowly the knives and forks sink from the upright. Down they get (Bob and Barbara), hold out hands stiffly; back again to their chairs, staring between the resumed mouthfuls. [But this we'll skip; ornaments, curtains, trefoil china plate, yellow oblongs of cheese, white squares of biscuit—skip, oh, but wait! Halfway through luncheon one of those shivers; Bob stares at her, spoon in mouth. "Get on with your pudding, Bob"; but Hilda disapproves. "Why *should* she twitch?" Skip, skip, till we reach the landing on the upper floor; stairs brass-bound; linoleum worn; oh, yes! little bedroom looking out over the roofs of Eastbourne—zigzagging roofs like the spines of caterpillars, this way, that way, striped red and yellow, with blue-black slating.] Now, Minnie, the door's shut; Hilda heavily descends to the basement; you unstrap the straps of your basket, lay on the bed a meagre nightgown, stand side by side furred felt slippers. The looking-glass—no, you avoid the looking-glass. Some methodical disposition of hat-pins. Perhaps the shell box has something in it? You shake it; its the pearl stud there was last year—that's all. And then the sniff, the sigh, the sitting by the window. Three o'clock on a December afternoon; the rain drizzling! one light low in the skylight of a drapery emporium; another high in a servant's bedroom—this one goes out. That gives her nothing to look at. A moment's blankness—then, what are you thinking? (Let me peep across at her opposite; she's asleep or pretending it; so what would she think about sitting at the window at three o'clock in the afternoon? Health, money, hills, her God?) Yes, sitting on the very edge of the chair looking over the roofs of Eastbourne, Minnie Marsh prays to God. That's all very well; and she may rub the pane too, as though to see God better; but what God does she see? Who's the God of Minnie Marsh, the God of the back streets of Eastbourne, the God of three o'clock in the afternoon? I, too, see roofs, I see sky; but, oh, dear—this seeing of Gods! More like President Kruger than Prince Albert—that's the best I can do for him; and I see him on a chair, in a black frock-coat, not so very high up either; I can manage a cloud or two for him to sit on; and then his hand trailing in the cloud holds a rod, a truncheon is it?—black, thick, thorned—a brutal old bully—Minnie's God! Did he send the itch and the patch and the twitch? Is that why she prays? What she rubs on the window is the stain of sin. Oh, she committed some crime!

I have my choice of crimes. The woods flit and fly—in summer there are bluebells; in the opening there, when spring comes, primroses. A parting, was it, twenty years ago? Vows broken? Not Minnie's! . . . She was faithful. How she nursed her mother! All her savings on the tombstone—wreaths under glass—daffodils in jars. But I'm off the track. A crime. . . . They would say she kept her sorrow, suppressed her secret—her sex, they'd say—the scientific people. But what flummery to saddle *her* with sex! No—more like this. Passing down the streets of Croydon twenty years ago, the violet loops of ribbon in the draper's window spangled in the electric light catch her eye. She lingers—past six. Still by running she can reach home. She pushes through the glass wing door. It's sale-time. Shallow trays brim with ribbons. She pauses, pulls this, fingers that with the raised roses on it—no need to choose, no need to buy, and each tray with its surprises. "We don't shut till seven," and then it *is* seven. She runs, she rushes, home she reaches, but too late. Neighbours—the doctor—baby brother—the kettle—scalded—hospital—dead—or only the shock of it, the blame? Ah, but the detail matters nothing! It's what she carries with her; the spot, the crime, the thing to expiate, always there between her shoulders. "Yes," she seems to nod to me, "it's the thing I did."

Whether you did, or what you did, I don't mind; it's not the thing I want. The draper's window looped with violet—that'll do; a little cheap perhaps, a little commonplace—since one has a choice of crimes, but then so many (let me peep across again—still sleeping, or pretending sleep! white, worn, the mouth closed—a touch of obstinacy, more than one would think—no hint of sex) —so many crimes aren't *your* crime; your crime was cheap, only the retribution solemn; for now the church door opens, the hard wooden pew receives her; on the brown tiles she kneels; every day, winter, summer, dusk, dawn (here she's at it) prays. All her sins fall, fall, for ever fall. The spot receives them. It's raised, it's red, it's burning. Next she twitches. Small boys point. "Bob at lunch today"—But elderly women are the worst.

Indeed now you can't sit praying any longer. Kruger's sunk beneath the clouds—washed over as with a painter's brush of liquid grey, to which he adds a tinge of black—even the tip of the truncheon gone now. That's what always happens! Just as you've seen him, felt him, someone interrupts. It's Hilda now.

How you hate her! She'll even lock the bathroom door overnight, too, though it's only cold water you want, and sometimes when the night's been bad it seems as if washing helped. And John at breakfast —the children—meals are worst, and sometimes there are friends— ferns don't altogether hide 'em—they guess, too; so out you go along the front, where the waves are grey, and the papers blow, and the glass shelters green and draughty, and the chairs cost tuppence—too much—for there must be preachers along the sands. Ah, that's a nigger—that's a funny man—that's a man with parakeets—poor little creatures! Is there no one here who thinks of God?—just up there, over the pier, with his rod—but no—there's nothing but grey in the sky or if it's blue the white clouds hide him, and the music—it's military music—and what they are fishing for? Do they catch them? How the children stare! Well, then home a back way—"Home a back way!" The words have meaning; might have been spoken by the old man with whiskers—no, no, he didn't really speak; but everything has meaning—placards leaning against doorways—names above shop-windows—red fruit in baskets—women's heads in the hairdresser's— all say "Minnie Marsh!" But here's a jerk. "Eggs are cheaper!" That's what always happens! I was heading her over the waterfall, straight for madness, when, like a flock of dream sheep, she turns t'other way and runs between my fingers, Eggs are cheaper. Tethered to the shores of the world, none of the crimes, sorrows, rhapsodies, or insanities for poor Minnie Marsh; never late for luncheon; never caught in a storm without a mackintosh; never utterly unconscious of the cheapness of eggs. So she reaches home—scrapes her boots.

Have I read you right? But the human face—the human face at the top of the fullest sheet of print holds more, withholds more. Now, eyes open, she looks out; and in the human eye—how d'you define it?—there's a break—a division—so that when you've grasped the stem the butterfly's off—the moth that hangs in the evening over the yellow flower—move, raise your hand, off, high, away. I won't raise my hand. Hang still, then, quiver, life, soul, spirit, whatever you are of Minnie Marsh—I, too, on my flower—the hawk over the down—

alone, or what were the worth of life? To rise; hang still in the evening, in the midday; hang still over the down. The flicker of a hand—off, up! then poised again. Alone, unseen; seeing all so still down there, all so lovely. None seeing, none caring. The eyes of others our prisons; their thoughts our cages. Air above, air below. And the moon and immortality. . . . Oh, but I drop to the turf! Are you down too, you in the corner, what's your name—woman—Minnie Marsh; some such name as that? There she is, tight to her blossom; opening her hand-bag, from which she takes a hollow shell—an egg—who was saying that eggs were cheaper? You or I? Oh, it was you who said it on the way home, you remember, when the old gentleman, suddenly opening his umbrella—or sneezing was it? Anyhow, Kruger went, and you came "home a back way," and scraped your boots. Yes. And now you lay across your knees a pocket-handkerchief into which drop little angular fragments of eggshell—fragments of a map—a puzzle. I wish I could piece them together! If you would only sit still. She's moved her knees—the map's in bits again. Down the slopes of the Andes the white blocks of marble go bounding and hurtling, crushing to death a whole troop of Spanish muleteers, with their convoy—Drake's booty, gold and silver. But to return—

To what, to where? She opened the door, and, putting her umbrella in the stand—that goes without saying; so, too, the whiff of beef from the basement; dot, dot, dot. But what I cannot thus eliminate, what I must, head down, eyes shut, with the courage of a battalion and the blindness of a bull, charge and disperse are, indubitably, the figures behind the ferns, commercial travellers. There, I've hidden them all this time in the hope that somehow they'd disappear, or better still emerge, as indeed they must, if the story's to go on gathering richness and rotundity, destiny and tragedy, as stories should, rolling along with it two, if not three, commercial travellers and a whole grove of aspidistra. "The fronds of the aspidistra only partly concealed the commercial traveller—" Rhododendrons would conceal him utterly, and into the bargain give me my fling of red and white, for which I starve and strive; but rhododendrons in Eastbourne—in December—on the Marshes' table—no, no, I dare not; it's all a matter of crusts and cruets, frills and ferns. Perhaps there'll be a moment later by the sea. Moreover, I feel, pleasantly pricking through the green fretwork and over the glacis of cut glass, a desire to peer and peep at the man opposite—one's as much as I can manage. James Moggridge is it, whom the Marshes call Jimmy? [Minnie, you must promise not to twitch till I've got this straight.] James Moggridge travels in—shall we say buttons?—but the time's not come for bringing *them* in—the big and the little on the long cards, some peacock-eyed, others dull gold; cairngorms some, and others coral sprays—but I say the time's not come. He travels, and on Thursdays, his Eastbourne day, takes his meals with the Marshes. His red face, his little steady eyes—by no means altogether commonplace—his enormous appetite (that's safe; he won't look at Minnie till the bread's swamped the gravy dry), napkin tucked diamond-wise—but this is primitive, and, whatever it may do the reader, don't take me in. Let's dodge to the Moggridge household, set that in motion. Well, the family boots are mended on Sundays by James himself. He reads *Truth*. But his passion? Roses—and his wife a retired hospital nurse—interesting—for God's sake let me have one woman with a name I like! But no; she's of the unborn children of the mind, illicit, none the less loved, like my rhododendrons. How many die in every novel that's written—the best, the dearest, while Moggridge lives. It's life's fault. Here's Minnie eating her egg at the moment opposite and at t'other end of the line—are we past Lewes?—there must be Jimmy—what's her twitch for?

There must be Moggridge—life's fault. Life imposes her laws; life blocks the way; life's behind the fern; life's the tyrant; oh, but not the bully! No, for I assure you I come willingly; I come wooed by Heaven knows what compulsion across ferns and cruets, table splashed and bottles smeared. I come irresistibly to lodge myself somewhere on the firm flesh, in the robust spine, wherever I can penetrate or find foothold on the person, in the soul, of Moggridge the man. The enormous stability of the fabric; the spine tough as whalebone, straight as oaktree; the ribs radiating branches; the flesh taut tarpaulin; the red hollows; the suck and regurgitation of the heart; while from above meat falls in brown cubes and beer gushes to be churned to blood again—and so we reach the eyes. Behind the aspidistra they see something: black, white, dismal; now the plate again; behind the aspidistra they see elderly woman; "Marsh's sister, Hilda's more my sort"; the tablecloth now. "Marsh would know what's wrong with Morrises . . ." talk that over; cheese has come; the plate again; turn it round—the enormous fingers; now the woman opposite. "Marsh's sister—not a bit like Marsh; wretched, elderly female. . . . You should feed your hens. . . . God's truth, what's set her twitching? Not what *I* said? Dear, dear, dear! these elderly women. Dear, dear!"

[Yes, Minnie; I know you've twitched, but one moment—James Moggridge.]

"Dear, dear, dear!" How beautiful the sound is! like the knock of a mallet on seasoned timber, like the throb of the heart of an ancient whaler when the seas press thick and the green is clouded. "Dear, dear!" what a passing bell for the souls of the fretful to soothe them and solace them, lap them in linen, saying, "So long. Good luck to you!" and then, "What's your pleasure?" for though Moggridge would pluck his rose for her, that's done, that's over. Now what's the next thing? "Madam, you'll miss your train," for they don't linger.

That's the man's way; that's the sound that reverberates; that's St. Paul's and the motor-omnibuses. But we're brushing the crumbs off. Oh, Moggridge, you won't stay? You must be off? Are you driving through Eastbourne this afternoon in one of those little carriages? Are you the man who's walled up in green cardboard boxes, and sometimes sits so solemn staring like a sphinx; and always there's a look of the sepulchral, something of the undertaker, the coffin, and the dusk about horse and driver? Do tell me—but the doors slammed. We shall never meet again. Moggridge, farewell!

Yes, yes, I'm coming. Right up to the top of the house. One moment I'll linger. How the mud goes round in the mind—what a swirl these monsters leave, the waters rocking, the weeds waving and green here, black there, striking to the sand, till by degrees the atoms reassemble, the deposit sifts itself, and again through the eyes one sees clear and still, and there comes to the lips some prayer for the departed, some obsequy for the souls of those one nods to, the people one never meets again.

James Moggridge is dead now, gone for ever. Well, Minnie—"I can face it no longer." If she said that— (Let me look at her. She is brushing the eggshell into deep declivities). She said it certainly, leaning against the wall of the bedroom, and plucking at the little balls which edge the claret-coloured curtain. But when the self speaks to the self, who is speaking?—the entombed soul, the spirit driven in, in, in to the central catacomb; the self that took the veil and left the world—a coward perhaps, yet somehow beautiful, as it flits with its lantern restlessly up and down the dark corridors. "I can bear it no longer," her spirit says. "That man at lunch—Hilda—the children." Oh, heavens, her sob! It's the spirit wailing its destiny, the spirit driven hither, thither, lodging on the diminishing carpets—meagre footholds—shrunken shreds of all the vanishing universe—love, life, faith, husband, children, I know not what splendours and pageantries glimpsed in girlhood. "Not for me—not for me."

But then—the muffins, the bald elderly dog? Bead mats I should fancy and the consolation of underlinen. If Minnie Marsh were run over and taken to hospital, nurses and doctors themselves would exclaim. . . . There's the vista and the vision—there's the distance—the blue blot at the end of the avenue, while, after all, the tea is rich, the muffin hot, and the dog—"Benny, to your basket, sir, and see what mother's brought you!" So, taking the glove with the worn thumb, defying once more the encroaching demon of what's called going in holes, you renew the fortifications, threading the grey wool, running it in and out.

Running it in and out, across and over, spinning a web through which God himself—hush, don't think of God! How firm the stitches are! You must be proud of your darning. Let nothing disturb her. Let the light fall gently, and the clouds show an inner vest of the first green leaf. Let the sparrow perch on the twig and shake the raindrop hanging to the twig's elbow. . . . Why look up? Was it a sound, a thought? Oh, heavens! Back again to the thing you did, the plate glass with the violet loops? But Hilda will come. Ignominies, humiliations, oh! Close the breach.

Having mended her glove, Minnie Marsh lays it in the drawer. She shuts the drawer with decision. I catch sight of her face in the glass. Lips are pursed. Chin held high. Next she laces her shoes. Then she touches her throat. What's your brooch? Mistletoe or merrythought? And what is happening? Unless I'm much mistaken, the pulse's quickened, the moment's coming, the threads are racing, Niagara's ahead. Here's the crisis! Heaven be with you! Down she goes. Courage, courage! Face it, be it! For God's sake don't wait on the mat now! There's the door! I'm on your side. Speak! Confront her, confound her soul!

"Oh, I beg your pardon! Yes, this is Eastbourne. I'll reach it down for you. Let me try the handle." [But Minnie, though we keep up pretences, I've read you right—I'm with you now.]

"That's all your luggage?"

"Much obliged, I'm sure."

(But why do you look about you? Hilda won't come to the station, nor John; and Moggridge is driving at the far side of Eastbourne.)

"I'll wait by my bag, ma'am, that's safest. He said he'd meet me. . . . Oh, there he is! That's my son."

So they walk off together.

Well, but I'm confounded. . . . Surely, Minnie, you know better! A strange young man. . . . Stop! I'll tell him—Minnie!—Miss Marsh!—I don't know though. There's something queer in her cloak as it blows. Oh, but it's untrue, it's indecent. . . . Look how he bends as they reach the gateway. She finds her ticket. What's the joke? Off they go, down the road, side by side. . . . Well, my world's done for! What do I stand on? What do I know? That's not Minnie. There never was Moggridge. Who am I? Life's bare as bone.

And yet the last look of them—he stepping from the kerb and she following him round the edge of the big building brims me with wonder—floods me anew. Mysterious figures! Mother and son. Who are you? Why do you walk down the street? Where tonight will you sleep, and then, tomorrow? Oh, how it whirls and surges—floats me afresh! I start after them. People drive this way and that. The white light splutters and pours. Plate-glass windows. Carnations; chrysanthemums. Ivy in dark gardens. Milk carts at the door. Wherever I go, mysterious figures, I see you, turning the corner, mothers and sons;

you, you, you. I hasten, I follow. This, I fancy, must be the sea. Grey is the landscape; dim as ashes; the water murmurs and moves. If I fall on my knees, if I go through the ritual, the ancient antics, it's you, unknown figures, you I adore; if I open my arms, it's you I embrace, you I draw to me—adorable world!

QUESTIONS

1. If Minnie Marsh is a creation of the narrator, how is it that the narrator imagines precisely the story she does—of an isolated woman near madness? Whose story are we hearing? (See Preface, pp. 1–11.)
2. Why, when the narrator learns that her story is false, does she feel "life's bare as bone"? What does she expect? Why does she need it?
3. At one moment she wants to know the woman's mysteries, at another she respects the isolated soul free from the "prison" of the "eyes of others," at still another she speaks of the isolated soul as "entombed"—dead. Discuss.
4. The story deals with the process of fiction trying to know reality. What does the narrator conclude about the process? Why does she, even at the end, continue? (See Preface, pp. 29–32.)
5. Is there anything of reality in the story the narrator invents? Do we sense anything of life? If so, what? And where does it come from?

JAMES JOYCE

(1882-1941)

Joyce, who is often regarded as this century's most important writer in the English language, was born of a middle-class family in Dublin, Ireland, in 1882. His father began to drink away his money, lose positions, sink in the social order; but Joyce was able to complete a good education under the Jesuits and go to University College. From early on he saw himself as a potential artist; before he had published, before he had even written very much poetry or prose, he knew that he was a genius and that his calling as an artist was certain. Still, he also worked on careers in medicine and concert singing before leaving for Paris and a writer's career. He returned to Ireland when his mother was dying, but stayed only a year. He fell in love with Nora Barnacle, his lifelong companion, and then looked for a job abroad, feeling that Ireland would suffocate his spirit and reject his art.

He obtained a teaching position in Zurich, but when he got there he found the position nonexistent and had to settle in Trieste, where he taught English for Berlitz and wrote—a hard life, with no acknowledgment for his art. His book of stories, *Dubliners*, written when Joyce was still in Dublin and completed in Trieste, terrified his publisher. In spite of pleas and offers to eliminate offensive passages, it was not until 1914 that the book was published.

Dubliners was decried not only because of its specific references to contemporary Ireland and its frank language and hints of sexuality, but also because of its bleak picture of Dublin as a stagnant pond that smothered all life, a city in which dead people deceived themselves into pretending they were alive, a city ruled by a repressive but moribund church.

In Trieste he wrote a mammoth novel, *Stephen Hero*, which he reduced and tightened into *A Portrait of the Artist as a Young Man,* published in 1916. Like Lawrence's *Sons and Lovers* (see p. 348), *Portrait* is autobiographical. But far more than Lawrence, Joyce retains an ironic detachment from the sensitive, spoiled, arrogant young man he had been. It is a strange "portrait," written not in a realistic style like *Dubliners* (see the following stories), but in a style which reflects the consciousness of its protagonist, and which changes as that consciousness changes.

By now he had won the admiration of Ezra Pound, who helped him win financial support from wealthy patrons. Joyce settled in Zurich in 1915, in Paris in 1920, where he became famous for a novel privately circulated but not yet published—*Ulysses*. When it was published, in 1922, it was banned not only in Ireland but in the United States as well, because of its language and descriptions of sexuality, and it became a necessary part of an American's European tour to smuggle the book through United States Customs. *Ulysses* is a massive novel about a single day in Dublin, June 16, 1904; it explores the ongoing consciousness of the major characters: Leopold Bloom, his wife Molly, and Stephen Dedalus, the young man who had been the protagonist of *Portrait*. Joyce dazzles the reader with a collection of styles, from witty questions and answers to newspaper clippings to stream of consciousness.

For the rest of his life Joyce wrote the amazing, complex *Work in Progress,* finally entitled *Finnegans Wake* when it was published in 1939, two years before Joyce's death. By now, he was a hero of literary culture; his *Wake,* Joyce said, took twenty years to write and ought to take twenty years to read. Critics have been reading it ever since, but it has remained very much a literary property, incomprehensible to most readers.

The stories in this anthology, "Araby," "Counterparts," and "Clay," are all taken from *Dubliners*. Brilliant examples of ironic realism, they also foreshadow Joyce's later writing, concerned as they are with finding intense significance in the commonplace, with finding overtones of myth and sacred reality in ordinary life.

[See Preface: "Clay," p. 25 (tone); "Araby," pp. 26–27 (tone).]

Araby

JAMES JOYCE

North Richmond Street, being blind, was a quiet street except at the hour when the Christian Brothers' School set the boys free. An uninhabited house of two stories stood at the blind end, detached from its neighbours in a square ground. The other houses of the street, conscious of decent lives within them, gazed at one another with brown imperturbable faces.

The former tenant of our house, a priest, had died in the back drawing-room. Air, musty from having been long enclosed, hung in all the rooms, and the waste room behind the kitchen was littered with old useless papers. Among these I found a few paper-covered books, the pages of which were curled and damp: *The Abbot,* by Walter Scott, *The Devout Communicant,* and *The Memoirs of Vidocq.* I liked the last best because its leaves were yellow. The wild garden behind the house contained a central apple tree and a few straggling bushes under one of which I found the late tenant's rusty bicycle pump. He had been a very charitable priest; in his will he had left all his money to institutions and the furniture of his house to his sister.

When the short days of winter came dusk fell before we had well eaten our dinners. When we met in the street the houses had grown sombre. The space of sky above us was the colour of ever-changing violet and towards it the lamps of the street lifted their feeble lanterns. The cold air stung us and we played till our bodies glowed. Our shouts echoed in the silent street. The career of our play brought us through the dark muddy lanes behind the houses where we ran the gauntlet of the rough tribes from the cottages, to the back doors of the dark dripping gardens where odours arose from the ash-pits, to the dark odorous stables where a coachman smoothed and combed the horse or shook music from the buckled harness. When we re-turned to the street, light from the kitchen windows had filled the areas. If my uncle was seen turning the corner we hid in the shadow until we had seen him safely housed. Or if Mangan's sister came out on the doorstep to call her brother in to his tea we watched her from our shadow peer up and down the street. We waited to see whether she would remain or go in and, if she remained, we left our shadow and walked up to Mangan's steps resignedly. She was waiting for us, her figure defined by the light from the half-opened door. Her brother always teased her before he obeyed and I stood by the railings looking at her. Her dress swung as she moved her body and the soft rope of her hair tossed from side to side.

Every morning I lay on the floor in the front parlour watching her door. The blind was pulled down to within an inch of the sash so that I could not be seen. When she came out on the doorstep my heart leaped. I ran to the hall, seized my books and followed her. I kept her brown figure always in my eye and, when we came near the point at which our ways diverged, I quickened my pace and passed her. This happened morning after morning. I had never spoken to her, except for a few casual words, and yet her name was like a summons to all my foolish blood.

Her image accompanied me even in places the most hostile to romance. On Saturday evenings when my aunt went marketing I had to go to carry some of the parcels. We walked through the flaring streets, jostled by drunken men and bargaining women, amid the curses of labourers, the shrill litanies of shop-boys who stood on guard by the barrels of pigs' cheeks, the nasal chanting of street-singers, who sang a *come-all-you* about O'Donovan Rossa, or a ballad about the troubles in our native land. These noises converged in a single sensation of life for me: I imagined that I bore my chalice safely through a throng of foes. Her name sprang to my lips at moments in strange prayers and praises which I myself did not understand. My eyes were often full of tears (I could not tell why) and at times a flood from my heart seemed to pour itself out into my bosom. I thought little of the future. I did not know whether I would ever speak to her or not or, if I spoke to her, how I could tell her of my confused adoration. But my body was like a harp and her words and gestures were like fingers running upon the wires.

One evening I went into the back drawing-room in which the priest had died. It was a dark rainy evening and there was no sound in the house. Through one of the broken panes I heard the rain impinge upon the earth, the fine incessant needles of water playing in the sodden beds. Some distant lamp or lighted window gleamed below me. I was thankful that I could see so little. All my senses seemed to desire to veil themselves and, feeling that I was about to slip from them, I pressed the palms of my hands together until they trembled, murmuring: *"O love! O love!"* many times.

At last she spoke to me. When she addressed the first words to me I was so confused that I did not know what to answer. She asked me was I going to *Araby*. I forgot whether I answered yes or no. It would be a splendid bazaar, she said she would love to go.

"And why can't you?" I asked.

While she spoke she turned a silver bracelet round and round her wrist. She could not go, she said, because there would be a retreat that week in her convent. Her brother and two other boys were fighting for their caps and I was alone at the railings. She held one of the spikes, bowing her head towards me. The light from the lamp opposite our door caught the white curve of her neck, lit up her hair that rested there and, falling, lit up the hand upon the railing. It fell over one side of her dress and caught the white border of a petticoat, just visible as she stood at ease.

"It's well for you," she said.

"If I go," I said, "I will bring you something."

What innumerable follies laid waste my waking and sleeping thoughts after the evening! I wished to annihilate the tedious intervening days. I chafed against the work of school. At night in my bedroom and by day in the classroom her image came between me and the page I strove to read. The syllables of the word *Araby* were called to me through the silence in which my soul luxuriated and cast an Eastern enchantment over me. I asked for leave to go to the bazaar on Saturday night. My aunt was surprised and hoped it was not some Freemason affair. I answered few questions in class. I watched my master's face pass from amiability to sternness; he hoped I was not beginning to idle, I could not call my wandering thoughts together. I had hardly any patience with the serious work of life which, now that it stood between me and my desire, seemed to me child's play, ugly monotonous child's play.

On Saturday morning I reminded my uncle that I wished to go to the bazaar in the evening. He was fussing at the hall-stand, looking for the hat brush, and answered me curtly:

"Yes, boy, I know."

As he was in the hall I could not go into the front parlour and lie at the window. I left the house in bad humour and walked slowly towards the school. The air was pitilessly raw and already my heart misgave me.

When I came home to dinner my uncle had not yet been home. Still it was early. I sat staring at the clock for some time and, when its ticking began to irritate me, I left the room. I mounted the staircase and gained the upper part of the house. The high cold empty gloomy rooms liberated me and I went from room to room singing. From the front window I saw my companions playing below in the street. Their cries reached me weakened and indistinct and, leaning my forehead against the cool glass, I looked over at the dark house where she lived. I may have stood there for an hour, seeing nothing but the brown-clad figure cast by my imagination, touched discreetly by the lamplight at the curved neck, at the hand upon the railings and at the border below the dress.

When I came downstairs again I found Mrs. Mercer sitting at the fire. She was an old garrulous woman, a pawnbroker's widow, who collected used stamps for some pious purpose. I had to endure the gossip of the tea-table. The meal was prolonged beyond an hour and still my uncle did not come. Mrs. Mercer stood up to go: she was sorry she couldn't wait any longer, but it was after eight o'clock and she did not like to be out late, as the night air was bad for her. When she had gone I began to walk up and down the room, clenching my fists. My aunt said:

"I'm afraid you may put off your bazaar for this night of Our Lord."

At nine o'clock I heard my uncle's latchkey in the hall-door. I heard him talking to himself and heard the hall-stand rocking when it had received the weight of his overcoat. I could interpret these signs. When he was midway through his dinner I asked him to give me the money to go to the bazaar. He had forgotten.

"The people are in bed and after their first sleep now," he said.

I did not smile. My aunt said to him energetically:

"Can't you give him the money and let him go? You've kept him late enough as it is."

My uncle said he was very sorry he had forgotten. He said he believed in the old saying: "All work and no play makes Jack a dull boy." He asked me where I was going and, when I had told him a second time, he asked me did I know *The Arab's Farewell to his Steed*. When I left the kitchen he was about to recite the opening lines of the piece to my aunt.

I held a florin tightly in my hand as I strode down Buckingham Street towards the station. The sight of the streets thronged with buyers and glaring with gas recalled to me the purpose of my journey. I took my seat in a third-class carriage of a deserted train. After an intolerable delay the train moved out of the station slowly. It crept onward among ruinous houses and over the twinkling river. At Westland Row Station a crowd of people pressed to the carriage doors; but the porters moved them back, saying that it was a special train for the bazaar. I remained alone in the bare carriage. In a few minutes the train drew up beside an improvised wooden platform. I passed out on the road and saw by the lighted dial of a clock that it was ten minutes to ten. In front of me was a large building which displayed the magical name.

I could not find any sixpenny entrance and, fearing that the bazaar would be closed, I passed in quickly through a turnstile, handing a shilling to a weary-looking man. I found myself in a big hall girdled at half its height by a gallery. Nearly all the stalls were closed and the greater part of the hall was in darkness. I recognized a silence like that which pervades a church after a service. I walked into the center of the bazaar timidly. A few people were gathered about the stalls which were still open. Before a curtain, over which the words *Café Chantant* were written in coloured lamps, two men were counting money on a salver. I listened to the fall of the coins.

Remembering with difficulty why I had come I went over to one of the stalls and examined porcelain vases and flowered tea-sets. At the door of the stall a young lady was talking and laughing with two young gentlemen. I remarked their English accents and listened vaguely to their conversation.

"O, I never said such a thing!"

"O, but you did!"

"O, but I didn't!"

"Didn't she say that?"

"Yes. I heard her."

"O, there's a . . . fib!"

Observing me, the young lady came over and asked me did I wish to buy anything. The tone of her voice was not encouraging; she seemed to have spoken to me out of a sense of duty. I looked humbly at the great jars that stood like eastern guards at either side of the dark entrance to the stall and murmured:

"No, thank you."

The young lady changed the position of one of the vases and went back to the two young men. They began to talk of the same subject. Once or twice the young lady glanced at me over her shoulder.

I lingered before her stall, though I knew my stay was useless, to make my interest in her wares seem the more real. Then I turned away slowly and walked down the middle of the bazaar. I allowed the two pennies to fall against the sixpence in my pocket. I heard a voice call from one end of the gallery that the light was out. The upper part of the hall was now completely dark.

Gazing up into the darkness I saw myself as a creature driven and derided by vanity; and my eyes burned with anguish and anger.

QUESTIONS

1. Often a setting can do more than tell the reader where the action is taking place and convey the atmosphere; it can express a quality of life. "The other houses of the street, conscious of decent lives within them, gazed at one another with brown imperturbable faces." What does this sentence do besides define physical space? What does it say about Dublin? (See Preface, pp. 18–21.)

2. How are the boys unlike the houses? Why does Joyce establish this contrast?

3. "Her dress swung as she moved her body and the soft rope of her hair tossed from side to side." We never hear her described more fully. "The light from the lamp opposite our door caught the white curve of her neck,

lit up her hair that rested there and, falling, lit up the hand upon the railing." How can the reader manage to experience what the boy experiences with such slight description? What does Joyce gain? How is the description psychologically right for the character?

4. "I imagined that I bore my chalice safely through a throng of foes." Why *chalice?* Note other religious images. Discuss their significance with regard to *theme.* (See Preface, pp. 27–28.)

5. What magic does the name of the fair, *Araby,* hold for the boy?

6. Joyce's narrator speaks about his old playmates: "From the front window I saw my companions playing below in the street. Their cries reached me weakened and indistinct. . . ." How does this view of his friends function in the story?

7. We hear fragmentary dialogue between a saleslady at Araby and two young men. Describe the quality of the dialogue. Why does Joyce include it? What is its impact on the boy?

8. At the end, the light in the bazaar is out. Discuss.

9. From what angle of vision is the story told? What is the relation between the narrator and the boy? Are they exactly the same person? Discuss.

Counterparts

JAMES JOYCE

The bell rang furiously and, when Miss Parker went to the tube, a furious voice called out in a piercing North of Ireland accent: "Send Farrington here!"

Miss Parker returned to her machine, saying to a man who was writing at a desk: "Mr. Alleyne wants you upstairs."

The man muttered *"Blast* him!" under his breath and pushed back his chair to stand up. When he stood up he was tall and of great bulk. He had a hanging face, dark wine-colored, with fair eyebrows and mustache: his eyes bulged forward slightly and the whites of them were dirty. He lifted up the counter and, passing by the clients, went out of the office with a heavy step.

He went heavily upstairs until he came to the second landing, where a door bore a brass plate with the inscription: MR. ALLEYNE. Here he halted, puffing with labor and vexation, and knocked. The shrill voice cried: "Come in!"

From *Dubliners* by James Joyce. Originally published by B. W. Huebsch, Inc. in 1916. Copyright © 1967 by the Estate of James Joyce. All Rights Reserved. Reprinted by permission of The Viking Press.

The man entered Mr. Alleyne's room. Simultaneously Mr. Alleyne, a little man wearing gold-rimmed glasses on a clean-shaven face, shot his head up over a pile of documents. The head itself was so pink and hairless it seemed like a large egg reposing on the papers. Mr. Alleyne did not lose a moment: "Farrington? What is the meaning of this? Why have I always to complain of you? May I ask you why you haven't made a copy of that contract between Bodley and Kirwan? I told you it must be ready by four o'clock."

"But Mr. Shelley said, sir—"

"*Mr. Shelley said, sir* . . . Kindly attend to what I say and not to what *Mr. Shelley says, sir.* You have always some excuse or another for shirking work. Let me tell you that if the contract is not copied before this evening I'll lay the matter before Mr. Crosbie. . . . Do you hear me now?"

"Yes, sir."

"Do you hear me now? . . . Ay, and another little matter! I might as well be talking to the wall as talking to you. Understand once for all that you get a half an hour for your lunch and not an hour and a half. How many courses do you want, I'd like to know. . . . Do you mind me now?"

"Yes, sir."

Mr. Alleyne bent his head again upon his pile of papers. The man stared fixedly at the polished skull which directed the affairs of Crosbie & Alleyne, gauging its fragility. A spasm of rage gripped his throat for a few moments and then passed, leaving after it a sharp sensation of thirst. The man recognized the sensation and felt that he must have a good night's drinking. The middle of the month was passed and, if he could get the copy done in time, Mr. Alleyne might give him an order on the cashier. He stood still, gazing fixedly at the head upon the pile of papers. Suddenly Mr. Alleyne began to upset all the papers, searching for something. Then, as if he had been unaware of the man's presence till that moment, he shot up his head again, saying: "Eh? Are you going to stand there all day? Upon my word, Farrington, you take things easy!"

"I was waiting to see—"

"Very good, you needn't wait to see. Go downstairs and do your work."

The man walked heavily toward the door, and as he went out of the room he heard Mr. Alleyne cry after him that if the contract was not copied by evening Mr. Crosbie would hear of the matter.

He returned to his desk in the lower office and counted the sheets which remained to be copied. He took up his pen and dipped it in the ink, but he continued to stare stupidly at the last words he had written: "In no case shall the said Bernard Bodley be" . . . The evening was falling, and in a few minutes they would be lighting the gas: then he could write. He felt that he must slake the thirst in his throat. He stood up from his desk and, lifting the counter as before, passed out of the office. As he was passing out the chief clerk looked at him inquiringly.

"It's all right, Mr. Shelley," said the man, pointing with his finger to indicate the objective of his journey.

The chief clerk glanced at the hatrack, but, seeing the row complete, offered no remark. As soon as he was on the landing the man pulled a shepherd's-plaid cap out of his pocket, put it on his head, and ran quickly down the rickety stairs. From the street door he walked on furtively on the inner side of the path toward the corner and all at once dived into a doorway. He was now safe in the dark snug of O'Neill's shop, and filling up the little window that looked into the bar with his inflamed face, the color of dark wine or dark meat, he called out: "Here, Pat, give us a G.P., like a good fellow."

The curate brought him a glass of plain porter. The man drank it at a gulp and asked for a caraway seed. He put his penny on the counter and, leaving the curate to grope for it in the gloom, retreated out of the snug as furtively as he had entered it.

Darkness, accompanied by a thick fog, was gaining upon the dusk of February, and the lamps in Eustace Street had been lit. The man went up by the houses until he reached the door of the office, wondering whether he could finish his copy in time. On the stairs a moist, pungent odor of perfumes saluted his nose: evidently Miss Delacour had come while he was out in O'Neill's. He crammed his cap back again into his pocket and re-entered the office, assuming an air of absent-mindedness.

"Mr. Alleyne has been calling for you," said the chief clerk severely. "Where were you?"

The man glanced at the two clients who were standing at the counter as if to intimate that their presence prevented him from answering. As the clients were both male the chief clerk allowed himself a laugh.

"I know that game," he said. "Five times in one day is a little bit. . . . Well, you better look sharp and get a copy of our correspondence in the Delacour case for Mr. Alleyne."

This address in the presence of the public, his run upstairs, and the porter he had gulped down so hastily confused the man, and as he sat down at his desk to get what was required he realized how hopeless was the task of finishing his copy of the contract before half past five. The dark damp night was coming and he longed to spend it in the bars, drinking with his friends amid the glare of gas and the clatter of glasses. He got out the Delacour correspondence and passed out of the office. He hoped Mr. Alleyne would not discover that the last two letters were missing.

The moist, pungent perfume lay all the way up to Mr. Alleyne's room. Miss Delacour was a middle-aged woman of Jewish appearance. Mr. Alleyne was said to be sweet on her or on her money. She came to the office often and stayed a long time when she came. She was sitting beside his desk now in an aroma of perfumes, smoothing the handle of her umbrella and nodding the great black feather in her hat. Mr. Alleyne had swiveled his chair round to face her and thrown his right foot jauntily upon his left knee. The man put the correspondence on the desk and bowed respectfully, but neither Mr. Alleyne nor Miss Delacour took any notice of his bow. Mr. Alleyne tapped a finger on the correspondence and then flicked it toward him as if to say: "That's all right: you can go."

The man returned to the lower office and sat down again at his desk. He stared intently at the incomplete phrase: "In no case shall the said Bernard Bodley be" . . . and thought how strange it was that the last three words began with the same letter. The chief clerk began to hurry Miss Parker, saying she would never have the letters typed in time for post. The man listened to the clicking of the machine for a few minutes and then set to work to finish his copy. But his head was not clear, and his mind wandered away to the glare and rattle of the public house. It was a night for hot punches. He struggled on with his copy, but when the clock struck five he had still fourteen pages to write. Blast it! He couldn't finish it in time. He longed to execrate aloud, to bring his fist down on something violently. He was so enraged that he wrote "Bernard Bernard" instead of "Bernard Bodley" and had to begin again on a clean sheet.

He felt strong enough to clear out the whole office singlehanded. His body ached to do something, to rush out and revel in violence. All the indignities of his life enraged him. . . . Could he ask the cashier privately for an advance? No, the cashier was no good, no damn good: he wouldn't give an advance. . . . He knew where he would meet the boys: Leonard and O'Halloran and Nosey Flynn. The barometer of his emotional nature was set for a spell of riot.

His imagination had so abstracted him that his name was called twice before he answered. Mr. Alleyne and Miss Delacour were standing outside the counter, and all the clerks had turned round in anticipation of something. The man got up from his desk. Mr. Alleyne began a tirade of abuse, saying that two letters were missing. The man answered that he knew nothing about them, that he had made a faithful copy. The tirade continued: it was so bitter and violent that the man could hardly restrain his fist from descending upon the head of the manikin before him.

"I know nothing about any other two letters," he said stupidly.

"*You—know—nothing.* Of course you know nothing," said Mr. Alleyne. "Tell me," he added, glancing first for approval to the lady beside him, "do you take me for a fool? Do you think me an utter fool?"

The man glanced from the lady's face to the little egg-shaped head and back again, and almost before he was aware of it, his tongue had found a felicitous moment: "I don't think, sir," he said, "that that's a fair question to put to me."

There was a pause in the very breathing of the clerks. Everyone was astounded (the author of the witticism no less than his neighbors), and Miss Delacour, who was a stout, amiable person, began to smile broadly. Mr. Alleyne flushed to the hue of a wild rose, and his mouth twitched with a dwarf's passion. He shook his fist in the man's face till it seemed to vibrate like the knob of some electric machine: "You impertinent ruffian! You impertinent ruffian! I'll make short work of you! Wait till you see! You'll apologize to me for your impertinence or you'll quit the office instanter! You'll quit this, I'm telling you, or you'll apologize to me!"

He stood in a doorway opposite the office, watching to see if the cashier would come out alone. All the clerks passed out, and finally the cashier came out with the chief clerk. It was no use trying to say a word to him when he was with the chief clerk. The man felt that his position was bad enough. He had been obliged to offer an abject apology to Mr. Alleyne for his impertinence, but he knew what a hornet's nest the office would be for him. He could remember the way in which Mr. Alleyne had hounded little Peake out of the office in order to make room for his own nephew. He felt savage and thirsty and revengeful, annoyed with himself and with everyone else. Mr. Alleyne would never give him an hour's rest; his life would be a hell to him. He had made a proper fool of himself this time. Could he not keep his tongue in his cheek? But they had never pulled together from the first, he and Mr. Alleyne, ever since the day Mr. Alleyne had overheard him mimicking his North of Ireland accent to amuse Higgins and Miss Parker: that had been the beginning of it. He might have tried Higgins for the money, but sure, Higgins never had anything for himself. A man with two establishments to keep up, of course he couldn't. . . .

He felt his great body again aching for the comfort of the public house. The fog had begun to chill him, and he wondered could he touch Pat in O'Neill's. He could not touch him for more than a bob—and a bob was no use. Yet he must get money somewhere or other: he had spent his last penny for the G.P., and soon it would be too late for getting money anywhere. Suddenly, as he was fingering his watch chain, he thought of Terry Kelly's pawn office in Fleet Street. That was the dart! Why didn't he think of it sooner? He went through the narrow alley of Temple Bar quickly, muttering to himself that they could all go to hell, because he was going to have a good night of it. The clerk in Terry Kelly's said a crown, but the consignor held out for six shillings; and in the end the six shillings was allowed him literally. He came out of the pawn office joyfully, making a little cylinder of the coins between his thumb and fingers. In Westmoreland Street the footpaths were crowded with young men and woman returning from business, and ragged urchins ran here and there yelling out the names of the evening editions. The man passed through the crowd, looking on the spectacle generally with proud satisfaction and staring masterfully at the office girls. His head was full of the noises of tram gongs and swishing trolleys, and his nose already sniffed the curling fumes of punch. As he walked on he preconsidered the terms in which he would narrate the incident to the boys:

"So I just looked at him—coolly, you know, and looked at her. Then I looked back at him again—taking my time, you know. 'I don't think that that's a fair question to put to me,' says I."

Nosey Flynn was sitting up in his usual corner of Davy Byrne's, and when he heard the story he stood Farrington a half one, saying it was as smart a thing as ever he heard. Farrington stood a drink in his turn. After a while O'Halloran and Paddy Leonard came in, and the story was repeated to them. O'Halloran stood tailors of malt, hot, all round, and told the story of the retort he had made to the chief clerk when he was in Callan's of Fownes's Street; but as the retort was after the manner of the liberal shepherds in the eclogues, he had to admit that it was not as clever as Farrington's retort. At this Farrington told the boys to polish off that and have another.

Just as they were naming their poisons who should come in but Higgins! Of course he had to join in with the others. The men asked him to give his version of it, and he did so with great vivacity; for the sight of five small hot whiskies was very exhilarating. Everyone roared laughing when he showed the way in which Mr. Alleyne shook his fist in Farrington's face. Then he imitated Farrington, saying, "And here was my nabs, as cool as you please," while Farrington looked at the company out of his heavy, dirty eyes, smiling and at times drawing forth stray drops of liquor from his mustache with the aid of his lower lip.

When that round was over there was a pause. O'Halloran had money, but neither of the other two seemed to have any; so the whole party left the shop somewhat regretfully. At the corner of Duke Street, Higgins and Nosey Flynn beveled off to the left, while the other three turned back toward the city. Rain was drizzling down on the cold streets, and when they reached the Ballast Office, Farrington suggested the Scotch House. The bar was full of men and loud with the noise of tongues and glasses. The three men pushed past the whining matchsellers at the door and formed a little party at the corner of the counter. They began to exchange stories. Leonard introduced them to a young fellow named Weathers who was performing at the Tivoli as an acrobat and knockabout *artiste*. Farrington stood a drink all round. Weathers said he would take a small Irish and Apollinaris. Farrington, who had definite notions of what was what, asked the boys would they have an Apollinaris too; but the boys told Tim to make theirs hot. The talk became theatrical. O'Halloran stood a round, and then Farrington stood another round, Weathers protesting that the hospitality was too Irish. He promised to get them in behind the scenes and introduce them to some nice girls. O'Halloran said that he and Leonard would go but that Farrington wouldn't go, because he was a married man; and Farrington's heavy, dirty eyes leered at the company in token that he understood he was being chaffed. Weathers made them all have just one little tincture at his expense and promised to meet them later on at Mulligan's in Poolbeg Street.

When the Scotch House closed they went round to Mulligan's. They went into the parlor at the back, and O'Halloran ordered small hot specials all around. They were all beginning to feel mellow. Farrington was just standing another round when Weathers came back. Much to Farrington's relief, he drank a glass of bitter this time. Funds were getting low, but they had enough to keep them going. Presently two young women with big hats and a young man in a check suit came in and sat at a table close by. Weathers saluted them and told the company that they were out of the Tivoli. Farrington's eyes wandered at every moment in the direction of one of the young women. There was something striking in her appearance. An immense scarf of peacockblue muslin was wound round her hat and knotted in a great bow under her chin, and she wore bright yellow gloves, reaching to the elbow. Farrington gazed admiringly at the plump arm which she moved very often and with much grace, and when, after a little time, she answered his gaze, he admired still more her large dark brown eyes. The oblique, staring expression in them fascinated him. She glanced at him once or twice, and when the party was leaving the room, she brushed against his chair and said, "Oh, pardon!" in a London accent. He watched her leave the room in the hope that she would look back at him, but he was disappointed. He cursed his want of money and cursed all the rounds he had stood, particularly all the whiskies and Apollinaris which he had stood to Weathers. If there was one thing that he hated, it was a sponge. He was so angry that he lost count of the conversation of his friends.

When Paddy Leonard called him, he found that they were talking about feats of strength. Weathers was showing his biceps muscle to the company and boasting so much that the other two had called on

Farrington to uphold the national honor. Farrington pulled up his sleeve accordingly and showed his biceps muscle to the company. The two arms were examined and compared, and finally it was agreed to have a trial of strength. The table was cleared, and the two men rested their elbows on it, clasping hands. When Paddy Leonard said "Go!" each was to try to bring down the other's hand on to the table. Farrington looked very serious and determined.

The trial began. After about thirty seconds Weathers brought his opponent's hand slowly down on to the table. Farrington's dark wine-colored face flushed darker still with anger and humiliation at having been defeated by such a stripling.

"You're not to put the weight of your body behind it. Play fair," he said.

"Who's not playing fair?" said the other.

"Come on again. The two best out of three."

The trial began again. The veins stood out on Farrington's forehead, and the pallor of Weathers' complexion changed to peony. Their hands and arms trembled under the stress. After a long struggle Weathers again brought his opponent's hand slowly on to the table. There was a murmur of applause from the spectators. The curate, who was standing beside the table, nodded his red head towards the victor and said with stupid familiarity: "Ah! that's the knack!"

"What the hell do you know about it?" said Farrington fiercely, turning on the man. "What do you put in your gab for?"

"Sh, sh!" said O'Halloran, observing the violent expression of Farrington's face. "Pony up, boys. We'll have just one little smahan more and then we'll be off."

A very sullen-faced man stood at the corner of O'Connell Bridge waiting for the little Sandymount tram to take him home. He was full of smoldering anger and revengefulness. He felt humiliated and discontented; he did not even feel drunk; and he had only twopence in his pocket. He cursed everything. He had done for himself in the office, pawned his watch, spent all his money; and he had not even got drunk. He began to feel thirsty again, and he longed to be back again in the hot, reeking public house. He had lost his reputation as a strong man, having been defeated twice by a mere boy. His heart swelled with fury, and when he thought of the woman in the big hat who had brushed against him and said "Pardon!" his fury nearly choked him.

His tram let him down at Shelbourne Road, and he steered his great body along in the shadow of the wall of the barracks. He loathed returning to his home. When he went in by the side door he found the kitchen empty and the kitchen fire nearly out. He bawled upstairs: "Ada! Ada!"

His wife was a little sharp-faced woman who bullied her husband when he was sober and was bullied by him when he was drunk. They had five children. A little boy came running down the stairs.

"Who is that?" said the man, peering through the darkness.

"Me, Pa."

"Who are you? Charlie?"

"No, Pa. Tom."

"Where's your mother?"

"She's out at the chapel."

"That's right. . . . Did she think of leaving any dinner for me?"

"Yes, Pa. I—"

"Light the lamp. What do you mean by having the place in darkness? Are the other children in bed?"

The man sat down heavily on one of the chairs while the little boy lit the lamp. He began to mimic his son's flat accent, saying half to himself: " 'At the chapel.' 'At the chapel,' if you please!" When the lamp was lit he banged his fist on the table and shouted: "What's for my dinner?"

"I'm going to . . . cook it, Pa," said the little boy.

The man jumped up furiously and pointed to the fire. "On that fire! You let the fire out! By God, I'll teach you to do that again!" He took a step to the door and seized the walking stick which was standing behind it. "I'll teach you to let the fire out!" he said, rolling up his sleeves in order to give his arm free play.

The little boy cried, "Oh, Pa!" and ran whimpering round the table, but the man followed him and caught him by the coat. The little boy looked about him wildly but, seeing no way of escape, fell upon his knees.

"Now, you'll let the fire out the next time!" said the man, striking at him vigorously with the stick. "Take that, you little whelp!"

The boy uttered a squeal of pain as the stick cut his thigh. He clasped his hands together in the air, and his voice shook with fright.

"Oh, Pa!" he cried. "Don't beat me, Pa! And I'll . . . I'll say a Hail Mary for you . . . I'll say a Hail Mary for you, Pa, if you don't beat me . . . I'll say a Hail Mary . . ."

QUESTIONS

1. "A spasm of rage gripped his throat for a few moments and then passed, leaving after it a sharp sensation of thirst." What connection is Joyce making between Farrington's condition and his drinking?

2. Compare and contrast Farrington's response to meaningless work as a copyist to that of Bartleby in Melville's "Bartleby the Scrivener."
3. "His body ached to do something, to rush out and revel in violence." Where does this violence come from? Where is it finally directed? Why? What are the "counterparts"?
4. How does Farrington change the story of his retort in the telling?
5. Why does Farrington, poor as he is, buy drinks for his friends?
6. What is the effect on you of the scene in the pubs? Do you experience it as joyful? What is the attitude of the author toward Farrington?
7. What is the effect on you of the boy's final cry? How would it have been different if the boy had said, "I'll be good, Pa"?
8. What is the theme of "Counterparts"? How do you know? (See Preface, pp. 27–28.)
9. Is this story just a "slice of life"? Does it have a traditional dramatic form (exposition, conflict, rising action, climax, falling action, denouement)? (See Preface, pp. 11–13.)
10. What is the function of the lady with the London accent?
11. Some readers find the story just a description of an ignorant lout and bully. Would you agree?
12. Compare the story to "Araby." The two protagonists are very different. What similarities can you find?

Clay

JAMES JOYCE

The matron had given her leave to go out as soon as the women's tea was over and Maria looked forward to her evening out. The kitchen was spick and span: the cook said you could see yourself in the big copper boilers. The fire was nice and bright and on one of the side-tables were four very big barmbracks. These barmbracks seemed uncut; but if you went closer you would see that they had been cut into long thick even slices and were ready to be handed round at tea. Maria had cut them herself.

Maria was a very, very small person indeed but she had a very long nose and a very long chin. She talked a little through her nose, always soothingly: *Yes, my dear,* and *No, my dear.* She was always sent for when the women quarrelled over their tubs and always succeeded in making peace. One day the matron had said to her:

—Maria, you are a veritable peace-maker!

And the sub-matron and two of the Board ladies had heard the compliment. And Ginger Mooney was always saying what she wouldn't do to the dummy who had charge of the irons if it wasn't for Maria. Everyone was so fond of Maria.

The women would have their tea at six o'clock and she would be able to get away before seven. From Ballsbridge to the Pillar, twenty minutes; from the Pillar to Drumcondra, twenty minutes; and twenty minutes to buy the things. She would be there before eight. She took out her purse with the silver clasps and read again the words *A Present from Belfast*. She was very fond of that purse because Joe had brought it to her five years before when he and Alphy had gone to Belfast on a Whit-Monday trip. In the purse were two half-crowns and some coppers. She would have five shillings clear after paying tram fare. What a nice evening they would have, all the children singing! Only she hoped that Joe wouldn't come in drunk. He was so different when he took any drink.

Often he had wanted her to go and live with them; but she would have felt herself in the way (though Joe's wife was ever so nice with her) and she had become accustomed to the life of the laundry. Joe was a good fellow. She had nursed him and Alphy too; and Joe used often say:

—Mamma is mamma but Maria is my proper mother.

After the break-up at home the boys had got her that position in the *Dublin by Lamplight* laundry, and she liked it. She used to have such a bad opinion of Protestants but now she thought they were very nice people, a little quiet and serious, but still very nice people to live with. Then she had her plants in the conservatory and she liked looking after them. She had lovely ferns and wax-plants and, whenever anyone came to visit her, she always gave the visitor one or two slips from her conservatory. There was one thing she didn't like and that was the tracts on the walls; but the matron was such a nice person to deal with, so genteel.

When the cook told her everything was ready she went into the women's room and began to pull the big bell. In a few minutes the women began to come in by twos and threes, wiping their steaming hands in their petticoats and pulling down the sleeves of their blouses over their red steaming arms. They settled down before their huge mugs which the cook and the dummy filled up with hot tea, already mixed with milk and sugar in huge tin cans. Maria super-intended the distribution of the barmbrack and saw that every woman got her four slices. There was a great deal of laughing and joking during the meal. Lizzie Fleming said Maria was sure to get the ring and, though Fleming had said that for so many Hallow Eves, Maria had to laugh and say she didn't want any ring or man either;

and when she laughed her grey-green eyes sparkled with disappointed shyness and the tip of her nose nearly met the tip of her chin. Then Ginger Mooney lifted up her mug of tea and proposed Maria's health while all the other women clattered with their mugs on the table, and said she was sorry she hadn't a sup of porter to drink it in. And Maria laughed again till the tip of her nose nearly met the tip of her chin and till her minute body nearly shook itself asunder because she knew that Mooney meant well though, of course, she had the notions of a common woman.

But wasn't Maria glad when the women had finished their tea and the cook and the dummy had begun to clear away the tea-things! She went into her little bedroom and, remembering that the next morning was a mass morning, changed the hand of the alarm from seven to six. Then she took off her working skirt and her house-boots and laid her best skirt out on the bed and her tiny dress-boots beside the foot of the bed. She changed her blouse too and, as she stood before the mirror, she thought of how she used to dress for mass on Sunday morning when she was a young girl; and she looked with quaint affection at the diminutive body which she had so often adorned. In spite of its years she found it a nice tidy little body.

When she got outside the streets were shining with rain and she was glad of her old brown raincloak. The tram was full and she had to sit on the little stool at the end of the car, facing all the people, with her toes barely touching the floor. She arranged in her mind all she was going to do and thought how much better it was to be independent and to have your own money in your pocket. She hoped they would have a nice evening. She was sure they would but she could not help thinking what a pity it was Alphy and Joe were not speaking. They were always falling out now but when they were boys together they used to be the best of friends: but such was life.

She got out of her tram at the Pillar and ferreted her way quickly among the crowds. She went into Downes's cakeshop but the shop was so full of people that it was a long time before she could get herself attended to. She bought a dozen of mixed penny cakes, and at last came out of the shop laden with a big bag. Then she thought what else would she buy: she wanted to buy something really nice. They would be sure to have plenty of apples and nuts. It was hard to know what to buy and all she could think of was cake. She decided to buy some plumcake but Downes's plumcake had not enough almond icing on top of it so she went over to a shop in Henry Street. Here she was a long time in suiting herself and the stylish young lady behind the counter, who was evidently a little annoyed by her, asked her was it wedding-cake she wanted to buy. That made Maria blush and smile at the young lady; but the young lady took it all very seriously and finally cut a thick slice of plumcake, parcelled it up and said:

—Two-and-four, please.

She thought she would have to stand in the Drumcondra tram because none of the young men seemed to notice her but an elderly gentleman made room for her. He was a stout gentleman and he wore a brown hard hat; he had a square red face and a greyish moustache. Maria thought he was a colonel-looking gentleman and she reflected how much more polite he was than the young men who simply stared straight before them. The gentleman began to chat with her about Hallow Eve and the rainy weather. He supposed the bag was full of good things for the little ones and said it was only right that the youngsters should enjoy themselves while they were young. Maria agreed with him and favoured him with demure nods and hems. He was very nice with her, and when she was getting out at the Canal Bridge she thanked him and bowed, and he bowed to her and raised his hat and smiled agreeably; and while she was going up along the terrace, bending her tiny head under the rain, she thought how easy it was to know a gentleman even when he has a drop taken.

Everybody said: *O, here's Maria!* when she came to Joe's house. Joe was there, having come home from business, and all the children had their Sunday dresses on. There were two big girls in from next door and games were going on. Maria gave the bag of cakes to the eldest boy, Alphy, to divide and Mrs. Donnelly said it was too good of her to bring such a big bag of cakes and made all the children say:

—Thanks, Maria.

But Maria said she had brought something special for papa and mamma, something they would be sure to like, and she began to look for her plumcake. She tried in Downes's bag and then in the pockets of her raincloak and then on the hall-stand but nowhere could she find it. Then she asked all the children had any of them eaten it—by mistake, of course—but the children all said no and looked as if they did not like to eat cakes if they were to be accused of stealing. Everybody had a solution for the mystery and Mrs. Donnelly said it was plain that Maria had left it behind her in the tram. Maria, remembering how confused the gentleman with the greyish moustache had made her, coloured with shame and vexation and disappointment. At the thought of the failure of her little surprise and of the two and four-pence she had thrown away for nothing she nearly cried outright.

But Joe said it didn't matter and made her sit down by the fire. He was very nice with her. He told her all that went on in his office, repeating for her a smart answer which he had made to the manager. Maria did not understand why Joe laughed so much over the answer he had made but she said that the manager must have been a very overbearing person to deal with. Joe said he wasn't so bad when you knew how to take him, that he was a decent sort so long as you didn't rub him the wrong way. Mrs. Donnelly played the piano for the children and they danced and sang. Then the two next-door girls handed round the nuts. Nobody could find the nutcrackers and Joe was nearly getting cross over it and asked how did they expect Maria to crack nuts without a nutcracker. But Maria said she didn't like nuts and that they weren't to bother about her. Then Joe asked would she take a bottle of stout and Mrs. Donnelly said there was port wine too in the house if she would prefer that. Maria said she would rather they didn't ask her to take anything: but Joe insisted.

So Maria let him have his way and they sat by the fire talking over old times and Maria thought she would put in a good word for Alphy. But Joe cried that God might strike him stone dead if ever he spoke a word to his brother again and Maria said she was sorry she had mentioned the matter. Mrs. Donnelly told her husband it was a great shame for him to speak that way of his own flesh and blood but Joe said that Alphy was no brother of his and there was nearly being a row on the head of it. But Joe said he would not lose his temper on account of the night it was and asked his wife to open some more stout. The two next-door girls had arranged some Hallow Eve games and soon everything was merry again. Maria was delighted to see the children so merry and Joe and his wife in such good spirits. The next-door girls put some saucers on the table and then led the children up to the table, blindfold. One got the prayer-book and the other three got the water; and when one of the next-door girls got the ring Mrs. Donnelly shook her finger at the blushing girl as much as to say: *O, I know all about it!* They insisted then on blindfolding Maria and leading her up to the table to see what she would get; and, while they were putting on the bandage, Maria laughed and laughed again till the tip of her nose nearly met the tip of her chin.

They led her up to the table amid laughing and poking and she put her hand out in the air as she was told to do. She moved her hand about here and there in the air and descended on one of the saucers. She felt a soft wet substance with her fingers and was surprised that nobody spoke or took off her bandage. There was a pause for a few seconds; and then a great deal of scuffling and whispering. Somebody said something about the garden, and at last Mrs. Donnelly said something very cross to one of the next-door girls and told her to throw it out at once: that was no play. Maria understood that it was wrong that time and so she had to do it over again: and this time she got the prayer-book.

After that Mrs. Donnelly played Miss McCloud's Reel for the children and Joe made Maria take a glass of wine. Soon they were all quite merry again and Mrs. Donnelly said Maria would enter a convent before the year was out because she had got the prayer-book. Maria had never seen Joe so nice to her as he was that night, so full of pleasant talk and reminiscences. She said they were all very good to her.

At last the children grew tired and sleepy and Joe asked Maria would she not sing some little song before she went, one of the old songs. Mrs. Donnelly said *Do, please, Maria!* and so Maria had to get up and stand beside the piano. Mrs. Donnelly bade the children be quiet and listen to Maria's song. Then she played the prelude and said *Now, Maria!* and Maria, blushing very much, began to sing in a tiny quavering voice. She sang *I Dreamt that I Dwelt,* and when she came to the second verse she sang again:

> I dreamt that I dwelt in marble halls
>   With vassals and serfs at my side
> And of all who assembled within those walls
>   That I was the hope and the pride.
> I had riches too great to count, could boast
>   Of a high ancestral name,
> But I also dreamt, which pleased me most,
>   That you loved me still the same.

But no one tried to show her her mistake; and when she had ended her song Joe was very much moved. He said that there was no time like the long ago and no music for him like poor old Balfe, whatever other people might say; and his eyes filled up so much with tears that he could not find what he was looking for and in the end he had to ask his wife to tell him where the corkscrew was.

FRANZ KAFKA

(1883-1924)

Born in Prague, Czechoslovakia, the son of a well-to-do Jewish factory owner, Kafka grew up a sensitive, introverted, tortured soul unable either to become the son his father wanted or to revolt against his father's domination. His writing was his only pocket of quiet resistance. For most of his adult life he wrote only late at night; during the day he worked in his father's business, even taking over as director when called upon. But he loathed the work and longed for time to write his strange fiction. Feeling squashed by his father and living in his father's house, he could not become independent, could not marry or develop a relationship with a woman, could not grow up. He published very little work during his lifetime. After his death (by tuberculosis) he left instructions with his friend and editor Max Brod to burn his manuscripts; instead, Brod published them, including most of the works for which Kafka is now famous, *The Castle, The Trial, Amerika*. It was only after the Second World War, when the world was recovering from the bureaucratic terror of the Nazis and when intellectuals were exploring the nuances of guilt, self-deception, and the helplessness of the individual in the face of a seemingly absurd universe, that Kafka became a significant figure.

In "The Bucket-Rider" the freezing and starving narrator begs for a bit of coal and, rebuffed by the coal dealer's wife, is blown away on the empty coal bucket. It is possible to read the story as a metaphysical cry that goes unanswered, a cry not far removed from Crane's in "The Open Boat." But without forcing a rigid interpretive schema on the story, we still feel its cry of human need and the experience of rejection. And we feel at the same time its mad humor—the narrator, begging from his seat on the coal bucket, is funny at the same time that his predicament is painful. This mixture of tones is equally unnerving in "A Country Doctor," in which the narrator's voice treats in a matter-of-fact way events that are utterly fantastic: the result is at once comic and horrifying.

[To learn more about Kafka, turn to Roth's essay at the beginning of his "Looking at Kafka" (p. 747). And see Preface, pp. 29–30 (fantasy).]

The Bucket-Rider

FRANZ KAFKA

Coal all spent; the bucket empty, the shovel useless; the stove breathing out cold; the room freezing; the leaves outside the window rigid, covered with rime; the sky a silver shield against anyone who looks for help from it. I must have coal; I cannot freeze to death; behind me is the pitiless stove, before me the pitiless sky, so I must ride out between them and on my journey seek aid from the coal-dealer. But he has already grown deaf to ordinary appeals; I must prove irrefutably to him that I have not a single grain of coal left, and that he means to me the very sun in the firmament. I must approach like a beggar who, with the death-rattle already in his throat, insists on dying on the doorstep, and to whom the grand people's cook accordingly decides to give the dregs of the coffee-pot; just so must the coal-dealer, filled with rage, but acknowledging the command, "Thou shalt not kill," fling a shovelful of coal into my bucket.

My mode of arrival must decide the matter; so I ride off on the bucket. Seated on the bucket, my hands on the handle, the simplest kind of bridle, I propel myself with difficulty down the stairs; but once down below my bucket ascends, superbly, superbly; camels humbly squatting on the ground do not rise with more dignity, shaking themselves under the sticks of their drivers. Through the hard frozen streets we go at a regular canter; often I am upraised as high as the first story of a house; never do I sink as low as the house doors. And at last I float at an extraordinary height above the vaulted cellar of the dealer, whom I see far below crouching over his table, where he is writing; he has opened the door to let out the excessive heat.

"Coal-dealer!" I cry in a voice burned hollow by the frost and

Translated by Willa and Edwin Muir. Reprinted by permission of Schocken Books Inc. from *The Penal Colony* by Franz Kafka. Copyright © 1948 by Schocken Books Inc. Copyright renewed © 1975 by Schocken Books Inc.

muffled in the cloud made by my breath, "please, coal-dealer, give me a little coal. My bucket is so light that I can ride on it. Be kind. When I can I'll pay you."

The dealer puts his hand to his ear. "Do I hear rightly?" He throws the question over his shoulder to his wife. "Do I hear rightly? A customer."

"I hear nothing," says his wife, breathing in and out peacefully while she knits on, her back pleasantly warmed by the heat.

"Oh, yes, you must hear," I cry. "It's me; an old customer; faithful and true; only without means at the moment."

"Wife," says the dealer, "it's some one, it must be; my ears can't have deceived me so much as that; it must be an old, a very old customer, that can move me so deeply."

"What ails you, man?" says his wife, ceasing from her work for a moment and pressing her knitting to her bosom. "It's nobody, the street is empty, all our customers are provided for; we could close down the shop for several days and take a rest."

"But I'm sitting up here on the bucket," I cry, and unfeeling frozen tears dim my eyes, "please look up here, just once; you'll see me directly; I beg you, just a shovelful; and if you give me more it'll make me so happy that I won't know what to do. All the other customers are provided for. Oh, if I could only hear the coal clattering into the bucket!"

"I'm coming," says the coal-dealer, and on his short legs he makes to climb the steps of the cellar, but his wife is already beside him, holds him back by the arm and says: "You stay here; seeing you persist in your fancies I'll go myself. Think of the bad fit of coughing you had during the night. But for a piece of business, even if it's one you've only fancied in your head, you're prepared to forget your wife and child and sacrifice your lungs. I'll go."

"Then be sure to tell him all the kinds of coal we have in stock; I'll shout out the prices after you."

"Right," says his wife, climbing up to the street. Naturally she sees me at once. "Frau Coal-dealer," I cry, "my humblest greetings; just one shovelful of coal; here in my bucket; I'll carry it home myself. One shovelful of the worst you have. I'll pay you in full for it, of course, but not just now, not just now." What a knell-like sound the words "not just now" have, and how bewilderingly they mingle with the evening chimes that fall from the church steeple nearby!

"Well, what does he want?" shouts the dealer. "Nothing," his wife shouts back, "there's nothing here; I see nothing, I hear nothing; only six striking, and now we must shut up the shop. The cold is terrible; tomorrow we'll likely have lots to do again."

She sees nothing and hears nothing; but all the same she loosens her apron-strings and waves her apron to waft me away. She succeeds, unluckily. My bucket has all the virtues of a good steed except powers of resistance, which it has not; it is too light; a woman's apron can make it fly through the air.

"You bad woman!" I shout back, while she, turning into the shop, half-contemptuous, half-reassured, flourishes her fist in the air. "You bad woman! I begged you for a shovelful of the worst coal and you would not give me it." And with that I ascend into the regions of the ice mountains and am lost forever.

A Country Doctor

FRANZ KAFKA

I was in great perplexity; I had to start on an urgent journey; a seriously ill patient was waiting for me in a village ten miles off; a thick blizzard of snow filled all the wide spaces between him and me; I had a gig, a light gig with big wheels, exactly right for our country roads; muffled in furs, my bag of instruments in my hand, I was in the courtyard all ready for the journey; but there was no horse to be had, no horse. My own horse had died in the night, worn out by the fatigues of this icy winter; my servant girl was now running round the village trying to borrow a horse; but it was hopeless, I knew it, and I stood there forlornly, with the snow gathering more and more thickly upon me, more and more unable to move. In the gateway the girl appeared, alone, and waved the lantern; of course, who would lend a horse at this time for such a journey? I strode through the courtyard once more; I could see no way out; in my confused distress I kicked at the dilapidated door of the year-long uninhabited pigsty. It flew open and flapped to and fro on its hinges. A steam and smell as of horses came out from it. A dim stable lantern was swinging inside from a rope. A man, crouching on his hams in that low space, showed an open blue-eyed face. "Shall I yoke up?" he asked, crawling out on all fours. I did not know what to say and merely stooped down to see what else was in the sty. The servant girl was standing beside me. "You never know what you're going to find in your own house," she said, and we both laughed. "Hey there, Brother, hey there, Sister!" called the groom, and two horses,

Translated by Willa and Edwin Muir. Reprinted by permission of Schocken Books Inc. from *The Penal Colony* by Franz Kafka. Copyright © 1948 by Schocken Books Inc. Copyright renewed © 1975 by Schocken Books Inc.

enormous creatures with powerful flanks, one after the other, their legs tucked close to their bodies, each well-shaped head lowered like a camel's, by sheer strength of buttocking squeezed out through the door hole which they filled entirely. But at once they were standing up, their legs long and their bodies steaming thickly. "Give him a hand," I said, and the willing girl hurried to help the groom with the harnessing. Yet hardly was she beside him when the groom clipped hold of her and pushed his face against hers. She screamed and fled back to me; on her cheek stood out in red the marks of two rows of teeth. "You brute," I yelled in fury, "do you want a whipping?" but in the same moment reflected that the man was a stranger; that I did not know where he came from, and that of his own free will he was helping me out when everyone else had failed me. As if he knew my thoughts he took no offense at my threat but, still busied with the horses, only turned round once towards me. "Get in," he said then, and indeed everything was ready. A magnificent pair of horses, I observed, such as I had never sat behind, and I climbed in happily. "But I'll drive, you don't know the way," I said. "Of course," said he, "I'm not coming with you anyway, I'm staying with Rose." "No," shrieked Rose, fleeing into the house with a justified presentiment that her fate was inescapable; I heard the door chain rattle as she put it up; I heard the key turn in the lock; I could see, moreover, how she put out the lights in the entrance hall and in further flight all through the rooms to keep herself from being discovered. "You're coming with me," I said to the groom, "or I won't go, urgent as my journey is. I'm not thinking of paying for it by handing the girl over to you." "Gee up!" he said; clapped his hands; the gig whirled off like a log in a freshet; I could just hear the door of my house splitting and bursting as the groom charged at it and then I was deafened and blinded by a storming rush that steadily buffeted all my senses. But this only for a moment, since, as if my patient's farmyard had opened out just before my courtyard gate, I was already there; the horses had come quietly to a standstill; the blizzard had stopped; moonlight all around; my patient's parents hurried out of the house, his sister behind them; I was almost lifted out of the gig; from their confused ejaculations I gathered not a word; in the sickroom the air was almost unbreathable; the neglected stove was smoking; I wanted to push open a window; but first I had to look at my patient. Gaunt, without any fever, not cold, not warm, with vacant eyes, without a shirt, the youngster heaved himself up from under the feather bedding, threw his arms round my neck, and whispered in my ear: "Doctor, let me die." I glanced round the room; no one had heard it; the parents were leaning forward in silence waiting for my verdict; the sister had set a chair for my handbag; I opened the bag and hunted among my instruments; the boy kept clutching at me from his bed to remind me of his entreaty; I picked up a pair of tweezers, examined them in the candlelight and laid them down again. "Yes," I thought blasphemously, "in cases like this the gods are helpful, send the missing horse, add to it a second because of the urgency, and to crown everything bestow even a groom—" And only now did I remember Rose again; what was I to do, how could I rescue her, how could I pull her away from under that groom at ten miles' distance, with a team of horses I couldn't control. These horses, now, they had somehow slipped the reins loose, pushed the windows open from outside, I did not know how; each of them had stuck a head in at a window and, quite unmoved by the startled cries of the family, stood eyeing the patient. "Better go back at once," I thought, as if the horses were summoning me to the return journey, yet I permitted the patient's sister, who fancied that I was dazed by the heat, to take my fur coat from me. A glass of rum was poured out for me, the old man clapped me on the shoulder, a familiarity justified by this offer of his treasure. I shook my head; in the narrow confines of the old man's thoughts I felt ill; that was my only reason for refusing the drink. The mother stood by the bedside and cajoled me towards it; I yielded, and, while one of the horses whinnied loudly to the ceiling, laid my head to the boy's breast, which shivered under my wet beard. I confirmed what I already knew; the boy was quite sound, something a little wrong with his circulation, saturated with coffee by his solicitous mother, but sound and best turned out of bed with one shove. I am no world reformer and so I let him lie. I was the district doctor and did my duty to the uttermost, to the point where it became almost too much. I was badly paid and yet generous and helpful to the poor. I had still to see that Rose was all right, and then the boy might have his way and I wanted to die too. What was I doing there in that endless winter! My horse was dead, and not a single person in the village would lend me another. I had to get my team out of the pigsty; if they hadn't chanced to be horses I should have had to travel with swine. That was how it was. And I nodded to the family. They knew nothing about it, and, had they known, would not have believed it. To write prescriptions is easy, but to come to an understanding with people is hard. Well, this should be the end of my visit, I had once more been called out needlessly, I was used to that, the whole district made my life a torment with my night bell, but that I should have to sacrifice Rose this time as well, the pretty girl who had lived in my house for years almost without my noticing her—that sacrifice was too much to ask, and I had somehow to get it reasoned out in my head with the help of what craft I could muster, in order not to let fly at this family, which with the best will in the world could not restore Rose to me. But as I shut my bag and put an arm out for my fur coat, the family meanwhile standing together, the father sniffing at the glass of rum in his hand, the mother, apparently disappointed in me—why, what do people expect?—biting her lips with tears in her eyes, the sister fluttering a blood-soaked towel, I was somehow ready to admit conditionally that the boy might be ill after all. I went toward him, he welcomed me smiling as if I were bringing him the most nourishing invalid broth—ah, now both horses were whinnying together; the noise, I suppose, was ordained by heaven to assist my examination of the patient—and this time I discovered that the boy was indeed ill. In his right side, near the hip, was an open wound as big as the palm of my hand. Rose-red, in many variations of shade, dark in the hollows, lighter at the edges, softly granulated, with irregular clots of blood, open as a surface mine to the daylight. That was how it looked from a distance. But on a closer inspection there was another complication. I could not help a low whistle of surprise. Worms, as thick and as long as my little finger, themselves rose-red and blood-spotted as well, were wriggling from their fastness in the interior of the wound towards the light, with small white heads and many little legs. Poor boy, you were past helping. I had discovered your great wound; this blossom in your side was destroying you. The family was pleased; they saw me busying myself; the sister told the mother, the mother the father, the father told several guests who were coming in, through the moonlight at the open door, walking on tiptoe, keeping their balance with outstretched arms. "Will you save me?" whispered the boy with a sob, quite blinded by the life within his wound. That is what people are like in my district. Always expecting the impossible from the doctor. They have lost their ancient beliefs; the parson sits at home and unravels his vestments, one after another; but the doctor is supposed to be omnipotent with his merciful surgeon's hand. Well, as it pleases them; I have not thrust my services on them; if they misuse me for sacred ends, I let that happen to me too; what better do I want, old country doctor that I am, bereft of my servant girl! And so they came, the family and the village elders, and stripped my clothes off me; a school choir with the teacher at the head of it stood before the house and sang these words to an utterly simple tune:

> Strip his clothes off, then he'll heal us,
> If he doesn't, kill him dead!
> Only a doctor, only a doctor.

Then my clothes were off and I looked at the people quietly, my fingers in my beard and my head cocked to one side. I was altogether composed and equal to the situation and remained so, although it was no help to me, since they now took me by the head and feet and carried me to the bed. They laid me down in it next to the wall, on the side of the wound. Then they all left the room; the door was shut; the singing stopped; clouds covered the moon; the bedding was warm around me; the horses' heads in the open windows wavered like shadows. "Do you know," said a voice in my ear, "I have very little confidence in you. Why, you were only blown in here, you didn't come on your own feet. Instead of helping me, you're cramping me on my deathbed. What I'd like best is to scratch your eyes out." "Right," I said, "it is a shame. And yet I am a doctor. What am I to do? Believe me, it is not too easy for me either." "Am I supposed to be content with this apology? Oh, I must be, I can't help it. I always have to put up with things. A fine wound is all I brought into the world; that was my sole endowment." "My young friend," said I, "your mistake is: you have not a wide enough view. I have been in all the sickrooms, far and wide, and I tell you: your wound is not so bad. Done in a tight corner with two strokes of the ax. Many a one proffers his side and can hardly hear the ax in the forest, far less that it is coming nearer to him." "Is that really so, or are you deluding me in my fever?" "It is really so, take the word of honor of an official doctor." And he took it and lay still. But now it was time for me to think of escaping. The horses were still standing faithfully in their places. My clothes, my fur coat, my bag were quickly collected; I didn't want to waste time dressing; if the horses raced home as they had come, I should only be springing as it were, out of this bed into my own. Obediently a horse backed away from the window; I threw my bundle into the gig; the fur coat missed its mark and was caught on a hook only by the sleeve. Good enough. I swung myself onto the horse. With the reins loosely trailing, one horse barely fastened to the other, the gig swaying behind, my fur coat last of all in the snow. "Gee up!" I said, but there was no galloping; slowly, like old men, we crawled through the snowy wastes; a long time echoed behind us the new but faulty song of the children:

> O be joyful, all you patients,
> The doctor's laid in bed beside you!

Never shall I reach home at this rate; my flourishing practice is done for; my successor is robbing me, but in vain, for he cannot take my place; in my house the disgusting groom is raging; Rose is his victim; I do not want to think about it any more. Naked, exposed to the frost of this most unhappy of ages, with an earthly vehicle, unearthly horses, old man that I am, I wander astray. My fur coat is hanging from the back of the gig, but I cannot reach it, and none of my limber pack of patients lifts a finger. Betrayed! Betrayed! A false alarm on the night bell once answered—it cannot be made good, not ever.

D. H. LAWRENCE

(1885-1930)

David Herbert Lawrence was born in a coal-mining district in England, his father a miner, his mother the educated daughter of a middle-class family. Caught between the class values of his parents, he grew close to his mother, who treated him as her only recompense for life with a man who could not understand her.

Encouraged by his mother and by his friend Jessie Chambers, he painted and wrote, and a year after his mother's death, he published *The White Peacock* (1911). While he was working on *Sons and Lovers*, an autobiographical novel, he met Frieda, wife of a former professor. They left her children behind and ran off to the continent. With her help, he finished *Sons and Lovers* and published it in 1913. It is a magnificent realistic novel about the development of a young man caught, as Lawrence himself was caught, between his mother and his father, between spirituality and physicality; the development of a young man unable to grow up because of the sway of his mother, living and dead, over him.

Returning to England, he and Frieda married on the eve of the First World War. Frieda was a Von Richtofen, sister of the famous German pilot, and Lawrence's position in England with a German wife was difficult. At one point during the war they were forced to leave Cornwall because neighbors and the military suspected them of signaling to German ships. Lawrence, a pacifist during the war, was called up for a physical examination, but his lungs were very bad, and he stayed out of the service.

During this period he wrote *The Rainbow* and *Women in Love*. *The Rainbow* spans three generations of an English family, from the closeness to work and to the earth of the grandparents to the dislocated, alienated self-consciousness of the grandchildren. But in each generation the same conflicts reappear in different ways. At the end the novel points towards some new integration, new life. *Women in Love* is more pessimistic. Two ways of life—self-conscious and sterile versus instinctive and life-affirming—are contrasted. The modern world is seen as a place of death; at the end of the novel, in the midst of cold and death, the protagonists move towards life, if only for themselves. *Women in Love* is one of the finest critiques of modern life in our literature.

In self-appointed exile after the war, Lawrence lived in Italy, in New Mexico, in Mexico, following the sun of life and instinct, only occasionally returning to England. Rejected in England and published mostly in the United States, Lawrence grew bitter, and his fiction of this period is often strained and doctrinaire: he saw himself as the prophet of life in the midst of a dying society. Both the stories included in this anthology, "The Blind Man" and "The Rocking-Horse Winner," were written during the 1920's, and both are very powerful expressions of a choice between life and death: between intellectuality, will, and possessiveness on the one hand, and the body, instinct, and open connection with the earth on the other.

During the late 1920's Lawrence was dying of tuberculosis. Still, he wrote furiously—three versions of *Lady Chatterley's Lover,* a number of poems, and the long story *The Man Who Died.* If during the early 1920's Lawrence had in bitterness turned to doctrines of power and hoped for a great leader to save society, toward the end of his life he turned back to a theme deeper in him—human sexual love, tenderness, touch. The lovers in *Lady Chatterley's Lover* cannot change the world, but they can survive its pressures; the Jesus figure of *The Man Who Died* has to flee, alone, but he has left his seed in the body and spirit of his woman. Lawrence has been accused of being fascist, sexist, and pseudo-mystical. He has also been praised for creating a model of the world that can counter the model of literary modernism; he makes the reader experience a new reverence for life, a new sense of its sacredness.

[See Preface: "The Blind Man," p. 14 (conflict); "The Rocking-Horse Winner," p. 14 (rising action and climax), p. 15 (exposition), p. 28 (vision).]

The Blind Man

D. H. LAWRENCE

Isabel Pervin was listening for two sounds—for the sound of wheels on the drive outside and for the noise of her husband's footsteps in the hall. Her dearest and oldest friend, a man who seemed almost indispensable to her living, would drive up in the rainy dusk of the closing November day. The trap had gone to fetch him from the station. And her husband, who had been blinded in Flanders, and who had a disfiguring mark on his brow, would be coming in from the outhouses.

He had been home for a year now. He was totally blind. Yet they had been very happy. The Grange was Maurice's own place. The back was a farmstead, and the Wernhams, who occupied the rear premises, acted as farmers. Isabel lived with her husband in the handsome rooms in front. She and he had been almost entirely alone together since he was wounded. They talked and sang and read together in a wonderful and unspeakable intimacy. Then she reviewed books for a Scottish newspaper, carrying on her old interest, and he occupied himself a good deal with the farm. Sightless, he could still discuss everything with Wernham, and he could also do a good deal of work about the place—menial work, it is true, but it gave him satisfaction. He milked the cows, carried in the pails, turned the separator, attended to the pigs and horses. Life was still very full and strangely serene for the blind man, peaceful with the almost incomprehensible peace of immediate contact in darkness. With his wife he had a whole world, rich and real and invisible.

They were newly and remotely happy. He did not even regret the loss of his sight in these times of dark, palpable joy. A certain exultance swelled his soul.

But as time wore on, sometimes the rich glamour would leave them. Sometimes, after months of this intensity, a sense of burden overcame Isabel, a weariness, a terrible ennui, in that silent house approached between a colonnade of tall-shafted pines. Then she felt she would go mad, for she could not bear it. And sometimes he had devastating fits of depression, which seemed to lay waste his whole being. It was worse than depression—a black misery, when his own life was a torture to him, and when his presence was unbearable to his wife. The dread went down to the roots of her soul as these black days recurred. In a kind of panic she tried to wrap herself up still further in her husband. She forced the old spontaneous cheerfulness and joy to continue. But the effort it cost her was almost too much. She knew she could not keep it up. She felt she would scream with the strain, and would give anything, anything, to escape. She longed to possess her husband utterly; it gave her inordinate joy to have him entirely to herself. And yet, when again he was gone in a black and massive misery, she could not bear him, she could not bear herself; she wished she could be snatched away off the earth altogether, anything rather than live at this cost.

Dazed, she schemed for a way out. She invited friends, she tried to give him some further connection with the outer world. But it was no good. After all their joy and suffering, after their dark, great year of blindness and solitude and unspeakable nearness, other people seemed to them both shallow, rattling, rather impertinent. Shallow prattle seemed presumptuous. He became impatient and irritated, she was wearied. And so they lapsed into their solitude again. For they preferred it.

But now, in a few weeks' time, her second baby would be born. The first had died, an infant, when her husband first went out to France. She looked with joy and relief to the coming of the second. It would be her salvation. But also she felt some anxiety. She was thirty years old, her husband was a year younger. They both wanted the child very much. Yet she could not help feeling afraid. She had her husband on her hands, a terrible joy to her, and a terrifying burden. The child would occupy her love and attention. And then, what of Maurice? What would he do? If only she could feel that he, too, would be at peace and happy when the child came! She did so want to luxuriate in a rich, physical satisfaction of maternity. But the man, what would he do? How could she provide for him, how avert those shattering black moods of his, which destroyed them both?

She sighed with fear. But at this time Bertie Reid wrote to Isabel. He was her old friend, a second or third cousin, a Scotchman, as she was a Scotchwoman. They had been brought up near to one another, and all her life he had been her friend, like a brother, but better than her own brothers. She loved him—though not in the marrying sense. There was a sort of kinship between them, an affinity. They understood one another instinctively. But Isabel would never have thought of marrying Bertie. It would have seemed like marrying in her own family.

Bertie was a barrister and a man of letters, a Scotchman of the intellectual type, quick, ironical, sentimental, and on his knees before the woman he adored but did not want to marry. Maurice Pervin was different. He came of a good old country family—the

Grange was not a very great distance from Oxford. He was passionate, sensitive, perhaps over-sensitive, wincing—a big fellow with heavy limbs and a forehead that flushed painfully. For his mind was slow, as if drugged by the strong provincial blood that beat in his veins. He was very sensitive to his own mental slowness, his feelings being quick and acute. So that he was just the opposite to Bertie, whose mind was much quicker than his emotions, which were not so very fine.

From the first the two men did not like each other. Isabel felt that they ought to get on together. But they did not. She felt that if only each could have the clue to the other there would be such a rare understanding between them. It did not come off, however. Bertie adopted a slightly ironical attitude, very offensive to Maurice, who returned the Scotch irony with English resentment, a resentment which deepened sometimes into stupid hatred.

This was a little puzzling to Isabel. However, she accepted it in the course of things. Men were made freakish and unreasonable. Therefore, when Maurice was going out to France for the second time, she felt that, for her husband's sake, she must discontinue her friendship with Bertie. She wrote to the barrister to this effect. Bertram Reid simply replied that in this, as in all other matters, he must obey her wishes, if these were indeed her wishes.

For nearly two years nothing had passed between the two friends. Isabel rather gloried in the fact; she had no compunction. She had one great article of faith, which was, that husband and wife should be so important to one another, that the rest of the world simply did not count. She and Maurice were husband and wife. They loved one another. They would have children. Then let everybody and everything else fade into insignificance outside this connubial felicity. She professed herself quite happy and ready to receive Maurice's friends. She was happy and ready: the happy wife, the ready woman in possession. Without knowing why, the friends retired abashed, and came no more. Maurice, of course, took as much satisfaction in this connubial absorption as Isabel did.

He shared in Isabel's literary activities, she cultivated a real interest in agriculture and cattle-raising. For she, being at heart perhaps an emotional enthusiast, always cultivated the practical side of life and prided herself on her mastery of practical affairs. Thus the husband and wife had spent the five years of their married life. The last had been one of blindness and unspeakable intimacy. And now Isabel felt a great indifference coming over her, a sort of lethargy. She wanted to be allowed to bear her child in peace, to nod by the fire and drift vaguely, physically, from day to day. Maurice was like an ominous thunder-cloud. She had to keep waking up to remember him.

When a little note came from Bertie, asking if he were to put up a tombstone to their dead friendship, and speaking of the real pain he felt on account of her husband's loss of sight, she felt a pang, a fluttering agitation of reawakening. And she read the letter to Maurice.

"Ask him to come down," he said.

"Ask Bertie to come here!" she re-echoed.

"Yes—if he wants to."

Isabel paused for a few moments.

"I know he wants to—he'd only be too glad," she replied. "But what about you, Maurice? How should you like it?"

"I should like it."

"Well—in that case—But I thought you didn't care for him—"

"Oh, I don't know. I might think differently of him now," the blind man replied. It was rather abstruse to Isabel.

"Well, dear," she said, "if you're quite sure—"

"I'm sure enough. Let him come," said Maurice.

So Bertie was coming, coming this evening, in the November rain and darkness. Isabel was agitated, racked with her old restlessness and indecision. She had always suffered from this pain of doubt, just an agonizing sense of uncertainty. It had begun to pass off, in the lethargy of maternity. Now it returned, and she resented it. She struggled as usual to maintain her calm, composed, friendly bearing, a sort of mask she wore over all her body.

A woman had lighted a tall lamp beside the table and spread the cloth. The long dining-room was dim, with its elegant but rather severe pieces of old furniture. Only the round table glowed softly under the light. It had a rich, beautiful effect. The white cloth glistened and dropped its heavy, pointed lace corners almost to the carpet, the china was old and handsome, creamy-yellow, with a blotched pattern of harsh red and deep blue, the cups large and bell-shaped, the teapot gallant. Isabel looked at it with superficial appreciation.

Her nerves were hurting her. She looked automatically again at the high, uncurtained windows. In the last dusk she could just perceive outside a huge fir-tree swaying its boughs: it was as if she thought it rather than saw it. The rain came flying on the window panes. Ah, why had she no peace? These two men, why did they tear at her? Why did they not come—why was there this suspense?

She sat in a lassitude that was really suspense and irritation. Maurice, at least, might come in—there was nothing to keep him out. She rose to her feet. Catching sight of her reflection in a mirror, she glanced at herself with a slight smile of recognition, as if she were an old friend to herself. Her face was oval and calm, her nose a little arched. Her neck made a beautiful line down to her shoulder. With hair knotted loosely behind, she had something of a warm, maternal look. Thinking this of herself, she arched her eyebrows and her rather heavy eyelids, with a little flicker of a smile, and for a moment her gray eyes looked amused and wicked, a little sardonic, out of her transfigured Madonna face.

Then, resuming her air of womanly patience—she was really fatally, self-determined—she went with a little jerk towards the door. Her eyes were slightly reddened.

She passed down the wide hall and through a door at the end. Then she was in the farm premises. The scent of dairy, and of farm-kitchen, and of farm-yard and of leather almost overcame her: but particularly the scent of dairy. They had been scalding out the pans. The flagged passage in front of her was dark, puddled, and wet. Light came out from the open kitchen door. She went forward and stood in the doorway. The farm-people were at tea, seated at a little distance from her, round a long, narrow table, in the centre of which stood a white lamp. Ruddy faces, ruddy hands holding food, red mouths working, heads bent over the tea-cups: men, landgirls, boys: it was tea-time, feeding-time. Some faces caught sight of her. Mrs. Wernham, going round behind the chairs with a large black teapot, halting slightly in her walk, was not aware of her for a moment. Then she turned suddenly.

"Oh, it is Madam!" she exclaimed. "Come in, then, come in! We're at tea." And she dragged forward a chair.

"No, I won't come in," said Isabel. "I'm afraid I interrupt your meal."

"No—no—not likely, Madame, not likely."

"Hasn't Mr. Pervin come in, do you know?"

"I'm sure I couldn't say! Missed him, have you, Madam?"

"No, I only wanted him to come in," laughed Isabel, as if shyly.

"Wanted him, did ye? Get up, boy—get up, now—"

Mrs. Wernham knocked one of the boys on the shoulder. He began to scrape to his feet, chewing largely.

"I believe he's in top stable," said another face from the table.

"Ah! No, don't get up. I'm going myself," said Isabel.

"Don't you go out on a dirty night like this. Let the lad go. Get along wi' ye, boy," said Mrs. Wernham.

"No, no," said Isabel, with a decision that was always obeyed. "Go on with your tea, Tom. I'd like to go across to the stable, Mrs. Wernham."

"Did ever you hear tell!" exclaimed the woman.

"Isn't the trap late?" asked Isabel.

"Why, no," said Mrs. Wernham, peering into the distance at the tall, dim clock. "No, Madam—we can give it another quarter or twenty minutes yet, good—yes, every bit of a quarter."

"Ah! It seems late when darkness falls so early," said Isabel.

"It do, that it do. Bother the days, that they draw in so," answered Mrs. Wernham. "Proper miserable!"

"They are," said Isabel, withdrawing.

She pulled on her overshoes, wrapped a large tartan shawl around her, put on a man's felt hat, and ventured out along the causeways of the first yard. It was very dark. The wind was roaring in the great elms behind the outhouses. When she came to the second yard the darkness seemed deeper. She was unsure of her footing. She wished she had brought a lantern. Rain blew against her. Half she liked it, half she felt unwilling to battle.

She reached at last the just visible door of the stable. There was no sign of a light anywhere. Opening the upper half, she looked in: into a simple well of darkness. The smell of horses and ammonia, and of warmth was startling to her, in that full night. She listened with all her ears but could hear nothing save the night, and the stirring of a horse.

"Maurice!" she called, softly and musically, though she was afraid. "Maurice—are you there?"

Nothing came from the darkness. She knew the rain and wind blew in upon the horses, the hot animal life. Feeling it wrong, she entered the stable and drew the lower half of the door shut, holding the upper part close. She did not stir, because she was aware of the presence of the dark hind-quarters of the horses, though she could not see them, and she was afraid. Something wild stirred in her heart.

She listened intensely. Then she heard a small noise in the distance—far away, it seemed—the chink of a pan, and a man's voice speaking a brief word. It would be Maurice, in the other part of the stable. She stood motionless, waiting for him to come through the partition door. The horses were so terrifyingly near to her, in the invisible.

The loud jarring of the inner door-latch made her start; the door was opened. She could hear and feel her husband entering and invisibly passing among the horses near to her, darkness as they were, actively intermingled. The rather low sound of his voice as he spoke to the horses came velvety to her nerves. How near he was, and how invisible! The darkness seemed to be in a strange swirl of violent life, just upon her. She turned giddy.

Her presence of mind made her call quietly and musically:

"Maurice! Maurice—dear-ar!"

"Yes," he answered. "Isabel?"

She saw nothing, and the sound of his voice seemed to touch her.

"Hello!" she answered cheerfully, straining her eyes to see him. He was still busy, attending to the horses near her, but she saw only darkness. It made her almost desperate.

"Won't you come in, dear?" she said.

"Yes, I'm coming. Just half a minute. Stand over—now! Trap's not come, has it?"

"Not yet," said Isabel.

His voice was pleasant and ordinary, but it had a slight suggestion of the stable to her. She wished he would come away. Whilst he was so utterly invisible, she was afraid of him.

"How's the time?" he asked.

"Not yet six," she replied. She disliked to answer into the dark. Presently he came very near to her, and she retreated out of doors.

"The weather blows in here," he said, coming steadily forward, feeling for the doors. She shrank away. At last she could dimly see him.

"Bertie won't have much of a drive," he said, as he closed the doors.

"He won't indeed!" said Isabel calmly, watching the dark shape at the door.

"Give me your arm dear," she said.

She pressed his arm close to her, as she went. But she longed to see him, to look at him. She was nervous. He walked erect, with face rather lifted, but with a curious tentative movement of his powerful, muscular legs. She could feel the clever, careful, strong contact of his feet with the earth, as she balanced against him. For a moment he was a tower of darkness to her, as if he rose out of the earth.

In the house-passage he wavered and went cautiously, with a curious look of silence about him as he felt for the bench. Then he sat down heavily. He was a man with rather sloping shoulders, but with heavy limbs, powerful legs that seemed to know the earth. His head was small, usually carried high and light. As he bent down to unfasten his gaiters and boots he did not look blind. His hair was brown and crisp, his hands were large, reddish, intelligent, the veins stood out in the wrists; and his thighs and knees seemed massive. When he stood up his face and neck were surcharged with blood, the veins stood out on his temples. She did not look at his blindness.

Isabel was always glad when they had passed through the dividing door into their own regions of repose and beauty. She was a little afraid of him, out there in the animal grossness of the back. His bearings also changed, as he smelt the familiar indefinable odour that pervaded his wife's surroundings, a delicate, refined scent, very faintly spicy. Perhaps it came from the potpourri bowls.

He stood at the foot of the stairs, arrested, listening. She watched him, and her heart sickened. He seemed to be listening to fate.

"He's not here yet," he said. "I'll go up and change."

"Maurice," she said, "you're not wishing he wouldn't come, are you?"

"I couldn't quite say," he answered. "I feel myself rather on the qui vive."

"I can see you are," she answered. And she reached up and kissed his cheek. She saw his mouth relax into a slow smile.

"What are you laughing at?" she said roguishly.

"You consoling me," he answered.

"Nay," she answered. "Why should I console you? You know we love each other—you know how married we are! What does anything else matter?"

"Nothing at all, my dear."

He felt for her face and touched it, smiling.

"You're all right, aren't you?" he asked anxiously.

"I'm wonderfully all right, love," she answered. "It's you I am a little troubled about, at times."

"Why me?" he said, touching her cheeks delicately with the tips of his fingers. The touch had an almost hypnotizing effect on her.

He went away upstairs. She saw him mount into the darkness, unseeing and unchanging. He did not know that the lamps on the upper corridor were unlighted. He went on into the darkness with unchanging step. She heard him in the bath-room.

Pervin moved about almost unconsciously in his familiar surroundings, dark though everything was. He seemed to know the presence of objects before he touched them. It was a pleasure to him to rock thus through a world of things, carried on the flood in a sort of blood-prescience. He did not think much or trouble much. So long as he kept this sheer immediacy of blood-contact with the substantial world he was happy, he wanted no intervention of visual consciousness. In this state there was a certain rich positivity, bordering sometimes on rapture. Life seemed to move in him like a tide lapping, lapping, and advancing, enveloping all things darkly. It was a pleasure to stretch forth the hand and meet the unseen object, clasp it, and possess it in pure contact. He did not try to remember, to visualize. He did not want to. The new way of consciousness substituted itself in him.

The rich suffusion of this state generally kept him happy, reaching its culmination in the consuming passion for his wife. But at times the flow would seem to be checked and thrown back. Then it would beat inside him like a tangled sea, and he was tortured in the shattered chaos of his own blood. He grew to dread this arrest, this throw-back, this chaos inside himself, when he seemed merely at the mercy of his own powerful and conflicting elements. How to get some measure of control or surety, this was the question. And when the question rose maddening in him, he would clench his fists as if he would compel the whole universe to submit to him. But it was in vain. He could not even compel himself.

Tonight, however, he was still serene, though little tremors of unreasonable exasperation ran through him. He had to handle the razor very carefully, as he shaved, for it was not at one with him, he was afraid of it. His hearing also was too much sharpened. He heard the woman lighting the lamps on the corridor, and attending to the fire in the visitors' room. And then, as he went to his room, he heard the trap arrive. Then came Isabel's voice, lifted and calling, like a bell ringing:

"Is it you, Bertie? Have you come?"

And a man's voice answered out of the wind:

"Hello, Isabel! There you are."

"Have you had a miserable drive? I'm so sorry we couldn't send a closed carriage. I can't see you at all, you know."

"I'm coming. No, I liked the drive—it was like Perthshire. Well, how are you? You're looking fit as ever, as far as I can see."

"Oh, yes," said Isabel. "I'm wonderfully well. How are you? Rather thin, I think—"

"Worked to death—everybody's old cry. But I'm all right, Ciss. How's Pervin?—isn't he here?"

"Oh, yes, he's upstairs changing. Yes, he's awfully well. Take off your wet things; I'll send them to be dried."

"And how are you both, in spirits? He doesn't fret?"

"No—no, not at all. No, on the contrary, really. We've been wonderfully happy, incredibly. It's more than I can understand—so wonderful: the nearness, and the peace—"

"Ah! Well, that's awfully good news—"

They moved away. Pervin heard no more. But a childish sense of desolation had come over him, as he heard their brisk voices. He seemed shut out—like a child that is left out. He was aimless and excluded, he did not know what to do with himself. The helpless desolation came over him. He fumbled nervously as he dressed himself, in a state almost of childishness. He disliked the Scotch accent in Bertie's speech, and the slight response it found on Isabel's tongue. He disliked the slight purr of complacency in the Scottish speech. He disliked intensely the glib way in which Isabel spoke of their happiness and nearness. It made him recoil. He was fretful and beside himself like a child, he had almost a childish nostalgia to be included in the life circle. And at the same time he was a man, dark and powerful and infuriated by his own weakness. By some fatal flaw, he could not be by himself, he had to depend on the support of another. And this very dependence enraged him. He hated Bertie Reid, and at the same time he knew the hatred was nonsense, he knew it was the outcome of his own weakness.

He went downstairs. Isabel was alone in the dining-room. She watched him enter, head erect, his feet tentative. He looked so strong-blooded and healthy and, at the same time, cancelled. Cancelled—that was the word that flew across her mind. Perhaps it was his scar suggested it.

"You heard Bertie come, Maurice?" she said.

"Yes—isn't he here?"

"He's in his room. He looks very thin and worn."

"I suppose he works himself to death."

A woman came in with a tray—and after a few minutes Bertie came down. He was a little dark man, with a very big forehead, thin, wispy hair, and sad, large eyes. His expression was inordinately sad—almost funny. He had odd, short legs.

Isabel watched him hesitate under the door, and glance nervously at her husband. Pervin heard him and turned.

"Here you are, now," said Isabel. "Come, let us eat."

Bertie went across to Maurice.

"How are you, Pervin?" he said, as he advanced.

The blind man stuck his hand out into space, and Bertie took it.

"Very fit. Glad you've come," said Maurice.

Isabel glanced at them, and glanced away, as if she could not bear to see them.

"Come," she said. "Come to table. Aren't you both awfully hungry? I am, tremendously."

"I'm afraid you waited for me," said Bertie, as they sat down.

Maurice had a curious monolithic way of sitting in a chair, erect and distant. Isabel's heart always beat when she caught sight of him thus.

"No," she replied to Bertie. "We're very little later than usual. We're having a sort of high tea, not dinner. Do you mind? It gives us such a nice long evening, uninterrupted."

"I like it," said Bertie.

Maurice was feeling, with curious little movements, almost like a cat kneading her bed, for his plate, his knife and fork, his napkin. He was getting the whole geography of his cover into his consciousness. He sat erect and inscrutable, remote-seeming. Bertie watched the static figure of the blind man, the delicate tactile discernment of the large, ruddy hands, and the curious mindless silence of the brow, above the scar. With difficulty he looked away, and without knowing what he did, picked up a little crystal bowl of violets from the table, and held them to his nose.

"They are sweet-scented," he said. "Where do they come from?"

"From the garden—under the windows," said Isabel.

"So late in the year—and so fragrant! Do you remember the violets under Aunt Bell's south wall?"

The two friends looked at each other and exchanged a smile, Isabel's eyes lighting up.

"Don't I?" she replied. "Wasn't she queer!"

"A curious old girl," laughed Bertie. "There's a streak of freakishness in the family, Isabel."

"Ah—but not in you and me, Bertie," said Isabel. "Give them to Maurice, will you?" she added, as Bertie was putting down the flowers. "Have you smelled the violets, dear? Do!—they are so scented."

Maurice held out his hand, and Bertie placed the tiny bowl against his large, warm-looking fingers. Maurice's hand closed over the thin white fingers of the barrister. Bertie carefully extricated himself. Then the two watched the blind man smelling the violets. He bent his head and seemed to be thinking. Isabel waited.

"Aren't they sweet, Maurice?" she said at last, anxiously.

"Very," he said. And he held out the bowl. Bertie took it. Both he and Isabel were a little afraid, and deeply disturbed.

The meal continued. Isabel and Bertie chatted spasmodically. The blind man was silent. He touched his food repeatedly, with quick, delicate touches of his knife-point, then cut irregular bits. He could not bear to be helped. Both Isabel and Bertie suffered: Isabel wondered why. She did not suffer when she was alone with Maurice. Bertie made her conscious of a strangeness.

After the meal the three drew their chairs to the fire, and sat down to talk. The decanters were put on a table near at hand. Isabel knocked the logs on the fire, and clouds of brilliant sparks went up the chimney. Bertie noticed a slight weariness in her bearing.

"You will be glad when your child comes now, Isabel?" he said.

She looked up to him with a quick wan smile.

"Yes, I shall be glad," she answered. "It begins to seem long. Yes, I shall be very glad. So will you, Maurice, won't you?" she added.

"Yes, I shall," replied her husband.

"We are both looking forward so much to having it," she said.

"Yes, of course," said Bertie.

He was a bachelor, three or four years older than Isabel. He lived in beautiful rooms overlooking the river, guarded by a faithful Scottish manservant. And he had his friends among the fair sex—not lovers, friends. So long as he could avoid any danger of courtship or marriage, he adored a few good women with constant and unfailing homage, and he was chivalrously fond of quite a number. But if they seemed to encroach on him, he withdrew and detested them.

Isabel knew him very well, knew his beautiful constancy, and kindness, also his incurable weakness, which made him unable ever to enter into close contact of any sort. He was ashamed of himself because he could not marry, could not approach women physically. He wanted to do so. But he could not. At the centre of him he was afraid, helplessly and even brutally afraid. He had given up hope, had ceased to expect any more that he could escape his own weakness. Hence he was a brilliant and successful barrister, also a litterateur of high repute, a rich man, and a great social success. At the centre he felt himself neuter, nothing.

Isabel knew him well. She despised him even while she admired him. She looked at his sad face, his little short legs, and felt contempt of him. She looked at his dark grey eyes, with their uncanny, almost childlike, intuition, and she loved him. He understood amazingly— but she had no fear of his understanding. As a man she patronized him.

And she turned to the impassive, silent figure of her husband. He sat leaning back, with folded arms, and face a little uptilted. His knees were straight and massive. She sighed, picked up the poker, and again began to prod the fire, to rouse the clouds of soft brilliant sparks.

"Isabel tells me," Bertie began suddenly, "that you have not suffered unbearably from the loss of sight."

Maurice straightened himself to attend but kept his arms folded.

"No," he said, "not unbearably. Now and again one struggles against it, you know. But there are compensations."

"They say it is much worse to be stone deaf," said Isabel.

"I believe it is," said Bertie. "Are there compensations?" he added to Maurice.

"Yes. You cease to bother about a great many things." Again Maurice stretched his figure, stretched the strong muscles of his back, and leaned backwards, with uplifted face.

"And that is a relief," said Bertie. "But what is there in place of the bothering? What replaces the activity?"

There was a pause. At length the blind man replied, as out of a negligent, unattentive thinking:

"Oh, I don't know. There's a good deal when you're not active."

"Is there?" said Bertie. "What exactly? It always seems to me that when there is no thought and no action, there is nothing."

Again Maurice was slow in replying.

"There is something," he replied. "I couldn't tell you what it is."

And the talk lapsed once more, Isabel and Bertie chatting gossip and reminiscence, the blind man silent.

At length Maurice rose restlessly, a big obtrusive figure. He felt tight and hampered. He wanted to go away.

"Do you mind," he said, "if I go and speak to Wernham?"

"No—go along, dear," said Isabel.

And he went out. A silence came over the two friends. At length Bertie said:

"Nevertheless, it is a great deprivation, Cissie."

"It is, Bertie. I know it is."

"Something lacking all the time," said Bertie.

"Yes, I know. And yet—and yet—Maurice is right. There is something else, something there, which you never knew was there, and which you can't express."

"What is there?" asked Bertie.

"I don't know—it's awfully hard to define it—but something strong and immediate. There's something strange in Maurice's presence—indefinable—but I couldn't do without it. I agree that it seems to put one's mind to sleep. But when we're alone I miss nothing; it seems awfully rich, almost splendid, you know."

"I'm afraid I don't follow," said Bertie.

They talked desultorily. The wind blew loudly outside, rain chattered on the window-panes, making a sharp drum-sound because of the closed, mellow-golden shutters inside. The logs burned slowly, with hot, almost invisible small flames. Bertie seemed uneasy, there were dark circles round his eyes. Isabel, rich with her approaching maternity, leaned looking into the fire. Her hair curled in odd, loose strands, very pleasing to the man. But she had a curious feeling of old woe in her heart, old timeless night-woe.

"I suppose we're all deficient somewhere," said Bertie.

"I suppose so," said Isabel wearily.

"Damned, sooner or later."

"I don't know," she said, rousing herself. "I feel quite all right, you know. The child coming seems to make me indifferent to everything, just placid. I can't feel that there's anything to trouble about, you know."

"A good thing, I should say," he replied slowly.

"Well, there it is. I suppose it's just Nature. If only I felt I needn't trouble about Maurice, I should be perfectly content—"

"But you feel you must trouble about him?"

"Well—I don't know—" She even resented this much effort.

The night passed slowly. Isabel looked at the clock. "I say," she said. "It's nearly ten o'clock. Where can Maurice be? I'm sure they're all in bed at the back. Excuse me a moment."

She went out, returning almost immediately.

"It's all shut up and in darkness," she said. "I wonder where he is. He must have gone out to the farm—"

Bertie looked at her.

"I suppose he'll come in," he said.

"I suppose so," she said. "But it's unusual for him to be out now."

"Would you like me to go out and see?"

"Well—if you wouldn't mind. I'd go, but—" She did not want to make the physical effort.

Bertie put on an old overcoat and took a lantern. He went out from the side door. He shrank from the wet and roaring night. Such weather had a nervous effect on him: too much moisture everywhere made him feel almost imbecile. Unwilling, he went through it all. A dog barked violently at him. He peered in all the buildings. At last, as he opened the upper door of a sort of intermediate barn, he heard a grinding noise, and looking in, holding up his lantern, saw Maurice, in his shirtsleeves, standing listening, holding the handle of a turnip-pulper. He had been pulping sweet roots, a pile of which lay dimly heaped in a corner behind him.

"That you, Wernham?" said Maurice, listening.

"No, it's me," said Bertie.

A large, half-wild grey cat was rubbing at Maurice's leg. The blind man stooped to rub its sides. Bertie watched the scene, then unconsciously entered and shut the door behind him. He was in a high sort of barn-place, from which, right and left, ran off the corridors in front of the stalled cattle. He watched the slow, stooping motion of the other man, as he caressed the great cat.

Maurice straightened himself.

"You came to look for me?" he said.

"Isabel was a little uneasy," said Bertie.

"I'll come in. I like messing about doing these jobs."

The cat had reared her sinister, feline length against his leg, clawing at his thigh affectionately. He lifted her claws out of his flesh.

"I hope I'm not in your way at all at the Grange here," said Bertie, rather shy and stiff.

"My way? No, not a bit. I'm glad Isabel has somebody to talk to. I'm afraid it's I who am in the way. I know I'm not very lively company. Isabel's all right, don't you think? She's not unhappy, is she?"

"I don't think so."

"What does she say?"

"She says she's very content—only a little troubled about you."

"Why me?"

"Perhaps afraid that you might brood," said Bertie, cautiously.

"She needn't be afraid of that." He continued to caress the flattened grey head of the cat with his fingers. "What I am a bit afraid of," he resumed, "is that she'll find me a dead weight, always alone with me down here."

"I don't think you need think that," said Bertie, though this was what he feared himself.

"I don't know," said Maurice. "Sometimes I feel it isn't fair that she's saddled with me." Then he dropped his voice curiously. "I say," he asked, secretly struggling, "is my face much disfigured? Do you mind telling me?"

"There is the scar," said Bertie, wondering. "Yes, it is a disfigurement. But more pitiable than shocking."

"A pretty bad scar, though," said Maurice.

"Oh, yes."

There was a pause.

"Sometimes I feel I am horrible," said Maurice, in a low voice, talking as if to himself. And Bertie actually felt a quiver of horror.

"That's nonsense," he said.

Maurice again straightened himself, leaving the cat.

"There's no telling," he said. Then again, in an odd tone, he added: "I don't really know you, do I?"

"Probably not," said Bertie.

"Do you mind if I touch you?"

The lawyer shrank away instinctively. And yet, out of very philanthropy, he said, in a small voice: "Not at all."

But he suffered as the blind man stretched out a strong, naked hand to him. Maurice accidentally knocked off Bertie's hat.

"I thought you were taller," he said, starting. Then he laid his hand on Bertie Reid's head, closing the dome of the skull in a soft, firm grasp, gathering it, as it were; then, shifting his grasp and softly closing again, with a fine, close pressure, till he had covered the skull and the face of the smaller man, tracing the brows, and touching the full, closed eyes, touching the small nose and the nostrils, the rough, short moustache, the mouth, the rather strong chin. The hand of the blind man grasped the shoulder, the arm, the hand of the other man. He seemed to take him, in the soft, travelling grasp.

"You seem young," he said quietly, at last.

The lawyer stood almost annihilated, unable to answer.

"Your head seems tender, as if you were young," Maurice repeated. "So do your hands. Touch my eyes, will you?—touch my scar."

Now Bertie quivered with revulsion. Yet he was under the power of the blind man, as if hypnotized. He lifted his hand, and laid the fingers on the scar, on the scarred eyes. Maurice suddenly covered them with his own hand, pressed the fingers of the other man upon his disfigured eye-sockets, trembling in every fibre, and rocking slightly, slowly, from side to side. He remained thus for a minute or more, whilst Bertie stood as if in a swoon, unconscious, imprisoned.

Then suddenly Maurice removed the hand of the other man from his brow, and stood holding it in his own.

"Oh, my God," he said, "we shall know each other now, shan't we? We shall know each other now."

Bertie could not answer. He gazed mute and terrorstruck, overcome by his own weakness. He knew he could not answer. He had an unreasonable fear lest the other man should suddenly destroy him. Whereas Maurice was actually filled with hot, poignant love, the passion of friendship. Perhaps it was this very passion of friendship which Bertie shrank from most.

"We're all right together now, aren't we?" said Maurice. "It's all right now, as long as we live, so far as we're concerned?"

"Yes," said Bertie, trying by any means to escape.

Maurice stood with head lifted, as if listening. The new delicate fulfilment of mortal friendship had come as a revelation and surprise to him, something exquisite and unhoped-for. He seemed to be listening to hear if it were real.

Then he turned for his coat.

"Come," he said, "we'll go to Isabel."

Bertie took the lantern and opened the door. The cat disappeared. The two men went in silence along the causeways. Isabel, as they came, thought their footsteps sounded strange. She looked up pathetically and anxiously for their entrance. There seemed a curious elation about Maurice. Bertie was haggard, with sunken eyes.

"What is it?" she asked.

"We've become friends," said Maurice, standing with his feet apart, like a strange colossus.

"Friends!" re-echoed Isabel. And she looked again at Bertie. He met her eyes with a furtive, haggard look; his eyes were as if glazed with misery.

"I'm so glad," she said, in sheer perplexity.

"Yes," said Maurice.

He was indeed so glad. Isabel took his hand with both hers, and held it fast.

"You'll be happier now, dear," she said.

But she was watching Bertie. She knew that he had one desire—to escape from this intimacy, this friendship, which had been thrust upon him. He could not bear it that he had been touched by the blind man, his insane reserve broken in. He was like a mollusc whose shell is broken.

QUESTIONS

1. Lawrence often connects sight with *intellect,* touch with *instinct.* Is "The Blind Man" a story of the conflict between them? (See Preface, pp. 3, 14–15.)

2. The locale is divided between farm and house. Discuss the contrast and relate the opposition to the conflict and theme of the story. (See Preface, pp. 27–28.)

3. Isabel is in the middle—between Bertie, a cousin, and Maurice, her husband. How do they represent the poles of her character? What is Lawrence's attitude toward Isabel?

4. "At the centre of him he was afraid, helplessly and even brutally afraid." Lawrence seems to tell us this as an omniscient author, not through Bertie's angle of vision. He tells us what characters deeply feel but could never acknowledge: "At the centre he felt himself neuter, nothing." He speaks like a prophet. How does this tone affect the theme of the story?

5. " 'I suppose we're all deficient somewhere,' said Bertie." How are Bertie and his way of life deficient? Paradoxically, the blind man seems generally more complete, more at peace. Discuss.

6. Consider the brilliant final scene: the question about the scar, the lie, the request, the touch by Bertie, then by Maurice. What happens to Bertie in this scene? Why? When they return to the house, what does each of the three experience? What does Isabel see? What is the meaning of the confrontation? Consider with regard to the theme.

The Rocking-Horse Winner

D. H. LAWRENCE

There was a woman who was beautiful, who started with all the advantages, yet she had no luck. She married for love, and the love turned to dust. She had bonny children, yet she felt they had been thrust upon her, and she could not love them. They looked at her coldly, as if they were finding fault with her. And hurriedly she felt she must cover up some fault in herself. Yet what it was that she must cover up she never knew. Nevertheless, when her children were present, she always felt the centre of her heart go hard. This troubled her, and in her manner she was all the more gentle and anxious for her children, as if she loved them very much. Only she herself knew that at the centre of her heart was a hard little place that could not feel love, no, not for anybody. Everybody else said of her: "She is such a good mother. She adores her children." Only she herself, and

From *The Complete Short Stories of D. H. Lawrence,* Volume III. Copyright 1933 by the Estate of D. H. Lawrence, © 1961 by Angelo Ravagli and C. M. Weekley, Executors of the Estate of Frieda Lawrence Ravagli. Reprinted by permission of The Viking Press.

her children themselves, knew it was not so. They read it in each other's eyes.

There were a boy and two little girls. They lived in a pleasant house, with a garden, and they had discreet servants, and felt themselves superior to anyone in the neighbourhood.

Although they lived in style, they felt always an anxiety in the house. There was never enough money. The mother had a small income, and the father had a small income, but not nearly enough for the social position which they had to keep up. The father went into town to some office. But though he had good prospects, these prospects never materialized. There was always the grinding sense of the shortage of money, though the style was always kept up.

At last the mother said: "I will see if I can't make something." But she did not know where to begin. She racked her brains, and tried this thing and the other, but could not find anything successful. The failure made deep lines come into her face. Her children were growing up, they would have to go to school. There must be more money, there must be more money. The father, who was always very handsome and expensive in his tastes, seemed as if he never would be able to do anything worth doing. And the mother, who had a great belief in herself, did not succeed any better, and her tastes were just as expensive.

And so the house came to be haunted by the unspoken phrase: There must be more money! There must be more money! The children could hear it all the time, though nobody said it aloud. They heard it at Christmas, when the expensive and splendid toys filled the nursery. Behind the shining modern rocking horse, behind the smart doll's-house, a voice would start whispering: "There must be more money! There must be more money!" And the children would stop playing, to listen for a moment. They would look into each other's eyes, to see if they had all heard. And each one saw in the eyes of the other two that they too had heard. "There must be more money! There must be more money!"

It came whispering from the springs of the still-swaying rocking horse, and even the horse, bending his wooden, champing head, heard it. The big doll, sitting so pink and smirking in her new pram, could hear it quite plainly, and seemed to be smirking all the more self-consciously because of it. The foolish puppy, too, that took the place of the Teddy bear, he was looking so extraordinarily foolish for no other reason but that he heard the secret whisper all over the house: "There must be more money!"

Yet nobody ever said it aloud. The whisper was everywhere, and therefore no one spoke it. Just as no one ever says: "We are breathing!" in spite of the fact that breath is coming and going all the time.

"Mother," said the boy Paul one day, "why don't we keep a car of our own? Why do we always use uncle's, or else a taxi?"

"Because we're the poor members of the family," said the mother.

"But why are we, mother?"

"Well—I suppose," she said slowly and bitterly, "it's because your father has no luck."

The boy was silent for some time.

"Is luck money, mother?" he asked, rather timidly.

"No, Paul. Not quite. It's what causes you to have money."

"Oh!" said Paul vaguely. "I thought when Uncle Oscar said filthy lucker, it meant money."

"Filthy lucre does mean money," said the mother. "But it's lucre, not luck."

"Oh!" said the boy. "Then what is luck, mother?"

"It's what causes you to have money. If you're lucky you have money. That's why it's better to be born lucky than rich. If you're rich, you may lose your money. But if you're lucky, you will always get more money."

"Oh! Will you? And is father not lucky?"

"Very unlucky, I should say," she said bitterly.

The boy watched her with unsure eyes.

"Why?" he asked.

"I don't know. Nobody ever knows why one person is lucky and another unlucky."

"Don't they? Nobody at all? Does nobody know?"

"Perhaps God. But He never tells."

"He ought to, then. And aren't you lucky either, mother?"

"I can't be, if I married an unlucky husband."

"But by yourself, aren't you?"

"I used to think I was, before I married. Now I think I am very unlucky indeed."

"Why?"

"Well—never mind! Perhaps I'm not really," she said.

The child looked at her, to see if she meant it. But he saw, by the lines of her mouth, that she was only trying to hide something from him.

"Well, anyhow," he said stoutly, "I'm a lucky person."

"Why?" said his mother, with a sudden laugh.

He stared at her. He didn't even know why he had said it.

"God told me," he asserted, brazening it out.

"I hope He did, dear!" she said, again with a laugh, but rather bitter.

"He did, mother!"

"Excellent!" said the mother, using one of her husband's exclamations.

The boy saw she did not believe him; or, rather, that she paid no attention to his assertion. This angered him somewhat, and made him want to compel her attention.

He went off by himself, vaguely, in a childish way, seeking for the clue to "luck." Absorbed, taking no heed of other people, he went about with a sort of stealth, seeking inwardly for luck. He wanted luck, he wanted it, he wanted it. When the two girls were playing dolls in the nursery, he would sit on his big rocking horse, charging madly into space, with a frenzy that made the little girls peer at him uneasily. Wildly the horse careered, the waving dark hair of the boy tossed, his eyes had a strange glare in them. The little girls dared not speak to him.

When he had ridden to the end of his mad little journey, he climbed down and stood in front of his rocking horse, staring fixedly into its lowered face. Its red mouth was slightly open, its big eye was wide and glassy-bright.

"Now!" he would silently command the snorting steed. "Now, take me to where there is luck! Now take me!"

And he would slash the horse on the neck with the little whip he had asked Uncle Oscar for. He knew the horse could take him to where there was luck, if only he forced it. So he would mount again, and start on his furious ride, hoping at last to get there. He knew he could get there.

"You'll break your horse, Paul!" said the nurse.

"He's always riding like that! I wish he'd leave off!" said his elder sister Joan.

But he only glared down on them in silence. Nurse gave him up. She could make nothing of him. Anyhow he was growing beyond her.

One day his mother and his Uncle Oscar came in when he was on one of his furious rides. He did not speak to them.

"Hallo, you young jockey! Riding a winner?" said his uncle.

"Aren't you growing too big for a rocking horse? You're not a very little boy any longer, you know," said his mother.

But Paul only gave a blue glare from his big, rather close-set eyes. He would speak to nobody when he was in full tilt. His mother watched him with an anxious expression on her face.

At last he suddenly stopped forcing his horse into the mechanical gallop, and slid down.

"Well, I got there!" he announced fiercely, his blue eyes still flaring, and his sturdy long legs straddling apart.

"Where did you get to?" asked his mother.

"Where I wanted to go," he flared back at her.

"That's right, son!" said Uncle Oscar. "Don't you stop till you get there. What's the horse's name?"

"He doesn't have a name," said the boy.

"Gets on without all right?" asked the uncle.

"Well, he has different names. He was called Sansovino last week."

"Sansovino, eh? Won the Ascot. How did you know his name?"

"He always talks about horse races with Bassett," said Joan.

The uncle was delighted to find that his small nephew was posted with all the racing news. Bassett, the young gardener, who had been wounded in the left foot in the war and had got his present job through Oscar Cresswell, whose batman he had been, was a perfect blade of the "turf." He lived in the racing events, and the small boy lived with him.

Oscar Cresswell got it all from Bassett.

"Master Paul comes and asks me, so I can't do more than tell him, sir," said Bassett, his face terribly serious, as if he were speaking of religious matters.

"And does he ever put anything on a horse he fancies?"

"Well—I don't want to give him away—he's a young sport, a fine sport, sir. Would you mind asking him yourself? He sort of takes a pleasure in it, and perhaps he'd feel I was giving him away, sir, if you don't mind."

Bassett was serious as a church.

The uncle went back to his nephew, and took him off for a ride in the car.

"Say, Paul, old man, do you ever put anything on a horse?" the uncle asked.

The boy watched the handsome man closely.

"Why, do you think I oughtn't to?" he parried.

"Not a bit of it! I thought perhaps you might give me a tip for the Lincoln."

The car sped on into the country, going down to Uncle Oscar's place in Hampshire.

"Honour bright?" said the nephew.

"Honour bright, son!" said the uncle.

"Well, then, Daffodil."

"Daffodil! I doubt it, sonny. What about Mirza?"

"I only know the winner," said the boy. "That's Daffodil."

"Daffodil, eh?"

There was a pause. Daffodil was an obscure horse comparatively.

"Uncle!"

"Yes, son?"

"You won't let it go any further, will you? I promised Bassett."

"Bassett be damned, old man! What's he got to do with it?"

"We're partners. We've been partners from the first. Uncle, he lent me my first five shillings, which I lost. I promised him, honour bright, it was only between me and him; only you gave me that ten-shilling note I started winning with, so I thought you were lucky. You won't let it go any further, will you?"

The boy gazed at his uncle from those big, hot, blue eyes, set rather close together. The uncle stirred and laughed uneasily.

"Right you are, son! I'll keep your tip private. Daffodil, eh? How much are you putting on him?"

"All except twenty pounds," said the boy. "I keep that in reserve."

The uncle thought it a good joke.

"You keep twenty pounds in reserve, do you, you young romancer? What are you betting, then?"

"I'm betting three hundred," said the boy gravely. "But it's between you and me, Uncle Oscar! Honour bright?"

The uncle burst into a roar of laughter.

"It's between you and me all right, you young Nat Gould," he said, laughing. "But where's your three hundred?"

"Bassett keeps it for me. We're partners."

"You are, are you! And what is Bassett putting on Daffodil?"

"He won't go quite as high as I do, I expect. Perhaps he'll go a hundred and fifty."

"What, pennies?" laughed the uncle.

"Pounds," said the child, with a surprised look at his uncle. "Bassett keeps a bigger reserve than I do."

Between wonder and amusement Uncle Oscar was silent. He pursued the matter no further, but he determined to take his nephew with him to the Lincoln races.

"Now, son," he said, "I'm putting twenty on Mirza, and I'll put five for you on any horse you fancy. What's your pick?"

"Daffodil, uncle."

"No, not the fiver on Daffodil!"

"I should if it was my own fiver," said the child.

"Good! Good! Right you are! A fiver for me and a fiver for you on Daffodil."

The child had never been to a race meeting before, and his eyes were blue fire. He pursed his mouth tight, and watched. A Frenchman just in front had put his money on Lancelot. Wild with excitement, he flayed his arms up and down, yelling "Lancelot! Lancelot!" in his French accent.

Daffodil came in first, Lancelot second, Mirza third. The child, flushed and with eyes blazing, was curiously serene. His uncle brought him four five-pound notes, four to one.

"What am I to do with these?" he cried, waving them before the boy's eyes.

"I suppose we'll talk to Bassett," said the boy. "I expect I have fifteen hundred now; and twenty in reserve; and this twenty."

His uncle studied him for some moments.

"Look here, son!" he said. "You're not serious about Bassett and that fifteen hundred, are you?"

"Yes, I am. But it's between you and me, uncle. Honour bright!"

"Honour bright all right, son! But I must talk to Bassett."

"If you'd like to be a partner, uncle, with Bassett and me, we could all be partners. Only, you'd have to promise, honour bright, uncle, not to let it go beyond us three. Bassett and I are lucky, and you must be lucky, because it was your ten shillings I started winning with . . ."

Uncle Oscar took both Bassett and Paul into Richmond Park for an afternoon, and there they talked.

"It's like this, you see, sir," Bassett said. "Master Paul would get me talking about racing events, spinning yarns, you know, sir. And he was always keen on knowing if I'd made or if I'd lost. It's about a year since, now, that I put five shillings on Blush of Dawn for him—and we lost. Then the luck turned, with that ten shillings he had from you, that we put on Singhalese. And since that time, it's been pretty steady, all things considering. What do you say, Master Paul?"

"We're all right when we're sure," said Paul. "It's when we're not quite sure that we go down."

"Oh, but we're careful then," said Bassett.

"But when are you sure?" smiled Uncle Oscar.

"It's Master Paul, sir," said Bassett, in a secret, religious voice. "It's as if he had it from heaven. Like Daffodil, now, for the Lincoln. That was as sure as eggs."

"Did you put anything on Daffodil?" asked Oscar Cresswell.

"Yes, sir, I made my bit."

"And my nephew?"

Bassett was obstinately silent, looking at Paul.

"I made twelve hundred, didn't I, Bassett? I told uncle I was putting three hundred on Daffodil."

"That's right," said Bassett, nodding.

"But where's the money?" asked the uncle.

"I keep it safe locked up, sir. Master Paul he can have it any minute he likes to ask for it."

"What, fifteen hundred pounds?"

"And twenty! and forty, that is, with the twenty he made on the course."

"It's amazing!" said the uncle.

"If Master Paul offers you to be partners, sir, I would, if I were you; if you'll excuse me," said Bassett.

Oscar Cresswell thought about it.

"I'll see the money," he said.

They drove home again, and sure enough, Bassett came round to the garden-house with fifteen hundred pounds in notes. The twenty pounds reserve was left with Joe Glee, in the Turf Commission deposit.

"You see, it's all right, uncle, when I'm sure! Then we go strong, for all we're worth. Don't we, Bassett?"

"We do that, Master Paul."

"And when are you sure?" said the uncle, laughing.

"Oh, well, sometimes I'm absolutely sure, like about Daffodil," said the boy; "and sometimes I have an idea; and sometimes I haven't even an idea, have I, Bassett? Then we're careful, because we mostly go down."

"You do, do you! And when you're sure, like about Daffodil, what makes you sure, sonny?"

"Oh, well, I don't know," said the boy uneasily. "I'm sure, you know, uncle; that's all."

"It's as if he had it from heaven, sir," Bassett reiterated.

"I should say so!" said the uncle.

But he became a partner. And when the Leger was coming on, Paul was "sure" about Lively Spark, which was a quite inconsiderable horse. The boy insisted on putting a thousand on the horse, Bassett went for five hundred, and Oscar Cresswell two hundred. Lively Spark came in first, and the betting had been ten to one against him. Paul had made ten thousand.

"You see," he said, "I was absolutely sure of him."

Even Oscar Cresswell had cleared two thousand.

"Look here, son," he said, "this sort of thing makes me nervous."

"It needn't, uncle! Perhaps I shan't be sure again for a long time."

"But what are you going to do with your money?" asked the uncle.

"Of course," said the boy, "I started it for mother. She said she had no luck, because father is unlucky, so I thought if I was lucky, it might stop whispering."

"What might stop whispering?"

"Our house. I hate our house for whispering."

"What does it whisper?"

"Why—why"—the boy fidgeted—"why, I don't know. But it's always short of money, you know, uncle."

"I know it, son, I know it."

"You know people send mother writs, don't you, uncle?"

"I'm afraid I do," said the uncle.

"And then the house whispers, like people laughing at you behind your back. It's awful, that is! I thought if I was lucky . . ."

"You might stop it," added the uncle.

The boy watched him with big blue eyes that had an uncanny cold fire in them, and he said never a word.

"Well, then!" said the uncle. "What are we doing?"

"I shouldn't like mother to know I was lucky," said the boy.

"Why not, son?"

"She'd stop me."

"I don't think she would."

"Oh!"—and the boy writhed in an odd way—"I don't want her to know, uncle."

"All right, son! We'll manage it without her knowing."

They managed it very easily. Paul, at the other's suggestion, handed over five thousand pounds to his uncle, who deposited it with the family lawyer, who was then to inform Paul's mother that a relative had put five thousand pounds into his hands, which sum was to be paid out a thousand pounds at a time, on the mother's birthday, for the next five years.

"So she'll have a birthday present of a thousand pounds for five successive years," said Uncle Oscar. "I hope it won't make it all the harder for her later."

Paul's mother had her birthday in November. The house had been "whispering" worse than ever lately, and, even in spite of his luck, Paul could not bear up against it. He was very anxious to see the effect of the birthday letter, telling his mother about the thousand pounds.

When there were no visitors, Paul now took his meals with his parents, as he was beyond the nursery control. His mother went into town nearly every day. She had discovered that she had an odd knack of sketching furs and dress materials, so she worked secretly in the studio of a friend who was the chief "artist" for the leading drapers. She drew the figures of ladies in furs and ladies in silk and sequins for the newspaper advertisements. This young woman artist earned several thousand pounds a year, but Paul's mother only made several hundreds, and she was again dissatisfied. She so wanted to be first in something, and she did not suceed, even in making sketches for drapery advertisements.

She was down to breakfast on the morning of her birthday. Paul watched her face as she read her letters. He knew the lawyer's letter. As his mother read it, her face hardened and became more expressionless. Then a cold, determined look came on her mouth. She hid the letter under the pile of others, and said not a word about it.

"Didn't you have anything nice in the post for your birthday, mother?" said Paul.

"Quite moderately nice," she said, her voice cold and absent.

She went away to town without saying more.

But in the afternoon Uncle Oscar appeared. He said Paul's mother had had a long interview with the lawyer, asking if the whole five thousand could be advanced at once, as she was in debt.

"What do you think, uncle?" said the boy.

"I leave it to you, son."

"Oh, let her have it, then! We can get some more with the other," said the boy.

"A bird in the hand is worth two in the bush, laddie!" said Uncle Oscar.

"But I'm sure to know for the Grand National; or the Lincolnshire; or else the Derby. I'm sure to know for one of them," said Paul.

So Uncle Oscar signed the agreement, and Paul's mother touched the whole five thousand. Then something very curious happened. The voices in the house suddenly went mad, like a chorus of frogs on a spring evening. There were certain new furnishings, and Paul had a tutor. He was really going to Eton, his father's school, in the following autumn. There were flowers in the winter, and a blossoming of the luxury Paul's mother had been used to. And yet the voices in the house, behind the sprays of mimosa and almond blossom, and from under the piles of iridescent cushions, simply trilled and screamed in a sort of ecstasy: "There must be more money! Oh-h-h, there must be more money. Oh, now, now-w! Now-w-w—there must be more money—more than ever! More than ever!"

It frightened Paul terribly. He studied away at his Latin and Greek with his tutors. But his intense hours were spent with Bassett. The Grand National had gone by: he had not "known," and had lost a hundred pounds. Summer was at hand. He was in agony for the Lincoln. But even for the Lincoln he didn't "know" and he lost fifty pounds. He became wild-eyed and strange, as if something were going to explode in him.

"Let it alone, son! Don't you bother about it!" urged Uncle Oscar. But it was as if the boy couldn't really hear what his uncle was saying.

"I've got to know for the Derby! I've got to know for the Derby!" the child reiterated, his big blue eyes blazing with a sort of madness.

His mother noticed how overwrought he was.

"You'd better go to the seaside. Wouldn't you like to go now to the seaside, instead of waiting? I think you'd better," she said, looking down at him anxiously, her heart curiously heavy because of him.

But the child lifted his uncanny blue eyes.

"I couldn't possibly go before the Derby, mother!" he said. "I couldn't possibly!"

"Why not?" she said, her voice becoming heavy when she was opposed. "Why not? You can still go from the seaside to see the

Derby with your Uncle Oscar, if that's what you wish. No need for you to wait here. Besides, I think you care too much about these races. It's a bad sign. My family has been a gambling family, and you won't know till you grow up how much damage it has done. But it has done damage. I shall have to send Bassett away, and ask Uncle Oscar not to talk racing to you, unless you promise to be reasonable about it; go away to the seaside and forget it. You're all nerves!"

"I'll do what you like, mother, so long as you don't send me away till after the Derby," the boy said.

"Send you away from where? Just from this house?"

"Yes," he said, gazing at her.

"Why, you curious child, what makes you care about this house so much, suddenly? I never knew you loved it."

He gazed at her without speaking. He had a secret within a secret, something he had not divulged, even to Bassett or to his Uncle Oscar.

But his mother, after standing undecided and a little bit sullen for some moments, said:

"Very well, then! Don't go to the seaside till after the Derby, if you don't wish it. But promise me you won't let your nerves go to pieces. Promise you won't think so much about horse racing and events, as you call them!"

"Oh, no," said the boy casually. "I won't think much about them, mother. You needn't worry. I wouldn't worry, mother, if I were you."

"If you were me and I were you," said his mother, "I wonder what we should do!"

"But you know you needn't worry, mother, don't you?" the boy repeated.

"I should be awfully glad to know it," she said wearily.

"Oh, well, you can, you know. I mean, you ought to know you needn't worry," he insisted.

"Ought I? Then I'll see about it," she said.

Paul's secret of secrets was his wooden horse, that which had no name. Since he was emancipated from a nurse and a nursery-governess, he had had his rocking horse removed to his own bedroom at the top of the house.

"Surely, you're too big for a rocking horse!" his mother had remonstrated.

"Well, you see, mother, till I can have a real horse, I like to have some sort of animal about," had been his quaint answer.

"Do you feel he keeps you company?" she laughed.

"Oh, yes! He's very good, he always keeps me company, when I'm there," said Paul.

So the horse, rather shabby, stood in an arrested prance in the boy's bedroom.

The Derby was drawing near, and the boy grew more and more tense. He hardly heard what was spoken to him, he was very frail, and his eyes were really uncanny. His mother had sudden seizures of uneasiness about him. Sometimes, for half-an-hour, she would feel a sudden anxiety about him that was almost anguish. She wanted to rush to him at once, and know he was safe.

Two nights before the Derby, she was at a big party in town, when one of her rushes of anxiety about her boy, her first-born, gripped her heart till she could hardly speak. She fought with the feeling, might and main, for she believed in common sense. But it was too strong. She had to leave the dance and go downstairs to telephone to the country. The children's nursery-governess was terribly surprised and startled at being rung up in the night.

"Are the children all right, Miss Wilmot?"

"Oh, yes, they are quite all right."

"Master Paul? Is he all right?"

"He went to bed as right as a trivet. Shall I run up and look at him?"

"No," said Paul's mother reluctantly. "No! Don't trouble. It's all right. Don't sit up. We shall be home fairly soon." She did not want her son's privacy intruded upon.

"Very good," said the governess.

It was about one o'clock when Paul's mother and father drove up to their house. All was still. Paul's mother went to her room and slipped off her white fur coat. She had told her maid not to wait up for her. She heard her husband downstairs, mixing a whisky-and-soda.

And then, because of the strange anxiety at her heart, she stole upstairs to her son's room. Noiselessly she went along the upper corridor. Was there a faint noise? What was it?

She stood, with arrested muscles, outside his door, listening. There was a strange, heavy, and yet not loud noise. Her heart stood still. It was a soundless noise, yet rushing and powerful. Something huge, in violent, hushed motion. What was it? What in God's name was it? She ought to know. She felt that she knew the noise. She knew what it was.

Yet she could not place it. She couldn't say what it was. And on and on it went, like a madness.

Softly, frozen with anxiety and fear, she turned the door handle.

The room was dark. Yet in the space near the window, she heard and saw something plunging to and fro. She gazed in fear and amazement.

Then suddenly she switched on the light, and saw her son, in his green pyjamas, madly surging on the rocking horse. The blaze of light suddenly lit him up, as he urged the wooden horse, and lit her up, as she stood, blonde, in her dress of pale green and crystal, in the doorway.

"Paul!" she cried. "Whatever are you doing?"

"It's Malabar!" he screamed, in a powerful, strange voice. "It's Malabar."

His eyes blazed at her for one strange and senseless second, as he ceased urging his wooden horse. Then he fell with a crash to the ground, and she, all her tormented motherhood flooding upon her, rushed to gather him up.

But he was unconscious, and unconscious he remained, with some brain-fever. He talked and tossed, and his mother sat stonily by his side.

"Malabar! It's Malabar! Bassett, Bassett, I know it! It's Malabar!"

So the child cried, trying to get up and urge the rocking horse that gave him his inspiration.

"What does he mean by Malabar?" asked the heart-frozen mother.

"I don't know," said the father stonily.

"What does he mean by Malabar?" she asked her brother Oscar.

"It's one of the horses running for the Derby," was the answer.

And, in spite of himself, Oscar Cresswell spoke to Bassett, and himself put a thousand on Malabar: at fourteen to one.

The third day of the illness was critical: they were waiting for a change. The boy, with his rather long, curly hair, was tossing ceaselessly on the pillow. He neither slept nor regained consciousness, and his eyes were like blue stones. His mother sat, feeling her heart had gone, turned actually into a stone.

In the evening, Oscar Cresswell did not come, but Bassett sent a message, saying could he come up for one moment, just one moment? Paul's mother was very angry at the intrusion, but on second thought she agreed. The boy was the same. Perhaps Bassett might bring him to consciousness.

The gardener, a shortish fellow with a little brown moustache, and sharp little brown eyes, tiptoed into the room, touched his imaginary cap to Paul's mother, and stole to the bedside, staring with glittering, smallish eyes, at the tossing, dying child.

"Master Paul!" he whispered. "Master Paul! Malabar come in first all right, a clean win. I did as you told me. You've made over seventy thousand pounds, you have; you've got over eighty thousand. Malabar came in all right, Master Paul."

"Malabar! Malabar! Did I say Malabar, mother? Did I say Malabar? Do you think I'm lucky, mother? I knew Malabar, didn't I? Over eighty thousand pounds! I call that lucky, don't you, mother?

Over eighty thousand pounds! I knew, didn't I know I knew? Malabar came in all right. If I ride my horse till I'm sure, then I tell you, Bassett, you can go as high as you like. Did you go for all you were worth, Bassett?"

"I went a thousand on it, Master Paul."

"I never told you, mother, that if I can ride my horse, and get there, then I'm absolutely sure—oh, absolutely! Mother, did I ever tell you? I'm lucky."

"No, you never did," said the mother.

But the boy died in the night.

And even as he lay dead, his mother heard her brother's voice saying to her: "My God, Hester, you're eighty-odd thousand to the good and a poor devil of a son to the bad. But, poor devil, poor devil, he's best gone out of a life where he rides his rocking horse to find a winner."

QUESTIONS

1. Why is Lawrence unwilling to turn this story into a comedy of magical good fortune? (See Preface, p. 28.)
2. Discuss Lawrence's role as an omniscient author in the story. Why does he want to play the role? Why not have the story told over the shoulder of the boy? (See Preface, pp. 5–11, 15.)
3. Why does Lawrence choose to make the rocking horse "shining" and "modern"? Think of the ordinary use to which a rocking horse is put. What does Paul's uncle mean when he says, "poor devil, poor devil, he's best gone out of a life where he rides his rocking horse to find a winner"? What kind of life is Lawrence condemning in this story? What kind of family, what kind of society?
4. What builds up the magical atmosphere of the story?
5. Where does Paul get his power? What qualities in society are associated with these qualities?
6. What is Lawrence's attitude toward Paul? Toward Paul's mother?
7. "Do you think I'm lucky, mother?" Discuss.

ISAAC BABEL

(1894-1941?)

Babel died in a Soviet prison in the Stalinist era, although he had been an active participant in the Revolution. A Jew, born in Odessa in 1894, he was always an alien, knowing that a *pogrom* against Jews was around the next corner. A sensitive boy with glasses, Babel watched the powerful Jewish gangster kings of Odessa with awe, and it was with awe and envy, mixed with horror, that he regarded the Cossack soldiers who were his comrades in the Red Army. "My First Goose" comes out of that experience. Babel paints an intense picture of the horrors of the Revolution at the same time that he believed in its aims.

Babel, like Chekhov, told the truth of his experience, told it precisely and with no excess. He was a meticulous craftsman, going over and over his stories as often as twenty times until each sentence resonated for him. Even in translation there is more power in this tiny story than in most novels.

"My First Goose" deals with an initiation into the real world paid for with cruelty. You may want to compare this story with "Homage to Isaac Babel" by Doris Lessing.

[See Preface, p. 10 (narrator as character), p. 19 (figurative language).]

My First Goose

ISAAC BABEL

Savitsky, Commander of the VI Division, rose when he saw me, and I wondered at the beauty of his giant's body. He rose, the purple of his riding breeches and the crimson of his little tilted cap and the decorations stuck on his chest cleaving the hut as a standard cleaves the sky. A smell of scent and the sickly sweet freshness of soap emanated from him. His long legs were like girls sheathed to the neck in shining riding boots.

He smiled at me, struck his riding whip on the table, and drew toward him an order that the Chief of Staff had just finished dictating. It was an order for Ivan Chesnokov to advance on Chugunov-Dobryvodka with the regiment entrusted to him, to make contact with the enemy and destroy the same.

"For which destruction," the Commander began to write, smearing the whole sheet, "I make this same Chesnokov entirely responsible, up to and including the supreme penalty, and will if necessary strike him down on the spot; which you, Chesnokov, who have been working with me at the front for some months now, cannot doubt."

The Commander signed the order with a flourish, tossed it to his orderlies and turned upon me gray eyes that danced with merriment.

I handed him a paper with my appointment to the Staff of the Division.

"Put it down in the Order of the Day," said the Commander. "Put him down for every satisfaction save the front one. Can you read and write?"

"Yes, I can read and write," I replied, envying the flower and iron of that youthfulness. "I graduated in law from St. Petersburg University."

"Oh, are you one of those grinds?" he laughed. "Specs on your nose, too! What a nasty little object! They've sent you along without making any enquiries; and this is a hot place for specs. Think you'll get on with us?"

"I'll get on all right," I answered, and went off to the village with the quartermaster to find a billet for the night.

The quartermaster carried my trunk on his shoulder. Before us stretched the village street. The dying sun, round and yellow as a pumpkin, was giving up its roseate ghost to the skies.

We went up to a hut painted over with garlands. The quartermaster stopped, and said suddenly, with a guilty smile:

"Nuisance with specs. Can't do anything to stop it, either. Not a life for the brainy type here. But you go and mess up a lady, and a good lady too, and you'll have the boys patting you on the back."

He hesitated, my little trunk on his shoulder; then he came quite close to me, only to dart away again despairingly and run to the nearest yard. Cossacks were sitting there, shaving one another.

"Here, you soldiers," said the quartermaster, setting my little trunk down on the ground. "Comrade Savitsky's orders are that you're to take this chap in your billets, so no nonsense about it, because the chap's been through a lot in the learning line."

The quartermaster, purple in the face, left us without looking back. I raised my hand to my cap and saluted the Cossacks. A lad with long straight flaxen hair and the handsome face of the Ryazan Cossacks went over to my little trunk and tossed it out at the gate. Then he turned his back on me and with remarkable skill emitted a series of shameful noises.

"To your guns—number double-zero!" an older Cossack shouted at him, and burst out laughing. "Running fire!"

His guileless art exhausted, the lad made off. Then, crawling over the ground, I began to gather together the manuscript and tattered garments that had fallen out of the trunk. I gathered them up and carried them to the other end of the yard. Near the hut, on a brick stove, stood a cauldron in which pork was cooking. The steam that rose from it was like the far-off smoke of home in the village, and it mingled hunger with desperate loneliness in my head. Then I covered my little broken trunk with hay, turning it into a pillow, and lay down on the ground to read in *Pravda* Lenin's speech at the Second Congress of the Comintern. The sun fell upon me from behind the toothed hillocks, the Cossacks trod on my feet, the lad made fun of me untiringly, the beloved lines came toward me along a thorny path and could not reach me. Then I put aside the paper and went out to the landlady, who was spinning on the porch.

"Landlady," I said, "I've got to eat."

The old woman raised to me the diffused whites of her purblind eyes and lowered them again.

"Comrade," she said, after a pause, "what with all this going on, I want to go and hang myself."

"Christ!" I muttered, and pushed the old woman in the chest with my fist. "You don't suppose I'm going to go into explanations with you, do you?"

And turning around I saw somebody's sword lying within reach. A severe-looking goose was waddling about the yard, inoffensively preening its feathers. I overtook it and pressed it to the ground. Its head cracked beneath my boot, cracked and emptied itself. The white neck lay stretched out in the dung, the wings twitched.

"Christ!" I said, digging into the goose with my sword. "Go and cook it for me, landlady."

Her blind eyes and glasses glistening, the old woman picked up the slaughtered bird, wrapped it in her apron, and started to bear it off toward the kitchen.

"Comrade," she said to me, after a while, "I want to go and hang myself." And she closed the door behind her.

The Cossacks in the yard were already sitting around their cauldron. They sat motionless, stiff as heathen priests at a sacrifice, and had not looked at the goose.

"The lad's all right," one of them said, winking and scooping up the cabbage soup with his spoon.

The Cossacks commenced their supper with all the elegance and restraint of peasants who respect one another. And I wiped the sword with sand, went out at the gate, and came in again, depressed. Already the moon hung above the yard like a cheap earring.

"Hey, you," suddenly said Surovkov, an older Cossack. "Sit down and feed with us till your goose is done."

He produced a spare spoon from his boot and handed it to me. We supped up the cabbage soup they had made, and ate the pork.

"What's in the newspaper?" asked the flaxen-haired lad, making room for me.

"Lenin writes in the paper," I said, pulling out *Pravda*. "Lenin writes that there's a shortage of everything."

And loudly, like a triumphant man hard of hearing, I read Lenin's speech out to the Cossacks.

Evening wrapped about me the quickening moisture of its twilight sheets; evening laid a mother's hand upon my burning forehead. I read on and rejoiced, spying out exultingly the secret curve of Lenin's straight line.

"Truth tickles everyone's nostrils," said Surovkov, when I had come to the end. "The question is, how's it to be pulled from the heap. But he goes and strikes at it straight off like a hen pecking at a grain!"

This remark about Lenin was made by Surovkov, platoon commander of the Staff Squadron; after which we lay down to sleep in the hayloft. We slept, all six of us, beneath a wooden roof that let in the stars, warming one another, our legs intermingled. I dreamed: and in my dreams saw women. But my heart, stained with bloodshed, grated and brimmed over.

F. SCOTT FITZGERALD

(1896-1940)

Fitzgerald, born in St. Paul, Minnesota, was the child of a middle-class father who failed as a businessman, and a mother from an old, wealthy family. Fitzgerald grew up between these poles: his wealthy grandmother sent him to prep school and Princeton, but he didn't have the money to live well there. Always the very rich were magical to Fitzgerald; always he felt the specter of failure close by him. He never forgot his academic, athletic, and social failures at college; without graduating, he joined the army in 1917. Returning to civilian life and early success as a writer, he was haunted by a sense of disintegration; even when he had just published *This Side of Paradise* and was able to marry his dream, Zelda, he wept to think that they would never be so happy again. In the middle of writing *Gatsby*, his best novel, he felt he was on the decline as an artist.

Enormous pain over beauty that is lost is the theme of "Babylon Revisited." One of his most exquisite, most beautiful stories, it looks over the shoulder of an American expatriate returning to Paris, the scene of the destruction of his life, as he struggles to recapture not only his child but the child within him.

A chronicler in this and other stories of the American expatriate community in Europe, Fitzgerald during the twenties foretold—wrote the script for—his own end. By the time *Tender Is the Night* was published in 1934, Fitzgerald was alcoholic, cared for by a nurse, with his wife in a sanitarium for the rest of her life. Trying to piece himself together, he wrote scripts for the movies; he was working on a novel about Hollywood, *The Last Tycoon*, when he died of a heart attack in 1940.

Babylon Revisited

F. SCOTT FITZGERALD

I

"And where's Mr. Campbell?" Charlie asked.

"Gone to Switzerland. Mr. Campbell's a pretty sick man, Mr. Wales."

"I'm sorry to hear that. And George Hardt?" Charlie inquired.

"Back in America, gone to work."

"And where is the Snow Bird?"

"He was in here last week. Anyway, his friend, Mr. Schaeffer, is in Paris."

Two familiar names from the long list of a year and a half ago. Charlie scribbled an address in his notebook and tore out the page.

"If you see Mr. Schaeffer, give him this," he said. "It's my brother-in-law's address. I haven't settled on a hotel yet."

He was not really disappointed to find Paris was so empty. But the stillness in the Ritz bar was strange and portentous. It was not an American bar any more—he felt polite in it, and not as if he owned it. It had gone back into France. He felt the stillness from the moment he got out of the taxi and saw the doorman, usually in a frenzy of activity at this hour, gossiping with a *chasseur* by the servant's entrance.

Passing through the corridor, he heard only a single, bored voice in the once-clamorous women's room. When he turned into the bar he traveled the twenty feet of green carpet with his eyes fixed straight ahead by old habit; and then, with his foot firmly on the rail, he turned and surveyed the room, encountering only a single pair of eyes that fluttered up from a newspaper in the corner. Charlie asked for the head barman, Paul, who in the latter days of the bull market had come to work in his own custom-built car—disembarking, however, with due nicety at the nearest corner. But Paul was at his country house today and Alix giving him information.

"No, no more," Charlie said, "I'm going slow these days."

Alix congratulated him: "You were going pretty strong a couple of years ago."

"I'll stick to it all right," Charlie assured him. "I've stuck to it for over a year and a half now."

"How do you find conditions in America?"

"I haven't been to America for months. I'm in business in Prague, representing a couple of concerns there. They don't know about me down there."

Alix smiled.

"Remember the night of George Hardt's bachelor dinner here?" said Charlie. "By the way, what's become of Claude Fessenden?"

Alix lowered his voice confidentially: "He's in Paris, but he doesn't come here any more. Paul doesn't allow it. He ran up a bill of thirty thousand francs, charging all his drinks and his lunches, and usually his dinner, for more than a year. And when Paul finally told him he had to pay, he gave him a bad check."

Alix shook his head sadly.

"I don't understand it, such a dandy fellow. Now he's all bloated up—" He made a plump apple of his hands.

Charlie watched a group of strident queens installing themselves in a corner.

"Nothing affects them," he thought. "Stocks rise and fall, people loaf or work, but they go on forever." The place oppressed him. He called for the dice and shook with Alix for the drink.

"Here for long, Mr. Wales?"

"I'm here for four or five days to see my little girl."

"Oh-h! You have a little girl?"

Outside, the fire-red, gas-blue, ghost-green signs shone smokily through the tranquil rain. It was late afternoon and the streets were in movement; the *bistros* gleamed. At the corner of the Boulevard des Capucines he took a taxi. The Place de la Concorde moved by in pink majesty; they crossed the logical Seine, and Charlie felt the sudden provincial quality of the left bank.

Charlie directed his taxi to the Avenue de l'Opera, which was out of his way. But he wanted to see the blue hour spread over the magnificent façade, and imagine that the cab horns, playing endlessly the first few bars of *Le Plus que Lent,* were the trumpets of the Second Empire. They were closing the iron grill in front of Brentano's Book-store, and people were already at dinner behind the trim little bourgeois hedge of Duval's. He had never eaten at a really cheap restaurant in Paris. Five-course dinner, four francs fifty, eighteen cents, wine included. For some odd reason he wished that he had.

As they rolled on to the Left Bank and he felt its sudden provincialism, he thought, "I spoiled this city for myself. I didn't realize it, but the days came along one after another, and then two years were gone, and everything was gone, and I was gone."

He was thirty-five, and good to look at. The Irish mobility of his face was sobered by a deep wrinkle between his eyes. As he rang his brother-in-law's bell in the Rue Palatine, the wrinkle deepened till it pulled down his brows; he felt a cramping sensation in his belly. From behind the maid who opened the door darted a lovely little girl of nine who shrieked "Daddy!" and flew up, struggling like a fish, into his arms. She pulled his head around by one ear and set her cheek against his.

"My old pie," he said.

"Oh, daddy, daddy, daddy, daddy, dads, dads, dads!"

She drew him into the salon, where the family waited, a boy and a girl his daughter's age, his sister-in-law and her husband. He greeted Marion with his voice pitched carefully to avoid feigned enthusiasm or dislike, but her response was more frankly tepid, though she minimized her expression of unalterable distrust by directing her regard toward his child. The two men clasped hands in a friendly way and Lincoln Peters rested his for a moment on Charlie's shoulder.

The room was warm and comfortably American. The three children moved intimately about, playing through the yellow oblongs that led to other rooms; the cheer of six o'clock spoke in the eager smacks of the fire and the sounds of French activity in the kitchen. But Charlie did not relax; his heart sat up rigidly in his body and he drew confidence from his daughter, who from time to time came close to him, holding in her arms the doll he had brought.

"Really extremely well," he declared in answer to Lincoln's question. "There's a lot of business there that isn't moving at all, but we're doing even better than ever. In fact, damn well. I'm bringing my sister over from America next month to keep house for me. My income last year was bigger than it was when I had money. You see, the Czechs—"

His boasting was for a specific purpose; but after a moment, seeing a faint restiveness in Lincoln's eye, he changed the subject:

"Those are fine children of yours, well brought up, good manners."

"We think Honoria's a great little girl too."

Marion Peters came back from the kitchen. She was a tall woman with worried eyes, who had once possessed a fresh American loveliness. Charlie had never been sensitive to it and was always surprised when people spoke of how pretty she had been. From the first there had been an instinctive antipathy between them.

"Well, how do you find Honoria?" she asked.

"Wonderful. I was astonished how much she's grown in ten months. All the children are looking well."

"We haven't had a doctor for a year. How do you like being back in Paris?"

"It seems very funny to see so few Americans around."

"I'm delighted," Marion said vehemently. "Now at least you can go into a store without their assuming you're a millionaire. We've suffered like everybody, but on the whole it's a good deal pleasanter."

"But it was nice while it lasted," Charlie said. "We were a sort of royalty, almost infallible, with a sort of magic around us. In the bar this afternoon"—he stumbled, seeing his mistake—"there wasn't a man I knew."

She looked at him keenly. "I should think you'd have had enough of bars."

"I only stayed a minute. I take one drink every afternoon, and no more."

"Don't you want a cocktail before dinner?" Lincoln asked.

"I take only one drink every afternoon, and I've had that."

"I hope you keep to it," said Marion.

Her dislike was evident in the coldness with which she spoke, but Charlie only smiled; he had larger plans. Her very aggressiveness gave him an advantage, and he knew enough to wait. He wanted them to initiate the discussion of what they knew had brought him to Paris.

At dinner he couldn't decide whether Honoria was most like him or her mother. Fortunate if she didn't combine the traits of both that had brought them to disaster. A great wave of protectiveness went over him. He thought he knew what to do for her. He believed in character; he wanted to jump back a whole generation and trust in character again as the eternally valuable element. Everything else wore out.

He left soon after dinner, but not to go home. He was curious to see Paris by night with clearer and more judicious eyes than those of other days. He bought a *strapontin* for the Casino and watched Josephine Baker go through her chocolate arabesques.

After an hour he left and strolled toward Montmartre, up the Rue Pigalle into the Place Blanche. The rain had stopped and there were a few people in evening clothes disembarking from taxis in front of cabarets, and *cocottes* prowling singly or in pairs, and many Negroes. He passed a lighted door from which issued music, and stopped with the sense of familiarity; it was Bricktop's, where he had parted with so many hours and so much money. A few doors farther on he found another ancient rendezvous and incautiously put his head inside. Immediately an eager orchestra burst into sound, a pair of professional dancers leaped to their feet and a maître d'hôtel swooped toward him, crying, "Crowd just arriving, sir!" But he withdrew quickly.

"You have to be damn drunk," he thought.

Zelli's was closed, the bleak and sinister cheap hotels surrounding it were dark; up in the Rue Blanche there was more light and a local, colloquial French crowd. The Poet's Cave had disappeared, but the two great mouths of the Café of Heaven and the Café of Hell still yawned—even devoured, as he watched, the meager contents of a tourist bus—a German, a Japanese, and an American couple who glanced at him with frightened eyes.

So much for the effort and ingenuity of Montmartre. All the catering to vice and waste was on an utterly childish scale, and he suddenly realized the meaning of the word "dissipate"—to dissipate into thin air; to make nothing out of something. In the little hours of the night every move from place to place was an enormous human jump, an increase of paying for the privilege of slower and slower motion.

He remembered thousand-franc notes given to an orchestra for playing a single number, hundred-franc notes tossed to a doorman for calling a cab.

But it hadn't been given for nothing.

It had been given, even the most wildly squandered sum, as an offering to destiny that he might not remember the things most worth remembering, the things that now he would always remember—his child taken from his control, his wife escaped to a grave in Vermont.

In the glare of a *brasserie* a woman spoke to him. He bought her some eggs and coffee, and then, eluding her encouraging stare, gave her a twenty-franc note and took a taxi to his hotel.

II

He woke upon a fine fall day—football weather. The depression of yesterday was gone and he liked the people on the streets. At noon he sat opposite Honoria at Le Grand Vatel, the only restaurant he could think of not reminiscent of champagne dinners and long luncheons that began at two and ended in a blurred and vague twilight.

"Now, how about vegetables? Oughtn't you to have some vegetables?"

"Well, yes."

"Here's *épinards* and *chou-fleur* and carrots and *haricots*."

"I'd like *chou-fleur*."

"Wouldn't you like to have two vegetables?"

"I usually only have one at lunch."

The waiter was pretending to be inordinately fond of children. *"Qu'elle est mignonne la petite! Elle parle exactement comme une Française."*

"How about dessert? Shall we wait and see?"

The waiter disappeared. Honoria looked at her father expectantly.

"What are we going to do?"

"First, we're going to that toy store in the Rue Saint-Honoré and buy you anything you like. And then we're going to the vaudeville at the Empire."

She hesitated. "I like it about the vaudeville, but not the toy store."

"Why not?"

"Well, you brought me this doll." She had it with her. "And I've got lots of things. And we're not rich any more, are we?"

"We never were. But today you are to have anything you want."

"All right," she agreed resignedly.

When there had been her mother and a French nurse he had been inclined to be strict; now he extended himself, reached out for a new tolerance; he must be both parents to her and not shut any of her out of communication.

"I want to get to know you," he said gravely. "First let me introduce myself. My name is Charles J. Wales, of Prague."

"Oh, daddy!" her voice cracked with laughter.

"And who are you, please?" he persisted, and she accepted a rôle immediately: "Honoria Wales, Rue Palatine, Paris."

"Married or single?"

"No, not married. Single."

He indicated the doll. "But I see you have a child, madame."

Unwilling to disinherit it, she took it to her heart and thought quickly: "Yes, I've been married, but I'm not married now. My husband is dead."

He went on quickly, "And the child's name?"

"Simone. That's after my best friend at school."

"I'm very pleased that you're doing so well at school."

"I'm third this month," she boasted. "Elsie"—that was her cousin—"is only about eighteenth, and Richard is about at the bottom."

"You like Richard and Elsie, don't you?"

"Oh, yes, I like Richard quite well and I like her all right."

Cautiously and casually he asked: "And Aunt Marion and Uncle Lincoln—which do you like best?"

"Oh, Uncle Lincoln, I guess."

He was increasingly aware of her presence. As they came in, a murmur of ". . . adorable" followed them, and now the people at the next table bent all their silences upon her, staring as if she were something no more conscious than a flower.

"Why don't I live with you?" she asked suddenly. "Because mamma's dead?"

"You must stay here and learn more French. It would have been hard for daddy to take care of you so well."

"I don't really need much taking care of any more. I do everything for myself."

Going out of the restaurant, a man and a woman unexpectedly hailed him.

"Well, the old Wales!"

"Hello there, Lorraine. . . . Dunc."

Sudden ghosts out of the past: Duncan Schaeffer, a friend from college. Lorraine Quarrles, a lovely, pale blonde of thirty; one of a crowd who had helped them make months into days in the lavish times of three years ago.

"My husband couldn't come this year," she said, in answer to his question. "We're poor as hell. So he gave me two hundred a month and told me I could do my worst on that. . . . This your little girl?"

"What about coming back and sitting down?" Duncan asked.

"Can't do it." He was glad for an excuse. As always, he felt Lorraine's passionate, provocative attraction, but his own rhythm was different now.

"Well, how about dinner?" she asked

"I'm not free. Give me your address and let me call you."

"Charlie, I believe you're sober," she said judicially. "I honestly believe he's sober, Dunc. Pinch him and see if he's sober."

Charlie indicated Honoria with his head. They both laughed.

"What's your address?" said Duncan skeptically.

He hesitated, unwilling to give the name of his hotel.

"I'm not settled yet. I'd better call you. We're going to see the vaudeville at the Empire."

"There! That's what I want to do," Lorraine said. "I want to see some clowns and acrobats and jugglers. That's just what we'll do, Dunc."

"We've got to do an errand first," said Charlie. "Perhaps we'll see you there."

"All right, you snob. . . . Good-by, beautiful little girl."

"Good-by."

Honoria bobbed politely.

Somehow, an unwelcome encounter. They liked him because he was functioning, because he was serious; they wanted to see him, because he was stronger than they were now, because they wanted to draw a certain sustenance from his strength.

At the Empire, Honoria proudly refused to sit upon her father's folded coat. She was already an individual with a code of her own, and Charlie was more and more absorbed by the desire of putting a little of himself into her before she crystallized utterly. It was hopeless to try to know her in so short a time.

Between the acts they came upon Duncan and Lorraine in the lobby where the band was playing.

"Have a drink?"

"All right, but not up at the bar. We'll take a table."

"The perfect father."

Listening abstractedly to Lorraine, Charlie watched Honoria's eyes leave their table, and he followed them wistfully about the room, wondering what they saw. He met her glance and she smiled.

"I liked that lemonade," she said.

What had she said? What had he expected? Going home in a taxi afterward, he pulled her over until her head rested against his chest.

"Darling, do you ever think about your mother?"

"Yes, sometimes," she answered vaguely.

"I don't want you to forget her. Have you got a picture of her?"

"Yes, I think so. Anyhow, Aunt Marion has. Why don't you want me to forget her?"

"She loved you véry much."

"I loved her too."

They were silent for a moment.

"Daddy, I want to come and live with you," she said suddenly.

His heart leaped; he had wanted it to come like this.

"Aren't you perfectly happy?"

"Yes, but I love you better than anybody. And you love me better than anybody, don't you, now that mummy's dead?"

"Of course I do. But you won't always like me best, honey. You'll grow up and meet somebody your own age and go marry him and forget you ever had a daddy."

"Yes, that's true," she agreed tranquilly.

He didn't go in. He was coming back at nine o'clock and he wanted to keep himself fresh and new for the thing he must say then.

"When you're safe inside, just show yourself in that window."

"All right. Good-by, dads, dads, dads, dads."

He waited in the dark street until she appeared, all warm and glowing, in the window above and kissed her fingers out into the night.

III

They were waiting. Marion sat behind the coffee service in a dignified black dinner dress that just faintly suggested mourning. Lincoln was walking up and down with the animation of one who had already been talking. They were as anxious as he was to get into the question. He opened it almost immediately:

"I suppose you know what I want to see you about—why I really came to Paris."

Marion played with the black stars on her necklace and frowned.

"I'm awfully anxious to have a home," he continued. "And I'm awfully anxious to have Honoria in it. I appreciate your taking in Honoria for her mother's sake, but things have changed now"—he hesitated and then continued more forcibly—"changed radically with me, and I want to ask you to reconsider the matter. It would be silly for me to deny that about three years ago I was acting badly—"

Marion looked up at him with hard eyes.

"—but all that's over. As I told you, I haven't had more than a drink a day for over a year, and I take that drink deliberately, so that the idea of alcohol won't get too big in my imagination. You see the idea?"

"No," said Marion succinctly.

"It's a sort of stunt I set myself. It keeps the matter in proportion."

"I get you," said Lincoln. "You don't want to admit it's got any attraction for you."

"Something like that. Sometimes I forget and don't take it. But I try to take it. Anyhow, I couldn't afford to drink in my position. The people I represent are more than satisfied with what I've done, and I'm bringing my sister over from Burlington to keep house for me, and I want awfully to have Honoria too. You know that even when her mother and I weren't getting along well we never let anything that happened touch Honoria. I know she's fond of me and I know I'm able to take care of her and—well, there you are. How do you feel about it?"

He knew that now he would have to take a beating. It would last an hour or two hours, and it would be difficult, but if he modulated his inevitable resentment to the chastened attitude of the reformed sinner, he might win his point in the end.

Keep your temper, he told himself. You don't want to be justified. You want Honoria.

Lincoln spoke first: "We've been talking it over ever since we got your letter last month. We're happy to have Honoria here. She's a dear little thing, and we're glad to be able to help her, but of course that isn't the question—"

Marion interrupted suddenly. "How long are you going to stay sober Charlie?" she asked.

"Permanently, I hope."

"How can anybody count on that?"

"You know I never did drink heavily until I gave up business and came over here with nothing to do. Then Helen and I began to run around with—"

"Please leave Helen out of it. I can't bear to hear you talk about her like that."

He stared at her grimly; he had never been certain how fond of each other the sisters were in life.

"My drinking only lasted about a year and a half—from the time we came over until I—collapsed."

"It was time enough."

"It was time enough," he agreed.

"My duty is entirely to Helen," she said. "I try to think what she would have wanted me to do. Frankly, from the night you did that terrible thing you haven't really existed for me. I can't help that. She was my sister."

"Yes."

"When she was dying she asked me to look out for Honoria. If you hadn't been in a sanitarium then, it might have helped matters."

He had no answer.

"I'll never in my life be able to forget the morning when Helen knocked at my door, soaked to the skin and shivering and said you'd locked her out."

Charlie gripped the sides of the chair. This was more difficult than he expected; he wanted to launch out into a long expostulation and explanation, but he only said: "The night I locked her out—" and she interrupted. "I don't feel up to going over that again."

After a moment's silence Lincoln said: "We're getting off the subject. You want Marion to set aside her legal guardianship and give you Honoria. I think the main point for her is whether she has confidence in you or not."

"I don't blame Marion," Charlie said slowly, "but I think she can have entire confidence in me. I had a good record up to three years ago. Of course, it's within human possibilities I might go wrong any time. But if we wait much longer I'll lose Honoria's childhood and my chance for a home." He shook his head, "I'll simply lose her, don't you see?"

"Yes, I see," said Lincoln.

"Why didn't you think of all this before?" Marion asked.

"I suppose I did, from time to time, but Helen and I were getting along badly. When I consented to the guardianship, I was flat on my back in a sanitarium and the market had cleaned me out. I knew I'd acted badly, and I thought if it would bring any peace to Helen, I'd agree to anything. But now it's different. I'm functioning, I'm behaving damn well, so far as—"

"Please don't swear at me," Marion said.

He looked at her, startled. With each remark the force of her dislike became more and more apparent. She had built up all her fear of life into one wall and faced it toward him. This trivial reproof was possibly the result of some trouble with the cook several hours before. Charlie became increasingly alarmed at leaving Honoria in this atmosphere of hostility against himself; sooner or later it would come out, in a word here, a shake of the head there, and some of that distrust would be irrevocably implanted in Honoria. But he pulled his temper down out of his face and shut it up inside him; he had won a point, for Lincoln realized the absurdity of Marion's remark and asked her lightly since when she had objected to the word "damn."

"Another thing," Charlie said: "I'm able to give her certain advantages now. I'm going to take a French governess to Prague with me. I've got a lease on a new apartment—"

He stopped, realizing that he was blundering. They couldn't be expected to accept with equanimity the fact that his income was again twice as large as their own.

"I suppose you can give her more luxuries than we can," said Marion. "When you were throwing away money we were living along watching every ten francs. . . . I suppose you'll start doing it again."

"Oh, no," he said. "I've learned. I worked hard for ten years, you know—until I got lucky in the market, like so many people. Terribly lucky. It won't happen again."

There was a long silence. All of them felt their nerves straining, and for the first time in a year Charlie wanted a drink. He was sure now that Lincoln Peters wanted him to have his child.

Marion shuddered suddenly; part of her saw that Charlie's feet were planted on the earth now, and her own maternal feeling recognized the naturalness of his desire; but she had lived for a long time with a prejudice—a prejudice founded on a curious disbelief in her sister's happiness, and which, in the shock of one terrible night, had turned to hatred for him. It had all happened at a point in her life where the discouragement of ill health and adverse circumstances made it necessary for her to believe in tangible villainy and a tangible villain.

"I can't help what I think!" she cried out suddenly. "How much you were responsible for Helen's death, I don't know. It's something you'll have to square with your own conscience."

An electric current of agony surged through him; for a moment he was almost on his feet, an unuttered sound echoing in his throat. He hung on to himself for a moment, another moment.

"Hold on there," said Lincoln uncomfortably. "I never thought you were responsible for that."

"Helen died of heart trouble," Charlie said dully.

"Yes, heart trouble." Marion spoke as if the phrase had another meaning for her.

Then, in the flatness that followed her outburst, she saw him plainly and she knew he had somehow arrived at control over the situation. Glancing at her husband, she found no help from him, and as abruptly as if it were a matter of no importance, she threw up the sponge.

"Do what you like!" she cried, springing up from her chair. "She's your child. I'm not the person to stand in your way. I think if it were my child I'd rather see her—" She managed to check herself. "You two decide it. I can't stand this. I'm sick. I'm going to bed."

She hurried from the room; after a moment Lincoln said:

"This has been a hard day for her. You know how strongly she feels—" His voice was almost apologetic: "When a woman gets an idea in her head."

"Of course."

"It's going to be all right. I think she sees now that you—can provide for the child, and we can't very well stand in your way or Honoria's way."

"Thank you, Lincoln."

"I'd better go along and see how she is."

"I'm going."

He was still trembling when he reached the street, but a walk down the Rue Bonaparte to the *quais* set him up, and as he crossed the Seine, fresh and new by the *quai* lamps, he felt exultant. But back in his room he couldn't sleep. The image of Helen haunted him. Helen whom he had loved so until they had senselessly begun to abuse each other's love, tear it into shreds. On that terrible February night that Marion remembered so vividly, a slow quarrel had gone on for hours. There was a scene at the Florida, and then he attempted to take her home, and then she kissed young Webb at a table; after that there was what she had hysterically said. When he arrived home alone he turned the key in the lock in wild anger. How could he know she would arrive an hour later alone, that there would be a snowstorm in which she wandered about in slippers, too confused to find a taxi? Then the aftermath, her escaping pneumonia by a miracle, and all the attendant horror. They were "reconciled," but that was the beginning of the end, as Marion, who had seen with her own eyes and who imagined it to be one of many scenes from her sister's martyrdom, never forgot.

Going over it again brought Helen nearer, and in the white, soft light that steals upon half sleep near morning he found himself talking to her again. She said that he was perfectly right about Honoria and that she wanted Honoria to be with him. She said she was glad he was being good and doing better. She said a lot of other things—very friendly things—but she was in a swing in a white dress, and swinging faster and faster all the time, so that at the end he could not hear clearly all that she said.

IV

He woke up feeling happy. The door of the world was open again. He made plans, vistas, futures for Honoria and himself, but suddenly he grew sad, remembering all the plans he and Helen had made. She had not planned to die. The present was the thing—work to do and someone to love. But not to love too much, for he knew the injury that a father can do to a daughter or a mother to a son by attaching them too closely: afterward, out in the world, the child would seek in the marriage partner the same blind tenderness and, failing probably to find it, turn against love and life.

It was another bright, crisp day. He called Lincoln Peters at the bank where he worked and asked if he could count on taking Honoria when he left for Prague. Lincoln agreed that there was no reason for delay. One thing—the legal guardianship. Marion wanted to retain that a while longer. She was upset by the whole matter, and it would oil things if she felt that the situation was still in her control for another year. Charlie agreed, wanting only the tangible, visible child.

Then the question of a governess. Charles sat in a gloomy agency and talked to a cross Béarnaise and to a buxom Breton peasant, neither of whom he could have endured. There were others whom he would see tomorrow.

He lunched with Lincoln Peters at Griffons, trying to keep down his exultation.

"There's nothing quite like your own child," Lincoln said. "But you understand how Marion feels too."

"She's forgotten how hard I worked for seven years there," Charlie said. "She just remembers one night."

"There's another thing." Lincoln hesitated. "While you and Helen were tearing around Europe throwing money away, we were just getting along. I didn't touch any of the prosperity because I never got ahead enough to carry anything but my insurance. I think Marion felt there was some kind of injustice in it—you not even working toward the end, and getting richer and richer."

"It went just as quick as it came," said Charlie.

"Yes, a lot of it stayed in the hands of *chasseurs* and saxophone players and maîtres d'hôtel—well, the big party's over now. I just said that to explain Marion's feeling about those crazy years. If you drop in about six o'clock tonight before Marion's too tired, we'll settle the details on the spot."

Back at his hotel, Charlie found a *pneumatique* that had been redirected from the Ritz bar where Charlie had left his address for the purpose of finding a certain man.

"DEAR CHARLIE:

"You were so strange when we saw you the other day that I wondered if I did something to offend you. If so, I'm not conscious of it. In fact, I have thought about you too much for the last year, and it's always been in the back of my mind that I might see you if I came over here. We *did* have such good times that crazy spring, like the night you and I stole the butcher's tricycle, and the time we tried to call on the president and you had the old derby rim and the wire cane. Everybody seems so old lately, but I don't feel old a bit. Couldn't we get together some time today for old time's sake? I've got a vile hang-over for the moment, but will be feeling better this afternoon and will look for you about five in the sweatshop at the Ritz.

"Always devotedly,

"LORRAINE."

His first feeling was one of awe that he had actually, in his mature years, stolen a tricycle and pedaled Lorraine all over the Étoile between the small hours and dawn. In retrospect it was a nightmare. Locking out Helen didn't fit in with any other act of his life, but the tricycle incident did—it was one of many. How many weeks or months of dissipation to arrive at that condition of utter irresponsibility?

He tried to picture how Lorraine had appeared to him then—very attractive; Helen was unhappy about it, though she said nothing. Yesterday, in the restaurant, Lorraine had seemed trite, blurred, worn away. He emphatically did not want to see her, and he was glad Alix had not given away his hotel address. It was a relief to think, instead, of Honoria, to think of Sundays spent with her and of saying good morning to her and of knowing she was there in his house at night, drawing her breath in the darkness.

At five he took a taxi and bought presents for all the Peters—a piquant cloth doll, a box of Roman soldiers, flowers for Marion, big linen handkerchiefs for Lincoln.

He saw, when he arrived in the apartment, that Marion had accepted the inevitable. She greeted him now as though he were a recalcitrant member of the family, rather than a menacing outsider. Honoria had been told she was going; Charlie was glad to see that her tact made her conceal her excessive happiness. Only on his lap did she whisper her delight and the question "When?" before she slipped away with the other children.

He and Marion were alone for a minute in the room, and on an impulse he spoke out boldly:

"Family quarrels are bitter things. They don't go according to any rules. They're not like aches or wounds; they're more like splits in the skin that won't heal because there's not enough material. I wish you and I could be on better terms."

"Some things are hard to forget," she answered. "It's a question of confidence." There was no answer to this and presently she asked, "When do you propose to take her?"

"As soon as I can get a governess. I hoped the day after tomorrow."

"That's impossible. I've got to get her things in shape. Not before Saturday."

He yielded. Coming back into the room, Lincoln offered him a drink.

"I'll take my daily whiskey," he said.

It was warm here, it was a home, people together by a fire. The children felt very safe and important; the mother and father were serious, watchful. They had things to do for the children more important than his visit here. A spoonful of medicine was, after all, more important than the strained relations between Marion and himself. They were not dull people, but they were very much in the grip of life and circumstances. He wondered if he couldn't do something to get Lincoln out of his rut at the bank.

A long peal at the door-bell; the *bonne à tout faire* passed through and went down the corridor. The door opened upon another long ring, and then voices, and the three in the salon looked up expectantly; Richard moved to bring the corridor within his range of vision, and Marion rose. Then the maid came back along the corridor, closely followed by the voices, which developed under the light into Duncan Schaeffer and Lorraine Quarrles.

They were gay, they were hilarious, they were roaring with laughter. For a moment Charlie was astounded; unable to understand how they ferreted out the Peters' address.

"Ah-h-h!" Duncan wagged his finger roguishly at Charlie. "Ah-h-h!"

They both slid down another cascade of laughter. Anxious and at a loss, Charlie shook hands with them quickly and presented them to Lincoln and Marion. Marion nodded, scarcely speaking. She had drawn back a step toward the fire; her little girl stood beside her, and Marion put an arm about her shoulder.

With growing annoyance at the intrusion, Charlie waited for them to explain themselves. After some concentration Duncan said:

"We came to invite you out to dinner. Lorraine and I insist that all this shishi, cagy business 'bout your address got to stop."

Charlie came closer to them, as if to force them backward down the corridor.

"Sorry, but I can't. Tell me where you'll be and I'll phone you in half an hour."

This made no impression. Lorraine sat down suddenly on the side of a chair, and focusing her eyes on Richard, cried, "Oh, what a nice little boy! Come here, little boy." Richard glanced at his mother, but did not move. With a perceptible shrug of her shoulders, Lorraine turned back to Charlie:

"Come and dine. Sure your cousins won' mine. See you so sel'om. Or solemn."

"I can't," said Charlie sharply. "You two have dinner and I'll phone you."

Her voice became suddenly unpleasant. "All right, we'll go. But I remember once when you hammered on my door at four A.M. I was enough of a good sport to give you a drink. Come on, Dunc."

Still in slow motion, with blurred, angry faces, with uncertain feet, they retired along the corridor.

"Good night," Charlie said.

"Good night!" responded Lorraine emphatically.

When he went back into the salon Marion had not moved, only now her son was standing in the circle of her other arm. Lincoln was still swinging Honoria back and forth like a pendulum from side to side.

"What an outrage!" Charlie broke out. "What an absolute outrage!"

Neither of them answered. Charlie dropped into an armchair, picked up his drink, set it down again and said:

"People I haven't seen for two years having the colossal nerve—"

He broke off. Marion had made the sound "Oh!" in one swift, furious breath, turned her body from him with a jerk and left the room.

Lincoln set down Honoria carefully.

"You children go in and start your soup," he said, and when they obeyed he said to Charlie:

"Marion's not well and she can't stand shocks. That kind of people make her really physically sick."

"I didn't tell them to come here. They wormed your name out of somebody. They deliberately—"

"Well, it's too bad. It doesn't help matters. Excuse me a minute."

Left alone, Charlie sat tense in his chair. In the next room he could hear the children eating, talking in monosyllables, already oblivious to the scene between their elders. He heard a murmur of conversation from a farther room and then the ticking bell of a telephone receiver picked up, and in a panic he moved to the other side of the room and out of earshot.

In a minute Lincoln came back. "Look here, Charlie. I think we'd better call off dinner for tonight. Marion's in bad shape."

"Is she angry with me?"

"Sort of," he said, almost roughly. "She's not strong and—"

"You mean she's changed her mind about Honoria?"

"She's pretty bitter right now. I don't know. You phone me at the bank tomorrow."

"I wish you'd explain to her I never dreamed these people would come here. I'm just as sore as you are."

"I couldn't explain anything to her now."

Charlie got up. He took his coat and hat and started down the corridor. Then he opened the door of the dining room and said in a strange voice, "Good night, children."

Honoria rose and ran around the table to hug him.

"Good night, sweetheart," he said vaguely, and then trying to make his voice more tender, trying to conciliate something, "Good night, dear children."

V

Charlie went directly to the Ritz bar with the furious idea of finding Lorraine and Duncan, but they were not there, and he realized that in any case there was nothing he could do. He had not touched his drink at the Peters, and now he ordered a whisky-and-soda. Paul came over to say hello.

"It's a great change," he said sadly. "We do about half the business we did. So many fellows I hear about back in the States lost everything, maybe not in the first crash, but then in the second. Your friend George Hardt lost every cent, I hear. Are you back in the States?"

"No, I'm in business in Prague."

"I heard that you lost a lot in the crash."

"I did," and he added grimly, "but I lost everything I wanted in the boom."

"Selling short."

"Something like that."

Again the memory of those days swept over him like a nightmare—the people they had met travelling; the people who couldn't add a row of figures or speak a coherent sentence. The little man Helen had consented to dance with at the ship's party, who had insulted her ten feet from the table; the women and girls carried screaming with drinks or drugs out of public places—

—The men who locked their wives out in the snow, because the snow of twenty-nine wasn't real snow. If you didn't want it to be snow, you just paid some money.

He went to the phone and called the Peters' apartment; Lincoln answered.

"I called up because this thing is on my mind. Has Marion said anything definite?"

"Marion's sick," Lincoln answered shortly. "I know this thing isn't altogether your fault, but I can't have her go to pieces about it. I'm afraid we'll have to let it slide for six months; I can't take the chance of working her up to this state again."

"I see."

"I'm sorry, Charlie."

He went back to his table. His whisky glass was empty, but he shook his head when Alix looked at it questionably. There wasn't much he could do now except send Honoria some things; he would send her a lot of things tomorrow. He thought rather angrily that this was just money—he had given so many people money. . . .

"No, no more," he said to another waiter. "What do I owe you?"

He would come back some day; they couldn't make him pay forever. But he wanted his child, and nothing was much good now, beside that fact. He wasn't young any more, with a lot of nice things and dreams to have by himself. He was absolutely sure Helen wouldn't have wanted him to be so alone.

WILLIAM FAULKNER

(1897-1962)

Faulkner was brought up in Mississippi, where his great-grandfather had been a Civil War hero and his father was treasurer of the state university. Although respected, the family was no longer wealthy. In 1918 he enrolled in the Canadian Royal Flying Corps but never saw service. Back in Mississippi he went to the university, then to New Orleans, where he became friends with Sherwood Anderson, already an established writer, who encouraged him and helped get his first novel, *Soldier's Pay*, published. While he wrote, he worked at odd jobs.

In 1929 he wrote—in a few months—the magnificent experimental novel *The Sound and the Fury*, whose characters are the same as in "That Evening Sun." Faulkner, like the nineteenth-century French novelist Balzac, used the same characters in many works; those who are minor in one story will be major in another. Essentially Faulkner created a whole "county"—Yoknapatawpha County—with a special history, significant families, legends. Novels and stories about Yoknapatawpha County include *Light in August, As I Lay Dying, Absalom, Absalom!, The Hamlet,* and *Go Down Moses.*

Faulkner's style is excellent for the unfolding of layers of overlapping reality, for themes that repeat themselves in different generations, for consciousness struggling to understand the past. The stories that follow, "That Evening Sun" and "A Rose for Emily," are not difficult to read. But notice the unusual use of angle of vision in both; notice the juggling of chronology in "A Rose for Emily" and the intertwining of children's world and adults' world in "That Evening Sun."

Though Faulkner deals with history in his fiction, his characters often try to eliminate it—to stop time, to stay fixed in a mythologized, aristocratic past. In *Light in August,* for example, Reverend

Hightower feels that his life ended generations before he was born, on the afternoon his ancestor rode on a wild cavalry raid through town during the Civil War. Emily, in "A Rose for Emily," also needs to stop time, to pretend that change hasn't occurred.

To an extent Faulkner shares his characters' love for tradition and traditional values. In his famous Nobel Prize speech in 1949, he argues that the writer must leave "no room in his workshop for anything but the old verities and truths of the heart, the old universal truths lacking which any story is ephemeral and doomed—love and honor and pity and pride and compassion and sacrifice." Faulkner uses these "universal truths" as the yardstick against which to measure actions.

That Evening Sun

WILLIAM FAULKNER

I

Monday is no different from any other weekday in Jefferson now. The streets are paved now, and the telephone and electric companies are cutting down more and more of the shade trees—the water oaks, the maples and locusts and elms—to make room for iron poles bearing clusters of bloated and ghostly and bloodless grapes; and we have a city laundry which makes the rounds on Monday morning, gathering the bundles of clothes into bright-colored, specially-made motorcars: the soiled wearing of a whole week now flees apparition-like behind alert and irritable electric horns, with a long diminishing noise of rubber and asphalt like tearing silk, and even the Negro women who still take in white people's washing after the old custom, fetch and deliver it in automobiles.

But fifteen years ago, on Monday morning the quiet, dusty, shady streets would be full of Negro women with, balanced on their steady, turbaned heads, bundles of clothes tied up in sheets, almost as large as cotton bales, carried so without touch of hand between the kitchen door of the white house and the blackened washpot beside a cabin door in Negro Hollow.

Nancy would set her bundle on the top of her head, then upon the bundle in turn she would set the black straw sailor hat which she wore winter and summer. She was tall, with a high, sad face sunken a little where her teeth were missing. Sometimes we would go a part of the way down the lane and across the pasture with her, to watch the balanced bundle and the hat that never bobbed nor wavered, even when she walked down into the ditch and up the other side and stooped through the fence. She would go down on her hands and knees and crawl through the gap, her head rigid, uptilted, the bundle steady as a rock or a balloon, and rise to her feet again and go on.

Sometimes the husbands of the washing women would fetch and deliver the clothes, but Jesus never did that for Nancy, even before Father told him to stay away from our house, even when Dilsey was sick and Nancy would come to cook for us.

And then about half the time we'd have to go down the lane to Nancy's cabin and tell her to come on and cook breakfast. We would stop at the ditch, because Father told us not to have anything to do with Jesus—he was a short black man, with a razor scar down his face—and we would throw rocks at Nancy's house until she came to the door, leaning her head around it without any clothes on.

"What yawl mean, chunking my house?" Nancy said. "What you little devils mean?"

"Father says for you to come on and get breakfast," Caddy said. "Father says it's over a half an hour now, and you've got to come this minute."

"I ain't studying no breakfast," Nancy said. "I going to get my sleep out."

"I bet you're drunk," Jason said. "Father says you're drunk. Are you drunk, Nancy?"

"Who says I is?" Nancy said. "I got to get my sleep out. I ain't studying no breakfast."

So after a while we quit chunking the cabin and went back home. When she finally came, it was too late for me to go to school. So we thought it was whiskey until that day they arrested her again and they were taking her to jail and they passed Mr. Stovall. He was the cashier in the bank and a deacon in the Baptist church, and Nancy began to say:

"When you going to pay me, white man? When you going to pay me, white man? It's been three times now since you paid me a cent—" Mr. Stovall knocked her down, but she kept on saying, "When you going to pay me, white man? It's been three times now since—" until Mr. Stovall kicked her in the mouth with his heel and the marshal caught Mr. Stovall back, and Nancy lying in the street, laughing. She turned her head and spat out some blood and teeth and said, "It's been three times now since he paid me a cent."

That was how she lost her teeth, and all that day they told about Nancy and Mr. Stovall, and all that night the ones that passed the jail could hear Nancy singing and yelling. They could see her hands holding to the window bars, and a lot of them stopped along the fence, listening to her and to the jailer trying to make her stop. She didn't shut up until almost daylight, when the jailer began to hear a bumping and scraping upstairs and he went up there and found Nancy hanging from the window bar. He said that it was cocaine and not whiskey, because no nigger would try to commit suicide unless he was full of cocaine, because a nigger full of cocaine wasn't a nigger any longer.

The jailer cut her down and revived her; then he beat her, whipped her. She had hung herself with her dress. She had fixed it all right, but when they arrested her she didn't have on anything except a dress and so she didn't have anything to tie her hands with and she couldn't make her hands let go of the window ledge. So the jailer heard the noise and ran up there and found Nancy hanging from the window, stark naked, her belly already swelling out a little, like a little balloon.

When Dilsey was sick in her cabin and Nancy was cooking for us, we could see her apron swelling out; that was before Father told Jesus to stay away from the house. Jesus was in the kitchen, sitting behind the stove, with his razor scar on his black face like a piece of dirty string. He said it was a watermelon that Nancy had under her dress.

"It never come off of your vine, though," Nancy said.

"Off of what vine?" Caddy said.

"I can cut down the vine it did come off of," Jesus said.

"What makes you want to talk like that before these chillen?" Nancy said. "Whyn't you go on to work? You done et. You want Mr. Jason to catch you hanging around his kitchen, talking that way before these chillen?"

"Talking what way?" Caddy said. "What vine?"

"I can't hang around white man's kitchen," Jesus said. "But white man can hang around mine. White man can come in my house, but I can't stop him. When white man want to come in my house, I ain't got no house. I can't stop him, but he can't kick me outen it. He can't do that."

Dilsey was still sick in her cabin. Father told Jesus to stay off our place. Dilsey was still sick. It was a long time. We were in the library after supper.

"Isn't Nancy through in the kitchen yet?" Mother said. "It seems to me that she has had plenty of time to have finished the dishes."

"Let Quentin go and see," Father said. "Go and see if Nancy is through, Quentin. Tell her she can go on home."

I went to the kitchen. Nancy was through. The dishes were put away and the fire was out. Nancy was sitting in a chair, close to the cold stove. She looked at me.

"Mother wants to know if you are through," I said.

"Yes," Nancy said. She looked at me. "I done finished." She looked at me.

"What is it?" I said. "What is it?"

"I ain't nothing but a nigger," Nancy said. "It ain't none of my fault."

She looked at me, sitting in the chair before the cold stove, the sailor hat on her head. I went back to the library. It was the cold stove and all, when you think of a kitchen being warm and busy and cheerful. And with a cold stove and the dishes all put away, and nobody wanting to eat at that hour.

"Is she through?" Mother said.

"Yessum," I said.

"What is she doing?" Mother said.

"She's not doing anything. She's through."

"I'll go and see," Father said.

"Maybe she's waiting for Jesus to come and take her home," Caddy said.

"Jesus is gone," I said. Nancy told us how one morning she woke up and Jesus was gone.

"He quit me," Nancy said. "Done gone to Memphis, I reckon. Dodging them city *po*-lice for a while, I reckon."

"And a good riddance," Father said. "I hope he stays there."

"Nancy's scaired of the dark," Jason said.

"So are you," Caddy said.

"I'm not," Jason said.

"Scairy cat," Caddy said.

"I'm not," Jason said.

"You, Candace!" Mother said. Father came back.

"I am going to walk down the lane with Nancy," he said. "She says that Jesus is back."

"Has she seen him?" Mother said.

"No. Some Negro sent her word that he was back in town. I won't be long."

"You'll leave me alone, to take Nancy home?" Mother said. "Is her safety more precious to you than mine?"

"I won't be long," Father said.

"You'll leave these children unprotected, with that Negro about?"

"I'm going too," Caddy said. "Let me go, Father."

"What would he do with them, if he were unfortunate enough to have them?" Father said.

"I want to go, too," Jason said.

"Jason!" Mother said. She was speaking to Father. You could tell that by the way she said the name. Like she believed that all day Father had been trying to think of doing the thing she wouldn't like the most, and that she knew all the time that after a while he would think of it. I stayed quiet, because Father and I both knew that Mother would want him to make me stay with her if she just thought of it in time. So Father didn't look at me. I was the oldest. I was nine and Caddy was seven and Jason was five.

"Nonsense," Father said. "We won't be long."

Nancy had her hat on. We came to the lane. "Jesus always been good to me," Nancy said. "Whenever he had two dollars, one of them was mine." We walked in the lane. "If I can just get through the lane," Nancy said, "I be all right then."

The lane was always dark. "This is where Jason got scaired on Hallowe'en," Caddy said.

"I didn't," Jason said.

"Can't Aunt Rachel do anything with him?" Father said. Aunt Rachel was old. She lived in a cabin beyond Nancy's, by herself. She had white hair and she smoked a pipe in the door, all day long; she didn't work any more. They said she was Jesus' mother. Sometimes she said she was and sometimes she said she wasn't any kin to Jesus.

"Yes you did," Caddy said. "You were scairder than Frony. You were scairder than T.P. even. Scairder than niggers."

"Can't nobody do nothing with him," Nancy said. "He say I done woke up the devil in him and ain't but one thing going to lay it down again."

"Well, he's gone now," Father said. "There's nothing for you to be afraid of now. And if you'd just let white men alone."

"Let what white men alone?" Caddy said. "How let them alone?"

"He ain't gone nowhere," Nancy said. "I can feel him. I can feel him now in this lane. He hearing us talk, every word, hid somewhere, waiting. I ain't seen him, and I ain't going to see him again but once more, with that razor in his mouth. That razor on that string down his back, inside his shirt. And then I ain't going to be even surprised."

"I wasn't scaired," Jason said.

"If you'd behave yourself, you'd have kept out of this," Father said. "But it's all right now. He's probably in Saint Louis now. Probably got another wife by now and forgot all about you."

"If he has, I better not find out about it," Nancy said. "I'd stand there right over them, and every time he wropped her, I'd cut that arm off. I'd cut his head off and I'd slit her belly and I'd shove—"

"Hush," Father said.

"Slit whose belly, Nancy?" Caddy said.

"I wasn't scaired," Jason said. "I'd walk right down this lane by myself."

"Yah," Caddy said. "You wouldn't dare to put your foot down in it if we were not here too."

II

Dilsey was still sick, so we took Nancy home every night until Mother said, "How much longer is this going on? I to be left alone in this big house while you take home a frightened Negro?"

We fixed a pallet in the kitchen for Nancy. One night we waked up, hearing the sound. It was not singing and it was not crying, coming up the dark stairs. There was a light in Mother's room and we heard Father going down the hall, down the back stairs, and Caddy and I went into the hall. The floor was cold. Our toes curled away from it while we listened to the sound. It was like singing and it wasn't like singing, like the sound that Negroes make.

Then it stopped and we heard Father going down the back stairs, and we went to the head of the stairs. Then the sound began again, in the stairway, not loud, and we could see Nancy's eyes halfway up the stairs, against the wall. They looked like cat's eyes do, like a big cat against the wall, watching us. When we came down the steps to where she was, she quit making the sound again, and we stood there until Father came back up from the kitchen, with his pistol in his hand. He went back down with Nancy and they came back with Nancy's pallet.

We spread the pallet in our room. After the light in Mother's room went off, we could see Nancy's eyes again. "Nancy," Caddy whispered, "are you asleep, Nancy?"

Nancy whispered something. It was oh or no, I don't know which. Like nobody had made it, like it came from nowhere and went nowhere, until it was like Nancy was not there at all; that I had looked so hard at her eyes on the stairs that they had got printed on my eyeballs, like the sun does when you have closed your eyes and there is no sun. "Jesus," Nancy whispered. "Jesus."

"Was it Jesus?" Caddy said. "Did he try to come into the kitchen?"

"Jesus," Nancy said. Like this: Jeeeeeeeeeeeeeeeesus, until the sound went out, like a match or a candle does.

"It's the other Jesus she means," I said.

"Can you see us, Nancy?" Caddy whispered. "Can you see our eyes too?"

"I ain't nothing but a nigger," Nancy said. "God knows. **God** knows."

"What did you see down there in the kitchen?" Caddy whispered. "What tried to get in?"

"God knows," Nancy said. We could see her eyes. "God knows."

Dilsey got well. She cooked dinner. "You'd better stay in bed a day or two longer," Father said.

"What for?" Dilsey said. "If I had been a day later, this place would be to rack and ruin. Get on out of here now, and let me get my kitchen straight again."

Dilsey cooked supper too. And that night, just before dark, Nancy came into the kitchen.

"How do you know he's back?" Dilsey said. "You ain't seen him."

"Jesus is a nigger," Jason said.

"I can feel him," Nancy said. "I can feel him laying yonder in the ditch."

"Tonight?" Dilsey said. "Is he there tonight?"

"Dilsey's a nigger too," Jason said.

"You try to eat something," Dilsey said.

"I don't want nothing," Nancy said.

"I ain't a nigger," Jason said.

"Drink some coffee," Dilsey said. She poured a cup of coffee for Nancy. "Do you know he's out there tonight? How come you know it's tonight?"

"I know," Nancy said. "He's there, waiting. I know. I done lived with him too long. I know what he is fixing to do fore he know it himself."

"Drink some coffee," Dilsey said. Nancy held the cup to her mouth and blew into the cup. Her mouth pursed out like a spreading adder's, like a rubber mouth, like she had blown all the color out of her lips with blowing the coffee.

"I ain't a nigger," Jason said. "Are you a nigger, Nancy?"

"I hellborn, child," Nancy said. "I won't be nothing soon. I going back where I come from soon."

III

She began to drink the coffee. While she was drinking, holding the cup in both hands, she began to make the sound again. She made the sound into the cup and the coffee sploshed out onto her hands and her dress. Her eyes looked at us and she sat there, her elbows on her knees, holding the cup in both hands, looking at us across the wet cup, making the sound.

"Look at Nancy," Jason said. "Nancy can't cook for us now. Dilsey's got well now."

"You hush up," Dilsey said. Nancy held the cup in both hands, looking at us, making the sound, like there were two of them: one looking at us and the other making the sound. "Whyn't you let Mr. Jason telefoam the marshal?" Dilsey said. Nancy stopped then, holding the cup in her long brown hands. She tried to drink some coffee again, but it sploshed out of the cup, onto her hands and her dress, and she put the cup down. Jason watched her.

"I can't swallow it," Nancy said. "I swallows but it won't go down me."

"You go down to the cabin," Dilsey said. "Frony will fix you a pallet and I'll be there soon."

"Won't no nigger stop him," Nancy said.

"I ain't a nigger," Jason said. "Am I, Dilsey?"

"I reckon not," Dilsey said. She looked at Nancy. "I don't reckon so. What you going to do, then?"

Nancy looked at us. Her eyes went fast, like she was afraid there wasn't time to look, without hardly moving at all. She looked at us, at all three of us at one time. "You member that night I stayed in yawls' room?" she said. She told about how we waked up early the next morning, and played. We had to play quiet, on her pallet, until Father woke up and it was time to get breakfast. "Go and ask your maw to let me stay here tonight," Nancy said. "I won't need no pallet. We can play some more."

Caddy asked Mother. Jason went too. "I can't have Negroes sleeping in the bedrooms," Mother said. Jason cried. He cried until Mother said he couldn't have any dessert for three days if he didn't stop. Then Jason said he would stop if Dilsey would make a chocolate cake. Father was there.

"Why don't you do something about it?" Mother said. "What do we have officers for?"

"Why is Nancy afraid of Jesus?" Caddy said. "Are you afraid of Father, Mother?"

"What could the officers do?" Father said. "If Nancy hasn't seen him, how could the officers find him?"

"Then why is she afraid?" Mother said

"She says he is there. She says she knows he is there tonight."

"Yet we pay taxes," Mother said. "I must wait here alone in this big house while you take a Negro woman home."

"You know that I am not lying outside with a razor," Father said.

"I'll stop if Dilsey will make a chocolate cake," Jason said. Mother told us to go out and Father said he didn't know if Jason would get a chocolate cake or not, but he knew what Jason was going to get in about a minute. We went back to the kitchen and told Nancy.

"Father said for you to go home and lock the door, and you'll be all right," Caddy said. "All right from what, Nancy? Is Jesus mad at you?" Nancy was holding the coffee cup in her hands again, her elbows on her knees and her hands holding the cup between her knees. She was looking into the cup. "What have you done that made Jesus mad?" Caddy said. Nancy let the cup go. It didn't break on the floor, but the coffee spilled out, and Nancy sat there with her hands still making the shape of the cup. She began to make the sound again, not loud. Not singing and not unsinging. We watched her.

"Here," Dilsey said. "You quit that, now. You get aholt of yourself. You wait here. I going to get Versh to walk home with you." Dilsey went out.

We looked at Nancy. Her shoulders kept shaking, but she quit making the sound. We watched her.

"What's Jesus going to do to you?" Caddy said. "He went away."

Nancy looked at us. "We had fun that night I stayed in yawls' room, didn't we?"

"I didn't," Jason said. "I didn't have any fun."

"You were asleep in Mother's room," Caddy said. "You were not there."

"Let's go down to my house and have some more fun," Nancy said.

"Mother won't let us," I said. "It's too late now."

"Don't bother her," Nancy said. "We can tell her in the morning. She won't mind."

"She wouldn't let us," I said.

"Don't ask her now," Nancy said. "Don't bother her now."

"She didn't say we couldn't go," Caddy said.

"We didn't ask," I said.

"If you go, I'll tell," Jason said.

"We'll have fun," Nancy said. "They won't mind, just to my house. I been working for yawl a long time. They won't mind."

"I'm not afraid to go," Caddy said. "Jason is the one that's afraid. He'll tell."

"I'm not," Jason said.

"Yes, you are," Caddy said. "You'll tell."

"I won't tell," Jason said. "I'm not afraid."

"Jason ain't afraid to go with me," Nancy said. "Is you, Jason?"

"Jason is going to tell," Caddy said. The lane was dark. We passed the pasture gate. "I bet if something was to jump out from behind that gate, Jason would holler."

"I wouldn't," Jason said. We walked down the lane. Nancy was talking loud.

"What are you talking so loud for, Nancy?" Caddy said.

"Who, me?" Nancy said. "Listen at Quentin and Caddy and Jason saying I'm talking loud."

"You talk like there was five of us here," Caddy said. "You talk like Father was here too."

"Who; me talking loud, Mr. Jason?" Nancy said.

"Nancy called Jason 'Mister,' " Caddy said.

"Listen how Caddy and Quentin and Jason talk," Nancy said.

"We're not talking loud," Caddy said. "You're the one that's talking like Father—"

"Hush," Nancy said; "hush, Mr. Jason."

"Nancy called Jason 'Mister' aguh—"

"Hush," Nancy said. She was talking loud when we crossed the ditch and stooped through the fence where she used to stoop through with the clothes on her head. Then we came to her house. We were going fast then. She opened the door. The smell of the house was like the lamp and the smell of Nancy was like the wick, like they were waiting for one another to begin to smell. She lit the lamp and closed the door and put the bar up. Then she quit talking loud, looking at us.

"What're we going to do?" Caddy said.

"What do yawl want to do?" Nancy said.

"You said we would have some fun," Caddy said.

There was something about Nancy's house; something you could smell besides Nancy and the house. Jason smelled it, even. "I don't want to stay here," he said. "I want to go home."

"Go home, then," Caddy said.

"I don't want to go by myself," Jason said.

"We're going to have some fun," Nancy said.

"How?" Caddy said.

Nancy stood by the door. She was looking at us, only it was like she had emptied her eyes, like she had quit using them. "What do you want to do?" she said.

"Tell us a story," Caddy said. "Can you tell a story?"

"Yes," Nancy said.

"Tell it," Caddy said. We looked at Nancy. "You don't know any stories."

"Yes," Nancy said. "Yes I do."

She came and sat in a chair before the hearth. There was a little fire there. Nancy built it up, when it was already hot inside. She built a good blaze. She told a story. She talked like her eyes looked, like her eyes watching us and her voice talking to us did not belong to her. Like she was living somewhere else, waiting somewhere else. She was outside the cabin. Her voice was inside and the shape of her, the Nancy that could stoop under a barbed wire fence with a bundle of clothes balanced on her head as though without weight, like a balloon, was there. But that was all. "And so this here queen come walking up to the ditch, where that bad man was hiding. She was walking up to the ditch, and she say, 'If I can just get past this here ditch,' was what she say . . ."

"What ditch?" Caddy said. "A ditch like that one out there? Why did a queen want to go into a ditch?"

"To get to her house," Nancy said. She looked at us. "She had to cross the ditch to get into her house quick and bar the door."

"Why did she want to go home and bar the door?" Caddy said.

IV

Nancy looked at us. She quit talking. She looked at us. Jason's legs stuck straight out of his pants where he sat on Nancy's lap. "I don't think that's a good story," he said. "I want to go home."

"Maybe we had better," Caddy said. She got up from the floor. "I bet they are looking for us right now." She went toward the door.

"No," Nancy said. "Don't open it." She got up quick and passed Caddy. She didn't touch the door, the wooden bar.

"Why not?" Caddy said.

"Come back to the lamp," Nancy said. "We'll have fun. You don't have to go."

"We ought to go," Caddy said. "Unless we have a lot of fun." She and Nancy came back to the fire, the lamp.

"I want to go home," Jason said. "I'm going to tell."

"I know another story," Nancy said. She stood close to the lamp. She looked at Caddy, like when your eyes look up at a stick balanced on your nose. She had to look down to see Caddy, but her eyes looked like that, like when you are balancing a stick.

"I won't listen to it," Jason said. "I'll bang on the floor."

"It's a good one," Nancy said. "It's better than the other one."

"What's it about?" Caddy said. Nancy was standing by the lamp. Her hand was on the lamp, against the light, long and brown.

"Your hand is on that hot globe," Caddy said. "Don't it feel hot to your hand?"

Nancy looked at her hand on the lamp chimney. She took her hand away, slow. She stood there, looking at Caddy, wringing her long hand as though it were tied to her wrist with a string.

"Let's do something else," Caddy said.

"I want to go home," Jason said.

"I got some popcorn," Nancy said. She looked at Caddy and then at Jason and then at me and then at Caddy again. "I got some popcorn."

"I don't like popcorn," Jason said. "I'd rather have candy."

Nancy looked at Jason. "You can hold the popper." She was still wringing her hand; it was long and limp and brown.

"All right," Jason said. "I'll stay a while if I can do that. Caddy can't hold it. I'll want to go home again if Caddy holds the popper."

Nancy built up the fire. "Look at Nancy putting her hands in the fire," Caddy said. "What's the matter with you, Nancy?"

"I got popcorn," Nancy said. "I got some." She took the popper from under the bed. It was broken. Jason began to cry.

"Now we can't have any popcorn," he said.

"We ought to go home, anyway," Caddy said. "Come on, Quentin."

"Wait," Nancy said; "wait. I can fix it. Don't you want to help me fix it?"

"I don't think I want any," Caddy said. "It's too late now."

"You help me, Jason," Nancy said. "Don't you want to help me?"

"No," Jason said. "I want to go home."

"Hush," Nancy said; "hush. Watch. Watch me. I can fix it so Jason can hold it and pop the corn." She got a piece of wire and fixed the popper.

"It won't hold good," Caddy said.

"Yes it will," Nancy said. "Yawl watch. Yawl help me shell some corn."

The popcorn was under the bed too. We shelled it into the popper and Nancy helped Jason hold the popper over the fire.

"It's not popping," Jason said. "I want to go home."

"You wait," Nancy said. "It'll begin to pop. We'll have fun then."

She was sitting close to the fire. The lamp was turned up so high it was beginning to smoke. "Why don't you turn it down some?" I said.

"It's all right," Nancy said. "I'll clean it. Yawl wait. The popcorn will start in a minute."

"I don't believe it's going to start," Caddy said. "We ought to start home, anyway. They'll be worried."

"No," Nancy said. "It's going to pop. Dilsey will tell um yawl with me. I been working for yawl long time. They won't mind if yawl at my house. You wait, now. It'll start popping any minute now."

Then Jason got some smoke in his eyes and he began to cry. He dropped the popper into the fire. Nancy got a wet rag and wiped Jason's face, but he didn't stop crying.

"Hush," she said. "Hush." But he didn't hush. Caddy took the popper out of the fire.

"It's burned up," she said. "You'll have to get some more popcorn, Nancy."

"Did you put all of it in?" Nancy said.

"Yes," Caddy said. Nancy looked at Caddy. Then she took the popper and opened it and poured the cinders into her apron and began to sort the grains, her hands long and brown, and we watching her.

"Haven't you got any more?" Caddy said.

"Yes," Nancy said; "yes. Look. This here ain't burnt. All we need to do is—"

"I want to go home," Jason said. "I'm going to tell."

"Hush," Caddy said. We all listened. Nancy's head was already turned toward the barred door, her eyes filled with red lamplight. "Somebody is coming," Caddy said.

Then Nancy began to make that sound again, not loud, sitting there above the fire, her long hands dangling between her knees; all of a sudden water began to come out on her face in big drops, running down her face, carrying in each one a little turning ball of firelight like a spark until it dropped off her chin. "She's not crying," I said.

"I ain't crying," Nancy said. Her eyes were closed. "I ain't crying. Who is it?"

"I don't know," Caddy said. She went to the door and looked out. "We've got to go now," she said. "Here comes Father."

"I'm going to tell," Jason said. "Yawl made me come."

The water still ran down Nancy's face. She turned in her chair. "Listen. Tell him. Tell him we going to have fun. Tell him I take good care of yawl until in the morning. Tell him to let me come home with yawl and sleep on the floor. Tell him I won't need no pallet. We'll have fun. You member last time how we had so much fun?"

"I didn't have fun," Jason said. "You hurt me. You put smoke in my eyes. I'm going to tell."

V

Father came in. He looked at us. Nancy did not get up.

"Tell him," she said.

"Caddy made us come down here," Jason said. "I didn't want to."

Father came to the fire. Nancy looked up at him. "Can't you go to Aunt Rachel's and stay?" he said. Nancy looked up at Father, her hands between her knees. "He's not here," Father said. "I would have seen him. There's not a soul in sight."

"He in the ditch," Nancy said. "He waiting in the ditch yonder."

"Nonsense," Father said. He looked at Nancy. "Do you know he's there?"

"I got the sign," Nancy said.

"What sign?"

"I got it. It was on the table when I come in. It was a hog-bone, with blood meat still on it, laying by the lamp. He's out there. When yawl walk out that door, I gone."

"Gone where, Nancy?" Caddy said.

"I'm not a tattletale," Jason said.

"Nonsense," Father said.

"He out there," Nancy said. "He looking through that window this minute, waiting for yawl to go. Then I gone."

"Nonsense," Father said. "Lock up your house and we'll take you on to Aunt Rachel's."

" 'Twon't do no good," Nancy said. She didn't look at Father now, but he looked down at her, at her long, limp, moving hands. "Putting it off won't do no good."

"Then what do you want to do?" Father said.

"I don't know," Nancy said. "I can't do nothing. Just put it off. And that don't do no good. I reckon it belong to me. I reckon what I going to get ain't no more than mine."

"Get what?" Caddy said. "What's yours?"

"Nothing," Father said. "You all must get to bed."

"Caddy made me come," Jason said.

"Go on to Aunt Rachel's," Father said.

"It won't do no good," Nancy said. She sat before the fire, her elbows on her knees, her long hands between her knees. "When even your own kitchen wouldn't do no good. When even if I was sleeping on the floor in the room with your chillen, and the next morning there I am, and blood—"

"Hush," Father said. "Lock the door and put out the lamp and go to bed."

"I scaired of the dark," Nancy said. "I scaired for it to happen in the dark."

"You mean you're going to sit right here with the lamp lighted?" Father said. Then Nancy began to make the sound again, sitting before the fire, her long hands between her knees. "Ah, damnation," Father said. "Come along, chillen. It's past bedtime."

"When yawl go home, I gone," Nancy said. She talked quieter now, and her face looked quiet, like her hands. "Anyway, I got my coffin money saved up with Mr. Lovelady." Mr. Lovelady was a short, dirty man who collected the Negro insurance, coming around to the cabins or the kitchens every Saturday morning, to collect fifteen cents. He and his wife lived at the hotel. One morning his wife committed suicide. They had a child, a little girl. He and the child went away. After a week or two he came back alone. We would see him going along the lanes and the back streets on Saturday mornings.

"Nonsense," Father said. "You'll be the first thing I'll see in the kitchen tomorrow morning."

"You'll see what you'll see, I reckon," Nancy said. "But it will take the Lord to say what that will be."

VI

We left her sitting before the fire.

"Come and put the bar up," Father said. But she didn't move. She didn't look at us again, sitting quietly there between the lamp and the fire. From some distance down the lane we could look back and see her through the open door.

"What, Father?" Caddy said. "What's going to happen?"

"Nothing," Father said. Jason was on Father's back, so Jason was the tallest of all of us. We went down into the ditch. I looked at it, quiet. I couldn't see much where the moonlight and the shadows tangled.

"If Jesus *is* hid here, he can see us, can't he?" Caddy said.

"He's not there," Father said. "He went away a long time ago."

"You made me come," Jason said, high; against the sky it looked like Father had two heads, a little one and a big one. "I didn't want to."

We went up out of the ditch. We could still see Nancy's house and the open door, but we couldn't see Nancy now, sitting before the fire with the door open, because she was tired. "I just done got tired," she said. "I just a nigger. It ain't no fault of mine."

But we could hear her, because she began just after we came up out of the ditch, the sound that was not singing and not unsinging. "Who will do our washing now, Father?" I said.

"I'm not a nigger," Jason said, high and close above Father's head.

"You're worse," Caddy said, "you are a tattletale. If something was to jump out, you'd be scairder than a nigger."

"I wouldn't," Jason said.

"You'd cry," Caddy said.

"Caddy," Father said.

"I wouldn't!" Jason said.

"Scairy cat," Caddy said.

"Candace!" Father said.

A Rose for Emily

WILLIAM FAULKNER

I

When Miss Emily Grierson died, our whole town went to her funeral: the men through a sort of respectful affection for a fallen monument, the women mostly out of curiosity to see the inside of her house, which no one save an old man-servant—a combined gardener and cook—had seen in at least ten years.

It was a big, squarish frame house that had once been white, decorated with cupolas and spires, and scrolled balconies in the heavily lightsome style of the seventies, set on what had once been our most select street. But garages and cotton gins had encroached and obliterated even the august names of that neighborhood; only Miss Emily's house was left, lifting its stubborn and coquettish decay above the cotton wagons and the gasoline pumps—an eyesore among eyesores. And now Miss Emily had gone to join the representatives of those august names where they lay in the cedar-bemused cemetery among the ranked and anonymous graves of Union and Confederate soldiers who fell at the battle of Jefferson.

Alive, Miss Emily had been a tradition, a duty, and a care; a sort of hereditary obligation upon the town, dating from that day in 1894 when Colonel Sartoris, the mayor—he who fathered the edict that no Negro woman should appear on the street without an apron—remitted her taxes, the dispensation dating from the death of her father on into perpetuity. Not that Miss Emily would have accepted charity. Colonel Sartoris invented an involved tale to the effect that Miss Emily's father had loaned money to the town, which the town, as a matter of business, preferred this way of repaying. Only a man of Colonel Sartoris' generation and thought could have invented it, and only a woman could have believed it.

When the next generation, with its more modern ideas, became mayors and aldermen, this arrangement created some little dissatisfaction. On the first of the year they mailed her a tax notice. February came, and there was no reply. They wrote her a formal letter, asking her to call at the sheriff's office at her convenience. A week later the mayor wrote her himself, offering to call or to send his car for her, and received in reply a note on paper of an archaic shape, in a thin, flowing calligraphy in faded ink, to the effect that she no longer went out at all. The tax notice was also enclosed, without comment.

They called a special meeting of the Board of Aldermen. A deputation waited upon her, knocked at the door through which no visitor had passed since she ceased giving china-painting lessons eight or ten years earlier. They were admitted by the old Negro into a dim hall from which a stairway mounted into still more shadow. It smelled of dust and disuse—a close, dank smell. The Negro led them into the parlor. It was furnished in heavy, leather-covered furniture. When the Negro opened the blinds of one window, they could see that the leather was cracked; and when they sat down, a faint dust rose sluggishly about their thighs, spinning with slow motes in the single sun-ray. On a tarnished gilt easel before the fireplace stood a crayon portrait of Miss Emily's father.

They rose when she entered—a small, fat woman in black, with a thin gold chain descending to her waist and vanishing into her belt, leaning on an ebony cane with a tarnished gold head. Her skeleton was small and spare; perhaps that was why what would have been merely plumpness in another was obesity in her. She looked bloated, like a body long submerged in motionless water, and of that pallid hue. Her eyes, lost in the fatty ridges of her face, looked like two small pieces of coal pressed into a lump of dough as they moved from one face to another while the visitors stated their errand.

She did not ask them to sit. She just stood in the door and listened quietly until the spokesman came to a stumbling halt. Then they could hear the invisible watch ticking at the end of the gold chain.

Her voice was dry and cold. "I have no taxes in Jefferson. Colonel Sartoris explained it to me. Perhaps one of you can gain access to the city records and satisfy yourselves."

"But we have. We are the city authorities, Miss Emily. Didn't you get a notice from the sheriff, signed by him?"

"I received a paper, yes," Miss Emily said. "Perhaps he considers himself the sheriff . . . I have no taxes in Jefferson."

"But there is nothing on the books to show that, you see. We must go by the—"

"See Colonel Sartoris. I have no taxes in Jefferson."

"But Miss Emily—"

"See Colonel Sartoris." (Colonel Sartoris had been dead almost ten years.) "I have no taxes in Jefferson. Tobe!" The Negro appeared. "Show these gentlemen out."

II

So she vanquished them, horse and foot, just as she had vanquished their fathers thirty years before about the smell. That was two years after her father's death and a short time after her sweetheart—the one we believed would marry her—had deserted her. After her father's death she went out very little; after her sweetheart went away, people hardly saw her at all. A few of the ladies had the temerity to call, but were not received, and the only sign of life about the place was the Negro man—a young man then—going in and out with a market basket.

"Just as if a man—any man—could keep a kitchen properly," the ladies said; so they were not surprised when the smell developed. It was another link between the gross, teeming world and the high and mighty Griersons.

A neighbor, a woman, complained to the mayor, Judge Stevens, eighty years old.

"But what will you have me do about it, madam?" he said.

"Why, send her word to stop it," the woman said. "Isn't there a law?"

"I'm sure that won't be necessary," Judge Stevens said. "It's probably just a snake or a rat that nigger of hers killed in the yard. I'll speak to him about it."

The next day he received two more complaints, one from a man who came in diffident deprecation. "We really must do something about it, Judge. I'd be the last one in the world to bother Miss Emily, but we've got to do something." That night the Board of Aldermen met—three graybeards and one younger man, a member of the rising generation.

"It's simple enough," he said. "Send her word to have her place cleaned up. Give her a certain time do it in, and if she don't . . ."

"Dammit, sir," Judge Stevens said, "will you accuse a lady to her face of smelling bad?"

So the next night, after midnight, four men crossed Miss Emily's lawn and slunk about the house like burglars, sniffing along the base of the brickwork and at the cellar openings while one of them performed a regular sowing motion with his hand out of a sack slung from his shoulder. They broke open the cellar door and sprinkled lime there, and in all the outbuildings. As they recrossed the lawn, a window that had been dark was lighted and Miss Emily sat in it, the light behind her, and her upright torso motionless as that of an idol. They crept quietly across the lawn and into the shadow of the locusts that lined the street. After a week or two the smell went away.

That was when people had begun to feel really sorry for her. People in our town, remembering how old lady Wyatt, her great-aunt, had gone completely crazy at last, believed that the Griersons held themselves a little too high for what they really were. None of the young men were quite good enough for Miss Emily and such. We had long thought of them as a tableau, Miss Emily a slender figure in white in the background, her father a spraddled silhouette in the foregound, his back to her and clutching a horsewhip, the two of them framed by the backflung front door. When she got to be thirty and was still single, we were not pleased exactly, but vindicated; even with insanity in the family she wouldn't have turned down all of her chances if they had really materialized.

When her father died, it got about that the house was all that was left to her; and in a way, people were glad. At last they could pity Miss Emily. Being left alone, and a pauper, she had become humanized. Now she too would know the old thrill and the old despair of a penny more or less.

The day after his death all the ladies prepared to call at the house and offer condolence and aid, as is our custom. Miss Emily met them at the door, dressed as usual and with no trace of grief on her face. She told them that her father was not dead. She did that for three days, with the ministers calling on her, and the doctors, trying to persuade her to let them dispose of the body. Just as they were about to resort to law and force, she broke down, and they buried her father quickly.

We did not say she was crazy then. We believed she had to do that. We remembered all the young men her father had driven away, and we knew that with nothing left, she would have to cling to that which had robbed her, as people will.

III

She was sick for a long time. When we saw her again, her hair was cut short, making her look like a girl, with a vague resemblance to those angels in colored church windows—sort of tragic and serene.

The town had just let the contracts for paving the sidewalks, and in the summer after her father's death they began the work. The construction company came with niggers and mules and machinery, and a foreman named Homer Barron, a Yankee—a big, dark, ready man, with a big voice and eyes lighter than his face. The little boys would follow in groups to hear him cuss the niggers, and the niggers singing in time to the rise and fall of picks. Pretty soon he knew everybody in town. Whenever you heard a lot of laughing anywhere about the square, Homer Barron would be in the center of the group.

Presently we began to see him and Miss Emily on Sunday afternoons driving in the yellow-wheeled buggy and the matched team of bays from the livery stable.

At first we were glad that Miss Emily would have an interest, because the ladies all said, "Of course a Grierson would not think seriously of a Northerner, a day laborer." But there were still others, older people, who said that even grief could not cause a real lady to forget *noblesse oblige*—without calling it *noblesse oblige*. They just said, "Poor Emily. Her kinsfolk should come to her." She had some kin in Alabama; but years ago her father had fallen out with them over the estate of old Lady Wyatt, the crazy woman, and there was no communication between the two families. They had not even been represented at the funeral.

And as soon as the old people said, "Poor Emily," the whispering began. "Do you suppose it's really so?" they said to one another. "Of course it is. What else could . . ." This behind their hands; rustling of craned silk and satin behind jalousies closed upon the sun of Sunday afternoon as the thin, swift clop-clop-clop of the matched team passed: "Poor Emily."

She carried her head high enough—even when we believed that she was fallen. It was as if she demanded more than ever the recognition of her dignity as the last Grierson; as if it had wanted that touch of earthiness to reaffirm her imperviousness. Like when she bought the rat poison, the arsenic. That was over a year after they had begun to say "Poor Emily," and while the two female cousins were visiting her.

"I want some poison," she said to the druggist. She was over thirty then, still a slight woman, though thinner than usual, with cold, haughty black eyes in a face the flesh of which was strained across the temples and about the eye-sockets as you imagine a lighthouse-keeper's face ought to look. "I want some poison," she said.

"Yes, Miss Emily. What kind? For rats and such? I'd recom—"

"I want the best you have. I don't care what kind."

The druggist named several. "They'll kill anything up to an elephant. But what you want is—"

"Arsenic," Miss Emily said. "Is that a good one?"

"Is . . . arsenic? Yes, ma'am. But what you want—"

"I want arsenic."

The druggist looked down at her. She looked back at him, erect, her face like a strained flag. "Why, of course," the druggist said. "If that's what you want. But the law requires you to tell what you are going to use it for."

Miss Emily just stared at him, her head tilted back in order to look him eye for eye, until he looked away and went and got the arsenic and wrapped it up. The Negro delivery boy brought her the package; the druggist didn't come back. When she opened the package at home there was written on the box, under the skull and bones: "For rats."

IV

So the next day we all said, "She will kill herself"; and we said it would be the best thing. When she had first begun to be seen with Homer Barron, we had said, "She will marry him." Then we said, "She will persuade him yet," because Homer himself had remarked—he liked men, and it was known that he drank with the younger men in the Elks' Club—that he was not a marrying man. Later we said, "Poor Emily" behind the jalousies as they passed on Sunday afternoon in the glittering buggy, Miss Emily with her head high and Homer Barron with his hat cocked and cigar in his teeth, reins and whip in a yellow glove.

Then some of the ladies began to say that it was a disgrace to the town and a bad example to the young people. The men did not want to interfere, but at last the ladies forced the Baptist minister— Miss Emily's people were Episcopal—to call upon her. He would never divulge what happened during that interview, but he refused to go back again. The next Sunday they again drove about the streets, and the following day the minister's wife wrote to Miss Emily's relations in Alabama.

So she had blood-kin under her roof again and we sat back to watch developments. At first nothing happened. Then we were sure that they were to be married. We learned that Miss Emily had been to the jeweler's and ordered a man's toilet set in silver, with the letters H. B. on each piece. Two days later we learned that she had bought a complete outfit of men's clothing, including a nightshirt, and we said, "They are married." We were really glad. We were glad because the two female cousins were even more Grierson than Miss Emily had ever been.

So we were not surprised when Homer Barron—the streets had been finished some time since—was gone. We were a little disappointed that there was not a public blowing-off, but we believed that he had gone on to prepare for Miss Emily's coming, or to give her a chance to get rid of the cousins. (By that time it was a cabal, and we were all Miss Emily's allies to help circumvent the cousins.) Sure enough, after another week they departed. And, as we had expected all along, within three days Homer Barron was back in town. A neighbor saw the Negro man admit him at the kitchen door at dusk one evening.

And that was the last we saw of Homer Barron. And of Miss Emily for some time. The Negro man went in and out with the market basket, but the front door remained closed. Now and then we would see her at a window for a moment, as the men did that night when they sprinkled the lime, but for almost six months she did not appear on the streets. Then we knew that this was to be expected too; as if that quality of her father which had thwarted her woman's life so many times had been too virulent and too furious to die.

When we next saw Miss Emily, she had grown fat and her hair was turning gray. During the next few years it grew grayer and grayer until it attained an even pepper-and-salt iron-gray, when it ceased turning. Up to the day of her death at seventy-four it was still that vigorous iron-gray, like the hair of an active man.

From that time on her front door remained closed, save for a period of six or seven years, when she was about forty, during which she gave lessons in china-painting. She fitted up a studio in one of the downstairs rooms, where the daughters and granddaughters of Colonel Sartoris' contemporaries were sent to her with the same regularity and in the same spirit that they were sent to church on Sunday with a twenty-five-cent piece for the collection plate. Meanwhile her taxes had been remitted.

Then the newer generation became the backbone and the spirit of the town, and the painting pupils grew up and fell away and did not send their children to her with boxes of color and tedious brushes and pictures cut from the ladies' magazines. The front door closed upon the last one and remained closed for good. When the town got free postal delivery, Miss Emily alone refused to let them fasten the metal numbers above her door and attach a mailbox to it. She would not listen to them.

Daily, monthly, yearly we watched the Negro grow grayer and more stooped, going in and out with the market basket. Each December we sent her a tax notice, which would be returned by the post office a week later, unclaimed. Now and then we would see her in one of the downstairs windows—she had evidently shut up the top floor of the house—like the carven torso of an idol in a niche, looking or not looking at us, we could never tell which. Thus she passed from generation to generation—dear, inescapable, impervious, tranquil, and perverse.

And so she died. Fell ill in the house filled with dust and shadows, with only a doddering Negro man to wait on her. We did not even know she was sick; we had long since given up trying to get any information from the Negro. He talked to no one, probably not even to her, for his voice had grown harsh and rusty, as if from disuse.

She died in one of the downstairs rooms, in a heavy walnut bed with a curtain, her gray head propped on a pillow yellow and moldy with age and lack of sunlight.

V

The Negro met the first of the ladies at the front door and let them in, with their hushed, sibilant voices and their quick, curious glances, and then he disappeared. He walked right through the house and out the back and was not seen again.

The two female cousins came at once. They held the funeral on the second day, with the town coming to look at Miss Emily beneath a mass of bought flowers, with the crayon face of her father musing profoundly above the bier and the ladies sibilant and macabre; and the very old men—some in their brushed Confederate uniforms—on the porch and the lawn, talking of Miss Emily as if she had been a contemporary of theirs, believing that they had danced with her and courted her perhaps, confusing time with its mathematical progression, as the old do, to whom all the past is not a diminishing road but, instead, a huge meadow which no winter ever quite touches, divided from them now by the narrow bottle-neck of the most recent decade of years.

Already we knew that there was one room in that region above stairs which no one had seen in forty years, and which would have to be forced. They waited until Miss Emily was decently in the ground before they opened it.

The violence of breaking down the door seemed to fill this room with pervading dust. A thin, acrid pall of the tomb seemed to lie everywhere upon this room decked and furnished as for a bridal: upon the valance curtains of faded rose color, upon the rose-shaded lights, upon the dressing table, upon the delicate array of crystal and the man's toilet things backed with tarnished silver, silver so tarnished that the monogram was obscured. Among them lay a collar and tie, as if they had just been removed, which, lifted, left upon the surface a pale crescent in the dust. Upon a chair hung the suit, carefully folded; beneath it the two mute shoes and the discarded socks.

The man himself lay in the bed.

For a long while we just stood there, looking down at the profound and fleshless grin. The body had apparently once lain in the attitude of an embrace, but now the long sleep that outlasts love, that conquers even the grimace of love, had cuckolded him. What was left of him, rotted beneath what was left of the nightshirt, had become inextricable from the bed in which he lay; and upon him and upon the pillow beside him lay that even coating of the patient and biding dust.

Then we noticed that in the second pillow was the indentation of a head. One of us lifted something from it, and leaning forward, that faint and invisible dust dry and acrid in the nostrils, we saw a long strand of iron-gray hair.

ERNEST HEMINGWAY

(1899-1961)

Hemingway was born in Oak Park, Illinois, in 1899, the son of a small town doctor. After high school he worked on the *Kansas City Star* but left to enter the First World War as an ambulance driver, before the United States joined in. Wounded in Italy, he returned home, married, and served as European correspondent for the *Toronto Star.*

But soon he gave up journalism to struggle as a writer. In Paris he was helped by Gertrude Stein, the American experimentalist, to shape his prose style, and by Ezra Pound (great modern poet, who also helped James Joyce and T. S. Eliot), and he became a friend of F. Scott Fitzgerald. (Hemingway, forty years later, remembered this period in a beautiful collection of memoirs, *A Moveable Feast.*) His first published works were fine short stories, most of them about the boyhood and young manhood of Nick Adams. They are stories of growing up, stories of the destructiveness of illusions and the attempt to survive without illusions in a world that demolishes the individual. In 1926 he published *The Sun Also Rises,* with the famous epigraph by Gertrude Stein, "You are all a lost generation." It is a novel about the postwar experience, about people disconnected from life, who suck at the lives of other people. The function of the narrator, made impotent by his war wound, is to observe, to experience revulsion, to reject the emptiness of the characters' lives. The natural world—here, the traditional world of the Spanish—is rich; the world of tourists is sterile, empty. In 1929 Hemingway went back behind this emptiness to its root metaphor—the First World War— with his novel *A Farewell to Arms.* There Frederick Henry, an American volunteer, tells of his wound, his separation from the war, the death of his love. At the end of the novel, as at the end of many of the Nick Adams stories, we are faced with a universe not just *indifferent,* as in Crane, but actively *hostile.* The only response is to live in it simply, live for the moment, with courage and without expectations.

During the 1930's Hemingway wrote a number of powerful stories, including "The Snows of Kilimanjaro." In a sense, "Snows" is all of Hemingway squeezed into one story; he acknowledged that in writing it he "wasted" many potentially interesting stories. As they appear in "Snows" they serve as extended metaphors (see Preface, pp. 18–21) for the condition of human existence—full of pain unless covered by illusions or anesthetized by a deadening of feeling. Harry has lost feeling—not only in his gangrenous leg but in his response to a world too terrible to bear. He has stopped writing, betraying himself and his experience in order to live without pain. This is the story of a man trying to recover something at the last moment; in that sense it is very much like Tolstoy's "The Death of Iván Ilých."

In 1940 Hemingway's magnificent novel of the Spanish Civil War was published. *For Whom the Bell Tolls* is not the novel of a man trying to eliminate life because it is too painful to bear; if Frederick Henry, in *A Farewell to Arms,* makes a "separate peace," Robert Jordan commits himself to the Loyalist cause, while recognizing the ironies of the war and rejecting the ideology of the Communists. In the novel Jordan is haunted by the death of his father, who, like Hemingway's own father, shot himself. Jordan rejects suicide for himself but dies a hero's death protecting his woman and friends.

During the Spanish Civil War Hemingway was not a demolitions expert like Robert Jordan but a journalist; during the Second World War he became part journalist, part private army, leading his own small band through France. Increasingly a legend, he also grew increasingly troubled, explosive. Most of his later work was rejected by the critics, and he grew stormy and sullen. In 1952 *The Old Man and the Sea* was published, which won him critical and popular acclaim. In 1954 he won the Nobel Prize for Literature. In 1961, broken in health and mind, he shot himself.

[See Preface, p. 20 (figurative language), pp. 21–24 (dialogue and vision).]

The Snows of Kilimanjaro

ERNEST HEMINGWAY

> *Kilimanjaro is a snow covered mountain 19,710 feet high, and is said to be the highest mountain in Africa. Its western summit is called the Masai "Ngàje Ngài," the House of God. Close to the western summit there is the dried and frozen carcass of a leopard. No one has explained what the leopard was seeking at that altitude.*

"The marvellous thing is that it's painless," he said. "That's how you know when it starts."

"Is it really?"

"Absolutely. I'm awfully sorry about the odor though. That must bother you."

"Don't! Please don't."

"Look at them," he said. "Now is it sight or is it scent that brings them like that?"

The cot the man lay on was in the wide shade of a mimosa tree and as he looked out past the shade onto the glare of the plain there were three of the big birds squatted obscenely, while in the sky a dozen more sailed, making quick-moving shadows as they passed.

"They've been there since the day the truck broke down," he said. "Today's the first time any have lit on the ground. I watched the way they sailed very carefully at first in case I ever wanted to use them in a story. That's funny now."

"I wish you wouldn't," she said.

"I'm only talking," he said. "It's much easier if I talk. But I don't want to bother you."

"You know it doesn't bother me," she said. "It's that I've gotten so very nervous not being able to do anything. I think we might make it as easy as we can until the plane comes."

"Or until the plane doesn't come."

"Please tell me what I can do. There must be something I can do."

"You can take the leg off and that might stop it, though I doubt it. Or you can shoot me. You're a good shot now. I taught you to shoot didn't I?"

"Please don't talk that way. Couldn't I read to you?"

"Read what?"

"Anything in the book bag that we haven't read."

"I can't listen to it," he said. "Talking is the easiest. We quarrel and that makes the time pass."

"I don't quarrel. I never want to quarrel. Let's not quarrel any more. No matter how nervous we get. Maybe they will be back with another truck today. Maybe the plane will come."

"I don't want to move," the man said. "There is no sense in moving now except to make it easier for you."

"That's cowardly."

"Can't you let a man die as comfortably as he can without calling him names? What's the use of slanging me?"

"You're not going to die."

"Don't be silly. I'm dying now. Ask those bastards." He looked over to where the huge, filthy birds sat, their naked heads sunk in the hunched feathers. A fourth planed down, to run quick-legged and then waddle slowly toward the others.

"They are around every camp. You never notice them. You can't die if you don't give up."

"Where did you read that? You're such a bloody fool."

"You might think about some one else."

"For Christ's sake," he said, "That's been my trade."

He lay then and was quiet for a while and looked across the heat shimmer of the plain to the edge of the bush. There were a few Tommies that showed minute and white against the yellow and, far off, he saw a herd of zebra, white against the green of the bush. This was a pleasant camp under big trees against a hill, with good water, and close by, a nearly dry water hole where sand grouse flighted in the mornings.

"Wouldn't you like me to read?" she asked. She was sitting on a canvas chair beside his cot. "There's a breeze coming up."

"No thanks."

"Maybe the truck will come."

"I don't give a damn about the truck."

"I do."

"You give a damn about so many things that I don't."

"Not so many, Harry."

"What about a drink?"

"It's supposed to be bad for you. It said in Black's to avoid all alcohol. You shouldn't drink."

"Molo!" he shouted.

"Yes Bwana."

"Bring whiskey-soda."

"Yes Bwana."

"You shouldn't," she said. "That's what I mean by giving up. It says it's bad for you. I know it's bad for you."

"No," he said. "It's good for me."

So now it was all over, he thought. So now he would never have a chance to finish it. So this was the way it ended in a bickering over a drink. Since the gangrene started in his right leg he had no pain and with the pain the horror had gone and all he felt now was a great tiredness and anger that this was the end of it. For this, that now was coming, he had very little curiosity. For years it had obsessed him; but now it meant nothing in itself. It was strange how easy being tired enough made it.

Now he would never write the things that he had saved to write until he knew enough to write them well. Well, he would not have to fail at trying to write them either. Maybe you could never write them, and that was why you put them off and delayed the starting. Well he would never know, now.

"I wish we'd never come," the woman said. She was looking at him holding the glass and biting her lip. "You never would have gotten anything like this in Paris. You always said you loved Paris. We could have stayed in Paris or gone anywhere. I'd have gone anywhere. I said I'd go anywhere you wanted. If you wanted to shoot we could have gone shooting in Hungary and been comfortable."

"Your bloody money," he said.

"That's not fair," she said. "It was always yours as much as mine. I left everything and I went wherever you wanted to go and I've done what you wanted to do. But I wish we'd never come here."

"You said you loved it."

"I did when you were all right. But now I hate it. I don't see why that had to happen to your leg. What have we done to have that happen to us?"

"I suppose what I did was to forget to put iodine on it when I first scratched it. Then I didn't pay any attention to it because I never infect. Then, later, when it got bad, it was probably using that weak carbolic solution when the other antiseptics ran out that paralyzed the minute blood vessels and started the gangrene." He looked at her, "What else?"

"I don't mean that."

"If we would have hired a good mechanic instead of a half baked kikuyu driver, he would have checked the oil and never burned out that bearing in the truck."

"I don't mean that."

"If you hadn't left your own people, your goddamned Old Westbury, Saratoga, Palm Beach people to take me on—"

"Why, I loved you. That's not fair. I love you now. I'll always love you. Don't you love me?"

"No," said the man. "I don't think so. I never have."

"Harry, what are you saying? You're out of your head."

"No. I haven't any head to go out of."

"Don't drink that," she said. "Darling, please don't drink that. We have to do everything we can."

"You do it," he said. "I'm tired."

Now in his mind he saw a railway station at Karagatch and he was standing with his pack and that was the headlight of the Simplon-Orient cutting the dark now and he was leaving Thrace then after the retreat. That was one of the things he had saved to write, with, in the morning at breakfast, looking out the window and seeing snow on the mountains in Bulgaria and Nansen's Secretary asking the old man if it were snow and the old man looking at it and saying, No, that's not snow. It's too early for snow. And the Secretary repeating to the other girls, No, you see. It's not snow and them all saying, It's not snow we were mistaken. But it was the snow all right and he sent them on into it when he evolved exchange of populations. And it was snow they tramped along in until they died that winter.

It was snow too that fell all Christmas week that year up in the Gauertal, that year they lived in the woodcutter's house with the big square porcelain stove that filled half the room, and they slept on mattresses filled with beech leaves, the time the deserter came with his feet bloody in the snow. He said the police were right behind him and they gave him woolen socks and held the gendarmes talking until the tracks had drifted over.

In Schrunz, on Christmas day, the snow was so bright it hurt your eyes when you looked out from the weinstube and saw every one coming home from church. That was where they walked up the sleigh-smoothed urine-yellowed road along the river with the steep pine hills, skis heavy on the shoulder, and where they ran that great run down the glacier above the Madlener-haus, the snow as smooth to see as cake frosting and as light as powder and he remembered the noiseless rush the speed made as you dropped down like a bird.

They were snow-bound a week in the Madlener-haus that time in the blizzard playing cards in the smoke by the lantern light and the stakes were higher all the time as Herr Lent lost more. Finally he lost it all. Everything, the skischule money and all the season's profit and then his capital. He could see him with his long nose, picking up the cards and then opening, "Sans Voir." There was always gambling then. When there was no snow you gambled and when there was too much you gambled. He thought of all the time in his life he had spent gambling.

But he had never written a line of that, nor of that cold, bright Christmas day with the mountains showing across the plain that Barker had flown across the lines to bomb the Austrian officers' leave train, machine-gunning them as they scattered and ran. He remem-

bered Barker afterwards coming into the mess and starting to tell about it. And how quiet it got and then somebody saying, "You bloody murderous bastard."

Those were the same Austrians they killed then that he skied with later. No not the same. Hans, that he skied with all that year, had been in the Kaiser-Jägers and when they went hunting hares to-gether up the little valley above the saw-mill they had talked of the fighting on Pasubio and of the attack on Pertica and Asalone and he had never written a word of that. Nor of Monte Corno, nor the Siete Commum, nor of Arsiedo.

How many winters had he lived in the Voralberg and the Arlberg? It was four and then he remembered the man who had the fox to sell when they had walked into Bludenz, that time to buy presents, and the cherry-pit taste of good kirsch, the fast-slipping rush of running powder-snow on crust, singing "Hi! Ho! said Rolly!" as you ran down the last stretch to the steep drop, taking it straight, then running the orchard in three turns and out across the ditch and onto the icy road behind the inn. Knocking your bindings loose, kicking the skis free and leaning them up against the wooden wall of the inn, the lamplight coming from the window, where inside, in the smoky, new-wine smelling warmth, they were playing the accordion.

"Where did we stay in Paris?" he asked the woman who was sitting by him in a canvas chair, now, in Africa.

"At the Crillon. You know that."

"Why do I know that?"

"That's where we always stayed."

"No. Not always."

"There and at the Pavillion Henri-Quatre in St. Germain. You said you loved it there."

"Love is a dunghill," said Harry. "And I'm the cock that gets on it to crow."

"If you have to go away," she said, "is it absolutely necessary to kill off everything you leave behind? I mean do you have to take away everything? Do you have to kill your horse, and your wife and burn your saddle and your armour?"

"Yes," he said. "Your damned money was my armour. My Swift and my Armour."

"Don't."

"All right. I'll stop that. I don't want to hurt you."

"It's a little bit late now."

"All right then. I'll go on hurting you. It's more amusing. The only thing I ever really liked to do with you I can't do now."

"No, that's not true. You liked to do many things and everything you wanted to do I did."

"Oh, for Christ sake stop bragging, will you?"

He looked at her and saw her crying.

"Listen," he said. "Do you think that it is fun to do this? I don't know why I'm doing it. It's trying to kill to keep yourself alive, I imagine. I was all right when we started talking. I didn't mean to start this, and now I'm crazy as a coot and being as cruel to you as I can be. Don't pay any attention, darling, to what I say. I love you, really. You know I love you. I've never loved any one else the way I love you."

He slipped into the familiar lie he made his bread and butter by.

"You're sweet to me."

"You bitch," he said. "You rich bitch. That's poetry. I'm full of poetry now. Rot and poetry. Rotten poetry."

"Stop it. Harry, why do you have to turn into a devil now?"

"I don't like to leave anything," the man said. "I don't like to leave things behind."

✳

It was evening now and he had been asleep. The sun was gone behind the hill and there was a shadow all across the plain and the small animals were feeding close to camp; quick dropping heads and switching tails, he watched them keeping well out away from the bush now. The birds no longer waited on the ground. They were all perched heavily in a tree. There were many more of them. His personal boy was sitting by the bed.

"Memsahib's gone to shoot," the boy said. "Does Bwana want?"

"Nothing."

She had gone to kill a piece of meat and, knowing how he liked to watch the game, she had gone well away so she would not disturb this little pocket of the plain that he could see. She was always thoughtful, he thought. On anything she knew about, or had read, or that she had ever heard.

It was not her fault that when he went to her he was already over. How could a woman know that you meant nothing that you said; that you spoke only from habit and to be comfortable? After he no longer meant what he said, his lies were more successful with women than when he had told them the truth.

It was not so much that he lied as that there was no truth to tell. He had had his life and it was over and then he went on living it again with different people and more money, with the best of the same places, and some new ones.

You kept from thinking and it was all marvellous. You were equipped with good insides so that you did not go to pieces that way, the way most of them had, and you made an attitude that you cared nothing for the work you used to do, now that you could no longer do it. But, in yourself, you said that you would write about these people; about the very rich; that you were really not of them but a spy in their country; that you would leave it and write of it and for once it would be written by some one who knew what he was writing of. But he would never do it, because each day of not writing, of comfort, of being that which he despised, dulled his ability and softened his will to work so that, finally, he did no work at all. The people he knew now were all much more comfortable when he did not work. Africa was where he had been happiest in the good time of his life, so he had come out here to start again. They had made this safari with the minimum of comfort. There was no hardship; but there was no luxury and he had thought that he could get back into training that way. That in some way he could work the fat off his soul the way a fighter went into the mountains to work and train in order to burn it out of his body.

She had liked it. She said she loved it. She loved anything that was exciting, that involved a change of scene, where there were new people and where things were pleasant. And he had felt the illusion of returning strength of will to work. Now if this was how it ended, and he knew it was, he must not turn like some snake biting itself because its back was broken. It wasn't this woman's fault. If it had not been she it would have been another. If he lived by a lie he should try to die by it. He heard a shot beyond the hill.

She shot very well this good, this rich bitch, this kindly caretaker and destroyer of his talent. Nonsense. He had destroyed his talent himself. Why should he blame this woman because she kept him well? He had destroyed his talent by not using it, by betrayals of himself and what he believed in, by drinking so much that he blunted the edge of his perceptions, by laziness, by sloth, and by snobbery, by pride and by prejudice, by hook and by crook. What was this? A catalogue of old books? What was his talent anyway? It was a talent all right but instead of using it, he had traded on it. It was never what he had done, but always what he could do. And he had chosen to make his living with something else instead of a pen or a pencil. It was strange, too, wasn't it, that when he fell in love with another woman, that woman should always have more money than the last one? But when he no longer was in love, when he was only lying, as to this woman, now, who had the most money of all, who had all the money there was, who had had a husband and children, who had taken lovers and been dissatisfied with them, and who loved him dearly as a writer, as a man, as a companion and as a proud possession; it was strange that when he did not love her at all and was lying, that he should be able to give her more for her money than when he had really loved.

We must all be cut out for what we do, he thought. However you make your living is where your talent lies. He had sold vitality, in one form or another, all his life and when your affections are not too involved you give much better value for the money. He had found that out but he would never write that, now, either. No, he would not write that, although it was well worth writing.

Now she came in sight, walking across the open toward the camp. She was wearing jodphurs and carrying her rifle. The two boys had a Tommie slung and they were coming along behind her. She was still a good-looking woman, he thought, and she had a pleasant body. She had a great talent and appreciation for the bed, she was not pretty, but he liked her face, she read enormously, liked to ride and shoot and, certainly, she drank too much. Her husband had died when she was still a comparatively young woman and for a while she had devoted herself to her two just-grown children, who did not need her and were embarrassed at having her about, to her stable of horses, to books, and to bottles. She liked to read in the evening before dinner and she drank Scotch and soda while she read. By dinner she was fairly drunk and after a bottle of wine at dinner she was usually drunk enough to sleep.

That was before the lovers. After she had the lovers she did not drink so much because she did not have to be drunk to sleep. But the lovers bored her. She had been married to a man who had never bored her and these people bored her very much.

Then one of her two children was killed in a plane crash and after that was over she did not want the lovers, and drink being no anæsthetic she had to make another life. Suddenly, she had been acutely frightened of being alone. But she wanted some one that she respected with her.

It had begun very simply. She liked what he wrote and she had always envied the life he led. She thought he did exactly what he wanted to. The steps by which she had acquired him and the way in which she had finally fallen in love with him were all part of a regular progression in which she had built herself a new life and he had traded away what remained of his old life.

He had traded it for security, for comfort too, there was no deny-ing that, and for what else? He did not know. She would have bought him anything he wanted. He knew that. She was a damned nice woman too. He would as soon be in bed with her as any one; rather with her, because she was richer, because she was very pleasant and appreciative and because she never made scenes. And now this life that she had built again was coming to a term because he had not used iodine two weeks ago when a thorn had scratched his knee as they moved forward trying to photograph a herd of waterbuck standing, their heads up, peering while their nostrils searched the air, their ears spread wide to hear the first noise that would send them rushing into the bush. They had bolted, too, before he got the picture.

Here she came now.

He turned his head on the cot to look toward her. "Hello," he said.

"I shot a Tommy ram," she told him. "He'll make you good broth and I'll have them mash some potatoes with the Klim. How do you feel?"

"Much better."

"Isn't that lovely? You know I thought perhaps you would. You were sleeping when I left."

"I had a good sleep. Did you walk far?"

"No. Just around behind the hill. I made quite a good shot on the Tommy."

"You shoot marvellously, you know."

"I love it. I've loved Africa. Really. If *you're* all right it's the most fun that I've ever had. You don't know the fun it's been to shoot with you. I've loved the country."

"I love it too."

"Darling, you don't know how marvellous it is to see you feeling better. I couldn't stand it when you felt that way. You won't talk to me like that again, will you? Promise me?"

"No," he said. "I don't remember what I said."

"You don't have to destroy me. Do you? I'm only a middle-aged woman who loves you and wants to do what you want to do. I've been destroyed two or three times already. You wouldn't want to destroy me again, would you?"

"I'd like to destroy you a few times in bed," he said.

"Yes. That's the good destruction. That's the way we're made to be destroyed. The plane will be here tomorrow."

"How do you know?"

"I'm sure. It's bound to come. The boys have the wood all ready and the grass to make the smudge. I went down and looked at it again today. There's plenty of room to land and we have the smudges ready at both ends."

"What makes you think it will come tomorrow?"

"I'm sure it will. It's overdue now. Then, in town, they will fix up your leg and then we will have some good destruction. Not that dreadful talking kind."

"Should we have a drink? The sun is down."

"Do you think you should?"

"I'm having one."

"We'll have one together. *Molo, letti dui whiskey-soda!*" she called.

"You'd better put on your mosquito boots," he told her.

"I'll wait till I bathe . . ."

While it grew dark they drank and just before it was dark and there was no longer enough light to shoot, a hyena crossed the open on his way around the hill.

"That bastard crosses there every night," the man said. "Every night for two weeks."

"He's the one makes the noise at night. I don't mind it. They're a filthy animal though."

Drinking together, with no pain now except the discomfort of lying in the one position, the boys lighting a fire, its shadow jumping on the tents, he could feel the return of acquiescence in this life of pleasant surrender. She *was* very good to him. He had been cruel and unjust in the afternoon. She was a fine woman, marvellous really. And just then it occurred to him that he was going to die.

It came with a rush; not as a rush of water nor of wind; but of a sudden evil-smelling emptiness and the odd thing was that the hyena slipped lightly along the edge of it.

"What is it, Harry?" she asked him.

"Nothing," he said. "You had better move over to the other side. To windward."

"Did Molo change the dressing?"

"Yes. I'm just using the boric now."

"How do you feel?"

"A little wobbly."

"I'm going in to bathe," she said. "I'll be right out. I'll eat with you and then we'll put the cot in."

So, he said to himself, we did well to stop the quarrelling. He had never quarrelled much with this woman, while with the women that he loved he had quarrelled so much they had finally, always, with the corrosion of the quarrelling, killed what they had together. He had loved too much, demanded too much, and he wore it all out.

He thought about alone in Constantinople that time, having quarrelled in Paris before he had gone out. He had whored the whole time and then, when that was over, and he had failed to kill his loneliness, but only made it worse, he had written her, the first one, the one who left him, a letter telling her how he had never been able to kill it. . . . How when he thought he saw her outside the Regence *one time it made him go all faint and sick inside, and that he would follow a woman who looked like her in some way, along the Boulevard, afraid to see it was not she, afraid to lose the feeling it gave him. How every one he had slept with had only made him miss her more. How what she had done could never matter since he knew he could not cure himself of loving her. He wrote this letter at the Club, cold sober, and mailed it to New York asking her to write him* at the office in Paris. That seemed safe. And that night missing her so much it made him feel hollow sick inside, he wandered up past Taxim's, picked a girl up and took her out to supper. He had gone to a place to dance with her afterward, she danced badly, and left her for a hot Armenian slut, that swung her belly against him so it almost scalded. He took her away from a British gunner subaltern after a row. The gunner asked him outside and they fought in the street on the cobbles in the dark. He'd hit him twice, hard, on the side of the jaw and when he didn't go down he knew he was in for a fight. The gunner hit him in the body, then beside his eye. He swung with his left again and landed and the gunner fell on him and grabbed his coat and tore the sleeve off and he clubbed him twice behind the ear and then smashed him with his right as he pushed him away. When the gunner went down his head hit first and he ran with the girl because they heard the M.P.'s coming. They got into a taxi and drove out to Rimmily Hissa along the Bosphorus, and around, and back in the cool night and went to bed and she felt as over-ripe as she looked but smooth, rose-petal, syrupy, smooth-bellied, big-breasted and needed no pillow under her buttocks, and he left her before she was awake looking blousy enough in the first daylight and turned up at the Pera Palace with a black eye, carrying his coat because one sleeve was missing.

That same night he left for Anatolia and he remembered, later on that trip, riding all day through fields of the poppies that they raised for opium and how strange it made you feel, finally, and all the distances seemed wrong, to where they had made the attack with the newly arrived Constantine officers, that did not know a god-damned thing, and the artillery had fired into the troops and the British observer had cried like a child.

That was the day he'd first seen dead men wearing white ballet skirts and upturned shoes with pompons on them. The Turks had come steadily and lumpily and he had seen the skirted men running and the officers shooting into them and running themselves and he and the British observer had run too until his lungs ached and his mouth was full of the taste of pennies and they stopped behind some rocks and there were the Turks coming as lumpily as ever. Later he had seen the things that he could never think of and later still he had seen much worse. So when he got back to Paris that time he could not talk about it or stand to have it mentioned. And there in the café as he passed was that American poet with a pile of saucers in front of him and a stupid look on his potato face talking about the Dada movement with a Roumanian who said his name was Tristan Tzara, who always wore a monocle and had a headache, and, back at the apartment with his wife that now he loved again, the quarrel all

*over, the madness all over, glad to be home, the office sent his mail up
to the flat. So then the letter in answer to the one he'd written came
in on a platter one morning and when he saw the handwriting he
went cold all over and tried to slip the letter underneath another.
But his wife said, "Who is that letter from, dear?" and that was the
end of the beginning of that.*

*He remembered the good times with them all, and the quarrels.
They always picked the finest places to have the quarrels. And why
had they always quarrelled when he was feeling best? He had never
written any of that because, at first, he never wanted to hurt any one
and then it seemed as though there was enough to write without it.
But he had always thought that he would write it finally. There was
so much to write. He had seen the world change; not just the events;
although he had seen many of them and had watched the people, but
he had seen the subtler change and he could remember how the
people were at different times. He had been in it and he had watched
it and it was his duty to write of it; but now he never would.*

"How do you feel?" she said. She had come out from the tent now
after her bath.

"All right."

"Could you eat now?" He saw Molo behind her with the folding
table and the other boy with the dishes.

"I want to write," he said.

"You ought to take some broth to keep your strength up."

"I'm going to die tonight," he said. "I don't need my strength
up."

"Don't be melodramatic, Harry, please," she said.

"Why don't you use your nose? I'm rotted half way up my thigh
now. What the hell should I fool with broth for? Molo bring whiskey-
soda."

"Please take the broth," she said gently.

"All right."

The broth was too hot. He had to hold it in the cup until it cooled
enough to take it and then he just got it down without gagging.

"You're a fine woman," he said. "Don't pay any attention to
me."

She looked at him with her well-known, well-loved face from *Spur*
and *Town and Country,* only a little the worse for drink, only a little
the worse for bed, but *Town and Country* never showed those good
breasts and those useful thighs and those lightly small-of-back-caress-
ing hands, and as he looked and saw her well known pleasant smile,
he felt death come again. This time there was no rush. It was a puff,
as of a wind that makes a candle flicker and the flame go tall.

"They can bring my net out later and hang it from the tree and build the fire up. I'm not going in the tent tonight. It's not worth moving. It's a clear night. There won't be any rain." ·

So this was how you died, in whispers that you did not hear. Well, there would be no more quarrelling. He could promise that. The one experience that he had never had he was not going to spoil now. He probably would. You spoiled everything. But perhaps he wouldn't.

"You can't take dictation, can you?"

"I never learned," she told him.

"That's all right."

There wasn't time, of course, although it seemed as though it telescoped so that you might put it all into one paragraph if you could get it right.

There was a log house, chinked white with mortar, on a hill above the lake. There was a bell on a pole by the door to call the people in to meals. Behind the house were fields and behind the fields was the timber. A line of lombardy poplars ran from the house to the dock. Other poplars ran along the point. A road went up to the hills along the edge of the timber and along that road he picked blackberries. Then that log house was burned down and all the guns that had been on deer foot racks above the open fire place were burned and afterwards their barrels, with the lead melted in the magazines, and the stocks burned away, lay out on the heap of ashes that were used to make lye for the big iron soap kettles, and you asked Grandfather if you could have them to play with, and he said, no. You see they were his guns still and he never bought any others. Nor did he hunt any more. The house was rebuilt in the same place out of lumber now and painted white and from its porch you saw the poplars and the lake beyond; but there were never any more guns. The barrels of the guns that had hung on the deer feet on the wall of the log house lay out there on the heap of ashes and no one ever touched them.

In the Black Forest, after the war, we rented a trout stream and there were two ways to walk to it. One was down the valley from Triberg and around the valley road in the shade of the trees that bordered the white road, and then up a side road that went up through the hills past many small farms, with the big Schwarzwald houses, until that road crossed the stream. That was where our fishing began.

The other way was to climb steeply up to the edge of the woods and then go across the top of the hills through the pine woods, and then out to the edge of a meadow and down across this meadow to the bridge. There were birches along the stream and it was not big, but narrow, clear and fast, with pools where it had cut under the roots of the birches. At the Hotel in Triberg the proprietor had a fine season. It was very pleasant and we were all great friends. The next year came the inflation and the money he had made the year before was not enough to buy supplies to open the hotel and he hanged himself.

You could dictate that, but you could not dictate the Place Contrescarpe where the flower sellers dyed their flowers in the street and the dye ran over the paving where the autobus started and the old men and the women, always drunk on wine and bad marc; and the children with their noses running in the cold; the smell of dirty sweat and poverty and drunkenness at the Café des Amateurs and the whores at the Bal Musette they lived above. The Concierge who entertained the trooper of the Garde Republicaine in her loge, his horse-hair-plumed helmet on a chair. The locataire across the hall whose husband was a bicycle racer and her joy that morning at the Cremerie when she had opened L'Auto and seen where he placed third in Paris-Tours, his first big race. She had blushed and laughed and then gone upstairs crying with the yellow sporting paper in her hand. The husband of the woman who ran the Bal Musette drove a taxi and when he, Harry, had to take an early plane the husband knocked upon the door to wake him and they each drank a glass of white wine at the zinc of the bar before they started. He knew his neighbors in that quarter then because they all were poor.

Around that Place there were two kinds; the drunkards and the sportifs. The drunkards killed their poverty that way; the sportifs took it out in exercise. They were the descendants of the Communards and it was no struggle for them to know their politics. They knew who had shot their fathers, their relatives, their brothers, and their friends when the Versailles troops came in and took the town after the Commune and executed any one they could catch with calloused hands, or who wore a cap, or carried any other sign he was a working man. And in that poverty, and in that quarter across the street from a Boucherie Chevaline and a wine co-operative he had written the start of all he was to do. There never was another part of Paris that he loved like that, the sprawling trees, the old white plastered houses painted brown below, the long green of the autobus in that round square, the purple flower dye upon the paving, the sudden drop down the hill of the rue Cardinal Lemoine to the River, and the other way the narrow crowded world of the rue Mouffetard. The street that ran up toward the Pantheon and the other that he always took with the bicycle, the only asphalted street in all that quarter, smooth under the tires, with the high narrow houses and the cheap tall hotel where Paul Verlaine had died. There were only two rooms in the apartments where they lived and he had a room on the top floor of that hotel that cost him sixty francs a month where he did his writing, and from it he could see the roofs and chimney pots and all the hills of Paris.

From the apartment you could only see the wood and coal man's place. He sold wine too, bad wine. The golden horse's head outside the Boucherie Chevaline where the carcasses hung yellow gold and red in the open window, and the green painted co-operative where they bought their wine; good wine and cheap. The rest was plaster walls and the windows of the neighbors. The neighbors who, at night, when some one lay drunk in the street, moaning and groaning in that typical French ivresse that you were propaganded to believe did not exist, would open their windows and then the murmur of talk.

"Where is the policeman? When you don't want him the bugger is always there. He's sleeping with some concierge. Get the Agent." Till some one threw a bucket of water from a window and the moaning stopped. "What's that? Water. Ah, that's intelligent." And the windows shutting. Marie, his femme de menage, protesting against the eight-hour day saying, "If a husband works until six he gets only a little drunk on the way home and does not waste too much. If he works only until five he is drunk every night and one has no money. It is the wife of the working man who suffers from this shortening of hours."

"Wouldn't you like some more broth?" the woman asked him now.

"No, thank you very much. It is awfully good."

"Try just a little."

"I would like a whiskey-soda."

"It's not good for you."

"No. It's bad for me. Cole Porter wrote the words and the music. This knowledge that you're going mad for me."

"You know I like you to drink."

"Oh yes. Only it's bad for me."

When she goes, he thought. I'll have all I want. Not all I want but all there is. Ayee he was tired. Too tired. He was going to sleep a little while. He lay still and death was not there. It must have gone around another street. It went in pairs, on bicycles, and moved absolutely silently on the pavements.

No, he had never written about Paris. Not the Paris that he cared about. But what about the rest that he had never written?

What about the ranch and the silvered gray of the sage brush, the quick, clear water in the irrigation ditches, and the heavy green of the alfalfa. The trail went up into the hills and the cattle in the *summer were shy as deer. The bawling and the steady noise and slow moving mass raising a dust as you brought them down in the fall. And behind the mountains, the clear sharpness of the peak in the evening light and, riding down along the trail in the moonlight, bright across the valley. Now he remembered coming down through the timber in the dark holding the horse's tail when you could not see and all the stories that he meant to write.*

About the half-wit chore boy who was left at the ranch that time and told not to let any one get any hay, and that old bastard from the Forks who had beaten the boy when he had worked for him stopping to get some feed. The boy refusing and the old man saying he would beat him again. The boy got the rifle from the kitchen and shot him when he tried to come into the barn and when they came back to the ranch he'd been dead a week, frozen in the corral, and the dogs had eaten part of him. But what was left you packed on a sled wrapped in a blanket and roped on and you got the boy to help you haul it, and the two of you took it out over the road on skis, and sixty miles down to town to turn the boy over. He having no idea that he would be arrested. Thinking he had done his duty and that you were his friend and he would be rewarded. He'd helped to haul the old man in so everybody could know how bad the old man had been and how he'd tried to steal some feed that didn't belong to him, and when the sheriff put the handcuffs on the boy he couldn't believe it. Then he'd started to cry. That was one story he had saved to write. He knew at least twenty good stories from out there and he had never written one. Why?

"You tell them why," he said.

"Why what, dear?"

"Why nothing."

She didn't drink so much, now, since she had him. But if he lived he would never write about her, he knew that now. Nor about any of them. The rich were dull and they drank too much, or they played too much backgammon. They were dull and they were repetitious. He remembered poor Julian and his romantic awe of them and how he had started a story once that began, "The very rich are different from you and me." And how some one had said to Julian, Yes, they have more money. But that was not humorous to Julian. He thought they were a special glamourous race and when he found they weren't it wrecked him just as much as any other thing that wrecked him.

He had been contemptuous of those who wrecked. You did not have to like it because you understood it. He could beat anything, he thought, because no thing could hurt him if he did not care.

All right. Now he would not care for death. One thing he had always dreaded was the pain. He could stand pain as well as any

man, until it went on too long, and wore him out, but here he had
something that had hurt frightfully and just when he had felt it
breaking him, the pain had stopped.

*He remembered long ago when Williamson, the bombing officer,
had been hit by a stick bomb some one in a German patrol had
thrown as he was coming in through the wire that night and, screaming, had begged every one to kill him. He was a fat man, very brave,
and a good officer, although addicted to fantastic shows. But that
night he was caught in the wire, with a flare lighting him up and his
bowels spilled out into the wire, so when they brought him in, alive,
they had to cut him loose. Shoot me, Harry. For Christ sake shoot me.
They had had an argument one time about our Lord never sending
you anything you could not bear and some one's theory had been
that meant that at a certain time the pain passed you out automatically. But he had always remembered Williamson, that night. Nothing passed out Williamson until he gave him all his morphine tablets
that he had always saved to use himself and then they did not work
right away.*

Still this now, that he had, was very easy; and if it was no worse as
it went on there was nothing to worry about. Except that he would
rather be in better company.

He thought a little about the company that he would like to
have.

No, he thought, when everything you do, you do too long, and do
too late, you can't expect to find the people still there. The people all
are gone. The party's over and you are with your hostess now.

I'm getting as bored with dying as with everything else, he
thought.

"It's a bore," he said out loud.

"What is, my dear?"

"Anything you do too bloody long."

He looked at her face between him and the fire. She was leaning
back in the chair and the firelight shone on her pleasantly lined face
and he could see that she was sleepy. He heard the hyena make a
noise just outside the range of the fire.

"I've been writing," he said. "But I got tired."

"Do you think you will be able to sleep?"

"Pretty sure. Why don't you turn in?"

"I like to sit here with you."

"Do you feel anything strange?" he asked her.

"No. Just a little sleepy."

"I do," he said.

He had just felt death come by again.

"You know the only thing I've never lost is curiosity," he said to her.

"You've never lost anything. You're the most complete man I've ever known."

"Christ," he said. "How little a woman knows. What is that? Your intuition?"

Because, just then, death had come and rested its head on the foot of the cot and he could smell its breath.

"Never believe any of that about a scythe and a skull," he told her. "It can be two bicycle policemen as easily, or be a bird. Or it can have a wide snout like a hyena."

It had moved up on him now, but it had no shape any more. It simply occupied space.

"Tell it to go away."

It did not go away but moved a little closer.

"You've got a hell of a breath," he told it. "You stinking bastard."

It moved up closer to him still and now he could not speak to it, and when it saw he could not speak it came a little closer, and now he tried to send it away without speaking, but it moved in on him so its weight was all upon his chest, and while it crouched there and he could not move, or speak, he heard the woman say, "Bwana is asleep now. Take the cot up very gently and carry it into the tent."

He could not speak to tell her to make it go away and it crouched now, heavier, so he could not breathe. And then, while they lifted the cot, suddenly it was all right and the weight went from his chest.

It was morning and had been morning for some time and he heard the plane. It showed very tiny and then made a wide circle and the boys ran out and lit the fires, using kerosene, and piled on grass so there were two big smudges at each end of the level place and the morning breeze blew them toward the camp and the plane circled twice more, low this time, and then glided down and levelled off and landed smoothly and, coming walking toward him, was old Compton in slacks, a tweed jacket and a brown felt hat.

"What's the matter, old cock?" Compton said.

"Bad leg," he told him. "Will you have some breakfast?"

"Thanks. I'll just have some tea. It's the Puss Moth you know. I won't be able to take the Memsahib. There's only room for one. Your lorry is on the way."

Helen had taken Compton aside and was speaking to him. Compton came back more cheery than ever.

"We'll get you right in," he said. "I'll be back for the Mem. Now I'm afraid I'll have to stop at Arusha to refuel. We'd better get going."

"What about the tea?"

"I don't really care about it you know."

The boys had picked up the cot and carried it around the green tents and down along the rock and out onto the plain and along past the smudges that were burning brightly now, the grass all consumed, and the wind fanning the fire, to the little plane. It was difficult getting him in, but once in he lay back in the leather seat, and the leg was stuck straight out to one side of the seat where Compton sat. Compton started the motor and got in. He waved to Helen and to the boys and, as the clatter moved into the old familiar roar, they swung around with Compie watching for wart-hog holes and roared, bumping, along the stretch between the fires and with the last bump rose and he saw them all standing below, waving, and the camp beside the hill, flattening now, and the plain spreading, clumps of trees, and the bush flattening, while the game trails ran now smoothly to the dry waterholes, and there was a new water that he had never known of. The zebra, small rounded backs now, and the wildebeeste, big-headed dots seeming to climb as they moved in long fingers across the plain, now scattering as the shadow came toward them, they were tiny now, and the movement had no gallop, and the plain as far as you could see, gray-yellow now and ahead old Compie's tweed back and the brown felt hat. Then they were over the first hills and the wildebeeste were trailing up them, and then they were over mountains with sudden depths of green-rising forest and the solid bamboo slopes, and then the heavy forest again, sculptured into peaks and hollows until they crossed, and hills sloped down and then another plain, hot now, and purple brown, bumpy with heat and Compie looking back to see how he was riding. Then there were other mountains dark ahead.

And then instead of going on to Arusha they turned left, he evidently figured that they had the gas, and looking down he saw a pink sifting cloud, moving over the ground, and in the air, like the first snow in a blizzard, that comes from nowhere, and he knew the locusts were coming up from the South. Then they began to climb and they were going to the East it seemed, and then it darkened and they were in a storm, the rain so thick it seemed like flying through a waterfall, and then they were out and Compie turned his head and grinned and pointed and there, ahead, all he could see, as wide as all the world, great, high, and unbelievably white in the sun, was the square top of Kilimanjaro. And then he knew that there was where he was going.

Just then the hyena stopped whimpering in the night and started to make a strange, human, almost crying sound. The woman heard it and stirred uneasily. She did not wake. In her dream she was at the house on Long Island and it was the night before her daughter's début. Somehow her father was there and he had been very rude. Then the noise the hyena made was so loud she woke and for a moment she did not know where she was and she was very afraid. Then she took the flashlight and shone it on the other cot that they had carried in after Harry had gone to sleep. She could see his bulk under the mosquito bar but somehow he had gotten his leg out and it hung down alongside the cot. The dressings had all come down and she could not look at it.

"Molo," she called, "Molo! Molo!"

Then she said, "Harry, Harry!" Then her voice rising, "Harry! Please, Oh Harry!"

There was no answer and she could not hear him breathing.

Outside the tent the hyena made the same strange noise that had awakened her. But she did not hear him for the beating of her heart.

QUESTIONS

1. Discuss the motif of *pain* and *painlessness*. (See Preface, p. 20.)
2. This is a story about a man dying; like Iván Ilých he realizes how much of his life has been a sham, how much he has avoided. Develop the comparison between Hemingway's and Tolstoy's use of approaching death.
3. Harry has not written many things. Is his desire to write them the vanity of an unsuccessful writer?
4. Hemingway has often been accused of sexism. Is his portrayal of the woman sexist? (See Preface, pp. 5–11.)
5. What is the significance of the italicized passages? Examine their content. What do you find?
6. Discuss the motif of *lying* and *truth telling* in the story.
7. How does Hemingway communicate exposition? (See Preface, pp. 15–16.) Why is there so much of the *past* here? Why isn't it boring?
8. Write a parody of the dialogue Hemingway writes. (See Preface, pp. 21–24.) Describe the quality of the dialogue.
9. "There wasn't time, of course, although it seemed as though it telescoped so that you might put it all into one paragraph if you could get it right." What is *it*? Discuss Harry's wish here. If he could write it, what would he say?
10. Examine closely the story of Williamson, the officer whose bowels spilled out onto the barbed wire. What is the connection between that story and Harry's story?
11. What is the meaning of the *two* endings of the story? Compare to the double ending of "The Death of Iván Ilých." Why, if Harry's dying and stinking in the heat, should Hemingway end the story (the first ending) rising to the cool mountain, Kilimanjaro?

CONTEMPORARY FICTION

JOHN STEINBECK

(1902-1968)

Steinbeck lived out a number of American myths about the writer. Born in Salinas and growing up near Monterey, California, he wrote about this land in his fiction, including "The Chrysanthemums." He knew the people: fishermen, farmers, eccentrics, poor. He was himself fruit picker, caretaker, newspaperman, and his fiction reflects this experience. In the 1930's he published *Tortilla Flat, In Dubious Battle,* and *The Grapes of Wrath.* In *The Grapes of Wrath,* which made him famous, we identify with the Joad family, among the thousands who, forced off their dustbowl farms in the midwest and southwest, go to California in search of jobs. At the end, Tom Joad goes off to be a labor organizer. But while Steinbeck sympathized with the worker, he never became a Communist in the 1930's, and the party attacked his (generally sympathetic) description of a party-led strike in *In Dubious Battle.* It seems fair to say that Steinbeck was more concerned with the lonely, the outcast, the uprooted, than with social action. His later novels include *Cannery Row* and *East of Eden.* In 1962, six years before his death, Steinbeck was awarded the Nobel Prize for Literature.

[See Preface, pp. 10–11 (mixed angle of vision), p. 13 (conflict), p. 18 (imagery), p. 28 (vision).]

The Chrysanthemums

JOHN STEINBECK

The high grey-flannel fog of winter closed off the Salinas Valley from the sky and from all the rest of the world. On every side it sat like a lid on the mountains and made of the great valley a closed pot. On the broad, level land floor the gang plows bit deep and left the black earth shining like metal where the shares had cut. On the foothill ranches across the Salinas River, the yellow stubble fields seemed to be bathed in pale cold sunshine, but there was no sunshine in the valley now in December. The thick willow scrub along the river flamed with sharp and positive yellow leaves.

It was a time of quiet and of waiting. The air was cold and tender. A light wind blew up from the southwest so that the farmers were mildly hopeful of a good rain before long; but fog and rain do not go together.

Across the river, on Henry Allen's foothill ranch there was little work to be done, for the hay was cut and stored and the orchards were plowed up to receive the rain deeply when it should come. The cattle on the higher slopes were becoming shaggy and rough-coated.

Elisa Allen, working in her flower garden, looked down across the yard and saw Henry, her husband, talking to two men in business suits. The three of them stood by the tractor shed, each man with one foot on the side of the little Fordson. They smoked cigarettes and studied the machine as they talked.

Elisa watched them for a moment and then went back to her work. She was thirty-five. Her face was lean and strong and her eyes were as clear as water. Her figure looked blocked and heavy in her gardening costume, a man's black hat pulled low down over her eyes, clod-hopper shoes, a figured print dress almost completely covered by a big corduroy apron with four big pockets to hold the snips, the trowel and scratcher, the seeds and the knife she worked with. She wore heavy leather gloves to protect her hands while she worked.

She was cutting down the old year's chrysanthemum stalks with a pair of short and powerful scissors. She looked down toward the men by the tractor shed now and then. Her face was eager and mature and handsome; even her work with the scissors was over-eager, over-powerful. The chrysanthemum stems seemed too small and easy for her energy.

She brushed a cloud of hair out of her eyes with the back of her glove, and left a smudge of earth on the cheek in doing it. Behind her stood the neat white farm house with red geraniums close-banked around it as high as the windows. It was a hard-swept looking little house, with hard-polished windows, and a clean mud-mat on the front steps.

Elisa cast another glance toward the tractor shed. The strangers were getting into their Ford coupe. She took off a glove and put her strong fingers down into the forest of new green chrysanthemum sprouts that were growing around the old roots. She spread the leaves and looked down among the close-growing stems. No aphids were there, no sowbugs or snails or cutworms. Her terrier fingers destroyed such pests before they could get started.

Elisa started at the sound of her husband's voice. He had come near quietly, and he leaned over the wire fence that protected her flower garden from cattle and dogs and chickens.

"At it again," he said. "You've got a strong new crop coming."

Elisa straightened her back and pulled on the gardening glove again. "Yes. They'll be strong this coming year." In her tone and on her face there was a little smugness.

"You've got a gift with things," Henry observed. "Some of those yellow chrysanthemums you had this year were ten inches across. I wish you'd work out in the orchard and raise some apples that big."

Her eyes sharpened. "Maybe I could do it, too. I've a gift with things, all right. My mother had it. She could stick anything in the ground and make it grow. She said it was having planters' hands that knew how to do it."

"Well, it sure works with flowers," he said.

"Henry, who were those men you were talking to?"

"Why, sure, that's what I came to tell you. They were from the Western Meat Company. I sold those thirty head of three-year-old steers. Got nearly my own price, too."

"Good," she said. "Good for you."

"And I thought," he continued, "I thought how it's Saturday afternoon, and we might go to Salinas for dinner at a restaurant, and then to a picture show—to celebrate, you see."

"Good," she repeated. "Oh, yes. That will be good."

Henry put on his joking tone. "There's fights tonight. How'd you like to go to the fights?"

"Oh, no," she said breathlessly. "No, I wouldn't like fights."

"Just fooling, Elisa. We'll go to a movie. Let's see. It's two now. I'm going to take Scotty and bring down those steers from the hill. It'll take us maybe two hours. We'll go in town about five and have dinner at the Cominos Hotel. Like that?"

"Of course I'll like it. It's good to eat away from home."

"All right, then. I'll go get up a couple of horses."

She said, "I'll have plenty of time to transplant some of these sets, I guess."

She heard her husband calling Scotty down by the barn. And a little later she saw the two men ride up the pale yellow hillside in search of the steers.

There was a little square sandy bed kept for rooting the chrysanthemums. With her trowel she turned the soil over and over, and smoothed it and patted it firm. Then she dug ten parallel trenches to receive the sets. Back at the chrysanthemum bed she pulled out the little crisp shoots, trimmed off the leaves of each one with her scissors and laid it on a small orderly pile.

A squeak of wheels and plod of hoofs came from the road. Elisa looked up. The country road ran along the dense bank of willows and cottonwoods that bordered the river, and up this road came a curious vehicle, curiously drawn. It was an old spring-wagon, with a round canvas top on it like the cover of a prairie schooner. It was drawn by an old bay horse and a little grey-and-white burro. A big stubble-bearded man sat between the cover flaps and drove the crawling team. Underneath the wagon, between the hind wheels, a lean and rangy mongrel dog walked sedately. Words were painted on the canvas in clumsy, crooked letters. "Pots, pans, knives, sisors, lawn mores. Fixed." Two rows of articles and the triumphantly definitive "Fixed" below. The black paint had run down in little sharp points beneath each letter.

Elisa, squatting on the ground, watched to see the crazy, loose-jointed wagon pass by. But it didn't pass. It turned into the farm road in front of her house, crooked old wheels skirling and squeaking. The rangy dog darted from between the wheels and ran ahead. Instantly the two ranch shepherds flew out at him. Then all three stopped, and with stiff and quivering tails, with taut straight legs, with ambassadorial dignity, they slowly circled, sniffing daintily. The caravan pulled up to Elisa's wire fence and stopped. Now the newcomer dog, feeling outnumbered, lowered his tail and retired under the wagon with raised hackles and bared teeth.

The man on the wagon seat called out. "That's a bad dog in a fight when he gets started."

Elisa laughed. "I see he is. How soon does he generally get started?"

The man caught up her laughter and echoed it heartily. "Sometimes not for weeks and weeks," he said. He climbed stiffly down, over the wheel. The horse and the donkey drooped like unwatered flowers.

Elisa saw that he was a very big man. Although his hair and beard were greying, he did not look old. His worn black suit was wrinkled and spotted with grease. The laughter had disappeared from his face and eyes the moment his laughing voice ceased. His eyes were dark and they were full of the brooding that gets in the eyes of teamsters and of sailors. The calloused hands he rested on the wire fence were cracked, and every crack was a black line. He took off his battered hat.

"I'm off my general road, ma'am," he said. "Does this dirt road cut over across the river to the Los Angeles highway?"

Elisa stood up and shoved the thick scissors in her apron pocket. "Well, yes, it does, but it winds around and then fords the river. I don't think your team could pull through the sand."

He replied with some asperity, "It might surprise you what them beasts can pull through."

"When they get started?" she asked.

He smiled for a second. "Yes. When they get started."

"Well," said Elisa, "I think you'll save time if you go back to the Salinas road and pick up the highway there."

He drew a big finger down the chicken wire and made it sing. "I ain't in any hurry, ma'am. I go from Seattle to San Diego and back every year. Takes all my time. About six months each way. I aim to follow nice weather."

Elisa took off her gloves and stuffed them in the apron pocket with the scissors. She touched the under edge of her man's hat, searching for fugitive hairs. "That sounds like a nice kind of a way to live," she said.

He leaned confidentially over the fence. "Maybe you noticed the writing on my wagon. I mend pots and sharpen knives and scissors. You got any of them things to do?"

"Oh, no," she said quickly. "Nothing like that." Her eyes hardened with resistance.

"Scissors is the worst thing," he explained. "Most people just ruin scissors trying to sharpen 'em, but I know how. I got a special tool. It's a little bobbit kind of thing, and patented. But it sure does the trick."

"No. My scissors are all sharp."

"All right, then. Take a pot," he continued earnestly, "a bent pot, or a pot with a hole. I can make it like new so you don't have to buy no new ones. That's a saving for you."

"No," she said shortly. "I tell you I have nothing like that for you to do."

His face fell to an exaggerated sadness. His voice took on a whining undertone. "I ain't had a thing to do today. Maybe I won't have no supper tonight. You see I'm off my regular road. I know folks on the highway clear from Seattle to San Diego. They save their things for me to sharpen up because they know I do it so good and save them money."

"I'm sorry," Elisa said irritably. "I haven't anything for you to do."

His eyes left her face and fell to searching the ground. They roamed about until they came to the chrysanthemum bed where she had been working. "What's them plants, ma'am?"

The irritation and resistance melted from Elisa's face. "Oh, those are chrysanthemums, giant whites and yellows. I raise them every year, bigger than anybody around here."

"Kind of a long-stemmed flower? Looks like a quick puff of colored smoke?" he asked.

"That's it. What a nice way to describe them."

"They smell kind of nasty till you get used to them," he said.

"It's a good bitter smell," she retorted, "not nasty at all."

He changed his tone quickly. "I like the smell myself."

"I had ten-inch blooms this year," she said.

The man leaned farther over the fence. "Look. I know a lady down the road a piece, has got the nicest garden you ever seen. Got nearly every kind of flower but no chrysanthemums. Last time I was mending a copper-bottom washtub for her (that's a hard job but I do it good), she said to me, 'If you ever run acrost some nice chrysanthemums I wish you'd try to get me a few seeds.' That's what she told me."

Elisa's eyes grew alert and eager. "She couldn't have known much about chrysanthemums. You can raise them from seed, but it's much easier to root the little sprouts you see there."

"Oh," he said. "I s'pose I can't take none to her, then."

"Why yes you can," Elisa cried. "I can put some in damp sand, and you can carry them right along with you. They'll take root in the pot if you keep them damp. And then she can transplant them."

"She'd sure like to have some, ma'am. You say they're nice ones?"

"Beautiful," she said. "Oh, beautiful." Her eyes shone. She tore off the battered hat and shook out her dark pretty hair. "I'll put them in a flower pot, and you can take them right with you. Come into the yard."

While the man came through the picket gate Elisa ran excitedly along the geranium-bordered path to the back of the house. And she returned carrying a big red flower pot. The gloves were forgotten now. She kneeled on the ground by the starting bed and dug up the sandy soil with her fingers and scooped it into the bright new flower pot. Then she picked up the little pile of shoots she had prepared. With her strong fingers she pressed them into the sand and tamped around them with her knuckles. The man stood over her. "I'll tell you what to do," she said. "You remember so you can tell the lady."

"Yes, I'll try to remember."

"Well, look. These will take root in about a month. Then she must set them out, about a foot apart in good rich earth like this, see?" She lifted a handful of dark soil for him to look at. "They'll grow fast and tall. Now remember this. In July tell her to cut them down, about eight inches from the ground."

"Before they bloom?" he asked.

"Yes, before they bloom." Her face was tight with eagerness. "They'll grow right up again. About the last of September the buds will start."

She stopped and seemed perplexed. "It's the budding that takes the most care," she said hesitantly. "I don't know how to tell you." She looked deep into his eyes, searchingly. Her mouth opened a little, and she seemed to be listening. "I'll try to tell you," she said. "Did you ever hear of planting hands?"

"Can't say I have, ma'am."

"Well, I can only tell you what it feels like. It's when you're picking off the buds you don't want. Everything goes right down into your fingertips. You watch your fingers work. They do it themselves. You can feel how it is. They pick and pick the buds. They never make a mistake. They're with the plant. Do you see? Your fingers and the plant. You can feel that, right up your arm. They know. They never make a mistake. You can feel it. When you're like that you can't do anything wrong. Do you see that? Can you understand that?"

She was kneeling on the ground looking up at him. Her breast swelled passionately.

The man's eyes narrowed. He looked away self-consciously. "Maybe I know," he said. "Sometimes in the night in the wagon there—"

Elisa's voice grew husky. She broke in on him. "I've never lived as you do, but I know what you mean. When the night is dark—why, the stars are sharp-pointed, and there's quiet. Why, you rise up and up! Every pointed star gets driven into your body. It's like that. Hot and sharp and—lovely."

Kneeling there, her hand went out toward his legs in the greasy black trousers. Her hesitant fingers almost touched the cloth. Then her hand dropped to the ground. She crouched low like a fawning dog.

He said, "It's nice, just like you say. Only when you don't have no dinner, it ain't."

She stood up then, very straight, and her face was ashamed. She held the flower pot out to him and placed it gently in his arms. "Here. Put it in your wagon, on the seat, where you can watch it. Maybe I can find something for you to do."

At the back of the house she dug in the can pile and found two old and battered aluminum saucepans. She carried them back and gave them to him. "Here, maybe you can fix these."

His manner changed. He became professional. "Good as new I can fix them." At the back of his wagon he set a little anvil, and out of an oily tool box dug a small machine hammer. Elisa came through the gate to watch him while he pounded out the dents in the kettles. His mouth grew sure and knowing. At a difficult part of the work he sucked his under-lip.

"You sleep right in the wagon?" Elisa asked.

"Right in the wagon, ma'am. Rain or shine I'm dry as a cow in there."

"It must be nice," she said. "It must be very nice. I wish women could do such things."

"It ain't the right kind of a life for a woman."

Her upper lip raised a little, showing her teeth. "How do you know? How can you tell?" she said.

"I don't know ma'am," he protested. "Of course I don't know. Now here's your kettles, done. You don't have to buy no new ones."

"How much?"

"Oh, fifty cents'll do. I keep my prices down and my work good. That's why I have all them satisfied customers up and down the highway."

Elisa brought him a fifty-cent piece from the house and dropped it in his hand. "You might be surprised to have a rival some time. I can sharpen scissors, too. And I can beat the dents out of little pots. I could show you what a woman might do."

He put his hammer back in the oily box and shoved the little anvil out of sight. "It would be a lonely life for a woman, ma'am, and a scarey life, too, with animals creeping under the wagon all night." He climbed over the single-tree, steadying himself with a hand on the burro's white rump. He settled himself in the seat, picked up the lines. "Thank you kindly, ma'am," he said. "I'll do like you told me; I'll go back and catch the Salinas road."

"Mind," she called, "if you're long in getting there, keep the sand damp."

"Sand, ma'am? . . . Sand? Oh, sure. You mean round the chrysanthemums. Sure I will." He clucked his tongue. The beasts leaned luxuriously into their collars. The mongrel dog took his place between the back wheels. The wagon turned and crawled out the entrance road and back the way it had come, along the river.

Elisa stood in front of her wire fence watching the slow progress of the caravan. Her shoulders were straight, her head thrown back, her eyes half-closed, so that the scene came vaguely into them. Her lips moved silently, forming the words "Good-bye—good-bye." Then she whispered, "That's a bright direction. There's a glowing there." The sound of her whisper startled her. She shook herself free and looked about to see whether anyone had been listening. Only the dogs had heard. They lifted their heads toward her from their sleeping in the dust, and then stretched out their chins and settled asleep again. Elisa turned and ran hurriedly into the house.

In the kitchen she reached behind the stove and felt the water tank. It was full of hot water from the noonday cooking. In the bathroom she tore off her soiled clothes and flung them into the corner. And then she scrubbed herself with a little block of pumice, legs and thighs, loins and chest and arms, until her skin was scratched and red. When she had dried herself she stood in front of a mirror in her bedroom and looked at her body. She tightened her stomach and threw out her chest. She turned and looked over her shoulder at her back.

After a while she began to dress, slowly. She put on her newest under-clothing and her nicest stockings and the dress which was the symbol of her prettiness. She worked carefully on her hair, pencilled her eyebrows and rouged her lips.

Before she was finished she heard the little thunder of hoofs and the shouts of Henry and his helper as they drove the red steers into the corral. She heard the gate bang shut and set herself for Henry's arrival.

His step sounded on the porch. He entered the house calling "Elisa, where are you?"

"In my room, dressing. I'm not ready. There's hot water for your bath. Hurry up. It's getting late."

When she heard him splashing in the tub, Elisa laid his dark suit on the bed, and shirt and socks and tie beside it. She stood his polished shoes on the floor beside the bed. Then she went to the porch and sat primly and stiffly down. She looked toward the river road where the willow-line was still yellow with frosted leaves so that under the high grey fog they seemed a thin band of sunshine. This was the only color in the grey afternoon. She sat unmoving for a long time. Her eyes blinked rarely.

Henry came banging out of the door, shoving his tie inside his vest as he came. Elisa stiffened and her face grew tight. Henry stopped short and looked at her. "Why—why, Elisa. You look so nice!"

"Nice? You think I look nice? What do you mean by 'nice?' "

Henry blundered on. "I don't know. I mean you look different, strong and happy."

"I am strong? Yes, strong. What do you mean 'strong?' "

He looked bewildered. "You're playing some kind of a game," he said helplessly. "It's a kind of a play. You look strong enough to break a calf over your knee, happy enough to eat it like watermelon."

For a second she lost her rigidity. "Henry! Don't talk like that. You didn't know what you said." She grew complete again. "I'm strong," she boasted. "I never knew before how strong."

Henry looked down toward the tractor shed, and when he brought his eyes back to her, they were his own again. "I'll get out the car. You can put on your coat while I'm starting."

Elisa went into the house. She heard him drive to the gate and idle down his motor, and then she took a long time to put on her hat. She pulled it here and pressed it there. When Henry turned the motor off she slipped into her coat and went out.

The little roadster bounced along on the dirt road by the river, raising the birds and driving the rabbits into the brush. Two cranes flapped heavily over the willow-line and dropped into the river-bed.

Far ahead on the road Elisa saw a dark speck. She knew.

She tried not to look as they passed it, but her eyes would not obey. She whispered to herself sadly. "He might have thrown them off the road. That wouldn't have been much trouble, not very much. But he kept the pot," she explained. "He had to keep the pot. That's why he couldn't get them off the road."

The roadster turned a bend and she saw the caravan ahead. She swung full around toward her husband so she could not see the little covered wagon and the mismatched team as the car passed them.

In a moment it was over. The thing was done. She did not look back. She said loudly, to be heard above the motor, "It will be good, tonight, a good dinner."

"Now you're changed again," Henry complained. He took one hand from the wheel and patted her knee. "I ought to take you in to dinner oftener. It would be good for both of us. We get so heavy out on the ranch."

"Henry," she asked, "could we have wine at dinner?"

"Sure we could. Say! That will be fine."

She was silent for a little while; then she said, "Henry, at those prize fights, do the men hurt each other very much?"

"Sometimes a little, not often. Why?"

"Well, I've read how they break noses, and blood runs down their chests. I've read how the fighting gloves get heavy and soggy with blood."

He looked around at her. "What's the matter, Elisa? I didn't know you read things like that." He brought the car to a stop, then turned to the right over the Salinas River bridge.

"Do any women ever go to the fights?" she asked.

"Oh, sure, some. What's the matter, Elisa? Do you want to go? I don't think you'd like it, but I'll take you if you really want to go."

She relaxed limply in the seat. "Oh, no. No. I don't want to go. I'm sure I don't." Her face was turned away from him. "It will be enough if we can have wine. It will be plenty." She turned up her coat collar so he could not see that she was crying weakly—like an old woman.

RICHARD WRIGHT

(1906-1960)

Born in Mississippi in 1908, Wright grew up with his mother after his father deserted the family. He was trouble as a child: at five, angry at his mother, bored, and frustrated, he touched a flaming straw to the window curtains and burned down his cabin. In one sense it was an accident, the result of ignorance and curiosity; in another sense it was Wright's first act of rebellion. At his grandparents' home he was willful and rebellious, refusing to learn the lesson of "humility" that permitted blacks in the South to survive. He came north to Chicago in 1928, joined the Communist party, and wrote regularly in party publications. "Bright and Morning Star" comes from *Uncle Tom's Children* (1938), which won him a reputation. In 1940 a much more brutal, even more powerful work, *Native Son,* was published, a novel in which his anger was fully expressed for the first time. His autobiography, *Black Boy,* appeared in 1955. By now he had left the Communist party and was mistrusted by Communists as well as by reactionary whites in the United States. From 1947 until his death in 1960 he was an exile in Paris, where he wrote *The Outsider* and works on Pan Africanism and black power. Wright is one of the greatest American writers of this century and the spiritual father of many black writers who followed him.

Bright and Morning Star

RICHARD WRIGHT

I

She stood with her black face some six inches from the moist windowpane and wondered when on earth would it ever stop raining. It might keep up like this all week, she thought. She heard rain
droning upon the roof and high up in the wet sky her eyes followed
the silent rush of a bright shaft of yellow that swung from the
airplane beacon in far off Memphis. Momently she could see it
cutting through the rainy dark; it would hover a second like a
gleaming sword above her head, then vanish. She sighed, troubling,
Johnny-Boys been trampin in this slop all day wid no decent shoes on
his feet. . . . Through the window she could see the rich black earth
sprawling outside in the night. There was more rain than the clay
could soak up; pools stood everywhere. She yawned and mumbled:
"Rains good n bad. It kin make seeds bus up thu the ground, er it
kin bog things down lika watah-soaked coffin." Her hands were
folded loosely over her stomach and the hot air of the kitchen traced
a filmy vein of sweat on her forehead. From the cook stove came the
soft singing of burning wood and now and then a throaty bubble
rose from a pot of simmering greens.

"Shucks, Johnny-Boy coulda let somebody else do all tha runnin
in the rain. Theres others bettah fixed fer it than he is. But, naw!
Johnny-Boy ain the one t trust nobody t do nothin. Hes gotta do it
all hissef. . . ."

She glanced at a pile of damp clothes in a zinc tub. Waal, Ah
bettah git t work. She turned, lifted a smoothing iron with a thick
pad of cloth, touched a spit-wet finger to it with a quick, jerking
motion: *smiiitz!* Yeah; its hot! Stooping, she took a blue work-shirt
from the tub and shook it out. With a deft twist of her shoulders she
caught the iron in her right hand; the fingers of her left hand took a
piece of wax from a tin box and a frying sizzle came as she smeared
the bottom. She was thinking of nothing now; her hands followed a
life-long ritual of toil. Spreading a sleeve, she ran the hot iron to and
fro until the wet cloth became stiff. She was deep in the midst of her
work when a song rose up out of the far off days of her childhood and
broke through half-parted lips:

> Hes the Lily of the Valley, the Bright n Mawnin Star
> Hes the Fairest of Ten Thousan t ma soul . . .

A gust of wind dashed rain against the window. Johnny-Boy oughta c mon home n eat his suppah. Aw, Lawd! Itd be fine ef Sug could eat wid us tonight! Itd be like ol times! Mabbe aftah all it wont be long fo he comes back. Tha lettah Ah got from im last week said *Don give up hope.* . . . Yeah; we gotta live in hope. Then both of her sons, Sug and Johnny-Boy, would be back with her.

With an involuntary nervous gesture, she stopped and stood still, listening. But the only sound was the lulling fall of rain. Shucks, ain no usa me ackin this way, she thought. Ever time they gits ready to hol them meetings Ah gits jumpity. Ah been a lil scared ever since Sug went t jail. She heard the clock ticking and looked. Johnny-Boys a *hour* late! He sho must be havin a time doin all tha trampin, trampin thu the mud. . . . But her fear was a quiet one; it was more like an intense brooding than a fear; it was a sort of hugging of hated facts so closely that she could feel their grain, like letting cold water run over her hand from a faucet on a winter morning.

She ironed again, faster now, as if she felt the more she engaged her body in work the less she would think. But how could she forget Johnny-Boy out there on those wet fields rounding up white and black Communists for a meeting tomorrow? And that was just what Sug had been doing when the sheriff had caught him, beat him, and tried to make him tell who and where his comrades were. Po Sug! They sho musta beat the boy somethin awful! But, thank Gawd, he didnt talk! He ain no weaklin, Sug ain! Hes been lion-hearted all his life long.

That had happened a year ago. And now each time those meetings came around the old terror surged back. While shoving the iron a cluster of toiling days returned; days of washing and ironing to feed Johnny-Boy and Sug so they could do party work; days of carrying a hundred pounds of white folks' clothes upon her head across fields sometimes wet and sometimes dry. But in those days a hundred pounds was nothing to carry carefully balanced upon her head while stepping by instinct over the corn and cotton rows. The only time it had seemed heavy was when she had heard of Sug's arrest. She had been coming home one morning with a bundle upon her head, her hands swinging idly by her sides, walking slowly with her eyes in front of her, when Bob, Johnny-Boy's pal, had called from across the fields and had come and told her that the sheriff had got Sug. That morning the bundle had become heavier than she could ever remember.

And with each passing week now, though she spoke of it to no one, things were becoming heavier. The tubs of water and the smoothing iron and the bundles of clothes were becoming harder to lift, with her back aching so; and her work was taking longer, all because Sug was gone and she didn't know just when Johnny-Boy would be taken too. To ease the ache of anxiety that was swelling her heart, she hummed, then sang softly:

> He walks wid me, He talks wid me
> He tells me Ahm His own. . . .

Guiltily, she stopped and smiled. *Looks like Ah jus cant seem t fergit them ol songs, no mattah how hard Ah tries.* . . . She had learned them when she was a little girl living and working on a farm. Every Monday morning from the corn and cotton fields the slow strains had floated from her mother's lips, lonely and haunting; and later, as the years had filled with gall, she had learned their deep meaning. Long hours of scrubbing floors for a few cents a day had taught her who Jesus was, what a great boon it was to cling to Him, to be like Him and suffer without a mumbling word. She had poured the yearning of her life into the songs, feeling buoyed with a faith beyond this world. The figure of the Man nailed in agony to the Cross, His burial in a cold grave, His transfigured Resurrection, His being breath and clay, God and Man—all had focused her feelings upon an imagery which had swept her life into a wondrous vision.

But as she had grown older, a cold white mountain, the white folks and their laws, had swum into her vision and shattered her songs and their spell of peace. To her that white mountain was temptation, something to lure her from her Lord, a part of the world God had made in order that she might endure it and come through all the stronger, just as Christ had risen with greater glory from the tomb. The days crowded with trouble had enhanced her faith and she had grown to love hardship with a bitter pride; she had obeyed the laws of the white folks with a soft smile of secret knowing.

After her mother had been snatched up to heaven in a chariot of fire, the years had brought her a rough workingman and two black babies, Sug and Johnny-Boy, all three of whom she had wrapped in the charm and magic of her vision. Then she was tested by no less than God; her man died, a trial which she bore with the strength shed by the grace of her vision; finally even the memory of her man faded into the vision itself, leaving her with two black boys growing tall, slowly into manhood.

Then one day grief had come to her heart when Johnny-Boy and Sug had walked forth demanding their lives. She had sought to fill their eyes with her vision, but they would have none of it. And she had wept when they began to boast of the strength shed by a new and terrible vision.

But she had loved them, even as she loved them now; bleeding, her heart had followed them. She could have done no less, being an old woman in a strange world. And day by day her sons had ripped from her startled eyes her old vision, and image by image had given her a new one, different, but great and strong enough to fling her into the light of another grace. The wrongs and sufferings of black men had taken the place of Him nailed to the Cross; the meager beginnings of the party had become another Resurrection; and the hate of those who would destroy her new faith had quickened in her a hunger to feel how deeply her new strength went.

"Lawd, Johnny-Boy," she would sometimes say, "Ah just wan them white folks t try t make me tell *who* is *in* the party n who *ain!* Ah jus wan em t try, Ahll show em somethin they never thought a black woman could have!"

But sometimes like tonight, while lost in the forgetfulness of work, the past and the present would become mixed in her; while toiling under a strange star for a new freedom the old songs would slip from her lips with their beguiling sweetness.

The iron was getting cold. She put more wood into the fire, stood again at the window and watched the yellow blade of light cut through the wet darkness. *Johnny-Boy ain here yit* . . . Then, before she was aware of it, she was still, listening for sounds. Under the drone of rain she heard the slosh of feet in mud. *Tha ain Johnny-Boy.* She knew his long, heavy footsteps in a million. She heard feet come on the porch. *Some woman.* . . . She heard bare knuckles knock three times, then once. *Thas some of them comrades!* She unbarred the door, cracked it a few inches, and flinched from the cold rush of damp wind.

"Whos tha?"

"Its me!"

"Who?"

"Me, Reva!"

She flung the door open.

"Lawd, chile, c mon in!"

She stepped to one side and a thin, blond-haired white girl ran through the door; as she slid the bolt she heard the girl gasping and shaking her wet clothes. *Somethings wrong! Reva wouldna walked a mil t mah house in all this slop fer nothin! That gals stuck onto Johnny-Boy. Ah wondah ef anythin happened t im?*

"Git on inter the kitchen, Reva, where its warm."

"Lawd, Ah sho is wet!"

"How yuh reckon yuhd be, in all tha rain?"

"Johnny-Boy ain here *yit?*" asked Reva.

"Naw! N ain no usa yuh worryin bout im. Jus yuh git them shoes off! Yuh wanna ketch vo deatha col?" She stood looking absently.

Yeah; its somethin about the party er Johnny-Boy thas gone wrong. Lawd, Ah wondah ef her pa knows how she feels bout Johnny-Boy?

"Honey, yuh hadn't oughta come out in sloppy weather like this."

"Ah had t come, An Sue."

She led Reva to the kitchen.

"Git them shoes off n git close t the stove so yuhll git dry!"

"An Sue, Ah got somethin t tell yuh . . ."

The words made her hold her breath. Ah bet its somethin bout Johnny-Boy!

"Whut, honey?"

"The sheriff wuz by our house tonight. He come t see pa."

"Yeah?"

"He done got word from somewheres bout tha meetin tomorrow."

"Is it Johnny-Boy, Reva?"

"Aw, naw, An Sue! Ah ain hearda word bout im. Ain yuh seen im tonight?"

"He ain come home t eat yit."

"Where kin he be?"

"Lawd knows, chile."

"Somebodys gotta tell them comrades that meetins off," said Reva. "The sheriffs got men watchin our house. Ah had t slip out t git here widout em followin me."

"Reva?"

"Hunh?"

"Ahma ol woman n Ah wans yuh t tell me the truth."

"Whut, An Sue?"

"Yuh ain tryin t fool me, is yuh?"

"*Fool* yuh?"

"Bout Johnny-Boy?"

"Lawd, naw, An Sue!"

"Ef theres anythin wrong jus tell me, chile. Ah kin stan it."

She stood by the ironing board, her hands as usual folded loosely over her stomach, watching Reva pull off her water-clogged shoes. She was feeling that Johnny-Boy was already lost to her; she was feeling the pain that would come when she knew it for certain; and she was feeling that she would have to be brave and bear it. She was like a person caught in a swift current of water and knew where the water was sweeping her and did not want to go on but had to go on to the end.

"It ain nothin bout Johnny-Boy, An Sue," said Reva. "But we gotta do somethin er we'll all git inter trouble."

"How the sheriff know about tha meetin?"

"Thas whut pa wants t know."

"Somebody done turned Judas."

"Sho looks like it."

"Ah bet it wuz some of them new ones," she said.

"Its hard t tell," said Reva.

"Lissen, Reva, yuh oughta stay here n git dry, but yuh bettah git back n tell yo pa Johnny-Boy ain here n Ah don know when hes gonna show up. *Some*bodys gotta tell them comrades t stay erway from yo pas house."

She stood with her back to the window, looking at Reva's wide, blue eyes. Po critter! Gotta go back thu all tha slop! Though she felt sorry for Reva, not once did she think that it would not have to be done. Being a woman, Reva was not suspect; she would *have* to go. It was just as natural for Reva to go back through the cold rain as it was for her to iron night and day, or for Sug to be in jail. Right now, Johnny-Boy was out there on those dark fields trying to get home. Lawd, don let em git im tonight! In spite of herself her feelings became torn. She loved her son and, loving him, she loved what he was trying to do. Johnny-Boy was happiest when he was working for the party, and her love for him was for his happiness. She frowned, trying hard to fit something together in her feelings: for her to try to stop Johnny-Boy was to admit that all the toil of years meant nothing; and to let him go meant that sometime or other he would be caught, like Sug. In facing it this way she felt a little stunned, as though she had come suddenly upon a blank wall in the dark. But outside in the rain were people, white and black, whom she had known all her life. Those people depended upon Johnny-Boy, loved him and looked to him as a man and leader. Yeah; hes gotta keep on; he cant stop now. . . . She looked at Reva; she was crying and pulling her shoes back on with reluctant fingers.

"Whut yuh carryin on tha way fer, chile?"

"Yuh done los Sug, now yuh sendin Johnny-Boy . . ."

"Ah got t, honey."

She was glad she could say that. Reva believed in black folks and not for anything in the world would she falter before her. In Reva's trust and acceptance of her she had found her first feelings of humanity; Reva's love was her refuge from shame and degradation. If in the early days of her life the white mountain had driven her back from the earth, then in her last days Reva's love was drawing her toward it, like the beacon that swung through the night outside. She heard Reva sobbing.

"Hush, honey!"

"Mah brothers in jail too! Ma cries ever day . . ."

"Ah know, honey."

She helped Reva with her coat; her fingers felt the scant flesh of the girl's shoulders. She don git ernuff t eat, she thought. She slipped her arms around Reva's waist and held her close for a moment.

"Now, yuh stop that cryin."

"A-a-ah c-c-cant hep it. . . ."

"Everythingll be awright; Johnny-Boyll be back."

"Yuh think so?"

"Sho, chile. Cos he will."

Neither of them spoke again until they stood in the doorway. Outside they could hear water washing through the ruts of the street.

"Be sho n send Johnny-Boy t tell the folks t stay erway from pas house," said Reva.

"Ahll tell im. Don yuh worry."

"Good-bye!"

"Good-bye!"

Leaning against the door jamb, she shook her head slowly and watched Reva vanish through the falling rain.

II

She was back at her board, ironing, when she heard feet sucking in the mud of the back yard; feet she knew from long years of listening were Johnny-Boy's. But tonight, with all the rain and fear, his coming was like a leaving, was almost more than she could bear. Tears welled to her eyes and she blinked them away. She felt that he was coming so that she could give him up; to see him now was to say good-bye. But it was a good-bye she knew she could never say; they were not that way toward each other. All day long they could sit in the same room and not speak; she was his mother and he was her son. Most of the time a nod or a grunt would carry all the meaning that she wanted to convey to him, or he to her. She did not even turn her head when she heard him come stomping into the kitchen. She heard him pull up a chair, sit, sigh, and draw off his muddy shoes; they fell to the floor with heavy thuds. Soon the kitchen was full of the scent of his drying socks and his burning pipe. Tha boys hongry! She paused and looked at him over her shoulder; he was puffing at his pipe with his head tilted back and his feet propped up on the edge of the stove; his eyelids drooped and his wet clothes steamed from the heat of the fire. Lawd, tha boy gits mo like his pa ever day he lives, she mused, her lips breaking in a slow, faint smile. Hols tha pipe in his mouth just like his pa usta hol his. Wondah how they woulda got erlong ef his pa hada lived? They oughta liked each other, they so mucha like. She wished there could have been other children besides Sug, so Johnny-Boy would not have to be so much alone. A man needs a woman by his side. . . . She thought of Reva; she liked Reva; the brightest glow her heart had ever known was when she had learned that Reva loved Johnny-Boy. But beyond Reva were cold white faces. Ef theys caught it means *death*. . . . She jerked around when she heard Johnny-Boy's pipe clatter to the floor. She saw him pick it up, smile sheepishly at her, and wag his head.

"Gawd, Ahm sleepy," he mumbled.

She got a pillow from her room and gave it to him.

"Here," she said.

"Hunh," he said, putting the pillow between his head and the back of the chair.

They were silent again. Yes, she would have to tell him to go back out into the cold rain and slop; maybe to get caught; maybe for the last time; she didn't know. But she would let him eat and get dry before telling him that the sheriff knew of the meeting to be held at Lem's tomorrow. And she would make him take a big dose of soda before he went out; soda always helped to stave off a cold. She looked at the clock. It was eleven. Theres time yit. Spreading a newspaper on the apron of the stove, she placed a heaping plate of greens upon it, a knife, a fork, a cup of coffee, a slab of cornbread, and a dish of peach cobbler.

"Yo suppahs ready," she said.

"Yeah," he said.

He did not move. She ironed again. Presently, she heard him eating. When she could no longer hear his knife tinkling against the edge of the plate, she knew he was through. It was almost twelve now. She would let him rest a little while longer before she told him. Till one er'clock, mabbe. Hes so tired. . . . She finished her ironing, put away the board, and stacked the clothes in her dresser drawer. She poured herself a cup of black coffee, drew up a chair, sat down and drank.

"Yuh almos dry," she said, not looking around.

"Yeah," he said, turning sharply to her.

The tone of voice in which she had spoken had let him know that more was coming. She drained her cup and waited a moment longer.

"Reva wuz here."

"Yeah?"

"She lef bout a hour ergo."

"Whut she say?"

"She said ol man Lem hada visit from the sheriff today."

"Bout the meetin?"

She saw him stare at the coals glowing red through the crevices of the stove and run his fingers nervously through his hair. She knew he was wondering how the sheriff had found out. In the silence he would ask a wordless question and in the silence she would answer wordlessly. Johnny-Boys too trustin, she thought. Hes trying t make the party big n hes takin in folks fastern he kin git t know em. You cant trust ever white man yuh meet. . . .

"Yuh know, Johnny-Boy, yuh been takin in a lotta them white folks lately . . ."

"Aw, ma!"

"But, Johnny-Boy . . ."

"Please, dont talk t me bout tha now, ma."

"Yuh ain t ol t lissen n learn, son," she said.

"Ah know whut yuh gonna say, ma. N yuh wrong. Yuh cant judge folks just by how yuh feel bout em n by how long yuh done knowed em. Ef we start that we wouldnt have *no*body in the party. When folks pledge they word t be with us, then we gotta take em in. Wes too weak to be choosy."

He rose abruptly, rammed his hands into his pockets, and stood facing the window; she looked at his back in a long silence. She knew his faith; it was deep. He had always said that black men could not fight the rich bosses alone; a man could not fight with every hand against him. But he believes so hard hes blind, she thought. At odd times they had had these arguments before; always she would be pitting her feelings against the hard necessity of his thinking, and always she would lose. She shook her head. Po Johnny-Boy; he don know . . .

"But ain nona our folks tol, Johnny-Boy," she said.

"How yuh know?" he asked. His voice came low and with a tinge of anger. He still faced the window and now and then the yellow blade of light flicked across the sharp outline of his black face.

"Cause Ah know em," she said.

"*Any*body mighta tol," he said.

"It wuznt nona *our* folks," she said again.

She saw his hand sweep in a swift arc of disgust.

"*Our* folks! Ma, who in Gawds name is *our* folks?"

"The folks we wuz born n raised wid, son. The folks we *know!*"

"We cant make the party grow tha way, ma."

"It mighta been Booker," she said.

"Yuh don know."

". . . er Blattberg . . ."

"Fer Chrissakes!"

". . . er any of the fo-five others whut joined las week."

"Ma, yuh jus don wan me t go out tonight," he said.

"Yo ol ma wans yuh t be careful, son."

"Ma, when yuh start doubtin folks in the party, then there ain no end."

"Son, Ah knows ever black man n woman in this parta the county," she said, standing too. "Ah watched em grow up; Ah even heped birth n nurse some of em; Ah knows em *all* from way back. There ain none of em that *coulda* tol! The folks Ah know jus don open

they dos n ast death t walk in! Son, it wuz some of them *white* folks!
Yuh just mark mah word n wait n see!"

"Why is it gotta be *white* folks?" he asked. "Ef they tol, then theys
jus Judases, thas all."

"Son, look at whuts befo yuh."

He shook his head and sighed.

"Ma, Ah done tol yuh a hundred times. Ah cant see white n Ah
cant see black," he said. "Ah sees rich men n Ah sees po men."

She picked up his dirty dishes and piled them in a pan. Out of the
corners of her eyes she saw him sit and pull on his wet shoes. Hes
goin! When she put the last dish away he was standing fully dressed,
warming his hands over the stove. Jus a few mo minutes now n hell
be gone, like Sug, mabbe. Her throat tightened. This black mans
fight takes *ever*thin! Looks like Gawd put us in this world jus t beat
us down!

"Keep this, ma," he said.

She saw a crumpled wad of money in his outstretched fingers.

"Naw, yuh keep it. Yuh might need it."

"It ain mine, ma. It berlongs t the party."

"But, Johnny-Boy, yuh might hafta go erway!"

"Ah kin make out."

"Don fergit yosef too much, son."

"Ef Ah don come back theyll need it."

He was looking at her face and she was looking at the money.

"Yuh keep tha," she said slowly. "Ahll give em the money."

"From where?"

"Ah got some."

"Where yuh git it from?"

She sighed.

"Ah been savin a dollah a week fer Sug ever since hes been in
jail."

"Lawd, ma!"

She saw the look of puzzled love and wonder in his eyes. Clumsily,
he put the money back into his pocket.

"Ahm gone," he said.

"Here; drink this glass of soda watah."

She watched him drink, then put the glass away.

"Waal," he said.

"Take the stuff outta yo pockets!"

She lifted the lid of the stove and he dumped all the papers from
his pocket into the fire. She followed him to the door and made him
turn around.

"Lawd, yuh tryin to maka revolution n yuh cant even keep yo coat
buttoned." Her nimble fingers fastened his collar high around his
throat. "There!"

He pulled the brim of his hat low over his eyes. She opened the door and with the suddenness of the cold gust of wind that struck her face, he was gone. She watched the black fields and the rain take him, her eyes burning. When the last faint footstep could no longer be heard, she closed the door, went to her bed, lay down, and pulled the cover over her while fully dressed. Her feelings coursed with the rhythm of the rain: Hes gone! Lawd, Ah *knows* hes gone! Her blood felt cold.

III

She was floating in a grey void somewhere between sleeping and dreaming and then suddenly she was wide awake, hearing and feeling in the same instant the thunder of the door crashing in and a cold wind filling the room. It was pitch black and she stared, resting on her elbows, her mouth open, not breathing, her ears full of the sound of tramping feet and booming voices. She knew at once: They lookin fer im! Then, filled with her will, she was on her feet, rigid, waiting, listening.

"The lamps burnin!"

"Yuh see her?"

"Naw!"

"Look in the kitchen!"

"Gee, this place smells like niggers!"

"Say, somebodys here er been here!"

"Yeah; theres fire in the stove!"

"Mabbe hes been here n gone?"

"Boy, look at these jars of jam!"

"Niggers make good jam!"

"Git some bread!"

"Heres some cornbread!"

"Say, lemme git some!"

"Take it easy! Theres plenty here!"

"Ahma take some of this stuff home!"

"Look, heres a pota greens!"

"N some hot cawffee!"

"Say, yuh guys! C mon! Cut it out! We didn't come here fer a feas!"

She walked slowly down the hall. They lookin fer im, but they ain got im yit! She stopped in the doorway, her gnarled, black hands as always folded over her stomach, but tight now, so tightly the veins bulged. The kitchen was crowded with white men in glistening raincoats. Though the lamp burned, their flashlights still glowed in red fists. Across her floor she saw the muddy tracks of their boots.

"Yuh white folks git outta mah house!"

There was a quick silence; every face turned toward her. She saw a sudden movement, but did not know what it meant until something hot and wet slammed her squarely in the face. She gasped, but did not move. Cálmly, she wiped the warm, greasy liquor of greens from her eyes with her left hand. One of the white men had thrown a handful of greens out of the pot at her.

"How they taste, ol bitch?"

"Ah ast yuh t git outta mah house!"

She saw the sheriff detach himself from the crowd and walk toward her.

"Now, Anty . . ."

"White man, don yuh *Ant*y me!"

"Yuh ain got the right sperit!"

"Sperit hell! Yuh git these men outta mah house!"

"Yuh ack like yuh don like it!"

"Naw, Ah don like it, n yuh knows dam waal Ah don!"

"What yuh gonna do about it?"

"Ahm telling yuh t git outta mah house!"

"Gittin sassy?"

"Ef telling yuh t git outta mah house is sass, then Ahm sassy!"

Her words came in a tense whisper; but beyond, back of them, she was watching, thinking, judging the men.

"Listen, Anty," the sheriff's voice came soft and low. "Ahm here t hep yuh. How come yuh wanna ack this way?"

"Yuh ain never heped yo *own* sef since yuh been born," she flared. "How kin the likes of yuh hep me?"

One of the white men came forward and stood directly in front of her.

"Lissen, nigger woman, yuh talkin t *white* men!"

"Ah don care who Ahm talkin t!"

"Yuhll wish some day yuh did!"

"Not t the likes of yuh!"

"Yuh need somebody t teach yuh how t be a good nigger!"

"*Yuh* cant teach it t me!"

"Yuh gonna change yo tune."

"Not longs mah bloods warm!"

"Don git smart now!"

"Yuh git outta mah house!"

"Spose we don go?" the sheriff asked.

They were crowded around her. She had not moved since she had taken her place in the doorway. She was thinking only of Johnny-Boy as she stood there giving and taking words; and she knew that they, too, were thinking of Johnny-Boy. She knew they wanted him, and her heart was daring them to take him from her.

"Spose we don go?" the sheriff asked again.

"Twenty of yuh runnin over one ol woman! Now, ain yuh white men glad yuh so brave?"

The sheriff grabbed her arm.

"C mon, now! Yuh don did ernuff sass fer one night. Wheres tha nigger son of yos?"

"Don yuh wished yuh knowed?"

"Yuh wanna git slapped?"

"Ah ain never seen one of yo kind that wuznt too low fer . . ."

The sheriff slapped her straight across her face with his open palm. She fell back against a wall and sank to her knees.

"Is tha whut white men do t nigger women?"

She rose slowly and stood again, not even touching the place that ached from his blow, her hands folded over her stomach.

"Ah ain never seen one of yo kind tha wuznt too low fer . . ."

He slapped her again; she reeled backward several feet and fell on her side.

"Is tha whut we too low t do?"

She stood before him again, dry-eyed, as though she had not been struck. Her lips were numb and her chin was wet with blood.

"Aw, let her go! Its the nigger we wan!" said one.

"Wheres that nigger son of yos?" the sheriff asked.

"Find im," she said.

"By Gawd, ef we hafta find im well kill im!"

"He wont be the only nigger yuh ever killed," she said.

She was consumed with a bitter pride. There was nothing on this earth, she felt then, that they could not do to her but that she could take. She stood on a narrow plot of ground from which she would die before she was pushed. And then it was, while standing there feeling warm blood seeping down her throat, that she gave up Johnny-Boy, gave him up to the white folks. She gave him up because they had come tramping into her heart demanding him, thinking they could get him by beating her, thinking they could scare her into making her tell where he was. She gave him up because she wanted them to know that they could not get what they wanted by bluffing and killing.

"Wheres this meetin gonna be?" the sheriff asked.

"Don yuh wish yuh knowed?"

"Ain there gonna be a meetin?"

"How come yuh astin me?"

"There *is* gonna be a meetin," said the sheriff.

"Is it?"

"Ah gotta great mind t choke it outta yuh!"

"Yuh so smart," she said.

"We ain playing wid yuh!"

"Did Ah say yuh wuz?"

"Tha nigger son of yos is erroun here somewheres n Ah aim to find im," said the sheriff. "Ef yuh tell us where he is n ef he talks, mabbe hell git off easy. But ef we hafta find im, well kill im! Ef we hafta find im, then yuh git a sheet t put over im in the mawnin, see? Git yuh a sheet, cause hes gonna be dead!"

"He wont be the only nigger yuh ever killed," she said again.

The sheriff walked past her. The others followed. Yuh didnt git whut yuh wanted! she thought exultingly. N yuh ain gonna *never* git it! Hotly, something ached in her to make them feel the intensity of her pride and freedom; her heart groped to turn the bitter hours of her life into words of a kind that would make them feel that she had taken all they had done to her in stride and could still take more. Her faith surged so strongly in her she was all but blinded. She walked behind them to the door, knotting and twisting her fingers. She saw them step to the muddy ground. Each whirl of the yellow beacon revealed glimpses of slanting rain. Her lips moved, then she shouted:

"Yuh didnt git whut yuh wanted! N yuh ain gonna nevah git it!"

The sheriff stopped and turned; his voice came low and hard.

"Now, by Gawd, thas ernuff outta yuh!"

"Ah know when Ah done said ernuff!"

"Aw, naw, yuh don!" he said. "Yuh don know when yuh done said ernuff, but Ahma teach yuh ternight!"

He was up the steps and across the porch with one bound. She backed into the hall, her eyes full on his face.

"Tell me when yuh gonna stop talkin!" he said, swinging his fist.

The blow caught her high on the cheek; her eyes went blank; she fell flat on her face. She felt the hard heel of his wet shoes coming into her temple and stomach.

"Lemme hear yuh talk some mo!"

She wanted to, but could not; pain numbed and choked her. She lay still and somewhere out of the grey void of unconsciousness she heard someone say: *Aw fer chrissakes leave her erlone, its the nigger we wan. . . .*

IV

She never knew how long she had lain huddled in the dark hallway. Her first returning feeling was of a nameless fear crowding the inside of her, then a deep pain spreading from her temple downward over her body. Her ears were filled with the drone of rain and she shuddered from the cold wind blowing through the door. She opened her eyes and at first saw nothing. As if she were imagining it, she knew she was half lying and half sitting in a corner against a wall.

With difficulty she twisted her neck and what she saw made her hold her breath—a vast white blur was suspended directly above her. For a moment she could not tell if her fear was from the blur or if the blur was from her fear. Gradually the blur resolved itself into a huge white face that slowly filled her vision. She was stone still, conscious really of the effort to breathe, feeling somehow that she existed only by the mercy of that white face. She had seen it before; its fear had gripped her many times; it had for her the fear of all the white faces she had ever seen in her life. *Sue* . . . As from a great distance, she heard her name being called. She was regaining consciousness now, but the fear was coming with her. She looked into the face of a white man, wanting to scream out for him to go; yet accepting his presence because she felt she had to. Though some remote part of her mind was active, her limbs were powerless. It was as if an invisible knife had split her in two, leaving one half of her lying there helpless, while the other half shrank in dread from a forgotten but familiar enemy. *Sue its me Sue its me* . . . Then all at once the voice came clearly.

"Sue, its me! Its Booker!"

And she heard an answering voice speaking inside of her. Yeah, its Booker . . . The one whut jus joined . . . She roused herself, struggling for full consciousness; and as she did so she transferred to the person of Booker the nameless fear she felt. It seemed that Booker towered above her as a challenge to her right to exist upon the earth.

"Yuh awright?"

She did not answer; she started violently to her feet and fell.

"Sue, yuh hurt!"

"Yeah," she breathed.

"Where they hit yuh?"

"Its mah head," she whispered.

She was speaking even though she did not want to; the fear that had hold of her compelled her.

"They beat yuh?"

"Yeah."

"Them bastards! Them Gawddam bastards!"

She heard him saying it over and over; then she felt herself being lifted.

"Naw!" she gasped.

"Ahma take yuh t the kitchen!"

"Put me down!"

"But yuh cant stay here like this!"

She shrank in his arms and pushed her hands against his body; when she was in the kitchen she freed herself, sank into a chair, and held tightly to its back. She looked wonderingly at Booker. There was nothing about him that should frighten her so, but even that did not ease her tension. She saw him go to the water bucket, wet his handkerchief, wring it, and offer it to her. Distrustfully, she stared at the damp cloth.

"Here; put this on yo fohead . . ."

"Naw!"

"C mon; itll make yuh feel bettah!"

She hesitated in confusion. What right had she to be afraid when someone was acting as kindly as this toward her? Reluctantly, she leaned forward and pressed the damp cloth to her head. It helped. With each passing minute she was catching hold of herself, yet wondering why she felt as she did.

"Whut happened?"

"Ah don know."

"Yuh feel bettah?"

"Yeah."

"Who all wuz here?"

"Ah don know," she said again.

"Yo head still hurt?"

"Yeah."

"Gee, Ahm sorry."

"Ahm awright," she sighed and buried her face in her hands.

She felt him touch her shoulder.

"Sue, Ah got some bad news fer yuh . . ."

She knew; she stiffened and grew cold. It had happened; she stared dry-eyed, with compressed lips.

"Its mah Johnny-Boy," she said.

"Yeah; Ahm awful sorry t hafta tell yuh this way. But Ah thought yuh oughta know . . ."

Her tension eased and a vacant place opened up inside of her. A voice whispered, Jesus, hep me!

"W-w-where is he?"

"They got im out t Foleys Woods tryin t make him tell who the others is."

"He ain gonna tell," she said. "They jus as waal kill im, cause he ain gonna nevah tell."

"Ah hope he don," said Booker. "But he didnt have a chance t tell the others. They grabbed im jus as he got t the woods."

Then all the horror of it flashed upon her; she saw flung out over the rainy countryside an array of shacks where white and black comrades were sleeping; in the morning they would be rising and going to Lem's; then they would be caught. And that meant terror, prison, and death. The comrades would have to be told; she would have to tell them; she could not entrust Johnny-Boy's work to another, and especially not to Booker as long as she felt toward him as

she did. Gripping the bottom of the chair with both hands, she tried
to rise; the room blurred and she swayed. She found herself resting in
Booker's arms.

"Lemme go!"

"Sue, yuh too weak t walk!"

"Ah gotta tell em!" she said.

"Set down, Sue! Yuh hurt! Yuh sick!"

When seated, she looked at him helplessly.

"Sue, lissen! Johnny-Boys caught. Ahm here. Yuh tell me who they
is n Ahll tell em."

She stared at the floor and did not answer. Yes; she was too weak to
go. There was no way for her to tramp all those miles through the
rain tonight. But should she tell Booker? If only she had somebody
like Reva to talk to! She did not want to decide alone; she must
make no mistake about this. She felt Booker's fingers pressing on her
arm and it was as though the white mountain was pushing her to the
edge of a sheer height; she again exclaimed inwardly. Jesus, hep me!
Booker's white face was at her side, waiting. Would she be doing
right to tell him? Suppose she did not tell and then the comrades
were caught? She could not ever forgive herself for doing a thing like
that. But maybe she was wrong; maybe her fear was what Johnny-
Boy had always called "jus foolishness." She remembered his saying,
Ma, we cant make the party grow ef we start doubtin everbody. . . .

"Tell me who they is, Sue, n Ahll tell em. Ah jus joined n Ah don
know who they is."

"Ah don know who they is," she said.

"Yuh *gotta* tell me who they is, Sue!"

"Ah tol yuh Ah don know!"

"Yuh *do* know! C mon! Set up n talk!"

"Naw!"

"Yuh wan em all t git *killed?*"

She shook her head and swallowed. Lawd, Ah don believe in this
man!

"Lissen, Ahll call the names n yuh tell me which ones is in the
party n which ones ain, see?"

"Naw!"

"Please, Sue!"

"Ah don know," she said.

"Sue, yuh ain doin right by em. Johnny-Boy wouldnt wan yuh t be
this way. Hes out there holdin up his end. Les hol up ours . . ."

"Lawd, Ah don know . . ."

"Is yuh scared a me cause Ahm *white?* Johnny-Boy ain like tha.
Don let all the work we done go fer nothin."

She gave up and bowed her head in her hands.

"Is it Johnson? Tell me, Sue?"

"Yeah," she whispered in horror; a mounting horror of feeling herself being undone.

"Is it Green?"

"Yeah."

"Murphy?"

"Lawd, Ah don know!"

"Yuh gotta tell me, Sue!"

"Mistah Booker, please leave me erlone . . ."

"Is it Murphy?"

She answered yes to the names of Johnny-Boy's comrades; she answered until he asked her no more. Then she thought, How he know the sheriffs men is watchin Lems house? She stood up and held onto her chair, feeling something sure and firm within her.

"How yuh know bout Lem?"

"Why . . . How Ah know?"

"Whut yuh doin here this tima night? How yuh know the sheriff got Johnny-Boy?"

"Sue, don yuh believe in me?"

She did not, but she could not answer. She stared at him until her lips hung open; she was searching deep within herself for certainty.

"You meet Reva?" she asked.

"Reva?"

"Yeah; Lems gal?"

"Oh, yeah. Sho, Ah met Reva."

"She tell yuh?"

She asked the question more of herself than of him; she longed to believe.

"Yeah," he said softly. "Ah reckon Ah oughta be goin t tell em now."

"Who?" she asked. "Tell *who*?"

The muscles of her body were stiff as she waited for his answer; she felt as though life depended upon it.

"The comrades," he said.

"Yeah," she sighed.

She did not know when he left; she was not looking or listening. She just suddenly saw the room empty and from her the thing that had made her fearful was gone.

V

For a space of time that seemed to her as long as she had been upon the earth, she sat huddled over the cold stove. One minute she would say to herself, They both gone now; Johnny-Boy n Sug . . . Mabbe Ahll never see em ergin. Then a surge of guilt would blot out her longing. "Lawd, Ah shouldna tol!" she mumbled. "But no man kin be so low-down as to do a thing like that . . ." Several times she had an impulse to try to tell the comrades herself; she was feeling a little better now. But what good would that do? She had told Booker the names. He jus couldnt be a Judas to po folks like us . . . He *couldnt!*

"An Sue!"

Thas Reva! Her heart leaped with an anxious gladness. She rose without answering and limped down the dark hallway. Through the open door, against the background of rain, she saw Reva's face lit now and then to whiteness by the whirling beams of the beacon. She was about to call, but a thought checked her. Jesus, hep me! Ah gotta tell her bout Johnny-Boy . . . Lawd, Ah cant!

"An Sue, yuh there?"

"C mon in, chile!"

She caught Reva and held her close for a moment without speaking.

"Lawd, Ahm sho glad yuh here," she said at last.

"Ah thought somethin had happened t yuh," said Reva, pulling away. "Ah saw the do open . . . Pa tol me to come back n stay wid yuh tonight . . ." Reva paused and started, "W-w-whuts the mattah?"

She was so full of having Reva with her that she did not understand what the question meant.

"Hunh?"

"Yo neck . . ."

"Aw, it ain nothin, chile. C mon in the kitchen."

"But theres blood on yo neck!"

"The sheriff wuz here . . ."

"Them fools! Whut they wanna bother yuh fer? Ah could kill em! So hep me Gawd, Ah could!"

"It ain nothin," she said.

She was wondering how to tell Reva about Johnny-Boy and Booker. Ahll wait a lil while longer, she thought. Now that Reva was here, her fear did not seem as awful as before.

"C mon, lemme fix yo head, An Sue. Yuh hurt."

They went to the kitchen. She sat silent while Reva dressed her scalp. She was feeling better now; in just a little while she would tell Reva. She felt the girl's finger pressing gently upon her head.

"Tha hurt?"

"A lil, chile."

"Yuh po thing."

"It ain nothin."

"Did Johnny-Boy come?"

She hesitated.

"Yeah."

"He done gone t tell the others?"

Reva's voice sounded so clear and confident that it mocked her. Lawd, Ah cant tell this chile . . .

"Yuh tol im, didnt yuh, An Sue?"

"Y-y-yeah . . ."

"Gee! Thas good! Ah tol pa he didnt hafta worry ef Johnny-Boy got the news. Mabbe thingsll come out awright."

"Ah hope . . ."

She could not go on; she had gone as far as she could. For the first time that night she began to cry.

"Hush, An Sue! Yuh awways been brave. Itll be awright!"

"Ain nothin awright, chile. The worls jus too much fer us, Ah reckon."

"Ef yuh cry that way itll make me cry."

She forced herself to stop. Naw; Ah cant carry on this way in fronta Reva . . . Right now she had a deep need for Reva to believe in her. She watched the girl get pine-knots from behind the stove, rekindle the fire, and put on the coffee pot.

"Yuh wan some cawffee?" Reva asked.

"Naw, honey."

"Aw, c mon, An Sue."

"Jusa lil, honey."

"Thas the way to be. Oh, say, Ah fergot," said Reva, measuring out spoonsful of coffee. "Pa tol me t tell yuh t watch out fer tha Booker man. Hes a stool."

She showed not one sign of outward movement or expression, but as the words fell from Reva's lips she went limp inside.

"Pa tol me soon as Ah got back home. He got word from town . . ."

She stopped listening. She felt as though she had been slapped to the extreme outer edge of life, into a cold darkness. She knew now what she had felt when she had looked up out of her fog of pain and had seen Booker. It was the image of all the white folks, and the fear that went with them, that she had seen and felt during her lifetime. And again, for the second time that night, something she had felt had come true. All she could say to herself was, Ah didnt like im! Gawd knows. Ah didnt! Ah tol Johnny-Boy it wuz some of them white folks . . .

"Here; drink yo cawffee . . ."

She took the cup; her fingers trembled, and the steaming liquid spilt onto her dress and leg.

"Ahm sorry, An Sue!"

Her leg was scalded, but the pain did not bother her.

"Its awright," she said.

"Wait; lemme put some lard on tha burn!"

"It don hurt."

"Yuh worried bout somethin."

"Naw, honey."

"Lemme fix yuh so mo cawffee."

"Ah don wan nothin now, Reva."

"Waal, buck up. Don be tha way . . ."

They were silent. She heard Reva drinking. No; she would not tell Reva; Reva was all she had left. But she had to do something, some way, somehow. She was undone too much as it was; and to tell Reva about Booker or Johnny-Boy was more than she was equal to; it would be too coldly shameful. She wanted to be alone and fight this thing out with herself.

"Go t bed, honey. Yuh tired."

"Naw; Ahm awright, An Sue."

She heard the bottom of Reva's empty cup clank against the top of the stove. Ah *got* t make her go t bed! Yes; Booker would tell the names of the comrades to the sheriff. If she could only stop him some way! That was the answer, the point, the star that grew bright in the morning of new hope. Soon, maybe half an hour from now, Booker would reach Foleys Woods. Hes boun t go the long way, cause he don know no short cut, she thought. Ah could wade the creek n beat im there. . . . But what would she do after that?

"Reva, honey, go t bed. Ahm awright. Yuh need res."

"Ah ain sleepy, An Sue."

"Ah knows whuts bes fer yuh, chile. Yuh tired n wet."

"Ah wanna stay up wid yuh."

She forced a smile and said:

"Ah don think they gonna hurt Johnny-Boy . . ."

"Fer *real,* An Sue?"

"Sho, honey."

"But Ah wanna wait up wid yuh."

"Thas mah job, honey. Thas whut a mas fer, t wait up fer her chullun."

"Good night, An Sue."

"Good night, honey."

She watched Reva pull up and leave the kitchen; presently she heard the shucks in the mattress whispering, and she knew that Reva had gone to bed. She was alone. Through the cracks of the stove she saw the fire dying to grey ashes; the room was growing cold again. The yellow beacon continued to flit past the window and the rain still drummed. Yes; she was alone; she had done this awful thing alone; she must find some way out, alone. Like touching a festering sore, she put her finger upon that moment when she had shouted her defiance to the sheriff, when she had shouted to feel her strength. She had lost Sug to save others; she had let Johnny-Boy go to save others; and then in a moment of weakness that came from too much strength she had lost all. If she had not shouted to the sheriff, she would have been strong enough to have resisted Booker; she would have been able to tell the comrades herself. Something tightened in her as she remembered and understood the fit of fear she had felt on coming to herself in the dark hallway. A part of her life she thought she had done away with forever had had hold of her then. She had thought the soft, warm past was over; she had thought that it did not mean much when now she sang: *"Hes the Lily of the Valley, the Bright n Mawnin Star"* . . . The days when she had sung that song were the days when she had not hoped for anything on this earth, the days when the cold mountain had driven her into the arms of Jesus. She had thought that Sug and Johnny-Boy had taught her to forget Him, to fix her hope upon the fight of black men for freedom. Through the gradual years she had believed and worked with them, had felt strength shed from the grace of their terrible vision. That grace had been upon her when she had let the sheriff slap her down; it had been upon her when she had risen time and again from the floor and faced him. But she had trapped herself with her own hunger; to water the long, dry thirst of her faith; her pride had made a bargain which her flesh could not keep. Her having told the names of Johnny-Boy's comrades was but an incident in a deeper horror. She stood up and looked at the floor while call and counter-call, loyalty and counter-loyalty struggled in her soul. Mired she was between two abandoned worlds, living, but dying without the strength of the grace that either gave. The clearer she felt it the fuller did something well up from the depths of her for release; the more urgent did she feel the need to fling into her black sky another star, another hope, one more terrible vision to give her the strength to live and act. Softly and restlessly she walked about the kitchen, feeling herself naked against the night, the rain, the world; and shamed whenever the thought of Reva's love crossed her mind. She lifted her empty hands and looked at her writhing fingers, Lawd, whut kin Ah do now? She could still wade the creek and get to Foleys Woods before Booker. And then what? How could she manage to see Johnny-Boy or Booker? Again she heard the sheriff's threatening voice: Git yuh a sheet, cause hes gonna be dead! The sheet! Thas it, the *sheet!* Her whole being leaped with will; the long years of her life bent toward a moment of focus, a point. Ah kin go wid mah sheet! Ahll be doin whut he said! Lawd Gawd in Heaven, Ahma go lika nigger woman wid mah windin sheet t git mah dead son! But then what? She stood straight and smiled grimly; she had in her heart the whole meaning of her life; her entire personality was poised on the brink of a total act. Ah know! Ah *know!* She thought of Johnny-Boy's gun in the dresser drawer. Ahll hide the gun in the sheet n go aftah Johnny-Boys body. . . . She tiptoed to her room, eased out the dresser drawer, and got a sheet. Reva was sleeping; the darkness was filled with her quiet breathing. She groped in the drawer and found the gun. She wound the gun in the sheet and held them both under her apron. Then she stole to the bedside and watched Reva. Lawd, hep her! But mabbe shes bettah off. This had t happen sometime . . . She n Johnny-Boy couldna been together in this here South . . . N Ah couldn't tell her about Booker. Itll come out awright n she wont nevah know. Reva's trust would never be shaken. She caught her breath as the shucks in the mattress rustled dryly; then all was quiet and she breathed easily again. She tiptoed to the door, down the hall, and stood on the porch. Above her the yellow beacon whirled through the rain. She went over muddy ground, mounted a slope, stopped and looked back at her house. The lamp glowed in her window, and the yellow beacon that swung every few seconds seemed to feed it with light. She turned and started across the fields, holding the gun and sheet tightly, thinking, Po Reva . . . Po critter . . . Shes fas ersleep . . .

VI

For the most part she walked with her eyes half shut, her lips tightly compressed, leaning her body against the wind and the driving rain, feeling the pistol in the sheet sagging cold and heavy in her fingers. Already she was getting wet; it seemed that her feet found every puddle of water that stood between the corn rows.

She came to the edge of the creek and paused, wondering at what point was it low. Taking the sheet from under her apron, she wrapped the gun in it so that her finger could be upon the trigger. Ahll cross here, she thought. At first she did not feel the water; her feet were already wet. But the water grew cold as it came up to her knees; she gasped when it reached her waist. Lawd, this creeks high! When she had passed the middle, she knew that she was out of danger. She came out of the water, climbed a grassy hill, walked on, turned a bend and saw the lights of autos gleaming ahead. Yeah; theys still there! She hurried with her head down. Wondah did Ah beat im here? Lawd, Ah *hope* so! A vivid image of Booker's white face hovered a moment before her eyes and a surging will rose up in her so hard and strong that it vanished. She was among the autos now. From nearby came the hoarse voices of the men.

"Hey, yuh!"

She stopped, nervously clutching the sheet. Two white men with shotguns came toward her.

"What in hell yuh doin out here?"

She did not answer.

"Didnt yuh hear somebody speak t yuh?"

"Ahm comin aftah mah son," she said humbly.

"Yo *son?*"

"Yessuh."

"What yo son doin out here?"

"The sheriffs got im."

"Holy Scott! Jim, its the niggers ma!"

"Whut yuh got there?" asked one.

"A sheet."

"A *sheet?*"

"Yessuh."

"Fer whut?"

"The sheriff tol me t bring a sheet t git his body."

"Waal, waal . . ."

"Now, ain tha somethin?"

The white men looked at each other.

"These niggers sho love one ernother," said one.

"N tha ain no lie," said the other.

"Take me t the sheriff," she begged.

"Yuh ain givin us *orders*, is yuh?"

"Nawsuh."

"Well take yuh when wes good n ready."

"Yessuh."

"So yuh wan his body?"

"Yessuh."

"Waal, he ain dead yit."

"They gonna kill im," she said.

"Ef he talks they wont."

"He ain gonna talk," she said.

"How yuh know?"

"Cause he ain."

"We got ways of makin niggers talk."

"Yuh ain got no way fer im."

"Yuh thinka lot of that black Red, don yuh?"

"Hes mah son."

"Why don yuh teach im some sense?"

"Hes mah son," she said again.

"Lissen, ol nigger woman, yuh stand there wid yo hair white. Yuh got bettah sense than t believe tha niggers kin make a revolution . . ."

"A black republic," said the other one, laughing.

"Take me t the sheriff," she begged.

"Yuh his ma," said one. "Yuh kin make im talk n tell whose in this thing wid im."

"He ain gonna talk," she said.

"Don yuh wan im t live?"

She did not answer.

"C mon, les take her t Bradley."

They grabbed her arms and she clutched hard at the sheet and gun; they led her toward the crowd in the woods. Her feelings were simple; Booker would not tell; she was there with the gun to see to that. The louder became the voices of the men the deeper became her feeling of wanting to right the mistake she had made; of wanting to fight her way back to solid ground. She would stall for time until Booker showed up. Oh, ef theyll only lemme git close t Johnny-Boy! As they led her near the crowd she saw white faces turning and looking at her and heard a rising clamor of voices.

"Whose tha?"

"A nigger woman!"

"Whut she doin out here?"

"This is his ma!" called one of the men.

"Whut she wans?"

"She brought a sheet t cover his body!"

"He ain dead yit!"

"They tryin t make im talk!"

"But he will be dead soon ef he don open up!"

"Say, look! The niggers ma brought a sheet t cover up his body!"

"Now, ain that sweet?"

"Mabbe she wans t hol a prayer meetin!"

"Did she git a preacher?"

"Say, go git Bradley!"

"O.K.!"

The crowd grew quiet. They looked at her curiously; she felt their cold eyes trying to detect some weakness in her. Humbly, she stood with the sheet covering the gun. She had already accepted all that they could do to her.

The sheriff came.

"So yuh brought yuh sheet, hunh?"

"Yessuh," she whispered.

"Looks like them slaps we gave yuh learned yuh some sense, didnt they?"

She did not answer.

"Yuh don need tha sheet. Yo son ain dead yit," he said, reaching toward her.

She backed away, her eyes wide.

"Naw!"

"Now, lissen, Anty!" he said. "There ain no use in yuh ackin a fool! Go in there n tell tha nigger son of yos t tell us whos in this wid im, see? Ah promise we wont kill im ef he talks. We'll let im git outta town."

"There ain nothin Ah kin tell im," she said.

"Yuh wan us t kill im?"

She did not answer. She saw someone lean toward the sheriff and whisper.

"Bring her erlong," the sheriff said.

They led her to a muddy clearing. The rain streamed down through the ghostly glare of the flashlights. As the men formed a semicircle she saw Johnny-Boy lying in a trough of mud. He was tied with rope; he lay hunched and one side of his face rested in a pool of black water. His eyes were staring questioningly at her.

"Speak t im," said the sheriff.

If she could only tell him why she was here! But that was impossible; she was close to what she wanted and she stared straight before her with compressed lips.

"Say, nigger!" called the sheriff, kicking Johnny-Boy. "Heres yo ma!"

Johnny-Boy did not move or speak. The sheriff faced her again.

"Lissen, Anty," he said. "Yuh got mo say wid im than anybody. Tell im t talk n hava chance. Whut he wanna pertect the other niggers n white folks fer?"

She slid her finger about the trigger of the gun and looked stonily at the mud.

"Go t him," said the sheriff.

She did not move. Her heart was crying out to answer the amazed question in Johnny-Boy's eyes. But there was no way now.

"Waal, yuhre astin fer it. By Gawd, we gotta way to *make* yuh talk t im," he said, turning away. "Say, Tim, git one of them logs n turn that nigger upside-down n put his legs on it!"

A murmur of assent ran through the crowd. She bit her lips; she knew what that meant.

"Yuh wan yo nigger son crippled?" she heard the sheriff ask.

She did not answer. She saw them roll the log up; they lifted Johnny-Boy and laid him on his face and stomach, then they pulled his legs over the log. His kneecaps rested on the sheer top of the log's back and the toes of his shoes pointed groundward. So absorbed was she in watching that she felt that it was she who was being lifted and made ready for torture.

"Git a crowbar!" said the sheriff.

A tall, lank man got a crowbar from a nearby auto and stood over the log. His jaws worked slowly on a wad of tobacco.

"Now, its up t yuh, Anty," the sheriff said. "Tell the man whut t do!"

She looked into the rain. The sheriff turned.

"Mebbe she think wes playin. Ef she don say nothin, then break em at the kneecaps!"

"O.K., Sheriff!"

She stood waiting for Booker. Her legs felt weak; she wondered if she would be able to wait much longer. Over and over she said to herself, Ef he came now Ahd kill em both!

"She ain sayin nothin, Sheriff!"

"Waal, Gawddammit, let im have it!"

The crowbar came down and Johnny-Boy's body lunged in the mud and water. There was a scream. She swayed, holding tight to the gun and sheet.

"Hol im! Git the other leg!"

The crowbar fell again. There was another scream.

"Yuh break em?" asked the sheriff.

The tall man lifted Johnny-Boy's legs and let them drop limply again, dropping rearward from the kneecaps. Johnny-Boy's body lay still. His head had rolled to one side and she could not see his face.

"Jus lika broke sparrow wing," said the man, laughing softly.

Then Johnny-Boy's face turned to her; he screamed.

"Go way, ma! Go way!"

It was the first time she had heard his voice since she had come out to the woods; she all but lost control of herself. She started violently forward, but the sheriff's arm checked her.

"Aw, naw! Yuh had yo chance!" He turned to Johnny-Boy. "She kin go ef yuh talk."

"Mistah, he ain gonna talk," she said.

"Go way, ma!" said Johnny-Boy.

"Shoot im! Don make im suffah so," she begged.

"He'll either talk or he'll never hear yuh ergin," the sheriff said. "Theres other things we kin do t im."

She said nothing.

"Whut yuh come here fer, ma?" Johnny-Boy sobbed.

"Ahm gonna split his eardrums," the sheriff said. "Ef yuh got anythin to say t im yuh bettah say it *now!*"

She closed her eyes. She heard the sheriff's feet sucking in mud. Ah could save im! She opened her eyes; there were shouts of eagerness from the crowd as it pushed in closer.

"Bus em, Sheriff!"

"Fix im so he cant hear!"

"He knows how t do it, too!"

"He busted a Jew boy tha way once!"

She saw the sheriff stoop over Johnny-Boy, place his flat palm over one ear and strike his fist against it with all his might. He placed his palm over the other ear and struck again. Johnny-Boy moaned, his head rolling from side to side, his eyes showing white amazement in a world without sound.

"Yuh wouldnt talk t im when yuh had the chance," said the sheriff. "Try n talk now."

She felt warm tears on her cheeks. She longed to shoot Johnny-Boy and let him go. But if she did that they would take the gun from her, and Booker would tell who the others were. Lawd, help me! The men were talking loudly now, as though the main business was over. It seemed ages that she stood there watching Johnny-Boy roll and whimper in his world of silence.

"Say, Sheriff, heres somebody lookin fer yuh!"

"Who is it?"

"Ah don know!"

"Bring em in!"

She stiffened and looked around wildly, holding the gun tight. Is tha Booker? Then she held still, feeling that her excitement might betray her. Mabbe Ah kin shoot em both! Mabbe Ah kin shoot *twice!* The sheriff stood in front of her, waiting. The crowd parted and she saw Booker hurrying forward.

"Ah know em all, Sheriff!" he called.

He came full into the muddy clearing where Johnny-Boy lay.

"Yuh mean yuh got the names?"

"Sho! The ol nigger . . ."

She saw his lips hang open and silent when he saw her. She stepped forward and raised the sheet.

"Whut . . ."

She fired, once; then, without pausing, she turned, hearing them yell. She aimed at Johnny-Boy, but they had their arms around her, bearing her to the ground, clawing at the sheet in her hand. She glimpsed Booker lying sprawled in the mud, on his face, his hands stretched out before him; then a cluster of yelling men blotted him out. She lay without struggling, looking upward through the rain at the white faces above her. And she was suddenly at peace; they were not a white mountain now; they were not pushing her any longer to the edge of life. Its awright . . .

"She shot Booker!"

"She hada gun in the sheet!"

"She shot im right thu the head!"

"Whut she shoot im fer?"

"Kill the bitch!"

"Ah *thought* somethin wuz wrong bout her!"

"Ah wuz fer givin it t her from the firs!"

"Thas whut yuh git fer treatin a nigger nice!"

"Say, Bookers dead!"

She stopped looking into the white faces, stopped listening. She waited, giving up her life before they took it from her; she had done what she wanted. Ef only Johnny-Boy . . . She looked at him; he lay looking at her with tired eyes. Ef she could only tell im! But he lay already buried in a grave of silence.

"Whut yuh kill im fer, hunh?"

It was the sheriff's voice; she did not answer.

"Mabbe she wuz shootin at yuh, Sheriff?"

"Whut yuh kill im fer?"

She felt the sheriff's foot come into her side; she closed her eyes.

"Yuh black bitch!"

"Let her have it!"

"Yuh reckon she foun out bout Booker?"

"She mighta."

"Jesus Chris, whut yuh dummies *waitin* on!"

"Yeah; kill her!"

"Kill em *both!*"

"Let her know her nigger sons dead firs!"

She turned her head toward Johnny-Boy; he lay looking puzzled in a world beyond the reach of voices. At leas he cant hear, she thought.

"C'mon, let im have it!"

She listened to hear what Johnny-Boy could not. They came, two of them, one right behind the other; so close together that they sounded like one shot. She did not look at Johnny-Boy now; she looked at the white faces of the men, hard and wet in the glare of the flashlights.

"Yuh hear tha, nigger woman?"

"Did tha surprise im? Hes in hell now wonderin whut hit im!"

"C mon! Give it t her, Sheriff!"

"Lemme shoot her, Sheriff! It wuz mah pal she shot!"

"Awright, Pete! Thas fair ernuff!"

She gave up as much of her life as she could before they took it from her. But the sound of the shot and the streak of fire that tore its way through her chest forced her to live again, intensely. She had not moved, save for the slight jarring impact of the bullet. She felt the heat of her own blood warming her cold, wet back. She yearned suddenly to talk. "Yuh didnt git whut yuh wanted! N yuh ain gonna nevah git it! Yuh didnt kill me; Ah come here by mahsef . . ." She felt rain falling into her wide-open, dimming eyes and heard faint voices. Her lips moved soundlessly. *Yuh didnt git yuh didnt yuh didnt . . .* Focused and pointed she was, buried in the depths of her star, swallowed in its peace and strength; and not feeling her flesh growing cold, cold as the rain that fell from the invisible sky upon the doomed living and the dead that never dies.

ALBERT CAMUS

(1913-1960)

Camus was born in Algeria, then a French colony, and Algeria is the background for much of his fiction, including *The Stranger, The Plague,* and the following short story, "The Guest." In France Camus wrote *The Stranger* and *The Myth of Sisyphus* at the start of the Second World War. Then he became deeply involved in the Resistance, emerging as a great literary and political hero at the end of the war. As an existentialist and a writer close to Sartre, Camus deals with people facing a life that has no "meaning" given it by a God or Nature or Reason, a life to which they have to give their own meaning. And while they choose a life and meaning they are tumbling toward a death that defeats them and ignores their meaning. *The Plague* (1947), about responses to bubonic plague in a small Algerian city, has overtones of the plague of Nazis as well as the metaphysical plague of death itself. In the late 1940's Camus broke from Sartre, refusing to support the Soviet Union and the Communist party in France. Still dealing with questions of conscience, he wrote the powerful, strange, first person novel *The Fall,* and in 1957 published a fine collection of short fiction, *The Exile and the Kingdom.* Camus was awarded the Nobel Prize for Literature in 1957. Three years later he was killed in an automobile accident.

The Guest

ALBERT CAMUS

The schoolmaster was watching the two men climb toward him. One was on horseback, the other on foot. They had not yet tackled the abrupt rise leading to the schoolhouse built on the hillside. They were toiling onward, making slow progress in the snow, among the stones, on the vast expanse of the high, deserted plateau. From time to time the horse stumbled. He could not be heard yet but the breath issuing from his nostrils could be seen. The schoolmaster calculated that it would take them a half hour to get onto the hill. It was cold; he went back into the school to get a sweater.

He crossed the empty, frigid classroom. On the blackboard the four rivers of France, drawn with four different colored chalks, had been flowing toward their estuaries for the past three days. Snow had suddenly fallen in mid-October after eight months of drought without the transition of rain, and the twenty pupils, more or less, who lived in the villages scattered over the plateau had stopped coming. With fair weather they would return. Daru now heated only the single room that was his lodging, adjoining the classroom. One of the windows faced, like the classroom windows, the south. On that side the school was a few kilometers from the point where the plateau began to slope toward the south. In clear weather the purple mass of the mountain range where the gap opened onto the desert could be seen.

Somewhat warmed, Daru returned to the window from which he had first noticed the two men. They were no longer visible. Hence they must have tackled the rise. The sky was not so dark, for the snow had stopped falling during the night. The morning had dawned with a dirty light which had scarcely become brighter as the ceiling of clouds lifted. At two in the afternoon it seemed as if the day were merely beginning. But still this was better than those three days when the thick snow was falling amidst unbroken darkness with little gusts of wind that rattled the double door of the classroom. Then Daru had spent long hours in his room, leaving it only to go to the shed and feed the chickens or get some coal. Fortunately the delivery truck from Tadjid, the nearest village to the north, had brought his supplies two days before the blizzard. It would return in forty-eight hours.

Besides, he had enough to resist a siege, for the little room was cluttered with bags of wheat that the administration had left as a supply to distribute to those of his pupils whose families had suffered from the drought. Actually they had all been victims because they were all poor. Every day Daru would distribute a ration to the children. They had missed it, he knew, during these bad days. Possibly one of the fathers or big brothers would come this afternoon and he could supply them with grain. It was just a matter of carrying them over to the next harvest. Now shiploads of wheat were arriving from France and the worst was over. But it would be hard to forget that poverty, that army of ragged ghosts wandering in the sunlight, the plateaus burned to a cinder month after month, the earth shriveled up little by little, literally scorched, every stone bursting into dust under one's foot. The sheep had died then by thousands, and even a few men, here and there, sometimes without anyone's knowing.

In contrast with such poverty, he who lived almost like a monk, in his remote schoolhouse, had felt like a lord with his whitewashed walls, his narrow couch, his unpainted shelves, his well, and his weekly provisioning with water and food. And suddenly this snow, without warning, without the foretaste of rain. This is the way the region was, cruel to live in, even without men, who didn't help matters either. But Daru had been born here. Everywhere else, he felt exiled.

He went out and stepped forward on the terrace in front of the schoolhouse. The two men were now halfway up the slope. He recognized the horseman to be Balducci, the old gendarme he had known for a long time. Balducci was holding at the end of a rope an Arab walking behind him with hands bound and head lowered. The gendarme waved a greeting to which Daru did not reply, lost as he was in contemplation of the Arab dressed in a faded blue *jellaba*, his feet in sandals but covered with socks of heavy raw wool, his head crowned with a narrow, short *chèche*. Balducci was holding back his horse in order not to hurt the Arab, and the group was advancing slowly.

Within earshot, Balducci shouted, "One hour to do the three kilometers from El Ameur!" Daru did not answer. Short and square in his thick sweater, he watched them climb. Not once had the Arab raised his head. "Hello," said Daru when they got up onto the terrace. "Come in and warm up." Balducci painfully got down from his horse without letting go of the rope. He smiled at the schoolmaster from under his bristling mustache. His little dark eyes, deep-set under a tanned forehead, and his mouth surrounded with wrinkles made him look attentive and studious. Daru took the bridle, led the horse to the shed, and came back to the two men who were now waiting for him in the school. He led them into his room. "I am going to heat up the classroom," he said. "We'll be more comfortable there."

When he entered the room again, Balducci was on the couch. He had undone the rope tying him to the Arab, who had squatted near the stove. His hands still bound, the *chèche* pushed back on his head, the Arab was looking toward the window. At first Daru noticed only his huge lips, fat, smooth, almost Negroid; yet his nose was straight, his eyes dark and full of fever. The *chèche* uncovered an obstinate forehead and, under the weathered skin now rather discolored by the cold, the whole face had a restless and rebellious look. "Go into the other room," said the schoolmaster, "and I'll make you some mint tea." "Thanks," Balducci said. "What a chore! How I long for retirement." And addressing his prisoner in Arabic, he said, "Come on, you." The Arab got up and, slowly, holding his bound wrists in front of him, went into the classroom.

With the tea, Daru brought a chair. But Balducci was already sitting in state at the nearest pupil's desk, and the Arab had squatted against the teacher's platform facing the stove, which stood between the desk and the window. When he held out the glass of tea to the prisoner, Daru hesitated at the sight of his bound hands. "He might perhaps be untied." "Sure," said Balducci. "That was for the trip." He started to get to his feet. But Daru, setting the glass on the floor, had knelt beside the Arab. Without saying anything, the Arab watched him with his feverish eyes. Once his hands were free, he rubbed his swollen wrists against each other, took the glass of tea and sucked up the burning liquid in swift little sips.

"Good," said Daru. "And where are you headed?"

Balducci withdrew his mustache from the tea. "Here, son."

"Odd pupils! And you're spending the night?"

"No. I'm going back to El Ameur. And you will deliver this fellow to Tinguit. He is expected at police headquarters."

Balducci was looking at Daru with a friendly little smile.

"What's this story?" asked the schoolmaster. "Are you pulling my leg?"

"No, son. Those are the orders."

"The orders? I'm not . . ." Daru hesitated, not wanting to hurt the old Corsican. "I mean, that's not my job."

"What! What's the meaning of that? In wartime people do all kinds of jobs."

"Then I'll wait for the declaration of war!"

Balducci nodded. "O.K. But the orders exist and they concern you too. Things are bubbling, it appears. There is talk of a forthcoming revolt. We are mobilized, in a way."

Daru still had his obstinate look.

"Listen, son," Balducci said. "I like you and you've got to understand. There's only a dozen of us at El Ameur to patrol the whole territory of a small department and I must be back in a hurry. He couldn't be kept there. His village was beginning to stir; they wanted to take him back. You must take him to Tinguit tomorrow before the day is over. Twenty kilometers shouldn't faze a husky fellow like you. After that, all will be over. You'll come back to your pupils and your comfortable life."

Behind the wall the horse could be heard snorting and pawing the earth. Daru was looking out the window. Decidedly the weather was clearing and the light was increasing over the snowy plateau. When all the snow was melted, the sun would take over again and once more would burn the fields of stone. For days still, the unchanging sky would shed its dry light on the solitary expanse where nothing had any connection with man.

"After all," he said, turning around toward Balducci, "what did he do?" And, before the gendarme had opened his mouth, he asked, "Does he speak French?"

"No, not a word. We had been looking for him for a month, but they were hiding him. He killed his cousin."

"Is he against us?"

"I don't think so. But you can never be sure."

"Why did he kill?"

"A family squabble, I think. One owed grain to the other, it seems. It's not at all clear. In short, he killed his cousin with a billhook. You know, like a sheep, *kreezk!*"

Balducci made the gesture of drawing a blade across his throat, and the Arab, his attention attracted, watched him with a sort of anxiety. Daru felt a sudden wrath against the man, against all men with their rotten spite, their tireless hates, their blood lust.

But the kettle was singing on the stove. He served Balducci more tea, hesitated, then served the Arab again, who drank avidly a second time. His raised arms made the *jellaba* fall open, and the schoolmaster saw his thin, muscular chest.

"Thanks, son," Balducci said. "And now I'm off."

He got up and went toward the Arab, taking a small rope from his pocket.

"What are you doing?" Daru asked dryly.

Balducci, disconcerted, showed him the rope.

"Don't bother."

The old gendarme hesitated. "It's up to you. Of course, you are armed?"

"I have my shotgun."

"Where?"

"In the trunk."

"You ought to have it near your bed."

"Why? I have nothing to fear."

"You're crazy, son. If there's an uprising, no one is safe; we're all in the same boat."

"I'll defend myself. I'll have time to see them coming."

Balducci began to laugh, then suddenly the mustache covered the white teeth. "You'll have time? O.K. That's just what I was saying. You always have been a little cracked. That's why I like you; my son was like that."

At the same time he took out his revolver and put it on the desk. "Keep it; I don't need two weapons from here to El Ameur."

The revolver shone against the black paint of the table. When the gendarme turned toward him, the schoolmaster caught his smell of leather and horseflesh.

"Listen, Balducci," Daru said suddenly, "all this disgusts me, beginning with your fellow here. But I won't hand him over. Fight, yes, if I have to. But not that."

The old gendarme stood in front of him and looked at him severely.

"You're being a fool," he said slowly. "I don't like it either. You don't get used to putting a rope on a man even after years of it, and you're even ashamed—yes, ashamed. But you can't let them have their way."

"I won't hand him over," Daru said again.

"It's an order, son, and I repeat it."

"That's right. Repeat to them what I've said to you: I won't hand him over."

Balducci made a visible effort to reflect. He looked at the Arab and at Daru. At last he decided.

"No, I won't tell them anything. If you want to drop us, go ahead; I'll not denounce you. I have an order to deliver the prisoner and I'm doing so. And now you'll just sign this paper for me."

"There's no need. I'll not deny that you left him with me."

"Don't be mean with me. I know you'll tell the truth. You're from around these parts and you are a man. But you must sign; that's the rule."

Daru opened his drawer, took out a little square bottle of purple ink, the red wooden penholder with the "sergeant-major" pen he used for models of handwriting, and signed. The gendarme carefully folded the paper and put it into his wallet. Then he moved toward the door.

"I'll see you off," Daru said.

"No," said Balducci. "There's no use being polite. You insulted me."

He looked at the Arab, motionless in the same spot, sniffed peevishly, and turned away toward the door. "Good-by, son," he said. The door slammed behind him. His footsteps were muffled by the snow. The horse stirred on the other side of the wall and several chickens fluttered in fright. A moment later Balducci reappeared outside the window leading the horse by the bridle. He walked toward the little rise without turning around and disappeared from sight with the horse following him.

Daru walked back toward the prisoner, who, without stirring, never took his eyes off him. "Wait," the schoolmaster said in Arabic and went toward the bedroom. As he was going through the door, he had a second thought, went to the desk, took the revolver, and stuck it in his pocket. Then, without looking back, he went into his room.

For some time he lay on his couch watching the sky gradually close over, listening to the silence. It was this silence that had seemed painful to him during the first days here, after the war. He had requested a post in the little town at the base of the foothills separating the upper plateaus from the desert. There rocky walls, green and black to the north, pink and lavender to the south, marked the frontier of eternal summer. He had been named to a post farther north, on the plateau itself. In the beginning, the solitude and the silence had been hard for him on these wastelands peopled only by stones. Occasionally, furrows suggested cultivation, but they had been dug to uncover a certain kind of stone good for building. The only plowing here was to harvest rocks. Elsewhere a thin layer of soil accumulated in the hollows would be scraped out to enrich paltry village gardens. This is the way it was: bare rock covered three quarters of the region. Towns sprang up, flourished, then disappeared; men came by, loved one another or fought bitterly, then died. No one in this desert, neither he nor his guest, mattered. And yet, outside this desert neither of them, Daru knew, could have really lived.

When he got up, no noise came from the classroom. He was amazed at the unmixed joy he derived from the mere thought that the Arab might have fled and that he would be alone with no decision to make. But the prisoner was there. He had merely stretched out between the stove and the desk and he was staring at the ceiling. In that position, his thick lips were particularly notice-able, giving him a pouting look. "Come," said Daru. The Arab got up and followed him. In the bedroom the schoolmaster pointed to a chair near the table under the window. The Arab sat down without ceasing to watch Daru.

"Are you hungry?"

"Yes," the prisoner said.

Daru set the table for two. He took flour and oil, shaped a cake in a frying pan, and lighted the little stove that functioned on bottled gas. While the cake was cooking, he went out to the shed to get cheese, eggs, dates, and condensed milk. When the cake was done he set it on the window sill to cool, heated some condensed milk diluted with water, and beat up the eggs into an omelette. In one of his motions he bumped into the revolver stuck in his right pocket. He set the bowl down, went into the classroom, and put the revolver in his desk drawer. When he came back to the room, night was falling. He put on the light and served the Arab. "Eat," he said. The Arab took a piece of the cake, lifted it eagerly to his mouth, and stopped short.

"And you?" he asked.

"After you. I'll eat too."

The thick lips opened slightly. The Arab hesitated, then bit into the cake determinedly.

The meal over, the Arab looked at the schoolmaster. "Are you the judge?"

"No, I'm simply keeping you until tomorrow."

"Why do you eat with me?"

"I'm hungry."

The Arab fell silent. Daru got up and went out. He brought back a camp cot from the shed and set it up between the table and the stove, at right angles to his own bed. From a large suitcase which, upright in a corner, served as a shelf for papers, he took two blankets and arranged them on the cot. Then he stopped, felt useless, and sat down on his bed. There was nothing more to do or to get ready. He had to look at this man. He looked at him therefore, trying to imagine his face bursting with rage. He couldn't do so. He could see nothing but the dark yet shining eyes and the animal mouth.

"Why did you kill him?" he asked in a voice whose hostile tone surprised him.

The Arab looked away. "He ran away. I ran after him."

He raised his eyes to Daru again and they were full of a sort of woeful interrogation. "Now what will they do to me?"

"Are you afraid?"

The Arab stiffened, turning his eyes away.

"Are you sorry?"

The Arab stared at him openmouthed. Obviously he did not understand. Daru's annoyance was growing. At the same time he felt awkward and self-conscious with his big body wedged between the two beds.

"Lie down there," he said impatiently. "That's your bed."

The Arab didn't move. He cried out, "Tell me!"

The schoolmaster looked at him.

"Is the gendarme coming back tomorrow?"

"I don't know."

"Are you coming with us?"

"I don't know. Why?"

The prisoner got up and stretched out on top of the blankets, his feet toward the window. The light from the electric bulb shone straight into his eyes and he closed them at once.

"Why?" Daru repeated, standing beside the bed.

The Arab opened his eyes under the blinding light and looked at him, trying not to blink. "Come with us," he said.

In the middle of the night, Daru was still not asleep. He had gone to bed after undressing completely; he generally slept naked. But when he suddenly realized that he had nothing on, he wondered. He felt vulnerable and the temptation came to him to put his clothes back on. Then he shrugged his shoulders; after all, he wasn't a child and, if it came to that, he could break his adversary in two. From his bed, he could observe him lying on his back, still motionless, his eyes closed under the harsh light. When Daru turned out the light, the darkness seemed to congeal all of a sudden. Little by little, the night came back to life in the window where the starless sky was stirring gently. The schoolmaster soon made out the body lying at his feet. The Arab was still motionless but his eyes seemed open. A faint wind was prowling about the schoolhouse. Perhaps it would drive away the clouds and the sun would reappear.

During the night the wind increased. The hens fluttered a little and then were silent. The Arab turned over on his side with his back to Daru, who thought he heard him moan. Then he listened for his guest's breathing, which had become heavier and more regular. He listened to that breathing so close to him and mused without being able to go to sleep. In the room where he had been sleeping alone for a year, this presence bothered him. But it bothered him also because it imposed on him a sort of brotherhood he refused to accept in the present circumstances; yet he was familiar with it. Men who share the same rooms, soldiers or prisoners, develop a strange alliance as if, having cast off their armor with their clothing, they fraternized every evening, over and above their differences, in the ancient community of dream and fatigue. But Daru shook himself; he didn't like such musings, and it was essential for him to sleep.

A little later, however, when the Arab stirred slightly, the schoolmaster was still not asleep. When the prisoner made a second move, he stiffened, on the alert. The Arab was lifting himself slowly on his arms with almost the motion of a sleepwalker. Seated upright in bed, he waited motionless without turning his head toward Daru, as if he were listening attentively. Daru did not stir; it had just occurred to him that the revolver was still in the drawer of his desk. It was better to act at once. Yet he continued to observe the prisoner, who, with the same slithery motion, put his feet on the ground, waited again, then stood up slowly. Daru was about to call out to him when the Arab began to walk, in a quite natural but extraordinarily silent way. He was heading toward the door at the end of the room that opened into the shed. He lifted the latch with precaution and went out, pushing the door behind him but without shutting it.

Daru had not stirred. "He is running away," he merely thought. "Good riddance!" Yet he listened attentively. The hens were not fluttering; the guest must be on the plateau. A faint sound of water reached him, and he didn't know what it was until the Arab again stood framed in the doorway, closed the door carefully, and came back to bed without a sound. Then Daru turned his back on him and fell asleep. Still later he seemed, from the depths of his sleep, to hear furtive steps around the schoolhouse. "I'm dreaming! I'm dreaming!" he repeated to himself. And he went on sleeping.

When he awoke, the sky was clear; the loose window let in a cold, pure air. The Arab was asleep, hunched up under the blankets now, his mouth open, utterly relaxed. But when Daru shook him he started dreadfully, staring at Daru with wild eyes as if he had never seen him and with such a frightened expression that the schoolmaster stepped back. "Don't be afraid. It is I. You must eat." The Arab nodded his head and said yes. Calm had returned to his face, but his expression was vacant and listless.

The coffee was ready. They drank it seated together on the cot as they munched their pieces of the cake. Then Daru led the Arab under the shed and showed him the faucet where he washed. He went back into the room, folded the blankets on the cot, made his own bed, and put the room in order. Then he went through the classroom and out onto the terrace. The sun was already rising in the blue sky; a soft, bright light enveloped the deserted plateau. On the ridge the snow was melting in spots. The stones were about to reappear. Crouched on the edge of the plateau, the schoolmaster looked at the deserted expanse. He thought of Balducci. He had hurt him, for he had sent him off as though he didn't want to be associated with him. He could still hear the gendarme's farewell and, without knowing why, he felt strangely empty and vulnerable.

At that moment, from the other side of the schoolhouse, the prisoner coughed. Daru listened to him almost despite himself and then, furious, threw a pebble that whistled through the air before sinking into the snow. That man's stupid crime revolted him, but to hand him over was contrary to honor; just thinking of it made him boil with humiliation. He simultaneously cursed his own people who had sent him this Arab and the Arab who had dared to kill and not managed to get away. Daru got up, walked in a circle on the terrace, waited motionless, and then went back into the schoolhouse.

The Arab, leaning over the cement floor of the shed, was washing his teeth with two fingers. Daru looked at him and said, "Come." He went back into the room ahead of the prisoner. He slipped a hunting jacket on over his sweater and put on walking shoes. Standing, he waited until the Arab had put on his *chèche* and sandals. They went into the classroom, and the schoolmaster pointed to the exit saying, "Go ahead." The fellow didn't budge. "I'm coming," said Daru. The Arab went out. Daru went back into the room and made a package with pieces of rusk, dates, and sugar in it. In the classroom, before going out, he hesitated a second in front of his desk, then crossed the threshold and locked the door. "That's the way," he said. He started toward the east, followed by the prisoner. But a short distance from the schoolhouse he thought he heard a slight sound behind him. He retraced his steps and examined the surroundings of the house; there was no one there. The Arab watched him without seeming to understand. "Come on," said Daru.

They walked for an hour and rested beside a sharp needle of limestone. The snow was melting faster and faster and the sun was drinking up the puddles just as quickly, rapidly cleaning the plateau, which gradually dried and vibrated like the air itself. When they resumed walking, the ground rang under their feet. From time to time a bird rent the space in front of them with a joyful cry. Daru felt a sort of rapture before the vast familiar expanse, now almost entirely yellow under its dome of blue sky. They walked an hour more, descending toward the south. They reached a sort of flattened elevation made up of crumbly rocks. From there on, the plateau sloped down—eastward toward a low plain on which could be made out a few spindly trees, and to the south toward outcroppings of rock that gave the landscape a chaotic look.

Daru surveyed the two directions. Not a man could be seen. He turned toward the Arab, who was looking at him blankly. Daru offered the package to him. "Take it," he said. "There are dates, bread, and sugar. You can hold out for two days. Here are a thousand francs too."

The Arab took the package and the money but kept his full hands at chest level as if he didn't know what to do with what was being given him.

"Now look," the schoolmaster said as he pointed in the direction of the east, "there's the way to Tinguit. You have a two-hour walk. At Tinguit are the administration and the police. They are expecting you."

The Arab looked toward the east, still holding the package and the money against his chest. Daru took his elbow and turned him rather roughly toward the south. At the foot of the elevation on which they stood could be seen a faint path. "That's the trail across the plateau. In a day's walk from here you'll find pasturelands and the first nomads. They'll take you in and shelter you according to their law."

The Arab had now turned toward Daru, and a sort of panic was visible in his expression. "Listen," he said.

Daru shook his head. "No, be quiet. Now I'm leaving you." He turned his back on him, took two long steps in the direction of the school, looked hesitantly at the motionless Arab, and started off again. For a few minutes he heard nothing but his own step resounding on the cold ground, and he did not turn his head. A moment later, however, he turned around. The Arab was still there on the edge of the hill, his arms hanging now, and he was looking at the schoolmaster. Daru felt something rise in his throat. But he swore with impatience, waved vaguely, and started off again. He had already gone a distance when he again stopped and looked. There was no longer anyone on the hill.

Daru hesitated. The sun was now rather high in the sky and beginning to beat down on his head. The schoolmaster retraced his steps, at first somewhat uncertainly, then with decision. When he reached the little hill, he was bathed in sweat. He climbed it as fast as he could and stopped, out of breath, on the top. The rock fields to the south stood out sharply against the blue sky, but on the plain to the east a steamy heat was rising. And in that slight haze, Daru, with heavy heart, made out the Arab walking slowly on the road to prison.

A little later, standing before the window of the classroom, the schoolmaster was watching the clear light bathing the whole surface of the plateau. Behind him on the blackboard, among the winding French rivers, sprawled the clumsily chalked up words he had just read: "You handed over our brother. You will pay for this." Daru looked at the sky, the plateau, and, beyond, the invisible lands stretching all the way to the sea. In this vast landscape he had loved so much, he was alone.

TILLIE OLSEN

(1913—)

"I Stand Here Ironing" comes from a beautiful collection of stories, *Tell Me a Riddle,* which won the O'Henry Award for Fiction in 1959 but only became well known with the growth of the women's movement in the early 1970's. Olsen deals with the struggles of women, the struggles of working people, to live up to their potential in the midst of an environment that sucks their lives away. A working-class wife and mother, Olsen only at the age of forty could begin to squeeze out the time to sit down and write, and these struggles are very much her own.

[See Preface, p. 1 (realism), pp.12 and 17 (focus), p. 28 (vision).]

I Stand Here Ironing

TILLIE OLSEN

I stand here ironing, and what you asked me moves tormented back and forth with the iron.

"I wish you would manage the time to come in and talk with me about your daughter. I'm sure you can help me understand her. She's a youngster who needs help and whom I'm deeply interested in helping."

"I Stand Here Ironing" originally appeared in *The Pacific Spectator* in 1956. Reprinted by permission.

"Who needs help." Even if I came, what good would it do? You think because I am her mother I have a key, or that in some way you could use me as a key? She has lived for nineteen years. There is all that life that has happened outside of me, beyond me.

And when is there time to remember, to sift, to weigh, to estimate, to total? I will start and there will be an interruption and I will have to gather it all together again. Or I will become engulfed with all I did or did not do, with what should have been and what cannot be helped.

She was a beautiful baby. The first and only one of our five that was beautiful at birth. You do not guess how new and uneasy her tenancy in her now-loveliness. You did not know her all those years she was thought homely, or see her poring over her baby pictures, making me tell her over and over how beautiful she had been—and would be, I would tell her—and was now, to the seeing eye. But the seeing eyes were few or nonexistent. Including mine.

I nursed her. They feel that's important nowadays. I nursed all the children, but with her, with all the fierce rigidity of first motherhood, I did like the books then said. Though her cries battered me to trembling and my breasts ached with swollenness, I waited till the clock decreed.

Why do I put that first? I do not even know if it matters, or if it explains anything.

She was a beautiful baby. She blew shining bubbles of sound. She loved motion, loved light, loved color and music and textures. She would lie on the floor in her blue overalls patting the surface so hard in ecstasy her hands and feet would blur. She was a miracle to me, but when she was eight months old I had to leave her daytimes with the woman downstairs to whom she was no miracle at all, for I worked or looked for work and for Emily's father, who "could no longer endure" (he wrote in his good-bye note) "sharing want with us."

I was nineteen. It was the pre-relief, pre-WPA world of the depression. I would start running as soon as I got off the streetcar, running up the stairs, the place smelling sour, and awake or asleep to startle awake, when she saw me she would break into a clogged weeping that could not be comforted, a weeping I can hear yet.

After a while I found a job hashing at night so I could be with her days, and it was better. But it came to where I had to bring her to his family and leave her.

It took a long time to raise the money for her fare back. Then she got chicken pox and I had to wait longer. When she finally came, I hardly knew her, walking quick and nervous like her father, looking like her father, thin, and dressed in a shoddy red that yellowed her skin and glared at the pockmarks. All the baby loveliness gone.

She was two. Old enough for nursery school they said, and I did not know then what I know now—the fatigue of the long day, and the lacerations of group life in nurseries that are only parking places for children.

  Except that it would have made no difference if I had known. It was the only place there was. It was the only way we could be together, the only way I could hold a job.

And even without knowing, I knew. I knew the teacher that was evil because all these years it has curdled into my memory, the little boy hunched in the corner, her rasp, "why aren't you outside, because Alvin hits you? that's no reason, go out, scaredy." I knew Emily hated it even if she did not clutch and implore "don't go Mommy" like the other children, mornings.

She always had a reason why we should stay home. Momma, you look sick, Momma. I feel sick. Momma, the teachers aren't there today, they're sick. Momma, we can't go, there was a fire there last night. Momma, it's a holiday today, no school, they told me.

But never a direct protest, never rebellion. I think of our others in their three-, four-year-oldness—the explosions, the tempers, the denunciations, the demands—and I feel suddenly ill. I put the iron down. What in me demanded that goodness in her? And what was the cost, the cost to her of such goodness?

The old man living in the back once said in his gentle way: "You should smile at Emily more when you look at her." What *was* in my face when I looked at her? I loved her. There were all the acts of love.

It was only with the others I remembered what he said, and it was the face of joy, and not of care or tightness or worry I turned to them—too late for Emily. She does not smile easily, let alone almost always as her brothers and sisters do. Her face is closed and sombre, but when she wants, how fluid. You must have seen it in her pantomimes, you spoke of her rare gift for comedy on the stage that rouses a laughter out of the audience so dear they applaud and applaud and do not want to let her go.

Where does it come from, that comedy? There was none of it in her when she came back to me that second time, after I had had to send her away again. She had a new daddy now to learn to love, and I think perhaps it was a better time.

Except when we left her alone nights, telling ourselves she was old enough.

"Can't you go some other time, Mommy, like tomorrow?" she would ask. "Will it be just a little while you'll be gone? Do you promise?"

The time we came back, the front door open, the clock on the floor in the hall. She rigid awake. "It wasn't just a little while. I didn't cry.

Three times I called you, just three times, and then I ran downstairs to open the door so you could come faster. The clock talked loud. I threw it away, it scared me what it talked."

She said the clock talked loud again that night I went to the hospital to have Susan. She was delirious with the fever that comes before red measles, but she was fully conscious all the week I was gone and the week after we were home when she could not come near the new baby or me.

She did not get well. She stayed skeleton thin, not wanting to eat, and night after night she had nightmares. She would call for me, and I would rouse from exhaustion to sleepily call back: "You're all right, darling, go to sleep, it's just a dream," and if she still called, in a sterner voice, "now go to sleep, Emily, there's nothing to hurt you." Twice, only twice, when I had to get up for Susan anyhow, I went in to sit with her.

Now when it is too late (as if she would let me hold and comfort her like I do the others) I get up and go to her at once at her moan or restless stirring. "Are you awake, Emily? Can I get you something?" And the answer is always the same: "No, I'm all right, go back to sleep, Mother."

They persuaded me at the clinic to send her away to a convalescent home in the country where "she can have the kind of food and care you can't manage for her, and you'll be free to concentrate on the new baby." They still send children to that place. I see pictures on the society page of sleek young women planning affairs to raise money for it, or dancing at the affairs, or decorating Easter eggs or filling Christmas stockings for the children.

They never have a picture of the children so I do not know if the girls still wear those gigantic red bows and the ravaged looks on the every other Sunday when parents can come to visit "unless otherwise notified"—as we were notified the first six weeks.

Oh it is a handsome place, green lawns and tall trees and fluted flower beds. High up on the balconies of each cottage the children stand, the girls in their red bows and white dresses, the boys in white suits and giant red ties. The parents stand below shrieking up to be heard and the children shriek down to be heard, and between them the invisible wall "Not To Be Contaminated by Parental Germs or Physical Affection."

There was a tiny girl who always stood hand in hand with Emily. Her parents never came. One visit she was gone. "They moved her to Rose College," Emily shouted in explanation. "They don't like you to love anybody here."

She wrote once a week, the labored writing of a seven-year-old. "I am fine. How is the baby. If I write my leter nicly I will have a star. Love." There never was a star. We wrote every other day, letters she could never hold or keep but only hear read—once. "We simply do not have room for children to keep any personal possessions," they patiently explained when we pieced one Sunday's shrieking together to plead how much it would mean to Emily, who loved so to keep things, to be allowed to keep her letters and cards.

Each visit she looked frailer. "She isn't eating," they told us.

(They had runny eggs for breakfast or mush with lumps, Emily said later, I'd hold it in my mouth and not swallow. Nothing ever tasted good, just when they had chicken.)

It took us eight months to get her released home, and only the fact that she gained back so little of her seven lost pounds convinced the social worker.

I used to try to hold and love her after she came back, but her body would stay stiff, and after a while she'd push away. She ate little. Food sickened her, and I think much of life too. Oh she had physical lightness and brightness, twinkling by on skates, bouncing like a ball up and down up and down over the jump rope, skimming over the hill; but these were momentary.

She fretted about her appearance, thin and dark and foreign-looking at a time when every little girl was supposed to look or thought she should look a chubby blonde replica of Shirley Temple. The doorbell sometimes rang for her, but no one seemed to come and play in the house or be a best friend. Maybe because we moved so much.

There was a boy she loved painfully through two school semesters. Months later she told me how she had taken pennies from my purse to buy him candy. "Licorice was his favorite and I brought him some every day, but he still liked Jennifer better'n me. Why, Mommy?" The kind of question for which there is no answer.

School was a worry to her. She was not glib or quick in a world where glibness and quickness were easily confused with ability to learn. To her overworked and exasperated teachers she was an over-conscientious "slow learner" who kept trying to catch up and was absent entirely too often.

I let her be absent, though sometimes the illness was imaginary. How different from my now-strictness about attendance with the others. I wasn't working. We had a new baby, I was home anyhow. Sometimes, after Susan grew old enough, I would keep her home from school, too, to have them all together.

Mostly Emily had asthma, and her breathing, harsh and labored, would fill the house with a curiously tranquil sound. I would bring the two old dresser mirrors and her boxes of collections to her bed. She would select beads and single earrings, bottle tops and shells, dried flowers and pebbles, old postcards and scraps, all sorts of oddments; then she and Susan would play Kingdom, setting up landscapes and furniture, peopling them with action.

Those were the only times of peaceful companionship between her and Susan. I have edged away from it, that poisonous feeling between them, that terrible balancing of hurts and needs I had to do between the two, and did so badly, those earlier years.

Oh there are conflicts between the others too, each one human, needing, demanding, hurting, taking—but only between Emily and Susan, no, Emily toward Susan that corroding resentment. It seems so obvious on the surface, yet it is not obvious. Susan, the second child, Susan, golden- and curly-haired and chubby, quick and articulate and assured, everything in appearance and manner Emily was not; Susan, not able to resist Emily's precious things, losing or sometimes clumsily breaking them; Susan telling jokes and riddles to company for applause while Emily sat silent (to say to me later: that was *my* riddle, Mother, I told it to Susan); Susan, who for all the five years' difference in age was just a year behind Emily in developing physically.

I am glad for that slow physical development that widened the difference between her and her contemporaries, though she suffered over it. She was too vulnerable for that terrible world of youthful competition, of preening and parading, of constant measuring of yourself against every other, of envy, "If I had that copper hair," "If I had that skin. . . ." She tormented herself enough about not looking like the others, there was enough of the unsureness, the having to be conscious of words before you speak, the constant caring—what are they thinking of me? without having it all magnified by the merciless physical drives.

Ronnie is calling. He is wet and I change him. It is rare there is such a cry now. That time of motherhood is almost behind me when the ear is not one's own but must always be racked and listening for the child cry, the child call. We sit for a while and I hold him, looking out over the city spread in charcoal with its soft aisles of light. *"Shoogily,"* he breathes and curls closer. I carry him back to bed, asleep. *Shoogily.* A funny word, a family word, inherited from Emily, invented by her to say: *comfort.*

In this and other ways she leaves her seal, I say aloud. And startle at my saying it. What do I mean? What did I start to gather together, to try and make coherent? I was at the terrible, growing years. War years. I do not remember them well. I was working, there were four smaller ones now, there was not time for her. She had to help be a mother, and housekeeper, and shopper. She had to set her seal. Mornings of crisis and near hysteria trying to get lunches packed, hair combed, coats and shoes found, everyone to school or Child Care on time, the baby ready for transportation. And always the paper scribbled on by a smaller one, the book looked at by Susan then mislaid, the homework not done. Running out to that huge school where she was one, she was lost, she was a drop; suffering over the unpreparedness, stammering and unsure in her classes.

There was so little time left at night after the kids were bedded down. She would struggle over books, always eating (it was in those years she developed her enormous appetite that is legendary in our family) and I would be ironing, or preparing food for the next day, or writing V-mail to Bill, or tending the baby. Sometimes, to make me laugh, or out of her despair, she would imitate happenings or types at school.

I think I said once: "Why don't you do something like this in the school amateur show?" One morning she phoned me at work, hardly understandable through the weeping: "Mother, I did it. I won, I won; they gave me first prize; they clapped and clapped and wouldn't let me go."

Now suddenly she was Somebody, and as imprisoned in her difference as she had been in anonymity.

She began to be asked to perform at other high schools, even in colleges, then at city and statewide affairs. The first one we went to, I only recognized her that first moment when thin, shy, she almost drowned herself into the curtains. Then: Was this Emily? The control, the command, the convulsing and deadly clowning, the spell, then the roaring, stamping audience, unwilling to let this rare and precious laughter out of their lives.

Afterwards: You ought to do something about her with a gift like that—but without money or knowing how, what does one do? We have left it all to her, and the gift has as often eddied inside, clogged and clotted, as been used and growing.

She is coming. She runs up the stairs two at a time with her light graceful step, and I know she is happy tonight. Whatever it was that occasioned your call did not happen today.

"Aren't you ever going to finish the ironing, Mother? Whistler painted his mother in a rocker. I'd have to paint mine standing over an ironing board." This is one of her communicative nights and she tells me everything and nothing as she fixes herself a plate of food out of the icebox.

She is so lovely. Why did you want me to come in at all? Why were you concerned? She will find her way.

She starts up the stairs to bed. "Don't get me up with the rest in the morning." "But I thought you were having midterms." "Oh, those," she comes back in, kisses me, and says quite lightly, "in a couple of years when we'll all be atom-dead they won't matter a bit."

She has said it before. She *believes* it. But because I have been dredging the past, and all that compounds a human being is so heavy and meaningful in me, I cannot endure it tonight.

I will never total it all. I will never come in to say: She was a child seldom smiled at. Her father left me before she was a year old. I had to work her first six years when there was work, or I sent her home and to his relatives. There were years she had care she hated. She was dark and thin and foreign-looking in a world where the prestige went to blondeness and curly hair and dimples, she was slow where glibness was prized. She was a child of anxious, not proud, love. We were poor and could not afford for her the soil of easy growth. I was a young mother, I was a distracted mother. There were the other children pushing up, demanding. Her younger sister seemed all that she was not. There were years she did not want me to touch her. She kept too much in herself, her life was such she had to keep too much in herself. My wisdom came too late. She has much to her and probably nothing will come of it. She is a child of her age, of depression, of war, of fear.

Let her be. So all that is in her will not bloom—but in how many does it? There is still enough left to live by. Only help her to know—help make it so there is cause for her to know—that she is more than this dress on the ironing board, helpless before the iron.

QUESTIONS

1. Tillie Olsen is not speaking. Who *is*? What do we know about her from the tone of her speech (see Preface, pp. 24–27)? Examine the quality of the language.
2. How is the story different from a sociological or psychological case study?
3. What is the conflict in the story? It isn't between the mother and Emily; it can hardly be between the mother and the teacher. Is it within the mother? Explain. (See Preface, pp. 13–14.)
4. How is it possible to write a seven-page story that covers nineteen years? (See Preface, pp. 13, 17.) How does Olsen keep the story more than a list of difficulties? (The answer to Question 3 will help here.)
5. Examine the *mother's* life. To what extent has she been like the dress on the ironing board, "helpless before the iron"? To what extent has she survived as a person? What about Emily? Do you find the story hopeful or hopeless?

BERNARD MALAMUD

(1914—)

A Jewish-American writer born in Brooklyn, Malamud uses his
Jewish background, speech patterns, and sensibility in his fiction to
create the atmosphere of a world in which life matters and in which
the magical and even the sacred hover just above the everyday. Both
"The Magic Barrel" and "Idiots First" are title stories of collections
of Malamud's short fiction, fiction that is among the most beautiful
of any contemporary writer's. His novels include *The Assistant, A
New Life,* and *The Fixer.*

[See Preface, "Idiots First," p. 2 (fantasy as reality), p. 15 (lack of
initial exposition); "The Magic Barrel," pp. 22–23 (dialogue and
vision).

The Magic Barrel

BERNARD MALAMUD

Not long ago there lived in uptown New York, in a small almost
meager room, though crowded with books, Leo Finkle, a rabbinical
student in the Yeshivah University. Finkle, after six years of study,
was to be ordained in June and had been advised by an acquaintance that he might find it easier to win himself a congregation if he
were married. Since he had no present prospects of marriage, after

two tormented days of turning it over in his mind, he called in Pinye Salzman, a marriage broker whose two-line advertisement he had read in the *Forward*.

The matchmaker appeared one night out of the dark fourth-floor hallway of the graystone rooming house where Finkle lived, grasping a black, strapped portfolio that had been worn thin with use. Salzman, who had been long in the business, was of slight but dignified build, wearing an old hat, and an overcoat too short and tight for him. He smelled frankly of fish, which he loved to eat, and although he was missing a few teeth, his presence was not displeasing, because of an amiable manner curiously contrasted with mournful eyes. His voice, his lips, his wisp of beard, his bony fingers were animated, but give him a moment of repose and his mild blue eyes revealed a depth of sadness, a characteristic that put Leo a little at ease although the situation, for him, was inherently tense.

He at once informed Salzman why he had asked him to come, explaining that his home was in Cleveland, and that but for his parents, who had married comparatively late in life, he was alone in the world. He had for six years devoted himself almost entirely to his studies, as a result of which, understandably, he had found himself without time for a social life and the company of young women. Therefore he thought it the better part of trial and error—of embarrassing fumbling—to call in an experienced person to advise him on these matters. He remarked in passing that the function of the marriage broker was ancient and honorable, highly approved in the Jewish community, because it made practical the necessary without hindering joy. Moreover, his own parents had been brought together by a matchmaker. They had made, if not a financially profitable marriage—since neither had possessed any worldly goods to speak of—at least a successful one in the sense of their everlasting devotion to each other. Salzman listened in embarrassed surprise, sensing a sort of apology. Later, however, he experienced a glow of pride in his work, an emotion that had left him years ago, and he heartily approved of Finkle.

The two went to their business. Leo had led Salzman to the only clear place in the room, a table near a window that overlooked the lamp-lit city. He seated himself at the matchmaker's side but facing him, attempting by an act of will to suppress the unpleasant tickle in his throat. Salzman eagerly unstrapped his portfolio and removed a loose rubber band from a thin packet of much-handled cards. As he flipped through them, a gesture and sound that physically hurt Leo, the student pretended not to see and gazed steadfastly out the window. Although it was still February, winter was on its last legs, signs of which he had for the first time in years begun to notice. He now observed the round white moon, moving high in the sky through a cloud menagerie, and watched with half-open mouth as it penetrated a huge hen, and dropped out of her like an egg laying itself. Salzman, though pretending through eyeglasses he had just slipped on, to be engaged in scanning the writing on the cards, stole occasional glances at the young man's distinguished face, noting with pleasure the long, severe scholar's nose, brown eyes heavy with learning, sensitive yet ascetic lips, and a certain almost hollow quality of the dark cheeks. He gazed around at shelves upon shelves of books and let out a soft, contented sigh.

When Leo's eyes fell upon the cards, he counted six spread out in Salzman's hand.

"So few?" he asked in disappointment.

"You wouldn't believe me how much cards I got in my office," Salzman replied. "The drawers are already filled to the top, so I keep them now in a barrel, but is every girl good for a new rabbi?"

Leo blushed at this, regretting all he had revealed of himself in a curriculum vitae he had sent to Salzman. He had thought it best to acquaint him with his strict standards and specifications, but in having done so, felt he had told the marriage broker more than was absolutely necessary.

He hesitantly inquired, "Do you keep photographs of your clients on file?"

"First comes family, amount of dowry, also what kind promises," Salzman replied, unbuttoning his tight coat and settling himself in the chair. "After comes pictures, rabbi."

"Call me Mr. Finkle. I'm not yet a rabbi."

Salzman said he would, but instead called him doctor, which he changed to rabbi when Leo was not listening too attentively.

Salzman adjusted his horn-rimmed spectacles, gently cleared his throat and read in an eager voice the contents of the top card:

"Sophie P. Twenty four years. Widow one year. No children. Educated high school and two years college. Father promises eight thousand dollars. Has wonderful wholesale business. Also real estate. On the mother's side comes teachers, also one actor. Well known on Second Avenue."

Leo gazed up in surprise. "Did you say a widow?"

"A widow don't mean spoiled, rabbi. She lived with her husband maybe four months. He was a sick boy she made a mistake to marry him."

"Marrying a widow has never entered my mind."

"This is because you have no experience. A widow, especially if she is young and healthy like this girl, is a wonderful person to marry. She will be thankful to you the rest of her life. Believe me, if I was looking now for a bride, I would marry a widow."

Leo reflected, then shook his head.

Salzman hunched his shoulders in an almost imperceptible gesture of disappointment. He placed the card down on the wooden table and began to read another:

"Lily H. High school teacher. Regular. Not a substitute. Has savings and new Dodge car. Lived in Paris one year. Father is successful dentist thirty-five years. Interested in professional man. Well Americanized family. Wonderful opportunity."

"I knew her personally," said Salzman. "I wish you could see this girl. She is a doll. Also very intelligent. All day you could talk to her about books and theyater and what not. She also knows current events."

"I don't believe you mentioned her age?"

"Her age?" Salzman said, raising his brows. "Her age is thirty-two years."

Leo said after a while, "I'm afraid that seems a little too old."

Salzman let out a laugh. "So how old are you, rabbi?"

"Twenty-seven."

"So what is the difference, tell me, between twenty-seven and thirty-two? My own wife is seven years older than me. So what did I suffer?—Nothing. If Rothschild's a daughter wants to marry you, would you say on account her age, no?"

"Yes," Leo said dryly.

Salzman shook off the no in the yes. "Five years don't mean a thing. I give you my word that when you will live with her for one week you will forget her age. What does it mean five years—that she lived more and knows more than somebody who is younger? On this girl, God bless her, years are not wasted. Each one that it comes makes better the bargain."

"What subject does she teach in high school?"

"Languages. If you heard the way she speaks French, you will think it is music. I am in the business twenty-five years, and I recommend her with my whole heart. Believe me, I know what I'm talking, rabbi."

"What's on the next card?" Leo said abruptly.

Salzman reluctantly turned up the third card:

"Ruth K. Nineteen years. Honor student. Father offers thirteen thousand cash to the right bridegroom. He is a medical doctor. Stomach specialist with marvelous practice. Brother in law owns own garment business. Particular people."

Salzman looked as if he had read his trump card.

"Did you say nineteen?" Leo asked with interest.

"On the dot."

"Is she attractive?" He blushed. "Pretty?"

Salzman kissed his finger tips. "A little doll. On this I give you my word. Let me call the father tonight and you will see what means pretty."

But Leo was troubled. "You're sure she's that young?"

"This I am positive. The father will show you the birth certificate."

"Are you positive there isn't something wrong with her?" Leo insisted.

"Who says there is wrong?"

"I don't understand why an American girl her age should go to a marriage broker."

A smile spread over Salzman's face.

"So for the same reason you went, she comes."

Leo flushed. "I am pressed for time."

Salzman, realizing he had been tactless, quickly explained. "The father came, not her. He wants she should have the best, so he looks around himself. When we will locate the right boy he will introduce him and encourage. This makes a better marriage than if a young girl without experience takes for herself. I don't have to tell you this."

"But don't you think this young girl believes in love?" Leo spoke uneasily.

Salzman was about to guffaw but caught himself and said soberly, "Love comes with the right person, not before."

Leo parted dry lips but did not speak. Noticing that Salzman had snatched a glance at the next card, he cleverly asked, "How is her health?"

"Perfect," Salzman said, breathing with difficulty. "Of course, she is a little lame on her right foot from an auto accident that it happened to her when she was twelve years, but nobody notices on account she is so brilliant and also beautiful."

Leo got up heavily and went to the window. He felt curiously bitter and upbraided himself for having called in the marriage broker. Finally, he shook his head.

"Why not?" Salzman persisted, the pitch of his voice rising.

"Because I detest stomach specialists."

"So what do you care what is his business? After you marry her do you need him? Who says he must come every Friday night in your house?"

Ashamed of the way the talk was going, Leo dismissed Salzman, who went home with heavy, melancholy eyes.

Though he had felt only relief at the marriage broker's departure, Leo was in low spirits the next day. He explained it as arising from Salzman's failure to produce a suitable bride for him. He did not care for his type of clientele. But when Leo found himself hesitating whether to seek out another matchmaker, one more polished than

Pinye, he wondered if it could be—his protestations to the contrary, and although he honored his father and mother—that he did not, in essence, care for the matchmaking institution? This thought he quickly put out of mind yet found himself still upset. All day he ran around in the woods—missed an important appointment, forgot to give out his laundry, walked out of a Broadway cafeteria without paying and had to run back with the ticket in his hand; had even not recognized his landlady in the street when she passed with a friend and courteously called out, "A good evening to you, Doctor Finkle." By nightfall, however, he had regained sufficient calm to sink his nose into a book and there found peace from his thoughts.

Almost at once there came a knock on the door. Before Leo could say enter, Salzman, commercial cupid, was standing in the room. His face was gray and meager, his expression hungry, and he looked as if he would expire on his feet. Yet the marriage broker managed, by some trick of the muscles, to display a broad smile.

"So good evening. I am invited?"

Leo nodded, disturbed to see him again, yet unwilling to ask the man to leave.

Beaming still, Salzman laid his portfolio on the table. "Rabbi, I got for you tonight good news."

"I've asked you not to call me rabbi. I'm still a student."

"Your worries are finished. I have for you a first-class bride."

"Leave me in peace concerning this subject." Leo pretended lack of interest.

"The world will dance at your wedding."

"Please, Mr. Salzman, no more."

"But first must come back my strength," Salzman said weakly. He fumbled with the portfolio straps and took out of the leather case an oily paper bag, from which he extracted a hard, seeded roll and a small, smoked white fish. With a quick motion of his hand he stripped the fish out of its skin and began ravenously to chew. "All day in a rush," he muttered.

Leo watched him eat.

"A sliced tomato you have maybe?" Salzman hesitantly inquired.

"No."

The marriage broker shut his eyes and ate. When he had finished he carefully cleaned up the crumbs and rolled up the remains of the fish, in the paper bag. His spectacled eyes roamed the room until he discovered, amid some piles of books, a one-burner gas stove. Lifting his hat he humbly asked, "A glass tea you got, rabbi?"

Conscience-stricken, Leo rose and brewed the tea. He served it with a chunk of lemon and two cubes of lump sugar, delighting Salzman.

After he had drunk his tea, Salzman's strength and good spirits were restored.

"So tell me, rabbi," he said amiably, "you considered some more the three clients I mentioned yesterday?"

"There was no need to consider."

"Why not?"

"None of them suits me."

"What then suits you?"

Leo let it pass because he could give only a confused answer.

Without waiting for a reply, Salzman asked, "You remember this girl I talked to you—the high school teacher?"

"Age thirty-two?"

But, surprisingly, Salzman's face lit in a smile. "Age twenty-nine."

Leo shot him a look. "Reduced from thirty-two?"

"A mistake," Salzman avowed. "I talked today with the dentist. He took me to his safety deposit box and showed me the birth certificate. She was twenty-nine years last August. They made her a party in the mountains where she went for her vacation. When her father spoke to me the first time I forgot to write the age and I told you thirty-two, but now I remember this was a different client, a widow."

"The same one you told me about? I thought she was twenty-four?"

"A different. Am I responsible that the world is filled with widows?"

"No, but I'm not interested in them, nor for that matter, in school teachers."

Salzman pulled his clasped hands to his breast. Looking at the ceiling he devoutly exclaimed, "Yiddishe kinder, what can I say to somebody that he is not interested in high school teachers? So what then you are interested?"

Leo flushed but controlled himself.

"In what else will you be interested," Salzman went on, "if you not interested in this fine girl that she speaks four languages and has personally in the bank ten thousand dollars? Also her father guarantees further twelve thousand. Also she has a new car, wonderful clothes, talks on all subjects, and she will give you a first-class home and children. How near do we come in our life to paradise?

"If she's so wonderful, why hasn't she married ten years ago?"

"Why?" said Salzman with a heavy laugh. "—Why? Because she is *partikiler*. This is why. She wants the *best*."

Leo was silent, amused at how he had entangled himself. But Salzman had aroused his interest in Lily H., and he began seriously to consider calling on her. When the marriage broker observed how intently Leo's mind was at work on the facts he had supplied, he felt certain they would soon come to an agreement.

Late Saturday afternoon, conscious of Salzman, Leo Finkle walked with Lily Hirschorn along Riverside Drive. He walked briskly and erectly, wearing with distinction the black fedora he had that morning taken with trepidation out of the dusty hat box on his closet shelf, and the heavy black Saturday coat he had thoroughly whisked clean. Leo also owned a walking stick, a present from a distant relative, but quickly put temptation aside and did not use it. Lily, petite and not unpretty, had on something signifying the approach of spring. She was au courant, animatedly, with all sorts of subjects, and he weighed her words and found her surprisingly sound—score another for Salzman, whom he uneasily sensed to be somewhere around, hiding perhaps high in a tree along the street, flashing the lady signals with a pocket mirror; or perhaps a cloven-hoofed Pan, piping nuptial ditties as he danced his invisible way before them, strewing wild buds on the walk and purple grapes in their path, symbolizing fruit of a union, though there was of course still none.

Lily startled Leo by remarking, "I was thinking of Mr. Salzman, a curious figure, wouldn't you say?"

Not certain what to answer, he nodded.

She bravely went on, blushing, "I for one am grateful for his introducing us. Aren't you?"

He courteously replied, "I am."

"I mean," she said with a little laugh—and it was all in good taste, or at least gave the effect of being not in bad—"do you mind that we came together so?"

He was not displeased with her honesty, recognizing that she meant to set the relationship aright, and understanding that it took a certain amount of experience in life, and courage, to want to do it quite that way. One had to have some sort of past to make that kind of beginning.

He said that he did not mind. Salzman's function was traditional and honorable—valuable for what it might achieve, which, he pointed out, was frequently nothing.

Lily agreed with a sigh. They walked on for a while and she said after a long silence, again with a nervous laugh, "Would you mind if I asked you something a little bit personal? Frankly, I find the subject fascinating." Although Leo shrugged, she went on half embarrassedly, "How was it that you came to your calling? I mean was it a sudden passionate inspiration?"

Leo, after a time, slowly replied, "I was always interested in the Law."

"You saw revealed in it the presence of the Highest?"

He nodded and changed the subject. "I understand that you spent a little time in Paris, Miss Hirschorn?"

"Oh, did Mr. Salzman tell you, Rabbi Finkle?" Leo winced but she went on, "It was ages ago and almost forgotten. I remember I had to return for my sister's wedding."

And Lily would not be put off. "When," she asked in a trembly voice, "did you become enamored of God?"

He stared at her. Then it came to him that she was talking not about Leo Finkle, but of a total stranger, some mystical figure, perhaps even passionate prophet that Salzman had dreamed up for her—no relation to the living or dead. Leo trembled with rage and weakness. The trickster had obviously sold her a bill of goods, just as he had him, who'd expected to become acquainted with a young lady of twenty-nine, only to behold, the moment he laid eyes upon her strained and anxious face, a woman past thirty-five and aging rapidly. Only his self control had kept him this long in her presence.

"I am not," he said gravely, "a talented religious person," and in seeking words to go on, found himself possessed by shame and fear. "I think," he said in a strained manner, "that I came to God not because I loved Him, but because I did not."

This confession he spoke harshly because its unexpectedness shook him.

Lily wilted. Leo saw a profusion of loaves of bread go flying like ducks high over his head, not unlike the winged loaves by which he had counted himself to sleep last night. Mercifully, then, it snowed, which he would not put past Salzman's machinations.

He was infuriated with the marriage broker and swore he would throw him out of the room the minute he reappeared. But Salzman did not come that night, and when Leo's anger had subsided, an unaccountable despair grew in its place. At first he thought this was caused by his disappointment in Lily, but before long it became evident that he had involved himself with Salzman without a true knowledge of his own intent. He gradually realized—with an emptiness that seized him with six hands—that he had called in the broker to find him a bride because he was incapable of doing it himself. This terrifying insight he had derived as a result of his meeting and conversation with Lily Hirschorn. Her probing questions had somehow irritated him into revealing—to himself more than her—the true nature of his relationship to God, and from that it had come upon him, with shocking force, that apart from his parents, he had never loved anyone. Or perhaps it went the other way, that he did not love God so well as he might, because he had not loved man. It seemed to Leo that his whole life stood starkly revealed and he saw himself for the first time as he truly was—unloved and loveless. This bitter but somehow not fully unexpected revelation brought him to a point of panic, controlled only by extraordinary effort. He covered his face with his hands and cried.

The week that followed was the worst of his life. He did not eat and lost weight. His beard darkened and grew ragged. He stopped attending seminars and almost never opened a book. He seriously considered leaving the Yeshivah, although he was deeply troubled at the thought of the loss of all his years of study—saw them like pages torn from a book, strewn over the city—and at the devastating effect of this decision upon his parents. But he had lived without knowledge of himself, and never in the Five Books and all the Commentaries—mea culpa—had the truth been revealed to him. He did not know where to turn, and in all this desolating loneliness there was no *to whom,* although he often thought of Lily but not once could bring himself to go downstairs and make the call. He became touchy and irritable, especially with his landlady, who asked him all manner of personal questions; on the other hand, sensing his own disagreeableness, he waylaid her on the stairs and apologized abjectly, until mortified, she ran from him. Out of this, however, he drew the consolation that he was a Jew and that a Jew suffered. But gradually, as the long and terrible week drew to a close, he regained his composure and some idea of purpose in life: to go on as planned. Although he was imperfect, the ideal was not. As for his quest of a bride, the thought of continuing afflicted him with anxiety and heartburn, yet perhaps with this new knowledge of himself he would be more successful than in the past. Perhaps love would now come to him and a bride to that love. And for this sanctified seeking who needed a Salzman?

The marriage broker, a skeleton with haunted eyes, returned that very night. He looked, withal, the picture of frustrated expectancy— as if he had steadfastly waited the week at Miss Lily Hirschorn's side for a telephone call that never came.

Casually coughing, Salzman came immediately to the point: "So how did you like her?"

Leo's anger rose and he could not refrain from chiding the matchmaker: "Why did you lie to me, Salzman?"

Salzman's pale face went dead white, the world had snowed on him.

"Did you not state that she was twenty-nine?" Leo insisted.

"I give you my word—"

"She was thirty-five, if a day. *At least* thirty-five."

"Of this don't be too sure. Her father told me—"

"Never mind. The worst of it was that you lied to her."

"How did I lie to her, tell me?"

"You told her things about me that weren't true. You made me out to be more, consequently less than I am. She had in mind a totally different person, a sort of semimystical Wonder Rabbi."

"All I said, you was a religious man."

"I can imagine."

Salzman sighed. "This is my weakness that I have," he confessed. "My wife says to me I shouldn't be a salesman, but when I have two fine people that they would be wonderful to be married, I am so happy that I talk too much." He smiled wanly. "This is why Salzman is a poor man."

Leo's anger left him. "Well, Salzman, I'm afraid that's all."

The marriage broker fastened hungry eyes on him.

"You don't want any more a bride?"

"I do," said Leo, "but I have decided to seek her in a different way. I am no longer interested in an arranged marriage. To be frank, I now admit the necessity of premarital love. That is, I want to be in love with the one I marry."

"Love?" said Salzman, astounded. After a moment he remarked, "For us, our love is our life, not for the ladies. In the ghetto they—"

"I know, I know," said Leo. "I've thought of it often. Love, I have said to myself, should be a by-product of living and worship rather than its own end. Yet for myself I find it necessary to establish the level of my need and fulfill it."

Salzman shrugged but answered, "Listen, rabbi, if you want love, this I can find for you also. I have such beautiful clients that you will love them the minute your eyes will see them."

Leo smiled unhappily. "I'm afraid you don't understand."

But Salzman hastily unstrapped his portfolio and withdrew a manila packet from it.

"Pictures," he said, quickly laying the envelope on the table.

Leo called after him to take the pictures away, but as if on the wings of the wind, Salzman had disappeared.

March came. Leo had returned to his regular routine. Although he felt not quite himself yet—lacked energy—he was making plans for a more active social life. Of course it would cost something, but he was an expert in cutting corners; and when there were no corners left he would make circles rounder. All the while Salzman's pictures had lain on the table, gathering dust. Occasionally as Leo sat studying, or enjoying a cup of tea, his eyes fell on the manila envelope, but he never opened it.

The days went by and no social life to speak of developed with a member of the opposite sex—it was difficult, given the circumstances of his situation. One morning Leo toiled up the stairs to his room and stared out the window at the city. Although the day was bright his view of it was dark. For some time he watched the people in the street below hurrying along and then turned with a heavy heart to his little room. On the table was the packet. With a sudden relentless gesture he tore it open. For a half-hour he stood by the table in a state of excitement, examining the photographs of the ladies Salzman had included. Finally, with a deep sigh he put them down. There were six, of varying degrees of attractiveness, but look at them long enough and they all became Lily Hirschorn: all past their prime, all starved behind bright smiles, not a true personality in the lot. Life, despite their frantic yoohooings, had passed them by; they were pictures in a brief case that stank of fish. After a while, however, as Leo attempted to return the photographs into the envelope, he found in it another, a snapshot of the type taken by a machine for a quarter. He gazed at it a moment and let out a cry.

Her face deeply moved him. Why, he could at first not say. It gave him the impression of youth—spring flowers, yet age—a sense of having been used to the bone, wasted; this came from the eyes, which were hauntingly familiar, yet absolutely strange. He had a vivid impression that he had met her before, but try as he might he could not place her although he could almost recall her name, as if he had read it in her own handwriting. No, this couldn't be; he would have remembered her. It was not, he affirmed, that she had an extraordinary beauty—no, though her face was attractive enough; it was that *something* about her moved him. Feature for feature, even some of the ladies of the photographs could do better; but she leaped forth to his heart—had *lived,* or wanted to—more than just wanted, perhaps regretted how she had lived—had somehow deeply suffered: it could be seen in the depths of those reluctant eyes, and from the way the light enclosed and shone from her, and within her, opening realms of possibility: this was her own. Her he desired. His head ached and eyes narrowed with the intensity of his gazing, then as if an obscure fog had blown up in the mind, he experienced fear of her and was aware that he had received an impression, somehow, of evil. He shuddered, saying softly, it is thus with us all. Leo brewed some tea in a small pot and sat sipping it without sugar, to calm himself. But before he had finished drinking, again with excitement he examined the face and found it good: good for Leo Finkle. Only such a one could understand him and help him seek whatever he was seeking. She might, perhaps, love him. How she had happened to be among the discards in Salzman's barrel he could never guess, but he knew he must urgently go find her.

Leo rushed downstairs, grabbed up the Bronx telephone book, and searched for Salzman's home address. He was not listed, nor was his office. Neither was he in the Manhattan book. But Leo remembered having written down the address on a slip of paper after he had read Salzman's advertisement in the "personals" column of the *Forward.* He ran up to his room and tore through his papers, without luck. It was exasperating. Just when he needed the matchmaker he was nowhere to be found. Fortunately Leo remembered to look in his wallet. There on a card he found his name written and a Bronx address. No phone number was listed, the reason—Leo now re-called—he had originally communicated with Salzman by letter. He got on his coat, put a hat on over his skull cap and hurried to the subway station. All the way to the far end of the Bronx he sat on the edge of his seat. He was more than once tempted to take out the picture and see if the girl's face was as he remembered it, but he refrained, allowing the snapshot to remain in his inside coat pocket, content to have her so close. When the train pulled into the station he was waiting at the door and bolted out. He quickly located the street Salzman had advertised.

The building he sought was less than a block from the subway, but it was not an office building, nor even a loft, nor a store in which one could rent office space. It was a very old tenement house. Leo found Salzman's name in pencil on a soiled tag under the bell and climbed three dark flights to his apartment. When he knocked, the door was opened by a thin, asthmatic, gray-haired woman, in felt slippers.

"Yes?" she said, expecting nothing. She listened without listening. He could have sworn he had seen her, too, before but he knew it was an illusion.

"Salzman—does he live here? Pinye Salzman," he said, "the match-maker?"

She stared at him a long minute. "Of course."

He felt embarrassed. "Is he in?"

"No." Her mouth, though left open, offered nothing more.

"The matter is urgent. Can you tell me where his office is?"

"In the air." She pointed upward.

"You mean he has no office?" Leo asked.

"In his socks."

He peered into the apartment. It was sunless and dingy, one large room divided by a half-open curtain, beyond which he could see a sagging metal bed. The near side of a room was crowded with rickety chairs, old bureaus, a three-legged table, racks of cooking utensils, and all the apparatus of a kitchen. But there was no sign of Salzman or his magic barrel, probably also a figment of the imagination. An odor of frying fish made Leo weak to the knees.

"Where is he?" he insisted. "I've got to see your husband."

At length she answered, "So who knows where he is? Every time he thinks a new thought he runs to a different place. Go home, he will find you."

"Tell him Leo Finkle."

She gave no sign she had heard.

He walked downstairs, depressed.

But Salzman, breathless, stood waiting at his door.

Leo was astounded and overjoyed. "How did you get here before me?"

"I rushed."

"Come inside."

They entered. Leo fixed tea, and a sardine sandwich for Salzman. As they were drinking he reached behind him for the packet of pictures and handed them to the marriage broker.

Salzman put down his glass and said expectantly, "You found somebody you like?"

"Not among these."

The marriage broker turned away.

"Here is the one I want." Leo held forth the snapshot.

Salzman slipped on his glasses and took the picture into his trembling hand. He turned ghastly and let out a groan.

"What's the matter?" cried Leo.

"Excuse me. Was an accident this picture. She isn't for you."

Salzman frantically shoved the manila packet into his portfolio. He thrust the snapshot into his pocket and fled down the stairs.

Leo, after momentary paralysis, gave chase and cornered the marriage broker in the vestibule. The landlady made hysterical outcries but neither of them listened.

"Give me back the picture, Salzman."

"No." The pain in his eyes was terrible.

"Tell me who she is then."

"This I can't tell you. Excuse me."

He made to depart, but Leo, forgetting himself, seized the matchmaker by his tight coat and shook him frenziedly.

"Please," sighed Salzman. *"Please."*

Leo ashamedly let him go. "Tell me who she is," he begged. "It's very important for me to know."

"She is not for you. She is a wild one—wild, without shame. This is not a bride for a rabbi."

"What do you mean wild?"

"Like an animal. Like a dog. For her to be poor was a sin. This is why to me she is dead now."

"In God's name, what do you mean?"

"Her I can't introduce to you," Salzman cried.

"Why are you so excited?"

"Why, he asks," Salzman said, bursting into tears. "This is my baby, my Stella, she should burn in hell."

Leo hurried up to bed and hid under the covers. Under the covers he thought his life through. Although he soon fell asleep he could not sleep her out of his mind. He woke, beating his breast. Though he prayed to be rid of her, his prayers went unanswered. Through days of torment he endlessly struggled not to love her; fearing success, he escaped it. He then concluded to convert her to goodness, himself to God. The idea alternately nauseated and exalted him.

He perhaps did not know that he had come to a final decision until he encountered Salzman in a Broadway cafeteria. He was sitting alone at a rear table, sucking the bony remains of a fish. The marriage broker appeared haggard, and transparent to the point of vanishing.

Salzman looked up at first without recognizing him. Leo had grown a pointed beard and his eyes were weighted with wisdom.

"Salzman," he said, "love has at last come to my heart."

"Who can love from a picture?" mocked the marriage broker.

"It is not impossible."

"If you can love her, then you can love anybody. Let me show you some new clients that they just sent me their photographs. One is a little doll."

"Just her I want," Leo murmured.

"Don't be a fool, doctor. Don't bother with her."

"Put me in touch with her, Salzman," Leo said humbly. "Perhaps I can be of service."

Salzman had stopped eating and Leo understood with emotion that it was now arranged.

Leaving the cafeteria, he was, however, afflicted by a tormenting suspicion that Salzman had planned it all to happen this way. Leo was informed by letter that she would meet him on a certain corner, and she was there one spring night, waiting under a street lamp. He appeared, carrying a small bouquet of violets and rosebuds. Stella stood by the lamp post, smoking. She wore white with red shoes, which fitted his expectations, although in a troubled moment he had imagined the dress red, and only the shoes white. She waited uneasily and shyly. From afar he saw that her eyes—clearly her father's—were filled with desperate innocence. He pictured, in her, his own redemption. Violins and lit candles revolved in the sky. Leo ran forward with flowers outthrust.

Around the corner, Salzman, leaning against a wall, chanted prayers for the dead.

QUESTIONS

1. Go back over the descriptions of Salzman as he enters scenes throughout the story. He seems increasingly wasted, increasingly unreal. What does this do to your reading of the story?
2. Do you see Salzman as a marriage salesman out for money? What does Malamud do to make him more than this?
3. What does Leo come to understand about his studies and his life? How does his new understanding affect the course of the story?

4. What is the conflict in the story? Is it really between Leo and Salzman?
5. Malamud uses strange imagery: for instance, "He now observed the round white moon, moving high in the sky through a cloud menagerie, and watched with half open mouth as it penetrated a huge hen, and dropped out of her like an egg laying itself." Note similar images. What effect do they have?
6. Think of the woman, Stella, whose picture he falls in love with. Why Stella? Think of her as some missing part of Leo. What part?
7. At the end Salzman is reciting prayers for the dead. In the light of the story as a whole, these prayers seem to have more than one meaning. Discuss.

Idiots First

BERNARD MALAMUD

The thick ticking of the tin clock stopped. Mendel, dozing in the dark, awoke in fright. The pain returned as he listened. He drew on his cold embittered clothing, and wasted minutes sitting at the edge of the bed.

"Isaac," he ultimately sighed.

In the kitchen, Isaac, his astonished mouth open, held six peanuts in his palm. He placed each on the table. "One . . . two . . . nine."

He gathered each peanut and appeared in the doorway. Mendel, in loose hat and long overcoat, still sat on the bed. Isaac watched with small eyes and ears, thick hair graying the sides of his head.

"Schlaf," he nasally said.

"No," muttered Mendel. As if stifling he rose. "Come, Isaac."

He wound his old watch though the sight of the stopped clock nauseated him.

Isaac wanted to hold it to his ear.

"No, it's late." Mendel put the watch carefully away. In the drawer he found the little paper bag of crumpled ones and fives and slipped it into his overcoat pocket. He helped Isaac on with his coat.

Isaac looked at one dark window, then at the other. Mendel stared at both blank windows.

They went slowly down the darkly lit stairs, Mendel first, Isaac watching the moving shadows on the wall. To one long shadow he offered a peanut.

"Hungrig."

In the vestibule the old man gazed through the thin glass. The November night was cold and bleak. Opening the door he cautiously thrust his head out. Though he saw nothing he quickly shut the door.

"Ginzburg, that he came to see me yesterday," he whispered in Isaac's ear.

Isaac sucked air.

"You know who I mean?"

Isaac combed his chin with his fingers.

"That's the one, with the black whiskers. Don't talk to him or go with him if he asks you."

Isaac moaned.

"Young people he don't bother so much," Mendel said in afterthought.

It was suppertime and the street was empty but the store windows dimly lit their way to the corner. They crossed the deserted street and went on. Isaac, with a happy cry, pointed to the three golden balls. Mendel smiled but was exhausted when they got to the pawnshop.

The pawnbroker, a red-bearded man with black horn-rimmed glasses, was eating a whitefish at the rear of the store. He craned his head, saw them, and settled back to sip his tea.

In five minutes he came forward, patting his shapeless lips with a large white handkerchief.

Mendel, breathing heavily, handed him the worn gold watch. The pawnbroker, raising his glasses, screwed in his eyepiece. He turned the watch over once. "Eight dollars."

The dying man wet his cracked lips. "I must have thirty-five."

"So go to Rothschild."

"Cost me myself sixty."

"In 1905." The pawnbroker handed back the watch. It had stopped ticking. Mendel wound it slowly. It ticked hollowly.

"Isaac must go to my uncle that he lives in California."

"It's a free country," said the pawnbroker.

Isaac, watching a banjo, snickered.

"What's the matter with him?" the pawnbroker asked.

"So let be eight dollars," muttered Mendel, "but where will I get the rest till tonight?"

"How much for my hat and coat?" he asked.

"No sale." The pawnbroker went behind the cage and wrote out a ticket. He locked the watch in a small drawer but Mendel still heard it ticking.

In the street he slipped the eight dollars into the paper bag, then searched in his pockets for a scrap of writing. Finding it, he strained to read the address by the light of the street lamp.

As they trudged to the subway, Mendel pointed to the sprinkled sky.

"Isaac, look how many stars are tonight."

"Eggs," said Isaac.

"First we will go to Mr. Fishbein, after we will eat."

They got off the train in upper Manhattan and had to walk several blocks before they located Fishbein's house.

"A regular palace," Mendel murmured, looking forward to a moment's warmth.

Isaac stared uneasily at the heavy door of the house.

Mendel rang. The servant, a man with long sideburns, came to the door and said Mr. and Mrs. Fishbein were dining and could see no one.

"He should eat in peace but we will wait till he finishes."

"Come back tomorrow morning. Tomorrow morning Mr. Fishbein will talk to you. He don't do business or charity at this time of the night."

"Charity I am not interested—"

"Come back tomorrow."

"Tell him it's life or death—"

"Whose life or death?"

"So if not his, then mine."

"Don't be such a big smart aleck."

"Look me in my face," said Mendel, "and tell me if I got time till tomorrow morning?"

The servant stared at him, then at Isaac, and reluctantly let them in.

The foyer was a vast high-ceilinged room with many oil paintings on the walls, voluminous silken draperies, a thick flowered rug at foot, and a marble staircase.

Mr. Fishbein, a paunchy bald-headed man with hairy nostrils and small patent leather feet, ran lightly down the stairs, a large napkin tucked under a tuxedo coat button. He stopped on the fifth step from the bottom and examined his visitors.

"Who comes on Friday night to a man that he has guests, to spoil him his supper?"

"Excuse me that I bother you, Mr. Fishbein," Mendel said. "If I didn't come now I couldn't come tomorrow."

"Without more preliminaries, please state your business. I'm a hungry man."

"Hungrig," wailed Isaac.

Fishbein adjusted his pince-nez. "What's the matter with him?"

"This is my son Isaac. He is like this all his life."

Isaac mewled.

"I am sending him to California."

"Mr. Fishbein don't contribute to personal pleasure trips."

"I am a sick man and he must go tonight on the train to my Uncle Leo."

"I never give to unorganized charity," Fishbein said, "but if you are hungry I will invite you downstairs in my kitchen. We having tonight chicken with stuffed derma."

"All I ask is thirty-five dollars for the train ticket to my uncle in California. I have already the rest."

"Who is your uncle? How old a man?"

"Eighty-one years, a long life to him."

Fishbein burst into laughter. "Eighty-one years and you are sending him this halfwit."

Mendel, flailing both arms, cried, "Please, without names."

Fishbein politely conceded.

"Where is open the door there we go in the house," the sick man said. "If you will kindly give me thirty-five dollars, God will bless you. What is thirty-five dollars to Mr. Fishbein? Nothing. To me, for my boy, is everything."

Fishbein drew himself up to his tallest height.

"Private contributions I don't make—only to institutions. This is my fixed policy."

Mendel sank to his creaking knees on the rug.

"Please, Mr. Fishbein, if not thirty-five, give maybe twenty."

"Levinson!" Fishbein angrily called.

The servant with the long sideburns appeared at the top of the stairs.

"Show this party where is the door—unless he wishes to partake food before leaving the premises."

"For what I got chicken won't cure it," Mendel said.

"This way if you please," said Levinson, descending.

Isaac assisted his father up.

"Take him to an institution," Fishbein advised over the marble balustrade. He ran quickly up the stairs and they were at once outside, buffeted by winds.

The walk to the subway was tedious. The wind blew mournfully. Mendel, breathless, glanced furtively at shadows. Isaac, clutching his peanuts in his frozen fist, clung to his father's side. They entered a small park to rest for a minute on a stone bench under a leafless two-branched tree. The thick right branch was raised, the thin left one hung down. A very pale moon rose slowly. So did a stranger as they approached the bench.

"Gut yuntif," he said hoarsely.

Mendel, drained of blood, waved his wasted arms. Isaac yowled sickly. Then a bell chimed and it was only ten. Mendel let out a piercing anguished cry as the bearded stranger disappeared into the bushes. A policeman came running, and though he beat the bushes with his nightstick, could turn up nothing. Mendel and Isaac hurried out of the little park. When Mendel glanced back the dead tree had its thin arm raised, the thick one down. He moaned.

They boarded a trolley, stopping at the home of a former friend, but he had died years ago. On the same block they went into a cafeteria and ordered two fried eggs for Isaac. The tables were crowded except where a heavy-set man sat eating soup with kasha. After one look at him they left in haste, although Isaac wept.

Mendel had another address on a slip of paper but the house was too far away, in Queens, so they stood in a doorway shivering.

What can I do, he frantically thought, in one short hour?

He remembered the furniture in the house. It was junk but might bring a few dollars. "Come, Isaac." They went once more to the pawnbroker's to talk to him, but the shop was dark and an iron gate—rings and gold watches glinting through it—was drawn tight across his place of business.

They huddled behind a telephone pole, both freezing. Isaac whimpered.

"See the big moon, Isaac. The whole sky is white."

He pointed but Isaac wouldn't look.

Mendel dreamed for a minute of the sky lit up, long sheets of light in all directions. Under the sky, in California, sat Uncle Leo drinking tea with lemon. Mendel felt warm but woke up cold.

Across the street stood an ancient brick synagogue.

He pounded on the huge door but no one appeared. He waited till he had breath and desperately knocked again. At last there were footsteps within, and the synagogue door creaked open on its massive brass hinges.

A darkly dressed sexton, holding a dripping candle, glared at them.

"Who knocks this time of night with so much noise on the synagogue door?"

Mendel told the sexton his troubles. "Please, I would like to speak to the rabbi."

"The rabbi is an old man. He sleeps now. His wife won't let you see him. Go home and come back tomorrow."

"To tomorrow I said goodbye already. I am a dying man."

Though the sexton seemed doubtful he pointed to an old wooden house next door. "In there he lives." He disappeared into the synagogue with his lit candle casting shadows around him.

Mendel, with Isaac clutching his sleeve, went up the wooden steps and rang the bell. After five minutes a big-faced, gray-haired bulky woman came out on the porch with a torn robe thrown over her nightdress. She emphatically said the rabbi was sleeping and could not be waked.

But as she was insisting, the rabbi himself tottered to the door. He listened a minute and said, "Who wants to see me let them come in."

They entered a cluttered room. The rabbi was an old skinny man with bent shoulders and a wisp of white beard. He wore a flannel nightgown and black skullcap; his feet were bare.

"Vey is mir," his wife muttered. "Put on shoes or tomorrow comes sure pneumonia." She was a woman with a big belly, years younger than her husband. Staring at Isaac, she turned away.

Mendel apologetically related his errand. "All I need more is thirty-five dollars."

"Thirty-five?" said the rabbi's wife. "Why not thirty-five thousand? Who has so much money? My husband is a poor rabbi. The doctors take away every penny."

"Dear friend," said the rabbi, "if I had I would give you."

"I got already seventy," Mendel said, heavy-hearted. "All I need more is thirty-five."

"God will give you," said the rabbi.

"In the grave," said Mendel. "I need tonight. Come, Isaac."

"Wait," called the rabbi.

He hurried inside, came out with a fur-lined caftan, and handed it to Mendel.

"Yascha," shrieked his wife, "not your new coat!"

"I got my old one. Who needs two coats for one body?"

"Yascha, I am screaming—"

"Who can go among poor people, tell me, in a new coat?"

"Yascha," she cried, "what can this man do with your coat? He needs tonight the money. The pawnbrokers are asleep."

"So let him wake them up."

"No." She grabbed the coat from Mendel.

He held on to a sleeve, wrestling her for the coat. Her I know, Mendel thought. "Shylock," he muttered. Her eyes glittered.

The rabbi groaned and tottered dizzily. His wife cried out as Mendel yanked the coat from her hands.

"Run," cried the rabbi.

"Run, Isaac."

They ran out of the house and down the steps.

"Stop, you thief," called the rabbi's wife. The rabbi pressed both hands to his temples and fell to the floor.

"Help!" his wife wept. "Heart attack! Help!"

But Mendel and Isaac ran through the streets with the rabbi's new fur-lined caftan. After them noiselessly ran Ginzburg.

It was very late when Mendel bought the train ticket in the only booth open.

There was no time to stop for a sandwich so Isaac ate his peanuts and they hurried to the train in the vast deserted station.

"So in the morning," Mendel gasped as they ran, "there comes a man that he sells sandwiches and coffee. Eat but get change. When reaches California the train, will be waiting for you on the station Uncle Leo. If you don't recognize him he will recognize you. Tell him I send best regards."

But when they arrived at the gate to the platform it was shut, the light out.

Mendel, groaning, beat on the gate with his fists.

"Too late," said the uniformed ticket collector, a bulky, bearded man with hairy nostrils and a fishy smell.

He pointed to the station clock. "Already past twelve."

"But I see standing there still the train," Mendel said, hopping in his grief.

"It just left—in one more minute."

"A minute is enough. Just open the gate."

"Too late I told you."

Mendel socked his bony chest with both hands. "With my whole heart I beg you this little favor."

"Favors you had enough already. For you the train is gone. You shoulda been dead already at midnight. I told you that yesterday. This is the best I can do."

"Ginzburg!" Mendel shrank from him.

"Who else?" The voice was metallic, eyes glittered, the expression amused.

"For myself," the old man begged, "I don't ask a thing. But what will happen to my boy?"

Ginzburg shrugged slightly. "What will happen happens. This isn't my responsibility. I got enough to think about without worrying about somebody on one cylinder."

"What then is your responsibility?"

"To create conditions. To make happen what happens. I ain't in the anthropomorphic business."

"Whatever business you in, where is your pity?"

"This ain't my commodity. The law is the law."

"Which law is this?"

"The cosmic universal law, goddamit, the one I got to follow myself."

"What kind of a law is it?" cried Mendel. "For God's sake, don't you understand what I went through in my life with this poor boy? Look at him. For thirty-nine years, since the day he was born, I wait for him to grow up, but he don't. Do you understand what this means in a father's heart? Why don't you let him go to his uncle?" His voice had risen and he was shouting.

Isaac mewled loudly.

"Better calm down or you'll hurt somebody's feelings," Ginzburg said with a wink toward Isaac.

"All my life," Mendel cried, his body trembling, "what did I have? I was poor. I suffered from my health. When I worked I worked too hard. When I didn't work was worse. My wife died a young woman. But I didn't ask from anybody nothing. Now I ask a small favor. Be so kind, Mr. Ginzburg."

The ticket collector was picking his teeth with a match stick.

"You ain't the only one, my friend, some got it worse than you. That's how it goes in this country."

"You dog you." Mendel lunged at Ginzburg's throat and began to choke. "You bastard, don't you understand what it means human?"

They struggled nose to nose, Ginzburg, though his astonished eyes bulged, began to laugh. "You pipsqueak nothing. I'll freeze you to pieces."

His eyes lit in rage and Mendel felt an unbearable cold like an icy dagger invading his body, all of his parts shriveling.

Now I die without helping Isaac.

A crowd gathered. Isaac yelped in fright.

Clinging to Ginzburg in his last agony, Mendel saw reflected in the ticket collector's eyes the depth of his terror. But he saw that Ginzburg, staring at himself in Mendel's eyes, saw mirrored in them the extent of his own awful wrath. He beheld a shimmering, starry, blinding light that produced darkness.

Ginzburg looked astounded. "Who me?"

His grip on the squirming old man slowly loosened, and Mendel, his heart barely beating, slumped to the ground.

"Go." Ginzburg muttered, "take him to the train."

"Let pass," he commanded a guard.

The crowd parted. Isaac helped his father up and they tottered down the steps to the platform where the train waited, lit and ready to go.

Mendel found Isaac a coach seat and hastily embraced him. "Help Uncle Leo, Isaakil. Also remember your father and mother."

"Be nice to him," he said to the conductor. "Show him where everything is."

He waited on the platform until the train began slowly to move. Isaac sat at the edge of his seat, his face strained in the direction of his journey. When the train was gone, Mendel ascended the stairs to see what had become of Ginzburg.

QUESTIONS

1. "The thick ticking of the tin clock stopped." This is not only a very beautiful sentence (read it aloud!) but one that carries a good deal of weight and attention. Why does Malamud choose to make the reader attend to the clock stopping? What other references to clocks do you see?
2. When do you first understand that Isaac is retarded?
3. Why does Malamud choose to call the son Isaac? How is this story different from the story of Abraham and Isaac?
4. Who is Ginzburg? Why doesn't Malamud tell us at once? Where does Ginzburg appear in the story?
5. Contrast Mr. Fishbein and the rabbi. Relate this contrast to the climax of the story, in which Ginzburg allows Mendel to take Isaac to the train.
6. Discuss the dialogue between Ginzburg and Mendel. Think about the looks they exchange as they grapple. What happens as a result of this moment? Discuss its significance.
7. Compare Malamud's stories to those of Peretz—"If Not Higher" and "Bontsha the Silent." Do similar values appear in both writers?

SAUL BELLOW

(1915—)

Bellow was born in Lachine, Quebec, in 1915 but grew up in Chicago in a Jewish household where he spoke Yiddish as well as English. A scholar-writer, he attended the University of Chicago, where now he is chairman of the Committee on Social Thought, an interdisciplinary program of study. Bellow has written a series of brilliant novels, beginning with *Dangling Man* (1944); *The Victim, The Adventures of Augie March, Seize the Day, Henderson the Rain King, Herzog, Mr. Sammler's Planet,* and *Humboldt's Gift* followed. He has won the National Book Award, the Pulitzer Prize, and, in 1976, the Nobel Prize for Literature.

Since the beginning of his career, Bellow has struggled against the cheapening of human life, against the "wasteland" attitude that sees human beings as living hollow, empty lives incapable of redemption. In a spiritual if not theological sense, Bellow yearns to believe in the possibility of redemption for ordinary people, and in "Looking for Mr. Green," written early in his career, he makes actual his quest for the meaningful reality of the person. It is as solidly realistic as anything by Steinbeck, yet vibrating through the realism is a visionary quality, a sense of something of value in the midst of broken towers and shutdown factories.

[See preface, p. 13 (Conflict).]

Looking for Mr. Green

SAUL BELLOW

> *Whatsoever thy hand findeth to do, do it with thy might. . . .*[1]

Hard work? No, it wasn't really so hard. He wasn't used to walking and stair-climbing, but the physical difficulty of his new job was not what George Grebe felt most. He was delivering relief checks in the Negro district, and although he was a native Chicagoan this was not a part of the city he knew much about—it needed a depression to introduce him to it. No, it wasn't literally hard work, not as reckoned in foot-pounds, but yet he was beginning to feel the strain of it, to grow aware of its peculiar difficulty. He could find the streets and numbers, but the clients were not where they were supposed to be, and he felt like a hunter inexperienced in the camouflage of his game. It was an unfavorable day, too—fall, and cold, dark weather, windy. But, anyway, instead of shells in his deep trenchcoat pocket he had the cardboard of checks, punctured for the spindles of the file, the holes reminding him of the holes in player-piano paper. And he didn't look much like a hunter, either; his was a city figure entirely, belted up in his Irish conspirator's coat. He was slender without being tall, stiff in the back, his legs looking shabby in a pair of old tweed pants gone through and fringy at the cuffs. With this stiffness, he kept his head forward, so that his face was red from the sharpness of the weather; and it was an indoors sort of face with gray eyes that persisted in some kind of thought and yet seemed to avoid definiteness of conclusion. He wore sideburns that surprised you somewhat by the tough curl of the blond hair and the effect of assertion in their length. He was not so mild as he looked, nor so youthful; and nevertheless there was no effort on his part to seem what he was not. He was an educated man; he was a bachelor; he was in some ways simple; without lushing, he liked a drink; his luck had not been good. Nothing was deliberately hidden.

He felt that his luck was better than usual today. When he had reported for work that morning he had expected to be shut up in the relief office at a clerk's job, for he had been hired downtown as a clerk, and he was glad to have, instead, the freedom of the streets and welcomed, at least at first, the vigor of the cold and even the blowing of the hard wind. But on the other hand he was not getting on with the distribution of the checks. It was true that it was a city job;

[1] *Whatsoever . . . might. . . .* See Ecclesiastes 9:10.

nobody expected you to push too hard at a city job. His supervisor, that young Mr. Raynor, had practically told him that. Still, he wanted to do well at it. For one thing, when he knew how quickly he could deliver a batch of checks, he would know also how much time he could expect to clip for himself. And then, too, the clients would be waiting for their money. That was not the most important consideration, though it certainly mattered to him. No, but he wanted to do well, simply for doing-well's sake, to acquit himself decently of a job because he so rarely had a job to do that required just this sort of energy. Of this peculiar energy he now had a superabundance; once it had started to flow, it flowed all too heavily. And, for the time being anyway, he was balked. He could not find Mr. Green.

So he stood in his big-skirted trenchcoat with a large envelope in his hand and papers showing from his pocket, wondering why people should be so hard to locate who were too feeble or sick to come to the station to collect their own checks. But Raynor had told him that tracking them down was not easy at first and had offered him some advice on how to proceed. "If you can see the postman, he's your first man to ask, and your best bet. If you can't connect with him, try the stores and tradespeople around. Then the janitor and the neighbors. But you'll find the closer you come to your man the less people will tell you. They don't want to tell you anything."

"Because I'm a stranger."

"Because you're white. We ought to have a Negro doing this, but we don't at the moment, and of course you've got to eat, too, and this is public employment. Jobs have to be made. Oh, that holds for me too. Mind you, I'm not letting myself out. I've got three years of seniority on you, that's all. And a law degree. Otherwise, you might be back of the desk and I might be going out into the field this cold day. The same dough pays us both and for the same, exact, identical reason. What's my law degree got to do with it? But you have to pass out these checks, Mr. Grebe, and it'll help if you're stubborn, so I hope you are."

"Yes, I'm fairly stubborn."

Raynor sketched hard with an eraser in the old dirt of his desk, left-handed, and said, "Sure, what else can you answer to such a question. Anyhow, the trouble you're going to have is that they don't like to give information about anybody. They think you're a plain-clothes dick or an installment collector, or summons-server or something like that. Till you've been seen around the neighborhood for a few months and people know you're only from the relief."

It was dark, ground-freezing, pre-Thanksgiving weather; the wind played hob with the smoke, rushing it down, and Grebe missed his gloves, which he had left in Raynor's office. And no one would admit knowing Green. It was past three o'clock and the postman had made his last delivery. The nearest grocer, himself a Negro, had never heard the name Tulliver Green, or said he hadn't. Grebe was inclined to think that it was true, that he had in the end convinced the man that he wanted only to deliver a check. But he wasn't sure. He needed experience in interpreting looks and signs and, even more, the will not to be put off or denied and even the force to bully if need be. If the grocer did know, he had got rid of him easily. But since most of his trade was with reliefers, why should he prevent the delivery of a check? Maybe Green, or Mrs. Green, if there was a Mrs. Green, patronized another grocer. And was there a Mrs. Green? It was one of Grebe's great handicaps that he hadn't looked at any of the case records. Raynor should have let him read files for a few hours. But he apparently saw no need for that, probably considering the job unimportant. Why prepare systematically to deliver a few checks?

But now it was time to look for the janitor. Grebe took in the building in the wind and gloom of the late November day—trampled, frost-hardened lots on one side; on the other, an automobile junk yard and then the infinite work of Elevated frames, weak-looking, gaping with rubbish fires; two sets of leaning brick porches three stories high and a flight of cement stairs to the cellar. Descending, he entered the underground passage, where he tried the doors until one opened and he found himself in the furnace room. There someone rose toward him and approached, scraping on the coal grit and bending under the canvas-jacketed pipes.

"Are you the janitor?"

"What do you want?"

"I'm looking for a man who's supposed to be living here. Green."

"What Green?"

"Oh, you maybe have more than one Green?" said Grebe with new, pleasant hope. "This is Tulliver Green."

"I don't think I c'n help you, mister. I don't know any."

"A crippled man."

The janitor stood bent before him. Could it be that he was crippled? Oh, God! what if he was. Grebe's gray eyes sought with excited difficulty to see. But no, he was only very short and stooped. A head awakened from meditation, a stronghaired beard, low, wide shoulders. A staleness of sweat and coal rose from his black shirt and the burlap sack he wore as an apron.

"Crippled how?"

Grebe thought and then answered with the light voice of unmixed candor, "I don't know. I've never seen him." This was damaging, but his only other choice was to make a lying guess, and he was not up to it. "I'm delivering checks for the relief to shut-in cases. If he weren't crippled he'd come to collect himself. That's why I said crippled. Bedridden, chairridden—is there anybody like that?"

This sort of frankness was one of Grebe's oldest talents, going back to childhood. But it gained him nothing here.

"No suh. I've got four buildin's same as this that I take care of. I don' know all the tenants, leave alone the tenants' tenants. The rooms turn over so fast, people movin' in and out every day. I can't tell you."

"Then where should I ask?"

The janitor opened his grimy lips but Grebe did not hear him in the piping of the valves and the consuming pull of air to flame in the body of the furnace. He knew, however, what he had said.

"Well, all the same, thanks. Sorry I bothered you. I'll prowl around upstairs again and see if I can turn up someone who knows him."

Once more in the cold air and early darkness he made the short circle from the cellarway to the entrance crowded between the brick-work pillars and began to climb to the third floor. Pieces of plaster ground under his feet; strips of brass tape from which the carpeting had been torn away marked old boundaries at the sides. In the passage, the cold reached him worse than in the street; it touched him to the bone. The hall toilets ran like springs. He thought grimly as he heard the wind burning around the building with a sound like that of the furnace, that this was a great piece of constructed shelter. Then he struck a match in the gloom and searched for names and numbers among the writings and scribbles on the walls. He saw WHOODY-DOODY GO TO JESUS, and zigzags, caricatures, sexual scrawls, and curses. So the sealed rooms of pyramids were also decorated, and the caves of human dawn.

The information on his card was, TULLIVER GREEN—APT 3D. There were no names, however, and no numbers. His shoulders drawn up, tears of cold in his eyes, breathing vapor, he went the length of the corridor and told himself that if he had been lucky enough to have the temperament for it he would bang on one of the doors and bawl out "Tulliver Green!" until he got results. But it wasn't in him to make an uproar and he continued to burn matches, passing the light over the walls. At the rear, in a corner off the hall, he discovered a door he had not seen before and he thought it best to investigate. It sounded empty when he knocked, but a young Negress answered, hardly more than a girl. She opened only a bit, to guard the warmth of the room.

"Yes suh?"

"I'm from the district relief station on Prairie Avenue. I'm looking for a man named Tulliver Green to give him his check. Do you know him?"

No, she didn't; but he thought she had not understood anything of what he had said. She had a dream-bound, dream-blind face, very soft and black, shut off. She wore a man's jacket and pulled the ends together at her throat. Her hair was parted in three directions, at the sides and transversely, standing up at the front in a dull puff.

"Is there somebody around here who might know?"

"I jus' taken this room las' week."

He observed that she shivered, but even her shiver was somnambu-listic and there was no sharp consciousness of cold in the big smooth eyes of her handsome face.

"All right, miss, thank you. Thanks," he said, and went to try another place.

Here he was admitted. He was grateful, for the room was warm. It was full of people, and they were silent as he entered—ten people, or a dozen, perhaps more, sitting on benches like a parliament. There was no light, properly speaking, but a tempered darkness that the window gave, and everyone seemed to him enormous, the men padded out in heavy work clothes and winter coats, and the women huge, too, in their sweaters, hats, and old furs. And, besides, bed and bedding, a black cooking range, a piano piled towering to the ceiling with papers, a dining-room table of the old style of prosperous Chicago. Among these people Grebe, with his cold-heightened fresh color and his smaller stature, entered like a schoolboy. Even though he was met with smiles and good will, he knew, before a single word was spoken, that all the currents ran against him and that he would make no headway. Nevertheless he began. "Does anybody here know how I can deliver a check to Mr. Tulliver Green?"

"Green?" It was the man that had let him in who answered. He was in short sleeves, in a checkered shirt and had a queer, high head, profusely overgrown and long as a shako; the veins entered it strongly from his forehead. "I never heard mention of him. Is this where he live?"

"This is the address they gave me at the station. He's a sick man, and he'll need his check. Can't anybody tell me where to find him?"

He stood his ground and waited for a reply, his crimson wool scarf wound about his neck and drooping outside his trenchcoat, pockets weighted with the block of checks and official forms. They must have realized that he was not a college boy employed afternoons by a bill collector, trying foxily to pass for a relief clerk, recognized that he was an older man who knew himself what need was, who had had more than an average seasoning in hardship. It was evident enough if you looked at the marks under his eyes and at the sides of his mouth.

"Anybody know this sick man?"

"No suh." On all sides he saw heads shaken and smiles of denial.

No one knew. And maybe it was true, he considered, standing silent in the earthen, musky human gloom of the place as the rumble continued. But he could never really be sure.

"What's the matter with this man?" said shako-head.

"I've never seen him. All I can tell you is that he can't come in person for his money. It's my first day in this district."

"Maybe they given you the wrong number?"

"I don't believe so. But where else can I ask about him?" He felt that his persistence amused them deeply, and in a way he shared their amusement that he should stand up so tenaciously to them. Though smaller, though slight, he was his own man, he retracted nothing about himself, and he looked back at them, gray-eyed, with amusement and also with a sort of courage. On the bench some man spoke in his throat, the words impossible to catch, and a woman answered with a wild, shrieking laugh, which was quickly cut off.

"Well, so nobody will tell me?"

"Ain't nobody who knows."

"At least, if he lives here, he pays rent to someone. Who manages the building?"

"Greatham Company. That's on Thirty-ninth Street."

Grebe wrote it in his pad. But, in the street again, a sheet of wind-driven paper clinging to his leg while he deliberated what direction to take next, it seemed a feeble lead to follow. Probably this Green didn't rent a flat, but a room. Sometimes there were as many as twenty people living in an apartment; the real-estate agent would know only the lessee. And not even the agent could tell you who the renters were. In some places the beds were even used in shifts, watchmen or jitney drivers or short-order cooks in night joints turning out after a day's sleep and surrendering their beds to a sister, a nephew, or perhaps a stranger, just off the bus. There were large numbers of newcomers in this terrific, blight-bitten portion of the city between Cottage Grove and Ashland, wandering from house to house and room to room. When you saw them, how could you know them? They didn't carry bundles on their backs or look picturesque. You only saw a man, a Negro, walking in the street or riding in the car, like everyone else, with his thumb closed on a transfer. And therefore how were you supposed to tell? Grebe thought the Greatham agent would only laugh at his question.

But how much it would have simplified the job to be able to say that Green was old, or blind, or consumptive. An hour in the files, taking a few notes, and he needn't have been at such a disadvantage. When Raynor gave him the block of checks he had asked, "How much should I know about these people?" Then Raynor had looked as though he were preparing to accuse him of trying to make the job more important than it was. He smiled, because by then they were on fine terms, but nevertheless he had been getting ready to say something like that when the confusion began in the station over Staika and her children.

Grebe had waited a long time for this job. It came to him through the pull of an old schoolmate in the Corporation Counsel's office. Never a close friend, but suddenly sympathetic and interested—pleased to show, moreover, how well he had done, how strongly he was coming on even in these miserable times. Well, he was coming through strongly, along with the Democratic administration itself. Grebe had gone to see him in City Hall and they had had a counter lunch or beers at least once a month for a year, and finally it had been possible to swing the job. He didn't mind being assigned the lowest clerical grade, nor even being a messenger, though Raynor thought he did.

This Raynor was an original sort of guy and Grebe had taken to him immediately. As was proper on the first day, Grebe had come early, but he waited long, for Raynor was late. At last he darted into his cubicle of an office as though he had just jumped from one of those hurtling huge red Indiana Avenue cars. His thin, rough face was wind-stung and he was grinning and saying something breathlessly to himself. In his hat, a small fedora and his coat, the velvet collar a neat fit about his neck, and his silk muffler that set off the nervous twist of his chin, he swayed and turned himself in his swivel chair, feet leaving the ground; so that he pranced a little as he sat. Meanwhile he took Grebe's measure out of his eyes, eyes of an unusual vertical length and slightly sardonic. So the two men sat for a while, saying nothing, while the supervisor raised his hat from his miscombed hair and put it in his lap. His cold-darkened hands were not clean. A steel beam passed through the little makeshift room, from which machine belts once had hung. The building was an old factory.

"I'm younger than you; I hope you won't find it hard taking orders from me," said Raynor. "But I don't make them up, either. You're how old, about?"

"Thirty-five."

"And you thought you'd be inside doing paper-work. But it so happens I have to send you out."

"I don't mind."

"And it's mostly a Negro load we have in this district."

"So I thought it would be."

"Fine. You'll get along. *C'est un bon boulot.*[2] Do you know French?"

---

[2] *C'est . . . boulot,* It's a good job.

"Some."

"I thought you'd be a university man."

"Have you been in France?" said Grebe.

"No, that's the French of the Berlitz School. I've been at it for more than a year, just as I'm sure people have been, all over the world, office boys in China and braves in Tanganyika. In fact, I damn well know it. Such is the attractive power of civilization. It's overrated, but what do you want? *Que voulez vous?*[3] I get *Le Rire*[4] and all the spicy papers, just like in Tanganyika. It must be mystifying, out there. But my reason is that I'm aiming at the diplomatic service. I have a cousin who's a courier, and the way he describes it is awfully attractive. He rides in the *wagon-lits*[5] and reads books. While we—What did you do before?"

"I sold."

"Where?"

"Canned meat at Stop and Shop. In the basement."

"And before that?"

"Window shades, at Goldblatt's."

"Steady work?"

"No, Thursdays and Saturdays. I also sold shoes."

"You've been a shoe-dog, too. Well. And prior to that? Here it is in your folder." He opened the record. "St. Olaf's College, instructor in classical languages. Fellow, University of Chicago, 1926–27. I've had Latin, too. Let's trade quotations—'*Dum spiro spero.*'"

"'*Da dextram misero.*'"

"'*Alea jacta est.*'"

"'*Excelsior.*'"[6]

Raynor shouted with laughter, and other workers came to look at him over the partition. Grebe also laughed, feeling pleased and easy. The luxury of fun on a nervous morning.

When they were done and no one was watching or listening, Raynor said rather seriously, "What made you study Latin in the first place. Was it for the priesthood?"

"No."

"Just for the hell of it? For the culture? Oh, the things people think they can pull!" He made his cry hilarious and tragic. "I ran my

---

[3] *Que voulez vous?* What do you want?

[4] *Le Rire*, a French comic magazine, literally "laughter."

[5] *wagon-lits*, sleeping cars.

[6] *Dum spiro spero*, While I breathe, I hope. *Da dextram misero*, Give your right hand to the wretched man. *Alea jacta est*, The die is cast, Caesar's remark on crossing the Rubicon on his return to Rome against the orders of the tribunes. *Excelsior*, Upward.

pants off so I could study for the bar, and I've passed the bar, so I get twelve dollars a week more than you as a bonus for having seen life straight and whole. I'll tell you, as a man of culture, that even though nothing looks to be real, and everything stands for something else, and that thing for another thing, and that thing for a still further one—there ain't any comparison between twenty-five and thirty-seven dollars a week, regardless of the last reality. Don't you think that was clear to your Greeks? They were a thoughtful people, but they didn't part with their slaves."

This was a great deal more than Grebe had looked for in his first interview with his supervisor. He was too shy to show all the astonishment he felt. He laughed a little, aroused, and brushed at the sunbeam that covered his head with its dust. "Do you think my mistake was so terrible?"

"Damn right it was terrible, and you know it now that you've had the whip of hard times laid on your back. You should have been preparing yourself for trouble. Your people must have been well off to send you to the university. Stop me, if I'm stepping on your toes. Did your mother pamper you? Did your father give in to you? Were you brought up tenderly, with permission to go out and find out what were the last things that everything else stands for while everybody else labored in the fallen world of appearances?"

"Well, no, it wasn't exactly like that." Grebe smiled. *The fallen world of appearances!* no less. But now it was his turn to deliver a surprise. "We weren't rich. My father was the last genuine English butler in Chicago—"

"Are you kidding?"

"Why should I be?"

"In a livery?"

"In livery. Up on the Gold Coast."

"And he wanted you to be educated like a gentleman?"

"He did not. He sent me to the Armour Institute to study chemical engineering. But when he died I changed schools."

He stopped himself, and considered how quickly Raynor had reached him. In no time he had your valise on the table and all your stuff unpacked. And afterward, in the streets, he was still reviewing how far he might have gone, and how much he might have been led to tell if they had not been interrupted by Mrs. Staika's great noise.

But just then a young woman, one of Raynor's workers, ran into the cubicle exlaiming, "Haven't you heard all the fuss?"

"We haven't heard anything."

"It's Staika, giving out with all her might. The reporters are coming. She said she phoned the papers, and you know she did."

"But what is she up to?" said Raynor.

"She brought her wash and she's ironing it here, with our current, because the relief won't pay her electric bill. She has her ironing board set up by the admitting desk, and her kids are with her, all six. They never are in school more than once a week. She's always dragging them around with her because of her reputation."

"I don't want to miss any of this," said Raynor, jumping up. Grebe, as he followed with the secretary, said, "Who is this Staika?"

"They call her the 'Blood Mother of Federal Street.' She's a professional donor at the hospitals. I think they pay ten dollars a pint. Of course it's no joke, but she makes a very big thing out of it and she and the kids are in the papers all the time."

A small crowd, staff and clients divided by a plywood barrier, stood in the narrow space of the entrance, and Staika was shouting in a gruff, mannish voice, plunging the iron on the board and slamming it on the metal rest.

"My father and mother came in a steerage, and I was born in our own house, Robey by Huron. I'm no dirty immigrant. I'm a US citizen. My husband is a gassed veteran from France with lungs weaker'n paper, that hardly can he go to the toilet by himself. These six children of mine, I have to buy the shoes for their feet with my own blood. Even a lousy little white communion necktie, that's a couple of drops of blood; a little piece of mosquito veil for my Vadja so she won't be ashamed in church for the other girls, they take my blood for it by Goldblatt. That's how I keep goin'. A fine thing if I had to depend on the relief. And there's plenty of people on the rolls—fakes! There's nothin' *they* can't get, that can go and wrap bacon at Swift and Armour any time. They're lookin' for them by the Yards. They never have to be out of work. Only they rather lay in their lousy beds and eat the public's money." She was not afraid, in a predominantly Negro station, to shout this way about Negroes.

Grebe and Raynor worked themselves forward to get a closer view of the woman. She was flaming with anger and with pleasure at herself, broad and huge, a golden-headed woman who wore a cotton cap laced with pink ribbon. She was barelegged and had on black gym-shoes, her hoover apron[7] was open and her great breasts, not much restrained by a man's undershirt, hampered her arms as she worked at the kid's dress on the ironing board. And the children, silent and white, with a kind of locked obstinacy, in sheepskins and lumberjackets, stood behind her. She had captured the station, and

---

7 *hoover apron,* so-called because it became popular during World War I for working in vegetable gardens; a loose overall dresslike garment with a tie and reversible fronts.

the pleasure this gave her was enormous. Yet her grievances were true grievances. She was telling the truth. But she behaved like a liar. The look of her small eyes was hidden, and while she raged she also seemed to be spinning and planning.

"They send me out college case-workers in silk pants to talk me out of what I got comin'. Are they better'n me? Who told them? Fire them. Let 'em go and get married, and then you won't have to cut electric from people's budget."

The chief supervisor, Mr. Ewing, couldn't silence her and he stood with folded arms at the head of his staff, bald, baldheaded, saying to his subordinates like the ex-school principal he was, "Pretty soon she'll be tired and go."

"No she won't," said Raynor to Grebe. "She'll get what she wants. She knows more about the relief even than Ewing. She's been on the rolls for years, and she always gets what she wants because she puts on a noisy show. Ewing knows it. He'll give in soon. He's only saving face. If he gets bad publicity, the Commissioner'll have him on the carpet, downtown. She's got him submerged; she'll submerge everybody in time, and that includes nations and governments."

Grebe replied with his characteristic smile, disagreeing completely. Who would take Staika's orders, and what changes could her yelling ever bring about?

No, what Grebe saw in her, the power that made people listen, was that her cry expressed the war of flesh and blood, perhaps turned a little crazy and certainly intensely ugly, on this place and this condition. And at first, when he went out, the spirit of Staika somehow presided over the whole district for him, and it took color from her; he saw her color, in the spotty curb-fires, and the fires under the El, the straight alley of flamey gloom. Later, too, when he went into a tavern for a shot of rye, the sweat of beer, association with West Side Polish streets, made him think of her again.

He wiped the corners of his mouth with his muffler, his handkerchief being inconvenient to reach for, and went out again to get on with the delivery of his checks. The air bit cold and hard and a few flakes of snow formed near him. A train struck by and left a quiver in the frames and a bristling icy hiss over the rails.

Crossing the street, he descended a flight of board steps into a basement grocery, setting off a little bell. It was a dark, long store and it caught you with its stinks of smoked meat, soap, dried peaches, and fish. There was a fire wrinkling and flapping in the little stove, and the proprietor was waiting, an Italian with a long, hollow face and stubborn bristles. He kept his hands warm under his apron.

No, he didn't know Green. You knew people, but not names. The same man might not have the same name twice. The police didn't know, either, and mostly didn't care. When somebody was shot or knifed they took the body away and didn't look for the murderer. In the first place, nobody would tell them anything. So they made up a name for the coroner and called it quits. And in the second place, they didn't give a goddam anyhow. But they couldn't get to the bottom of a thing even if they wanted to. Nobody would get to know even a tenth of what went on among these people. They stabbed and stole, they did every crime and abomination you ever heard of, men and men, women and women, parents and children, worse than the animals. They carried on their own way, and the horrors passed off like a smoke. There was never anything like it in the history of the whole world.

It was a long speech, deepening with every word in its fantasy and passion and becoming increasingly senseless and terrible: a swarm amassed by suggestion and invention, a huge, hugging, despairing knot, a human wheel of heads, legs, bellies, arms, rolling through his shop.

Grebe felt that he must interrupt him. He said sharply, "What are you talking about! All I asked was whether you knew this man."

"That isn't even the half of it. I been here six years. You probably don't want to believe this. But suppose it's true?"

"All the same," said Grebe, "there must be a way to find a person."

The Italian's close-spaced eyes had been queerly concentrated, as were his muscles, while he leaned across the counter trying to convince Grebe. Now he gave up the effort and sat down on his stool. "Oh—I suppose. Once in a while. But I been telling you, even the cops don't get anywhere."

"They're always after somebody. It's not the same thing."

"Well, keep trying if you want. I can't help you."

But he didn't keep trying. He had no more time to spend on Green. He slipped Green's check to the back of the block. The next name on the list was FIELD, WINSTON.

He found the back-yard bungalow without the least trouble; it shared a lot with another house, a few feet of yard between. Grebe knew these two-shack arrangements. They had been built in vast numbers in the days before the swamps were filled and the streets raised, and they were all the same—a boardwalk along the fence, well under street level, three or four ball-headed posts for clotheslines, greening wood, dead shingles, and a long, long flight of stairs to the rear door.

A twelve-year-old boy let him into the kitchen, and there the old man was, sitting by the table in a wheel chair.

"Oh, it's d'government man," he said to the boy when Grebe drew out his checks. "Go bring me my box of papers." He cleared a space on the table.

"Oh, you don't have to go to all that trouble," said Grebe. But Field laid out his papers: Social Security card, relief certification, letters from the state hospital in Manteno, and a naval discharge dated San Diego, 1920.

"That's plenty," Grebe said. "Just sign."

"You got to know who I am," the old man said. "You're from the government. It's not your check, it's a government check and you got no business to hand it over till everything is proved."

He loved the ceremony of it, and Grebe made no more objections. Field emptied his box and finished out the circle of cards and letters.

"There's everything I done and been. Just the death certificate and they can close book on me." He said this with a certain happy pride and magnificence. Still he did not sign; he merely held the little pen upright on the golden-green corduroy of his thigh. Grebe did not hurry him. He felt the old man's hunger for conversation.

"I got to get better coal," he said. "I send my little gran'son to the yard with my order and they fill his wagon with screening. The stove ain't made for it. It fall through the grate. The order says Franklin County egg-size coal."

"I'll report it and see what can be done."

"Nothing can be done, I expect. You know and I know. There ain't no little ways to make things better, and the only big thing is money. That's the only sunbeams, money. Nothing is black where it shines, and the only place you see black is where it ain't shining. What we colored have to have is our own rich. There ain't no other way."

Grebe sat, his reddened forehead bridged levelly by his close-cut hair and his cheeks lowered in the wings of his collar—the caked fire shone hard within the isinglass and iron frames but the room was not comfortable—sat and listened while the old man unfolded his scheme. This was to create one Negro millionaire a month by subscription. One clever, good-hearted young fellow elected every month would sign a contract to use the money to start a business employing Negroes. This would be advertised by chain letters and word of mouth, and every Negro wage-earner would contribute a dollar a month. Within five years there would be sixty millionaires.

"That'll fetch respect," he said with a throat-stopped sound that came out like a foreign syllable. "You got to take and organize all the money that gets thrown away on the policy wheel and horse race. As long as they can take it away from you, they got no respect for you. Money, that's d' sun of human kind!" Field was a Negro of mixed blood, perhaps Cherokee, or Natchez; his skin was reddish. And he sounded, speaking about a golden sun in this dark room, and looked, shaggy and slab-headed, with the mingled blood of his face and broad lips, the little pen still upright in his hand, like one of the underground kings of mythology, old judge Minos[8] himself.

And now he accepted the check and signed. Not to soil the slip, he held it down with his knuckles. The table budged and creaked, the center of the gloomy, heathen midden of the kitchen covered with bread, meat, and cans, and the scramble of papers.

"Don't you think my scheme'd work?"

"It's worth thinking about. Something ought to be done, I agree."

"It'll work if people will do it. That's all. That's the only thing, any time. When they understand it in the same way, all of them."

"That's true," said Grebe, rising. His glance met the old man's.

"I know you got to go," he said. "Well, God bless you, boy, you ain't been sly with me. I can tell it in a minute."

He went back through the buried yard. Someone nursed a candle in a shed, where a man unloaded kindling wood from a sprawl-wheeled baby buggy and two voices carried on a high conversation. As he came up the sheltered passage he heard the hard boost of the wind in the branches and against the house fronts, and then, reaching the sidewalk, he saw the needle-eye red of cable towers in the open icy height hundreds of feet above the river and the factories—those keen points. From here, his view was unobstructed all the way to the South Branch and its timber banks, and the cranes beside the water. Rebuilt after the Great Fire,[9] this part of the city was, not fifty years later, in ruins again, factories boarded up, buildings deserted or fallen, gaps of prairie between. But it wasn't desolation that this made you feel, but rather a faltering of organization that set free a huge energy, an escaped, unattached, unregulated power from the giant raw place. Not only must people feel it but, it seemed to Grebe, they were compelled to match it. In their very bodies. He no less than others, he realized. Say that his parents had been servants in their time, whereas he was not supposed to be one. He thought that they had never done any service like this, which no one visible asked for, and probably flesh and blood could not even perform. Nor could anyone show why it should be performed; or see where the performance would lead. That did not mean that he wanted to be released from it, he realized with a grimly pensive face. On the contrary. He had something to do. To be compelled to feel this energy and yet have no task to do—that was horrible; that was suffering; he knew what that was. It was now quitting time. Six o'clock. He could go home if he liked, to his room, that is, to wash in hot water, to pour a

---

8 *Minos,* a legendary king of Crete, after his death one of three judges of the dead in Hades.

9 *Great Fire,* in 1871.

drink, lie down on his quilt, read the paper, eat some liver paste on crackers before going out to dinner. But to think of this actually made him feel a little sick, as though he had swallowed hard air. He had six checks left, and he was determined to deliver at least one of these: Mr. Green's check.

So he started again. He had four or five dark blocks to go, past open lots, condemned houses, old foundations, closed schools, black churches, mounds, and he reflected that there must be many people alive who had once seen the neighborhood rebuilt and new. Now there was a second layer of ruins; centuries of history accomplished through human massing. Numbers had given the place forced growth; enormous numbers had also broken it down. Objects once so new, so concrete that it could never have occurred to anyone they stood for other things, had crumbled. Therefore, reflected Grebe, the secret of them was out. It was that they stood for themselves by agreement, and were natural and not unnatural by agreement, and when the things themselves collapsed the agreement became visible. What was it, otherwise, that kept cities from looking peculiar? Rome, that was almost permanent, did not give rise to thoughts like these. And was it abidingly real? But in Chicago, where the cycles were so fast and the familiar died out, and again rose changed, and died again in thirty years, you saw the common agreement or covenant, and you were forced to think about appearances and realities. (He remembered Raynor and he smiled. Raynor was a clever boy.) Once you had grasped this, a great many things became intelligible. For instance, why Mr. Field should conceive such a scheme. Of course, if people were to agree to create a millionaire, a real millionaire would come into existence. And if you wanted to know how Mr. Field was inspired to think of this, why, he had within sight of his kitchen window the chart, the very bones of a successful scheme—the El with its blue and green confetti of signals. People consented to pay dimes and ride the crash-box cars, and so it was a success. Yet how absurd it looked; how little reality there was to start with. And yet Yerkes,[10] the great financier who built it, had known that he could get people to agree to do it. Viewed as itself, what a scheme of a scheme it seemed, how close to an appearance. Then why wonder at Mr. Field's idea? He had grasped a principle. And then Grebe remembered, too, that Mr. Yerkes had established the Yerkes Observatory and endowed it with millions. Now how did the notion come to him in his New York

---

[10] *Yerkes,* Charles Tyson Yerkes (1837–1905), financier and traction magnate, donor of funds to The University of Chicago for the astronomical observatory named for him and built at Williams Point, Wisconsin. Dreiser based the hero of his *The Titan* on Yerkes.

museum of a palace or his Aegean-bound yacht to give money to astronomers? Was he awed perhaps by the success of his bizarre enterprise and therefore ready to spend money to find out where in the universe being and seeming were identical? Yes, he wanted to know what abides; and whether flesh is Bible-grass;[11] and he offered money to be burned in the fire of suns. Okay, then, Grebe thought further, these things exist because people consent to exist with them—we have got so far—and also there is a reality which doesn't depend on consent but within which consent is a game. But what about need, the need that keeps so many vast thousands in position? You tell me that, you *private* little gentleman and *decent* soul—he used these words against himself scornfully. Why is the consent given to misery? And why so painfully ugly? Because there is *something* that is dismal and permanently ugly? Here he sighed and gave it up, and thought it was enough for the present moment that he had a real check in his pocket for a Mr. Green who must be real beyond question. If only his neighbors didn't think they had to conceal him.

This time he stopped at the second floor. He struck a match and found a door. Presently a man answered his knock and Grebe had the check ready and showed it even before he began. "Does Tulliver Green live here? I'm from the relief."

The man narrowed the opening and spoke to someone at his back.

"Does he live here?"

"Uh-uh. No."

"Or anywhere in this building? He's a sick man and he can't come for his dough." He exhibited the check in the light, which was smoky—the air smelled of charred lard—and the man held off the brim of his cap to study it.

"Uh-uh. Never seen the name."

"There's nobody around here that uses crutches?"

He seemed to think, but it was Grebe's impression that he was simply waiting for a decent interval to pass.

"No, suh. Nobody I ever see."

"I've been looking for this man all afternoon," Grebe spoke out with sudden force, "and I'm going to have to carry this check back to the station. It seems strange not to be able to find a person to *give* him something when you're looking for him for a good reason. I suppose if I had bad news for him I'd find him quick enough."

There was a responsive motion in the other man's face. "That's right, I reckon."

---

11 *flesh is Bible-grass.* See I Peter 1:24.

"It almost doesn't do any good to have a name if you can't be found by it. It doesn't stand for anything. He might as well not have any," he went on, smiling. It was as much of a concession as he could make to his desire to laugh.

"Well, now, there's a little old knot-back man I see once in a while. He might be the one you lookin' for. Downstairs."

"Where? Right side or left? Which door?"

"I don't know which. Thin face little knot-back with a stick."

But no one answered at any of the doors on the first floor. He went to the end of the corridor, searching by matchlight, and found only a stairless exit to the yard, a drop of about six feet. But there was a bungalow near the alley, an old house like Mr. Field's. To jump was unsafe. He ran from the front door, through the underground passage and into the yard. The place was occupied. There was a light through the curtains, upstairs. The name on the ticket under the broken, scoopshaped mailbox was Green! He exultantly rang the bell and pressed against the locked door. Then the lock clicked faintly and a long staircase opened before him. Someone was slowly coming down—a woman. He had the impression in the weak light that she was shaping her hair as she came, making herself presentable, for he saw her arms raised. But it was for support that they were raised; she was feeling her way downward, down the walls, stumbling. Next he wondered about the pressure of her feet on the treads; she did not seem to be wearing shoes. And it was a freezing stairway. His ring had got her out of bed, perhaps, and she had forgotten to put them on. And then he saw that she was not only shoeless but naked; she was entirely naked, climbing down while she talked to herself, a heavy woman, naked and drunk. She blundered into him. The contact of her breasts, though they touched only his coat, made him go back against the door with a blind shock. See what he had tracked down, in his hunting game!

The woman was saying to herself, furious with insult, "So I cain't ——k, huh? I'll show that son-of-a-bitch kin I, cain't I."

What should he do now? Grebe asked himself. Why, he should go. He should turn away and go. He couldn't talk to this woman. He couldn't keep her standing naked in the cold. But when he tried he found himself unable to turn away.

He said, "Is this where Mr. Green lives?"

But she was still talking to herself and did not hear him.

"Is this Mr. Green's house?"

At last she turned her furious drunken glance on him. "What do you want?"

Again her eyes wandered from him; there was a dot of blood in their enraged brilliance. He wondered why she didn't feel the cold.

"I'm from the relief."

"Awright, what?"

"I've got a check for Tulliver Green."

This time she heard him and put out her hand.

"No, no, for *Mr.* Green. He's got to sign," he said. How was he going to get Green's signature tonight!

"I'll take it. He cain't."

He desperately shook his head, thinking of Mr. Field's precautions about identification. "I can't let you have it. It's for him. Are you Mrs. Green?"

"Maybe I is, and maybe I ain't. Who want to know?"

"Is he upstairs?"

"Awright. Take it up yourself, you goddam fool."

Sure, he was a goddamned fool. Of course he could not go up because Green would probably be drunk and naked, too. And perhaps he would appear on the landing soon. He looked eagerly upward. Under the light was a high narrow brown wall. Empty! It remained empty!

"Hell with you, then!" he heard her cry. To deliver a check for coal and clothes, he was keeping her in the cold. She did not feel it, but his face was burning with frost and self-ridicule. He backed away from her.

"I'll come tomorrow, tell him."

"Ah, hell with you. Don' never come. What you doin' here in the nighttime? Don' come back." She yelled so that he saw the breadth of her tongue. She stood astride in the long cold box of the hall and held on to the banister and the wall. The bungalow itself was shaped something like a box, a clumsy, high box pointing into the freezing air with its sharp, wintry lights.

"If you are Mrs. Green, I'll give you the check," he said, changing his mind.

"Give here, then." She took it, took the pen offered with it in her left hand, and tried to sign the receipt on the wall. He looked around, almost as though to see whether his madness was being observed, and came near believing that someone was standing on a mountain of used tires in the auto-junking shop next door.

"But are you Mrs. Green?" he now thought to ask. But she was already climbing the stairs with the check, and it was too late, if he had made an error, if he was now in trouble, to undo the thing. But he wasn't going to worry about it. Though she might not be Mrs. Green, he was convinced that Mr. Green was upstairs. Whoever she was, the woman stood for Green, whom he was not to see this time. Well, you silly bastard, he said to himself, so you think you found him. So what? Maybe you really did find him—what of it? But it was important that there was a real Mr. Green whom they could not keep him from reaching because he seemed to come as an emissary from hostile appearances. And though the self-ridicule was slow to diminish, and his face still blazed with it, he had, nevertheless, a feeling of elation, too. "For after all," he said, "he *could* be found!"

QUESTIONS

1. What makes a story out of a poor man's attempt to deliver a check? There's hardly a plot here. What are we interested in? How would you define the conflict? (See Preface, pp. 13–14.)
2. Raynor kids Grebe about trying to seek reality behind the "fallen world of appearances." This search recurs through the story. How is this more than a philosophical exercise? What is Bellow saying about the elevated trains created by Yerkes—about conventional aspects to reality?
3. Why is Staika, "the Blood Mother of Federal Street," in the story?
4. Mr. Field shows Grebe all his identification before he will accept his check. How is this gesture thematically connected to the rest of the story? (See Preface, pp. 27–28.)
5. What is the significance of Grebe's search?

CARSON McCULLERS

(1917-1967)

Melville uses Bartleby, strange and solitary character, as a repre-
sentation—exaggerated, and therefore more intense—of the human
condition. In the same way McCullers uses her strange, isolated
characters to express her vision of the lives of all of us. Born in
Georgia in 1917, McCullers at age twenty-two published *The Heart
Is a Lonely Hunter,* a brilliant novel which, like this lovely short
story, deals with a child learning about the struggle to love and to
communicate. Ten years later she wrote *A Member of the Wedding,*
and in 1951, *The Ballad of the Sad Café,* a collection including "A
Tree, A Rock, A Cloud."
[See Preface, p. 17 (focus).]

A Tree, A Rock, A Cloud

CARSON McCULLERS

It was raining that morning, and still very dark. When the boy
reached the streetcar café he had almost finished his route and he went
in for a cup of coffee. The place was an all-night café owned by a
bitter and stingy man called Leo. After the raw, empty street, the
café seemed friendly and bright; along the counter there were a

From the book *Collected Short Stories and the Novel, The Ballad of the Sad Café,*
by Carson McCullers. Reprinted by permission of Houghton Mifflin Company,
Boston. Copyright 1955 by Carson McCullers.

couple of soldiers, three spinners from the cotton mill, and in a corner a man who sat hunched over with his nose and half his face down in a beer mug. The boy wore a helmet such as aviators wear. When he went into the café he unbuckled the chin strap and raised the right flap up over his pink little ear; often as he drank his coffee someone would speak to him in a friendly way. But this morning Leo did not look into his face and none of the men were talking. He paid and was leaving the café when a voice called out to him:

"Son! Hey Son!"

He turned back and the man in the corner was crooking his finger and nodding to him. He had brought his face out of the beer mug and he seemed suddenly very happy. The man was long and pale, with a big nose and faded orange hair.

"Hey Son!"

The boy went toward him. He was an undersized boy of about twelve, with one shoulder drawn higher than the other because of the weight of the paper sack. His face was shallow, freckled, and his eyes were round child eyes.

"Yeah Mister?"

The man laid one hand on the paper boy's shoulders, then grasped the boy's chin and turned his face slowly from one side to the other. The boy shrank back uneasily.

"Say! What's the big idea?"

The boy's voice was shrill; inside the café it was suddenly very quiet.

The man said slowly, "I love you."

All along the counter the men laughed. The boy, who had scowled and sidled away, did not know what to do. He looked over the counter at Leo, and Leo watched him with a weary, brittle jeer. The boy tried to laugh also. But the man was serious and sad.

"I did not mean to tease you, Son," he said. "Sit down and have a beer with me. There is something I have to explain."

Cautiously, out of the corner of his eye, the paper boy questioned the men along the counter to see what he should do. But they had gone back to their beer or their breakfast and did not notice him. Leo put a cup of coffee on the counter and a little jug of cream.

"He is a minor," Leo said.

The paper boy slid himself up onto the stool. His ear beneath the upturned flap of the helmet was very small and red. The man was nodding at him soberly. "It is important," he said. Then he reached in his hip pocket and brought out something which he held up in the palm of his hand for the boy to see.

"Look very carefully," he said.

The boy stared, but there was nothing to look at very carefully. The man held in his big, grimy palm a photograph. It was the face of a woman, but blurred, so that only the hat and the dress she was wearing stood out clearly.

"See?" the man asked.

The boy nodded and the man placed another picture in his palm. The woman was standing on a beach in a bathing suit. The suit made her stomach very big, and that was the main thing you noticed.

"Got a good look?" He leaned over closer and finally asked: "You ever seen her before?"

The boy sat motionless, staring slantwise at the man. "Not so I know of."

"Very well." The man blew on the photographs and put them back into his pocket. "That was my wife."

"Dead?" the boy asked.

Slowly the man shook his head. He pursed his lips as though about to whistle and answered in a long-drawn way: "Nuuu—" he said. "I will explain."

The beer on the counter before the man was in a large brown mug. He did not pick it up to drink. Instead he bent down and, putting his face over the rim, he rested there for a moment. Then with both hands he tilted the mug and sipped.

"Some night you'll go to sleep with your big nose in a mug and drown," said Leo. "Prominent transient drowns in beer. That would be a cute death."

The paper boy tried to signal to Leo. While the man was not looking he screwed up his face and worked his mouth to question soundlessly: "Drunk?" But Leo only raised his eyebrows and turned away to put some pink strips of bacon on the grill. The man pushed the mug away from him, straightened himself, and folded his loose crooked hands on the counter. His face was sad as he looked at the paper boy. He did not blink, but from time to time the lids closed down with delicate gravity over his pale green eyes. It was nearing dawn and the boy shifted the weight of the paper sack.

"I am talking about love," the man said. "With me it is a science."

The boy half slid down from the stool. But the man raised his forefinger, and there was something about him that held the boy and would not let him go away.

"Twelve years ago I married the woman in the photograph. She was my wife for one year, nine months, three days, and two nights. I loved her. Yes. . . ." He tightened his blurred, rambling voice and said again: "I loved her. I thought also that she loved me. I was a railroad engineer. She had all home comforts and luxuries. It never crept into my brain that she was not satisfied. But do you know what happened?"

"Mgneeow!" said Leo.

The man did not take his eyes from the boy's face. "She left me. I came in one night and the house was empty and she was gone. She left me."

"With a fellow?" the boy asked.

Gently the man placed his palm down on the counter. "Why, naturally, Son. A woman does not run off like that alone."

The café was quiet, the soft rain black and endless in the street outside. Leo pressed down the frying bacon with the prongs of his long fork. "So you have been chasing the floozie for eleven years. You frazzled old rascal!"

For the first time the man glanced at Leo. "Please don't be vulgar. Besides, I was not speaking to you." He turned back to the boy and said in a trusting and secretive undertone, "Let's not pay any attention to him. O.K.?"

The paper boy nodded doubtfully.

"It was like this," the man continued. "I am a person who feels many things. All my life one thing after another has impressed me. Moonlight. The leg of a pretty girl. One thing after another. But the point is that when I had enjoyed anything there was a peculiar sensation as though it was laying around loose in me. Nothing seemed to finish itself up or fit in with the other things. Women? I had my portion of them. The same. Afterwards laying around loose in me. I was a man who had never loved."

Very slowly he closed his eyelids, and the gesture was like a curtain drawn at the end of a scene in a play. When he spoke again his voice was excited and the words came fast—the lobes of his large, loose ears seemed to tremble.

"Then I met this woman. I was fifty-one years old and she always said she was thirty. I met her at a filling station and we were married within three days. And do you know what it was like? I just can't tell you. All I had ever felt was gathered together around this woman. Nothing lay around loose in me any more but was finished up by her."

The man stopped suddenly and stroked his long nose. His voice sank down to a steady and reproachful undertone: "I'm not explaining this right. What happened was this. There were these beautiful feelings and loose little pleasures inside me. And this woman was something like an assembly line for my soul. I run these little pieces of myself through her and I come out complete. Now do you follow me?"

"What was her name?" the boy asked.

"Oh," he said. "I called her Dodo. But that is immaterial."

"Did you try to make her come back?"

The man did not seem to hear. "Under the circumstances you can imagine how I felt when she left me."

Leo took the bacon from the grill and folded two strips of it between a bun. He had a gray face, with slitted eyes, and a pinched nose saddled by faint blue shadows. One of the mill workers signaled for more coffee and Leo poured it. He did not give refills on coffee free. The spinner ate breakfast there every morning, but the better Leo knew his customers the stingier he treated them. He nibbled his own bun as though he grudged it to himself.

"And you never got hold of her again?"

The boy did not know what to think of the man, and his child's face was uncertain with mingled curiosity and doubt. He was new on the paper route; it was still strange to him to be out in the town in the black, queer early morning.

"Yes," the man said. "I took a number of steps to get her back. I went around trying to locate her. I went to Tulsa where she had folks. And to Mobile. I went to every town she had ever mentioned to me, and I hunted down every man she had formerly been connected with. Tulsa, Atlanta, Chicago, Cheehaw, Memphis. . . . For the better part of two years I chased around the country trying to lay hold of her."

"But the pair of them had vanished from the face of the earth!" said Leo.

"Don't listen to him," the man said confidentially. "And also just forget those two years. They are not important. What matters is that around the third year a curious thing begun to happen to me."

"What?" the boy asked.

The man leaned down and tilted his mug to take a sip of beer. But as he hovered over the mug his nostrils fluttered slightly; he sniffed the staleness of the beer and did not drink. "Love is a curious thing to begin with. At first I thought only of getting her back. It was a kind of mania. But then as time went on I tried to remember her. But do you know what happened?"

"No," the boy said.

"When I laid myself down on a bed and tried to think about her my mind became a blank. I couldn't see her. I would take out her pictures and look. No good. Nothing doing. A blank. Can you imagine it?"

"Say Mac!" Leo called down the counter. "Can you imagine this bozo's mind a blank?"

Slowly, as though fanning away flies, the man waved his hand. His green eyes were concentrated and fixed on the shallow little face of the paper boy.

"But a sudden piece of glass on a sidewalk. Or a nickel tune in a music box. A shadow on a wall at night. And I would remember. It might happen in a street and I would cry or bang my head against a lamppost. You follow me?"

"A piece of glass . . ." the boy said.

"Anything. I would walk around and I had no power of how and when to remember her. You think you can put up a kind of shield. But remembering don't come to a man face forward—it corners around sideways. I was at the mercy of everything I saw and heard. Suddenly instead of me combing the countryside to find her she began to chase me around in my very soul. *She* chasing *me,* mind you! and in my soul."

The boy asked finally: "What part of the country were you in then?"

"Ooh," the man groaned, "I was a sick mortal. It was like small-pox. I confess, Son, that I boozed. I fornicated. I committed any sin that suddenly appealed to me. I am loath to confess it but I will do so. When I recall that period it is all curdled in my mind, it was so terrible."

The man leaned his head down and tapped his forehead on the counter. For a few seconds he stayed bowed over in this position, the back of his stringy neck covered with orange furze, his hands with their long warped fingers held palm to palm in an attitude of prayer. Then the man straightened himself; he was smiling and suddenly his face was bright and tremulous and old.

"It was in the fifth year that it happened," he said. "And with it I started my science."

Leo's mouth jerked with a pale, quick grin. "Well none of we boys are getting any younger," he said. Then with sudden anger he balled up a dishcloth he was holding and threw it down hard on the floor. "You draggle-tailed old Romeo!"

"What happened?" the boy asked.

The old man's voice was high and clear: "Peace," he answered.

"Huh?"

"It is hard to explain scientifically, Son," he said. "I guess the logical explanation is that she and I had fleed around from each other for so long that finally we just got tangled up together and lay down and quit. Peace. A queer and beautiful blankness. It was spring in Portland and the rain came every afternoon. All evening I just stayed there on my bed in the dark. And that is how the science come to me."

The windows in the streetcar were pale blue with light. The two soldiers paid for their beers and opened the door—one of the soldiers combed his hair and wiped off his muddy puttees before they went outside. The three mill workers bent silently over their breakfasts. Leo's clock was ticking on the wall.

"It is this. And listen carefully. I meditated on love and reasoned it out. I realized what is wrong with us. Men fall in love for the first time. And what do they fall in love with?"

The boy's soft mouth was partly open and he did not answer.

"A woman," the old man said. "Without science, with nothing to go by, they undertake the most dangerous and sacred experience in God's earth. They fall in love with a woman. Is that correct, Son?"

"Yeah," the boy said faintly.

"They start at the wrong end of love. They begin at the climax. Can you wonder it is so miserable? Do you know how men should love?"

The old man reached over and grasped the boy by the collar of his leather jacket. He gave him a gentle shake and his green eyes gazed down unblinking and grave.

"Son, do you know how love should be begun?"

The boy sat small and listening and still. Slowly he shook his head. The old man leaned closer and whispered:

"A tree. A rock. A cloud."

It was still raining outside in the street: a mild, gray, endless rain. The mill whistle blew for the six o'clock shift and the three spinners paid and went away. There was no one in the café but Leo, the old man, and the little paper boy.

"The weather was like this in Portland," he said. "At the time my science was begun. I meditated and I started very cautious. I would pick up something from the street and take it home with me. I bought a goldfish and I concentrated on the goldfish and I loved it. I graduated from one thing to another. Day by day I was getting this technique. On the road from Portland to San Diego——"

"Aw shut up!" screamed Leo suddenly. "Shut up! Shut up!"

The old man still held the collar of the boy's jacket; he was trembling and his face was earnest and bright and wild. "For six years now I have gone around by myself and built up my science. And now I am a master. Son, I can love anything. No longer do I have to think about it even. I see a street full of people and a beautiful light comes in me. I watch a bird in the sky. Or I meet a traveler on the road. Everything, Son. And anybody. All strangers and all loved! Do you realize what a science like mine can mean?"

The boy held himself stiffly, his hands curled tight around the counter edge. Finally he asked: "Did you ever really find that lady?"

"What? What say, Son?"

"I mean," the boy asked timidly. "Have you fallen in love with a woman again?"

The old man loosened his grasp on the boy's collar. He turned away and for the first time his green eyes had a vague and scattered look. He lifted his mug from the counter, drank down the yellow beer. His head was shaking slowly from side to side. Then finally he answered: "No, Son. You see that is the last step in my science. I go cautious. And I am not quite ready yet."

"Well!" said Leo. "Well well well!"

The old man stood in the open doorway. "Remember," he said. Framed there in the gray damp light of the early morning he looked shrunken and seedy and frail. But his smile was bright. "Remember I love you," he said with a last nod. And the door closed quietly behind him.

The boy did not speak for a long time. He pulled down the bangs on his forehead and slid his grimy little forefinger around the rim of his empty cup. Then without looking at Leo he finally asked:

"Was he drunk?"

"No," said Leo shortly.

The boy raised his clear voice higher. "Then was he a dope fiend?"

"No."

The boy looked up at Leo, and his flat little face was desperate, his voice urgent and shrill. "Was he crazy? Do you think he was a lunatic?" The paper boy's voice dropped suddenly with doubt. "Leo? Or not?"

But Leo would not answer him. Leo had run a night café for fourteen years, and he held himself to be a critic of craziness. There were the town characters and also the transients who roamed in from the night. He knew the manias of all of them. But he did not want to satisfy the questions of the waiting child. He tightened his pale face and was silent.

So the boy pulled down the right flap of his helmet and as he turned to leave he made the only comment that seemed safe to him, the only remark that could not be laughed down and despised:

"He sure has done a lot of traveling."

SHIRLEY JACKSON

(1919-1965)

Shirley Jackson lived a quiet life in Bennington, Vermont, the wife
of a literary critic and teacher, mother of a family, and teller of tales,
some of them bizarre and terrifying. Humdrum realism and horror
combine in "The Lottery" (1949), the story of an anachronistic agri-
cultural rite of human sacrifice whose original meaning has been
forgotten in the ordinary New England town where the rite is still
practiced. Something in the story moves us, convinces us, in spite of
the incongruity; somehow Jackson seems to have touched a nerve—
something we know about each other, something we know about how
evil works, about the destructive power of the "way it used to be" or
"the way things are." Even without simple analogies like military
draft, "The Lottery" is a persuasive nightmare.

[See Preface, p. 7 (objective angle of vision).]

The Lottery

SHIRLEY JACKSON

The morning of June 27th was clear and sunny, with the fresh warmth of a full-summer day; the flowers were blossoming profusely and the grass was richly green. The people of the village began to gather in the square, between the post office and the bank, around ten o'clock; in some towns there were so many people that the lottery took two days and had to be started on June 26th, but in this village, where there were only about three hundred people, the whole lottery took less than two hours, so it could begin at ten o'clock in the morning and still be through in time to allow the villagers to get home for noon dinner.

The children assembled first, of course. School was recently over for the summer, and the feeling of liberty sat uneasily on most of them; they tended to gather together quietly for a while before they broke into boisterous play, and their talk was still of the classroom and the teacher, of books and reprimands. Bobby Martin had already stuffed his pockets full of stones, and the other boys soon followed his example, selecting the smoothest and roundest stones; Bobby and Harry Jones and Dickie Delacroix—the villagers pronounced this name "Dellacroy"—eventually made a great pile of stones in one corner of the square and guarded it against the raids of the other boys. The girls stood aside, talking among themselves, looking over their shoulders at the boys, and the very small children rolled in the dust or clung to the hands of their older brothers or sisters.

Soon the men began to gather, surveying their own children, speaking of planting and rain, tractors and taxes. They stood together, away from the pile of stones in the corner, and their jokes were quiet and they smiled rather than laughed. The women, wearing faded house dresses and sweaters, came shortly after their menfolk. They greeted one another and exchanged bits of gossip as they went to join their husbands. Soon the women, standing by their husbands, began to call to their children, and the children came reluctantly, having to be called four or five times. Bobby Martin ducked under his mother's grasping hand and ran, laughing, back to the pile of stones. His father spoke up sharply, and Bobby came quickly and took his place between his father and his oldest brother.

The lottery was conducted—as were the square dances, the teen-age club, the Halloween program—by Mr. Summers, who had time and energy to devote to civic activities. He was a round-faced, jovial man and he ran the coal business, and people were sorry for him, because he had no children and his wife was a scold. When he arrived in the square, carrying the black wooden box, there was a murmur of conversation among the villagers, and he waved and called, "Little late today, folks." The postmaster, Mr. Graves, followed him, carrying a three-legged stool, and the stool was put in the center of the square and Mr. Summers set the black box down on it. The villagers kept their distance, leaving a space between them-selves and the stool, and when Mr. Summers said, "Some of you fellows want to give me a hand?" there was a hesitation before two men, Mr. Martin and his oldest son, Baxter, came forward to hold the box steady on the stool while Mr. Summers stirred up the papers inside it.

The original paraphernalia for the lottery had been lost long ago, and the black box now resting on the stool had been put into use even before Old Man Warner, the oldest man in town, was born. Mr. Summers spoke frequently to the villagers about making a new box, but no one liked to upset even as much tradition as was represented by the black box. There was a story that the present box had been made with some pieces of the box that had preceded it, the one that had been constructed when the first people settled down to make a village here. Every year, after the lottery, Mr. Summers began talking again about a new box, but every year the subject was allowed to fade off without anything's being done. The black box grew shabbier each year; by now it was no longer completely black but splintered badly along one side to show the original wood color, and in some places faded or stained.

Mr. Martin and his oldest son, Baxter, held the black box securely on the stool until Mr. Summers had stirred the papers thoroughly with his hand. Because so much of the ritual had been forgotten or discarded, Mr. Summers had been successful in having slips of paper substituted for the chips of wood that had been used for generations. Chips of wood, Mr. Summers had argued, had been all very well when the village was tiny, but now that the population was more than three hundred and likely to keep on growing, it was necessary to use something that would fit more easily into the black box. The night before the lottery, Mr. Summers and Mr. Graves made up the slips of paper and put them in the box, and it was then taken to the safe of Mr. Summers' coal company and locked up until Mr. Summers was ready to take it to the square next morning. The rest of the year, the box was put away, sometimes one place, sometimes another; it had spent one year in Mr. Graves's barn and another year underfoot in the post office, and sometimes it was set on a shelf in the Martin grocery and left there.

There was a great deal of fussing to be done before Mr. Summers declared the lottery open. There were the lists to make up—of heads of families, heads of households in each family, members of each household in each family. There was the proper swearing-in of Mr. Summers by the postmaster, as the official of the lottery; at one time, some people remembered, there had been a recital of some sort, performed by the official of the lottery, a perfunctory, tuneless chant that had been rattled off duly each year; some people believed that the official of the lottery used to stand just so when he said or sang it, others believed that he was supposed to walk among the people, but years and years ago this part of the ritual had been allowed to lapse. There had been, also, a ritual salute, which the official of the lottery had had to use in addressing each person who came up to draw from the box, but this also had changed with time, until now it was felt necessary only for the official to speak to each person approaching. Mr. Summers was very good at all this; in his clean white shirt and blue jeans, with one hand resting carelessly on the black box. he seemed very proper and important as he talked interminably to Mr. Graves and the Martins.

Just as Mr. Summers finally left off talking and turned to the assembled villagers, Mrs. Hutchinson came hurriedly along the path to the square, her sweater thrown over her shoulders, and slid into place in the back of the crowd. "Clean forgot what day it was," she said to Mrs. Delacroix, who stood next to her, and they both laughed softly. "Thought my old man was out back stacking wood," Mrs. Hutchinson went on, "and then I looked out the window and the kids were gone, and then I remembered it was the twenty-seventh and came a-running." She dried her hands on her apron, and Mrs. Delacroix said, "You're in time, though. They're still talking away up there."

Mrs. Hutchinson craned her neck to see through the crowd and found her husband and children standing near the front. She tapped Mrs. Delacroix on the arm as a farewell and began to make her way through the crowd. The people separated good-humoredly to let her through; two or three people said, in voices just loud enough to be heard across the crowd, "Here comes your Missus, Hutchinson," and "Bill, she made it after all." Mrs. Hutchinson reached her husband, and Mr. Summers, who had been waiting, said cheerfully, "Thought we were going to have to get on without you, Tessie." Mrs. Hutchinson said, grinning, "Wouldn't have me leave m'dishes in the sink, now, would you, Joe?" and soft laughter ran through the crowd as the people stirred back into position after Mrs. Hutchinson's arrival.

"Well, now," Mr. Summers said soberly, "guess we better get started, get this over with, so's we can go back to work. Anybody ain't here?"

"Dunbar," several people said. "Dunbar, Dunbar."

Mr. Summers consulted his list. "Clyde Dunbar," he said. "That's right. He's broke his leg, hasn't he? Who's drawing for him?"

"Me, I guess," a woman said, and Mr. Summers turned to look at her. "Wife draws for her husband," Mrs. Summers said. "Don't you have a grown boy to do it for you, Janey?" Although Mr. Summers and everyone else in the village knew the answer perfectly well, it was the business of the official of the lottery to ask such questions formally. Mr. Summers waited with an expression of polite interest while Mrs. Dunbar answered.

"Horace's not but sixteen yet," Mrs. Dunbar said regretfully. "Guess I gotta fill in for the old man this year."

"Right," Mr. Summers said. He made a note on the list he was holding. Then he asked, "Watson boy drawing this year?"

A tall boy in the crowd raised his hand. "Here," he said. "I'm drawing for m'mother and me." He blinked his eyes nervously and ducked his head as several voices in the crowd said things like "Good fellow, Jack," and "Glad to see your mother's got a man to do it."

"Well," Mr. Summers said, "guess that's everyone. Old Man Warner make it?"

"Here," a voice said, and Mr. Summers nodded.

A sudden hush fell on the crowd as Mr. Summers cleared his throat and looked at the list. "All ready?" he called. "Now, I'll read the names—heads of families first—and the men come up and take a paper out of the box. Keep the paper folded in your hand without looking at it until everyone has had a turn. Everything clear?"

The people had done it so many times that they only half listened to the directions; most of them were quiet, wetting their lips, not looking around. Then Mr. Summers raised one hand high and said, "Adams." A man disengaged himself from the crowd and came forward. "Hi, Steve," Mr. Summers said, and Mr. Adams said, "Hi, Joe." They grinned at one another humorlessly and nervously. Then Mr. Adams reached into the black box and took out a folded paper. He held it firmly by one corner as he turned and went hastily back to his place in the crowd, where he stood a little apart from his family, not looking down at his hand.

"Allen," Mr. Summers said. "Anderson . . . Bentham."

"Seems like there's no time at all between lotteries any more," Mrs. Delacroix said to Mrs. Graves in the back row. "Seems like we got through with the last one only last week."

"Time sure goes fast," Mrs. Graves said.

"Clark . . . Delacroix."

"There goes my old man," Mrs. Delacroix said. She held her breath while her husband went forward.

"Dunbar," Mr. Summers said, and Mrs. Dunbar went steadily to the box while one of the women said, "Go on, Janey," and another said, "There she goes."

"We're next," Mrs. Graves said. She watched while Mr. Graves came around from the side of the box, greeted Mr. Summers gravely, and selected a slip of paper from the box. By now, all through the crowd there were men holding the small folded papers in their large hands, turning them over and over nervously. Mrs. Dunbar and her two sons stood together, Mrs. Dunbar holding the slip of paper.

"Harburt . . . Hutchinson."

"Get up there, Bill," Mrs. Hutchinson said, and the people near her laughed.

"Jones."

"They do say," Mr. Adams said to Old Man Warner, who stood next to him, "that over in the north village they're talking of giving up the lottery."

Old Man Warner snorted. "Pack of crazy fools," he said. "Listening to the young folks, nothing's good enough for *them*. Next thing you know, they'll be wanting to go back to living in caves, nobody work any more, live *that* way for a while. Used to be a saying about 'Lottery in June, corn be heavy soon.' First thing you know, we'd all be eating stewed chickweed and acorns. There's *always* been a lottery," he added petulantly. "Bad enough to see young Joe Summers up there joking with everybody."

"Some places have already quit lotteries," Mrs. Adams said.

"Nothing but trouble in *that*," Old Man Warner said stoutly. "Pack of young fools."

"Martin." And Bobby Martin watched his father go forward. "Overdyke . . . Percy."

"I wish they'd hurry," Mrs. Dunbar said to her older son. "I wish they'd hurry."

"They're almost through," her son said.

"You get ready to run tell Dad," Mrs. Dunbar said.

Mr. Summers called his own name and then stepped forward precisely and selected a slip from the box. Then he called, "Warner."

"Seventy-seventh year I been in the lottery," Old Man Warner said as he went through the crowd. "Seventy-seventh time."

"Watson." The tall boy came awkwardly through the crowd. Someone said, "Don't be nervous, Jack," and Mr. Summers said, "Take your time, son."

"Zanini."

After that, there was a long pause, a breathless pause, until Mr. Summers, holding his slip of paper in the air, said, "All right, fellows." For a minute, no one moved, and then all the slips of paper were opened. Suddenly, all the women began to speak at once, saying, "Who is it?" "Who's got it?" "Is it the Dunbars?" "Is it the Watsons?" Then the voices began to say, "It's Hutchinson. It's Bill," "Bill Hutchinson's got it."

"Go tell your father," Mrs. Dunbar said to her older son.

People began to look around to see the Hutchinsons. Bill Hutchinson was standing quiet, staring down at the paper in his hand. Suddenly, Tessie Hutchinson shouted to Mr. Summers, "You didn't give him time enough to take any paper he wanted. I saw you. It wasn't fair."

"Be a good sport, Tessie," Mrs. Delacroix called, and Mrs. Graves said, "All of us took the same chance."

"Shut up, Tessie," Bill Hutchinson said.

"Well, everyone," Mr. Summers said, "that was done pretty fast, and now we've got to be hurrying a little more to get done in time." He consulted his next list. "Bill," he said, "you draw for the Hutchinson family. You got any other households in the Hutchinsons?"

"There's Don and Eva," Mrs. Hutchinson yelled. "Make *them* take their chance!"

"Daughters draw with their husbands' families, Tessie," Mr. Summers said gently. "You know that as well as anyone else."

"It wasn't *fair*," Tessie said.

"I guess not, Joe," Bill Hutchinson said regretfully. "My daughter draws with her husband's family, that's only fair. And I've got no other family except the kids."

"Then, as far as drawing for families is concerned, it's you," Mr. Summers said in explanation, "and as far as drawing for households is concerned, that's you, too. Right?"

"Right," Bill Hutchinson said.

"How many kids, Bill?" Mr. Summers asked formally.

"Three," Bill Hutchinson said. "There's Bill, Jr., and Nancy, and little Dave. And Tessie and me."

"All right, then," Mr. Summers said. "Harry, you got their tickets back?"

Mr. Graves nodded and held up the slips of paper. "Put them in the box, then," Mr. Summers directed. "Take Bill's and put it in."

"I think we ought to start over," Mrs. Hutchinson said, as quietly as she could. "I tell you it wasn't *fair*. You didn't give him time enough to choose. *Every*body saw that."

Mr. Graves had selected the five slips and put them in the box, and he dropped all the papers but those onto the ground, where the breeze caught them and lifted them off.

"Listen, everybody," Mrs. Hutchinson was saying to the people around her.

"Ready, Bill?" Mr. Summers asked, and Bill Hutchinson, with one quick glance around at his wife and children, nodded.

"Remember," Mr. Summers said, "take the slips and keep them folded until each person has taken one. Harry, you help little Dave." Mr. Graves took the hand of the little boy, who came willingly with him up to the box. "Take a paper out of the box, Davy," Mr. Summers said. Davy put his hand into the box and laughed. "Take just *one* paper," Mr. Summers said. "Harry, you hold it for him." Mr. Graves took the child's hand and removed the folded paper from the tight fist and held it while little Dave stood next to him and looked up at him wonderingly.

"Nancy next," Mr. Summers said. Nancy was twelve, and her school friends breathed heavily as she went forward, switching her skirt, and took a slip daintily from the box. "Bill, Jr.," Mr. Summers said, and Billy, his face red and his feet over-large, nearly knocked the box over as he got a paper out. "Tessie," Mr. Summers said. She hesitated for a minute, looking around defiantly, and then set her lips and went up to the box. She snatched a paper out and held it behind her.

"Bill," Mr. Summers said, and Bill Hutchinson reached into the box and felt around, bringing his hand out at last with the slip of paper in it.

The crowd was quiet. A girl whispered, "I hope it's not Nancy," and the sound of the whisper reached the edges of the crowd.

"It's not the way it used to be," Old Man Warner said clearly. "People ain't the way they used to be."

"All right," Mr. Summers said. "Open the papers. Harry, you open little Dave's."

Mr. Graves opened the slip of paper and there was a general sigh through the crowd as he held it up and everyone could see that it was blank. Nancy and Bill, Jr., opened theirs at the same time, and both beamed and laughed, turning around to the crowd and holding their slips of paper above their heads.

"Tessie," Mr. Summers said. There was a pause, and then Mr. Summers looked at Bill Hutchinson, and Bill unfolded his paper and showed it. It was blank.

"It's Tessie," Mr. Summers said, and his voice was hushed. "Show us her paper, Bill."

Bill Hutchinson went over to his wife and forced the slip of paper out of her hand. It had a black spot on it, the black spot Mr. Summers had made the night before with the heavy pencil in the coal-company office. Bill Hutchinson held it up, and there was a stir in the crowd.

"All right, folks," Mr. Summers said. "Let's finish quickly."

Although the villagers had forgotten the ritual and lost the original black box, they still remembered to use stones. The pile of stones the boys had made earlier was ready; there were stones on the ground with the blowing scraps of paper that had come out of the box. Mrs. Delacroix selected a stone so large she had to pick it up with both hands and turned to Mrs. Dunbar. "Come on," she said. "Hurry up."

Mrs. Dunbar had small stones in both hands, and she said, gasping for breath, "I can't run at all. You'll have to go ahead and I'll catch up with you."

The children had stones already, and someone gave little Davy Hutchinson a few pebbles.

Tessie Hutchinson was in the center of a cleared space by now, and she held her hands out desperately as the villagers moved in on her. "It isn't fair," she said. A stone hit her on the side of the head.

Old Man Warner was saying, "Come on, come on, everyone." Steve Adams was in the front of the crowd of villagers, with Mrs. Graves beside him.

"It isn't fair, it isn't right," Mrs. Hutchinson screamed, and then they were upon her.

DORIS LESSING

(1919—)

Raised on a large farm in Rhodesia, Doris Lessing used her childhood, youthful marriage, and Communist organizing in Africa as material for her early stories and novels—*The Grass Is Singing* and the five novels of the Martha Quest series. In 1949 she moved to London, the locale of most action in her magnificent *The Golden Notebook* and *Four-Gated City*. Some of her recent fiction moves away from realism into science fiction, mysticism, and madness. "How I Finally Lost My Heart" has a hard-nosed realistic tone, witty, intellectual, cynical, but the material is as fantastic as Kafka's. "Homage for Isaac Babel" sets up the confrontation of the self-centered innocence of childhood with the painful vision of Babel's "My First Goose." Compare the two stories.

[See Preface, "How . . ." p. 2 (fantasy as reality).]

Homage for Isaac Babel

DORIS LESSING

The day I had promised to take Catherine down to visit my young
friend Philip at his school in the country, we were to leave at eleven,
but she arrived at nine. Her blue dress was new, and so were her
fashionable shoes. Her hair had just been done. She looked more
than ever like a pink and gold Renoir girl who expects everything
from life.

Catherine lives in a white house overlooking the sweeping brown
tides of the river. She helped me clean up my flat with a devotion
which said that she felt small flats were altogether more romantic than
large houses. We drank tea, and talked mainly about Philip, who,
being fifteen, has pure stern tastes in everything from food to music.
Catherine looked at the books lying around his room, and asked if
she might borrow the stories of Isaac Babel to read on the train.
Catherine is thirteen. I suggested she might find them difficult, but she
said: "Philip reads them, doesn't he?"

During the journey I read newspapers and watched her pretty
frowning face as she turned the pages of Babel, for she was
determined to let nothing get between her and her ambition to be
worthy of Philip.

At the school, which is charming, civilised, and expensive, the two
children walked together across green fields, and I followed, seeing
how the sun gilded their bright friendly heads turned towards each
other as they talked. In Catherine's left hand she carried the stories
of Isaac Babel.

After lunch we went to the pictures. Philip allowed it to be seen
that he thought going to the pictures just for the fun of it was not
worthy of intelligent people, but he made the concession, for our
sakes. For his sake we chose the more serious of the two films that were
showing in the little town. It was about a good priest who helped
criminals in New York. His goodness, however, was not enough to
prevent one of them from being sent to the gas chamber; and Philip
and I waited with Catherine in the dark until she had stopped crying
and could face the light of a golden evening.

At the entrance of the cinema the doorman was lying in wait for
anyone who had red eyes. Grasping Catherine by her suffering arm,

he said bitterly: "Yes, why are you crying? He had to be punished for his crime, didn't he?" Catherine stared at him, incredulous. Philip rescued her by saying with disdain: "Some people don't know right from wrong even when it's *demonstrated* to them." The doorman turned his attention to the next red-eyed emerger from the dark; and we went on together to the station, the children silent because of the cruelty of the world.

Finally Catherine said, her eyes wet again: "I think it's all absolutely beastly, and I can't bear to think about it." And Philip said: "But we've got to think about it, don't you see, because if we don't it'll just go on and *on,* don't you see?"

In the train going back to London I sat beside Catherine. She had the stories open in front of her, but she said: "Philip's awfully lucky. I wish I went to that school. Did you notice that girl who said hullo to him in the garden? They must be great friends. I wish my mother would let me have a dress like that, it's *not* fair."

"I thought it was too old for her."

"Oh, *did* you?"

Soon she bent her head again over the book, but almost at once lifted it to say: "Is he a very famous writer?"

"He's a marvellous writer, brilliant, one of the very best."

"Why?"

"Well, for one thing he's so simple. Look how few words he uses, and how strong his stories are."

"I see. Do you know him? Does he live in London?"

"Oh no, he's dead."

"Oh. Then why did you—I thought he was alive, the way you talked."

"I'm sorry, I suppose I wasn't thinking of him as dead."

"When did he die?"

"He was murdered. About twenty years ago, I suppose."

"Twenty years." Her hands began the movement of pushing the book over to me, but then relaxed. "I'll be fourteen in November," she stated, sounding threatened, while her eyes challenged me.

I found it hard to express my need to apologise, but before I could speak, she said, patiently attentive again: "You said he was murdered?"

"Yes."

"I expect the person who murdered him felt sorry when he discovered he had murdered a famous writer."

"Yes, I expect so."

"Was he old when he was murdered?"

"No, quite young really."

"Well, that was bad luck, wasn't it?"

"Yes, I suppose it was bad luck."

"Which do you think is the very best story here? I mean, in your honest opinion, the very very best one."

I chose the story about killing the goose. She read it slowly, while I sat waiting, wishing to take it from her, wishing to protect this charming little person from Isaac Babel.

When she had finished she said: "Well, some of it I don't understand. He's got a funny way of looking at things. Why should a man's legs in boots look like *girls?*" She finally pushed the book over at me, and said: "I think it's all morbid."

"But you have to understand the kind of life he had. First, he was a Jew in Russia. That was bad enough. Then his experience was all revolution and civil war and . . ."

But I could see these words bouncing off the clear glass of her fiercely denying gaze; and I said: "Look, Catherine, why don't you try again when you're older? Perhaps you'll like him better then?"

She said gratefully: "Yes, perhaps that would be best. After all, Philip is two years older than me, isn't he?"

A week later I got a letter from Catherine.

Thank you very much for being kind enough to take me to visit Philip at his school. It was the most lovely day in my whole life. I am extremely grateful to you for taking me. I have been thinking about the Hoodlum Priest. That was a film which demonstrated to me beyond any shadow of doubt that Capital Punishment is a Wicked Thing, and I shall never forget what I learned that afternoon, and the lessons of it will be with me all my life. I have been meditating about what you said about Isaac Babel, the famed Russian short story writer, and I now see that the conscious simplicity of his style is what makes him, beyond the shadow of a doubt, the great writer that he is, and now in my school compositions I am endeavouring to emulate him so as to learn a conscious simplicity which is the only basis for a really brilliant writing style. Love, Catherine. P.S. Has Philip said anything about my party? I wrote but he hasn't answered. Please find out if he is coming or if he just forgot to answer my letter. I hope he comes, because sometimes I feel I shall die if he doesn't. P.P.S. Please don't tell him I said anything, because I should die if he knew. Love, Catherine.

How I Finally Lost My Heart

DORIS LESSING

It would be easy to say that I picked up a knife, slit open my side, took my heart out, and threw it away; but unfortunately it wasn't as easy as that. Not that I, like everybody else, had not often wanted to do it. No, it happened differently, and not as I expected.

It was just after I had had a lunch and a tea with two different men. My lunch partner I had lived with for (more or less) four and seven-twelfths years. When he left me for new pastures, I spent two years, or was it three, half dead, and my heart was a stone, impossible to carry about, considering all the other things weighing on one. Then I slowly, and with difficulty, got free, because my heart cherished a thousand adhesions to my first love—though from another point of view he could be legitimately described as either my second *real* love (my father being the first) or my third (my brother intervening).

As the folk song has it:

> I have loved but three men in my life,
> My father, my brother, and the man that took my life.

But if one were going to look at the thing from outside, without insight, he could be seen as (perhaps, I forget) the thirteenth, but to do that means disregarding the inner emotional truth. For we all know that those affairs or entanglements one has between *serious* loves, though they may number dozens and stretch over years, *don't really count.*

This way of looking at things creates a number of unhappy people, for it is well known that what doesn't really count for me might very well count for you. But there is no way of getting over this difficulty, for a *serious* love is the most important business in life, or nearly so. At any rate, most of us are engaged in looking for it. Even when we are in fact being very serious indeed with one person we still have an eighth of an eye cocked in case some stranger unexpectedly encountered might turn out to be even more serious. We are all entirely in agreement that we are in the right to taste, test, sip and sample a thousand people on our way to the *real* one. It is not too much to say that in our circles tasting and sampling is probably the second most important activity, the first being earning money. Or to put it another way, "If you are serious about this thing, you go on laying everybody that offers until something clicks and you're all set to go."

I have digressed from an earlier point: that I regarded this man I had lunch with (we will call him A) as my first love; and still do, despite the Freudians, who insist on seeing my father as A and possibly my brother as B, making my (real) first love C. And despite, also, those who might ask: What about your two husbands and all those affairs?

What about them? I did not *really* love them, the way I loved A.

I had lunch with him. Then, quite by chance, I had tea with B. When I say B, here, I mean my *second* serious love, not my brother, or the little boys I was in love with between the ages of five and fifteen, if we are going to take fifteen (arbitrarily) as the point of no return . . . which last phrase is in itself a pretty brave defiance of the secular arbiters.

In between A and B (my count) there were a good many affairs, or samples, but they didn't score. B and I *clicked,* we went off like a bomb, though not quite as simply as A and I had clicked, because my heart was bruised, sullen, and suspicious because of A's throwing me over. Also there were all those ligaments and adhesions binding me to A still to be loosened, one by one. However, for a time B and I got on like a house on fire, and then we came to grief. My heart was again a ton weight in my side.

> If this were a stone in my side, a stone,
> I could pluck it out and be free. . . .

Having lunch with A, then tea with B, two men who between them had consumed a decade of my previous years (I am not counting the test or trial affairs in between) and, it is fair to say, had balanced all the delight (plenty and intense) with misery (oh Lord, Lord) —moving from one to the other, in the course of an afternoon, conversing amiably about this and that, with meanwhile my heart giving no more than slight reminiscent tugs, the fish of memory at the end of a long slack line. . . .

To sum up, it was salutary.

Particularly as that evening I was expecting to meet C, or someone who might very well turn out to be C—though I don't want to give too much emphasis to C, the truth is I can hardly remember what he looked like, but one can't be expected to remember the unimportant ones one has sipped or tasted in between. But after all, he might have turned out to be C, we might have *clicked,* and I was in that state of mind (in which we all so often are) of thinking: He might turn out to be the one. (I use a woman's magazine phrase deliberately here, instead of saying, as I might. *Perhaps it will be serious*.)

So there I was (I want to get the details and atmosphere right) standing at a window looking into a street (Great Portland Street, as a matter of fact) and thinking that while I would not dream of regretting my affairs, or experiences, with A and B (it is better to have loved and lost than never to have loved at all), my anticipation of the heart because of spending an evening with a possible C had a certain unreality, because there was no doubt that both A and B had caused me unbelievable pain. Why, therefore, was I looking forward to C? I should rather be running away as fast as I could.

It suddenly occurred to me that I was looking at the whole phenomenon quite inaccurately. My (or perhaps I am permitted to say our?) way of looking at it is that one must search for an A, or a B, or a C or a D with a certain combination of desirable or sympathetic qualities so that one may click, or spontaneously combust: or to put it differently, one needs a person who, like a saucer of water, allows one to float off on him/her, like a transfer. But this wasn't so at all. Actually one carries with one a sort of burning spear stuck in one's side, that one waits for someone else to pull out; it is something painful, like a sore or a wound, that one cannot wait to share with someone else.

I saw myself quite plainly in a moment of truth: I was standing at a window (on the third floor) with A and B (to mention only the mountain peaks of my emotional experience) behind me, a rather attractive woman, if I may say so, with a mellowness that I would be the first to admit is the sad harbinger of age, but is attractive by definition, because it is a testament to the amount of sampling and sipping (I nearly wrote simpling and sapping) I have done in my time . . . there I stood, brushed, dressed, red-lipped, kohl-eyed, all waiting for an evening with a possible C. And at another window overlooking (I think I am right in saying) Margaret Street, stood C, brushed, washed, shaved, smiling: an attractive man (I think), and *he* was thinking: Perhaps she will turn out to be D (or A or 3 or ? or %, or whatever symbol he used). We stood, separated by space, certainly, in identical conditions of pleasant uncertainty and anticipation, and we both held our hearts in our hands, all pink and palpitating and ready for pleasure and pain, and we were about to throw these hearts in each other's face like snowballs, or cricket balls (How's that?) or, more accurately, like great bleeding wounds: "Take my wound." Because the last thing one ever thinks at such moments is that he (or she) will say: Take *my* wound, please remove the spear from *my* side. No, not at all, one simply expects to get rid of one's own.

I decided I must go to the telephone and say C!—You know that joke about the joke-makers who don't trouble to tell each other jokes, but simply say Joke 1, or Joke 2, and everyone roars with laughter, or snickers, or giggles appropriately. . . . Actually one could reverse the game by guessing whether it was Joke C (b) or Joke A (d) according to what sort of laughter a person made to match the silent thought. . . . Well, C (I imagined myself saying), the analogy is for our instruction: Let's take the whole thing as read or said. Let's not lick each other's sores; let's keep our hearts to ourselves. Because just consider it, C, how utterly absurd—here we stand at our respective windows with our palpitating hearts in our hands. . . .

At this moment, dear reader, I was forced simply to put down the telephone with an apology. For I felt the fingers of my left hand push outwards around something rather large, light, and slippery—hard to describe this sensation, really. My hand is not large, and my heart was in a state of inflation after having had lunch with A, tea with B, and then looking forward to C. . . . Anyway, my fingers were stretching out rather desperately to encompass an unknown, largish, lightish object, and I said: Excuse me a minute, to C, looked down, and there was my heart, in my hand.

I had to end the conversation there.

For one thing, to find that one has achieved something so often longed for, so easily, is upsetting. It's not as if I had been trying. To get something one wants simply by accident—no, there's no pleasure in it, no feeling of achievement. So to find myself heart-whole, or, more accurately, heart-less, or at any rate, rid of the damned thing, and at such an awkward moment, in the middle of an imaginary telephone call with a man who might possibly turn out to be C, well, it was irritating rather than not.

For another thing, a heart, raw and bleeding and fresh from one's side, is not the prettiest sight. I'm not going into that at all. I was appalled, and indeed embarrassed that *that* was what had been loving and beating away all those years, because if I'd had any idea at all—well, enough of that.

My problem was how to get rid of it.

Simple, you'll say, drop it into the waste bucket.

Well, let me tell you, that's what I tried to do. I took a good look at this object, nearly died with embarrassment, and walked over to the rubbish can, where I tried to let it roll off my fingers. It wouldn't. It was stuck. There was my heart, a large red pulsing bleeding repulsive object, stuck to my fingers. What was I going to do? I sat down, lit a cigarette (with one hand, holding the matchbox between my knees), held my hand with the heart stuck on it over the side of the chair so that it could drip into a bucket, and considered.

> If this were a stone in my hand, a stone,
> I could throw it over a tree. . . .

When I had finished the cigarette, I carefully unwrapped some tin foil, of the kind used to wrap food in when cooking, and I fitted a sort of cover around my heart. This was absolutely and urgently necessary. First, it was smarting badly. After all, it had spent some forty years protected by flesh and ribs and the air was too much for it. Secondly, I couldn't have any Tom, Dick and Harry walking in and looking at it. Thirdly, I could not look at it for too long myself, it filled me with shame. The tin foil was effective, and indeed rather striking. It is quite pliable and now it seemed as if there were a stylised heart balanced on my palm, like a globe, in glittering, silvery substance. I almost felt I needed a sceptre in the other hand to balance it. . . . But the thing was, there is no other word for it, in bad taste. I then wrapped a scarf around hand and tin-foiled heart, and felt safer. Now it was a question of pretending to have hurt my hand until I could think of a way of getting rid of my heart altogether, short of amputating my hand.

Meanwhile I telephoned (really, not in imagination) C, who now would never be C. I could feel my heart, which was stuck so close to my fingers that I could feel every beat or tremor, give a gulp of resigned grief at the idea of this beautiful experience now never to be. I told him some idiotic lie about having flu. Well, he was all stiff and indignant, but concealing it urbanely, as I would have done, making a joke but allowing a tiny barb of sarcasm to rankle in the last well-chosen phrase. Then I sat down again to think out my whole situation.

There I sat.

What was I going to do?

There I sat.

I am going to have to skip about four days here, vital enough in all conscience, because I simply cannot go heartbeat by heartbeat through my memories. A pity, since I suppose this is what this story is about; but in brief: I drew the curtains, I took the telephone off the hook, I turned on the lights, I took the scarf off the glittering shape, then the tin foil, then I examined the heart. There were two-fifths of a century's experiences to work through, and before I had even got through the first night, I was in a state hard to describe. . . .

> Or if I could pull the nerves from my skin
> A quick red net to drag through a sea for fish. . . .

By the end of the fourth day I was worn out. By no act of will, or intention, or desire, could I move that heart by a fraction—on the contrary, it was not only stuck to my fingers, like a sucked boiled sweet, but was actually growing to the flesh of my fingers and my palm.

I wrapped it up again in tin foil and scarf, and turned out the lights and pulled up the blinds and opened the curtains. It was about ten in the morning, an ordinary London day, neither hot nor cold nor clear nor clouded nor wet nor fine. And while the street is interesting, it is not exactly beautiful, so I wasn't looking at it so much as waiting for something to catch my attention while thinking of something else.

Suddenly I heard a tap-tap-tapping that got louder, sharp and clear, and I knew before I saw her that this was the sound of high heels on a pavement though it might just as well have been a hammer against stone. She walked fast opposite my window and her heels hit the pavement so hard that all the noises of the street seemed absorbed into that single tap-tap-clang-clang. As she reached the corner at Great Portland Street two London pigeons swooped diagonally from the sky very fast, as if they were bullets aimed to kill her; and then as they saw her they swooped up and off at an angle. Meanwhile she had turned the corner. All this has taken time to write down, but the thing happening took a couple of seconds: the woman's body hitting the pavement bang-bang through her heels then sharply turning the corner in a right angle; and the pigeons making another acute angle across hers and intersecting it in a fast swoop of displaced air. Nothing to all that, of course, nothing—she had gone off down the street, her heels tip-tapping, and the pigeons landed on my windowsill and began cooing. All gone, all vanished, the marvellous exact coordination of sound and movement, but it had happened, it had made me happy and exhilarated, I had no problems in this world, and I realized that the heart stuck to my fingers was quite loose. I couldn't get it off altogether, though I was tugging at it under the scarf and the tin foil, but almost.

I understood that sitting and analysing each movement or pulse or beat of my heart through forty years was a mistake. I was on the wrong track altogether: this was the way to attach my red, bitter, delighted heart to my flesh forever and ever. . . .

> Ha! So you think I'm done! You think. . . .
> Watch, I'll roll my heart in a mesh of rage
> And bounce it like a handball off
> Walls, faces, railings, umbrellas and pigeons' backs. . . .

No, all that was no good at all, it just made things worse. What I must do is to take myself by surprise, as it were, the way I was taken by surprise over the woman and the pigeons and the sharp sounds of heels and silk wings.

I put on my coat, held my lumpy scarfed arm across my chest, so that if anyone said: What have you done with your hand? I could say: I've banged my finger in the door. Then I walked down into the street.

It wasn't easy to go among so many people, when I was worried that they were thinking: What has that woman done to her hand? because that made it hard to forget myself. And all the time it tingled and throbbed against my fingers, reminding me.

Now I was out I didn't know what to do. Should I go and have lunch with someone? Or wander in the park? Or buy myself a dress? I decided to go to the Round Pond, and walk around it by myself. I was tired after four days and nights without sleep. I went down into the Underground at Oxford Circus. Midday. Crowds of people. I felt self-conscious, but of course need not have worried. I swear you could walk naked down the street in London and no one would even turn round.

So I went down the escalator and looked at the faces coming up past me on the other side, as I always do; and wondered, as I always do, how strange it is that those people and I should meet by chance in such a way, and how odd that we would never see each other again, or, if we did, we wouldn't know it. And I went on to the crowded platform and looked at the faces as I always do, and got into the train, which was very full, and found a seat. It wasn't as bad as at rush hour, but all the seats were filled. I leaned back and closed my eyes, deciding to sleep a little, being so tired. I was just beginning to doze off, when I heard a woman's voice muttering, or rather, declaiming:

"A gold cigarette case, well, that's a nice thing, isn't it, I must say, a gold case, yes. . . ."

There was something about this voice which made me open my eyes: on the other side of the compartment, about eight persons away, sat a youngish woman, wearing a cheap green cloth coat, gloveless hands, flat brown shoes, and lisle stockings. She must be rather poor—a woman dressed like this is a rare sight, these days. But it was her posture that struck me. She was sitting half twisted in her seat, so that her head was turned over her left shoulder, and she was looking straight at the stomach of an elderly man next to her. But it was clear she was not seeing it: her young staring eyes were sightless, she was looking inwards.

She was so clearly alone, in the crowded compartment, that it was not as embarrassing as it might have been. I looked around, and people were smiling, or exchanging glances, or winking, or ignoring her, according to their natures, but she was oblivious of us all.

She suddenly aroused herself, turned so that she sat straight in her seat, and directed her voice and her gaze to the opposite seat:

"Well so that's what you think, you think that, you think that do you, well, you think I'm just going to wait at home for you, but you gave her a gold case and . . ."

And with a clockwork movement of her whole thin person, she turned her narrow pale-haired head sideways over her left shoulder, and resumed her stiff empty stare at the man's stomach. He was grinning uncomfortably. I leaned forward to look along the line of people in the row of seats I sat in, and the man opposite her, a young man, had exactly the same look of discomfort which he was determined to keep amused. So we all looked at her, the young, thin, pale woman in her private drama of misery, who was so completely unconscious of us that she spoke and thought out loud. And again, without particular warning or reason, in between stops, so it wasn't that she was disturbed from her dream by the train stopping at Bond Street, and then jumping forward again, she twisted her body frontways, and addressed the seat opposite her (the young man had got off, and a smart grey-curled matron had got in):

"Well I know about it now, don't I, and if you come in all smiling and pleased well then I know, don't I, you don't have to tell me, I know, and I've said to her, I've said, I know he gave you a gold cigarette case. . . ."

At which point, with the same clockwork impulse, she stopped, or was checked, or simply ran out, and turned herself half around to stare at the stomach—the same stomach, for the middle-aged man was still there. But we stopped at Marble Arch and he got out, giving the compartment, rather than the people in it, a tolerant half-smile which said: I am sure I can trust you to realize that this unfortunate woman is stark staring mad. . . .

His seat remained empty. No people got in at Marble Arch, and the two people standing waiting for seats did not want to sit by her to receive her stare.

We all sat, looking gently in front of us, pretending to ourselves and to each other that we didn't know the poor woman was mad and that in fact we ought to be doing something about it. I even wondered what I should say: Madam, you're mad—shall I escort you to your home? Or: Poor thing, don't go on like that, it doesn't do any good, you know—just leave him, that'll bring him to his senses. . . .

And behold, after the interval that was regulated by her inner mechanism had elapsed, she turned back and said to the smart matron who received this statement of accusation with perfect self-command:

"Yes, I know! Oh yes! And what about my shoes, what about them, a golden cigarette case is what she got, the filthy bitch, a golden case. . . ."

Stop. Twist. Stare. At the empty seat by her.

Extraordinary. Because it was a frozen misery, how shall I put it? A passionless passion—we were seeing unhappiness embodied, we were looking at the essence of some private tragedy—rather, Tragedy. There was no emotion in it. She was like an actress doing Accusation, or Betrayed Love, or Infidelity, when she has only just learned her lines and is not bothering to do more than get them right.

And whether she sat in her half-twisted position, her unblinking eyes staring at the greenish, furry, ugly covering of the train seat, or sat straight, directing her accusation to the smart woman opposite, there was a frightening immobility about her—yes, that was why she frightened us. For it was clear that she might very well (if the inner machine ran down) stay silent, forever, in either twisted or straight position, or at any point between them—yes, we could all imagine her, frozen perpetually in some arbitrary pose. It was as if we watched the shell of some woman going through certain predetermined motions.

For *she* was simply not there. *What* was there, who she was, it was impossible to tell, though it was easy to imagine her thin, gentle little face breaking into a smile in total forgetfulness of what she was enacting now. She did not know she was in a train between Marble Arch and Queensway, nor that she was publicly accusing her husband or lover, nor that we were looking at her.

And we, looking at her, felt an embarrassment and shame that was not on her account at all. . . .

Suddenly I felt, under the scarf and the tin foil, a lightening of my fingers, as my heart rolled loose.

I hastily took it off my palm, in case it decided to adhere there again, and I removed the scarf, leaving balanced on my knees a perfect stylised heart, like a silver heart on a Valentine card, though of course it was three-dimensional. This heart was not so much harmless, no that isn't the word, as artistic, but in very bad taste, as I said. I could see that the people in the train, now looking at me and the heart, and not at the poor madwoman, were pleased with it.

I got up, took the four or so paces to where she was, and laid the tin-foiled heart down on the seat so that it received her stare.

For a moment she did not react, then with a groan or a mutter of relieved and entirely theatrical grief, she leaned forward, picked up the glittering heart, and clutched it in her arms, hugging it and rocking it back and forth, even laying her cheek against it, while staring over its top at her husband as if to say: Look what I've got, I don't care about you and your cigarette case, I've got a silver heart.

I got up, since we were at Notting Hill Gate, and, followed by the pleased congratulatory nods and smiles of the people left behind, I went out onto the platform, up the escalators, into the street, and along to the park.

No heart. No heart at all. What bliss. What freedom. . . .

Hear that sound? That's laughter, yes.
That's me laughing, yes, that's me.

QUESTIONS

1. What sort of tone (see Preface, pp. 24–27) might you expect from a title like "How I Finally Lost My Heart"? What is the narrator's tone like instead? What evidence do you have?
2. How does the tone function in the story? What does it do for the narrator?
3. Where and how does the tone change in the course of the story?
4. What does it mean, *To lose your heart*? *To have your heart in your hand*? How is Lessing *using* (not falling prey to) cultural clichés about love?
5. What is the meaning of the fantasy? How does it relate to the tone?
6. Compare the woman in the subway with the woman in the train in Woolf's "An Unwritten Novel." Does Lessing's narrator *know* the woman? How does she function in the emotional life of the narrator? What is the significance of her taking the heart?
7. "No heart at all. What bliss. What freedom. . . ." Is the statement serious? Ironic? Both? Discuss.

JAMES BALDWIN

(1924—)

Baldwin is a master of short fiction, novel, play, and essay. Born in 1924 in New York City's Harlem, he was encouraged by Richard Wright, who helped him win a fellowship while Baldwin wrote his autobiographical novel *Go Tell It on the Mountain* (1953). Very prominent in the developing civil rights movement, he published *Notes of a Native Son, Nobody Knows My Name,* and *The Fire Next Time.* His novels include *Giovanni's Room, Another Country,* and *Tell Me How Long the Train's Been Gone.*

In both "Sonny's Blues" and "This Morning, This Evening, So Soon," Baldwin shows us a man who found himself in a world that wanted him to exist only in a false image. In both stories the man grows up to real maturity in *another country*—literally, in France, or spiritually, in the struggle against heroin addiction and through initiation into the world of jazz. Baldwin is dealing with levels of self-awareness most people never reach; yet he gives us the sense of understanding those levels, of being there with our lives in our hands.

[See Preface, "Sonny's Blues," p. 10 (first person narration).]

Sonny's Blues

JAMES BALDWIN

I read about it in the paper, in the subway, on my way to work. I read it, and I couldn't believe it, and I read it again. Then perhaps I just stared at it, at the newsprint spelling out his name, spelling out the story. I stared at it in the swinging lights of the subway car, and in the faces and bodies of the people, and in my own face, trapped in the darkness which roared outside.

It was not to be believed and I kept telling myself that as I walked from the subway station to the high school. And at the same time I couldn't doubt it. I was scared, scared for Sonny. He became real to me again. A great block of ice got settled in my belly and kept melting there slowly all day long, while I taught my classes algebra. It was a special kind of ice. It kept melting, sending trickles of ice water all up and down my veins, but it never got less. Sometimes it hardened and seemed to expand until I felt my guts were going to come spilling out or that I was going to choke or scream. This would always be at a moment when I was remembering some specific thing Sonny had once said or done.

When he was about as old as the boys in my classes his face had been bright and open, there was a lot of copper in it; and he'd had wonderfully direct brown eyes, and great gentleness and privacy. I wondered what he looked like now. He had been picked up, the evening before, in a raid on an apartment downtown, for peddling and using heroin.

I couldn't believe it: but what I mean by that is that I couldn't find any room for it anywhere inside me. I had kept it outside me for a long time. I hadn't wanted to know. I had had suspicions, but I didn't name them, I kept putting them away. I told myself that Sonny was wild, but he wasn't crazy. And he'd always been a good boy, he hadn't ever turned hard or evil or disrespectful, the way kids can, so quick, so quick, especially in Harlem. I didn't want to believe that I'd ever see my brother going down, coming to nothing, all that light in his face gone out, in the condition I'd already seen so many others. Yet it had happened and here I was, talking about algebra to a lot of boys who might, every one of them for all I knew, be popping off needles every time they went to the head. Maybe it did more for them than algebra could.

I was sure that the first time Sonny had ever had horse, he couldn't have been much older than these boys were now. These boys, now, were living as we'd been living then, they were growing up with a rush and their heads bumped abruptly against the low ceiling of their actual possibilities. They were filled with rage. All they really knew were two darknesses, the darkness of their lives, which was now closing in on them, and the darkness of the movies, which had blinded them to that other darkness, and in which they now, vindictively, dreamed, at once more together than they were at any other time, and more alone.

When the last bell rang, the last class ended, I let out my breath. It seemed I'd been holding it for all that time. My clothes were wet—I may have looked as though I'd been sitting in a steam bath, all dressed up, all afternoon. I sat alone in the classroom a long time. I listened to the boys outside, downstairs, shouting and cursing and laughing. Their laughter struck me for perhaps the first time. It was not the joyous laughter which—God knows why—one associates with children. It was mocking and insular, its intent was to denigrate. It was disenchanted, and in this, also, lay the authority of their curses. Perhaps I was listening to them because I was thinking about my brother and in them I heard my brother. And myself.

One boy was whistling a tune, at once very complicated and very simple, it seemed to be pouring out of him as though he were a bird, and it sounded very cool and moving through all that harsh, bright air, only just holding its own through all those other sounds.

I stood up and walked over to the window and looked down into the courtyard. It was the beginning of the spring and the sap was rising in the boys. A teacher passed through them every now and again, quickly, as though he or she couldn't wait to get out of that courtyard, to get those boys out of their sight and off their minds. I started collecting my stuff. I thought I'd better get home and talk to Isabel.

The courtyard was almost deserted by the time I got downstairs. I saw this boy standing in the shadow of a doorway, looking just like Sonny. I almost called his name. Then I saw that it wasn't Sonny, but somebody we used to know, a boy from around our block. He'd been Sonny's friend. He'd never been mine, having been too young for me, and, anyway, I'd never liked him. And now, even though he was a grown-up man, he still hung around that block, still spent hours on the street corner, was always high and raggy. I used to run into him from time to time and he'd often work around to asking me for a quarter or fifty cents. He always had some real good excuse, too, and I always gave it to him, I don't know why.

But now, abruptly, I hated him. I couldn't stand the way he looked at me, partly like a dog, partly like a cunning child. I wanted to ask him what the hell he was doing in the school courtyard.

He sort of shuffled over to me, and he said, "I see you got the papers. So you already know about it."

"You mean about Sonny? Yes, I already know about it. How come they didn't get you?"

He grinned. It made him repulsive and it also brought to mind what he'd looked like as a kid. "I wasn't there. I stay away from them people."

"Good for you." I offered him a cigarette and I watched him through the smoke. "You come all the way down here just to tell me about Sonny?"

"That's right." He was sort of shaking his head and his eyes looked strange, as though they were about to cross. The bright sun deadened his damp dark brown skin and it made his eyes look yellow and showed up the dirt in his conked hair. He smelled funky. I moved a little away from him and I said, "Well, thanks. But I already know about it and I got to get home."

"I'll walk you a little ways," he said. We started walking. There were a couple of kids still loitering in the courtyard and one of them said good night to me and looked strangely at the boy beside me.

"What're you going to do?" he asked me. "I mean, about Sonny?"

"Look. I haven't seen Sonny for over a year, I'm not sure I'm going to do anything. Anyway, what the hell *can* I do?"

"That's right," he said quickly, "ain't nothing you can do. Can't much help old Sonny no more, I guess."

It was what I was thinking and so it seemed to me he had no right to say it.

"I'm surprised at Sonny, though," he went on—he had a funny way of talking, he looked straight ahead as though he were talking to himself—"I thought Sonny was a smart boy, I thought he was too smart to get hung."

"I guess he thought so too," I said sharply, "and that's how he got hung. And how about you? You're pretty goddamn smart, I bet."

Then he looked directly at me, just for a minute. "I ain't smart," he said. "If I was smart, I'd have reached for a pistol a long time ago."

"Look. Don't tell *me* your sad story, if it was up to me, I'd give you one." Then I felt guilty—guilty, probably, for never having supposed that the poor bastard *had* a story of his own, much less a sad one, and I asked, quickly, "What's going to happen to him now?"

He didn't answer this. He was off by himself some place. "Funny thing," he said, and from his tone we might have been discussing the quickest way to get to Brooklyn, "when I saw the papers this morning, the first thing I asked myself was if I had anything to do with it. I felt sort of responsible."

I began to listen more carefully. The subway station was on the corner, just before us, and I stopped. He stopped, too. We were in front of a bar and he ducked slightly, peering in, but whoever he was looking for didn't seem to be there. The juke box was blasting away with something black and bouncy and I half watched the barmaid as she danced her way from the juke box to her place behind the bar. And I watched her face as she laughingly responded to something someone said to her, still keeping time to the music. When she smiled one saw the little girl, one sensed the doomed, still-struggling woman beneath the battered face of the semi-whore.

"I never *give* Sonny nothing," the boy said finally, "but a long time ago I come to school high and Sonny asked me how it felt." He paused, I couldn't bear to watch him, I watched the barmaid, and I listened to the music which seemed to be causing the pavement to shake. "I told him it felt great." The music stopped, the barmaid paused and watched the juke box until the music began again. "It did."

All this was carrying me some place I didn't want to go. I certainly didn't want to know how it felt. It filled everything, the people, the houses, the music, the dark, quicksilver barmaid, with menace; and this menace was their reality.

"What's going to happen to him now?" I asked again.

"They'll send him away some place and they'll try to cure him." He shook his head. "Maybe he'll even think he's kicked the habit. Then they'll let him loose"—he gestured, throwing his cigarette into the gutter. "That's all."

"What do you mean, that's *all?*"

But I knew what he meant.

"I *mean*, that's *all*." He turned his head and looked at me, pulling down the corners of his mouth. "Don't you know what I mean?" he asked softly.

"How the hell *would* I know what you mean?" I almost whispered it, I don't know why.

"That's right," he said to the air, "how would *he* know what I mean?" He turned toward me again, patient and calm, and yet I somehow felt him shaking, shaking as though he were going to fall apart. I felt that ice in my guts again, the dread I'd felt all afternoon; and again I watched the barmaid, moving about the bar, washing glasses, and singing. "Listen. They'll let him out and then it'll just start all over again. That's what I mean."

"You mean—they'll let him out. And then he'll just start working his way back in again. You mean he'll never kick the habit. Is that what you mean?"

"That's right," he said, cheerfully. *"You* see what I mean."

"Tell me," I said at last, "why does he want to die? He must want to die, he's killing himself, why does he want to die?"

He looked at me in surprise. He licked his lips. "He don't want to die. He wants to live. Don't nobody want to die, ever."

Then I wanted to ask him—too many things. He could not have answered, or if he had, I could not have borne the answers. I started walking. "Well, I guess it's none of my business."

"It's going to be rough on old Sonny," he said. We reached the subway station. "This is your station?" he asked. I nodded. I took one step down. "Damn!" he said, suddenly. I looked up at him. He grinned again. "Damn if I didn't leave all my money home. You ain't got a dollar on you, have you? Just for a couple of days, is all."

All at once something inside gave and threatened to come pouring out of me. I didn't hate him any more. I felt that in another moment I'd start crying like a child.

"Sure," I said. "Don't sweat." I looked in my wallet and didn't have a dollar, I only had a five. "Here," I said. "That hold you?"

He didn't look at it—he didn't want to look at it. A terrible, closed look came over his face, as though he were keeping the number on the bill a secret from him and me. "Thanks," he said, and now he was dying to see me go. "Don't worry about Sonny. Maybe I'll write him or something."

"Sure," I said. "You do that. So long."

"Be seeing you," he said. I went on down the steps.

And I didn't write Sonny or send him anything for a long time. When I finally did, it was just after my little girl died, he wrote me back a letter which made me feel like a bastard.

Here's what he said:

DEAR BROTHER,

You don't know how much I needed to hear from you. I wanted to write you many a time but I dug how much I must have hurt you and so I didn't write. But now I feel like a man who's been trying to climb up out of some deep, real deep and funky hole and just saw the sun up there, outside. I got to get outside.

I can't tell you much about how I got here. I mean I don't know how to tell you. I guess I was afraid of something or I was trying to escape from something and you know I have never been very strong in the head (smile). I'm glad Mama and Daddy are dead and can't see what's happened to their son and I swear if I'd known what I was doing I would never have hurt you so, you and a lot of other fine people who were nice to me and who believed in me.

I don't want you to think it had anything to do with me being a musician. It's more than that. Or maybe less than that. I can't get anything straight in my head down here and I try not to think about what's going to happen to me when I get outside again. Sometime I think I'm going to flip and *never* get outside and sometime I think I'll come straight back. I tell you one thing, though, I'd rather blow my brains out than go through this again. But that's what they all say, so they tell me. If I tell you when I'm coming to New York and if you could meet me, I sure would appreciate it. Give my love to Isabel and the kids and I was sorry to hear about little Gracie. I wish I could be like Mama and say the Lord's will be done, but I don't know it seems to me that trouble is the one thing that never does get stopped and I don't know what good it does to blame it on the Lord. But maybe it does some good if you believe it.

Your brother,

SONNY

Then I kept in constant touch with him and I sent him whatever I could and I went to meet him when he came back to New York. When I saw him many things I thought I had forgotten came flooding back to me. This was because I had begun, finally, to wonder about Sonny, about the life that Sonny lived inside. This life, whatever it was, had made him older and thinner and it had deepened the distant stillness in which he had always moved. He looked very unlike my baby brother. Yet, when he smiled, when we shook hands, the baby brother I'd never known looked out from the depths of his private life, like an animal waiting to be coaxed into the light.

"How you been keeping?" he asked me.

"All right. And you?"

"Just fine." He was smiling all over his face. "It's good to see you again."

"It's good to see you."

The seven years' difference in our ages lay between us like a chasm: I wondered if these years would ever operate between us as a bridge. I was remembering, and it made it hard to catch my breath, that I had been there when he was born; and I had heard the first words he had ever spoken. When he started to walk, he walked from our mother straight to me. I caught him just before he fell when he took the first steps he ever took in this world.

"How's Isabel?"

"Just fine. She's dying to see you."

"And the boys?"

"They're fine, too. They're anxious to see their uncle."

"Oh, come on. You know they don't remember me."

"Are you kidding? Of course they remember you."

He grinned again. We got into a taxi. We had a lot to say to each other, far too much to know how to begin.

As the taxi began to move, I asked, "You still want to go to India?"

He laughed. "You still remember that. Hell, no. This place is Indian enough for me."

"It used to belong to them," I said.

And he laughed again. "They damn sure knew what they were doing when they got rid of it."

Years ago, when he was around fourteen, he'd been all hipped on the idea of going to India. He read books about people sitting on rocks, naked, in all kinds of weather, but mostly bad, naturally, and walking barefoot through hot coals and arriving at wisdom. I used to say that it sounded to me as though they were getting away from wisdom as fast as they could. I think he sort of looked down on me for that.

"Do you mind," he asked, "if we have the driver drive alongside the park? On the west side—I haven't seen the city in so long."

"Of course not," I said. I was afraid that I might sound as though I were humoring him, but I hoped he wouldn't take it that way.

So we drove along, between the green of the park and the stony, lifeless elegance of hotels and apartment buildings, toward the vivid, killing streets of our childhood. These streets hadn't changed, though housing projects jutted up out of them now like rocks in the middle of a boiling sea. Most of the houses in which we had grown up had vanished, as had the stores from which we had stolen, the basements in which we had first tried sex, the rooftops from which we had hurled tin cans and bricks. But houses exactly like the houses of our past yet dominated the landscape, boys exactly like the boys we once had been found themselves smothering in these houses, came down into the streets for light and air and found themselves encircled by disaster. Some escaped the trap, most didn't. Those who got out always left something of themselves behind, as some animals amputate a leg and leave it in the trap. It might be said, perhaps, that I had escaped, after all, I was a school teacher; or that Sonny had, he hadn't lived in Harlem for years. Yet, as the cab moved uptown through streets which seemed, with a rush, to darken with dark people, and as I covertly studied Sonny's face, it came to me that what we both were seeking through our separate cab windows was that part of ourselves which had been left behind. It's always at the hour of trouble and confrontation that the missing member aches.

We hit 110th Street and started rolling up Lenox Avenue. And I'd known this avenue all my life, but it seemed to me again, as it had seemed on the day I'd first heard about Sonny's trouble, filled with a hidden menace which was its very breath of life.

"We almost there," said Sonny.

"Almost." We were both too nervous to say anything more.

We live in a housing project. It hasn't been up long. A few days after it was up it seemed uninhabitably new, now, of course, it's already run-down. It looks like a parody of the good, clean, faceless life—God knows the people who live in it do their best to make it a parody. The beat-looking grass lying around isn't enough to make their lives green, the hedges will never hold out the streets, and they know it. The big windows fool no one, they aren't big enough to make space out of no space. They don't bother with the windows, they watch the TV screen instead. The playground is most popular with the children who don't play at jacks, or skip rope, or roller skate, or swing, and they can be found in it after dark. We moved in partly because it's not too far from where I teach, and partly for the kids; but it's really just like the houses in which Sonny and I grew up. The same things happen, they'll have the same things to remember. The moment Sonny and I started into the house I had the feeling that I was simply bringing him back into the danger he had almost died trying to escape.

Sonny has never been talkative. So I don't know why I was sure he'd be dying to talk to me when supper was over the first night. Everything went fine, the oldest boy remembered him, and the youngest boy liked him, and Sonny had remembered to bring something for each of them; and Isabel, who is really much nicer than I am, more open and giving, had gone to a lot of trouble about dinner and was genuinely glad to see him. And she's always been able to tease Sonny in a way that I haven't. It was nice to see her face so vivid again and to hear her laugh and watch her make Sonny laugh. She wasn't, or, anyway, she didn't seem to be, at all uneasy or embarrassed. She chatted as though there were no subject which had to be avoided and she got Sonny past his first, faint stiffness. And thank God she was there, for I was filled with that icy dread again. Everything I did seemed awkward to me, and everything I said sounded freighted with hidden meaning. I was trying to remember everything I'd heard about dope addiction and I couldn't help watching Sonny for signs. I wasn't doing it out of malice. I was trying to find out something about my brother. I was dying to hear him tell me he was safe.

"Safe!" my father grunted, whenever Mama suggested trying to move to a neighborhood which might be safer for children. "Safe, hell! Ain't no place safe for kids, nor nobody."

He always went on like this, but he wasn't, ever, really as bad as he sounded, not even on weekends, when he got drunk. As a matter of fact, he was always on the lookout for "something a little better," but he died before he found it. He died suddenly, during a drunken weekend in the middle of the war, when Sonny was fifteen. He and Sonny hadn't ever got on too well. And this was partly because Sonny was the apple of his father's eye. It was because he loved Sonny so much and was frightened for him, that he was always fighting with him. It doesn't do any good to fight with Sonny. Sonny just moves back, inside himself, where he can't be reached. But the principal reason that they never hit it off is that they were so much alike. Daddy was big and rough and loud-talking, just the opposite of Sonny, but they both had—that same privacy.

Mama tried to tell me something about this, just after Daddy died. I was home on leave from the army.

This was the last time I ever saw my mother alive. Just the same, this picture gets all mixed up in my mind with pictures I had of her when she was younger. The way I always see her is the way she used to be on a Sunday afternoon, say, when the old folks were talking after the big Sunday dinner. I always see her wearing pale blue. She'd be sitting on the sofa. And my father would be sitting in the easy chair, not far from her. And the living room would be full of church folks and relatives. There they sit, in chairs all around the living room, and the night is creeping up outside, but nobody knows it yet. You can see the darkness growing against the window-panes and you hear the street noises every now and again, or maybe the jangling beat of a tambourine from one of the churches close by, but it's real quiet in the room. For a moment nobody's talking, but every face looks darkening, like the sky outside. And my mother rocks a little from the waist, and my father's eyes are closed. Everyone is looking at something a child can't see. For a minute they've forgotten the children. Maybe a kid is lying on the rug half asleep. Maybe somebody's got a kid on his lap and is absent-mindedly stroking the kid's head. Maybe there's a kid, quiet and big-eyed, curled up in a big chair in the corner. The silence, the darkness coming, and the darkness in the faces frightens the child obscurely. He hopes that the hand which strokes his forehead will never stop—will never die. He hopes that there will never come a time when the old folks won't be sitting around the living room, talking about where they've come from, and what they've seen, and what's happened to them and their kinfolk.

But something deep and watchful in the child knows that this is bound to end, is already ending. In a moment someone will get up and turn on the light. Then the old folks will remember the children and they won't talk any more that day. And when light fills the room, the child is filled with darkness. He knows that every time this happens he's moved just a little closer to that darkness outside. The darkness outside is what the old folks have been talking about. It's what they've come from. It's what they endure. The child knows that they won't talk any more because if he knows too much about what's happened to *them,* he'll know too much too soon, about what's going to happen to *him.*

The last time I talked to my mother, I remember I was restless. I wanted to get out and see Isabel. We weren't married then and we had a lot to straighten out between us.

There Mama sat, in black, by the window. She was humming an old church song, *Lord, you brought me from a long ways off.* Sonny was out somewhere. Mama kept watching the streets.

"I don't know," she said, "if I'll ever see you again, after you go off from here. But I hope you'll remember the things I tried to teach you."

"Don't talk like that," I said, and smiled. "You'll be here a long time yet."

She smiled, too, but she said nothing. She was quiet for a long time. And I said, "Mama, don't you worry about nothing. I'll be writing all the time, and you be getting the checks. . . ."

"I want to talk to you about your brother," she said, suddenly. "If anything happens to me he ain't going to have nobody to look out for him."

"Mama," I said, "ain't nothing going to happen to you *or* Sonny. Sonny's all right. He's a good boy and he's got good sense."

"It ain't a question of his being a good boy," Mama said, "nor of his having good sense. It ain't only the bad ones, nor yet the dumb ones that gets sucked under." She stopped, looking at me. "Your Daddy once had a brother," she said, and she smiled in a way that made me feel she was in pain. "You didn't never know that, did you?"

"No," I said, "I never knew that," and I watched her face.

"Oh, yes," she said, "your Daddy had a brother." She looked out of the window again. "I know you never saw your Daddy cry. But *I* did—many a time, through all these years."

I asked her, "What happened to his brother? How come nobody's ever talked about him?"

This was the first time I ever saw my mother look old.

"His brother got killed," she said, "when he was just a little younger than you are now. I knew him. He was a fine boy. He was maybe a little full of the devil, but he didn't mean nobody no harm."

Then she stopped and the room was silent, exactly as it had sometimes been on those Sunday afternoons. Mama kept looking out into the streets.

"He used to have a job in the mill," she said, "and, like all young folks, he just liked to perform on Saturday nights. Saturday nights, him and your father would drift around to different places, go to dances and things like that, or just sit around with people they knew, and your father's brother would sing, he had a fine voice, and play along with himself on his guitar. Well, this particular Saturday night, him and your father was coming home from some place, and they were both a little drunk and there was a moon that night, it was bright like day. Your father's brother was feeling kind of good, and he was whistling to himself, and he had his guitar slung over his shoulder. They was coming down a hill and beneath them was a road that turned off from the highway. Well, your father's brother, being always kind of frisky, decided to run down this hill, and he did, with that guitar banging and clanging behind him, and he ran across the road, and he was making water behind a tree. And your father was sort of amused at him and he was still coming down the hill, kind of slow. Then he heard a car motor and that same minute his brother stepped from behind the tree, into the road, in the moonlight. And he started to cross the road. And your father started to run down the hill, he says he don't know why. This car was full of white men. They was all drunk, and when they seen your father's brother they let out a great whoop and holler and they aimed the car straight at him. They was having fun, they just wanted to scare him, the way they do sometimes, you know. But they was drunk. And I guess the boy, being drunk, too, and scared, kind of lost his head. By the time he jumped it was too late. Your father says he heard his brother scream when the car rolled over him, and he heard the wood of that guitar when it give, and he heard them strings go flying, and he heard them white men shouting, and the car kept on a-going and it ain't stopped till this day. And, time your father got down the hill, his brother weren't nothing but blood and pulp."

Tears were gleaming on my mother's face. There wasn't anything I could say.

"He never mentioned it," she said, "because I never let him mention it before you children. Your Daddy was like a crazy man that night and for many a night thereafter. He says he never in his life seen anything as dark as that road after the lights of that car had gone away. Weren't nothing, weren't nobody on that road, just your Daddy and his brother and that busted guitar. Oh, yes. Your Daddy never did really get right again. Till the day he died he weren't sure but that every white man he saw was the man that killed his brother."

She stopped and took out her handkerchief and dried her eyes and looked at me.

"I ain't telling you all this," she said, "to make you scared or bitter or to make you hate nobody. I'm telling you this because you got a brother. And the world ain't changed."

I guess I didn't want to believe this. I guess she saw this in my face. She turned away from me, toward the window again, searching those streets.

"But I praise my Redeemer," she said at last, "that He called your Daddy home before me. I ain't saying it to throw no flowers at myself, but, I declare, it keeps me from feeling too cast down to know I helped your father get safely through this world. Your father always acted like he was the roughest, strongest man on earth. And everybody took him to be like that. But if he hadn't had *me* there—to see his tears!"

She was crying again. Still, I couldn't move. I said, "Lord, Lord, Mama, I didn't know it was like that."

"Oh, honey," she said, "there's a lot that you don't know. But you are going to find it out." She stood up from the window and came over to me. "You got to hold on to your brother," she said, "and don't let him fall, no matter what it looks like is happening to him and no matter how evil you gets with him. You going to be evil with him many a time. But don't you forget what I told you, you hear?"

"I won't forget," I said. "Don't you worry, I won't forget. I won't let nothing happen to Sonny."

My mother smiled as though she were amused at something she saw in my face. Then, "You may not be able to stop nothing from happening. But you got to let him know you's *there*."

Two days later I was married, and then I was gone. And I had a lot of things on my mind and I pretty well forgot my promise to Mama until I got shipped home on a special furlough for her funeral.

And, after the funeral, with just Sonny and me alone in the empty kitchen, I tried to find out something about him.

"What do you want to do?" I asked him.

"I'm going to be a musician," he said.

For he had graduated, in the time I had been away, from dancing to the juke box to finding out who was playing what, and what they were doing with it, and he had bought himself a set of drums.

"You mean, you want to be a drummer?" I somehow had the feeling that being a drummer might be all right for other people but not for my brother Sonny.

"I don't think," he said, looking at me very gravely, "that I'll ever be a good drummer. But I think I can play a piano."

I frowned. I'd never played the role of the older brother quite so seriously before, had scarcely ever, in fact, *asked* Sonny a damn thing. I sensed myself in the presence of something I didn't really know how to handle, didn't understand. So I made my frown a little deeper as I asked: "What kind of musician do you want to be?"

He grinned. "How many kinds do you think there are?"

"Be *serious*," I said.

He laughed, throwing his head back, and then looked at me. "I *am* serious."

"Well, then, for Christ's sake, stop kidding around and answer a serious question. I mean, do you want to be a concert pianist, you want to play classical music and all that, or—or what?" Long before I finished he was laughing again. "For Christ's *sake*, Sonny!"

He sobered, but with difficulty. "I'm sorry. But you sound so— *scared!*" and he was off again.

"Well, you may think it's funny now, baby, but it's not going to be so funny when you have to make your living at it, let me tell you *that*." I was furious because I knew he was laughing at me and I didn't know why.

"No," he said, very sober now, and afraid, perhaps, that he'd hurt me, "I don't want to be a classical pianist. That isn't what interests me. I mean"—he paused, looking hard at me, as though his eyes would help me to understand, and then gestured helplessly, as though perhaps his hand would help—"I mean, I'll have a lot of studying to do, and I'll have to study *everything*, but I mean, I want to play *with*—jazz musicians." He stopped. "I want to play jazz," he said.

Well, the word had never before sounded as heavy, as real, as it sounded that afternoon in Sonny's mouth. I just looked at him and I was probably frowning a real frown by this time. I simply couldn't see why on earth he'd want to spend his time hanging around night clubs, clowning around on bandstands, while people pushed each other around a dance floor. It seemed—beneath him, somehow. I had never thought about it before, had never been forced to, but I suppose I had always put jazz musicians in a class with what Daddy called "good-time people."

"Are you *serious?*"

"Hell, *yes,* I'm serious."

He looked more helpless than ever, and annoyed, and deeply hurt.

I suggested, helpfully: "You mean—like Louis Armstrong?"

His face closed as though I'd struck him. "No. I'm not talking about none of that old-time, down home crap."

"Well, look, Sonny, I'm sorry, don't get mad. I just don't alto-gether get it, that's all. Name somebody—you know, a jazz musician you admire."

"Bird."

"Who?"

"Bird! Charlie Parker! Don't they teach you nothing in the goddamn army?"

I lit a cigarette. I was surprised and then a little amused to discover that I was trembling. "I've been out of touch," I said, "You'll have to be patient with me. Now. Who's this Parker character?"

"He's just one of the greatest jazz musicians alive," said Sonny, sullenly, his hands in his pockets, his back to me. "Maybe *the* greatest," he added, bitterly, "that's probably why *you* never heard of him."

"All right," I said, "I'm ignorant. I'm sorry. I'll go out and buy all the cat's records right away, all right?"

"It don't," said Sonny, with dignity, "make any difference to me. I don't care what you listen to. Don't do me no favors."

I was beginning to realize that I'd never seen him so upset before. With another part of my mind I was thinking that this would probably turn out to be one of those things kids go through and that I shouldn't make it seem important by pushing it too hard. Still, I didn't think it would do any harm to ask: "Doesn't all this take a lot of time? Can you make a living at it?"

He turned back to me and half leaned, half sat, on the kitchen table. "Everything takes time," he said, "and—well, yes, sure, I can make a living at it. But what I don't seem to be able to make you understand is that it's the only thing I want to do."

"Well Sonny," I said, gently, "you know people can't always do exactly what they *want* to do—"

"*No,* I don't know that," said Sonny, surprising me. "I think people *ought* to do what they want to do, what else are they alive for?"

"You getting to be a big boy," I said desperately, "it's time you started thinking about your future."

"I'm thinking about my future," said Sonny, grimly. "I think about it all the time."

I gave up. I decided, if he didn't change his mind, that we could always talk about it later. "In the meantime," I said, "you got to finish school." We had already decided that he'd have to move in with Isabel and her folks. I knew this wasn't the ideal arrangement because Isabel's folks are inclined to be dicty and they hadn't especially wanted Isabel to marry me. But I didn't know what else to do. "And we have to get you fixed up at Isabel's."

There was a long silence. He moved from the kitchen table to the window. "That's a terrible idea. You know it yourself."

"Do you have a *better* idea?"

He just walked up and down the kitchen for a minute. He was as tall as I was. He had started to shave. I suddenly had the feeling that I didn't know him at all.

He stopped at the kitchen table and picked up my cigarettes. Looking at me with a kind of mocking, amused defiance, he put one between his lips. "You mind?"

"You smoking already?"

He lit the cigarette and nodded, watching me through the smoke. "I just wanted to see if I'd have the courage to smoke in front of you." He grinned and blew a great cloud of smoke to the ceiling. "It was easy." He looked at my face. "Come on, now. I bet you was smoking at my age, tell the truth."

I didn't say anything but the truth was on my face, and he laughed. But now there was something very strained in his laugh. "Sure. And I bet that ain't all you was doing."

He was frightening me a little. "Cut the crap," I said. "We already decided that you was going to go and live at Isabel's. Now what's got into you all of a sudden?"

"*You* decided it," he pointed out. "*I* didn't decide nothing." He stopped in front of me, leaning against the stove, arms loosely folded. "Look, brother. I don't want to stay in Harlem no more, I really don't." He was very earnest. He looked at me, then over toward the kitchen window. There was something in his eyes I'd never seen before, some thoughtfulness, some worry all his own. He rubbed the muscle of one arm. "It's time I was getting out of here."

"Where do you want to *go*, Sonny?"

"I want to join the army. Or the navy, I don't care. If I say I'm old enough they'll believe me."

Then I got mad. It was because I was so scared. "You must be crazy. You goddamn fool, what the hell do you want to go and join the *army* for?"

"I just told you. To get out of Harlem."

"Sonny, you haven't even finished *school*. And if you really want to be a musician, how do you expect to study if you're in the *army?*"

He looked at me, trapped, and in anguish. "There's ways. I might be able to work out some kind of deal. Anyway, I'll have the G.I. Bill when I come out."

"*If* you come out." We stared at each other. "Sonny, please. Be reasonable. I know the setup is far from perfect. But we got to do the best we can."

"I ain't learning nothing in school," he said. "Even when I go." He turned away from me and opened the window and threw his cigarette out into the narrow alley. I watched his back. "At least, I ain't learning nothing you'd want me to learn." He slammed the window so hard I thought the glass would fly out, and turned back to me. "And I'm sick of the stink of these garbage cans!"

"Sonny," I said, "I know how you feel. But if you don't finish school now, you're going to be sorry later that you didn't." I grabbed him by the shoulders. "And you only got another year. It ain't so bad. And I'll come back and I swear I'll help you do *whatever* you want to do. Just try to put up with it till I come back. Will you please do that? For me?"

He didn't answer and he wouldn't look at me.

"Sonny. You hear me?"

He pulled away. "I hear you. But you never hear anything *I* say."

I didn't know what to say to that. He looked out of the window and then back at me. "OK," he said, and sighed. "I'll try."

Then I said, trying to cheer him up a little, "They got a piano at Isabel's. You can practice on it."

And as a matter of fact, it did cheer him up for a minute. "That's right," he said to himself. "I forgot that." His face relaxed a little. But the worry, the thoughtfulness, played on it still, the way shadows play on a face which is staring into the fire.

But I thought I'd never hear the end of that piano. At first, Isabel would write me, saying how nice it was that Sonny was so serious about his music and how, as soon as he came in from school, or wherever he had been when he was supposed to be at school, he went straight to that piano and stayed there until suppertime. And, after supper, he went back to that piano and stayed there until everybody went to bed. He was at the piano all day Saturday and all day Sunday. Then he bought a record player and started playing records. He'd play one record over and over again, all day long sometimes, and he'd improvise along with it on the piano. Or he'd play one section of the record, one chord, one change, one progression, then he'd do it on the piano. Then back to the record. Then back to the piano.

Well, I really don't know how they stood it. Isabel finally confessed that it wasn't like living with a person at all, it was like living with sound. And the sound didn't make any sense to her, didn't make any sense to any of them—naturally. They began, in a way, to be afflicted by this presence that was living in their home. It was as though Sonny were some sort of god, or monster. He moved in an atmosphere which wasn't like theirs at all. They fed him and he ate, he washed himself, he walked in and out of their door; he certainly wasn't nasty or unpleasant or rude, Sonny isn't any of those things; but it was as though he were all wrapped up in some cloud, some fire, some vision all his own; and there wasn't any way to reach him.

At the same time, he wasn't really a man yet, he was still a child, and they had to watch out for him in all kinds of ways. They certainly couldn't throw him out. Neither did they dare to make a great scene about that piano because even they dimly sensed, as I sensed, from so many thousands of miles away, that Sonny was at that piano playing for his life.

But he hadn't been going to school. One day a letter came from the school board and Isabel's mother got it—there had, apparently, been other letters but Sonny had torn them up. This day, when Sonny came in, Isabel's mother showed him the letter and asked where he'd been spending his time. And she finally got it out of him that he'd been down in Greenwich Village, with musicians and other characters, in a white girl's apartment. And this scared her and she started to scream at him and what came up, once she began—though she denies it to this day—was what sacrifices they were making to give Sonny a decent home and how little he appreciated it.

Sonny didn't play the piano that day. By evening, Isabel's mother had calmed down but then there was the old man to deal with, and Isabel herself. Isabel says she did her best to be calm but she broke down and started crying. She says she just watched Sonny's face. She could tell, by watching him, what was happening with him. And what was happening was that they penetrated his cloud, they had reached him. Even if their fingers had been a thousand times more gentle than human fingers ever are, he could hardly help feeling that they had stripped him naked and were spitting on that nakedness. For he also had to see that his presence, that music, which was life or death to him, had been torture for them and that they had endured it, not at all for his sake, but only for mine. And Sonny couldn't take that. He can take it a little better today than he could then but he's still not very good at it and, frankly, I don't know anybody who is.

The silence of the next few days must have been louder than the sound of all the music ever played since time began. One morning, before she went to work, Isabel was in his room for something and she suddenly realized that all of his records were gone. And she knew for certain that he was gone. And he was. He went as far as the navy would carry him. He finally sent me a postcard from some place in Greece and that was the first I knew that Sonny was still alive. I didn't see him any more until we were both back in New York and the war had long been over.

He was a man by then, of course, but I wasn't willing to see it. He came by the house from time to time, but we fought almost every time we met. I didn't like the way he carried himself, loose and dreamlike all the time, and I didn't like his friends, and his music seemed to be merely an excuse for the life he led. It sounded just that weird and disordered.

Then we had a fight, a pretty awful fight, and I didn't see him for months. By and by I looked him up, where he was living, in a furnished room in the Village, and I tried to make it up. But there were lots of other people in the room and Sonny just lay on his bed, and he wouldn't come downstairs with me, and he treated these other people as though they were his family and I weren't. So I got mad and then he got mad, and then I told him that he might just as well be dead as live the way he was living. Then he stood up and he told me not to worry about him any more in life, that he *was* dead as far as I was concerned. Then he pushed me to the door and the other people looked on as though nothing were happening, and he slammed the door behind me. I stood in the hallway, staring at the door. I heard somebody laugh in the room and then the tears came to my eyes. I started down the steps, whistling to keep from crying, I kept whistling to myself, *You going to need me, baby, one of these cold, rainy days.*

I read about Sonny's trouble in the spring. Little Grace died in the fall. She was a beautiful little girl. But she only lived a little over two years. She died of polio and she suffered. She had a slight fever for a couple of days, but it didn't seem like anything and we just kept her in bed. And we would certainly have called the doctor, but the fever dropped, she seemed to be all right. So we thought it had just been a cold. Then, one day, she was up, playing, Isabel was in the kitchen fixing lunch for the two boys when they'd come in from school, and she heard Grace fall down in the living room. When you have a lot of children you don't always start running when one of them falls, unless they start screaming or something. And, this time, Grace was quiet. Yet, Isabel says that when she heard that *thump* and then that silence, something happened in her to make her afraid. And she ran to the living room and there was little Grace on the floor, all twisted up and the reason she hadn't screamed was that she couldn't get her breath. And when she did scream, it was the worst sound, Isabel says, that she'd ever heard in all her life, and she still hears it sometimes in her dreams. Isabel will sometimes wake me up with a low, moaning, strangled sound and I have to be quick to awaken her and hold her to me and where Isabel is weeping against me seems a mortal wound.

I think I may have written Sonny the very day that little Grace was buried. I was sitting in the living room in the dark, by myself, and I suddenly thought of Sonny. My trouble made his real.

One Saturday afternoon, when Sonny had been living with us, or, anyway, been in our house, for nearly two weeks, I found myself wandering aimlessly about the living room, drinking from a can of beer, and trying to work up the courage to search Sonny's room. He was out, he was usually out whenever I was home, and Isabel had taken the children to see their grandparents. Suddenly I was standing still in front of the living room window, watching Seventh Avenue. The idea of searching Sonny's room made me still. I scarcely dared to admit to myself what I'd be searching for. I didn't know what I'd do if I found it. Or if I didn't.

On the sidewalk across from me, near the entrance to a barbecue joint, some people were holding an old-fashioned revival meeting. The barbecue cook, wearing a dirty white apron, his conked hair reddish and metallic in the pale sun, and a cigarette between his lips, stood in the doorway, watching them. Kids and older people paused in their errands and stood there, along with some older men and a couple of very tough-looking women who watched everything that happened on the avenue, as though they owned it, or were maybe owned by it. Well, they were watching this, too. The revival was being carried on by three sisters in black, and a brother. All they had were their voices and their Bibles and a tambourine. The brother was testifying and while he testified two of the sisters stood together, seeming to say, Amen, and the third sister walked around with the tambourine outstretched and a couple of people dropped coins into it. Then the brother's testimony ended and the sister who had been taking up the collection dumped the coins into her palm and transferred them to the pocket of her long black robe. Then she raised both hands, striking the tambourine against the air, and then against one hand, and she started to sing. And the two other sisters and the brother joined in.

It was strange, suddenly, to watch, though I had been seeing these street meetings all my life. So, of course, had everybody else down there. Yet, they paused and watched and listened and I stood still at the window. *"Tis the old ship of Zion,"* they sang, and the sister with the tambourine kept a steady, jangling beat, *"It has rescued many a thousand!"* Not a soul under the sound of their voices was hearing this song for the first time, not one of them had been rescued. Nor had they seen much in the way of rescue work being done around them. Neither did they especially believe in the holiness of the three sisters and the brother, they knew too much about them, knew where they lived, and how. The woman with the tambourine, whose voice dominated the air, whose face was bright with joy, was divided by very little from the woman who stood watching her, a cigarette between her heavy, chapped lips, her hair a cuckoo's nest, her face scarred and swollen from many beatings, and her black eyes glittering like coal. Perhaps they both knew this, which was why, when, as rarely, they addressed each other, they addressed each other as Sister. As the singing filled the air the watching, listening faces underwent a change, the eyes focusing on something within; the music seemed to soothe a poison out of them; and time seemed, nearly, to fall away from the sullen, belligerent, battered faces, as though they were fleeing back to their first condition, while dreaming of their last. The barbecue cook half shook his head and smiled, and dropped his cigarette and disappeared into his joint. A man fumbled in his pockets for change and stood holding it in his hand impatiently, as though he had just remembered a pressing appointment further up the avenue. He looked furious. Then I saw Sonny, standing on the edge of the crowd. He was carrying a wide, flat notebook with a green cover, and it made him look, from where I was standing, almost like a schoolboy. The coppery sun brought out the copper in his skin, he was very faintly smiling, standing very still. Then the singing stopped, the tambourine turned into a collection plate again. The furious man dropped in his coins and vanished, so did a couple of the women, and Sonny dropped some change in the plate, looking directly at the woman with a little smile. He started across the avenue, toward the house. He has a slow, loping walk, something like the way Harlem hipsters walk, only he's imposed on this his own halfbeat. I had never really noticed it before.

I stayed at the window, both relieved and apprehensive. As Sonny disappeared from my sight, they began singing again. And they were still singing when his key turned in the lock.

"Hey," he said.

"Hey, yourself. You want some beer?"

"No. Well, maybe." But he came up to the window and stood beside me, looking out. "What a warm voice," he said.

They were singing *If I could only hear my mother pray again!*

"Yes," I said, "and she can sure beat that tambourine."

"But what a terrible song," he said, and laughed. He dropped his notebook on the sofa and disappeared into the kitchen. "Where's Isabel and the kids?"

"I think they went to see their grandparents. You hungry?"

"No." He came back into the living room with his can of beer. "You want to come some place with me tonight?"

I sensed, I don't know how, that I couldn't possibly say No. "Sure. Where?"

He sat down on the sofa and picked up his notebook and started leafing through it. "I'm going to sit in with some fellows in a joint in the Village."

"You mean, you're going to play, tonight?"

"That's right." He took a swallow of his beer and moved back to the window. He gave me a sidelong look. "If you can stand it."

"I'll try," I said.

He smiled to himself and we both watched as the meeting across the way broke up. The three sisters and the brother, heads bowed, were singing *God be with you till we meet again*. The faces around them were very quiet. Then the song ended. The small crowd dispersed. We watched the three women and the lone man walk slowly up the avenue.

"When she was singing before," said Sonny, abruptly, "her voice reminded me for a minute of what heroin feels like sometimes—when it's in your veins. It makes you feel sort of warm and cool at the same time. And distant. And—and sure." He sipped his beer, very deliberately not looking at me. I watched his face. "It makes you feel—in control. Sometimes you've got to have that feeling."

"Do you?" I sat down slowly in the easy chair.

"Sometimes." He went to the sofa and picked up his notebook again. "Some people do."

"In order," I asked, "to play?" And my voice was very ugly, full of contempt and anger.

"Well"—he looked at me with great, troubled eyes, as though, in fact, he hoped his eyes would tell me things he could never otherwise say—"they *think* so. And *if* they think so—!"

"And what do *you* think?" I asked.

He sat on the sofa and put his can of beer on the floor. "I don't know," he said, and I couldn't be sure if he were answering my question or pursuing his thoughts. His face didn't tell me. "It's not so much to *play*. It's to *stand* it, to be able to make it at all. On any level." He frowned and smiled: "In order to keep from shaking to pieces."

"But these friends of yours," I said, "they seem to shake themselves to pieces pretty goddamn fast."

"Maybe." He played with the notebook. And something told me that I should curb my tongue, that Sonny was doing his best to talk, that I should listen. "But of course you only know the ones that've gone to pieces. Some don't—or at least they haven't *yet* and that's just about all *any* of us can say." He paused. "And then there are some who just live, really, in hell, and they know it and they see what's happening and they go right on. I don't know." He sighed, dropped the notebook, folded his arms. "Some guys, you can tell from the way they play, they on something *all* the time. And you can see that, well, it makes something real for them. But of course," he picked up his beer from the floor and sipped it and put the can down again, "they *want* to, too, you've got to see that. Even some of them that say they don't—*some*, not all."

"And what about you?" I asked—I couldn't help it. "What about you? Do *you* want to?"

He stood up and walked to the window and remained silent for a long time. Then he sighed. "Me," he said. Then: "While I was downstairs before, on my way here, listening to that woman sing, it struck me all of a sudden how much suffering she must have had to go through—to sing like that. It's *repulsive* to think you have to suffer that much."

I said: "But there's no way not to suffer—is there, Sonny?"

"I believe not," he said, and smiled, "but that's never stopped anyone from trying." He looked at me. "Has it?" I realized, with this mocking look, that there stood between us, forever, beyond the power of time or forgiveness, the fact that I had held silence—so long!—when he had needed human speech to help him. He turned back to the window. "No, there's no way not to suffer. But you try all kinds of ways to keep from drowning in it, to keep on top of it, and to make it seem—well, like *you*. Like you did something, all right, and now you're suffering for it. You know?" I said nothing. "Well you know," he said, impatiently, "why *do* people suffer? Maybe it's better to do something to give it a reason, *any* reason."

"But we just agreed," I said, "that there's no way not to suffer. Isn't it better, then, just to—take it?"

"But nobody just takes it," Sonny cried, "that's what I'm telling you! *Everybody* tries not to. You're just hung up on the *way* some people try—it's not *your* way!"

The hair on my face began to itch, my face felt wet. "That's not true," I said, "that's not true. I don't give a damn what other people do, I don't even care how they suffer. I just care how *you* suffer." And he looked at me. "Please believe me," I said, "I don't want to see you—die—trying not to suffer."

"I won't," he said, flatly, "die trying not to suffer. At least, not any faster than anybody else."

"But there's no need," I said, trying to laugh, "is there? in killing yourself."

I wanted to say more, but I couldn't. I wanted to talk about will power and how life could be—well, beautiful. I wanted to say that it was all within; but was it? or, rather, wasn't that exactly the trouble? And I wanted to promise that I would never fail him again. But it would all have sounded—empty words and lies.

So I made the promise to myself and prayed that I would keep it.

"It's terrible sometimes, inside," he said, "that's what's the trouble. You walk these streets, black and funky and cold, and there's not really a living ass to talk to, and there's nothing shaking, and there's no way of getting it out—that storm inside. You can't talk it and you can't make love with it, and when you finally try to get with it and play it, you realize *nobody's* listening. So *you've* got to listen. You got to find a way to listen."

And then he walked away from the window and sat on the sofa again, as though all the wind had suddenly been knocked out of him. "Sometimes you'll do *anything* to play, even cut your mother's throat." He laughed and looked at me. "Or your brother's." Then he sobered. "Or your own." Then: "Don't worry. I'm all right now and I think I'll *be* all right. But I can't forget—where I've been. I don't mean just the physical place I've been, I mean where I've *been*. And *what* I've been."

"What have you been, Sonny?" I asked.

He smiled—but sat sideways on the sofa, his elbow resting on the back, his fingers playing with his mouth and chin, not looking at me. "I've been something I didn't recognize, didn't know I could be. Didn't know anybody could be." He stopped, looking inward, looking helplessly young, looking old. "I'm not talking about it now because I feel *guilty* or anything like that—maybe it would be better if I did, I don't know. Anyway, I can't really talk about it. Not to you, not to anybody," and now he turned and faced me. "Sometimes, you know, and it was actually when I was most *out* of the world, I felt that I was in it, and that I was *with* it, really, and I could play or I didn't really have to *play*, it just came out of me, it was there. And I don't know how I played, thinking about it now, but I know I did awful things, those times, sometimes, to people. Or it wasn't that I *did* anything to them—it was that they weren't real." He picked up the beer can; it was empty; he rolled it between his palms: "And other times—well, I needed a fix, I needed to find a place to lean, I needed to clear a space to *listen*—and I couldn't find it, and I—went crazy, I did terrible things to *me, I* was terrible *for* me." He began pressing the beer can between his hands, I watched the metal begin to give. It glittered, as he played with it, like a knife, and I was afraid he would cut himself, but I said nothing. "Oh well. I can never tell you. I was all by myself at the bottom of something, stinking and sweating and crying and shaking, and I smelled it, you know? *my* stink, and I thought I'd die if I couldn't get away from it and yet, all the same, I knew that everything I was doing was just locking me in with it. And I didn't know," he paused, still flattening the beer can, "I didn't know, I still *don't* know, something kept telling me that maybe it was good to smell your own stink, but I didn't think that *that* was what I'd been trying to do—and—who can stand it?" and he abruptly dropped the ruined beer can, looking at me with a small, still smile, and then rose, walking to the window as though it were the lodestone rock. I watched his face, he watched the avenue. "I couldn't tell you when Mama died—but the reason I wanted to leave Harlem so bad was to get away from drugs. And then, when I ran away, that's what I was running from—really. When I came back, nothing had changed, *I* hadn't changed, I was just—older." And he stopped, drumming with his fingers on the windowpane. The sun had vanished, soon darkness would fall. I watched his face. "It can come again," he said, almost as though speaking to himself. Then he turned to me. "It can come again," he repeated. "I just want you to know that."

"All right," I said, at last. "So it can come again. All right."

He smiled, but the smile was sorrowful. "I had to try to tell you," he said.

"Yes," I said. "I understand that."

"You're my brother," he said, looking straight at me, and not smiling at all.

"Yes," I repeated, "yes. I understand that."

He turned back to the window, looking out. "All that hatred down there," he said, "all that hatred and misery and love. It's a wonder it doesn't blow the avenue apart."

We went to the only night club on a short, dark street, downtown. We squeezed through the narrow, chattering, jam-packed bar to the entrance of the big room, where the bandstand was. And we stood there for a moment, for the lights were very dim in this room and we couldn't see. Then, "Hello, boy," said a voice and an enormous black man, much older than Sonny or myself, erupted out of all that atmospheric lighting and put an arm around Sonny's shoulder. "I been sitting right here," he said, "waiting for you."

He had a big voice, too, and heads in the darkness turned toward us.

Sonny grinned and pulled a little away, and said, "Creole, this is my brother. I told you about him."

Creole shook my hand. "I'm glad to meet you, son," he said, and it was clear that he was glad to meet me *there,* for Sonny's sake. And he smiled, "You got a real musician in *your* family," and he took his arm from Sonny's shoulder and slapped him, lightly, affectionately, with the back of his hand.

"Well. Now I've heard it all," said a voice behind us. This was another musician, and a friend of Sonny's, a coal-black, cheerful-looking man, built close to the ground. He immediately began confiding to me, at the top of his lungs, the most terrible things about Sonny, his teeth gleaming like a lighthouse and his laugh coming up out of him like the beginning of an earthquake. And it turned out that everyone at the bar knew Sonny, or almost everyone; some were musicians, working there, or nearby, or not working, some were simply hangers-on, and some were there to hear Sonny play. I was introduced to all of them and they were all very polite to me. Yet, it was clear that, for them, I was only Sonny's brother. Here, I was in Sonny's world. Or, rather: his kingdom. Here, it was not even a question that his veins bore royal blood.

They were going to play soon and Creole installed me, by myself, at a table in a dark corner. Then I watched them, Creole, and the little black man, and Sonny, and the others, while they horsed around, standing just below the bandstand. The light from the bandstand spilled just a little short of them and, watching them laughing and gesturing and moving about, I had the feeling that they, nevertheless, were being most careful not to step into that circle of light too suddenly: that if they moved into the light too suddenly, without thinking, they would perish in flame. Then, while I watched, one of them, the small, black man, moved into the light and crossed the bandstand and started fooling around with his drums. Then—being funny and being, also, extremely ceremonious—Creole took Sonny by the arm and led him to the piano. A woman's voice called Sonny's name and a few hands started clapping. And Sonny, also being funny and being ceremonious, and so touched, I think, that he could have cried, but neither hiding it nor showing it, riding it like a man, grinned, and put both hands to his heart and bowed from the waist.

Creole then went to the bass fiddle and a lean, very bright-skinned brown man jumped up on the bandstand and picked up his horn. So there they were, and the atmosphere on the bandstand and in the room began to change and tighten. Someone stepped up to the microphone and announced them. Then there were all kinds of murmurs. Some people at the bar shushed others. The waitress ran around, frantically getting in the last orders, guys and chicks got closer to each other, and the lights on the bandstand, on the quartet, turned to a kind of indigo. Then they all looked different there. Creole looked about him for the last time, as though he were making certain that all his chickens were in the coop, and then he—jumped and struck the fiddle. And there they were.

All I know about music is that not many people ever really hear it. And even then, on the rare occasions when something opens within, and the music enters, what we mainly hear, or hear corroborated, are personal private, vanishing evocations. But the man who creates the music is hearing something else, is dealing with the roar rising from the void and imposing order on it as it hits the air. What is evoked in him, then, is of another order, more terrible because it has no words, and triumphant, too, for that same reason. And his triumph, when he triumphs, is ours. I just watched Sonny's face. His face was troubled, he was working hard, but he wasn't with it. And I had the feeling that, in a way, everyone on the bandstand was waiting for him, both waiting for him and pushing him along. But as I began to watch Creole, I realized that it was Creole who held them all back. He had them on a short rein. Up there, keeping the beat with his whole body, wailing on the fiddle, with his eyes half closed, he was listening to everything, but he was listening to Sonny. He was having a dialogue with Sonny. He wanted Sonny to leave the shore line and strike out for the deep water. He was Sonny's witness that deep water and drowning were not the same thing—he had been there, and he knew. And he wanted Sonny to know. He was waiting for Sonny to do the things on the keys which would let Creole know that Sonny was in the water.

And, while Creole listened, Sonny moved, deep within, exactly like someone in torment. I had never before thought of how awful the relationship must be between the musician and his instrument. He has to fill it, this instrument, with the breath of life, his own. He has to make it do what he wants it to do. And a piano is just a piano. It's made out of so much wood and wires and little hammers and big ones, and ivory. While there's only so much you can do with it, the only way to find this out is to try and make it do everything.

And Sonny hadn't been near a piano for over a year. And he wasn't on much better terms with his life, not the life that stretched before him now. He and the piano stammered, started one way, got scared, stopped; started another way, panicked, marked time, started again; then seemed to have found a direction, panicked again, got stuck. And the face I saw on Sonny I'd never seen before. Everything had been burned out of it, and, at the same time, things usually hidden were being burned in, by the fire and fury of the battle which was occurring in him up there.

Yet, watching Creole's face as they neared the end of the first set, I had the feeling that something had happened, something I hadn't heard. Then they finished, there was scattered applause, and then, without an instant's warning, Creole started into something else, it was almost sardonic, it was *Am I Blue*. And, as though he commanded, Sonny began to play. Something began to happen. And Creole let out the reins. The dry, low, black man said something awful on the drums, Creole answered, and the drums talked back. Then the horn insisted, sweet and high, slightly detached perhaps, and Creole listened, commenting now and then, dry, and driving, beautiful and calm and old. Then they all came together again, and Sonny was part of the family again. I could tell this from his face. He seemed to have found, right there beneath his fingers, a damn brand-new piano. It seemed that he couldn't get over it. Then, for awhile, just being happy with Sonny, they seemed to be agreeing with him that brand-new pianos certainly were a gas.

Then Creole stepped forward to remind them that what they were playing was the blues. He hit something in all of them, he hit something in me, myself, and the music tightened and deepened, apprehension began to beat the air. Creole began to tell us what the blues were all about. They were not about anything very new. He and his boys up there were keeping it new, at the risk of ruin, destruction, madness, and death, in order to find new ways to make us listen. For, while the tale of how we suffer, and how we are delighted, and how we may triumph is never new, it always must be heard. There isn't any other tale to tell, it's the only light we've got in all this darkness.

And this tale, according to that face, that body, those strong hands on those strings, has another aspect in every country, and a new depth in every generation. Listen, Creole seemed to be saying, listen. Now these are Sonny's blues. He made the little black man on the drums know it, and the bright, brown man on the horn. Creole wasn't trying any longer to get Sonny in the water. He was wishing him Godspeed. Then he stepped back, very slowly, filling the air with the immense suggestion that Sonny speak for himself.

Then they all gathered around Sonny and Sonny played. Every now and again one of them seemed to say, Amen. Sonny's fingers filled the air with life, his life. But that life contained so many others. And Sonny went all the way back, he really began with the spare, flat statement of the opening phrase of the song. Then he began to make it his. It was very beautiful because it wasn't hurried and it was no longer a lament. I seemed to hear with what burning he had made it his, with what burning we had yet to make it ours, how we could cease lamenting. Freedom lurked around us and I understood, at last, that he could help us to be free if we would listen, that he would never be free until we did. Yet, there was no battle in his face now. I heard what he had gone through, and would continue to go through until he came to rest in earth. He had made it his: that long line, of which we knew only Mama and Daddy. And he was giving it back, as everything must be given back, so that, passing through death, it can live forever. I saw my mother's face again, and felt, for the first time, how the stones of the road she had walked on must have bruised her feet. I saw the moonlit road where my father's brother died. And it brought something else back to me, and carried me past it, I saw my little girl again and felt Isabel's tears again, and I felt my own tears begin to rise. And I was yet aware that this was only a moment, that the world waited outside, as hungry as a tiger, and that trouble stretched above us, longer than the sky.

Then it was over. Creole and Sonny let out their breath, both soaking wet, and grinning. There was a lot of applause and some of it was real. In the dark, the girl came by and I asked her to take drinks to the bandstand. There was a long pause, while they talked up there in the indigo light and after awhile I saw the girl put a Scotch and milk on top of the piano for Sonny. He didn't seem to notice it, but just before they started playing again, he sipped from it and looked toward me, and nodded. Then he put it back on top of the piano. For me, then, as they began to play again, it glowed and shook above my brother's head like the very cup of trembling.

QUESTIONS

1. Who is the narrator of "Sonny's Blues"? What do we learn about him? Why has Baldwin chosen this narrator?

2. Why does the story begin with the narrator teaching school? How does childhood function in the story?

3. "All this was carrying me some place I didn't want to go," the narrator says in the middle of his conversation with Sonny's friend. What does he mean?

4. The narrator says that he and Sonny, riding through the streets of New York, "both were seeking through our separate cab windows . . . that part of ourselves which had been left behind. It's always at the hour of trouble and confrontation that the missing member aches." (See Preface, pp. 18–21, imagery.) What has been amputated? What happens to the lost member during the course of the story?

5. According to the narrator and his family, what is it that happens to people, that destroys people? Who is destroyed and how?

6. What is the significance of jazz to Sonny?

7. Sonny's brother writes Sonny just after his own daughter dies. What connection can you see between these events?

8. Look carefully at the description of the spirituals sung in the street. What is the connection between them and Sonny's music?

9. Sonny has developed a certain wisdom from his experience. In this he seems able to teach his older brother, the teacher. Discuss. Relate this wisdom to his music.

10. "He wanted Sonny to leave the shore line and strike out for the deep water. He was Sonny's witness that deep water and drowning were not the same thing—he had been there, and he knew." Discuss this metaphor. Notice the word *witness*. It could come from legal terminology but in this story is has a different connotation. Discuss.

11. Baldwin seems to use the long, beautiful description of jazz as a way of expressing a vision of art and of life. (See Preface, pp. 1–5, 27–29.) Discuss this vision. Can it be translated into rational, analytical language without destroying it?

This Morning, This Evening, So Soon

JAMES BALDWIN

"You are full of nightmares," Harriet tells me. She is in her dressing gown and has cream all over her face. She and my older sister, Louisa, are going out to be girls together. I suppose they have many things to talk about—they have *me* to talk about, certainly—and they do not want my presence. I have been given a bachelor's evening. The director of the film which has brought us such incredible and troubling riches will be along later to take me out to dinner.

I watch her face. I know that it is quite impossible for her to be as untroubled as she seems. Her self-control is mainly for my benefit— my benefit, and Paul's. Harriet comes from orderly and progressive Sweden and has reacted against all the advanced doctrines to which she has been exposed by becoming steadily and beautifully old-fashioned. We never fought in front of Paul, not even when he was a baby. Harriet does not so much believe in protecting children as she does in helping them to build a foundation on which they can build and build again, each time life's high-flying steel ball knocks down everything they have built.

Whenever I become upset, Harriet becomes very cheerful and composed. I think she began to learn how to do this over eight years ago, when I returned from my only visit to America. Now, perhaps, it has become something she could not control if she wished to. This morning, at breakfast, when I yelled at Paul, she averted Paul's tears and my own guilt by looking up and saying, "My God, your father is cranky this morning, isn't he?"

Paul's attention was immediately distracted from his wounds, and the unjust inflicter of those wounds, to his mother's laughter. He watched her.

"It is because he is afraid they will not like his songs in New York. Your father is an *artiste, mon chou,* and they are very mysterious people, *les artistes.* Millions of people are waiting for him in New York, they are begging him to come, and they will give him a *lot* of money, but he is afraid they will not like him. Tell him he is wrong."

She succeeded in rekindling Paul's excitement about places he has

---

never seen. I was also, at once, reinvested with all my glamour. I think it is sometimes extremely difficult for Paul to realize that the face he sees on record sleeves and in the newspapers and on the screen is nothing more or less than the face of his father—who sometimes yells at him. Of course, since he is only seven—going on eight, he will be eight years old this winter—he cannot know that I am baffled, too.

"Of course, you are wrong, you are silly," he said with passion—and caused me to smile. His English is strongly accented and is not, in fact, as good as his French, for he speaks French all day at school. French is really his first language, the first he ever heard. "You are the greatest singer in France"—sounding exactly as he must sound when he makes this pronouncement to his schoolmates—"the greatest *American* singer"—this concession was so gracefully made that it was not a concession at all, it added inches to my stature, America being only a glamorous word for Paul. It is the place from which his father came, and to which he now is going, a place which very few people have ever seen. But his aunt is one of them and he looked over at her. "Mme. Dumont says so, and she says he is a *great actor, too.*" Louisa nodded, smiling. "And she has seen *Les Fauves Nous Attendent*—five times!" This clinched it, of course. Mme. Dumont is our concierge and she has known Paul all his life. I suppose he will not begin to doubt anything she says until he begins to doubt everything.

He looked over at me again. "So you are wrong to be afraid."

"I was wrong to yell at you, too. I won't yell at you any more today."

"All right." He was very grave.

Louisa poured more coffee. "He's going to knock them dead in New York. You'll see."

"Mais bien sur," said Paul, doubtfully. He does not quite know what "knock them dead" means, though he was sure, from her tone, that she must have been agreeing with him. He does not quite understand this aunt, whom he met for the first time two months ago, when she arrived to spend the summer with us. Her accent is entirely different from anything he has ever heard. He does not really understand why, since she is my sister and his aunt, she should be unable to speak French.

Harriet, Louisa, and I looked at each other and smiled. "Knock them dead," said Harriet, "means *d'avoir un succès fou*. But you will soon pick up all the American expressions." She looked at me and laughed. "So will I."

"That's what he's afraid of." Louisa grinned. "We have *got* some expressions, believe me. Don't let anybody ever tell you America hasn't got a culture. Our culture is as thick as clabber milk."

"Ah," Harriet answered, "I know. I know."

"I'm going to be practicing later," I told Paul.

His face lit up. *"Bon."* This meant that, later, he would come into my study and lie on the floor with his papers and crayons while I worked out with the piano and the tape recorder. He knew that I was offering this as an olive branch. All things considered, we get on pretty well, my son and I.

He looked over at Louisa again. She held a coffee cup in one hand and a cigarette in the other; and something about her baffled him. It was early, so she had not yet put on her face. Her short, thick, graying hair was rougher than usual, almost as rough as my own—later, she would be going to the hairdresser's; she is fairer than I, and better-looking; Louisa, in fact, caught all the looks in the family. Paul knows that she is my older sister and that she helped to raise me, though he does not, of course, know what this means. He knows that she is a schoolteacher in the *American* South, which is not, for some reason, the same place as South America. I could see him trying to fit all these exotic details together into a pattern which would explain her strangeness—strangeness of accent, strangeness of manner. In comparison with the people he has always known, Louisa must seem, for all her generosity and laughter and affection, peculiarly uncertain of herself, peculiarly hostile and embattled.

I wondered what he would think of his Uncle Norman, older and much blacker than I, who lives near the Alabama town in which we were born. Norman will meet us at the boat.

✳

Now Harriet repeats, "Nightmares, nightmares. Nothing ever turns out as badly as you think it will—in fact," she adds laughing, "I am happy to say that that would scarcely be possible."

Her eyes seek mine in the mirror—dark-blue eyes, pale skin, black hair. I had always thought of Sweden as being populated entirely by blondes, and I thought that Harriet was abnormally dark for a Swedish girl. But when we visited Sweden, I found out differently. "It is all a great racial salad, Europe, that is why I am sure that I will never understand your country," Harriet said. That was in the days when we never imagined that we would be going to it.

I wonder what she is really thinking. Still, she is right, in two days we will be on a boat, and there is simply no point in carrying around my load of apprehension. I sit down on the bed, watching her fix her face. I realize that I am going to miss this old-fashioned bedroom. For years, we've talked about throwing out the old junk which came with the apartment and replacing it with less massive, modern furniture. But we never have.

"Oh, everything will probably work out," I say. "I've been in a bad mood all day long. I just can't sing any more." We both laugh. She reaches for a wad of tissues and begins wiping off the cream. "I wonder how Paul will like it, if he'll make friends—that's all."

"Paul will like any place where you are, where we are. Don't you worry about Paul."

Paul has never been called any names, so far. Only, once he asked us what the word *métis* meant and Harriet explained to him that it meant mixed blood, adding that the blood of just about everybody in the world was mixed by now. Mme. Dumont contributed bawdy and detailed corroboration from her own family tree, the roots of which were somewhere in Corsica; the moral of the story, as she told it, was that women were weak, men incorrigible, and *le bon Dieu* appallingly clever. Mme. Dumont's version is the version I prefer, but it may not be, for Paul, the most utilitarian.

Harriet rises from the dressing table and comes over to sit in my lap. I fall back with her on the bed, and she smiles down into my face.

"Now, don't worry," she tells me, "please try not to worry. Whatever is coming, we will manage it all very well, you will see. We have each other and we have our son and we know what we want. So, we are luckier than most people."

I kiss her on the chin. "I'm luckier than most men."

"I'm a very lucky woman, too."

And for a moment we are silent, alone in our room, which we have shared so long. The slight rise and fall of Harriet's breathing creates an intermittent pressure against my chest, and I think how, if I had never left America, I would never have met her and would never have established a life of my own, would never have entered my own life. For everyone's life begins on a level where races, armies, and churches stop. And yet everyone's life is always shaped by races, churches, and armies; races, churches, armies menace, and have taken, many lives. If Harriet had been born in America, it would have taken her a long time, perhaps forever, to look on me as a man like other men; if I had met her in America, I would never have been able to look on her as a woman like all other women. The habits of public rage and power would also have been our private compulsions, and would have blinded our eyes. We would never have been able to love each other. And Paul would never have been born.

Perhaps, if I had stayed in America, I would have found another woman and had another son. But that other woman, that other son are in the limbo of vanished possibilities. I might also have become something else, instead of an actor-singer, perhaps a lawyer, like my brother, or a teacher, like my sister. But no, I am what I have become and this woman beside me is my wife, and I love her. All the sons I might have had mean nothing, since I *have* a son, I named him, Paul, for my father, and I love him.

I think of all the things I have seen destroyed in America, all the things that I have lost there, all the threats it holds for me and mine.

I grin up at Harriet. "Do you love me?"

"Of course not. I simply have been madly plotting to get to America all these years."

"What a patient wench you are."

"The Swedes are very patient."

She kisses me again and stands up. Louisa comes in, also in a dressing gown.

"I hope you two aren't sitting in here yakking about the *subject*." She looks at me. "My, you are the sorriest-looking celebrity I've ever seen. I've always wondered why people like you hired press agents. Now I know." She goes to Harriet's dressing table. "Honey, do you mind if I borrow some of that *mad* nail polish?"

Harriet goes over to the dressing table. "I'm not sure I know *which* mad nail polish you mean."

Harriet and Louisa, somewhat to my surprise, get on very well. Each seems to find the other full of the weirdest and most delightful surprises. Harriet has been teaching Louisa French and Swedish expressions, and Louisa has been teaching Harriet some of the saltier expressions of the black South. Whenever one of them is not playing straight man to the other's accent, they become involved in long speculations as to how a language reveals the history and the attitudes of a people. They discovered that all the European languages contain a phrase equivalent to "to work like a nigger." ("Of course," says Louisa, "they've had black men working for them for a long time.") "Language is experience and language is power," says Louisa, after regretting that she does not know any of the African dialects. "That's what I keep trying to tell those dicty bastards down South. They get their own experience into the language, we'll have a great language. But, no, they all want to talk like white folks." Then she leans forward, grasping Harriet by the knee. "I tell them, honey, white folks ain't saying *nothing*. Not a thing are they saying—and *some* of them know it, they *need* what you got, the whole world needs it." Then she leans back, in disgust. "You think they listen to me? Indeed they do not. They just go right on, trying to talk like white folks." She leans forward again, in tremendous indignation. "You know some of them folks are *ashamed* of Mahalia Jackson? *Ashamed* of her, one of the greatest singers alive! They think she's common." Then she looks about the room as though she held a bottle in her hand and were looking for a skull to crack.

I think it is because Louisa has never been able to talk like this to any white person before. All the white people she has ever met needed, in one way or another, to be reassured, consoled, to have their consciences pricked but not blasted; could not, could not afford to hear a truth which would shatter, irrevocably, their image of themselves. It is astonishing the lengths to which a person, or a people, will go in order to avoid a truthful mirror. But Harriet's necessity is precisely the opposite: it is of the utmost importance that she learn everything that Louisa can tell her, and then learn more, much more. Harriet is really trying to learn from Louisa how best to protect her husband and her son. This is why they are going out alone tonight. They will have, tonight, as it were, a final council of war. I may be moody, but they, thank God, are practical.

Now Louisa turns to me while Harriet rummages about on the dressing table. "What time is Vidal coming for you?"

"Oh, around seven-thirty, eight o'clock. He says he's reserved tables for us in some very chic place, but he won't say where." Louisa wriggles her shoulders, raises her eyebrows, and does a tiny bump and grind. I laugh. "That's right. And then I guess we'll go out and get drunk."

"I hope to God you do. You've been about as cheerful as a cemetery these last few days. And, that way, your hangover will keep you from bugging us tomorrow."

"What about *your* hangovers? I know the way you girls drink."

"Well, we'll be paying for our own drinks," says Harriet, "so I don't think we'll have that problem. But *you're* going to be feted, like an international movie star."

"You sure you don't want to change your mind and come out with Vidal and me?"

"We're sure," Louisa says. She looks down at me and gives a small, amused grunt. "An international movie star. And I used to change your diapers. I'll be damned." She is grave for a moment. "Mama'd be proud of you, you know that?" We look at each other and the air between us is charged with secrets which not even Harriet will ever know. "Now, get the hell out of here, so we can get dressed."

"I'll take Paul on down to Mme. Dumont's."

Paul is to have supper with her children and spend the night there.

"For the last time," says Mme. Dumont and she rubs her hand over Paul's violently curly black hair. *"Tu vas nous manquer, tu sais?"* Then she looks up at me and laughs. "He doesn't care. He is only interested in seeing the big ship and all the wonders of New York. Children are never sad to make journeys."

"I would be very sad to go," says Paul, "but my father must go to New York to work and he wants me to come with him."

Over his head, Mme. Dumont and I smile at each other. *"Il est malin, ton gosse!"* She looks down at him again. "And do you think, my little diplomat, that you will like New York?"

"We aren't only going to New York," Paul answers, "we are going to California, too."

"Well, do you think you will like California?"

Paul looks at me. "I don't know. If we don't like it, we'll come back."

"So simple. Just like that," says Mme. Dumont. She looks at me. "It is the best way to look at life. Do come back. You know, we feel that you belong to us, too, here in France."

"I hope you do," I say. "I hope you do. I have always felt—always felt at home here." I bend down and Paul and I kiss each other on the cheek. We have always done so—but will we be able to do so in America? American fathers never kiss American sons. I straighten, my hand on Paul's shoulder. "You be good. I'll pick you up for break-fast, or, if you get up first you come and pick me up and we can hang out together tomorrow, while your *Maman* and your Aunt Louisa finish packing. They won't want two men hanging around the house."

"D'accord. Where shall we hang out?" On the last two words he stumbles a little and imitates me.

"Maybe we can go to the zoo, I don't know. And I'll take you to lunch at the Eiffel Tower, would you like that?"

"Oh, yes," he says, "I'd love that." When he is pleased, he seems to glow. All the energy of his small, tough, concentrated being charges an unseen battery and adds an incredible luster to his eyes, which are large and dark brown—like mine—and to his skin, which always reminds me of the colors of honey and the fires of the sun.

"OK, then." I shake hands with Mme. Dumont. *"Bonsoir, Madame."* I ring for the elevator, staring at Paul. *"Caio, Pauli."*

"Bonsoir, Papa."

And Mme. Dumont takes him inside.

Upstairs, Harriet and Louisa are finally powdered, perfumed, and jeweled, and ready to go: dry martinis at the Ritz, supper, "in some *very* expensive little place," says Harriet, and perhaps the Folies Bergère afterwards. "A real cornball, tourist evening," says Louisa. "I'm working on the theory that if I can get Harriet to act like an American now, she won't have so much trouble later."

"I very much doubt," Harriet says, "that I will be able to endure the Folies Bergère for three solid hours."

"Oh, then we'll duck across town to Harry's New York bar and drink mint juleps," says Louisa.

I realize that, quite apart from everything else, Louisa is having as much fun as she has ever had in her life. Perhaps she, too, will be sad to leave Paris, even though she has only known it for such a short time.

"Do people drink those in New York?" Harriet asks. I think she is making a list of the things people do or do not do in New York.

"Some people do." Louisa winks at me. "Do you realize that this Swedish chick's picked up an Alabama drawl?"

We laugh together. The elevator chugs to a landing.

"We'll stop and say goodnight to Paul," Harriet says. She kisses me. "Give our best to Vidal."

"Right. Have a good time. Don't let any Frenchmen run off with Louisa."

"I did not come to Paris to be protected, and if I had, this wild chick *you* married couldn't do it. I just *might* upset everybody and come home with a French count." She presses the elevator button and the cage goes down.

⌘

I walk back into our dismantled apartment. It stinks of departure. There are bags and crates in the hall which will be taken away tomorrow, there are no books in the bookcases, the kitchen looks as though we never cooked a meal there, never dawdled there, in the early morning or late at night, over coffee. Presently, I must shower and shave but now I pour myself a drink and light a cigarette and step out on our balcony. It is dusk, the brilliant light of Paris is beginning to fade, and the green of the trees is darkening.

I have lived in this city for twelve years. This apartment is on the top floor of a corner building. We look out over the trees and the roof tops to the Champ de Mars, where the Eiffel Tower stands. Beyond this field is the river, which I have crossed so often, in so many states of mind. I have crossed every bridge in Paris, I have walked along every *quai*. I know the river as one finally knows a friend, know it when it is black, guarding all the lights of Paris in its depths, and seeming, in its vast silence, to be communing with the dead who lie beneath it; when it is yellow, evil, and roaring, giving a rough time to tugboats and barges, and causing people to remember that it has been known to rise, it has been known to kill; when it is peaceful, a slick dark, dirty green, playing host to rowboats and *les bateaux mouches* and throwing up from time to time an extremely unhealthy fish. The men who stand along the *quais* all summer with their fishing lines gratefully accept the slimy object and throw it in a rusty can. I have always wondered who eats those fish.

And I walk up and down, up and down, glad to be alone.

It is August, the month when all Parisians desert Paris and one has to walk miles to find a barbershop or a laundry open in some tree-shadowed, silent side street. There is a single person on the avenue, a paratrooper walking toward École Militaire. He is also walking, almost certainly, and rather sooner than later, toward Algeria. I have a friend, a good-natured boy who was aways hanging around the clubs in which I worked in the old days, who has just returned from Algeria, with a recurring, debilitating fever, and minus one eye. The government has set his pension at the sum, arbitrary if not occult, of fifty-three thousand francs every three months. Of course, it is quite impossible to live on this amount of money without working—but who will hire a half-blind invalid? This boy has been spoiled forever, long before his thirtieth birthday, and there are thousands like him all over France.

And there are fewer Algerians to be found on the streets of Paris now. The rug sellers, the peanut vendors, the postcard peddlers and money-changers have vanished. The boys I used to know during my first years in Paris are scattered—or corralled—the Lord knows where.

Most of them had no money. They lived three and four together in rooms with a single skylight, a single hard cot, or in buildings that seemed abandoned, with cardboard in the windows, with erratic plumbing in a wet, cobblestoned yard, in dark, dead-end alleys, or on the outer, chilling heights of Paris.

The Arab cafés are closed—those dark, acrid cafés in which I used to meet with them to drink tea, to get high on hashish, to listen to the obsessive, stringed music which has no relation to any beat, any time, that I have ever known. I once thought of the North Africans as my brothers and that is why I went to their cafés. They were very friendly to me, perhaps one or two of them remained really fond of me even after I could no longer afford to smoke Lucky Strikes and after my collection of American sport shirts had vanished—mostly into their wardrobes. They seemed to feel that they had every right to them, since I could only have wrested these things from the world by cunning—it meant nothing to say that I had had no choice in the matter; perhaps I had wrested these things from the world by treason, by refusing to be identified with the misery of my people. Perhaps, indeed, I identified myself with those who were responsible for this misery.

And this was true. Their rage, the only note in all their music which I could not fail to recognize, to which I responded, yet had the effect of setting us more than ever at a division. They were perfectly prepared to drive all Frenchmen into the sea, and to level the city of Paris. But I could not hate the French, because they left me alone.

And I love Paris, I will always love it, it is the city which saved my life. It saved my life by allowing me to find out who I am.

It was on a bridge, one tremendous, April morning, that I knew I had fallen in love. Harriet and I were walking hand in hand. The bridge was the Pont Royal, just before us was the great *horloge,* high and lifted up, saying ten to ten; beyond this, the golden statue of Joan of Arc, with her sword uplifted. Harriet and I were silent, for we had been quarreling about something. Now, when I look back, I think we had reached that state when an affair must either end or become something more than an affair.

I looked sideways at Harriet's face, which was still. Her dark-blue eyes were narrowed against the sun, and her full, pink lips were still slightly sulky, like a child's. In those days, she hardly ever wore make-up. I was in my shirt sleeves. Her face made me want to laugh and run my hand over her short dark hair. I wanted to pull her to me and say, *Baby, don't be mad at me,* and at that moment something tugged at my heart and made me catch my breath. There were millions of people all around us, but I was alone with Harriet. She was alone with me. Never, in all my life, until that moment, had I been alone with anyone. The world had always been with us, between us, defeating the quarrel we could not achieve, and making love impossible. During all the years of my life, until that moment, I had carried the menacing, the hostile, killing world with me everywhere. No matter what I was doing or saying or feeling, one eye had always been on the world—that world which I had learned to distrust almost as soon as I learned my name, that world on which I knew one could never turn one's back, the white man's world. And for the first time in my life I was free of it; it had not existed for me; I had been quarreling with my girl. It was our quarrel, it was entirely between us, it had nothing to do with anyone else in the world. For the first time in my life I had not been afraid of the patriotism of the mindless, in uniform or out, who would beat me up and treat the woman who was with me as though she were the lowest of untouchables. For the first time in my life I felt that no force jeopardized my right, my power, to possess and to protect a woman; for the first time, the first time, felt that the woman was not, in her own eyes or in the eyes of the world, degraded by my presence.

The sun fell over everything, like a blessing, people were moving all about us, I will never forget the feeling of Harriet's small hand in mine, dry and trusting, and I turned to her, slowing our pace. She looked up at me with her enormous, blue eyes, and she seemed to wait. I said, "Harriet. Harriet. *Tu sais, il y a quelque chose de très grave qui m'est arrivé. Je t'aime. Je t'aime. Tu me comprehends,* or shall I say it in English?"

This was eight years ago, shortly before my first and only visit home.

That was when my mother died. I stayed in America for three months. When I came back, Harriet thought that the change in me was due to my grief—I was very silent, very thin. But it had not been my mother's death which accounted for the change. I had known that my mother was going to die. I had not known what America would be like for me after nearly four years away.

I remember standing at the rail and watching the distance between myself and Le Havre increase. Hands fell, ceasing to wave, handkerchiefs ceased to flutter, people turned away, they mounted their bicycles or got into their cars and rode off. Soon, Le Havre was nothing but a blur. I thought of Harriet, already miles from me in Paris, and I pressed my lips tightly together in order not to cry.

Then, as Europe dropped below the water, as the days passed and passed, as we left behind us the skies of Europe and the eyes of everyone on the ship began, so to speak, to refocus, waiting for the first glimpse of America, my apprehension began to give way to a secret joy, a checked anticipation. I thought of such details as showers, which are rare in Paris, and I thought of such things as rich, cold, American milk and heavy, chocolate cake. I wondered about my friends, wondered if I had any left, and wondered if they would be glad to see me.

The Americans on the boat did not seem to be so bad, but I was fascinated, after such a long absence from it, by the nature of their friendliness. It was a friendliness which did not suggest, and was not intended to suggest, any possibility of friendship. Unlike Europeans, they dropped titles and used first names almost at once, leaving themselves, unlike the Europeans, with nowhere thereafter to go. Once one had become "Pete" or "Jane" or "Bill" all that could decently be known was known and any suggestion that there might be further depths, a person, so to speak, behind the name, was taken as a violation of that privacy which did not, paradoxically, since they trusted it so little, seem to exist among Americans. They apparently equated privacy with the unspeakable things they did in the bathroom or the bedroom, which they related only to the analyst, and then read about in the pages of best sellers. There was an eerie and unnerving irreality about everything they said and did, as though they were all members of the same team and were acting on orders from some invincibly cheerful and tirelessly inventive coach. I was fascinated by it. I found it oddly moving, but I cannot say that I was displeased. It had not occurred to me before that Americans, who had never treated me with any respect, had no respect for each other.

On the last night but one, there was a gala in the big ballroom and

I sang. It had been a long time since I had sung before so many Americans. My audience had mainly been penniless French students, in the weird, Left Bank bistros I worked in those days. Still, I was a great hit with them and by this time I had become enough of a drawing card, in the Latin quarter and in St. Germain des Prés, to have attracted a couple of critics, to have had my picture in *France-soir,* and to have acquired a legal work permit which allowed me to make a little more money. Just the same, no matter how industrious and brilliant some of the musicians had been, or how devoted my audience, they did not know, they could not know, what my songs came out of. They did not know what was funny about it. It was impossible to translate: It damn well better be funny, or Laughing to keep from crying, or What did *I* do to be so black and blue?

The moment I stepped out on the floor, they began to smile, something opened in them, they were ready to be pleased. I found in their faces, as they watched me, smiling, waiting, an artless relief, a profound reassurance. Nothing was more familiar to them than the sight of a dark boy, singing, and there were few things on earth more necessary. It was under cover of darkness, my own darkness, that I could sing for them of the joys, passions, and terrors they smuggled about with them like steadily depreciating contraband. Under cover of the midnight fiction that I was unlike them because I was black, they could stealthily gaze at those treasures which they had been mysteriously forbidden to possess and were never permitted to declare.

I sang *I'm Coming, Virginia,* and *Take This Hammer,* and *Precious Lord.* They wouldn't let me go and I came back and sang a couple of the oldest blues I knew. Then someone asked me to sing *Swanee River,* and I did, astonished that I could, astonished that this song, which I had put down long ago, should have the power to move me. Then, if only, perhaps, to make the record complete, I wanted to sing *Strange Fruit,* but, on this number, no one can surpass the great, tormented Billie Holiday. So I finished with *Great Getting-Up Morning* and I guess I can say that if I didn't stop the show I certainly ended it. I got a big hand and I drank at a few tables and I danced with a few girls.

After one more day and one more night, the boat landed in New York. I woke up, I was bright awake at once, and I thought, *We're here.* I turned on all the lights in my small cabin and I stared into the mirror as though I were committing my face to memory. I took a shower and I took a long time shaving and I dressed myself very carefully. I walked the long ship corridors to the dining room, looking at the luggage piled high before the elevators and beside the steps. The dining room was nearly half empty and full of a quick and joyous excitement which depressed me even more. People ate quickly, chattering to each other, anxious to get upstairs and go on deck. Was it my imagination or was it true that they seemed to avoid my eyes? A few people waved and smiled, but let me pass; perhaps it would have made them uncomfortable, this morning, to try to share their excitement with me; perhaps they did not want to know whether or not it was possible for me to share it. I walked to my table and sat down. I munched toast as dry as paper and drank a pot of coffee. Then I tipped my waiter, who bowed and smiled and called me "sir" and said that he hoped to see me on the boat again. "I hope so, too," I said.

And was it true, or was it my imagination, that a flash of wondering comprehension, a flicker of wry sympathy, then appeared in the waiter's eyes? I walked upstairs to the deck.

There was a breeze from the water but the sun was hot and made me remember how ugly New York summers could be. All of the deck chairs had been taken away and people milled about in the space where the deck chairs had been, moved from one side of the ship to the other, clambered up and down the steps, crowded the rails, and they were busy taking photographs—of the harbor, of each other, of the sea, of the gulls. I walked slowly along the deck, and an impulse stronger than myself drove me to the rail. There it was, the great, unfinished city, with all its towers blazing in the sun. It came toward us slowly and patiently, like some enormous, cunning, and murderous beast, ready to devour, impossible to escape. I watched it come closer and I listened to the people around me, to their excitement and their pleasure. There was no doubt that it was real. I watched their shining faces and wondered if I were mad. For a moment I longed, with all my heart, to be able to feel whatever they were feeling, if only to know what such a feeling was like. As the boat moved slowly into the harbor, they were being moved into safety. It was only I who was being floated into danger. I turned my head, looking for Europe, but all that stretched behind me was the sky, thick with gulls. I moved away from the rail. A big, sandy-haired man held his daughter on his shoulders, showing her the Statue of Liberty. I would never know what this statue meant to others, she had always been an ugly joke for me. And the American flag was flying from the top of the ship, above my head. I had seen the French flag drive the French into the most unspeakable frenzies, I had seen the flag which was nominally mine used to dignify the vilest purposes: now I would never, as long as I lived, know what others saw when they saw a flag. "There's no place like home," said a voice close by, and I thought, *There damn sure isn't.* I decided to go back to my cabin and have a drink.

There was a cablegram from Harriet in my cabin. It said: Be good.

Be quick. I'm waiting. I folded it carefully and put it in my breast pocket. Then I wondered if I would ever get back to her. How long would it take me to earn the money to get out of this land? Sweat broke out on my forehead and I poured myself some whiskey from my nearly empty bottle. I paced the tiny cabin. It was silent. There was no one down in the cabins now.

I was not sober when I faced the uniforms in the first-class lounge. There were two of them; they were not unfriendly. They looked at my passport, they looked at me. "You've been away a long time," said one of them.,

"Yes," I said, "it's been a while."

"What did you do over there all that time?"—with a grin meant to hide more than it revealed, which hideously revealed more than it could hide.

I said, "I'm a singer," and the room seemed to rock around me. I held on to what I hoped was a calm, open smile. I had not had to deal with these faces in so long that I had forgotten how to do it. I had once known how to pitch my voice precisely between curtness and servility, and known what razor's edge of a pickaninny's smile would turn away wrath. But I had forgotten all the tricks on which my life had once depended. Once I had been an expert at baffling these people, at setting their teeth on edge, and dancing just outside the trap laid for me. But I was not an expert now. These faces were no longer merely the faces of two white men, who were my enemies. They were the faces of two white people whom I did not understand, and I could no longer plan my moves in accordance with what I knew of their cowardice and their needs and their strategy. That moment on the bridge had undone me forever.

"That's right," said one of them, "that's what it says, right here on the passport. Never heard of you, though." They looked up at me. "Did you do a lot of singing over there?"

"Some."

"What kind—concerts?"

"No." I wondered what I looked like, sounded like. I could tell nothing from their eyes. "I worked a few nightclubs."

"Nightclubs, eh? I guess they liked you over there."

"Yes," I said, "they seemed to like me all right."

"Well"—and my passport was stamped and handed back to me— "let's hope they like you over here."

"Thanks." They laughed—was it at me, or was it my imagination? and I picked up the one bag I was carrying and threw my trench coat over one shoulder and walked out of the first-class lounge. I stood in the slow-moving, murmuring line which led to the gangplank. I looked straight ahead and watched heads, smiling faces, step up to the shadow of the gangplank awning and then swiftly descend out of sight. I put my passport back in my breast pocket—*Be quick. I'm waiting*—and I held my landing card in my hand. Then, suddenly, there I was, standing on the edge of the boat, staring down the long ramp to the ground. At the end of the plank, on the ground, stood a heavy man in a uniform. His cap was pushed back from his gray hair and his face was red and wet. He looked up at me. This was the face I remembered, the face of my nightmares; perhaps hatred had caused me to know this face better than I would ever know the face of any lover. "Come on, boy," he cried, "come on, come on!"

And I almost smiled. I was home. I touched my breast pocket. I thought of a song I sometimes sang, *When will I ever get to be a man?* I came down the gangplank, stumbling a little, and gave the man my landing card.

Much later in the day, a customs inspector checked my baggage and waved me away. I picked up my bags and started walking down the long stretch which led to the gate, to the city.

And I heard someone call my name.

I looked up and saw Louisa running toward me. I dropped my bags and grabbed her in my arms and tears came to my eyes and rolled down my face. I did not know whether the tears were for joy at seeing her, or from rage, or both.

"How are you? How are you? You look wonderful, but, oh, haven't you lost weight? It's wonderful to see you again."

I wiped my eyes. "It's wonderful to see you, too, I bet you thought I was never coming back."

Louisa laughed. "I wouldn't have blamed you if you hadn't. These people are just as corny as ever, I swear I don't believe there's any hope for them. How's your French? Lord, when I think that it was I who studied French and now I can't speak a word. And you never went near it and you probably speak it like a native."

I grinned. *"Pas mal. Je me défends pas mal."* We started down the wide steps into the street. "My God," I said. "New York." I was not aware of its towers now. We were in the shadow of the elevated highway but the thing which most struck me was neither light nor shade, but noise. It came from a million things at once, from trucks and tires and clutches and brakes and doors; from machines shuttling and stamping and rolling and cutting and pressing; from the building of tunnels, the checking of gas mains, the laying of wires, the digging of foundations; from the chattering of rivets, the scream of the pile driver, the clanging of great shovels; from the battering down and the raising up of walls; from millions of radios and television sets and juke boxes. The human voices distinguished themselves from the roar only by their note of strain and hostility. Another fleshy man, uniformed and red faced, hailed a cab for us and touched his cap politely but could only manage a peremptory growl: "Right this way, miss. Step up, sir." He slammed the cab door behind us. Louisa directed the driver to the New Yorker Hotel.

"Do they take us there?"

She looked at me. "They got laws in New York, honey, it'd be the easiest thing in the world to spend all your time in court. But over at the New Yorker, I believe they've already got the message." She took my arm. "You see? In spite of all this chopping and booming, this place hasn't really changed very much. You still can't hear yourself talk."

And I thought to myself, Maybe that's the point.

Early the next morning we checked out of the hotel and took the plane for Alabama.

I am just stepping out of the shower when I hear the bell ring. I dry myself hurriedly and put on a bathrobe. It is Vidal, of course, and very elegant he is, too, with his bushy gray hair quite lustrous, his swarthy, cynical, gypsylike face shaved and lotioned. Usually he looks just any old way. But tonight his brief bulk is contained in a dark-blue suit and he has an ironical pearl stickpin in his blue tie.

"Come in, make yourself a drink. I'll be with you in a second."

"I am, *hélas!*, on time. I trust you will forgive me for my thoughtlessness."

But I am already back in the bathroom. Vidal puts on a record: Mahalia Jackson, singing *I'm Going to Live the Life I Sing About in My Song.*

When I am dressed, I find him sitting in a chair before the open window. The daylight is gone, but it is not exactly dark. The trees are black now against the darkening sky. The lights in windows and the lights of motorcars are yellow and ringed. The street lights have not yet been turned on. It is as though, out of deference to the departed day, Paris waited a decent interval before assigning her role to a more theatrical but inferior performer.

Vidal is drinking a whiskey and soda. I pour myself a drink. He watches me.

"Well. How are you, my friend? You are nearly gone. Are you happy to be leaving us?"

"No." I say this with more force than I had intended. Vidal raises his eyebrows, looking amused and distant. "I never really intended to go back there. I certainly never intended to raise my kid there—"

"*Mais, mon cher,*" Vidal says, calmly, "you are an intelligent man, you must have known that you would probably be returning one day." He pauses. "And, as for Pauli—did it never occur to you that he might wish one day to see the country in which his father and his father's fathers were born?"

"To do that, really, he'd have to go to Africa."

"America will always mean more to him than Africa, you know that."

"I don't know." I throw my drink down and pour myself another. "Why should he want to cross all that water just to be called a nigger? America never gave him anything."

"It gave him his father."

I look at him. "You mean, his father escaped."

Vidal throws back his head and laughs. If Vidal likes you, he is certain to laugh at you and his laughter can be very unnerving. But the look, the silence which follows this laughter can be very unnerving, too. And, now, in the silence, he asks me, "Do you really think that you have escaped anything? Come. I know you for a better man than that." He walks to the table which holds the liquor. "In that movie of ours which has made you so famous, and, as I now see, so troubled, what are you playing, after all? What is the tragedy of this half-breed troubadour if not, precisely, that he has taken all the possible roads to escape and that all these roads have failed him?" He pauses, with the bottle in one hand, and looks at me. "Do you remember the trouble I had to get a performance out of you? How you hated me, you sometimes looked as though you wanted to shoot me! And do you remember when the role of Chico began to come alive?" He pours his drink. "Think back, remember. I am a very great director, *mais pardon!* I could not have got such a performance out of anyone but you. And what were you thinking of, what was in your mind, what nightmare were you living with when you began, at last, to play the role—truthfully?" He walks back to his seat.

Chico, in the film, is the son of a Martinique woman and a French *colon* who hates both his mother and his father. He flees from the island to the capital, carrying his hatred with him. This hatred has now grown, naturally, to include all dark women and all white men, in a word, everyone. He descends into the underworld of Paris, where he dies. *Les fauves*—the wild beasts—refers to the life he has fled and to the life which engulfs him. When I agreed to do the role, I felt that I could probably achieve it by bearing in mind the North Africans I had watched in Paris for so long. But this did not please Vidal. The blowup came while we were rehearsing a fairly simple, straightforward scene. Chico goes into a sleazy Pigalle dance hall to beg the French owner for a particularly humiliating job. And this Frenchman reminds him of his father.

"You are playing this boy as though you thought of him as the noble savage," Vidal said, icily. "*Ça vient d'où*—all these ghastly mannerisms you are using all the time?"

Everyone fell silent, for Vidal rarely spoke this way. This silence told me that everyone, the actor with whom I was playing the scene and all the people in the "dance hall," shared Vidal's opinion of my performance and were relieved that he was going to do something about it. I was humiliated and too angry to speak; but perhaps I also felt, at the very bottom of my heart, a certain relief, an unwilling respect.

"You are doing it all wrong," he said, more gently. Then, "Come, let us have a drink together."

We walked into his office. He took a bottle and two glasses out of his desk. "Forgive me, but you put me in mind of some of those English *lady* actresses who love to play *putain* as long as it is always absolutely clear to the audience that they are really ladies. So perhaps they read a book, not usually, *hélas!*, *Fanny Hill*, and they have their chauffeurs drive them through Soho once or twice—and they come to the stage with a performance so absolutely loaded with detail, every bit of it meaningless, that there can be no doubt that they are acting. It is what the British call a triumph." He poured two cognacs. "That is what you are doing. Why? Who do you think this boy is, what do you think he is feeling, when he asks for this job?" He watched me carefully and I bitterly resented his look. "You come from America. The situation is not so pretty there for boys like you. I know you may not have been as poor as—as some—but is it really impossible for you to understand what a boy like Chico feels? Have you never, yourself, been in a similar position?"

I hated him for asking the question because I knew he knew the answer to it. "I would have had to be a very lucky black man not to have been in such a position."

"You would have had to be a very lucky *man*."

"Oh, God," I said, "please don't give me any of this equality-in-anguish business."

"It is perfectly possible," he said, sharply, "that there is not another kind."

Then he was silent. He sat down behind his desk. He cut a cigar and lit it, puffing up clouds of smoke, as though to prevent us from seeing each other too clearly. "Consider this," he said. "I am a French director who has never seen your country. I have never done you any harm, except, perhaps, historically—I mean, because I am white—but I cannot be blamed for that—"

"But *I* can be," I said, "and I am! I've never understood why, if *I* have to pay for the history written in the color of my skin, *you* should get off scot-free!" But I was surprised at my vehemence, I had not known I was going to say these things, and by the fact that I was trembling and from the way he looked at me I knew that, from a professional point of view anyway, I was playing into his hands.

"What makes you think I *do?*" His face looked weary and stern. "I am a Frenchman. Look at France. You think that I—we—are not paying for our history?" He walked to the window, staring out at the rather grim little town in which the studio was located. "If it is revenge that you want, well, then, let me tell you, you will have it. You will probably have it, whether you want it or not, our stupidity will make it inevitable." He turned back into the room. "But I beg you not to confuse me with the happy people of your country, who scarcely know that there is such a thing as history and so, naturally, imagine that they can escape, as you put it, scot-free. That is what you are doing, that is what I was about to say. I was about to say that I am a French director and I have never been in your country and I have never done you any harm—but you are not talking to that man, in this room, now. You are not talking to Jean Luc Vidal, but to some other white man, whom you remember, who has nothing to do with me." He paused and went back to his desk. "Oh, most of the time you are not like this, I know. But it is there all the time, it must be, because when you are upset, this is what comes out. So you are not playing Chico truthfully, you are lying about him, and I will not let you do it. When you go back, now, and play this scene again, I want you to remember what has just happened in this room. You brought your past into this room. That is what Chico does when he walks into the dance hall. The Frenchman whom he begs for a job is not merely a Frenchman—he is the father who disowned and betrayed him and all the Frenchmen whom he hates." He smiled and poured me another cognac. "Ah! If it were not for *my* history, I would not have so much trouble to get the truth out of you." He looked into my face, half smiling. "And you, you are angry—are you not?—that I *ask* you for the truth. You think I have no right to ask." Then he said something which he knew would enrage me. "Who are you then, and what good has it done you to come to France, and how will you raise your son? Will you teach him never to tell the truth to anyone?" And he moved behind his desk and looked at me, as though from behind a barricade.

"You have no right to talk to me this way."

"Oh, yes, I do," he said. "I have a film to make and a reputation to maintain and I am going to get a performance out of you." He looked at his watch. "Let us go back to work."

I watch him now, sitting quietly in my living room, tough, cynical, crafty old Frenchman, and I wonder if he knows that the nightmare at the bottom of my mind, as I played the role of Chico, was all the possible fates of Paul. This is but another way of saying that I relived the disasters which had nearly undone me; but, because I was thinking of Paul, I discovered that I did not want my son ever to feel toward me as I had felt toward my own father. He had died when I was eleven, but I had watched the humiliations he had to bear, and I had pitied him. But was there not, in that pity, however painfully and unwillingly, also some contempt? For how could I *know* what he had borne? I knew only that I was his son. However he had loved me, whatever he had borne, I, his son, was despised. Even had he lived, he could have done nothing to prevent it, nothing to protect me. The best that he could hope to do was to prepare me for it; and even at that he had failed. How can one be prepared for the spittle in the face, all the tireless ingenuity which goes into the spite and fear of small, unutterably miserable people, whose greatest terror is the singular identity, whose joy, whose safety, is entirely dependent on the humiliation and anguish of others?

But for Paul, I swore it, such a day would never come. I would throw my life and my work between Paul and the nightmare of the world. I would make it impossible for the world to treat Paul as it had treated my father and me.

Mahalia's record ends. Vidal rises to turn it over. "Well?" He looks at me very affectionately. "Your nightmares, please!"

"Oh, I was thinking of that summer I spent in Alabama, when my mother died." I stop. "You know, but when we finally filmed that bar scene, I was thinking of New York. I was scared in Alabama, but I almost went crazy in New York. I was sure I'd never make it back here—back here to Harriet. And I knew if I didn't, it was going to be the end of me." Now Mahalia is singing *When the Saints Go Marching In.* "I got a job in the town as an elevator boy, in the town's big department store. It was a special favor, one of my father's white friends got it for me. For a long time, in the South, we all—depended —on the—*kindness*—of white friends." I take out a handkerchief and wipe my face. "But this man didn't like me. I guess I didn't seem grateful enough, wasn't enough like my father, what he thought my father was. And I couldn't get used to the town again, I'd been away too long, I hated it. It's a terrible town, anyway, the whole thing looks as though it's been built around a jailhouse. There's a room in the courthouse, a room where they beat you up. Maybe you're walking along the street one night, it's usually at night, but it happens in the daytime, too. And the police car comes up behind you and the cop says, 'Hey, boy. Come on over here.' So you go on over. He says, 'Boy, I believe you're drunk.' And, you see, if you say, 'No, no sir,' he'll beat you because you're calling him a liar. And if you say anything else, unless it's something to make him laugh, he'll take you in and beat you, just for fun. The trick is to think of some way for them to have their fun without beating you up."

The street lights of Paris click on and turn all the green leaves silver. "Or to go along with the ways *they* dream up. And they'll do anything, anything at all, to prove that you're no better than a dog and to make you feel like one. And they hated me because I'd been North and I'd been to Europe. People kept saying, I hope you didn't bring no foreign notions back here with you, boy. And I'd say, 'No sir,' or 'No ma'am,' but I never said it right. And there was a time, all of them remembered it, when I *had* said it right. But now they could tell that I despised them—I guess, no matter what, I wanted them to know that I despised them. But I didn't despise them any more than everyone else did, only the others never let it show. They knew how to keep the white folks happy, and it was easy—you just had to keep them feeling like they were God's favor to the universe. They'd walk around with great, big, foolish grins on their faces and the colored folks loved to see this, because they hated them so much. 'Just look at So-and-So,' somebody'd say. 'His white is *on* him today.' And when we didn't hate them, we pitied them. In America, that's usually what it means to have a white friend. You pity the poor bastard because he was born believing the world's a great place to be, and you know it's not, and you can see that he's going to have a terrible time getting used to this idea, if he ever gets used to it."

Then I think of Paul again, those eyes which still imagine that I can do anything, that skin, the color of honey and fire, his jet-black, curly hair. I look out at Paris again, and I listen to Mahalia. "Maybe it's better to have the terrible times first. I don't know. Maybe, then, you can have, *if* you live, a better life, a real life, because you had to fight so hard to get it away—you know?—from the mad dog who held it in his teeth. But then your life has all those tooth marks, too, all those tatters, and all that blood." I walk to the bottle and raise it. "One for the road?"

"Thank you," says Vidal.

I pour us a drink, and he watches me. I have never talked so much before, not about those things anyway. I know that Vidal has nightmares, because he knows so much about them, but he has never told me what his are. I think that he probably does not talk about his nightmares any more. I know that the war cost him his wife and his son, and that he was in prison in Germany. He very rarely refers to it. He has a married daughter who lives in England, and he rarely speaks of her. He is like a man who has learned to live on what is left of an enormous fortune.

We are silent for a moment.

"Please go on," he says, with a smile. "I am curious about the reality behind the reality of your performance."

"My sister, Louisa, never married," I say, abruptly, "because, once, years ago, she and the boy she was going with and two friends of theirs were out driving in a car and the police stopped them. The girl who was with them was very fair and the police pretended not to believe her when she said she was colored. They made her get out and stand in front of the headlights of the car and pull down her pants and raise her dress—they said that was the only way they could be sure. And you can imagine what they said, and what they did— and they were lucky, at that, that it didn't go any further. But none of the men could do anything about it. Louisa couldn't face the boy again, and I guess he couldn't face her." Now it is really growing dark in the room and I cross to the light switch. "You know, I know what that boy felt, I've felt it. They want you to feel that you're not a man, maybe that's the only way they can feel like men, I don't know. I walked around New York with Harriet's cablegram in my pocket as though it were some atomic secret, in *code,* and they'd kill me if they ever found out what it meant. You know, there's some- thing wrong with people like that. And thank God Harriet was here, she *proved* that the world was bigger than the world they wanted me to live in, I *had* to get back here, get to a place where people were too busy with their own lives, *their private lives,* to make fantasies about mine, to set up walls around mine." I look at him. The light in the room has made the night outside blue-black and golden and the great searchlight of the Eiffel Tower is turning in the sky. "That's what it's like in America, for me, anyway. I always feel that I don't exist there, except in someone else's—usually dirty—mind. I don't know if you know what that means, but I do, and I don't want to put Harriet through that and I don't want to raise Paul there."

"Well," he says at last, "you are not required to remain in America forever, are you? You will sing in that elegant club which apparently feels that it cannot, much longer, so much as open its doors without you, and you will probably accept the movie offer, you would be very foolish not to. You will make a lot of money. Then, one day, you will remember that airlines and steamship companies are still in business and that France still exists. *That* will certainly be cause for astonish- ment."

Vidal was a Gaulist before de Gaulle came to power. But he regrets the manner of de Gaulle's rise and he is worried about de Gaulle's regime. "It is not the fault of *mon général,*" he sometimes says, sadly. "Perhaps it is history's fault. I *suppose* it must be history which always arranges to bill a civilization at the very instant it is least prepared to pay."

Now he rises and walks out on the balcony, as though to reassure himself of the reality of Paris. Mahalia is singing *Didn't It Rain?* I walk out and stand beside him.

"You are a good boy—Chico," he says. I laugh. "You believe in love. You do not know all the things love cannot do, but"—he smiles—"love will teach you that."

We go, after dinner, to a Left Bank discothèque which can charge outrageous prices because Marlon Brando wandered in there one night. By accident, according to Vidal. "Do you know how many people in Paris are becoming rich—to say nothing of those, *hélas!*, who are going broke—on the off chance that Marlon Brando will lose his way again?"

He has not, presumably, lost his way tonight, but the discothèque is crowded with those strangely faceless people who are part of the night life of all great cities, and who always arrive, moments, hours, or decades late, on the spot made notorious by an event or a movement or a handful of personalities. So here are American boys, anything but beardless, scratching around for Hemingway; American girls, titillating themselves with Frenchmen and existentialism, while waiting for the American boys to shave off their beards; French painters, busily pursuing the revolution which ended thirty years ago; and the young, bored, perverted, American *arrivistes* who are buying their way into the art world via flattery and liquor, and the production of canvases as arid as their greedy little faces. Here are boys, of all nations, one step above the pimp, who are occasionally walked across a stage or trotted before a camera. And the girls, their enemies, whose faces are sometimes seen in ads, one of whom will surely have a tantrum before the evening is out.

In a corner, as usual, surrounded, as usual, by smiling young men, sits the drunken blonde woman who was once the mistress of a famous, dead painter. She is a figure of some importance in the art world, and so rarely has to pay for either her drinks or her lovers. An older Frenchman, who was once a famous director, is playing *quatre cent vingt-et-un* with the woman behind the cash register. He nods pleasantly to Vidal and me as we enter, but makes no move to join us, and I respect him for this. Vidal and I are obviously cast tonight in the role vacated by Brando: our entrance justifies the prices and sends a kind of shiver through the room. It is marvelous to watch the face of the waiter as he approaches, all smiles and deference and grace, not so much honored by our presence as achieving his reality from it; excellence, he seems to be saying, gravitates naturally toward excellence. We order two whiskey and sodas. I know why Vidal sometimes comes here. He is lonely. I do not think that he expects ever to love one woman again, and so he distracts himself with many.

Since this is a discothèque, jazz is blaring from the walls and record sleeves are scattered about with a devastating carelessness. Two of them are mine and no doubt, presently, someone will play the recording of the songs I sang in the film.

"I thought," says Vidal, with a malicious little smile, "that your farewell to Paris would not be complete without a brief exposure to the perils of fame. Perhaps it will help prepare you for America, where, I am told, the populace is yet more carnivorous than it is here."

I can see that one of the vacant models is preparing herself to come to our table and ask for an autograph, hoping, since she is pretty—she has, that is, the usual female equipment, dramatized in the usual, modern way—to be invited for a drink. Should the maneuver succeed, one of her boy friends or girl friends will contrive to come by the table, asking for a light or a pencil or a lipstick, and it will be extremely difficult not to invite this person to join us, too. Before the evening ends, we will be surrounded. I don't, now, know what I expected of fame, but I suppose it never occurred to me that the light could be just as dangerous, just as killing, as the dark.

"Well, let's make it brief," I tell him. "Sometimes I wish that you weren't quite so fond of me."

He laughs. "There are some very interesting people here tonight. Look."

Across the room from us, and now staring at our table, are a group of American Negro students, who are probably visiting Paris for the first time. There are four of them, two boys and two girls, and I suppose that they must be in their late teens or early twenties. One of the boys, a gleaming, curly-haired, golden-brown type—the color of his mother's fried chicken—is carrying a guitar. When they realize we have noticed them, they smile and wave—wave as though I were one of their possessions, as, indeed, I am. Golden-brown is a mime. He raises his guitar, drops his shoulders, and his face falls into the lugubrious lines of Chico's face as he approaches death. He strums a little of the film's theme music, and I laugh and the table laughs. It is as though we were all back home and had met for a moment, on a Sunday morning, say, before a church or a poolroom or a barbershop.

And they have created a sensation in the discothèque, naturally, having managed, with no effort whatever, to outwit all the gleaming boys and girls. Their table, which had been of no interest only a moment before, has now become the focus of a rather pathetic attention; their smiles have made it possible for the others to smile, and to nod in our direction.

"Oh," says Vidal, "he does that far better than you ever did, perhaps I will make him a star."

"Feel free, *m'sieu, le bon Dieu,* I got mine." But I can see that his attention has really been caught by one of the girls, slim, tense, and dark, who seems, though it is hard to know how one senses such things, to be treated by the others with a special respect. And, in fact, the table now seems to be having a council of war, to be demanding her opinion or her cooperation. She listens, frowning, laughing; the quality, the force of her intelligence causes her face to keep changing all the time, as though a light played on it. And, presently with a gesture she might once have used to scatter feed to chickens, she scoops up from the floor one of those dangling rag bags women love to carry. She holds it loosely by the drawstrings, so that it is banging somewhere around her ankle, and walks over to our table. She has an honest, forthright walk, entirely unlike the calculated, pelvic workout by means of which most women get about. She is small, but sturdily, economically, put together.

As she reaches our table, Vidal and I rise, and this throws her for a second. (It has been a long time since I have seen such an attractive girl.)

Also, everyone, of course, is watching us. It is really a quite curious moment. They have put on the record of Chico singing a sad, angry Martinique ballad; my own voice is coming at us from the walls as the girl looks from Vidal to me, and smiles.

"I guess you know," she says, "we weren't *about* to let you get out of here without bugging you just a little bit. We've only been in Paris just a couple of days and we thought for sure that we wouldn't have a chance of running into you anywhere, because it's in all the papers that you're coming home."

"Yes," I say, "yes. I'm leaving the day after tomorrow."

"Oh!" She grins. "Then we really *are* lucky." I find that I have almost forgotten the urchin-like grin of a colored girl. "I guess, before I keep babbling on, I'd better introduce myself. My name is Ada Holmes."

We shake hands. "This is Monsieur Vidal, the director of the film."

"I'm very honored to meet you, sir."

"Will you join us for a moment? Won't you sit down?" And Vidal pulls a chair out for her.

But she frowns contritely. "I really ought to get back to my friends." She looks at me. "I really just came over to say, for myself and all the kids, that we've got your records and we've seen your movie, and it means so much to us"—and she laughs, breathlessly, nervously, it is somehow more moving than tears—"more than I can say. Much more. And we wanted to know if you and your friend"— she looks at Vidal—"your *director,* Monsieur Vidal, would allow us to buy you a drink? We'd be very honored if you would."

"It is we who are honored," says Vidal, promptly, *"and* grateful.

We were getting terribly bored with one another, thank God you came along."

The three of us laugh, and we cross the room.

The three at the table rise, and Ada makes the introductions. The other girl, taller and paler than Ada, is named Ruth. One of the boys is named Talley—"short for Talliafero"—and Golden-brown's name is Pete. "Man," he tells me, "I dig you the most. You tore me up, baby, tore me *up*."

"You tore up a lot of people," Talley says, cryptically, and he and Ruth laugh. Vidal does not know, but I do, that Talley is probably referring to white people.

They are from New Orleans and Tallahassee and North Carolina; are college students, and met on the boat. They have been in Europe all summer, in Italy and Spain, but are only just getting to Paris.

"We meant to come sooner," says Ada, "but we could never make up our minds to leave a place. I thought we'd never pry Ruth loose from Venice."

"I resigned myself," says Pete, "and just sat in the Piazza San Marco, drinking gin fizz and being photographed with the pigeons, while Ruth had herself driven *all* up and down the Grand Canal." He looks at Ruth. "Finally, thank heaven, it rained."

"She was working off her hostilities," says Ada, with a grin. "We thought we might as well let her do it in Venice, the opportunities in North Carolina are really terribly limited."

"There are some very upset people walking around down there," Ruth says, "and a couple of tours around the Grand Canal might do them a world of good."

Pete laughs. "Can't you just see Ruth escorting them to the edge of the water?"

"I haven't lifted my hand in anger yet," Ruth says, "but, oh Lord," and she laughs, clenching and unclenching her fists.

"You haven't been back for a long time, have you?" Talley asks me.

"Eight years. I haven't really lived there for twelve years."

Pete whistles. "I fear you are in for some surprises, my friend. There have been some changes made." Then, "Are you afraid?"

"A little."

"We all are," says Ada, "that's why I was so glad to get away for a little while."

"Then you haven't been back since Black Monday," Talley says. He laughs. "That's how it's gone down in Confederate history." He turns to Vidal. "What do people think about it here?"

Vidal smiles, delighted. "It seems extraordinarily infantile behavior, even for Americans, from whom, I must say, I have never expected very much in the way of maturity." Everyone at the table laughs. Vidal goes on. "But I cannot really talk about it, I do not understand it. I have never really understood Americans; I am an old man now, and I suppose I never will. There is something very nice about them, something very winning, but they seem so ignorant—so ignorant of life. Perhaps it is strange, but the only people from your country with whom I have ever made contact are black people—like my good friend, my discovery here," and he slaps me on the shoulder. "Perhaps it is because we, in Europe, whatever else we do not know, or have forgotten, know about suffering. We have suffered here. You have suffered, too. But most Americans do not yet know what anguish is. It is too bad, because the life of the West is in their hands." He turns to Ada. "I cannot help saying that I think it is a scandal—and we may all pay very dearly for it—that a civilized nation should elect to represent it a man who is so simple that he thinks the world is simple." And silence falls at the table and the four young faces stare at him.

"Well," says Pete, at last, turning to me, "you won't be bored, man, when you get back there."

"It's much too nice a night," I say, "to stay cooped up in this place, where all I can hear is my own records." We laugh. "Why don't we get out of here and find a sidewalk café?" I tap Pete's guitar. "Maybe we can find out if you've got any talent."

"Oh, talent I've got," says Pete, "but character, man, I'm lacking."

So, after some confusion about the bill, for which Vidal has already made himself responsible, we walk out into the Paris night. It is very strange to feel that, very soon now, these boulevards will not exist for me. People will be walking up and down, as they are tonight, and lovers will be murmuring in the black shadows of the plane trees, and there will be these same still figures on the benches or in the parks—but they will not exist for me, I will not be here. For a long while Paris will no longer exist for me, except in my mind; and only in the minds of some people will I exist any longer for Paris. After departure, only invisible things are left, perhaps the life of the world is held together by invisible chains of memory and loss and love. So many things, so many people, depart! And we can only repossess them in our minds. Perhaps this is what the old folks meant, what my mother and my father meant, when they counseled us to keep the faith.

We have taken a table at the Deux Magots and Pete strums on his guitar and begins to play this song:

> Preach the word, preach the word, preach the word!
> If I never, never see you any more.
> Preach the word, preach the word.
> And I'll meet you on Canaan's shore.

He has a strong, clear, boyish voice, like a young preacher's, and he is smiling as he sings his song. Ada and I look at each other and grin, and Vidal is smiling. The waiter looks a little worried, for we are already beginning to attract a crowd, but it is a summer night, the gendarmes on the corner do not seem to mind, and there will be time, anyway, to stop us.

Pete was not there, none of us were, the first time this song was needed; and no one now alive can imagine what that time was like. But the song has come down the bloodstained ages. I suppose this to mean that the song is still needed, still has its work to do.

The others are all, visibly, very proud of Pete; and we all join him, and people stop to listen:

> Testify! Testify!
> If I never, never see you any more!
> Testify! Testify!
> I'll meet you on Canaan's shore!

In the crowd that has gathered to listen to us, I see a face I know, the face of a North African prize fighter, who is no longer in the ring. I used to know him well in the old days, but have not seen him for a long time. He looks quite well, his face is shining, he is quite decently dressed. And something about the way he holds himself, not quite looking at our table, tells me that he has seen me, but does not want to risk a rebuff. So I call him. "Boona!"

And he turns, smiling, and comes loping over to our table, his hands in his pockets. Pete is still singing and Ada and Vidal have taken off on a conversation of their own. Ruth and Talley look curiously, expectantly, at Boona. Now that I have called him over, I feel somewhat uneasy. I realize that I do not know what he is doing now, or how he will get along with any of these people, and I can see in his eyes that he is delighted to be in the presence of two young girls. There are virtually no North African women in Paris, and not even the dirty, rat-faced girls who live, apparently, in cafés are willing to go with an Arab. So Boona is always looking for a girl, and because he is so deprived and because he is not Western, his techniques can be very unsettling. I know he is relieved that the girls are not French and not white. He looks briefly at Vidal and Ada. Vidal, also, though for different reasons, is always looking for a girl.

But Boona has always been very nice to me. Perhaps I am sorry that I called him over, but I do not want to snub him.

He claps one hand to the side of my head, as is his habit. "*Comment vas-tu, mon frère?* I have not see you, oh, for long time." And he asks me, as in the old days, "You all right? Nobody bother you?" And he laughs. "Ah! *Tu as fait le chemin, toi!* Now you are *vedette,* big star—wonderful!" He looks around the table, made a little uncomfortable by the silence that has fallen, now that Pete has stopped singing. "I have seen you in the movies—you know?—and I tell everybody, I know *him!*" He points to me, and laughs, and Ruth and Talley laugh with him. "That's right, man, you make me real proud, you make me cry!"

"Boona, I want you to meet some friends of mine." And I go round the table: "Ruth, Talley, Ada, Pete"—and he bows and shakes hands, his dark eyes gleaming with pleasure—*"et Monsieur Vidal, le metteur en scène du film qui t'a arraché des larmes."*

"Enchanté." But his attitude toward Vidal is colder, more distrustful. "Of course I have heard of Monsieur Vidal. He is the director of many films, many of them made me cry." This last statement is utterly, even insolently, insincere.

But Vidal, I think, is relieved that I will now be forced to speak to Boona and will leave him alone with Ada.

"Sit down," I say, "have a drink with us, let me have your news. What's been happening with you, what are you doing with yourself these days?"

"Ah," he sits down, "nothing very brilliant, my brother." He looks at me quickly, with a little smile. "You know, we have been having hard times here."

"Where are you from?" Ada asks him.

His brilliant eyes take her in entirely, but she does not flinch. "I am from Tunis." He says it proudly, with a little smile.

"From Tunis. I have never been to Africa, I would love to go one day."

He laughs. "Africa is a big place. Very big. There are many countries in Africa, many"—he looks briefly at Vidal—"different kinds of people, many colonies."

"But Tunis," she continues, in her innocence, "is free? Freedom is happening all over Africa. That's why I would like to go there."

"I have not been back for a long time," says Boona, "but all the news I get from Tunis, from my people, is not good."

"Wouldn't you like to go back?" Ruth asks.

Again he looks at Vidal. "That is not so easy."

Vidal smiles. "You know what I would like to do? There's a wonderful Spanish place not far from here, where we can listen to live music and dance a little." He turns to Ada. "Would you like that?"

He is leaving it up to me to get rid of Boona, and it is, of course, precisely for this reason that I cannot do it. Besides, it is no longer so simple.

"Oh, I'd love that," says Ada, and she turns to Boona. "Won't you come, too?"

"Thank you, mam'selle," he says, softly, and his tongue flicks briefly over his lower lip, and he smiles. He is very moved, people are not often nice to him.

In the Spanish place there are indeed a couple of Spanish guitars, drums, castanets, and a piano, but the uses to which these are being put carry one back, as Pete puts it, to the levee. "These are the wailingest Spanish cats I ever heard," says Ruth. "They didn't learn how to do this in Spain, no, they didn't, they been rambling. You ever hear anything like this going on in Spain?" Talley takes her out on the dance floor, which is already crowded. A very handsome Frenchwoman is dancing with an enormous, handsome black man, who seems to be her lover, who seems to have taught her how to dance. Apparently, they are known to the musicians, who egg them on with small cries of *"Olé!"* It is a very good-natured crowd, mostly foreigners, Spaniards, Swedes, Greeks. Boona takes Ada out on the dance floor while Vidal is answering some questions put to him by Pete on the entertainment situation in France. Vidal looks a little put out, and I am amused.

We are there for perhaps an hour, dancing, talking, and I am, at last, a little drunk. In spite of Boona, who is a very good and tireless dancer, Vidal continues his pursuit of Ada, and I begin to wonder if he will make it and I begin to wonder if I want him to.

I am still puzzling out my reaction when Pete, who has disappeared, comes in through the front door, catches my eye, and signals to me. I leave the table and follow him into the streets.

He looks very upset. "I don't want to bug you, man," he says, "but I fear your boy has goofed."

I know he is not joking. I think he is probably angry at Vidal because of Ada, and I wonder what I can do about it and why he should be telling me.

I stare at him, gravely, and he says, "It looks like he stole some money."

"Stole *money?* Who, Vidal?"

And then, of course, I get it, in the split second before he says, impatiently, "No, are you kidding? Your friend, the Tunisian."

I do not know what to say or what to do, and so I temporize with questions. All the time I am wondering if this can be true and what I can do about it if it is. The trouble is, I know that Boona steals, he would probably not be alive if he didn't, but I cannot say so to these children, who probably still imagine that everyone who steals is a thief. But he has never, to my knowledge, stolen from a friend. It seems unlike him. I have always thought of him as being better than that, and smarter than that. And so I cannot believe it, but neither can I doubt it. I do not know anything about Boona's life, these days. This causes me to realize that I do not really know much about Boona.

"Who did he steal it from?"

"From Ada. Out of her bag."

"How much?"

"Ten dollars. It's not an awful lot of money, but"—he grimaces—"none of us *have* an awful lot of money."

"I know." The dark side street on which we stand is nearly empty. The only sound on the street is the muffled music of the Spanish club. "How do you know it was Boona?"

He anticipates my own unspoken rejoinder. "Who else could it be? Besides—somebody *saw* him do it."

"Somebody saw him?"

"Yes."

I do not ask him who this person is, for fear that he will say it is Vidal.

"Well," I say, "I'll try to get it back." I think that I will take Boona aside and then replace the money myself. "Was it in dollars or in francs?"

"In francs."

I have no dollars and this makes it easier. I do not know how I can possibly face Boona and accuse him of stealing money from my friends. I would rather give him the benefit of even the faintest doubt. But, "Who saw him?" I ask.

"Talley. But we didn't want to make a thing about it—"

"Does Ada know it's gone?"

"Yes." He looks at me helplessly. "I know this makes you feel pretty bad, but we thought we'd better tell you, rather than"—lamely—"anybody else."

Now, Ada comes out of the club, carrying her ridiculous handbag, and with her face all knotted and sad. "Oh," she says, "I hate to cause all this trouble, it's not worth it, not for ten lousy dollars." I am astonished to see that she has been weeping, and tears come to her eyes now.

I put my arm around her shoulder. "Come on, now. You're not causing anybody any trouble and, anyway, it's nothing to cry about."

"It isn't your fault, Ada," Pete says, miserably.

"Oh, I ought to get a sensible handbag," she says, "like you're always telling me to do," and she laughs a little, then looks at me. "Please don't try to do anything about it. Let's just forget it."

"What's happening inside?" I ask her.

"Nothing. They're just talking. I think Mr. Vidal is dancing with Ruth. He's a great dancer, that little Frenchman."

"He's a great talker, too," Pete says.

"Oh, he doesn't mean anything," says Ada, "he's just having fun. He probably doesn't get a chance to talk to many American girls."

"He certainly made up for lost time tonight."

"Look," I say, "if Talley and Boona are alone, maybe you better go back in. We'll be in in a minute. Let's try to keep this as quiet as we can."

"Yeah," he says, "okay. We're going soon anyway, okay?"

"Yes," she tells him, "right away."

But as he turns away, Boona and Talley step out into the street, and it is clear that Talley feels that he has Boona under arrest. I almost laugh, the whole thing is beginning to resemble one of those mad French farces with people flying in and out of doors; but Boona comes straight to me.

"They say I stole money, my friend. You know me, you are the only one here who knows me, you know I would not do such a thing."

I look at him and I do not know what to say. Ada looks at him with her eyes full of tears and looks away. I take Boona's arm.

"We'll be back in a minute," I say. We walk a few paces up the dark, silent street.

"She say I take her money," he says. He, too, looks as though he is about to weep—but I do not know for which reason. "You know me, you know me almost twelve years, you think I do such a thing?"

Talley saw you, I want to say, but I cannot say it. Perhaps Talley only thought he saw him. Perhaps it is easy to see a boy who looks like Boona with his hand in an American girl's purse.

"If you not believe me," he says, "search me. Search me!" And he opens his arms wide, theatrically, and now there are tears standing in his eyes.

I do not know what his tears mean, but I certainly cannot search him. I want to say, I know you steal, I know you have to steal. Perhaps you took the money out of this girl's purse in order to eat tomorrow, in order not to be thrown into the streets tonight, in order to stay out of jail. This girl means nothing to you, after all, she is only an American, an American like me. Perhaps, I suddenly think, no girl means anything to you, or ever will again, they have beaten you too hard and kept you out in the gutter too long. And I also think, if you would steal from her, then of course you would lie to me, neither of us means anything to you; perhaps, in your eyes, we are simply luckier gangsters in a world which is run by gangsters. But I cannot say any of these things to Boona. I cannot say, Tell me the truth, nobody cares about the money any more.

So I say, "Of course I will not search you." And I realize that he knew I would not.

"I think it is that Frenchman who say I am a thief. They think we all are thieves." His eyes are bright and bitter. He looks over my shoulder. "They have all come out of the club now."

I look around and they are all there, in a little dark knot on the sidewalk.

"Don't worry," I say. "It doesn't matter."

"You believe me? My brother?" And his eyes look into mine with a terrible intensity.

"Yes," I force myself to say, "yes, of course, I believe you. Someone made a mistake, that's all."

"You know, the way American girls run around, they have their sack open all the time, she could have lost the money anywhere. Why she blame me? Because I come from Africa?" Tears are glittering on his face. "Here she come now."

And Ada comes up the street with her straight, determined walk. She walks straight to Boona and takes his hand. "I am sorry," she says, "for everything that happened. Please believe me. It isn't worth all this fuss. I'm sure you're a very nice person, and"—she falters—"I must have lost the money, I'm sure I lost it." She looks at him. "It isn't worth hurting your feelings, and I'm terribly sorry about it."

"I no take your money," he says. "Really, truly, I no take it. Ask him"—pointing to me, grabbing me by the arm, shaking me—"he know me for years, he will tell you that I never, never steal!"

"I'm sure," she says. "I'm sure."

I take Boona by the arm again. "Let's forget it. Let's forget it all. We're all going home now, and one of these days we'll have a drink again and we'll forget all about it, all right?"

"Yes," says Ada, "let us forget it." And she holds out her hand.

Boona takes it wonderingly. His eyes take her in again. "You are a very nice girl. Really. A very nice girl."

"I'm sure you're a nice person, too." She pauses. "Goodnight."

"Goodnight," he says, after a long silence.

Then he kisses me on both cheeks. *Au revoir, mon frère.*

"Au revoir, Boona."

After a moment we turn and walk away, leaving him standing there.

"Did he take it?" asks Vidal.

"I tell you, I *saw* him," says Talley.

"Well," I say, "it doesn't matter now." I look back and see Boona's stocky figure disappearing down the street.

"No," says Ada, "it doesn't matter." She looks up. "It's almost morning."

"I would gladly," says Vidal, stammering, "gladly—"

But she is herself again. "I wouldn't think of it. We had a wonderful time tonight, a wonderful time, and I wouldn't think of it." She turns to me with that urchin-like grin. "It was wonderful meeting you. I hope you won't have too much trouble getting used to the States again."

"Oh, I don't think I will," I say. And then, "I hope you won't."

"No," she says, "I don't think anything they can do will surprise me anymore."

"Which way are we all going?" asks Vidal. "I hope someone will share my taxi with me."

But he lives in the sixteenth arrondissement, which is not in anyone's direction. We walk him to the line of cabs standing under the clock at Odéon.

And we look each other in the face, in the growing morning light. His face looks weary and lined and lonely. He puts both hands on my shoulders and then puts one hand on the nape of my neck. "Do not forget me, Chico," he says. "You must come back and see us, one of these days. Many of us depend on you for many things."

"I'll be back," I say. "I'll never forget you."

He raises his eyebrows and smiles. *"Alors, Adieu."*

"Adieu, Vidal."

"I was happy to meet all of you," he says. He looks at Ada. "Perhaps we will meet again before you leave."

"Perhaps," she says. "Goodby, Monsieur Vidal."

"Goodby."

Vidal's cab drives away. "I also leave you now," I say. "I must go home and wake up my son and prepare for our journey."

I leave them standing on the corner, under the clock, which points to six. They look very strange and lost and determined, the four of them. Just before my cab turns off the boulevard, I wave to them and they wave back.

Mme. Dumont is in the hall, mopping the floor.

"Did all my family get home?" I ask. I feel very cheerful, I do not know why.

"Yes," she says, "they are all here. Paul is still sleeping."

"May I go in and get him?"

She looks at me in surprise. "Of course."

So I walk into her apartment and walk into the room where Paul lies sleeping. I stand over his bed for a long time.

Perhaps my thoughts traveled—travel through to him. He opens his eyes and smiles up at me. He puts a fist to his eyes and raises his arms. *"Bonjour, Papa."*

I lift him up. *"Bonjour.* How do you feel today?"

"Oh, I don't know yet," he says.

I laugh. I put him on my shoulder and walk out into the hall. Mme. Dumont looks up at him with her radiant, aging face.

"Ah," she says, "you are going on a journey! How does it feel?"

"He doesn't know yet," I tell her. I walk to the elevator door and open it, dropping Paul down to the crook of my arm.

She laughs again. "He will know later. What a journey! *Jusqu'au nouveau monde!*"

I open the cage and we step inside. "Yes," I say, "all the way to the new world." I press the button and the cage, holding my son and me, goes up.

FLANNERY O'CONNOR

(1925-1964)

Like Carson McCullers, Flannery O'Connor was born in Georgia and like McCullers, the characters she wrote about were grotesques. But while McCullers' characters long to be understood and to love, O'Connor's struggle with the God that won't let them be, wildly rejecting Him with gestures of violence and cruelty but tortured in their rejection by His grace. A practicing Catholic, O'Connor sees "from the standpoint of Christian Orthodoxy. This means that for me the meaning of life is centered in our Redemption by Christ and that what I see in the world I see in its relation to that"—even the murder of a family by an escaped criminal, as in "A Good Man Is Hard to Find." But this story, like O'Connor's work in general, is not typical religious fiction. Its tone is of black humor, gallows humor, humor in the presence of grotesquerie and horror. In the face of comic daemonic nothingness she celebrates the power of God.

A Good Man Is Hard to Find

FLANNERY O'CONNOR

The grandmother didn't want to go to Florida. She wanted to visit some of her connections in east Tennessee and she was seizing at every chance to change Bailey's mind. Bailey was the son she lived with, her only boy. He was sitting on the edge of his chair at the table, bent over the orange sports section of the *Journal*. "Now look here, Bailey," she said, "see here, read this," and she stood with one hand on her thin hip and the other rattling the newspaper at his bald head. "Here this fellow that calls himself The Misfit is aloose from the Federal Pen and headed toward Florida and you read here what it says he did to these people. Just you read it. I wouldn't take my children in any direction with a criminal like that aloose in it. I couldn't answer to my conscience if I did."

Bailey didn't look up from his reading so she wheeled around then and faced the children's mother, a young woman in slacks, whose face was as broad and innocent as a cabbage and was tied round with a green head-kerchief that had two points on the top like rabbit's ears. She was sitting on the sofa, feeding the baby his apricots out of a jar. "The children have been to Florida before," the old lady said. "You all ought to take them somewhere else for a change so they would see different parts of the world and be broad. They never have been to east Tennessee."

The children's mother didn't seem to hear her but the eight-year-old boy, John Wesley, a stocky child with glasses, said, "If you don't want to go to Florida, why dontcha stay at home?" He and the little girl, June Star, were reading the funny papers on the floor.

"She wouldn't stay at home to be queen for a day," June Star said without raising her yellow head.

"Yes and what would you do if this fellow, The Misfit, caught you?" the grandmother asked.

"I'd smack his face," John Wesley said.

"She wouldn't stay at home for a million bucks," June Star said. "Afraid she'd miss something. She has to go everywhere we go."

"All right, Miss," the grandmother said. "Just remember that the next time you want me to curl your hair."

June Star said her hair was naturally curly.

The next morning the grandmother was the first one in the car, ready to go. She had her big black valise that looked like the head of a hippopotamus in one corner, and underneath it she was hiding a basket with Pitty Sing, the cat, in it. She didn't intend for the cat to be left alone in the house for three days because he would miss her too much and she was afraid he might brush against one of the gas burners and accidentally asphyxiate himself. Her son, Bailey, didn't like to arrive at a motel with a cat.

She sat in the middle of the back seat with John Wesley and June Star on either side of her. Bailey and the children's mother and the baby sat in the front and they left Atlanta at eight forty-five with the mileage on the car at 55890. The grandmother wrote this down because she thought it would be interesting to say how many miles they had been when they got back. It took them twenty minutes to reach the outskirts of the city.

The old lady settled herself comfortably, removing her white cotton gloves and putting them up with her purse on the shelf in front of the back window. The children's mother still had on slacks and still had her head tied up in a green kerchief, but the grandmother had on a navy blue straw sailor hat with a bunch of white violets on the brim and a navy blue dress with a small white dot in the print. Her collar and cuffs were white organdy trimmed with lace and at her neckline she had pinned a purple spray of cloth violets containing a sachet. In case of an accident, anyone seeing her dead on the highway would know at once that she was a lady.

She said she thought it was going to be a good day for driving, neither too hot nor too cold, and she cautioned Bailey that the speed limit was fifty-five miles an hour and that the patrolmen hid themselves behind billboards and small clumps of trees and sped out after you before you had a chance to slow down. She pointed out interesting details of the scenery: Stone Mountain; the blue granite that in some places came up to both sides of the highway; the brilliant red clay banks slightly streaked with purple; and the various crops that made rows of green lace-work on the ground. The trees were full of silver-white sunlight and the meanest of them sparkled. The children were reading comic magazines and their mother had gone back to sleep.

"Let's go through Georgia fast so we won't have to look at it much," John Wesley said.

"If I were a little boy," said the grandmother, "I wouldn't talk about my native state that way. Tennessee has the mountains and Georgia has the hills."

"Tennessee is just a hillbilly dumping ground," John Wesley said, "and Georgia is a lousy state too."

"You said it," June Star said.

"In my time," said the grandmother, folding her thin veined fingers, "children were more respectful of their native states and their parents and everything else. People did right then. Oh look at the cute little pickaninny!" she said and pointed to a Negro child standing in the door of a shack. "Wouldn't that make a picture, now?" she asked and they all turned and looked at the little Negro out of the back window. He waved.

"He didn't have any britches on," June said.

"He probably didn't have any," the grandmother explained. "Little niggers in the country don't have things like we do. If I could paint, I'd paint that picture," she said.

The children exchanged comic books.

The grandmother offered to hold the baby and the children's mother passed him over the front seat to her. She set him on her knee and bounced him and told him about the things they were passing. She rolled her eyes and screwed up her mouth and stuck her leathery thin face into his smooth bland one. Occasionally he gave her a faraway smile. They passed a large cotton field with five or six graves fenced in the middle of it, like a small island. "Look at the graveyard!" the grandmother said, pointing it out. "That was the old family burying ground. That belonged to the plantation."

"Where's the plantation?" John Wesley asked.

"Gone With the Wind," said the grandmother. "Ha. Ha."

When the children finished all the comic books they had brought, they opened the lunch and ate it. The grandmother ate a peanut butter sandwich and an olive and would not let the children throw the box and the paper napkins out the window. When there was nothing else to do they played a game by choosing a cloud and making the other two guess what shape it suggested. John Wesley took one the shape of a cow and June Star guessed a cow and John Wesley said, no, an automobile, and June Star said he didn't play fair, and they began to slap each other over the grandmother.

The grandmother said she would tell them a story if they would keep quiet. When she told a story, she rolled her eyes and waved her head and was very dramatic. She said once when she was a maiden lady she had been courted by a Mr. Edgar Atkins Teagarden from Jasper, Georgia. She said he was a very good-looking man and a gentleman and that he brought her a watermelon every Saturday afternoon with his initials cut in it, E. A. T. Well, one Saturday, she said, Mr. Teagarden brought the watermelon and there was nobody at home and he left it on the front porch and returned in his buggy to Jasper, but she never got the watermelon, she said, because a nigger boy ate it when he saw the initials, E. A. T.! This story tickled John Wesley's funny bone and he giggled and giggled but June Star didn't think it was any good. She said she wouldn't marry a man that just brought her a watermelon on Saturday. The grandmother said she would have done well to marry Mr. Teagarden because he was a gentleman and had bought Coca-Cola stock when it first came out and that he had died only a few years ago, a very wealthy man.

They stopped at The Tower for barbecued sandwiches. The Tower was a part stucco and part wood filling station and dance hall set in a clearing outside of Timothy. A fat man named Red Sammy Butts ran it and there were signs stuck here and there on the building and for miles up and down the highway saying, TRY RED SAMMY'S FAMOUS BARBECUE. NONE LIKE FAMOUS RED SAMMY'S! RED SAM! THE FAT BOY WITH THE HAPPY LAUGH. A VETERAN! SAMMY'S YOUR MAN!

Red Sammy was lying on the bare ground outside The Tower with his head under a truck while a gray monkey about a foot high, chained to a small chinaberry tree, chattered nearby. The monkey sprang back into the tree and got on the highest limb as soon as he saw the children jump out of the car and run toward him.

Inside, The Tower was a long dark room with a counter at one end and tables at the other and dancing space in the middle. They all sat down at a broad table next to the nickelodeon and Red Sam's wife, a tall burnt-brown woman with hair and eyes lighter than her skin, came and took their order. The children's mother put a dime in the machine and played "The Tennessee Waltz," and the grandmother said that tune always made her want to dance. She asked Bailey if he would like to dance but he only glared at her. He didn't have a naturally sunny disposition like she did and trips made him nervous. The grandmother's brown eyes were very bright. She swayed her head from side to side and pretended she was dancing in her chair. June Star said play something she could tap to so the children's mother put in another dime and played a fast number and June Star stepped out onto the dance floor and did her tap routine.

"Ain't she cute?" Red Sam's wife said, leaning over the counter. "Would you like to come be my little girl?"

"No I certainly wouldn't," June Star said. "I wouldn't live in a broken-down place like this for a million bucks!" and she ran back to the table.

"Ain't she cute?" the woman repeated, stretching her mouth politely.

"Aren't you ashamed?" hissed the grandmother.

Red Sam came in and told his wife to quit lounging on the counter and hurry with these people's order. His khaki trousers reached just to his hip bones and his stomach hung over them like a sack of meal swaying under his shirt. He came over and sat down at a table nearby and let out a combination sigh and yodel. "You can't win," he said. "You can't win," and he wiped his sweating red face off with a gray handkerchief. "These days you don't know who to trust," he said. "Ain't that the truth?"

"People are certainly not nice like they used to be," said the grandmother.

"Two fellers come in here last week," Red Sammy said, "driving a Chrysler. It was a old beat-up car but it was a good one and these boys looked all right to me. Said they worked at the mill and you know I let them fellers charge the gas they bought? Now why did I do that?"

"Because you're a good man!" the grandmother said at once.

"Yes'm, I suppose so," Red Sam said as if he were struck with the answer.

His wife brought the orders, carrying the five plates all at once without a tray, two in each hand and one balanced on her arm. "It isn't a soul in this green world of God's that you can trust," she said. "And I don't count anybody out of that, not nobody," she repeated, looking at Red Sammy.

"Did you read about that criminal, The Misfit, that's escaped?" asked the grandmother.

"I wouldn't be a bit surprised if he didn't attact this place right here," said the woman. "If he hears about it being here, I wouldn't be none surprised to see him. If he hears it's two cent in the cash register, I wouldn't be a tall surprised if he . . ."

"That'll do," Red Sam said. "Go bring these people their Co'Colas," and the woman went off to get the rest of the order.

"A good man is hard to find," Red Sammy said. "Everything is getting terrible. I remember the day you could go off and leave your screen door unlatched. Not no more."

He and the grandmother discussed better times. The old lady said that in her opinion Europe was entirely to blame for the way things were now. She said the way Europe acted you would think we were made of money and Red Sam said it was no use talking about it, she was exactly right. The children ran outside into the white sunlight and looked at the monkey in the lacy chinaberry tree. He was busy catching fleas on himself and biting each one carefully between his teeth as if it were a delicacy.

They drove off again into the hot afternoon. The grandmother took cat naps and woke up every few minutes with her own snoring. Outside of Toombsboro she woke up and recalled an old plantation that she had visited in this neighborhood once when she was a young lady. She said the house had six white columns across the front and that there was an avenue of oaks leading up to it and two little wooden trellis arbors on either side in front where you sat down with your suitor after a stroll in the garden. She recalled exactly which road to turn off to get to it. She knew that Bailey would not be willing to lose any time looking at an old house, but the more she talked about it, the more she wanted to see it once again and find out if the little twin arbors were still standing. "There was a secret panel in this house," she said craftily, not telling the truth but wishing that she were, "and the story went that all the family silver was hidden in it when Sherman came through but it was never found . . ."

"Hey!" John Wesley said. "Let's go see it! We'll find it! We'll poke all the woodwork and find it! Who lives there? Where do you turn off at? Hey Pop, can't we turn off there?"

"We never have seen a house with a secret panel!" June Star shrieked. "Let's go to the house with the secret panel! Hey, Pop, can't we go see the house with the secret panel!"

"It's not far from here, I know," the grandmother said. "It wouldn't take over twenty minutes."

Bailey was looking straight ahead. His jaw was as rigid as a horseshoe. "No," he said.

The children began to yell and scream that they wanted to see the house with the secret panel. John Wesley kicked the back of the front seat and June Star hung over her mother's shoulder and whined desperately into her ear that they never had any fun even on their vacation, and that they could never do what THEY wanted to do. The baby began to scream and John Wesley kicked the back of the seat so hard that his father could feel the blows in his kidney.

"All right!" he shouted, and drew the car to a stop at the side of the road. "Will you all shut up? Will you all just shut up for one second? If you don't shut up, we won't go anywhere."

"It would be very educational for them," the grandmother murmured.

"All right," Bailey said, "but get this: this is the only time we're going to stop for anything like this. This is the one and only time."

"The dirt road that you have to turn down is about a mile back," the grandmother directed. "I marked it when we passed."

"A dirt road," Bailey groaned.

After they had turned around and were headed toward the dirt road, the grandmother recalled other points about the house, the beautiful glass over the front doorway and the candle-lamp in the hall. John Wesley said that the secret panel was probably in the fireplace.

"You can't go inside this house," Bailey said. "You don't know who lives there."

"While you all talk to the people in front, I'll run around behind and get in a window," John Wesley suggested.

"We'll all stay in the car," his mother said.

They turned onto the dirt road and the car raced roughly along in a swirl of pink dust. The grandmother recalled the times when there were no paved roads and thirty miles was a day's journey. The dirt road was hilly and there were sudden washes in it and sharp curves on dangerous embankments. All at once they would be on a hill, looking down over the blue tops of trees for miles around, then the next minute, they would be in a red depression with the dust-coated trees looking down on them.

"This place had better turn up in a minute," Bailey said, "or I'm going to turn around."

The road looked as if no one had traveled on it in months.

"It's not much farther," the grandmother said and just as she said it, a horrible thought came to her. The thought was so embarrassing that she turned red in the face and her eyes dilated and her feet jumped up, upsetting her valise in the corner. The instant the valise moved, the newspaper top she had over the basket under it rose with a snarl and Pitty Sing, the cat, sprang onto Bailey's shoulder.

The children were thrown to the floor and their mother, clutching the baby, was thrown out the door onto the ground, the old lady was thrown into the front seat. The car turned over once and landed right-side-up in a gulch on the side of the road. Bailey remained in the driver's seat with the cat—gray-striped with a broad white face and an orange nose—clinging to his neck like a caterpillar.

As soon as the children saw they could move their arms and legs, they scrambled out of the car, shouting. "We've had an ACCIDENT!" The grandmother was curled up under the dashboard, hoping she was injured so that Bailey's wrath would not come down on her all at once. The horrible thought she had had before the accident was that the house she had remembered so vividly was not in Georgia but in Tennessee.

Bailey removed the cat from his neck with both hands and flung it out the window against the side of a pine tree. Then he got out of the car and started looking for the children's mother. She was sitting against the side of the red gutted ditch, holding the screaming baby, but she only had a cut down her face and a broken shoulder. "We've had an ACCIDENT!" the children screamed in a frenzy of delight.

"But nobody's killed," June Star said with disappointment as the grandmother limped out of the car, her hat still pinned to her head but the broken front brim standing up at a jaunty angle and the violet spray hanging off the side. They all sat down in the ditch, except the children, to recover from the shock. They were all shaking.

"Maybe a car will come along," said the children's mother hoarsely.

"I believe I have injured an organ," said the grandmother, pressing her side, but no one answered her. Bailey's teeth were clattering. He had on a yellow sport shirt with bright blue parrots designed in it and his face was as yellow as the shirt. The grandmother decided that she would not mention that the house was in Tennessee.

The road was about ten feet above and they could see only the tops of the trees on the other side of it. Behind the ditch they were sitting in there were more woods, tall and dark and deep. In a few minutes they saw a car some distance away on top of a hill, coming slowly as if the occupants were watching them. The grandmother stood up and waved both arms dramatically to attract their attention. The car continued to come on slowly, disappeared around a bend and appeared again, moving even slower, on top of the hill they had gone over. It was a big black battered hearse-like automobile. There were three men in it.

It came to a stop just over them and for some minutes, the driver looked down with a steady expressionless gaze to where they were sitting, and didn't speak. Then he turned his head and muttered something to the other two and they got out. One was a fat boy in black trousers and a red sweat shirt with a silver stallion embossed on the front of it. He moved around on the right side of them and stood staring, his mouth partly open in a kind of loose grin. The other had on khaki pants and a blue striped coat and a gray hat pulled down very low, hiding most of his face. He came around slowly on the left side. Neither spoke.

The driver got out of the car and stood by the side of it, looking down at them. He was an older man than the other two. His hair was just beginning to gray and he wore silver-rimmed spectacles that gave him a scholarly look. He had a long creased face and didn't have on any shirt or undershirt. He had on blue jeans that were too tight for him and was holding a black hat and a gun. The two boys also had guns.

"We've had an ACCIDENT!" the children screamed.

The grandmother had the peculiar feeling that the bespectacled man was someone she knew. His face was as familiar to her as if she had known him all her life but she could not recall who he was. He moved away from the car and began to come down the embankment, placing his feet carefully so that he wouldn't slip. He had on tan and white shoes and no socks, and his ankles were red and thin. "Good afternoon," he said. "I see you all had you a little spill."

"We turned over twice!" said the grandmother.

"Oncet," he corrected. "We seen it happen. Try their car and see will it run, Hiram," he said quietly to the boy with the gray hat.

"What you got that gun for?" John Wesley asked. "Whatcha gonna do with that gun?"

"Lady," the man said to the children's mother, "would you mind calling them children to sit down by you? Children make me ner-

vous. I want all you all to sit down right together there where you're
at."

"What are you telling us what to do for?" June Star asked.

Behind them the line of woods gaped like a dark open mouth.
"Come here," said their mother.

"Look here now," Bailey began suddenly, "we're in a predicament!
We're in . . ."

The grandmother shrieked. She scrambled to her feet and stood
staring. "You're The Misfit!" she said. "I recognized you at once."

"Yes'm," the man said, smiling slightly as if he were pleased in
spite of himself to be known, "but it would have been better for all
of you, lady, if you hadn't of reckernized me."

Bailey turned his head sharply and said something to his mother
that shocked even the children. The old lady began to cry and The
Misfit reddened.

"Lady," he said, "don't you get upset. Sometimes a man says things
he don't mean. I don't reckon he meant to talk to you thataway."

"You wouldn't shoot a lady, would you?" the grandmother said
and removed a clean handkerchief from her cuff and began to slap at
her eyes with it.

The Misfit pointed the toe of his shoe into the ground and made a
little hole and then covered it up again. "I would hate to have to,"
he said.

"Listen," the grandmother almost screamed, "I know you're a good
man. You don't look a bit like you have common blood. I know you
must come from nice people!"

"Yes mam," he said, "finest people in the world." When he smiled
he showed a row of strong white teeth. "God never made a finer
woman than my mother and my daddy's heart was pure gold," he
said. The boy with the red sweat shirt had come around behind them
and was standing with his gun at his hip. The Misfit squatted down
on the ground. "Watch them children, Bobby Lee," he said. "You
know they make me nervous." He looked at the six of them huddled
together in front of him and he seemed to be embarrassed as if he
couldn't think of anything to say. "Ain't a cloud in the sky," he
remarked, looking up at it. "Don't see no sun but don't see no cloud
neither."

"Yes, it's a beautiful day," said the grandmother. "Listen," she
said, "you shouldn't call yourself The Misfit because I know you're a
good man at heart. I can just look at you and tell."

"Hush!" Bailey yelled. "Hush! Everybody shut up and let me
handle this!" He was squatting in the position of a runner about to
sprint forward but he didn't move.

"I pre-chate that, lady," The Misfit said and drew a little circle in
the ground with the butt of his gun.

"It'll take a half a hour to fix this here car," Hiram called, looking over the raised hood of it.

"Well, first you and Bobby Lee get him and that little boy to step over yonder with you," The Misfit said, pointing to Bailey and John Wesley. "The boys want to ask you something," he said to Bailey. "Would you mind stepping back in them woods there with them?"

"Listen," Bailey began, "we're in a terrible predicament. Nobody realizes what this is," and his voice cracked. His eyes were as blue and intense as the parrots in his shirt and he remained perfectly still.

The grandmother reached up to adjust her hat brim as if she were going to the woods with him but it came off in her hand. She stood staring at it and after a second she let it fall on the ground. Hiram pulled Bailey up by the arm as if he were assisting an old man. John Wesley caught hold of his father's hand and Bobby Lee followed. They went off toward the woods and just as they reached the dark edge, Bailey turned and supporting himself against a gray naked pine trunk, he shouted, "I'll be back in a minute, Mamma, wait on me!"

"Come back this instant!" his mother shrilled but they all disappeared into the woods.

"Bailey Boy!" the grandmother called in a tragic voice but she found she was looking at The Misfit squatting on the ground in front of her. "I just know you're a good man," she said desperately. "You're not a bit common!"

"Nome, I ain't a good man," The Misfit said after a second as if he had considered her statement carefully, "but I ain't the worst in the world neither. My daddy said I was different breed of dog from my brothers and sisters. 'You know,' Daddy said, 'it's some that can live their whole life out without asking about it and it's others has to know why it is, and this boy is one of the latters. He's going to be into everything!' " He put on his black hat and looked up suddenly and then away deep into the woods as if he were embarrassed again. "I'm sorry I don't have on a shirt before you ladies," he said, hunching his shoulders slightly. "We buried our clothes that we had on when we escaped and we're just making do until we can get better. We borrowed these from some folks we met," he explained.

"That's perfectly all right," the grandmother said. "Maybe Bailey has an extra shirt in his suitcase."

"I'll look and see terrectly," The Misfit said.

"Where are they taking him?" the children's mother screamed.

"Daddy was a card himself," the Misfit said. "You couldn't put anything over on him. He never got in trouble with the Authorities though. Just had the knack of handling them."

"You could be honest too if you'd only try," said the grandmother. "Think how wonderful it would be to settle down and live a comfortable life and not have to think about somebody chasing you all the time."

The Misfit kept scratching in the ground with the butt of his gun as if he were thinking about it. "Yes'm, somebody is always after you," he murmured.

The grandmother noticed how thin his shoulder blades were just behind his hat because she was standing up looking down on him. "Do you ever pray?" she asked.

He shook his head. All she saw was the black hat wiggle between his shoulder blades. "Nome," he said.

There was a pistol shot from the woods, followed closely by another. Then silence. The old lady's head jerked around. She could hear the wind move through the tree tops like a long satisfied insuck of breath. "Bailey Boy!" she called.

"I was a gospel singer for a while," The Misfit said. "I been most everything. Been in the arm service, both land and sea, at home and abroad, been twict married, been an undertaker, been with the railroads, plowed Mother Earth, been in a tornado, seen a man burnt alive oncet," and he looked up at the children's mother and the little girl who were sitting close together, their faces white and their eyes glassy; "I even seen a woman flogged," he said.

"Pray, pray," the grandmother began, "pray, pray . . ."

"I never was a bad boy that I remember of," The Misfit said in an almost dreamy voice, "but somewheres along the line I done something wrong and got sent to the penitentiary. I was buried alive," and he looked up and held her attention to him by a steady stare.

"That's when you should have started to pray," she said. "What did you do to get sent to the penitentiary that first time?"

"Turn to the right, it was a wall," The Misfit said, looking up again at the cloudless sky. "Turn to the left, it was a wall. Look up it was a ceiling, look down it was a floor. I forgot what I done, lady. I set there and set there, trying to remember what it was I done and I ain't recalled it to this day. Oncet in a while, I would think it was coming to me, but it never come."

"Maybe they put you in by mistake," the old lady said vaguely.

"Nome," he said. "It wasn't no mistake. They had the papers on me."

"You must have stolen something," she said.

The Misfit sneered slightly. "Nobody had nothing I wanted," he said. "It was a head-doctor at the penitentiary said what I had done was kill my daddy but I know that for a lie. My daddy died in nineteen ought nineteen of the epidemic flu and I never had a thing to do with it. He was buried in the Mount Hopewell Baptist churchyard and you can go there and see for yourself."

"If you would pray," the old lady said, "Jesus would help you."

"That's right," The Misfit said.

"Well then, why don't you pray?" she asked trembling with delight suddenly.

"I don't want no hep," he said. "I'm doing all right by myself."

Bobby Lee and Hiram came ambling back from the woods. Bobby Lee was dragging a yellow shirt with bright blue parrots in it.

"Throw me that shirt, Bobby Lee," The Misfit said. The shirt came flying at him and landed on his shoulder and he put it on. The grandmother couldn't name what the shirt reminded her of. "No, lady," The Misfit said while he was buttoning it up. "I found out the crime don't matter. You can do one thing or you can do another, kill a man or take a tire off his car, because sooner or later you're going to forget what it was you done and just be punished for it."

The children's mother had begun to make heaving noises as if she couldn't get her breath. "Lady," he asked, "would you and that little girl like to step off yonder with Bobby Lee and Hiram and join your husband?"

"Yes, thank you," the mother said faintly. Her left arm dangled helplessly and she was holding the baby, who had gone to sleep, in the other. "Hep that lady up, Hiram," The Misfit said as she struggled to climb out of the ditch, "and Bobby Lee, you hold onto that little girl's hand."

"I don't want to hold hands with him," June Star said. "He reminds me of a pig."

The fat boy blushed and laughed and caught her by the arm and pulled her off into the woods after Hiram and her mother.

Alone with The Misfit, the grandmother found that she had lost her voice. There was not a cloud in the sky nor any sun. There was nothing around her but woods. She wanted to tell him that he must pray. She opened and closed her mouth several times before anything came out. Finally she found herself saying, "Jesus, Jesus," meaning Jesus will help you, but the way she was saying it, it sounded as if she might be cursing.

"Yes'm," The Misfit said as if he agreed. "Jesus thown everything off balance. It was the same case with Him as with me except He hadn't committed any crime and they could prove I had committed one because they had the papers on me. Of course," he said, "they never shown me any papers. That's why I sign myself now. I said long ago, you get you a signature and sign everything you do and keep a copy of it. Then you'll know what you done and you can hold up the crime to the punishment and see do they match and in the end you'll have something to prove you ain't been treated right. I call myself The Misfit," he said, "because I can't make what all I done wrong fit what all I gone through in punishment."

There was a piercing scream from the woods, followed closely by a pistol report. "Does it seem right to you, lady, that one is punished a heap and another ain't punished at all?"

"Jesus!" the old lady cried. "You've got good blood! I know you wouldn't shoot a lady! I know you come from nice people! Pray! Jesus, you ought not to shoot a lady. I'll give you all the money I've got!"

"Lady," The Misfit said, looking beyond her far into the woods, "there never was a body that give the undertaker a tip."

There were two more pistol reports and the grandmother raised her head like a parched old turkey hen crying for water and called, "Bailey Boy, Bailey Boy!" as if her heart would break.

"Jesus was the only One that ever raised the dead," The Misfit continued, "and He shouldn't have done it. He thown everything off balance. If He did what He said, then it's nothing for you to do but thow away everything and follow Him, and if He didn't, then it's nothing for you to do but enjoy the few minutes you got left the best way you can—by killing somebody or burning down his house or doing some other meanness to him. No pleasure but meanness," he said and his voice had become almost a snarl.

"Maybe He didn't raise the dead," the old lady mumbled, not knowing what she was saying and feeling so dizzy that she sank down in the ditch with her legs twisted under her.

"I wasn't there so I can't say He didn't," The Misfit said. "I wisht I had of been there," he said, hitting the ground with his fist. "It ain't right I wasn't there because if I had of been there I would of known. Listen lady," he said in a high voice, "if I had of been there I would of known and I wouldn't be like I am now." His voice seemed about to crack and the grandmother's head cleared for an instant. She saw the man's face twisted close to her own as if he were going to cry and she murmured, "Why you're one of my babies. You're one of my own children!" She reached out and touched him on the shoulder. The Misfit sprang back as if a snake had bitten him and shot her three times through the chest. Then he put his gun down on the ground and took off his glasses and began to clean them.

Hiram and Bobby Lee returned from the woods and stood over the ditch, looking down at the grandmother who half sat and half lay in a puddle of blood with her legs crossed under her like a child's and her face smiling up at the cloudless sky.

Without his glasses, The Misfit's eyes were red-rimmed and pale and defenseless-looking. "Take her off and thow her where you thown the others," he said, picking up the cat that was rubbing itself against his leg.

"She was a talker, wasn't she?" Bobby Lee said, sliding down the ditch with a yodel.

"She would of been a good woman," The Misfit said, "if it had been somebody there to shoot her every minute of her life."

"Some fun!" Bobby Lee said.

"Shut up, Bobby Lee," The Misfit said. "It's no real pleasure in life."

JOHN UPDIKE

(1932—)

"Separating" is one of a number of Updike stories about the Maples,
stories that describe with amazing precision the tensions and emotional complexities of middle-class relationships. The style is so careful, the tone so low-keyed, almost placid, in keeping with the emotional balance of the characters, that the final tearful question by
Dickie registers powerfully. (Compare this to the direct expression of
strong feeling in Olsen's "I Stand Here Ironing.")

Besides his numerous short stories, mostly published first in *The
New Yorker*, Updike has written a number of popular and critically
respected novels, including *Rabbit, Run; Couples;* and *Rabbit
Redux.*

Separating

JOHN UPDIKE

The day was fair. Brilliant. All that June the weather had mocked
the Maples' internal misery with solid sunlight—golden shafts and
cascades of green in which their conversations had wormed unseeing,
their sad murmuring selves the only stain in Nature. Usually by this
time of the year they had acquired tans; but when they met their
elder daughter's plane on her return from a year in England they

were almost as pale as she, though Judith was too dazzled by the sunny opulent jumble of her native land to notice. They did not spoil her homecoming by telling her immediately. Wait a few days, let her recover from jet lag, had been one of their formulations, in that string of gray dialogues—over coffee, over cocktails, over Cointreau—that had shaped the strategy of their dissolution, while the earth performed its annual stunt of renewal unnoticed beyond their closed windows. Richard had thought to leave at Easter; Joan had insisted they wait until the four children were at last assembled, with all exams passed and ceremonies attended, and the bauble of summer to console them. So he had drudged away, in love, in dread, repairing screens, getting the mowers sharpened, rolling and patching their new tennis court.

The court, clay, had come through its first winter pitted and windswept bare of redcoat. Years ago, the Maples had observed how often, among their friends, divorce followed a dramatic home improvement, as if the marriage were making one last twitchy effort to live; their own worst crisis had come amid the plaster dust and exposed plumbing of a kitchen renovation. Yet, a summer ago, as canary-yellow bulldozers gaily churned a grassy, daisy-dotted knoll into a muddy plateau, and a crew of pigtailed young men raked and tamped clay into a plane, this transformation did not strike them as ominous, but festive in its impudence; their marriage could rend the earth for fun. The next spring, waking each day at dawn to a sliding sensation as if the bed were being tipped, Richard found the barren tennis court, its net and tapes still rolled in the barn, an environment congruous with his mood of purposeful desolation, and the crumbling of handfuls of clay into cracks and holes (dogs had frolicked on the court in a thaw; rivulets had evolved trenches) an activity suitably elemental and interminable. In his sealed heart he hoped the day would never come.

Now it was here. A Friday. Judith was reacclimated; all four children were assembled, before jobs and camps and visits again scattered them. Joan thought they should be told one by one. Richard was for making an announcement at the table. She said, "I think just making an announcement is a cop-out. They'll start quarrelling and playing to each other instead of focussing. They're each individuals, you know, not just some corporate obstacle to your freedom."

"O.K., O.K. I agree." Joan's plan was exact. That evening, they were giving Judith a belated welcome-home dinner, of lobster and champagne. Then, the party over, they, the two of them, who nineteen years before would push her in a baby carriage along Tenth Street to Washington Square, were to walk her out of the house, to the bridge across the salt creek, and tell her, swearing her to secrecy.

Then Richard Jr., who was going directly from work to a rock concert in Boston, would be told, either late when he returned on the train or early Saturday morning before he went off to his job; he was seventeen and employed as one of a golf-course maintenance crew. Then the two younger children, John and Margaret, could, as the morning wore on, be informed.

"Mopped up, as it were," Richard said.

"Do you have any better plan? That leaves you the rest of Saturday to answer any questions, pack, and make your wonderful departure."

"No," he said, meaning he had no better plan, and agreed to hers, though it had an edge of false order, a plea for control in the semblance of its achievement, like Joan's long chore lists and financial accountings and, in the days when he first knew her, her too copious lecture notes. Her plan turned one hurdle for him into four—four knife-sharp walls, each with a sheer blind drop on the other side.

All spring he had been morbidly conscious of insides and outsides, of barriers and partitions. He and Joan stood as a thin barrier between the children and the truth. Each moment was a partition, with the past on one side and the future on the other, a future containing this unthinkable *now*. Beyond four knifelike walls a new life for him waited vaguely. His skull cupped a secret, a white face, a face both frightened and soothing, both strange and known, that he wanted to shield from tears, which he felt all about him, solid as the sunlight. So haunted, he had become obsessed with battening down the house against his absence, replacing screens and sash cords, hinges and latches—a Houdini making things snug before his escape.

The lock. He had still to replace a lock on one of the doors of the screened porch. The task, like most such, proved more difficult than he had imagined. The old lock, aluminum frozen by corrosion, had been deliberately rendered obsolete by manufacturers. Three hardware stores had nothing that even approximately matched the mortised hole its removal (surprisingly easy) left. Another hole had to be gouged, with bits too small and saws too big, and the old hole fitted with a block of wood—the chisels dull, the saw rusty, his fingers thick with lack of sleep. The sun poured down, beyond the porch, on a world of neglect. The bushes already needed pruning, the windward side of the house was shedding flakes of paint, rain would get in when he was gone, insects, rot, death. His family, all those he would lose, filtered through the edges of his awareness as he struggled with screw holes, splinters, opaque instructions, minutiae of metal.

Judith sat on the porch, a princess returned from exile. She regaled them with stories of fuel shortages, of bomb scares in the Underground, of Pakistani workmen loudly lusting after her as she walked past on her way to dance school. Joan came and went, in and out of the house, calmer than she should have been, praising his struggles with the lock as if this were one more and not the last of their chain of shared chores. The younger of his sons, John, now at fifteen suddenly, unwittingly handsome, for a few minutes held the rickety screen door while his father clumsily hammered and chiselled, each blow a kind of sob in Richard's ears. His younger daughter, having been at a slumber party, slept on the porch hammock through all the noise—heavy and pink, trusting and forsaken. Time, like the sunlight, continued relentlessly; the sunlight slowly slanted. Today was one of the longest days. The lock clicked, worked. He was through. He had a drink; he drank it on the porch, listening to his daughter. "It was so sweet," she was saying, "during the worst of it, how all the butcher's and bakery shops kept open by candlelight. They're all so plucky and cute. From the papers, things sounded so much worse here—people shooting people in gas lines, and everybody freezing."

Richard asked her, "Do you still want to live in England forever?" *Forever:* the concept, now a reality upon him, pressed and scratched at the back of his throat.

"No," Judith confessed, turning her oval face to him, its eyes still childishly far apart, but the lips set as over something succulent and satisfactory. "I was anxious to come home. I'm an American." She was a woman. They had raised her; he and Joan had endured together to raise her, alone of the four. The others had still some raising left in them. Yet it was the thought of telling Judith—the image of her, their first baby, walking between them arm in arm to the bridge—that broke him. The partition between himself and the tears broke. Richard sat down to the celebratory meal with the back of his throat aching; the champagne, the lobster seemed phases of sunshine; he saw them and tasted them through tears. He blinked, swallowed, croakily joked about hay fever. The tears would not stop leaking through; they came not through a hole that could be plugged but through a permeable spot in a membrane, steadily, purely, endlessly, fruitfully. They became, his tears, a shield for himself against these others—their faces, the fact of their assembly, a last time as innocents, at a table where he sat the last time as head. Tears dropped from his nose as he broke the lobster's back; salt flavored his champagne as he sipped it; the raw clench at the back of his throat was delicious. He could not help himself.

His children tried to ignore his tears. Judith, on his right, lit a cigarette, gazed upward in the direction of her too energetic, too sophisticated exhalation; on her other side, John earnestly bent his face to the extraction of the last morsels—legs, tail segments—from the scarlet corpse. Joan, at the opposite end of the table, glanced at him surprised, her reproach displaced by a quick grimace, of forgiveness, or of salute to his superior gift of strategy. Between them, Margaret, no longer called Bean, thirteen and large for her age, gazed from the other side of his pane of tears as if into a shopwindow at something she coveted—at her father, a crystalline heap of splinters and memories. It was not she, however, but John who, in the kitchen, as they cleared the plates and carapaces away, asked Joan the question: *"Why is Daddy crying?"*

Richard heard the question but not the murmured answer. Then he heard Bean cry, "Oh, no-oh!"—the faintly dramatized exclamation of one who had long expected it.

John returned to the table carrying a bowl of salad. He nodded tersely at his father and his lips shaped the conspiratorial words "She told."

"Told what?" Richard asked aloud, insanely.

The boy sat down as if to rebuke his father's distraction with the example of his own good manners and said quietly, "The separation."

Joan and Margaret returned; the child, in Richard's twisted vision, seemed diminished in size, and relieved, relieved to have had the boogeyman at last proved real. He called out to her—the distances at the table had grown immense—"You knew, you always knew," but the clenching at the back of his throat prevented him from making sense of it. From afar he heard Joan talking, levelly, sensibly, reciting what they had prepared: it was a separation for the summer, an experiment. She and Daddy both agreed it would be good for them; they needed space and time to think; they liked each other but did not make each other happy enough, somehow.

Judith, imitating her mother's factual tone, but in her youth off-key, too cool, said, "I think it's silly. You should either live together or get divorced."

Richard's crying, like a wave that has crested and crashed, had become tumultuous; but it was overtopped by another tumult, for John, who had been so reserved, now grew larger and larger at the table. Perhaps his younger sister's being credited with knowing set him off. "Why didn't you *tell* us?" he asked, in a large round voice quite unlike his own. "You should have *told* us you weren't getting along."

Richard was startled into attempting to force words through his tears. "We *do* get along, that's the trouble, so it doesn't show even to us—" "That we do not love each other" was the rest of the sentence; he couldn't finish it.

Joan finished for him, in her style. "And we've always, *especially,* loved our children."

John was not mollified. "What do you care about *us?*" he boomed. "We're just little things you *had.*" His sisters' laughing forced a laugh from him, which he turned hard and parodistic: "Ha ha *ha*." Richard and Joan realized simultaneously that the child was drunk, on Judith's homecoming champagne. Feeling bound to keep the center of the stage, John took a cigarette from Judith's pack, poked it into his mouth, let it hang from his lower lip, and squinted like a gangster.

"You're not little things we had," Richard called to him. "You're the whole point. But you're grown. Or almost."

The boy was lighting matches. Instead of holding them to his cigarette (for they had never seen him smoke; being "good" had been his way of setting himself apart), he held them to his mother's face, closer and closer, for her to blow out. Then he lit the whole folder—a hiss and then a torch, held against his mother's face. Prismed by his tears, the flame filled Richard's vision; he didn't know how it was extinguished. He heard Margaret say, "Oh stop showing off," and saw John, in response, break the cigarette in two and put the halves entirely into his mouth and chew, sticking out his tongue to display the shreds to his sister.

Joan talked to him, reasoning—a fountain of reason, unintelligible. "Talked about it for years . . . our children must help us . . . Daddy and I both want . . ." As the boy listened, he carefully wadded a paper napkin into the leaves of his salad, fashioned a ball of paper and lettuce, and popped it into his mouth, looking around the table for the expected laughter. None came. Judith said, "Be mature," and dismissed a plume of smoke.

Richard got up from this stifling table and led the boy outside. Though the house was in twilight, the outdoors still brimmed with light, the long waste light of high summer. Both laughing, he supervised John's spitting out the lettuce and paper and tobacco into the pachysandra. He took him by the hand—a square gritty hand, but for its softness a man's. Yet, it held on. They ran together up into the field, past the tennis court. The raw banking left by the bulldozers was dotted with daisies. Past the court and a flat stretch where they used to play family baseball stood a soft green rise glorious in the sun, each weed and species of grass distinct as illumination on parchment. "I'm sorry, so sorry," Richard cried. "You were the only one who ever tried to help me with all the goddam jobs around this place."

Sobbing, safe within his tears and the champagne, John explained, "It's not just the separation, it's the whole crummy year, I *hate* that school, you can't make any friends, the history teacher's a scud."

They sat on the crest of the rise, shaking and warm from their tears but easier in their voices, and Richard tried to focus on the child's sad year—the weekdays long with homework, the weekends spent in his room with model airplanes, while his parents murmured down below, nursing their separation. How selfish, how blind, Richard thought; his eyes felt scoured. He told his son, "We'll think about getting you transferred. Life's too short to be miserable."

They had said what they could, but did not want the moment to heal, and talked on, about the school, about the tennis court, whether it would ever again be as good as it had been that first summer. They walked to inspect it and pressed a few more tapes more firmly down. A little stiltedly, perhaps trying to make too much of the moment, to prolong it, Richard led the boy to the spot in the field where the view was best, of the metallic blue river, the emerald marsh, the scattered islands velvet with shadow in the low light, the white bits of beach far away. "See," he said. "It goes on being beautiful. It'll be here tomorrow."

"I know," John answered, impatiently. The moment had closed.

Back in the house, the others had opened some white wine, the champagne being drunk, and still sat at the table, the three females, gossiping. Where Joan sat had become the head. She turned, showing him a tearless face, and asked, "All right?"

"We're fine," he said, resenting it, though relieved, that the party went on without him.

In bed she explained, "I couldn't cry I guess because I cried so much all spring. It really wasn't fair. It's your idea, and you made it look as though I was kicking you out."

"I'm sorry," he said. "I couldn't stop. I wanted to but couldn't."

"You *didn't* want to. You loved it. You were having your way, making a general announcement."

"I love having it over," he admitted. "God, those kids were great. So brave and funny." John, returned to the house, had settled to a model airplane in his room, and kept shouting down to them, "I'm O.K. No sweat." "And the way," Richard went on, cozy in his relief, "they never questioned the reasons we gave. No thought of a third person. Not even Judith."

"That *was* touching," Joan said.

He gave her a hug. "You were great too. Thank you." Guiltily, he realized he did not feel separated.

"You still have Dickie to do," she told him. These words set before him a black mountain in the darkness; its cold breath, its near weight affected his chest. Of the four children Dickie was most nearly his conscience. Joan did not need to add, "That's one piece of your dirty work I won't do for you."

"I know. I'll do it. You go to sleep."

Within minutes, her breathing slowed, became oblivious and deep. It was quarter to midnight. Dickie's train from the concert would come in at one-fourteen. Richard set the alarm for one. He had slept atrociously for weeks. But whenever he closed his lids some glimpse of the last hours scorched them—Judith exhaling toward the ceiling in a kind of aversion, Bean's mute staring, the sunstruck growth of the field where he and John had rested. The mountain before him moved closer, moved within him; he was huge, momentous. The ache at the back of his throat felt stale. His wife slept as if slain beside him. When, exasperated by his hot lids, his crowded heart, he rose from bed and dressed, she awoke enough to turn over. He told her then, "If I could undo it all, I would."

"Where would you begin?" she asked. There was no place. Giving him courage, she was always giving him courage. He put on shoes without socks in the dark. The children were breathing in their rooms, the downstairs was hollow. In their confusion they had left lights burning. He turned off all but one, the kitchen overhead. The car started. He had hoped it wouldn't. He met only moonlight on the road; it seemed a diaphanous companion, flickering in the leaves along the roadside, haunting his rearview mirror like a pursuer, melting under his headlights. The center of town, not quite deserted, was eerie at this hour. A young cop in uniform kept company with a gang of T-shirted kids on the steps of the bank. Across from the railroad station, several bars kept open. Customers, mostly young, passed in and out of the warm night, savoring summer's novelty. Voices shouted from cars as they passed; an immense conversation seemed in progress. Richard parked and in his weariness put his head on the passenger seat, out of the commotion and wheeling lights. It was as when, in the movies, an assassin grimly carries his mission through the jostle of a carnival—except the movies cannot show the precipitous, palpable slope you cling to within. You cannot climb back down; you can only fall. The synthetic fabric of the car seat, warmed by his cheek, confided to him an ancient, distant scent of vanilla.

A train whistle caused him to lift his head. It was on time; he had hoped it would be late. The slender drawgates descended. The bell of approach tingled happily. The great metal body, horizontally fluted, rocked to a stop, and sleepy teen-agers disembarked, his son among them. Dickie did not show surprise that his father was meeting him at this terrible hour. He sauntered to the car with two friends, both taller than he. He said "Hi" to his father and took the passenger's seat with an exhausted promptness that expressed gratitude. The friends got into the back, and Richard was grateful; a few more minutes' postponement would be won by driving them home.

He asked, "How was the concert?"

"Groovy," one boy said from the back seat.

"It bit," the other said.

"It was O.K.," Dickie said, moderate by nature, so reasonable that in his childhood the unreason of the world had given him headaches, stomach aches, nausea. When the second friend had been dropped off at his dark house, the boy blurted, "Dad, my eyes are killing me with hay fever! I'm out there cutting that mothering grass all day!"

"Do we still have those drops?"

"They didn't do any good last summer."

"They might this." Richard swung a U-turn on the empty street. The drive home took a few minutes. The mountain was here, in his throat. "Richard," he said, and felt the boy, slumped and rubbing his eyes, go tense at his tone, "I didn't come to meet you just to make your life easier. I came because your mother and I have some news for you, and you're a hard man to get ahold of these days. It's sad news."

"That's O.K." The reassurance came out soft, but quick, as if released from the tip of a spring.

Richard had feared that his tears would return and choke him, but the boy's manliness set an example, and his voice issued forth steady and dry. "It's sad news, but it needn't be tragic news, at least for you. It should have no practical effect on your life, though it's bound to have an emotional effect. You'll work at your job, and go back to school in September. Your mother and I are really proud of what you're making of your life; we don't want that to change at all."

"Yeah," the boy said lightly, on the intake of his breath, holding himself up. They turned the corner; the church they went to loomed like a gutted fort. The home of the woman Richard hoped to marry stood across the green. Her bedroom light burned.

"Your mother and I," he said, "have decided to separate. For the summer. Nothing legal, no divorce yet. We want to see how it feels. For some years now, we haven't been doing enough for each other, making each other as happy as we should be. Have you sensed that?"

"No," the boy said. It was an honest, unemotional answer: true or false in a quiz.

Glad for the factual basis, Richard pursued, even garrulously, the details. His apartment across town, his utter accessibility, the split vacation arrangements, the advantages to the children, the added mobility and variety of the summer. Dickie listened, absorbing. "Do the others know?"

Richard described how they had been told.

"How did they take it?"

"The girls pretty calmly. John flipped out; he shouted and ate a cigarette and made a salad out of his napkin and told us how much he hated school."

His brother chuckled. "He did?"

"Yeah. The school issue was more upsetting for him than Mom and me. He seemed to feel better for having exploded."

"He did?" The repetition was the first sign that he was stunned.

"Yes. Dickie, I want to tell you something. This last hour, waiting for your train to get in, has been about the worst of my life. I hate this. *Hate* it. My father would have died before doing it to me." He felt immensely lighter, saying this. He had dumped the mountain on the boy. They were home. Moving swiftly as a shadow, Dickie was out of the car, through the bright kitchen. Richard called after him, "Want a glass of milk or anything?"

"No thanks."

"Want us to call the course tomorrow and say you're too sick to work?"

"No, that's all right." The answer was faint, delivered at the door to his room; Richard listened for the slam of a tantrum. The door closed normally. The sound was sickening.

Joan had sunk into the first deep trough of sleep and was slow to awake. Richard had to repeat, "I told him."

"What did he say?"

"Nothing much. Could you go say good night to him? Please."

She left their room, without putting on a bathrobe. He sluggishly changed back into his pajamas and walked down the hall. Dickie was already in bed, Joan was sitting beside him, and the boy's bedside clock radio was murmuring music. When she stood, an inexplicable light—the moon?—outlined her body through the nightie. Richard sat on the warm place she had indented on the child's narrow mattress. He asked him, "Do you want the radio on like that?"

"It always is."

"Doesn't it keep you awake? It would me."

"No."

"Are you sleepy?"

"Yeah."

"Good. Sure you want to get up and go to work? You've had a big night."

"I want to."

Away at school this winter he had learned for the first time that you can go short of sleep and live. As an infant he had slept with an immobile sweating intensity that had alarmed his babysitters. As the children aged, he became the first to go to bed, earlier for a time than his younger brother and sister. Even now, he would go slack in the middle of a television show, his sprawled legs hairy and brown. "O.K. Good boy. Dickie, listen. I love you so much, I never knew how much until now. No matter how this works out, I'll always be with you. Really."

Richard bent to kiss an averted face but his son, sinewy, turned and with wet cheeks embraced him and gave him a kiss, on the lips, passionate as a woman's. In his father's ear he moaned one word, the crucial, intelligent word: *"Why?"*

Why. It was a whistle of wind in a crack, a knife thrust, a window thrown open on emptiness. The white face was gone, the darkness was featureless. Richard had forgotten why.

RICHARD DOKEY

(1933—)

A contemporary Chicano writer born in California, Richard Dokey has worked in factories, in a shipyard, and on the railroad. He now teaches humanities and writes both poetry and fiction.

Like Faulkner's "A Rose for Emily," "Sánchez" deals with the loss of a traditional way of life—with uprootedness and the loss of dignity. But while Faulkner keeps us outside Emily as interested spectators, Dokey allows us to identify with Sánchez, to see America through his eyes. Sánchez has the tragic grandeur of the great Sioux teacher and visionary of *Black Elk Speaks*.

Sánchez

RICHARD DOKEY

That summer the son of Juan Sánchez went to work for the Flotill Cannery in Stockton. Juan drove with him to the valley in the old Ford.

While they drove, the boy, whose name was Jesús, told him of the greatness of the cannery, of the great aluminum buildings, the marvelous machines, and the belts of cans that never stopped running. He told him of the building on one side of the road where the cans were made and how the cans ran in a metal tube across the road to the cannery. He described the food machines, the sanitary precautions. He laughed when he spoke of the labeling. His voice was serious about the money.

When they got to Stockton, Jesús directed him to the central district of town, the skid row where the boy was to live while he worked for the Flotill. It was a cheap hotel on Center Street. The room smelled. There was a table with one chair. The floor was stained like the floor of a public urinal and the bed was soiled, as were the walls. There were no drapes on the windows. A pall spread out from the single light bulb overhead that was worked with a length of grimy string.

"I will not stay much in the room," Jesús said, seeing his father's face. "It is only for sleep. I will be working overtime, too. There is also the entertainment."

Jesús led him from the room and they went out into the street. Next to the hotel there was a vacant lot where a building had stood. The hole which was left had that recent, peculiar look of uprootedness. There were the remains of the foundation, the broken flooring, and the cracked bricks of tired red to which the gray blotches of mortar clung like dried phlegm. But the ground had not yet taken on the opaqueness of wear that the air and sun give it. It gleamed dully in the light and held to itself where it had been torn, as earth does behind a plow. Juan studied the hole for a time; then they walked up Center Street to Main, passing other empty lots, and then moved east toward Hunter Street. At the corner of Hunter and Main a wrecking crew was at work. An iron ball was suspended from the end of a cable and a tall machine swung the ball up and back and then whipped it forward against the building. The ball was very thick-looking, and when it struck the wall the building trembled, spurted dust, and seemed to cringe inward. The vertical lines of the building had gone awry. Juan shook each time the iron struck the wall.

"They are tearing down the old buildings," Jesús explained. "Redevelopment," he pronounced. "Even my building is to go someday."

Juan looked at his son. "And what of the men?" he asked. "Where do the men go when there are no buildings?"

Jesús, who was a head taller than his father, looked down at him and then shrugged in that Mexican way, the head descending and cocking while the shoulders rise as though on puppet strings. *"Quien sabe?"*

"And the large building there?" Juan said, looking across the rows of parked cars in Hunter Square. "The one whose roof rubs the sky. Of what significance?"

"That is the new courthouse," Jesús said.

"There are no curtains on the windows."

"They do not put curtains on such windows," Jesús explained.

"No," sighed Juan, "that is true."

They walked north on Hunter past the new Bank of America and entered an old building. They stood to one side of the entrance. Jesús smiled proudly and inhaled the stale air.

"This is the entertainment," he said.

Juan looked about. A bar was at his immediate left, and a bald man in a soiled apron stood behind it. Beyond the bar there were many thick-wooded tables covered with green material. Men crouched over them and cone-shaped lights hung low from the ceiling casting broad cones of light downward upon the men and tables. Smoke drifted and rolled in the light and pursued the men when they moved quickly. There was the breaking noise of balls striking together, the hard wooden rattle of the cues in the racks upon the wall, the humming slither of the scoring disks along the loose wires overhead, the explosive cursing of the men. The room was warm and dirty. Juan shook his head.

"I have become proficient at the game," Jesús said.

"This is the entertainment," Juan said, still moving his head.

Jesús turned and walked outside. Juan followed. The boy pointed across the parked cars past the courthouse to a marquee on Main Street. "There are also motion pictures," Jesús said.

Juan had seen a movie as a young man working in the fields near Fresno. He had understood no English then. He sat with his friends in the leather seats that had gum under the arms and watched the images move upon the white canvas. The images were dressed in expensive clothes. There was laughing and dancing. One of the men did kissing with two very beautiful women, taking turns with each when the other was absent. This had embarrassed Juan, the embracing and unhesitating submission of the women with so many unfamiliar people to watch. Juan loved his wife, was very tender and gentle with her before she died. He never went to another motion picture, even after he had learned English, and this kept him from the Spanish films as well.

"We will go to the cannery now," Jesús said, taking his father's arm. "I will show you the machines."

Juan permitted himself to be led away, and they moved back past the bank to where the men were destroying the building. A ragged hole, like a wound, had been opened in the wall. Juan stopped and watched. The iron ball came forward tearing at the hole, enlarging it, exposing the empty interior space that had once been a room. The floor of the room teetered at a precarious angle. The wood was splintered and very dry in the noon light.

"I do not think I will go to the cannery," Juan said.

The boy looked at his father like a child who has made a toy out of string and bottle caps only to have it ignored.

"But it is honorable work," Jesús said, suspecting his father. "And it pays well."

"Honor," Juan said. "Honor is a serious matter. It is not a question of honor. You are a man now. All that is needed is a room and a job at the Flotill. Your father is tired, that is all."

"You are disappointed," Jesús said, hanging his head.

"No," Juan said. "I am beyond disappointment. You are my son. Now you have a place in the world. You have the Flotill."

Nothing more was said, and they walked to the car. Juan got in behind the wheel. Jesús stood beside the door, his arms at his sides, the fingers spread. Juan looked up at him. The boy's eyes were big.

"You are my son," Juan said, "and I love you. Do not have disappointment. I am not of the Flotill. Seeing the machines would make it worse. You understand, *niño?*"

"*Sí*, Papa," Jesús said. He put a hand on his father's shoulder.

"It is a strange world, *niñito*," Juan said.

"I will earn money. I will buy a red car and visit you. All in Twin Pines will be envious of the son of Sánchez, and they will say that Juan Sánchez has a son of purpose."

"Of course, Jesús *mío*," Juan said. He bent and placed his lips against the boy's hand. "I will look for the bright car. I will write regardless." He smiled, showing yellowed teeth. "Goodbye, *querido*," he said. He started the car, raced the engine once too high, and drove off up the street.

When Juan Sánchez returned to Twin Pines, he drove the old Ford to the top of Bear Mountain and pushed it over. He then proceeded systematically to burn all that was of importance to him, all that was of nostalgic value, and all else that meant nothing in itself, like the extra chest of drawers he had kept after his wife's death, the small table in the bedroom, and the faded mahogany stand in which he kept his pipe and tobacco and which sat next to the stuffed chair in the front room. He broke all the dishes, cups, plates, discarded all the cooking and eating utensils in the same way. The fire rose in the blue wind carrying dust wafers of ash in quick, breathless spirals and then released them in a panoply of diluted smoke, from which they drifted and spun and fell like burnt snow. The forks, knives, and spoons became very black with a flaky crust of oxidized metal. Then Juan burned his clothing, all that was unnecessary, and the smoke dampened and took on a thick smell. Finally he threw his wife's rosary into the flames. It was a cheap one, made of wood, and disappeared immediately. He went into his room then and lay down on the bed. He went to sleep.

When he woke, it was dark and cool. He stepped outside, urinated, and then returned, shutting the door. The darkness was like a mammoth held breath, and he felt very awake listening to the beating of his heart. He would not be able to sleep now, and so he lay awake thinking.

He thought of his village in Mexico, the baked white clay of the small houses spread like little forts against the stillness of the bare mountains, the men with their great wide hats, their wide, white pants, and their naked, brown-skinned feet, splayed against the fine dust of the road. He saw the village cistern and the women all so big and slow, always with child, enervated by the earth and the unbearable sun, the enervation passing into their very wombs like the acceptance, slow, silent blood. The men walked bent as though carrying the air or sky, slept against the buildings in the shade like old dogs, ate dry, hot food that dried them inside and seemed to bake the moisture from the flesh, so that the men and women while still young had faces like eroded fields and fingers like stringy, empty stream beds. It was a hard land. It took the life of his father and mother before he was twelve and the life of his aunt, with whom he then lived, before he was sixteen.

When he was seventeen he went to Mexicali because he had heard much of America and the money to be obtained there. They took him in a truck with other men to work in the fields around Bakersfield, then in the fields near Fresno. On his return to Mexicali he met La Belleza, as he came to call her: loveliness. He married her when he was nineteen and she only fifteen. The following year she had a baby girl. It was stillborn and the birth almost killed her, for the doctor said the passage was oversmall. The doctor cautioned him (warned him, really) La Belleza could not have children and live, and he went outside into the moonlight and wept.

He had heard much of the loveliness of the Sierra Nevada above what was called the Mother Lode, and because he feared the land, believed almost that it possessed the power to kill him—as it had killed his mother and father, his aunt, was, in fact, slowly killing so many of his people—he wanted to run away from it to the high white cold of the California mountains, where he believed his heart would grow, his blood run and, perhaps, the passage of La Belleza might open. Two years later he was taken in the trucks to Stockton in the San Joaquin Valley to pick tomatoes, and he saw the Sierra Nevada above the Mother Lode.

It was from a distance, of course, and in the summer, so that there was no snow. But when he returned he told La Belleza about the blueness of the mountains in the warm, still dawn, the extension of them, the aristocracy of their unmoving height, and that they were only fifty miles away from where he had stood.

He worked very hard now and saved his money. He took La Belleza back to his village, where he owned the white clay house of his father. It was cheaper to live there while he waited, fearing the sun, the dust, and the dry, airless silence, for the money to accumulate. That fall La Belleza became pregnant again by an accident of passion and the pregnancy was very difficult. In the fifth month the doctor—who was an atheist—said that the baby would have to be taken or else the mother would die. The village priest, a very loud, dramatic man—an educated man who took pleasure in striking a pose—proclaimed the wrath of God in the face of such sacrilege. It was the child who must live, the priest cried. The pregnancy must go on. There was the immortal soul of the child to consider. But Juan decided for the atheist doctor, who did take the child. La Belleza lost much blood. At one point her heart had stopped beating. When the child was torn from its mother and Juan saw that it was a boy, he ran out of the clay house of his father and up the dusty road straight into a hideous red moon. He cursed the earth, the sky. He cursed his village, himself, the soulless indifference of the burnt mountains. He cursed God.

Juan was very afraid now, and though it cost more money, he had himself tied by the atheist doctor so that he could never again put the life of La Belleza in danger, for the next time, he knew with certainty, would kill her.

The following summer he went again on the trucks to the San Joaquin Valley. The mountains were still there, high and blue in the quiet dawn, turned to a milky pastel by the heat swirls and haze of midday. Sometimes at night he stepped outside the shacks in which the men were housed and faced the darkness. It was tragic to be so close to what you wanted, he would think, and be unable to possess it. So strong was the feeling in him, particularly during the hot, windless evenings, that he sometimes went with the other men into Stockton, where he stood on the street corners of skid row and talked, though he did not get drunk on cheap wine or go to the whores, as did the other men. Nor did he fight.

They rode in old tilted trucks covered with canvas and sat on rude benches staring out over the slats of the tail gate. The white glare of headlights crawled up and lay upon them, waiting to pass. They stared over the whiteness. When the lights swept out and by, the glass of the side windows shone. Behind the windows sometimes there would be the ghost flash of an upturned face, before the darkness clamped shut. Also, if one of the men had a relative who lived in the area, there was the opportunity to ride in a car.

He had done so once. He had watched the headlights of the car pale, then whiten the back of one of the trucks. He saw the faces of the men turned outward and the looks on the faces that seemed to float upon the whiteness of the light. The men sat forward, arms on knees, and looked over the glare into the darkness. After that he always rode in the trucks.

When he returned to his village after that season's harvest, he knew they could wait no longer. He purchased a dress of silk for La

Belleza and in a secondhand store bought an American suit for himself. He had worked hard, sold his father's house, saved all his money, and on a bright day in early September they crossed the border at Mexicali and caught the Greyhound for Fresno.

Juan got up from his bed to go outside. He stood looking up at the stars. The stars were pinned to the darkness, uttering little flickering cries of light, and as always he was moved by the nearness and profusion of their agony. His mother had told him the stars were a kind of purgatory in which souls burned in cold, silent repentance. He had wondered after her death if the earth too were not a star burning in loneliness, and he could never look at them later without thinking this and believing that the earth must be the brightest of all stars. He walked over to the remains of the fire. A dull heat came from the ashes and a column of limp smoke rose and then bent against the night wind. He studied the ashes for a time and then looked over the tall pine shapes to the southern sky. It was there all right. He could feel the dry char of its heat, that deeper, dryer burning. He imagined it, of course. But it was there nevertheless. He went back into the cabin and lay down, but now his thoughts were only of La Belleza and the beautiful Sierra Nevada.

From Fresno all the way up the long valley to Stockton they had been full with pride and expectation. They had purchased oranges and chocolate bars and they ate them laughing. The other people on the bus looked at them, shook their heads, and slept or read magazines. He and La Belleza gazed out the window at the land.

In Stockton they were helped by a man named Eugenio Mendez. Juan had met him while picking tomatoes in the delta. Eugenio had eight children and a very fat but very kind and tolerant wife named Anilla. He had helped them find a cheap room off Center Street, where they stayed while determining their next course of action. Eugenio had access to a car, and it was he who drove them finally to the mountains.

It was a day like no other day in his life: to be sitting in the car with La Belleza, to be in this moving car with his Belleza heading straight toward the high, lovely mountains. The car traveled from the flatness of the valley into the rolling brown swells of the foothills, where hundreds of deciduous and evergreen oaks grew, their puff-ball shapes like still pictures of exploding holiday rockets, only green, but spreading up and out and then around and down in nearly perfect canopies. At Jackson the road turned and began an immediate, constant climb upward.

It was as though his dream about it had materialized. He had never seen so many trees, great with dignity: pines that had gray bark twisted and stringy like hemp; others whose bark resembled dry, flat ginger cookies fastened with black glue about a drum, and others whose bark pulled easily away; and those called redwoods, standing stiff and tall, amber-hued with straight rolls of bark as thick as his fist, flinging out high above great arms of green. And the earth, rich red, as though the blood of scores of Indians had just flowed there and dried. Dark patches of shadow stunned with light, blue flowers, orange flowers, birds, even deer. They saw them all on that first day.

"*¿A dónde vamos?*" Eugenio had asked. "Where are we going?"

"*Bellísima,*" Juan replied. "Into much loveliness."

They did not reach Twin Pines that day. But on their return a week later they inquired in Jackson about the opportunity of buying land or a house in the mountains. The man, though surprised, told them of the sawmill town of Twin Pines, where there were houses for sale.

Their continued luck on that day precipitated the feeling in Juan that it was indeed the materialization of a dream. He had been able in all those years to save two thousand dollars, and a man had a small shack for sale at the far edge of town. He looked carefully at Juan, at La Belleza and Eugenio and said, "One thousand dollars," believing they could never begin to possess such a sum. When Juan handed him the money, the man was so struck that he made out a bill of sale. Juan Sanchez and his wife had their home in the Sierra.

When Juan saw the cabin close up, he knew the man had stolen their money. It was small, the roof slanted to one side, the door would not close evenly. The cabin was gradually falling downhill. But it was theirs and he could, with work, repair it. Hurriedly they drove back to Jackson, rented a truck, bought some cheap furniture and hauled it back to the cabin. When they had moved in, Juan brought forth a bottle of whiskey and for the first time in his life proceeded to get truly drunk.

Juan was very happy with La Belleza. She accepted his philosophy completely, understood his need, made it her own. In spite of the people of the town, they created a peculiar kind of joy. And anyway Juan had knowledge about the people.

Twin Pines had been founded, he learned by one Benjamin Carter, who lived with his daughter in a magnificent house on the hill overlooking town. This Benjamin Carter was a very wealthy man. He had come to the mountains thirty years before to save his marriage, for he had been poor once and loved when he was poor, but then he grew very rich because of oil discovered on his father's Ohio farm and he went away to the city and became incapable of love in the pursuit of money and power. When he at last married the woman whom he had loved, a barrier had grown between them, for Ben Carter had changed but the woman had not. Then the woman became ill and Ben Carter promised her he would take her West, all the way West away from the city so that it could be as it had been in the beginning of their love. But the woman was with child. And so Ben Carter rushed to the California mountains, bought a thousand acres of land, and hurried to build his house before the rain and snows came. He hired many men and the house was completed, except for the interior work and the furnishings. All that winter men he had hired worked in the snow to finish the house while Ben Carter waited with his wife in the city. When it was early spring they set out for California, Ben Carter, his wife, and the doctor, who strongly advised against the rough train trip and the still rougher climb by horse and wagon from Jackson to the house. But the woman wanted the child born properly, so they went. The baby came the evening of their arrival at the house, and the woman died all night having it. It was this Ben Carter who lived with that daughter now in the great house on the hill, possessing her to the point, it was said about his madness, that he had murdered a young man who had shown interest in her.

Juan learned all this from a Mexican servant who had worked at the great house from the beginning, and when he told the story to La Belleza she wept because of its sadness. It was a tragedy of love, she explained, and Juan—soaring to the heights of his imagination—believed that the town, all one hundred souls, had somehow been infected with the tragedy, as they were touched by the shadow of the house itself, which crept directly up the highway each night when the sun set. This was why they left dead chickens and fish on the porch of the cabin or dumped garbage into the yard. He believed he understood something profound and so did nothing about these incidents, which, after all, might have been the pranks of boys. He did not want the infection to touch him, nor the deeper infection of their prejudice because he was Mexican. He was not indifferent. He was simply too much in love with La Belleza and the Sierra Nevada. Finally the incidents stopped.

Now the life of Juan Sánchez entered its most beautiful time. When the first snows fell he became delirious, running through the pines, shouting, rolling on the ground, catching the flakes in his open mouth, bringing them in his cupped hands to rub in the hair of La Belleza, who stood in the doorway of their cabin laughing at him. He danced, made up a song about snowflakes falling on a desert and then a prayer which he addressed to the Virgin of Snowflakes. That night while the snow fluttered like wings against the bedroom window, he celebrated the coming of the whiteness with La Belleza.

He understood that first year in the mountains that love was an enlargement of himself, that it enabled him to be somehow more than he had ever been before, as though certain pores of his senses had only just been opened. Whereas before he had desired the Sierra Nevada for its beauty and contrast to his harsh fatherland, now he came to acquire a love for it, and he loved it as he loved La Belleza; he loved it as a woman. Also in that year he came to realize that there was a fear or dread about such love. It was more a feeling than anything else, something which reached thought now and then, particularly in those last moments before sleep. It was an absolutely minor thing. The primary knowledge was of the manner in which this love seemed to assimilate everything, rejecting all that would not yield. This love was a kind of blindness.

That summer Juan left La Belleza at times to pick the crops of the San Joaquin Valley. He had become good friends with the servant of the big house and this man had access to the owner's car, which he always drove down the mountain in a reckless but confident manner. After that summer Juan planned also to buy a car, not out of material desire, but simply because he believed this man would one day kill himself, and also because he did not wish to be dependent.

He worked in the walnuts near the town of Linden and again in the tomatoes of the rich delta. He wanted very much to have La Belleza with him, but that would have meant more money and a hotel room in the skid row, and that was impossible because of the pimps and whores, the drunks and criminals and the general despair, which the police always tapped at periodic intervals, as one does a vat of fermenting wine. The skid row was a place his love could not assimilate, but he could not ignore it because so many of his people were lost there. He stayed in the labor camps, which were also bad because of what the men did with themselves, but they were tolerable. He worked hard and as often as he could and gazed at the mountains, which he could always see clearly in the morning light. When tomato season was over he returned to La Belleza.

Though the town would never accept them as equals, it came that summer to tolerate their presence. La Belleza made straw baskets which she sold to the townspeople and which were desired for their beauty and intricacy of design. Juan carved animals, a skill he had acquired from his father, and these were also sold. The activity succeeded so well that Juan took a box of these things to Jackson, where they were readily purchased. The following spring he was able to buy the Ford.

Juan acquired another understanding that second year in the mountains. It was, he believed, that love, his love, was the single greatness of which he was capable, the thing which ennobled him and gave him honor. Love, he became convinced, was his only ability, the one success he had accomplished in a world of insignificance. It was a simple thing, after all, made so painfully simple each time he went to the valley to work with his face toward the ground, every time he saw the men in the fields and listened to their talk and watched them drive off to the skid row at night. After he had acquired this knowledge, the nights he had to spend away from La Belleza were occupied by a new kind of loneliness, as though a part of his body had been separated from the whole. He began also to understand something more of the fear or dread that seemed to trail behind love.

It happened late in the sixth year of their marriage. It was impossible, of course, and he spent many hours at the fire in their cabin telling La Belleza of the impossibility, for the doctor has assured him that all had been well tied. He had conducted himself on the basis of that assumption. But doctors can be wrong. Doctors can make mistakes. La Belleza was with child.

For the first five months the pregnancy was not difficult, and he came almost to believe that indeed the passage of La Belleza would open. He prayed to God. He prayed to the earth and sky. He prayed to the soul of his mother. But after the fifth month the true sickness began and he discarded prayer completely in favor of blasphemy. There was no God and never could be God in the face of such sickness, such unbelievable human sickness. Even when he had her removed to the hospital in Stockton, the doctors could not stop it, but it continued so terribly that he believed that La Belleza carried sickness itself in her womb.

After seven months the doctors decided to take the child. They brought La Belleza into a room with lights and instruments. They worked on her for a long time and she died there under the lights with the doctors cursing and perspiring above the large wound of her pain. They did not tell him of the child, which they had cleaned and placed in an incubator, until the next day. That night he sat in the Ford and tried to see it all, but he could only remember the eyes of La Belleza in the vortex of pain. They were of an almost eerie calmness. They had possessed calmness, as one possesses the truth. Toward morning he slumped sideways on the seat and went to sleep.

So he put her body away in the red earth of the town cemetery beyond the cabin. The pines came together overhead and in the heat of midday a shadow sprinkled with spires of light lay upon the ground so that the earth was cool and clean to smell. He did not even think of taking her back to Mexico, since, from the very beginning she had always been part of that dream he had dreamed. Now she would be always in the Sierra Nevada, with the orange and blue flowers, the quiet, deep whiteness of winter, and all that he ever was or could be was with her.

But he did not think these last thoughts then, as he did now. He had simply performed them out of instinct for their necessity, as he had performed the years of labor while waiting for the infant Jesús to grow to manhood. Jesús. Why had he named the boy Jesús? That, perhaps, had been instinct too. He had stayed after La Belleza's death for the boy, to be with him until manhood, to show him the loveliness of the Sierra Nevada, to instruct him toward true manhood. But Jesús. Ah, Jesús. Jesús the American. Jesús of the Flotill. Jesús understood nothing. Jesús, he believed, was forever lost to knowledge. That day with Jesús had been his own liberation.

For a truth had come upon him after the years of waiting, the ultimate truth that he understood only because La Belleza had passed through his life. Love was beauty, La Belleza and the Sierra Nevada, a kind of created or made thing. But there was another kind of love, a very profound, embracing love that he had felt of late blowing across the mountains from the south and that, he knew now, had always been there from the beginning of his life, disguised in the sun and wind. In this love there was blood and earth and, yes, even God, some kind of god, at least the power of a god. This love wanted him for its own. He understood it, that it had permitted him to have La Belleza and that without it there could have been no Belleza.

Juan placed an arm over his eyes and turned to face the wall. The old bed sighed. An image went off in his head and he remembered vividly the lovely body of La Belleza. In that instant the sound that loving had produced with the bed was alive in him like a forgotten melody, and his body seemed to swell and press against the ceiling. It was particularly cruel because it was so sudden, so intense, and came from so deep within him that he knew it must all still be alive somewhere, and that was the cruelest part of all. He wept softly and held the arm across his eyes.

In the dark morning the people of the town were awakened by the blaze of fire that was the house of Juan Sánchez. Believing that he had perished in the flames, several of the townspeople placed a marker next to the grave of his wife with his name on it. But, of course, on that score they were mistaken. Juan Sánchez had simply gone home.

QUESTIONS

1. How does Dokey lead us to identify with an old man so rigid in his rejection of modern American life?
2. What kind of life can Jesús look forward to?
3. Compare the demolition of houses at the beginning of the story to Sánchez' destruction of his car, dishes, household belongings. What is Sánchez doing?
4. Think about the images of flat land and mountain. How do they work in the story?
5. "Juan Sánchez had simply gone home," the story ends. Where is home?

JOHN J. CLAYTON

(1935—)

Clayton, born in New York City, got his B.A. at Columbia College and his Ph.D. at Indiana University. He has published short fiction in a number of quarterlies and a critical work, *Saul Bellow: In Defense of Man.* "Cambridge Is Sinking!" comes out of his work in the antiwar movement of the late 1960's and his sharing in the loss of that movement in the early 1970's. It was reprinted in the Martha Foley and O'Henry collections of short stories (1973, 1974). Clayton teaches at the University of Massachusetts in Amherst.

[See Preface, p. 18 (imagery).]

Cambridge Is Sinking!

JOHN J. CLAYTON

The Sunday night telephone call from Steve's parents: his mother sorrowed that such an educated boy couldn't find a job. She suggested kelp and brewer's yeast. His father told him, "What kind of economics did you study, so when I ask for the names of some stocks, which ones should I buy, you can't tell me?"

"It's true, Dad."

George rolled a joint and handed it to Steve. Steve shook his head. "But thanks anyway," he said to George, hand covering the phone.

Reprinted from *The Massachusetts Review,* © 1972 The Massachusetts Review, Inc.

"Man, you're becoming a Puritan," George said.

"Stevie, you're getting to be practically a vagrant." His father sighed.

Susan kissed him in a rush on the way out to her support meeting. Where was *his* support meeting? He closed his eyes and floated downstream. "Good-bye, baby."

A one-eyed cat pounced from cushion to cushion along the floor. He hooked his claws into the Indian bedspreads that were the flowing walls of the living room. The cat floated, purring, until Steve yelled:

"Che! For Christsakes!" and Che leaped off a gold flower into the lifeboat. It wasn't a lifeboat; really an inflated surplus raft of rubberized canvas; it floated in the lagoon of a Cambridge living room. It was Steve who nicknamed it "the Lifeboat" and christened it with a quart of beer.

Steve scratched the cat's ears and seduced him into his lap under Section 4 of the Sunday *New York Times:* The Week in Review. Burrowing underneath, Che bulged out Nixon's smiling face into a mask. Che made a rough sea out of Wages and Prices, Law and Order, Education. Steve stopped trying to read.

The *Times* on a Sunday! Travel and Resorts. *Voilà!* "A Guide to Gold in the Hills of France." Arts and Leisure. Business and Finance. Sports. Remember sports? My God. It was clear something was over.

All these years the *New York Times* was going on, not just a thing to clip articles from for a movement newspaper, but a thing people read. Truly, there were people who went to Broadway shows on the advice of Clive Barnes and Walter Kerr, who examined the rise and fall of mutual funds, who attended and supported the college and church of their choice, who visited Bermuda on an eight-day package plan, who discussed cybernetics and school architecture. People who had never had a second-hand millennial notion of where we were heading—only a vague anger and uneasiness.

Steve tried to telepathize all this to Che under the newspaper blanket: Che, it's over. Hey. John is making films, Fred lives with eight other people on a farm. But it isn't a *commune,* whatever that was. The experiment is over.

Look. When Nancy cleared out of the apartment with her stash of acid and peyote and speed and hash after being released from Mass Mental, cleared out and went home to Connecticut; when trippy Phil decided to campaign for George McGovern and nobody laughed; when the *Rolling Stone* subscription ran out; when Steve himself stopped buying the *Liberated Guardian* or worrying about its differences from the regular *Guardian;* when George—when *George—* stopped doing acid and got into a heavy wordless depression that he dulled with bottle after bottle of Tavola—and said he'd stop drinking "soon—and maybe get into yoga or a school thing"—something was finished, over.

Che purred.

The lifeboat floated like a bright orange H.M.S. *Queen Elizabeth* sofa in the middle of the sunset floor. Steve sat in the lifeboat on one of the inflated cushions reading Arts and Leisure and listening to Ray Charles through the wall of George's room. As long as it was Ray Charles he didn't bother to drown it out with the living room stereo. As if he had the energy. He sipped cranberry juice out of an Ocean Spray bottle and looked through this newspaper of strange science fiction planet aha.

Ray Charles whined to dead stop in midsong. George stood in the doorway and stood there with something to say and stood there and waited.

"Come aboard. I'm liking this old boat better and better."

George: hippo body, leonine face with a wild red mane. He ignored the boat. "Steve, I'm going back to school."

"School? To do what?"

"Get a masters."

"What in?"

"I haven't got that far yet. I'll let you know." The door closed. Ray Charles started up from where he left off.

Steve smiled. He stretched out in the lifeboat and let it float him downstream. They came to a rapids, he and Che and the *New York Times,* and he began negotiating the white water. George. George: school? Well, why not.

George. One day last year when George was tripping he found his Harvard diploma in the trunk under his bed: he ripped it into a lot of pieces and burned—or began to burn—the pieces one by one. But halfway through he chickened out and spent the rest of his trip on his knees staring into the jigsaw fragments as if they were the entrails of Homeric birds, *telling him something.* Yesterday, when Steve went into his room to retrieve his bathrobe, he found the fragments glued onto oak tag: half a B.A. on the wall. Nothing else was any different: unmade bed, unread books, undressed George, sacked out in the bathrobe. Steve burned a wooden match and with the cooled char wrote R.I.P. on George's forehead. George did.

Susan was gone for hours. Sunday night. Steve sat cross-legged in his lifeboat and made up lists on 3-by-5 cards.

It was a joke that began when he was doing his honors thesis at Harvard. On the backs of throwaway 3-by-5's he'd write

B–214:
Steve Kalman cites Marx—18th Brumaire—"Peasants shld be led into socialism by being asked to do housecleaning once a week."

He'd tape that to the bathroom mirror so the early morning peasants, recovering from dope and alcohol and speed, could hate him and get some adrenalin working. It was therapeutic.

Now the lists were different:

B–307:
Steve Kalman tells us in his definitive work on Engels' late period:

a) *learn karate*
b) *practice abdominal breathing while making love*
c) *read Marx's* Grundrisse
d) *read something through to the last page*
e) *"Be modest and prudent, guard against arrogance and rashness, and serve the . . . people heart and soul" (Mao)*
f) *specifically: fight racism, sexism, exploitation*
   (whew!)
g) *practice revolution*

When he felt it might be necessary to do something about an item on the list, he closed his eyes and meditated. Words sneaked in: what he might have said to Susan, what was the shortest route to Harvard Square, would he see his guru face to face the way Sam said he had, how many gallons would it take to do the kitchen. Aach, you should just get into the waiting, into this time without political meetings or leafletting at factory gates. Get into something.

In his mind's eye Steve saw Susan's face. All right, she wasn't Beatrice or Shri Krishna. But who was, nowadays?

⌘

She came in late from her support group; Steve was in a gloomy half sleep. She curled up behind him and touched her lips to the baby hairs on his back. He grunted and turned around: "And that's another thing—" He kissed her cheek, her nipple.

"What's another thing?"

"Your other nipple." Which he addressed himself to. "Listen. You come home after an exciting day at work while I've just swept the floors and wiped up the children's doodoo. Then you, you want to make love."

She held the cheeks of his ass and pressed him against her. They kissed. "Stephen, I don't have what you just said quite figured out, but I think you're making a sexist comment."

"Sexist? What sexist? I envy you your support group. You leave me nothing but the lifeboat and Chairman Mao."

"And a couple of years ago you'd have been up all night hammering out a 'position.' I think you're better off."

"We make love more, for sure."

"Let's make love, Steve."

And they did.

"Let's get out of Cambridge before it sinks. Cambridge is sinking."

Susan played with his curly black hair and beard, a Cambridge Dionysus. "You're silly. Cambridge is built on money. There are new banks all over the place."

"Then it's *us* who are sinking. We've got a lifeboat, let's go."

"Go where?"

"How about British Columbia? They need teachers. Or northern Ontario?"

"You'll get a lot of political thinking done up there."

"In exile? Look at Ho Chi Minh. Look at Lenin."

"Oh, baby. They were connected to a party."

"I love you. You're right. Let's go to Quebec and get away from politics."

"Away from politics? Quebec?"

"To Ontario."

"But, baby, you're away from 'politics' right here. That's what you're complaining about."

"But Cambridge is sinking."

At night in bed it was funny and they had each other. But daytime after they breakfasted and kissed good-bye and Susan would go off to teach her fourth-grade class and Steve would go off to the library to read Trotsky or Ian Fleming or he'd sub at a Cambridge junior high and sit dully in the faculty lounge waiting for his class to begin, then he'd think again, like the words of an irritating jingle that wouldn't stay quiet, about whether to go on for his doctorate in sociology so he could be unemployed as a Ph.D. instead of unemployed as an M.A.

❈

Susan was off at work. Steve washed the dishes this morning. M.A. Ph.D. The dishes. If you called it karma yoga it was better than dishwashing. But he envied Susan her nine-year-olds, even if she were being paid to socialize them into a society with no meaningful work, a society which—*watch it:* do the dishes and stop the words.

He did the dishes—then spent the rest of the morning at Widener Library reading Mao's *On Contradictions*.

He was to meet George for lunch. On his way Jeff Segal passed him a leaflet without looking up.

The press loves to boast that the student movement is dead. It's alive and fighting back. And SDS is in the forefront of that fight . . .

My God—SDS. (Which meant, in fact, PL.) Well, Steve felt happy that somebody considered themselves a Movement, even a handful of people using the rhetoric of 1950's ad men.

Steve passed through Harvard Square—past the straight-looking Jesus freaks and the bald Krishna freaks dancing in their saffron or white sheets and their insulated rubber boots. In the corner news store, across from the kiosk (Steve remembered when they "took" the Square and people got up on the kiosk and the cops came. So the freaks charged off in all directions busting windows—called "liberating the Square"—while he, Steve, who'd helped organize the march and rally, walked quietly away) —in the corner news and magazine store there was George reading the sex books at the rear of the store.

"Hey, George!"

They got out into the street and stood blinking at the noon light like a couple of junkies oozing out of a basement. George took out from his army coat lining the copy of *Fusion* he'd ripped off. He thumbed through the record reviews and he headed down Boylston to Minute Man Radio. "You stay here, Steve. I know what you think about my ripping off."

Steve watched the young women of Cambridge pass. A lot of fine lunchtime arrogance that he delighted in; but, he considered, not a hell of a lot in their eyes to back it up. One blonde on the other side of Boylston, tall, with a strong walk and no-bullshit eyes: Steve fell in love with her right away and they started living together but she had kids and he didn't get it on with them and she had perverse tastes in bed and didn't understand politics so by the time she actually crossed the street and passed by they'd separated it was too bad but anyway there was Susan to think of and so on. But they smiled at each other. Then George came out with Bob Dylan—*Greatest Hits Volume II*— and showed it to Steve when they'd sat down for lunch.

They ate in the Française under the painted pipes, ate their good quiche and drank French coffee. "George, I think this is a Hemingway memoir. I'm feeling nostalgia for this place while I'm still here. That's bad.

"I wonder where I'm going, George . . .

"I can't be Raskolnikov, George, as long as I can afford quiche for lunch. But it's the direction things are moving."

George ran his thick fingers through his wild red mane. "Not me. I decided. I don't want to be a casualty. I'm getting my M.A. in English and moving into a publishing house. I've got an uncle."

"Could you get your uncle to help you get your room cleaned up?"

"It's a pretty hip publishing house."

"I bet, George, that they make their profits off only the most freaky books."

"What's wrong with you, anyway?"

Steve bought George an espresso. "Here. Forgive me. This is so I can take our lunch off my taxes. I'm organizing you into our new revolutionary party."

"You couldn't organize your ass, lately."

Steve agreed. "I'm into getting my internal organs to communicate. I'm establishing dialogue at all levels."

After lunch Steve called Susan in the teachers' lounge at her school. "Hello, Baby? Cambridge is collapsing."

"Love, I can't do anything about that. Thirty-one kids is all I can handle."

"Pretend I'm a reporter from the *Times* and you're a terrific genius. 'Tell me, Miss French, how did you get to be such a terrific genius? I mean, here the city is falling down and nobody can stop snorting coke long enough to shore up a building, and here you are helping thirty-one human kids to survive. How, how, how, Miss French?' "

"Steve, you know better, you nut."

"Steve knows what he knows; me, I'm a reporter."

"Well," she cleared her throat, "I take vitamins, and I make love a lot with my friend Steve. And I ask his advice—"

"Ha! Fat chance!"

"—and I owe it to my sisters in the women's movement."

Steve didn't laugh. "It's true, it's true. Ah, anyway, love, I miss you."

Steve went up to the raised desk at the Booksmith on Brattle Street to ask the manager whether the one-volume reduction of Marx's *Grundrisse* was out in paper. The "manager"—long mustachios and shaggy hair like a riverboat gambler, fifty-dollar boots up on the desk where they could make a *statement*—aha, it turned out to be Phil. Hey, Phil.

Phil looked down from the counter, stopped picking his Mississippi teeth and grinned. "I've been meaning to stop by, Steve. You didn't know I had this gig, huh?"

"It's good to see you."

"Sure. I watch the motherfuckers on my closed-circuit swivel-eye

TV setup, dig it, and I check out the Square when things are slow. It's okay. I'm learning. In a couple of months I'm going out to Brattleboro, open a bookstore. A hip, a very hip bookstore."

"In Vermont?"

"There's a whole lot of freaks in Vermont."

"You doing a movement bookstore?"

Phil began picking his teeth like waiting to look at his hole card. Grinned his riverboat grin. "My uncle's setting me up, Steve. I want to make bread, man. As much as I can make in two, three years, and then I'll sell and split for someplace."

"Where?" Steve played at *naif* to Phil's heavy hipoisie.

"Lots of time to work that one out."

Steve forgot to ask about Marx. But Marx was all right. He found a *Capital* and when the camera had swiveled away, he slipped it into his bookbag. Then a Debray. A Ché. Mao's *Quotations*. A Kropotkin. Into the lining of his air force parka. If Phil noticed, he didn't say. They grinned hip gambler grins at one another and Phil said, "Later, Steve."

⌘

Marx, Mao, Ché, Debray, and Kropotkin. A complete infield, including catcher.

Steve pitched his winnings out of his lining, into the lifeboat.

"You, Steve?"

"Everybody's got an uncle, George. Wow. I remember Phil when we took the administration building. He was up on a car that night doing a Mario Savio. And now—" Steve told George about the *very* hip bookstore in Brattleboro.

"Everybody's got an uncle, huh?" George grunted. "And you're pure, huh?" He assimilated it into his computer; it fit. He swallowed once, then his massive moon face framed by red solar fire, his face relaxed. He went back to his room. Steve considered tacking up a 3-by-5 sign over the doorway: The Bestiary. Today he was a wall-eyed computer. Yesterday George was a griffin. Tomorrow he could expect a drunken red-haired cyclops.

What animal was Steve? Steve was *existentialops meshugenah.* Nearly extinct, thank God. Little survival value. Never looked down at the ground. Every bush a metaphor. Can't go for a picnic on a hillside without watching for a lion, a wolf, and a leopard.

He shrugged. Ask Chairman Mao. He opened the *Red Book* at random:

> We should rid our ranks of all impotent thinking. All views that over-
> estimate the strength of the enemy and underestimate the strength of
> the people are wrong.

Good advice. But, plagued by impotent thinking, he climbed into the lifeboat and hugged his knees and sulked. He sat there till George, hammering up another picture on his wall, got to him. "George, will you cool it? Cool it, George. I'm miserable. The sky's falling down."

He tossed Mao aft in the boat, fitted real oars to the real oarlocks, and began to row in the imaginary water. It was smoother and easier than in real water—there was no struggle, and so, no forward motion. All things proceed by contraries. Blake or Heraclitus or Hegel or Marx. He rowed.

He rowed. Aha! It began to make sense. He was expressing precisely the "contraries" he felt in this year of the Nixon: him pushing, nothing pushing back but hot air from the radiators.

So. He closed his eyes. There was a forest on both sides. Tactical Police were utterly lost in the woods. Maybe it was a beer commercial. Inside his head Steve did up a joint and floated, eyes closed. The Tactical Police were stoned. Then he turned inside out and floated into a deep jungle world. There was a fat parrot with iridescent yellow and green, red and blue wing feathers. It was as big as a tiger.

George had a real parrot in his room, and it was the only thing George took care of. Including George. It wasn't very beautiful, certainly not iridescent or big as a tiger. It liked dope, ice cream, and Cream of Wheat. Like George. But now Steve floated while a very different bird floated overhead like a bubble or helium-filled crystal ball. He watched for the Good Witch of the West. Or for the Wizard of the East. But before any such visitation, he fell asleep.

Cambridge is a lie. Doesn't exist never existed. I am in my cups. The moon a cracked saucer. We are hardly acquainted.

In the graveyard of the Unitarian Church, sixteen-year-old runaways slept, dreaming of breasts with amphetamine nipples. They are all the time tired. Cats prowl the graveyard lean and angry. They suck blood and fly moonwards. The Unitarians underground are coughing uneasily. They are pressed down by the weight.

He woke up. He pretended it was a Caribbean cruise, this was the ship's boat, his jeans were a dinner jacket and tuxedo trousers. Susan was off to the captain's table getting champagne cocktails.

When she came back they walked through the Square arm in arm with champagne glasses and a bottle of Mumm's. It was spring; they kissed in front of a Bogart poster and poured more champagne for a toast. The Beatles were on again at the Brattle. There was nobody else in the theater. All the psychedelic flowers were fading, wilting dingy, like the murals on WPA post office walls. The submarine had faded to a rusty chartreuse. Steve remembered when it was bright yellow and Lucy looked just like an acid lady. You used to get stoned or drop acid and get into the colors.

The lifeboat was getting full. Harpo was asleep on a raccoon coat, and George and his girl, very stoned, were examining a wind-up see-through clock they'd ripped off at DR. Steve could hardly spread out his newspaper. It was a rush-hour subway except everybody had suitcases and guitars with them. "Is this the way to Charles Street?" The sign over the door said DORCHESTER.

They held on and on, the subway was behaving like a bad little boy; they were disappointed and wrote a strong note home but his government didn't reply. They floated through Cambridge trying to find the exit. They shouted FIRE! but it wasn't a crowded theater, and so they were stuck, everyone with their own suitcase and their own piece of the action.

Susan's key turned in the lock.

"Susan—hey, Susan! Let's go get dinner!"

⌘

The neighborhood food cooperative operated out of Ellen's apartment. Her twins crawled among the market boxes and noshed grapes.

"Stop noshing grapes!" Ellen warned. Susan put an Angela Davis defense petition on the table for coop members to sign. Chairman Mao sat cross-legged on a cushion slicing a California avocado with his pocket knife. He ate slice after slice of the creamy green fruit.

Coop members started arriving to pick up their orders. Twenty-three member households came in; only five ordered Angela Davis. Steve threw up his hands: "Dare to struggle, dare to win!" Chairman Mao shrugged sympathetically. He'd had trouble of his own with Cambridge intellectual types. Ellen hugged her twins and said, "But it's people that count, not politics." She put a Paul Klee on the stereo and recited W. B. Yeats.

Early spring. Cambridge. Torpor, confusion, scattered energies. A return to sanity was advertised in *Life* and in the little magazines. Aha, you mean sanity's *in* again. Okay! The art show Steve and Susan took in after dinner so they could drink free wine and hold hands, it was all giant realistic figures and giant, colorful geometrics. He could imagine them in the lobby of the new, sane, John Hancock Building. They said EXPENSIVE, CAREFUL, INTELLIGENT, PURPOSEFUL, SERIOUS; but HIP. And look at the long hair on the doctors and PR men at the opening. Everyone was hip.

"They're into patchouli oil on their genitalia for sure!"

"Who're you kidding?" Susan laughed. "You don't want to see paintings, you came to kvetch. You're a silly man. I want a Baskin and Robbins ice-cream cone. And I'm willing to buy one for you, too."

"You're throwing your wealth up to me."

"Well"—Susan sighed and took his arm like a lady—"some of us have firm positions in the world. Only Harvard Square trash does substitute teaching. This is a free country. Anyone with a little guts and brains and in-i-sha-tiff—"

"All right, I want an ice-cream cone." He stopped and right there on Mass Avenue kissed her, because she was so fine, because her tight jeans made him want to rub her thighs, because she kept him going through the foolishness.

They walked by the Charles River with their bridges burned behind them. There was nothing but to shrug. An invisible demonstration passed them from 1969 waving red and black flags and shouting old slogans. So they marched too. Steve lifted a revolutionary first and shouted, "Take Harvard!" Susan said he sounded like a Princeton fan from the fifties.

"In the fifties I was a kid waiting for someone to push a button and end my having to go to school. I wouldn't blow up: just my school. The walls. Then in the sixties I expected us to tear down the walls."

"Well?"

"Now? Ah, Susan, where will we wind up?"

"In a clock factory?"

On the other side of the river the business students stood by the bank with almost long hair and fat empty pockets. They bought and sold dope and sincere greeting cards with pictures of couples walking almost naked by the edge of the sea. Since the bridges were burned, Steve could yell, "You think you smell any sweeter, baby?" The business majors at the bank ignored them. When they had their stock options, where would Susan and Steve be? In the bathtub making love? In their lifeboat on a stream in British Columbia trying to locate the Source?

They wanted to make love, so they went back to their lifeboat and opened a bottle of cheap champagne. "What should we toast?" she asked.

"The river that gets us out of here?"

Steve made love with Susan on a quilt in the bottom of the rubber boat, a raft made for saving downed fliers.

⌘

Tuesday at lunch George and Steve spent a bottle of beer mourning the casualties.

"I decided again this morning," George said. "Not to be a casualty."

"Terrific."

"It's been a war of attrition. You know, 'I have seen the best minds of my generation . . .' "

"And some of the worst," Steve said.

"Sure. But like last night. Lynne came in to crash at two A.M. She didn't want to ball, just have a place. I think Paul kicked her out. This morning I woke up to the smell of dope, and she was getting sexed up and so we balled, but she didn't even know I was here. I can't get into that sickness anymore."

"Well," Steve said, "afterwards Lynne came into the kitchen, you were still in bed, Susan was off at work. We had coffee. I asked about her children. Her mother is still taking care of them. 'But I'm really together, Steve.' She's told me that about three times this past year. 'I couldn't stay in that hospital; nobody knew anything about where I was coming from. My *supposed* therapist had never done acid, but he's telling me about drugs. But anyway, they detoxified me. Cleaned me out.'

"I asked her how much she'd been doing. 'Wow, too much,' she said. 'I was exploring heavy things, I was deep into myself. But back-to-back acid trips . . . Too much. I think the hospital was good. But this psychiatrist with long hair, you know? . . . About my father.' Her voice started fading out. 'I had to split. I had to get back to my kids . . .' So she signed herself out.

"I reminisced about her kids—one day Susan and I took Lynne and the kids out to the Children's Zoo. So I was blabbing and fixing coffee, I turned around, and Lynne was doing up a joint, and her clear blue eyes were really spaced out. She was fingering Nancy's old flute, recorder really, and she was talking to it: 'This side is blue, is Hegel, and the lower register is red, is Marx. The point is to listen down into the tone of God. Otherwise you're condemned to repeat the cycle.'

"I gave her a kiss on the cheek and went back to my lifeboat to read. I understand you about casualties, George."

The casualties. And what about Lynne's two little girls? Today Nixon was on TV from Mars. He toasted a new "long march" of the American and Martian people. Two years ago we thought it was all set to autodestruct: General Murders and Lying Johnson and Noxious Trixter and Spirococcus Agony and the Chase Banana Bank. Now we're out looking for jobs. Peter, who put me down for getting a degree. Offered a job at Michigan if he'd finish his dissertation. He refused, lived on welfare and organized at factory gates. Now he's still on welfare, but there's hardly a movement to support him. Two years ago he was right. Now he's another kind of casualty.

The bridge is burning while we stand in the middle. Our long hair is burning, wild and beautiful. We are the work of art we never had time to make.

I don't want to be a casualty.

✖

Feeling restless, uneasy, he sat cross-legged on a pillow in the orange boat. He tried paddling down a magic river of umbrella trees, giraffes with French horn necks, a translucent lady with humming-birds flying out of her third eye. But the film kept breaking. To placate him or perhaps to make things more difficult, the projection-ist flashed a scene out of his childhood: floating on a black rubber tube, a towel wrapped around the valve like the bathing suit that sheltered his own penis. He floated safe and self-sufficiently past the breaker rocks. Where nobody could touch him. Meanwhile his mother stood by the edge of the ocean waving a red kerchief she pulled out of the cleft between her heavy breasts. She called and called, she tried to interest the lifeguard in his case. Steve's lips and ears were sealed.

Steve opened his eyes. They burned a little from salt water al-though he was 24 years old, although this was a make-believe boat, a living room prop. He felt like a shmuck. Chairman Mao's face was red.

He didn't close his eyes again. "Hey, George? George!"

"I'm doing up a joint," George said from the other room. Then he came in and lit up. "Want a toke?"

"Listen, George—"

"I'm gonna get stoned and then get my room clean. Clean."

"George, first, come with me for a couple of hours. We'll wash our sins away in the tide."

They lifted the inflated rubber boat onto their heads like dis-located duck hunters. Through the French doors to the balcony, then by rope to the back yard. Steve lashed it to the top of George's '59 Cadillac. He wore a red blanket pinned at the collar, Indian style.

At the Harvard crew house they put the boat in the water and pushed off into the Charles. Metaphor of Indian so long ago no Prudential Center or Georgian architecture of Harvard. Nice to push off into the river wrapped in such a metaphor. But today there was oil and dirt on the surface of the Charles; perch, hypnotized or drugged, maintained freedom of consciousness by meditating on their own motion. Even the fish with hooks in their mouths were contemplating their Being and harking to a different drummer. That's all more metaphor, too, for who would go fishing in the Charles? Steve played a rinky-dink tune to the fish on Nancy's recorder, but they turned belly up and became free of their bodies and of the river. The smell was nasty.

George said he felt like Huck Finn. Steve thought that was possible. They floated under the Harvard footbridge and past the site of the future water purification plant to the River Street Bridge. Stench of traffic and *COCA-COLA* in two-story letters. The river curved. "I can see myself as Tom Sawyer," Steve said. "For me it wasn't quite real, getting Jim out of slavery. I always figured on Aunt Sally's investment firm to settle down into. But for you, George, it was a real plunge. You almost didn't come back out. You were almost a shaman who didn't return."

"What are you saying, you crazy fool?"

"We must steer the boat. Susan's school is by the left bank. She'll be getting out in fifteen minutes."

Kids in the playground on the other side of Memorial Drive waved at the young man in the bright red blanket. Steve leaned over the chain link fence: "Peace to white and black brothers," he said, spreading his arms. "Tell Princess Afterglow we have come." George and a small boy tossed a ball back and forth over the fence.

"You're silly," a little boy told the Indian.

"Call Miss French. Ask Miss French to come down to the fence."

Miss French came down to the fence. Two little girls held her hands as they led her to the fence. She laughed and laughed and gestured "ten minutes" with her fingers.

George took up the recorder. It squeaked. "Steve. Those kids. That's where it's at."

"George, I don't believe you said that. Listen, George. I may dig being crazy or playing at being a child, but I can tell you that won't save me. Or being a freak. Or being an Indian. Metaphor won't save me. I got to save my own ass, so to speak. I mean, it's not any kind of revolution to float down the Charles in an orange boat."

"It was your idea. And who's talking about revolution? You're getting incredibly straight."

"And there—see—you can't make it on categories like straight. It's all over—the time you could think of *them* as bread and wine. So everything turns to shit in your mouth. Is bound to." He tugged at George's matted hair. "Except I don't feel like that this afternoon. I feel pretty manic and joyful."

Susan leaned against her bookbag in the stern and stretched back, her face parallel to the sky, and took it all in.

"Just smell this water. Don't let's fall in, friends," Susan said. "We'd be pickled in a minute."

They paddled upstream towards Harvard. Downstream, upstream.

Circle Line sightseeing: on your right is Stop and Cop, and the Robert Hall Big Man Shop. Fer you, George. Harvard crews raced each other towards the lifeboat; alongside was the coach's motor launch. The coach, in trench coat, scarf trailing crimson in the wind, stood droning into a bullhorn. For a second Married Students' Housing was upside down in the water; then a gust of wind shattered it into an impressionist canvas.

The shells raced by and the orange lifeboat rocked in their wake and in the wake of the launch. They shared an apple left over from Susan's lunch and didn't fight the rocking.

They rowed. They were rowing home. Home because

> The cat has to be fed.
> And the parrot.
> Because we are hungry and
> the place needs to be cleaned up bad.
> There are lots of books at home, and a telephone.
> Home doesn't smell as bad as this river.

No wild crowds on shore cheered this. From the footbridge no Radcliffe girls dropped white roses on their heads. Farther on, even more to the point, no marchers cheered them with raised fists, with red flags in the spring breeze, with a bullhorn dropped down off the Anderson Bridge so that Steve and Susan and George could address the crowd:

"Well, it's been a terrific five years. We've all learned how to make love and posters. We can really get into the here and now at times and we've learned to respect our fantasies. Yum yum. We're glad to be going home. We hope to see all the old faces tomorrow right after the revolution is over so we can clean up the paper we dropped."

After this didn't happen they paddled up Memorial Drive some more. The gulls were fishing. The shells raced past them going the other way and they rocked and bobbed, like a floater for fish. They sang,

> Fish on a line
> all strung out.
> If I cry the moon will go away.
> Are you with me?
> Plenty of conditions
> Sold by the millions.
> Nice to tell you
> can't hold water.

They drew pictures of fish in the water like invisible ink to be recovered later and read.

"We can't get anywhere this way," Steve said.

"Just float, man. The trouble with you is you never learned to float." George shrugged and reversed his oar, so the boat circled after itself like a dog after tail, like Paulo and Francesca. Infinite longing unsatisfied. But this was merely parody. George knew better than to long. The river stank but he had a cold. Steve and Susan were kissing on the bottom of the boat. Who knows how this fairy tale goes?

Why are the bridges all falling down? Why are the boats floating against bars of Ivory soap and turning over? It doesn't matter how the words go. They wound me up and didn't give me directions, Steve groaned, playing wind-up toy. But when he finished kissing his friend Susan, he took up paddle and coaxed George into rowing upstream past Harvard to the boathouse.

⌘

Steve—oh God, Steve, you've got to stop torchereeing yrself, Steve decided painfully. China wasn't built in a day. Steve closed his eyes and meditated, cross-legged in the wet lifeboat, on the career of Mao Tse-tung.

Susan and George carried in a brass tray with what was left of the champagne. But Steve was meditating.

"Join us, why don't you? We've got some heavy pazoola here on a fancy gold tray," George like a six-foot-three, red-haired genie wheedled. "Cut the meditating."

"Who's meditating? I'm telephoning Mao Tse-tung in Peking. *Hello, Peking?*"

"Well, tell us what he says."

Chairman Mao, Chairman Mao, Steve said inside his head. Tell us what we can do in this year of the Nixon.

Ah, yes, Mister Nixon . . .

It's been a long winter, Chairman Mao.

With no leaves on the trees, the wind shrieks; when leaves fill the branches, the wind rustles.

I think, Steve said, inside his head, I get what you mean.

The important thing, Chairman Mao said, is to get outside your head. Open your eyes. What do you see?

The rubberized canvas sides of my orange raft and a print of Primavera on my wall. My friends are offering me champagne on a gold tray. A brass tray to be exact.

Chairman Mao supposed a difficulty in translation. You, you behave like a blind man groping for fish. Open your eyes. Study conditions conscientiously. Proceed from objective reality and not from subjective wishes. Conclusions invariably come after investigation, and not before. Open your eyes.

"Open your eyes and your mouth," Susan said. "Here it comes." She tilted a glass of champagne to his lips.

"Well, nobody can say those are elitist grapes. Those are the people's grapes," Steve said, pursing his mouth.

"Connoisseur! Drink up!"

Picking up the pieces. Picking up the check. Somebody got to pay before we split and all them lights go out. Ah, well, but it's time to clean up and start almost from scratch.

Susan and Steve helped George clean up his room: Two green plastic trash bags full of wine bottles and dustballs, molding plates of spaghetti, old *Rolling Stones,* socks with cat spray, insulating felt strips chewed up by the parrot, Kleenex and Tampax and a cracked copy of Bob Dylan's *Greatest Hits Volume I* and a few cracked *ands* that broke open like milkweed pods and had to be vacuumed up in a search and destroy operation.

When George's room was swept and scrubbed, George decided to wash away the Charles River effluvium in the bathtub. So Steve and Susan sat cross-legged in the bottom of the lifeboat. Wiped out.

Then Steve pulled the plug. The boat hissed disapproval, deflated, expired. They were sitting in their own space, for better or worse.

RECENT EXPERIMENTAL
FICTION

JORGE LUIS BORGES

(1899—)

Borges, born in Buenos Aires, Argentina, and educated in Europe, is as much an international as an Argentine writer. A classic in his own time, Borges became well known to Americans in the 1960's for *Labyrinths* and *Ficciones*. The stories are fantasies that create paradoxes, stories that vibrate in us and make us uncomfortable with our ordinary ways of seeing time and events. "The South" is simpler than most of Borges' fiction. But notice how this story of adventure ending in romantic death is exactly the story of Juan Dahlmann's own fantasy. It is as if he had written his own story, influenced in that writing by romantic literature. Is the section after the sanitarium all the dream of a man dying on the operating table, dying "under the knife"? Is it "real"? Perhaps the question, Borges would smile, is not important.

The South

JORGE LUIS BORGES

The man who landed in Buenos Aires in 1871 bore the name of Johannes Dahlmann and he was a minister in the Evangelical Church. In 1939, one of his grandchildren, Juan Dahlmann, was secretary of a municipal library on Calle Córdoba, and he considered himself profoundly Argentinian. His maternal grandfather had been that Francisco Flores, of the Second Line-Infantry Division, who had died on the frontier of Buenos Aires, run through with a lance by Indians from Catriel; in the discord inherent between his two lines of descent, Juan Dahlmann (perhaps driven to it by his Germanic blood) chose the line represented by his romantic ancestor, his ancestor of the romantic death. An old sword, a leather frame containing the daguerreotype of a blank-faced man with a beard, the dash and grace of certain music, the familiar strophes of *Martín Fierro,* the passing years, boredom and solitude, all went to foster this voluntary, but never ostentatious nationalism. At the cost of numerous small privations, Dahlmann had managed to save the empty shell of a ranch in the South which had belonged to the Flores family; he continually recalled the image of the balsamic eucalyptus trees and the great rose-colored house which had once been crimson. His duties, perhaps even indolence, kept him in the city. Summer after summer he contented himself with the abstract idea of possession and with the certitude that his ranch was waiting for him on a precise site in the middle of the plain. Late in February, 1939, something happened to him.

Blind to all fault, destiny can be ruthless at one's slightest distraction. Dahlmann had succeeded in acquiring, on that very afternoon, an imperfect copy of Weil's edition of *The Thousand and One Nights.* Avid to examine this find, he did not wait for the elevator but hurried up the stairs. In the obscurity, something brushed by his forehead: a bat, a bird? On the face of the woman who opened the door to him he saw horror engraved, and the hand he wiped across his face came away red with blood. The edge of a recently painted door which someone had forgotten to close had caused this wound. Dahlmann was able to fall asleep, but from the moment he awoke at dawn the savor of all things was atrociously poignant. Fever wasted him and the pictures in *The Thousand and One Nights* served to illustrate nightmares. Friends and relatives paid him visits and, with exaggerated smiles, assured him that they thought he looked fine. Dahlmann listened to them with a kind of feeble stupor and he marveled at their not knowing that he was in hell. A week, eight days passed, and they were like eight centuries. One afternoon, the usual doctor appeared, accompanied by a new doctor, and they carried him off to a sanitarium on the Calle Ecuador, for it was necessary to X-ray him. Dahlmann, in the hackney coach which bore them away, thought that he would, at last, be able to sleep in a room different from his own. He felt happy and communicative. When he arrived at his destination, they undressed him, shaved his head, bound him with metal fastenings to a stretcher; they shone bright lights on him until he was blind and dizzy, auscultated him, and a masked man stuck a needle into his arm. He awoke with a feeling of nausea, covered with a bandage, in a cell with something of a well about it; in the days and nights which followed the operation he came to realize that he had merely been, up until then, in a suburb of hell. Ice in his mouth did not leave the least trace of freshness. During these days Dahlmann hated himself in minute detail: he hated his identity, his bodily necessities, his humiliation, the beard which bristled upon his face. He stoically endured the curative measures, which were painful, but when the surgeon told him he had been on the point of death from septicemia, Dahlmann dissolved in tears of self-pity for his fate. Physical wretchedness and the incessant anticipation of horrible nights had not allowed him time to think of anything so abstract as death. On another day, the surgeon told him he was healing and that, very soon, he would be able to go to his ranch for convalescence. Incredibly enough, the promised day arrived.

Reality favors symmetries and slight anachronisms: Dahlmann had arrived at the sanitarium in a hackney coach and now a hackney coach was to take him to the Constitución station. The first fresh tang of autumn, after the summer's oppressiveness, seemed like a symbol in nature of his rescue and release from fever and death. The city, at seven in the morning, had not lost that air of an old house lent it by the night; the streets seemed like long vestibules, the plazas were like patios. Dahlmann recognized the city with joy on the edge of vertigo: a second before his eyes registered the phenomena themselves, he recalled the corners, the billboards, the modest variety of Buenos Aires. In the yellow light of the new day, all things returned to him.

Every Argentine knows that the South begins at the other side of Rivadavia. Dahlmann was in the habit of saying that this was no mere convention, that whoever crosses this street enters a more ancient and sterner world. From inside the carriage he sought out, among the new buildings, the iron grill window, the brass knocker, the arched door, the entrance way, the intimate patio.

At the railroad station he noted that he still had thirty minutes. He quickly recalled that in a café on the Calle Brazil (a few dozen feet from Yrigoyen's house) there was an enormous cat which allowed itself to be caressed as if it were a disdainful divinity. He entered the café. There was the cat, asleep. He ordered a cup of coffee, slowly stirred the sugar, sipped it (this pleasure had been denied him in the clinic), and thought, as he smoothed the cat's black coat, that this contact was an illusion and that the two beings, man and cat, were as good as separated by a glass, for man lives in time, in succession, while the magical animal lives in the present, in the eternity of the instant.

Along the next to the last platform the train lay waiting. Dahlmann walked through the coaches until he found one almost empty. He arranged his baggage in the network rack. When the train started off, he took down his valise and extracted, after some hesitation, the first volume of *The Thousand and One Nights*. To travel with this book, which was so much a part of the history of his ill-fortune, was a kind of affirmation that his ill-fortune had been annulled; it was a joyous and secret defiance of the frustrated forces of evil.

Along both sides of the train the city dissipated into suburbs; this sight, and then a view of the gardens and villas, delayed the beginning of his reading. The truth was that Dahlmann read very little. The magnetized mountain and the genie who swore to kill his benefactor are—who would deny it?—marvelous, but not so much more than the morning itself and the mere fact of being. The joy of life distracted him from paying attention to Scheherezade and her superfluous miracles. Dahlmann closed his book and allowed himself to live.

Lunch—the bouillon served in shining metal bowls, as in the remote summers of childhood—was one more peaceful and rewarding delight.

Tomorrow I'll wake up at the ranch, he thought, and it was as if he was two men at a time: the man who traveled through the autumn day and across the geography of the fatherland, and the other one, locked up in a sanitarium and subject to methodical servitude. He saw unplastered brick houses, long and angled, time-lessly watching the trains go by; he saw horsemen along the dirt roads; he saw gullies and lagoons and ranches; he saw great luminous clouds that resembled marble; and all these things were accidental, casual, like dreams of the plain. He also thought he recognized trees and crop fields; but he would not have been able to name them, for his actual knowledge of the countryside was quite inferior to his nostalgic and literary knowledge.

From time to time he slept, and his dreams were animated by the impetus of the train. The intolerable white sun of high noon had already become the yellow sun which precedes nightfall, and it would not be long before it would turn red. The railroad car was now also different; it was not the same as the one which had quit the station siding at Constitución; the plain and the hours had transfigured it. Outside, the moving shadow of the railroad car stretched toward the horizon. The elemental earth was not perturbed either by settlements or other signs of humanity. The country was vast but at the same time intimate and, in some measure, secret. The limitless country sometimes contained only a solitary bull. The solitude was perfect, perhaps hostile, and it might have occurred to Dahlmann that he was traveling into the past and not merely south. He was distracted from these considerations by the railroad inspector who, on reading his ticket, advised him that the train would not let him off at the regular station but at another: an earlier stop, one scarcely known to Dahlmann. (The man added an explanation which Dahlmann did not attempt to understand, and which he hardly heard, for the mechanism of events did not concern him.)

The train laboriously ground to a halt, practically in the middle of the plain. The station lay on the other side of the tracks; it was not much more than a siding and a shed. There was no means of conveyance to be seen, but the station chief supposed that the traveler might secure a vehicle from a general store and inn to be found some ten or twelve blocks away.

Dahlmann accepted the walk as a small adventure. The sun had already disappeared from view, but a final splendor exalted the vivid and silent plain, before the night erased its color. Less to avoid fatigue than to draw out his enjoyment of these sights, Dahlmann walked slowly, breathing in the odor of clover with sumptuous joy.

The general store at one time had been painted a deep scarlet, but the years had tempered this violent color for its own good. Something in its poor architecture recalled a steel engraving, perhaps one from an old edition of *Paul et Virginie*. A number of horses were hitched up to the paling. Once inside, Dahlmann thought he recognized the shopkeeper. Then he realized that he had been deceived by the man's resemblance to one of the male nurses in the sanitarium. When the shopkeeper heard Dahlmann's request, he said he would have the shay made up. In order to add one more event to that day and to kill time, Dahlmann decided to eat at the general store.

Some country louts, to whom Dahlmann did not at first pay any attention, were eating and drinking at one of the tables. On the floor, and hanging on to the bar, squatted an old man, immobile as an object. His years had reduced and polished him as water does a stone or the generations of men do a sentence. He was dark, dried up, diminutive, and seemed outside time, situated in eternity. Dahlmann noted with satisfaction the kerchief, the thick poncho, the long *chiripá*, and the colt boots, and told himself, as he recalled futile discussions with people from the Northern counties or from the province of Entre Rios, that gauchos like this no longer existed outside the South.

Dahlmann sat down next to the window. The darkness began overcoming the plain, but the odor and sound of the earth penetrated the iron bars of the window. The shop owner brought him sardines, followed by some roast meat. Dahlmann washed the meal down with several glasses of red wine. Idling, he relished the tart savor of the wine, and let his gaze, now grown somewhat drowsy, wander over the shop. A kerosene lamp hung from a beam. There were three customers at the other table: two of them appeared to be farm workers; the third man, whose features hinted at Chinese blood, was drinking with his hat on. Of a sudden, Dahlmann felt something brush lightly against his face. Next to the heavy glass of turbid wine, upon one of the stripes in the table cloth, lay a spit ball of bread-crumb. That was all: but someone had thrown it there.

The men at the other table seemed totally cut off from him. Perplexed, Dahlmann decided that nothing had happened, and he opened the volume of *The Thousand and One Nights*, by way of suppressing reality. After a few moments another little ball landed on his table, and now the *peones* laughed outright. Dahlmann said to himself that he was not frightened, but he reasoned that it would be a major blunder if he, a convalescent, were to allow himself to be dragged by strangers into some chaotic quarrel. He determined to leave, and had already gotten to his feet when the owner came up and exhorted him in an alarmed voice:

"*Señor* Dahlmann, don't pay any attention to those lads; they're half high."

Dahlmann was not surprised to learn that the other man, now, knew his name. But he felt that these conciliatory words served only to aggravate the situation. Previous to this moment, the *peones'* provocation was directed against an unknown face, against no one in particular, almost against no one at all. Now it was an attack against him, against his name, and his neighbors knew it. Dahlmann pushed the owner aside, confronted the *peones,* and demanded to know what they wanted of him.

The tough with a Chinese look staggered heavily to his feet. Almost in Juan Dahlmann's face he shouted insults, as if he had been a long way off. His game was to exaggerate his drunkenness, and this extravagance constituted a ferocious mockery. Between curses and obscenities, he threw a long knife into the air, followed it with his eyes, caught and juggled it, and challenged Dahlmann to a knife fight. The owner objected in a tremulous voice, pointing out that Dahlmann was unarmed. At this point, something unforeseeable occurred.

From a corner of the room, the old ecstatic gaucho—in whom Dahlmann saw a summary and cipher of the South (his South) — threw him a naked dagger, which landed at his feet. It was as if the South had resolved that Dahlmann should accept the duel. Dahlmann bent over to pick up the dagger, and felt two things. The first, that this almost instinctive act bound him to fight. The second, that the weapon, in his torpid hand, was no defense at all, but would merely serve to justify his murder. He had once played with a poniard, like all men, but his idea of fencing and knife-play did not go further than the notion that all strokes should be directed upwards, with the cutting edge held inwards. *They would not have allowed such things to happen to me in the sanitarium,* he thought.

"Let's get on our way," said the other man.

They went out and if Dahlmann was without hope, he was also without fear. As he crossed the threshold, he felt that to die in a knife fight, under the open sky, and going forward to the attack, would have been a liberation, a joy, and a festive occasion, on the first night in the sanitarium, when they stuck him with the needle. He felt that if he had been able to choose, then, or to dream his death, this would have been the death he would have chosen or dreamt.

Firmly clutching his knife, which he perhaps would not know how to wield, Dahlmann went out into the plain.

JOHN BARTH

(1930—)

Born in 1930 in Maryland, Barth was the age of his narrator Ambrose during World War II, the time of "Lost in the Funhouse." Barth tells us he feels sentimentally connected to the setting and to the story. And so one would expect a simple reflection of Barth's adolescence. Instead we get a brilliant, difficult story about storytelling as well as about the storyteller.

Barth is usually both entertaining and difficult. He has written a number of popular novels, including *Giles Goat Boy* and *The Sot Weed Factor*, books that are parodies of novels as this is a parody of short fiction. At the same time, "Lost in the Funhouse" is not simply *metafiction*—fiction about the process of fictionalizing—it is also a moving story about a boy trying to put himself together.

[See Preface, pp. 30–31 (fiction about fictionalizing).]

Lost in the Funhouse

JOHN BARTH

For whom is the funhouse fun? Perhaps for lovers. For Ambrose it is *a place of fear and confusion.* He has come to the seashore with his family for the holiday, *the occasion of their visit is Independence Day, the most important secular holiday of the United States of America.* A single straight underline is the manuscript mark for italic type, *which in turn* is the printed equivalent to oral emphasis of words and phrases as well as the customary type for titles of complete works, not to mention. Italics are also employed, in fiction stories especially, for "outside," intrusive, or artificial voices, such as radio announcements, the texts of telegrams and newspaper articles, et cetera. They should be used *sparingly.* If passages originally in roman type are italicized by someone repeating them, it's customary to acknowledge the fact. *Italics mine.*

Ambrose was "at that awkward age." His voice came out high-pitched as a child's if he let himself get carried away; to be on the safe side, therefore, he moved and spoke with *deliberate calm* and *adult gravity.* Talking soberly of unimportant or irrelevant matters and listening consciously to the sound of your own voice are useful habits for maintaining control in this difficult interval. *En route* to Ocean City he sat in the back seat of the family car with his brother Peter, age fifteen, and Magda G——, age fourteen, a pretty girl *an exquisite young lady,* who lived not far from them on B—— Street in the town of D——, Maryland. Initials, blanks, or both were often substituted for proper names in nineteenth-century fiction to enhance the illusion of reality. It is as if the author felt it necessary to delete the names for reasons of tact or legal liability. Interestingly, as with other aspects of realism, it is an *illusion* that is being enhanced, by purely artificial means. Is it likely, does it violate the principle of verisimilitude, that a thirteen-year-old boy could make such a sophisticated observation? A girl of fourteen is *the psychological coeval* of a boy of fifteen or sixteen; a thirteen-year-old boy, therefore, even one precocious in some other respects, might be three years *her emotional junior.*

Thrice a year—on Memorial, Independence, and Labor Days—the family visits Ocean City for the afternoon and evening. When Ambrose and Peter's father was their age, the excursion was made by train, as mentioned in the novel *The 42nd Parallel* by John Dos Passos. Many families from the same neighborhood used to travel together, with dependent relatives and often with Negro servants; schoolfuls of children swarmed through the railway cars; everyone shared everyone else's Maryland fried chicken, Virginia ham, deviled eggs, potato salad, beaten biscuits, iced tea. Nowadays (that is, in 19—, the year of our story) the journey is made by automobile— more comfortably and quickly though without the extra fun though without the *camaraderie* of a general excursion. It's all part of the deterioration of American life, their father declares; Uncle Karl supposes that when the boys take *their* families to Ocean City for the holidays they'll fly in Autogiros. Their mother, sitting in the middle of the front seat like Magda in the second, only with her arms on the seat-back behind the men's shoulders, wouldn't want the good old days back again, the steaming trains and stuffy long dresses; on the other hand she can do without Autogiros, too, if she has to become a grandmother to fly in them.

Description of physical appearance and mannerisms is one of several standard methods of characterization used by writers of fiction. It is also important to "keep the senses operating"; when a detail from one of the five senses, say visual, is "crossed" with a detail from another, say auditory, the reader's imagination is oriented to the scene, perhaps unconsciously. This procedure may be compared to the way surveyors and navigators determine their positions by two or more compass bearings, a process known as triangulation. The brown hair on Ambrose's mother's forearms gleamed in the sun like. Though right-handed, she took her left arm from the seat-back to press the dashboard cigar lighter for Uncle Karl. When the glass bead in its handle glowed red, the lighter was ready for use. The smell of Uncle Karl's cigar smoke reminded one of. The fragrance of the ocean came strong to the picnic ground where they always stopped for lunch, two miles inland from Ocean City. Having to pause for a full hour almost within sound of the breakers was difficult for Peter and Ambrose when they were younger; even at their present age it was not easy to keep their anticipation, *stimulated by the briny spume,* from turning into short temper. The Irish author James Joyce, in his unusual novel entitled *Ulysses,* now available in this country, uses the adjectives *snot-green* and *scrotum-tightening* to describe the sea. Visual, auditory, tactile, olfactory, gustatory. Peter and Ambrose's father, while steering their black 1936 LaSalle sedan with one hand, could with the other remove the first cigarette from a white pack of Lucky Strikes and, more remarkably, light it with a match forefingered from its book and thumbed against the flint paper without being detached. The matchbook cover merely advertised U. S. War Bonds and Stamps. A fine metaphor, simile, or other figure of speech, in addition to its obvious "first-order" relevance to the thing it describes, will be seen upon reflection to have a second order of significance: it may be drawn from the *milieu* of the action, for example, or be particularly appropriate to the sensibility of the narrator, even hinting to the reader things of which the narrator is unaware; or it may cast further and subtler lights upon the thing it describes, sometimes ironically qualifying the more evident sense of the comparison.

To say that Ambrose's and Peter's mother was *pretty* is to accomplish nothing; the reader may acknowledge the proposition, but his imagination is not engaged. Besides, Magda was also pretty, yet in an altogether different way. Although she lived on B—— Street she had very good manners and did better than average in school. Her figure was very well developed for her age. Her right hand lay casually on the plush upholstery of the seat, very near Ambrose's left leg, on which his own hand rested. The space between their legs, between her right and his left leg, was out of the line of sight of anyone sitting on the other side of Magda, as well as anyone glancing into the rear-view mirror. Uncle Karl's face resembled Peter's—rather, vice versa. Both had dark hair and eyes, short husky statures, deep voices. Magda's left hand was probably in a similar position on her left side. The boys' father is difficult to describe; no particular feature of his appearance or manner stood out. He wore glasses and was principal of a T—— County grade school. Uncle Karl was a masonry contractor.

Although Peter must have known as well as Ambrose that the latter, because of his position in the car, would be the first to see the electrical towers of the power plant at V——, the halfway point of their trip, he leaned forward and slightly toward the center of the car and pretended to be looking for them through the flat pinewoods and tuckahoe creeks along the highway. For as long as the boys could remember, "looking for the Towers" had been a feature of the first half of their excursions to Ocean City, "looking for the standpipe" of the second. Though the game was childish, their mother preserved the tradition of rewarding the first to see the Towers with a candy-bar or piece of fruit. She insisted now that Magda play the game; the prize, she said, was "something hard to get nowadays." Ambrose decided not to join in; he sat far back in his seat. Magda, like Peter, leaned forward. Two sets of straps were discernible through the shoulders of her sun dress; the inside right one, a brassiere-strap, was fastened or shortened with a small safety pin. The right armpit of her dress, presumably the left as well, was damp with perspiration. The simple strategy for being first to espy the Towers, which Ambrose had understood by the age of four, was to sit on the right-hand side of the

car. Whoever sat there, however, had also to put up with the worst of
the sun, and so Ambrose, without mentioning the matter, chose
sometimes the one and sometimes the other. Not impossibly Peter
had never caught on to the trick, or thought that his brother hadn't
simply because Ambrose on occasion preferred shade to a Baby Ruth
or tangerine.

The shade-sun situation didn't apply to the front seat, owing to
the windshield; if anything the driver got more sun, since the person
on the passenger side not only was shaded below by the door and
dashboard but might swing down his sunvisor all the way too.

"Is that them?" Magda asked. Ambrose's mother teased the boys
for letting Magda win, insinuating that "somebody [had] a girlfriend." Peter and Ambrose's father reached a long thin arm across
their mother to butt his cigarette in the dashboard ashtray, under the
lighter. The prize this time for seeing the Towers first was a banana.
Their mother bestowed it after chiding their father for wasting a half-
smoked cigarette when everything was so scarce. Magda, to take the
prize, moved her hand from so near Ambrose's that he could have
touched it as though accidentally. She offered to share the prize,
things like that were so hard to find; but everyone insisted it was hers
alone. Ambrose's mother sang an iambic trimeter couplet from a
popular song, femininely rhymed:

> "What's good is in the Army;
> What's left will never harm me."

Uncle Karl tapped his cigar ash out the ventilator window; some
particles were sucked by the slipstream back into the car through the
rear window on the passenger side. Magda demonstrated her ability
to hold a banana in one hand and peel it with her teeth. She still sat
forward; Ambrose pushed his glasses back onto the bridge of his nose
with his left hand, which he then negligently let fall to the seat
cushion immediately behind her. He even permitted the single hair,
gold, on the second joint of his thumb to brush the fabric of her skirt.
Should she have sat back at that instant, his hand would have been
caught under her.

Plush upholstery prickles uncomfortably through gabardine slacks
in the July sun. The function of the *beginning* of a story is to
introduce the principal characters, establish their initial relationships, set the scene for the main action, expose the background of the
situation if necessary, plant motifs and foreshadowings where appropriate, and initiate the first complication or whatever of the "rising
action." Actually, if one imagines a story called "The Funhouse," or
"Lost in the Funhouse," the details of the drive to Ocean City don't
seem especially relevant. The *beginning* should recount the events
between Ambrose's first sight of the funhouse early in the afternoon

and his entering it with Magda and Peter in the evening. The *middle* would narrate all relevant events from the time he goes in to the time he loses his way; middles have the double and contradictory function of delaying the climax while at the same time preparing the reader for it and fetching him to it. Then the *ending* would tell what Ambrose does while he's lost, how he finally finds his way out, and what everybody makes of the experience. So far there's been no real dialogue, very little sensory detail, and nothing in the way of a *theme*. And a long time has gone by already without anything happening; it makes a person wonder. We haven't even reached Ocean City yet: we will never get out of the funhouse.

The more closely an author identifies with the narrator, literally or metaphorically, the less advisable it is, as a rule, to use the first-person narrative viewpoint. Once three years previously the young people *aforementioned* played Niggers and Masters in the backyard; when it was Ambrose's turn to be Master and theirs to be Niggers Peter had to go serve his evening papers; Ambrose was afraid to punish Magda alone, but she led him to the whitewashed Torture Chamber between the woodshed and the privy in the Slaves Quarters; there she knelt sweating among bamboo rakes and dusty Mason jars, pleadingly embraced his knees, and while bees droned in the lattice as if on an ordinary summer afternoon, purchased clemency at a surprising price set by herself. Doubtless she remembered nothing of this event; Ambrose on the other hand seemed unable to forget the least detail of his life. He even recalled how, standing beside himself with awed impersonality in the reeky heat, he'd stared the while at an empty cigar box in which Uncle Karl kept stone-cutting chisels: beneath the words *El Producto*, a laureled, loose-toga'd lady regarded the sea from a marble bench; beside her, forgotten or not yet turned to, was a five-stringed lyre. Her shin reposed on the back of her right hand; her left depended negligently from the bencharm. The lower half of scene and lady was peeled away; the words EXAMINED BY —— were inked there into the wood. Nowadays cigar boxes are made of pasteboard. Ambrose wondered what Magda would have done, Ambrose wondered what Magda would do when she sat back on his hand as he resolved she should. Be angry. Make a teasing joke of it. Give no sign at all. For a long time she leaned forward, playing cowpoker with Peter against Uncle Karl and Mother and watching for the first sign of Ocean City. At nearly the same instant, picnic ground and Ocean City standpipe hove into view; an Amoco filling station on their side of the road cost Mother and Uncle Karl fifty cows and the game; Magda bounced back, clapping her right hand on Mother's right arm; Ambrose moved clear "in the nick of time."

At this rate our hero, at this rate our protagonist will remain in the funhouse forever. Narrative ordinarily consists of alternating dramatization and summarization. One symptom of nervous tension, paradoxically, is repeated and violent yawning; neither Peter nor Magda nor Uncle Karl nor Mother reacted in this manner. Although they were no longer small children, Peter and Ambrose were each given a dollar to spend on boardwalk amusements in addition to what money of their own they'd brought along. Magda too, though she protested she had ample spending money. The boys' mother made a little scene out of distributing the bills; she pretended that her sons and Magda were small children and cautioned them not to spend the sum too quickly or in one place. Magda promised with a merry laugh and, having both hands free, took the bill with her left. Peter laughed also and pledged in a falsetto to be a good boy. His imitation of a child was not clever. The boys' father was tall and thin, balding, fair-complexioned. Assertions of that sort are not effective; the reader may acknowledge the proposition, but. We should be much farther along than we are; something has gone wrong; not much of this preliminary rambling seems relevant. Yet everyone begins in the same place; how is it that most go along without difficulty but a few lose their way?

"Stay out from under the boardwalk," Uncle Karl growled from the side of his mouth. The boys' mother pushed his shoulder *in mock annoyance*. They were all standing before Fat May the Laughing Lady who advertised the funhouse. Larger than life, Fat May mechanically shook, rocked on her heels, slapped her thighs while recorded laughter—uproarious, female—came amplified from a hidden loudspeaker. It chuckled, wheezed, wept; tried in vain to catch its breath; tittered, groaned, exploded raucous and anew. You couldn't hear it without laughing yourself, no matter how you felt. Father came back from talking to a Coast-Guardsman on duty and reported that the surf was spoiled with crude oil from tankers recently torpedoed offshore. Lumps of it, difficult to remove, made tarry tidelines on the beach and stuck on swimmers. Many bathed in the surf nevertheless and came out speckled; others paid to use a municipal pool and only sunbathed on the beach. We would do the latter. We would do the latter.

Under the boardwalk, matchbook covers, grainy other things. What is the story's theme? Ambrose is ill. He perspires in the dark passages; candied apples-on-a-stick, delicious-looking, disappointing to eat. Funhouses need men's and ladies' rooms at intervals. Others perhaps have also vomited in corners and corridors; may even have had bowel movements liable to be stepped in in the dark. The word *fuck* suggests suction and/or and/or flatulence. Mother and Father; grandmothers and grandfathers on both sides; great-grandmothers and great-grandfathers on four sides, et cetera. Count a generation as thirty years: in approximately the year when Lord Baltimore was granted charter to the province of Maryland by Charles I, five hundred twelve women—English, Welsh, Bavarian, Swiss—of every class and character, received into themselves the penises the intromittent organs of five hundred twelve men, ditto, in every circumstance and posture, to conceive the five hundred twelve ancestors of the two hundred fifty-six ancestors of the et cetera et cetera et cetera et cetera et cetera et cetera et cetera et cetera of the author, of the narrator, of this story, *Lost in the Funhouse.* In alleyways, ditches, canopy beds, pinewoods, bridal suites, ships' cabins, coach-and-fours, coaches-and-four, sultry toolsheds; on the cold sand under boardwalks, littered with *El Producto* cigar butts, treasured with Lucky Strike cigarette stubs, Coca-Cola caps, gritty turds, cardboard lollipop sticks, matchbook covers warning that A Slip of the Lip Can Sink a Ship. The shluppish whisper, continuous as seawash round the globe, tidelike falls and rises with the circuit of dawn and dusk.

Magda's teeth. She *was* left-handed. Perspiration. They've gone all the way, through, Magda and Peter, they've been waiting for hours with Mother and Uncle Karl while Father searches for his lost son; they draw french-fried potatoes from a paper cup and shake their heads. They've named the children they'll one day have and bring to Ocean City on holidays. Can spermatozoa properly be thought of as male animalcules when there are no female spermatozoa? They grope through hot, dark windings, past Love's Tunnel's fearsome obstacles. Some perhaps lose their way.

Peter suggested then and there that they do the funhouse; he had been through it before, so had Magda, Ambrose hadn't and suggested, his voice cracking on account of Fat May's laughter, that they swim first. All were chuckling, couldn't help it; Ambrose's father, Ambrose's and Peter's father came up grinning like a lunatic with two boxes of syrup-coated popcorn, one for Mother, one for Magda; the men were to help themselves. Ambrose walked on Magda's right; being by nature lefthanded, she carried the box in her left hand. Up front the situation was reversed.

"What are you limping for?" Magda inquired of Ambrose. He supposed in a husky tone that his foot had gone to sleep in the car. Her teeth flashed. "Pins and needles?" It was the honeysuckle on the lattice of the former privy that drew the bees. Imagine being stung there. How long is this going to take?

The adults decided to forgo the pool; but Uncle Karl insisted they change into swimsuits and do the beach. "He wants to watch the pretty girls," Peter teased, and ducked behind Magda from Uncle Karl's pretended wrath. "You've got all the pretty girls you need right here," Magda declared, and Mother said: "Now that's the gospel truth." Magda scolded Peter, who reached over her shoulder to sneak some popcorn. "Your brother and father aren't getting any." Uncle Karl wondered if they were going to have fireworks that night, what with the shortages. It wasn't the shortages, Mr. M—— replied; Ocean City had fireworks from prewar. But it was too risky on account of the enemy submarines, some people thought.

"Don't seem like Fourth of July without fireworks," said Uncle Karl. The inverted tag in dialogue writing is still considered permissible with proper names or epithets, but sounds old-fashioned with personal pronouns. "We'll have 'em again soon enough," predicted the boys' father. Their mother declared she could do without fireworks: they reminded her too much of the real thing. Their father said all the more reason to shoot off a few now and again. Uncle Karl asked *rhetorically* who needed reminding, just look at people's hair and skin.

"The oil, yes," said Mrs. M——.

Ambrose had a pain in his stomach and so didn't swim but enjoyed watching the others. He and his father burned red easily. Magda's figure was exceedingly well developed for her age. She too declined to swim, and got mad, and became angry when Peter attempted to drag her into the pool. She always swam, he insisted; what did she mean not swim? Why did a person come to Ocean City?

"Maybe I want to lay here with Ambrose," Magda teased.

Nobody likes a pedant.

"Aha," said Mother. Peter grabbed Magda by one ankle and ordered Ambrose to grab the other. She squealed and rolled over on the beach blanket. Ambrose pretended to help hold her back. Her tan was darker than even Mother's and Peter's. "Help out, Uncle Karl!" Peter cried. Uncle Karl went to seize the other ankle. Inside the top of her swimsuit, however, you could see the line where the sunburn ended and, when she hunched her shoulders and squealed again, one nipple's auburn edge. Mother made them behave themselves. "*You* should certainly know," she said to Uncle Karl. Archly. "That when a lady says she doesn't feel like swimming, a gentleman doesn't ask questions." Uncle Karl said excuse *him;* Mother winked at Magda; Ambrose blushed; stupid Peter kept saying "Phooey on *feel like!*" and tugging at Magda's ankle; then even he got the point, and cannonballed with a holler into the pool.

"I swear," Magda said, in mock *in feigned* exasperation.

The diving would make a suitable literary symbol. To go off the high board you had to wait in a line along the poolside and up the ladder. Fellows tickled girls and goosed one another and shouted to the ones at the top to hurry up, or razzed them for bellyfloppers. Once on the springboard some took a great while posing or clowning or deciding on a dive or getting up their nerve; others ran right off. Especially among the younger fellows the idea was to strike the funniest pose or do the craziest stunt as you fell, a thing that got harder to do as you kept on and kept on. But whether you hollered *Geronimo!* or *Sieg heil!*, held your nose or "rode a bicycle," pretended to be shot or did a perfect jackknife or changed your mind halfway down and ended up with nothing, it was over in two seconds, after all that wait. Spring, pose, splash. Spring, neat-o, splash. Spring, aw fooey, splash.

The grown-ups had gone on; Ambrose wanted to converse with Magda; she was remarkably well developed for her age; it was said that that came from rubbing with a turkish towel, and there were other theories. Ambrose could think of nothing to say except how good a diver Peter was, who was showing off for her benefit. You could pretty well tell by looking at their bathing suits and arm muscles how far along the different fellows were. Ambrose was glad he hadn't gone in swimming, the cold water shrank you up so. Magda pretended to be uninterested in the diving; she probably weighed as much as he did. If you knew your way around in the funhouse like your own bedroom, you could wait until a girl came along and then slip away without ever getting caught, even if her boyfriend was right with her. She'd think *he* did it! It would be better to be the boyfriend, and act outraged, and tear the funhouse apart.

Not act; *be*.

"He's a master diver," Ambrose said. In feigned admiration. "You really have to slave away at it to get that good." What would it matter anyhow if he asked her right out whether she remembered, even teased her with it as Peter would have?

There's no point in going farther; this isn't getting anybody anywhere; they haven't even come to the funhouse yet. Ambrose is off the track, in some new or old part of the place that's not supposed to be used; he strayed into it by some one-in-a-million chance, like the time the roller-coaster car left the tracks in the nineteen-teens against all the laws of physics and sailed over the boardwalk in the dark. And they can't locate him because they don't know where to look. Even the designer and operator have forgotten this other part, that winds around on itself like a whelk shell. That winds around the right part like the snakes on Mercury's caduceus. Some people, perhaps, don't "hit their stride" until their twenties, when the growing-up business is over and women appreciate other things besides wisecracks and teasing and strutting. Peter didn't have one-tenth the imagination *he* had, not one-tenth. Peter did this naming-their-children thing as a joke, making up names like Aloysius and Murgatroyd, but Ambrose knew *exactly* how it would feel to be married and have children of your own, and be a loving husband and father, and go comfortably to work in the mornings and to bed with your wife at night, and wake up with her there. With a breeze coming through the sash and birds and mockingbirds singing in the Chinese-cigar trees. His eyes watered, there aren't enough ways to say that. He would be quite famous in his line of work. Whether Magda was his wife or not, one evening when he was wise-lined and gray at the temples he'd smile gravely, at a fashionable dinner party, and remind her of his youthful passion. The time they went with his family to Ocean City; the *erotic fantasies* he used to have about her. How long ago it seemed, and childish! Yet tender, too, *n'est-ce pas?* Would she have imagined that the world-famous whatever remembered how many strings were on the lyre on the bench beside the girl on the label of the cigar box he'd stared at in the toolshed at age ten while she, age eleven. Even then he had felt *wise beyond his years;* he'd stroked her hair and said in his deepest voice and correctest English, as to a dear child: "I shall never forget this moment."

But though he had breathed heavily, groaned as if ecstatic, what he'd really felt throughout was an odd detachment, as though someone else were Master. Strive as he might to be transported, he heard his mind take notes upon the scene: *This is what they call* passion. *I am experiencing it.* Many of the digger machines were out of order in the penny arcades and could not be repaired or replaced for the duration. Moreover the prizes, made now in USA, were less interesting than formerly, pasteboard items for the most part, and some of the machines wouldn't work on white pennies. The gypsy fortune-teller machine might have provided a foreshadowing of the climax of this story if Ambrose had operated it. It was even dilapidateder than most: the silver coating was worn off the brown metal handles, the glass windows around the dummy were cracked and taped, her kerchiefs and silks long-faded. If a man lived by himself, he could take a department-store mannequin with flexible joints and modify her in certain ways. *However:* by the time he was that old he'd have a real woman. There was a machine that stamped your name around a white-metal coin with a star in the middle: *A——.* His son would be the second, and when the lad reached thirteen or so he would put a strong arm around his shoulder and tell him calmly: "It is perfectly normal. We have all been through it. It will not last forever." Nobody knew how to be what they were right. He'd smoke a pipe, teach his son how to fish and softcrab, assure him he needn't worry about himself. Magda would certainly give, Magda would certainly yield a great deal of milk, although guilty of occasional solecisms. It don't taste so bad. Suppose the lights came on now!

The day wore on. You think you're yourself, but there are other persons in you. Ambrose gets hard when Ambrose doesn't want to, *and obversely.* Ambrose watches them disagree; Ambrose watches him watch. In the funhouse mirror-room you can't see yourself go on forever, because no matter how you stand, your head gets in the way.

Even if you had a glass periscope, the image of your eye would cover up the thing you really wanted to see. The police will come; there'll be a story in the papers. That must be where it happened. Unless he can find a surprise exit, an unofficial backdoor or escape hatch opening on an alley, say, and then stroll up to the family in front of the funhouse and ask where everybody's been; *he's* been out of the place for ages. That's just where it happened, in that last lighted room: Peter and Magda found the right exit; he found one that you weren't supposed to find and strayed off into the works somewhere. In a perfect funhouse you'd be able to go only one way, like the divers off the highboard; getting lost would be impossible; the doors and halls would work like minnow traps or the valves in veins.

On account of German U-boats, Ocean City was "browned out": streetlights were shaded on the seaward side; shop-windows and boardwalk amusement places were kept dim, not to silhouette tankers and Liberty-ships for torpedoing. In a short story about Ocean City, Maryland, during World War II, the author could make use of the image of sailors on leave in the penny arcades and shooting galleries, sighting through the crosshairs of toy machine guns at swastika'd subs, while out in the black Atlantic a U-boat skipper squints through his periscope at real ships outlined by the glow of penny arcades. After dinner the family strolled back to the amusement end of the boardwalk. The boys' father had burnt red as always and was masked with Noxzema, a minstrel in reverse. The grownups stood at the end of the boardwalk where the Hurricane of '33 had cut an inlet from the ocean to Assawoman Bay.

"Pronounced with a long *o*," Uncle Karl reminded Magda with a wink. His shirt sleeves were rolled up; Mother punched his brown biceps with the arrowed heart on it and said his mind was naughty. Fat May's laugh came suddenly from the funhouse, as if she'd just got the joke; the family laughed too at the coincidence. Ambrose went under the boardwalk to search for out-of-town matchbook covers with the aid of his pocket flashlight; he looked out from the edge of the North American continent and wondered how far their laughter carried over the water. Spies in rubber rafts; survivors in lifeboats. If the joke had been beyond his understanding, he could have said: "*The laughter was over his head.*" And let the reader see the serious wordplay on second reading.

He turned the flashlight on and then off at once even before the woman whooped. He sprang away, heart athud, dropping the light. What had the man grunted? Perspiration drenched and chilled him by the time he scrambled up to the family. "See anything?" his father asked. His voice wouldn't come; he shrugged and violently brushed sand from his pants legs.

"Let's ride the old flying horses!" Magda cried. I'll never be an author. It's been forever already, everybody's gone home, Ocean City's deserted, the ghost-crabs are tickling across the beach and down the littered cold streets. And the empty halls of clapboard hotels and abandoned funhouses. A tidal wave; an enemy air raid; a monster-crab swelling like an island from the sea. *The inhabitants fled in terror.* Magda clung to his trouser leg; he alone knew the maze's secret. "He gave his life that we might live," said Uncle Karl with a scowl of pain, as he. The fellow's hands had been tattooed; the woman's legs, the woman's fat white legs had. *An astonishing coincidence.* He yearned to tell Peter. He wanted to throw up for excitement. They hadn't even chased him. He wished he were dead.

One possible ending would be to have Ambrose come across another lost person in the dark. They'd match their wits together against the funhouse, struggle like Ulysses past obstacle after obstacle, help and encourage each other. Or a girl. By the time they found the exit they'd be closest friends, sweethearts if it were a girl; they'd know each other's inmost souls, be bound together *by the cement of shared adventure;* then they'd emerge into the light and it would turn out that his friend was a Negro. A blind girl. President Roosevelt's son. Ambrose's former archenemy.

Shortly after the mirror room he'd groped along a musty corridor, his heart already misgiving him at the absence of phosphorescent arrows and other signs. He'd found a crack of light—not a door, it turned out, but a seam between the plyboard wall panels—and squinting up to it, espied a small old man, *in appearance not unlike* the photographs at home of Ambrose's late grandfather, nodding upon a stool beneath a bare, speckled bulb. A crude panel of toggle- and knife-switches hung beside the open fuse box near his head; elsewhere in the little room were wooden levers and ropes belayed to boat cleats. At the time, Ambrose wasn't lost enough to rap or call; later he couldn't find that crack. Now it seemed to him that he'd possibly dozed off for a few minutes somewhere along the way; certainly he was exhausted from the afternoon's sunshine and the evening's problems; he couldn't be sure he hadn't dreamed part or all of the sight. Had an old black wall fan droned like bees and shimmied two flypaper streamers? Had the funhouse operator— gentle, somewhat sad and tired-appearing, in expression not unlike the photographs at home of Ambrose's late Uncle Konrad—murmured in his sleep? Is there really such a person as Ambrose, or is he a figment of the author's imagination? Was it Assawoman Bay or Sinepuxent? Are there other errors of fact in this fiction? Was there another sound besides the little slap slap of thigh on ham, like water sucking at the chine-boards of a skiff?

When you're lost, the smartest thing to do is stay put till you're found, hollering if necessary. But to holler guarantees humiliation as well as rescue; keeping silent permits some saving of face—you can act surprised at the fuss when your rescuers find you and swear you weren't lost, if they do. What's more you might find your own way yet, *however belatedly*.

"Don't tell me your foot's still asleep!" Magda exclaimed as the three young people walked from the inlet to the area set aside for ferris wheels, carrousels, and other carnival rides, they having decided in favor of the vast and ancient merry-go-round instead of the funhouse. What a sentence, everything was wrong from the outset. People don't know what to make of him, he doesn't know what to make of himself, he's only thirteen, *athletically and socially inept,* not astonishingly bright, but there are antennae; he has . . . some sort of receivers in his head; things speak to him, he understands more than he should, the world winks at him through its objects, grabs grinning at his coat. Everybody else is in on some secret he doesn't know; they've forgotten to tell him. Through simple *procrastination* his mother put off his baptism until this year. Everyone else had it done as a baby; he'd assumed the same of himself, as had his mother, so she claimed, until it was time for him to join Grace Methodist-Protestant and the oversight came out. He was mortified, but pitched sleepless through his private catechizing, intimidated by the ancient mysteries, a thirteen year old would never say that, resolved to experience conversion like St. Augustine. When the water touched his brow and Adam's sin left him, he contrived by a strain like defecation to bring tears into his eyes—but felt nothing. There was some simple, radical difference about him; he hoped it was genius, feared it was madness, devoted himself to amiability and inconspicuousness. Alone on the seawall near his house he was seized by the terrifying transports he'd thought to find in toolshed, in Communion-cup. The grass was alive! The town, the river, himself, were not imaginary; time roared in his ears like wind; the world was *going on!* This part ought to be dramatized. The Irish author James Joyce once wrote. Ambrose M—— is going to scream.

There is no *texture of rendered sensory detail,* for one thing. The faded distorting mirrors beside Fat May; the impossibility of choosing a mount when one had but a single ride on the great carrousel; the *vertigo attendant on his recognition* that Ocean City was worn out, the place of fathers and grandfathers, straw-boatered men and parasoled ladies survived by their amusements. Money spent, the three paused at Peter's insistence beside Fat May to watch the girls get their skirts blown up. The object was to tease Magda, who said: "I swear, Peter M——, you've got a one-track mind! Amby and me aren't *interested* in such things." In the tumbling-barrel, too, just inside the Devil's-mouth entrance to the funhouse, the girls were upended and their boyfriends and others could see up their dresses if they cared to. Which was the whole point, Ambrose realized. Of the entire funhouse! If you looked around, you noticed that almost all the people on the boardwalk were paired off into couples except the small children; in a way, that was the whole point of Ocean City! If you had X-ray eyes and could see everything going on at that instant under the boardwalk and in all the hotel rooms and cars and alleyways, you'd realize that all that normally *showed*, like restaurants and dance halls and clothing and test-your-strength machines, was merely preparation and intermission. Fat May screamed.

Because he watched the goings-on from the corner of his eye, it was Ambrose who spied the half-dollar on the boardwalk near the tumbling-barrel. Losers weepers. The first time he'd heard some people moving through a corridor not far away, just after he'd lost sight of the crack of light, he'd decided not to call to them, for fear they'd guess he was scared and poke fun; it sounded like roughnecks; he'd hoped they'd come by and he could follow in the dark without their knowing. Another time he'd heard just one person, unless he imagined it, bumping along as if on the other side of the plywood; perhaps Peter coming back for him, or Father, or Magda lost too. Or the owner and operator of the funhouse. He'd called out once, as though merrily: "Anybody know where the heck we are?" But the query was too stiff, his voice cracked, when the sounds stopped he was terrified: maybe it was a queer who waited for fellows to get lost, or a longhaired filthy monster that lived in some cranny of the funhouse. He stood rigid for hours it seemed like, scarcely respiring. His future was shockingly clear, in outline. He tried holding his breath to the point of unconsciousness. There ought to be a button you could push to end your life absolutely without pain; disappear in a flick, like turning out a light. He would push it instantly! He despised Uncle Karl. But he despised his father too, for not being what he was supposed to be. Perhaps his father hated *his* father, and so on, and his son would hate him, and so on. Instantly!

Naturally he didn't have nerve enough to ask Magda to go through the funhouse with him. With incredible nerve and to everyone's surprise he invited Magda, quietly and politely, to go through the funhouse with him. "I warn you, I've never been through it before," he added, *laughing easily;* "but I reckon we can manage somehow. The important thing to remember, after all, is that it's meant to be a *fun*house; that is, a place of amusement. If people really got lost or injured or too badly frightened in it, the owner'd go out of business. There'd even be lawsuits. No character in a work of fiction can make a speech this long without interruption or acknowledgment from the other characters."

Mother teased Uncle Karl: "Three's a crowd, I always heard." But actually Ambrose was relieved that Peter now had a quarter too.

Nothing was what it looked like. Every instant, under the surface of the Atlantic Ocean, millions of living animals devoured one another. Pilots were falling in flames over Europe; women were being forcibly raped in the South Pacific. His father should have taken him aside and said: "There is a simple secret to getting through the funhouse, as simple as being first to see the Towers. Here it is. Peter does not know it; neither does your Uncle Karl. You and I are different. Not surprisingly, you've often wished you weren't. Don't think I haven't noticed how unhappy your childhood has been! But you'll understand, when I tell you, why it had to be kept secret until now. And you won't regret not being like your brother and your uncle. *On the contrary!*" If you knew all the stories behind all the people on the boardwalk, you'd see that *nothing* was what it looked like. Husbands and wives often hated each other; parents didn't necessarily love their children; et cetera. A child took things for granted because he had nothing to compare his life to and everybody acted as if things were as they should be. Therefore each saw himself as the hero of the story, when the truth might turn out to be that he's the villain, or the coward. And there wasn't one thing you could do about it!

Hunchbacks, fat ladies, fools—that no one chose what he was was unbearable. In the movies he'd meet a beautiful young girl in the funhouse; they'd have hairs-breadth escapes from real dangers; he'd do and say the right things; she also; in the end they'd be lovers; their dialogue lines would match up; he'd be perfectly at ease; she'd not only like him well enough, she'd think he was *marvelous;* she'd lie awake thinking about *him,* instead of vice versa—the way *his* face looked in different lights and how he stood and exactly what he'd said—and yet that would be only one small episode in his wonderful life, among many many others. Not a *turning point* at all. What had happened in the toolshed was nothing. He hated, he loathed his parents! One reason for not writing a lost-in-the-funhouse story is that either everybody's felt what Ambrose feels, in which case it goes without saying, or else no normal person feels such things, in which case Ambrose is a freak. "Is anything more tiresome, in fiction, than the problems of sensitive adolescents?" And it's all too long and rambling, as if the author. For all a person knows the first time through, the end could be just around any corner; perhaps, *not impossibly* it's been within reach any number of times. On the other hand he may be scarcely past the start, with everything yet to get through, an intolerable idea.

Fill in: His father's raised eyebrows when he announced his decision to do the funhouse with Magda. Ambrose understands now, but didn't then, that his father was wondering whether he knew what the funhouse was *for*—especially since he didn't object, as he should have, when Peter decided to come along too. The ticket-woman, witchlike, mortifying him when inadvertently he gave her his name-coin instead of the half-dollar, then unkindly calling Magda's attention to the birthmark on his temple: "Watch out for him, girlie, he's a marked man!" She wasn't even cruel, he understood, only vulgar and insensitive. Somewhere in the world there was a young woman with such splendid understanding that she'd see him entire, like a poem or story, and find his words so valuable after all that when he confessed his apprehensions she would explain why they were in fact the very things that made him precious to her . . . and to Western Civilization! There was no such girl, the simple truth being. Violent yawns as they approached the mouth. Whispered advice from an old-timer on a bench near the barrel: "Go crabwise and ye'll get an eyeful without upsetting!" Composure vanished at the first pitch: Peter hollered joyously, Magda tumbled, shrieked, clutched her skirt; Ambrose scrambled crabwise, tight-lipped with terror, was soon out, watched his dropped name-coin slide among the couples. Shame-faced he saw that to get through expeditiously was not the point; Peter feigned assistance in order to trip Magda up, shouted "I see Christmas!" when her legs went flying. The old man, his latest betrayer, cackled approval. A dim hall then of black-thread cobwebs and recorded gibber: he took Magda's elbow to steady her against revolving discs set in the slanted floor to throw your feet out from under, and explained to her in a calm, deep voice his theory that each phase of the funhouse was triggered either automatically, by a series of photoelectric devices, or else manually by operators stationed at peepholes. But he lost his voice thrice as the discs unbalanced him; Magda was anyhow squealing; but at one point she clutched him about the waist to keep from falling, and her right cheek pressed for a moment against his belt-buckle. Heroically he drew her up, it was his chance to clutch her close as if for support and say: "I love you." He even put an arm lightly about the small of her back before a sailor-and-girl pitched into them from behind, sorely treading his left big toe and knocking Magda asprawl with them. The sailor's girl was a string-haired hussy with a loud laugh and light blue drawers; Ambrose realized that he wouldn't have said "I love you" anyhow, and was smitten with self-contempt. How much better it would be to be that common sailor! A wiry little Seaman 3rd, the fellow squeezed a girl to each side and stumbled hilarious into the mirror room, closer to Magda in thirty seconds than Ambrose had got in thirteen years. She giggled at something the fellow said to Peter; she drew her hair from her eyes with a movement so womanly it struck Ambrose's heart; Peter's smacking her backside then seemed particularly coarse. But Magda made a pleased indignant face and cried, "All right for *you,* mister!" and pursued Peter into the maze without a backward glance. The sailor followed after, leisurely, drawing his girl against his hip; Ambrose understood not only that they were all so relieved to be rid of his burdensome company that they didn't even notice his absence, but that he himself shared their relief. Stepping from the treacherous passage at last into the mirror-maze, he saw once again, more clearly than ever, how readily he deceived himself into supposing he was a person. He even foresaw, wincing at his dreadful self-knowledge, that he would repeat the deception, at ever-rarer intervals, all his wretched life, so fearful were the alternatives. Fame, madness, suicide; perhaps all three. It's not believable that so young a boy could articulate that reflection, and in fiction the merely true must always yield to the plausible. Moreover, the symbolism is in places heavy-footed. Yet Ambrose M—— understood, as few adults do, that the famous loneliness of the great was no popular myth but a general truth—furthermore, that it was as much cause as effect.

All the preceding except the last few sentences is exposition that should've been done earlier or interspersed with the present action instead of lumped together. No reader would put up with so much with such *prolixity*. It's interesting that Ambrose's father, though presumably an intelligent man (as indicated by his role as grade-school principal), neither encouraged nor discouraged his sons at all in any way—as if he either didn't care about them or cared all right but didn't know how to act. If this fact should contribute to one of them's becoming a celebrated but wretchedly unhappy scientist, was it a good thing or not? He too might someday face the question; it would be useful to know whether it had tortured his father for years, for example, or never once crossed his mind.

In the maze two important things happened. First, our hero found a name-coin someone else had lost or discarded: *AMBROSE,* suggestive of the famous lightship and of his late grandfather's favorite dessert, which his mother used to prepare on special occasions out of coconut, oranges, grapes, and what else. Second, as he wondered at the endless replication of his image in the mirrors, second, as he *lost himself in the reflection* that the necessity for an observer makes perfect observation impossible, better make him eighteen at least, yet that would render other things unlikely, he heard Peter and Magda chuckling somewhere together in the maze. "Here!" "No, here!" they shouted to each other; Peter said, "Where's Amby?" Magda murmured. "Amb?" Peter called. In a pleased, friendly voice. He didn't reply. The truth was, his brother was a *happy-go-lucky youngster* who'd've been better off with a regular brother of his own, but who seldom complained of his lot and was generally cordial. Ambrose's throat ached; there aren't enough different ways to say that. He stood quietly while the two young people giggled and thumped through the glittering maze, hurrah'd their discovery of its exit, cried out in joyful alarm at what next beset them. Then he set his mouth and followed after, as he supposed, took a wrong turn, strayed into the pass *wherein he lingers yet.*

The action of conventional dramatic narrative may be represented by a diagram called Freitag's Triangle:

or more accurately by a variant of that diagram:

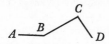

in which *AB* represents the exposition, *B* the introduction of conflict, *BC* the "rising action," complication, or development of the conflict, *C* the climax, or turn of the action, *CD* the dénouement, or resolution of the conflict. While there is no reason to regard this pattern as an absolute necessity, like many other conventions it became conventional because great numbers of people over many years learned by trial and error that it was effective; one ought not to forsake it, therefore, unless one wishes to forsake as well the effect of drama or has clear cause to feel that deliberate violation of the "normal" pattern can better can better effect that effect. This can't go on much longer; it can go on forever. He died telling stories to himself in the dark; years later, when that vast unsuspected area of the funhouse came to light, the first expedition found his skeleton in one of its labyrinthine corridors and mistook it for part of the entertainment. He died of starvation telling himself stories in the dark; but unbeknownst unbeknownst to him, an assistant operator of the funhouse, happening to overhear him, crouched just behind the plyboard partition and wrote down his every word. The operator's daughter, an exquisite young woman with a figure unusually well developed for her age, crouched just behind the partition and transcribed his every word. Though she had never laid eyes on him, she recognized that here was one of Western Culture's truly great imaginations, the eloquence of whose suffering would be an inspiration to unnumbered. And her heart was torn between her love for the misfortunate young man (yes, she loved him, though she had never laid though she knew him only—but how well!—through his words, and the deep, calm voice in which he spoke them) between her love et cetera and her womanly intuition that only in suffering and isolation could he give voice et cetera. Lone dark dying. Quietly she kissed the rough plyboard, and a tear fell upon the page. Where she had written in shorthand *Where she had written in shorthand* Where she had written in shorthand *Where she* et cetera. A long time ago we should have passed the apex of Freitag's Triangle and made brief work of the *dénouement;* the plot doesn't rise by meaningful steps but winds upon itself, digresses, retreats, hesitates, sighs, collapses, expires. The climax of the story must be its protagonist's discovery of a way to get through the funhouse. But he has found none, may have ceased to search.

What relevance does the war have to the story? Should there be fireworks outside or not?

Ambrose wandered, languished, dozed. Now and then he fell into his habit of rehearsing to himself the unadventurous story of his life, narrated from the third-person point of view, from his earliest memory parenthesis of maple leaves stirring in the summer breath of tidewater Maryland end of parenthesis to the present moment. Its principal events, on this telling, would appear to have been *A, B, C,* and *D*.

He imagined himself years hence, successful, married, at ease in the world, the trials of his adolescence far behind him. He has come to the seashore with his family for the holiday: how Ocean City has changed! But at one seldom at one ill-frequented end of the board-walk a few derelict amusements survive from times gone by: the great carrousel from the turn of the century, with its monstrous griffins and mechanical concert band; the roller coaster rumored since 1916 to have been condemned; the mechanical shooting gallery in which only the image of our enemies changed. His own son laughs with Fat May and wants to know what a funhouse is; Ambrose hugs the sturdy lad close and smiles around his pipestem at his wife.

The family's going home. Mother sits between Father and Uncle Karl, who teases him good-naturedly who chuckles over the fact that the comrade with whom he'd fought his way shoulder to shoulder through the funhouse had turned out to be a blind Negro girl—to their mutual discomfort, as they'd opened their souls. But such are the walls of custom, which even. Whose arm is where? How must it feel. He dreams of a funhouse vaster by far than any yet constructed; but by then they may be out of fashion, like steamboats and ex-cursion trains. Already quaint and seedy: the draperied ladies on the frieze of the carrousel are his father's father's mooncheeked dreams; if he thinks of it more he will vomit his apple-on-a-stick.

He wonders: will he become a regular person? Something has gone wrong; his vaccination didn't take; at the Boy-Scout initiation camp-fire he only pretended to be deeply moved, as he pretends to this hour that it is not so bad after all in the funhouse, and that he has a little limp. How long will it last? He envisions a truly astonishing funhouse, incredibly complex yet utterly controlled from a great central switchboard like the console of a pipe organ. Nobody had enough imagination. He could design such a place himself, wiring and all, and he's only thirteen years old. He would be its operator: panel lights would show what was up in every cranny of its cunning of its multifarious vastness; a switch-flick would ease this fellow's way, complicate that's, to balance things out; if anyone seemed lost or frightened, all the operator had to do was.

He wishes he had never entered the funhouse. But he has. Then he wishes he were dead. But he's not. Therefore he will construct funhouses for others and be their secret operator—though he would rather be among the lovers for whom funhouses are designed.

QUESTIONS

1. Who is speaking? It can't be John Barth, for Barth wouldn't write, "The Irish author James Joyce, in his unusual novel entitled *Ulysses*. . . ." Barth would simply write, "Joyce, in *Ulysses*. . . ." There is a naiveté in the speaking voice. We must imagine that the voice we hear is that of a dramatized narrator (see Preface, pp. 5–11). Essentially, there are two stories—the one the narrator is trying, clumsily, to tell, and the story of someone trying to clarify his identity, trying to put himself together, trying to tell a story. "Ambrose understands now, but didn't then. . . ." Apparently the narrator is some years older than the thirteen-year-old Ambrose. Discuss.

2. Why does the narrator have such a difficult time telling a simple story? Why does he feel so false? Why does he feel uncomfortable using stand-ard narrative devices?

3. The narrator tells us that "talking soberly of unimportant or irrelevant matters and listening to the sound of your own voice are useful habits for maintaining control in this difficult interval." He is talking about a boy's attempt to deal with his emotions. What does it also tell you about the form of the story and about the motivation for creating the form, the emotional needs of the narrator? Note: Remember, the narrator is not Barth.

4. List the ways in which the story breaks from the traditional short story that could have been written.

5. List the ways in which, while examining them, the narrator uses standard fictional techniques.

6. Examine three incidents of emotional demand: the sexual encounter at age ten with Magda, the baptism, the Boy Scout initiation. How does Ambrose feel during each? What does he do—and why? How does his response to these incidents explain the strange form of this story?

7. The *funhouse* is analogous to the life of Ambrose and to the form of fiction. Discuss. What alternative image might you invent for a tradi-tional story form and for a traditional sense of a life?

8. Ambrose feels unreal. He feels he is not a real person but an actor. How do these feelings explain the form of the story?

9. How does authentic, spontaneous feeling slip through in this story in spite of Ambrose? Examine the scene of the couple under the boardwalk,

notice the imagery of sexuality. What is the significance of the sexual genealogy?

10. Discuss at some length the image of Ambrose's head getting in the way of his observation. How does this apply to the process of fiction? See Woolf, "An Unwritten Novel" (p. 308). Like Woolf's narrator, the narrator of "Funhouse" asks, "Is there really such a person as Ambrose, or is he a figment of the author's imagination?" Take this in two senses: (1) What is the reality of a character, even one in an autobiography (see Preface, pp. 3–5)? (2) What is the reality of a *person,* created to "meet the faces that he meets"? See Fort's story, "The Coal Shoveller" (p. 763).

11. Ambrose seeks the secret of his reality under the world of appearances. Discuss in relation to his life and to fictional form.

12. Does your life fit Freitag's Triangle? Can you make it fit? What is the relation between fiction and ongoing experience?

13. This story is a kind of *Portrait of the Artist as a Young Man* (see the sketch of James Joyce, pp. 318–319). If you've read *Portrait,* compare and contrast the exploration of the artist figure. Compare the funhouse to the labyrinth Stephen flies out from.

14. Discuss the final paragraph. What does it tell you about Ambrose and about the artist?

15. How is "Lost in the Funhouse" more than a clever exercise? Is it also a moving story? Discuss.

DONALD BARTHELME

(1931—)

Barthelme was born in Philadelphia and grew up in Texas. He has worked as a newspaper reporter, museum director, and editor of a literary magazine. His fiction is published regularly in *The New Yorker*. His collections of sad and comic short fiction include *Come Back, Dr. Caligari; Unspeakable Practices, Unnatural Acts;* and *City Life;* he has written one strange novel, *Snow White*.

If there is a New York avant-garde (it is probably a literary creation), Barthelme is at its center. To make up a story like "Balloon" is very much the same as to make a fantastic balloon like the one inside the story. Both the story itself and the balloon represent a preference for an art of playful energy, an art which does not signify anything, which has no message, no linear structure, no meaning—a creation that offers a model for freedom. The story, then, *is* (paradoxically) meaningful, satirical of people who read meaning into a work of art, who seeks purposes instead of porpoises.

The Balloon

DONALD BARTHELME

The balloon, beginning at a point on Fourteenth Street, the exact location of which I cannot reveal, expanded northward all one night, while people were sleeping, until it reached the Park. There, I stopped it; at dawn the northernmost edges lay over the Plaza; the free-hanging motion was frivolous and gentle. But experiencing a faint irritation at stopping, even to protect the trees, and seeing no reason the balloon should not be allowed to expand upward, over the parts of the city it was already covering, into the "air space" to be found there, I asked the engineers to see to it. This expansion took place throughout the morning, soft imperceptible sighing of gas through the valves. The balloon then covered forty-five blocks north-south and an irregular area east-west, as many as six crosstown blocks on either side of the Avenue in some places. That was the situation, then.

But it is wrong to speak of "situations," implying sets of circumstances leading to some resolution, some escape of tension; there were no situations, simply the balloon hanging there—muted heavy grays and browns for the most part, contrasting with walnut and soft yellows. A deliberate lack of finish, enhanced by skillful installation, gave the surface a rough, forgotten quality; sliding weights on the inside, carefully adjusted, anchored the great, vari-shaped mass at a number of points. Now we have had a flood of original ideas in all media, works of singular beauty as well as significant milestones in the history of inflation, but at that moment there was only *this balloon,* concrete particular, hanging there.

There were reactions. Some people found the balloon "interesting." As a response this seemed inadequate to the immensity of the balloon, the suddenness of its appearance over the city; on the other hand, in the absence of hysteria or other societally-induced anxiety, it must be judged a calm, "mature" one. There was a certain amount of initial argumentation about the "meaning" of the balloon; this subsided, because we have learned not to insist on meanings, and they are rarely even looked for now, except in cases involving the simplest, safest phenomena. It was agreed that since the meaning of the balloon could never be known absolutely, extended discussion was pointless, or at least less purposeful than the activities of those who, for example, hung green and blue paper lanterns from the warm gray underside, in certain streets, or seized the occasion to write messages on the surface, announcing their availability for the performance of unnatural acts, or the availability of acquaintances.

Daring children jumped, especially at those points where the balloon hovered close to a building, so that the gap between balloon and building was a matter of a few inches, or points where the balloon actually made contact, exerting an ever-so-slight pressure against the side of a building, so that balloon and building seemed a unity. The upper surface was so structured that a "landscape" was presented, small valleys as well as slight knolls, or mounds; once atop the balloon, a stroll was possible, or even a trip, from one place to another. There was pleasure in being able to run down an incline, then up the opposing slope, both gently graded, or in making a leap from one side to the other. Bouncing was possible, because of the pneumaticity of the surface, and even falling, if that was your wish. That all these varied motions, as well as others, were within one's possibilities, in experiencing the "up" side of the balloon, was extremely exciting for children, accustomed to the city's flat, hard skin. But the purpose of the balloon was not to amuse children.

Too, the number of people, children and adults, who took advantage of the opportunities described was not so large as it might have been: a certain timidity, lack of trust in the balloon, was seen. There was, furthermore, some hostility. Because we had hidden the pumps, which fed helium to the interior, and because the surface was so vast that the authorities could not determine the point of entry—that is, the point at which the gas was injected—a degree of frustration was evidenced by those city officers into whose province such manifestations normally fell. The apparent purposelessness of the balloon was vexing (as was the fact that it was "there" at all). Had we painted, in great letters, "LABORATORY TESTS PROVE" OR "18% MORE EFFECTIVE" on the sides of the balloon, this difficulty would have been circumvented. But I could not bear to do so. On the whole, these officers were remarkably tolerant, considering the dimensions of the anomaly, this tolerance being the result of, first, secret tests conducted by night that convinced them that little or nothing could be done in the way of removing or destroying the balloon, and, secondly, a public warmth that arose (not uncolored by touches of the aforementioned hostility) toward the balloon, from ordinary citizens.

As a single balloon must stand for a lifetime of thinking about balloons, so each citizen expressed, in the attitude he chose, a complex of attitudes. One man might consider that the balloon had to do with the notion *sullied,* as in the sentence *The big balloon sullied the otherwise clear and radiant Manhattan sky.* That is, the balloon was, in this man's view, an imposture, something inferior to the sky that had formerly been there, something interposed between the people and their "sky." But in fact it was January, the sky was dark and ugly; it was not a sky you could look up into, lying on your back in the street, with pleasure, unless pleasure, for you, proceeded from having been threatened, from having been misused. And the underside of the balloon was a pleasure to look up into, we had seen to that, muted grays and browns for the most part, contrasted with walnut and soft, forgotten yellows. And so, while this man was thinking *sullied,* still there was an admixture of pleasurable cognition in his thinking, struggling with the original perception.

Another man, on the other hand, might view the balloon as if it were part of a system of unanticipated rewards, as when one's employer walks in and says, "Here, Henry, take this package of money I have wrapped for you, because we have been doing so well in the business here, and I admire the way you bruise the tulips, without which bruising your department would not be a success, or at least not the success that it is." For this man the balloon might be a brilliantly heroic "muscle and pluck" experience, even if an experience poorly understood.

Another man might say, "Without the example of ———, it is doubtful that ——— would exist today in its present form," and find many to agree with him, or to argue with him. Ideas of "bloat" and "float" were introduced, as well as concepts of dream and responsibility. Others engaged in remarkably detailed fantasies having to do with a wish either to lose themselves in the balloon, or to engorge it. The private character of these wishes, of their origins, deeply buried and unknown, was such that they were not much spoken of; yet there is evidence that they were widespread. It was also argued that what was important was what you felt when you stood under the balloon; some people claimed that they felt sheltered, warmed, as never before, while enemies of the balloon felt, or reported feeling, constrained, a "heavy" feeling.

Critical opinion was divided:

"monstrous pourings"

"harp"

XXXXXXX "certain contrasts with darker portions"

"inner joy"

"large, square corners"

"conservative eclecticism that has so far governed modern balloon design"

::::::: "abnormal vigor"

"warm, soft, lazy passages"

"Has unity been sacrificed for a sprawling quality?"

"Quelle catastrophe!"

"munching"

People began, in a curious way, to locate themselves in relation to aspects of the balloon: "I'll be at that place where it dips down into Forty-seventh Street almost to the sidewalk, near the Alamo Chile House," or, "Why don't we go stand on top, and take the air, and maybe walk about a bit, where it forms a tight, curving line with the façade of the Gallery of Modern Art—" Marginal intersections offered entrances within a given time duration, as well as "warm, soft, lazy passages" in which . . . But it is wrong to speak of "marginal intersections," each intersection was crucial, none could be ignored (as if, walking there, you might not find someone capable of turning your attention, in a flash, from old exercises to new exercises, risks and escalations). Each intersection was crucial, meeting of balloon and building, meeting of balloon and man, meeting of balloon and balloon.

It was suggested that what was admired about the balloon was finally this: that it was not limited, or defined. Sometimes a bulge, blister, or sub-section would carry all the way east to the river on its own initiative, in the manner of an army's movements on a map, as seen in a headquarters remote from the fighting. Then that part would be, as it were, thrown back again, or would withdraw into new dispositions; the next morning, that part would have made another sortie, or disappeared altogether. This ability of the balloon to shift its shape, to change, was very pleasing, especially to people whose lives were rather rigidly patterned, persons to whom change, although desired, was not available. The balloon, for the twenty-two days of its existence, offered the possibility, in its randomness, of mislocation of the self, in contradistinction to the grid of precise, rectangular pathways under our feet. The amount of specialized training currently needed, and the consequent desirability of long-term commitments, has been occasioned by the steadily growing importance of complex machinery, in virtually all kinds of operations; as this tendency increases, more and more people will turn, in bewildered inadequacy, to solutions for which the balloon may stand as a prototype, or "rough draft."

I met you under the balloon, on the occasion of your return from Norway; you asked if it was mine; I said it was. The balloon, I said, is a spontaneous autobiographical disclosure, having to do with the unease I felt at your absence, and with sexual deprivation, but now that your visit to Bergen has been terminated, it is no longer necessary or appropriate. Removal of the balloon was easy; trailer trucks carried away the depleted fabric, which is now stored in West Virginia, awaiting some other time of unhappiness, sometime, perhaps, when we are angry with one another.

PHILIP ROTH

(1933—)

Best known for his first book of stories, *Goodby Columbus,* Roth has written a number of celebrated, sometimes scandalous, novels, including *Letting Go, When She Was Good, Portnoy's Complaint,* and *The Breast.* Where Kafka, in "The Metamorphosis," changes his character into a beetle, Roth, playing on Kafka, turns *his* character into a breast. So in "Looking at Kafka" Roth looks at a writer closely connected to him. In this idiosyncratic story he uses both essay and fiction-posing-as-autobiography to immerse himself in Kafka and to examine his own life. Like Woolf, Barth, and Fort, Roth is laying open to the reader the process of writing fiction and its meaning in the writer's life.

"I Always Wanted You to Admire My Fasting"; or, Looking at Kafka

PHILIP ROTH

To the students of English 275, University of Pennsylvania, Fall 1972

> *"I always wanted you to admire my fasting," said the hunger artist. "We do admire it," said the overseer, affably. "But you shouldn't admire it," said the hunger artist. "Well then we don't admire it," said the overseer, "but why shouldn't we admire it?" "Because I have to fast, I can't help it," said the hunger artist. "What a fellow you are," said the overseer, "and why can't you help it?" "Because," said the hunger artist, lifting his head a little and speaking, with his lips pursed, as if for a kiss, right into the overseer's ear, so that no syllable might be lost, "because I couldn't find the food I liked. If I had found it, believe me, I should have made no fuss and stuffed myself like you or anyone else." These were his last words, but in his dimming eyes remained the firm though no longer proud persuasion that he was still continuing to fast.*
>
> *—"A Hunger Artist," Franz Kafka*

1

I am looking, as I write of Kafka, at the photograph taken of him at the age of forty (my age)—it is 1924, as sweet and hopeful a year as he may ever have known as a man, and the year of his death. His face is sharp and skeletal, a burrower's face: pronounced cheekbones made even more conspicuous by the absence of sideburns; the ears shaped and angled on his head like angel wings; an intense, creaturely gaze of startled composure—enormous fears, enormous control; a black towel of Levantine hair pulled close around the skull the only sensuous feature; there is a familiar Jewish flare in the bridge of the nose, the nose itself is long and weighted slightly at the tip—the nose of half the Jewish boys who were my friends in high school. Skulls chiseled like this one were shoveled by the thousands from the ovens; had he lived, his would have been among them, along with the skulls of his three younger sisters. Of course it is no more horrifying to think of Franz Kafka in Auschwitz than to think of anyone in Auschwitz—to paraphrase Tolstoy, it is just horrifying in its own way. But he died too soon for the holocaust. Had he lived, perhaps he would have escaped with his good friend and great advocate Max Brod, who eventually found refuge in Palestine, a citizen of Israel until his death there in 1970. But *Kafka* escaping? It seems unlikely for one so fascinated by entrapment and careers that culminate in anguished death. Still, there is Karl Rossman, his American greenhorn. Having imagined Karl's escape to America and his mixed luck here, could not Kafka have found a way to execute an escape for himself? The New School for Social Research in New York becoming *his* Great Nature Theater of Oklahoma? Or perhaps through the influence of Thomas Mann, a position in the German department at Princeton . . . But then had Kakfa lived it is not at all certain that the books of his which Mann celebrated from *his* refuge in New Jersey would ever have been published; eventually Kafka might either have destroyed those manuscripts that he had once bid Max Brod to dispose of at his death, or, at the least, continued to keep them his secret. The Jewish refugee arriving in America in 1938 would not then have been Mann's "religious humorist," but a frail and bookish fifty-five-year-old bachelor, formerly a lawyer for a government insurance firm in Prague, retired on a pension in Berlin at the time of Hitler's rise to power—an author, yes, but of a few eccentric stories, mostly about animals, stories no one in America had ever heard of and only a handful in Europe had read; a homeless K., but without K.'s willfulness and purpose, a homeless Karl, but without Karl's youthful spirit and resilience; just a Jew lucky enough to have escaped with his life, in his possession a suitcase containing some clothes, some family photos, some Prague mementos, and the manuscripts, still unpublished and in pieces, of *Amerika, The Trial, The Castle,* and (stranger things happen) three more fragmented novels, no less remarkable than the bizarre masterworks that he keeps to himself out of Oedipal timidity, perfectionist madness, and insatiable longings for solitude and spiritual purity.

July, 1923: Eleven months before he will die in a Vienna sanatorium, Kafka somehow finds the resolve to leave Prague and his father's home for good. Never before has he even remotely succeeded in living apart, independent of his mother, his sisters and his father, nor has he been a writer other than in those few hours when he is not working in the legal department of the Workers' Accident Insurance Office in Prague; since taking his law degree at the university, he has been by all reports the most dutiful and scrupulous of employees, though he finds the work tedious and enervating. But in June of 1923—having some months earlier been pensioned from his job because of his illness—he meets a young Jewish girl of nineteen at a seaside resort in Germany, Dora Dymant, an employee at the vacation camp of the Jewish People's Home of Berlin. Dora has left her

Orthodox Polish family to make a life of her own (at half Kafka's age); she and Kafka—who has just turned forty—fall in love . . . Kafka has by now been engaged to two somewhat more conventional Jewish girls—twice to one of them—hectic, anguished engagements wrecked largely by his fears. "I am mentally incapable of marrying," he writes his father in the forty-five-page letter he gave to his mother to deliver, ". . . the moment I make up my mind to marry I can no longer sleep, my head burns day and night, life can no longer be called life." He explains why. "Marrying is barred to me," he tells his father, "because it is your domain. Sometimes I imagine the map of the world spread out and you stretched diagonally across it. And I feel as if I could consider living in only those regions that either are not covered by you or are not within your reach. And in keeping with the conception I have of your magnitude, these are not many and not very comforting regions—and marriage is not among them." The letter explaining what is wrong between this father and this son is dated November, 1919; the mother thought it best not even to deliver it, perhaps for lack of courage, probably, like the son, for lack of hope.

During the following two years Kafka attempts to wage an affair with Milena Jesenská-Pollak, an intense young woman of twenty-four who has translated a few of his stories into Czech and is most unhappily married in Vienna; his affair with Milena, conducted feverishly, but by and large through the mails, is even more demoralizing to Kafka than the fearsome engagements to the nice Jewish girls. They aroused only the paterfamilias longings that he dared not indulge, longings inhibited by his exaggerated awe of his father—"spellbound," says Brod, "in the family circle"—and the hypnotic spell of his own solitude; but the Czech Milena, impetuous, frenetic, indifferent to conventional restraints, a woman of appetite and anger, arouses more elemental yearnings and more elemental fears. According to a Prague critic, Rio Preisner, Milena was "psychopathic"; according to Margaret Buber-Neumann, who lived two years beside her in the German concentration camp where Milena died following a kidney operation in 1944, she was powerfully sane, extraordinarily humane and courageous. Milena's obituary for Kafka was the only one of consequence to appear in the Prague press; the prose is strong, so are the claims she makes for Kafka's accomplishment. She is still only in her twenties, the dead man is hardly known as a writer beyond his small circle of friends—yet Milena writes, "His knowledge of the world was exceptional and deep, and he was a deep and exceptional world in himself . . . [He had] a delicacy of feeling bordering on the miraculous and a mental clarity that was terrifyingly uncompromising, and in turn he loaded on to his illness the whole burden of his mental fear of life . . . He wrote the most important books in recent German literature." One can imagine this vibrant young woman stretched diagonally across the bed, as awesome to Kafka as his own father spread out across the map of the world. His letters to her are disjointed, unlike anything else of his in print; the word fear, frequently emphasized, appears on page after page. "We are both married, you in Vienna, I to my Fear in Prague." He yearns to lay his head upon her breast; he calls her "Mother Milena"; during at least one of their two brief rendezvous, he is hopelessly impotent. At last he has to tell her to leave him be, an edict that Milena honors though it leaves her hollow with grief. "Do not write," Kafka tells her, "and let us not see each other; I ask you only to quietly fulfill this request of mine; only on those conditions is survival possible for me; everything else continues the process of destruction."

Then in the early summer of 1923, during a visit to his sister who is vacationing with her children by the Baltic Sea, he finds young Dora Dymant, and within a month Franz Kafka has gone off to live with her in two rooms in a suburb of Berlin, out of reach at last of the "claws" of Prague and home. How can it be? How can he, in his illness, have accomplished so swiftly and decisively the leave-taking that was so beyond him in his healthiest days? The impassioned letter-writer who could equivocate interminably about which train to catch to Vienna to meet with Milena (if he should meet with her for the weekend at all); the bourgeois suitor in the high collar, who, during his drawn-out agony of an engagement with the proper Fräulein Bauer, secretly draws up a memorandum for himself, countering the arguments "for" marriage with the arguments "against"; the poet of the ungraspable and the unresolved, whose belief in the immovable barrier separating the wish from its realization is at the heart of his excruciating visions of defeat, the Kafka whose fictions refute every easy, touching, humanish daydream of salvation and justice and fulfillment with densely imagined counter-dreams that mock all solutions and escapes—this Kafka, escapes! Overnight! K. penetrates the Castle walls—Joseph K. evades his indictment—"a breaking away from it altogether, a mode of living completely outside the jurisdiction of the court." Yes, the possibility of which Joseph K. has just a glimmering in the Cathedral, but can neither fathom nor effectuate —"not . . . some influential manipulation of the case, but . . . a circumvention of it"—Kafka realizes in the last year of his life.

Was it Dora Dymant or was it death that pointed the new way? Perhaps it could not have been one without the other. We know that the "illusory emptiness" at which K. gazed upon first entering the village and looking up through the mist and the darkness to the Castle was no more vast and incomprehensible than was the idea of himself as husband and father to the young Kafka; but now it seems the prospect of a Dora forever, of a wife, home, and children everlasting, is no longer the terrifying, bewildering prospect it would once have been, for now "everlasting" is undoubtedly not much more than a matter of months. Yes, the dying Kafka is determined to marry, and writes to Dora's Orthodox father for his daughter's hand. But the imminent death that has resolved all contradictions and uncertainties in Kafka is the very obstacle placed in his path by the young girl's father. The request of Franz Kafka, a dying man, to bind to him in his invalidism Dora Dymant, a healthy young girl, is— denied!

If there is not one father standing in Kafka's way, there is another—and, to be sure, another beyond him. Dora's father, writes Max Brod in his biography of Kafka, "set off with [Kafka's] letter to consult the man he honored most, whose authority counted more than anything else for him, the 'Gerer Rebbe.' The rabbi read the letter, put it to one side, and said nothing more than the single syllable, 'No.' " *No.* Klamm himself could have been no more abrupt—or any more removed from the petitioner. *No.* In its harsh finality, as telling and inescapable as the curselike threat delivered by his father to Georg Bendemann, that thwarted fiancé: "Just take your bride on your arm and try getting in my way. I'll sweep her from your very side, you don't know how!" *No.* Thou shalt not have, say the fathers, and Kafka agrees that he shall not. The habit of obedience and renunciation; also his own distaste for the diseased and reverence for strength, appetite, and health. " 'Well, clear this out now!' said the overseer, and they buried the hunger artist, straw and all. Into the cage they put a young panther. Even the most insensitive felt it refreshing to see this wild creature leaping around the cage that had so long been dreary. The panther was all right. The food he liked was brought him without hesitation by the attendants; he seemed not even to miss his freedom; his noble body, furnished almost to the bursting point with all that it needed, seemed to carry freedom around with it too; somewhere in his jaws it seemed to lurk; and the joy of life streamed with such ardent passion from his throat that for the onlookers it was not easy to stand the shock of it. But they braced themselves, crowded around the cage, and did not want ever to move away." So no is no; he knew as much himself. A healthy young girl of nineteen cannot, *should* not, be given in matrimony to a sickly man twice her age, who spits up blood ("I sentence you," cries Georg Bendemann's father, "to death by drowning!") and shakes in his bed with fevers and chills. What sort of un-Kafka-like dream had Kafka been dreaming?

And those nine months spent with Dora have still other "Kafkaesque" elements: a fierce winter in quarters inadequately heated; the inflation that makes a pittance of his own meager pension, and sends into the streets of Berlin the hungry and needy whose sufferings, says Dora, turn Kafka "ash-gray"; and his tubercular lungs, flesh transformed and punished. Dora cares as devotedly and tenderly for the diseased writer as does Gregor Samsa's sister for her brother, the bug. Gregor's sister plays the violin so beautifully that Gregor "felt as if the way were opening before him to the unknown nourishment he craved"; he dreams, in his condition, of sending his gifted sister to the Conservatory! Dora's music is Hebrew, which she reads aloud to Kafka, and with such skill that, according to Brod, "Franz recognized her dramatic talent; on his advice and under his direction she later educated herself in the art . . ."

Only Kafka is hardly vermin to Dora Dymant, *or to himself*. Away from Prague and his father's home, Kafka, in his fortieth year, seems at last to have been delivered from the self-loathing, the self-doubt, and those guilt-ridden impulses to dependence and self-effacement that had nearly driven him mad throughout his twenties and thirties; all at once he seems to have shed the pervasive sense of hopeless despair that informs the great punitive fantasies of *The Trial,* "The Penal Colony," and "The Metamorphosis." Years earlier, in Prague, he had directed Max Brod to destroy all his papers, including three unpublished novels, upon his death; now, in Berlin, when Brod introduces him to a German publisher interested in his work, Kafka consents to the publication of a volume of four stories, and consents, says Brod, "without much need of long arguments to persuade him." With Dora to help, he diligently resumes his study of Hebrew; despite his illness and the harsh winter, he travels to the Berlin Academy for Jewish Studies to attend a series of lectures on the Talmud—a very different Kafka from the estranged melancholic who once wrote in his diary, "What have I in common with the Jews? I have hardly anything in common with myself and should stand very quietly in a corner, content that I can breathe." And to further mark the change, there is ease and happiness with a woman: with this young and adoring companion, he is playful, he is pedagogical, and one would guess, in light of his illness (*and* his happiness), he is chaste. If not a husband (such as he had striven to be to the conventional Fräulein Bauer), if not a lover (as he struggled hopelessly to be with Milena), he would seem to have become something no less miraculous in his scheme of things: a father, a kind of father to this sisterly, mothering daughter. *As Franz Kafka awoke one morning from uneasy dreams he found himself transformed in his bed into a father, a writer, and a Jew.*

"I have completed the construction of my burrow," begins the long, exquisite, and tedious story that he wrote that winter in Berlin, "and it seems to be successful. . . . Just the place where, according to my calculations, the Castle Keep should be, the soil was very loose and sandy and had literally to be hammered and pounded into a firm state to serve as a wall for the beautifully vaulted chamber. But for such tasks the only tool I possess is my forehead. So I had to run with my forehead thousands and thousands of times, for whole days and nights, against the ground, and I was glad when the blood came, for that was proof that the walls were beginning to harden; in that way, as everybody must admit, I richly paid for my Castle Keep."

"The Burrow" is the story of an animal with a keen sense of peril whose life is organized around the principle of defense, and whose deepest longings are for security and serenity; with teeth and claws— *and* forehead—the burrower constructs an elaborate and ingeniously intricate system of underground chambers and corridors that are designed to afford it some peace of mind; however, while this burrow does succeed in reducing the sense of danger from without, its maintenance and protection are equally fraught with anxiety: "these anxieties are different from ordinary ones, prouder, richer in content, often long repressed, but in their destructive effects they are perhaps much the same as the anxieties that existence in the outer world gives rise to." The story (whose ending is lost) terminates with the burrower fixated upon distant subterranean noises that cause it "to assume the existence of a great beast," itself burrowing in the direction of the Castle Keep.

Another grim tale of entrapment, and of obsession so absolute that no distinction is possible between character and predicament. Yet this fiction imagined in the last "happy" months of his life is touched with a spirit of personal reconciliation and sardonic self-acceptance, with a tolerance for one's own brand of madness, that is not apparent in "The Metamorphosis"; the piercing masochistic irony of the early animal story—as of "The Judgment" and *The Trial*—has given way here to a critique of the self and its preoccupations that, though bordering on mockery, no longer seeks to resolve itself in images of the uttermost humiliation and defeat . . . But there is more here than a metaphor for the insanely defended ego, whose striving for invulnerability produces a defensive system that must in its turn become the object of perpetual concern—there is also a very unromantic and hard-headed fable about how and why art is made, a portrait of the artist in all his ingenuity, anxiety, isolation, dissatisfaction, relentlessness, obsessiveness, secretiveness, paranoia, and self-addiction, a portrait of the magical thinker at the end of his tether, Kafka's Prospero . . . It is an infinitely suggestive story, this story of life in a hole. For, finally, remember the proximity of Dora Dymant during the months that Kafka was at work on "The Burrow" in the two underheated rooms that was their illicit home. Certainly a dreamer like Kafka need never have entered the young girl's body for her tender presence to kindle in him a fantasy of a hidden orifice that promises "satisfied desire," "achieved ambition," and "profound slumber," but that once penetrated and in one's possession, arouses the most terrifying and heartbreaking fears of retribution and loss. "For the rest I try to unriddle the beast's plans. Is it on its wanderings, or is it working on its own burrow? If it is on its wanderings then perhaps an understanding with it might be possible. If it should really break through to the burrow I shall give it some of my stores and it will go on its way again. It will go on its way again, a fine story! Lying in my heap of earth I can naturally dream of all sorts of things, even of an understanding with the beast, though I know well enough that no such thing can happen, and that at the instant when we see each other, more, at the moment when we merely guess at each other's presence, we shall blindly bare our claws and teeth . . ."

He died of tuberculosis of the lungs and the larynx a month short of his forty-first birthday, June 3, 1924. Dora, inconsolable, whispers for days afterward, "My love, my love, my good one . . ."

2

1942. I am nine; my Hebrew school teacher, Dr. Kafka, is fifty-nine. To the little boys who must attend his "four to five" class each afternoon, he is known—in part because of his remote and melancholy foreignness, but largely because we vent on him our resentment at having to learn an ancient calligraphy at the very hour we should be out screaming our heads off on the ballfield—he is known as Dr. Kishka. Named, I confess, by me. His sour breath, spiced with intestinal juices by five in the afternoon, makes the Yiddish word for "insides" particularly telling, I think. Cruel, yes, but in truth I would have cut out my tongue had I ever imagined the name would become legend. A coddled child, I do not yet think of myself as persuasive, nor, quite yet, as a literary force in the world. My jokes don't hurt, how could they, I'm so adorable. And if you don't believe me, just ask my family and the teachers in school. Already at nine, one foot in Harvard, the other in the Catskills. Little Borscht Belt comic that I am outside the classroom, I amuse my friends Schlossman and Ratner on the dark walk home from Hebrew school with an imitation of Kishka, his precise and finicky professorial manner, his German accent, his cough, his gloom. "Doctor *Kishka!*" cries Schlossman, and hurls himself savagely against the newsstand that belongs to the candy store owner whom Schlossman drives just a little crazier each night. "Doctor Franz—Doctor Franz—Doctor Franz—*Kishka!*" screams Ratner, and my chubby little friend who lives upstairs from me on nothing but chocolate milk and Mallomars does not stop laughing until, as is his wont (his mother has asked me "to keep an eye on him" for just this reason), he wets his pants. Schlossman takes the occasion of Ratner's humiliation to pull the little boy's paper out of his notebook and wave it in the air—it is the assignment Dr. Kafka has just returned to us, graded; we were told to make up an alphabet of our own, out of straight lines and curved lines and dots. "That is all an alphabet is," he had explained. "That is all Hebrew is. That is all English is. Straight lines and curved lines and dots." Ratner's alphabet, for which he received a C, looks like twenty-six skulls strung in a row. I received my A for a curlicued alphabet inspired largely (as Dr. Kafka would seem to have surmised from his comment at the top of the page) by the number eight. Schlossman received an F for forgetting even to do it—and a lot he seems to care, too. He is content—he is *overjoyed*—with things as they are. Just waving a piece of paper in the air, and screaming, *"Kishka! Kishka!"* makes him deliriously happy. We should all be so lucky.

At home, alone in the glow of my goose-necked "desk" lamp (plugged after dinner into an outlet in the kitchen, my study) the vision of our refugee teacher, sticklike in a fraying three-piece blue suit, is no longer very funny—particularly after the entire beginner's Hebrew class, of which I am the most studious member, takes the name "Kishka" to its heart. My guilt awakens redemptive fantasies of heroism. I have them often about "the Jews in Europe." I must save him. If not me, who? The demonic Schlossman? The babyish Ratner? And if not now, when? For I have learned in the ensuing weeks that Dr. Kafka lives in "a room" in the house of an elderly Jewish lady on the shabby lower stretch of Avon Avenue, where the trolley still runs, and the poorest of Newark's Negroes shuffle meekly up and down the street, for all they seem to know still back in Mississippi. A *room*. And *there*! My family's apartment is no palace, but it is ours at least, so long as we pay the thirty-eight-fifty a month in rent; and though our neighbors are not rich, they refuse to be poor and they refuse to be meek. Tears of shame and sorrow in my eyes, I rush into the living room to tell my parents what I have heard (though not that I heard it during a quick game of "aces up" played a minute before class against the synagogue's rear wall—worse, played directly beneath a stained glass window embossed with the names of the dead): "My Hebrew teacher lives in a *room*."

My parents go much further than I could imagine anybody going in the real world. Invite him to dinner, my mother says. *Here*? Of course here—Friday night; I'm sure he can stand a home-cooked meal and a little pleasant company. Meanwhile my father gets on the phone to call my Aunt Rhoda, who lives with my grandmother and tends her and her potted plants in the apartment house at the corner of our street. For nearly two decades now my father has been introducing my mother's forty-year-old "baby" sister to the Jewish bachelors and widowers of New Jersey. No luck so far. Aunt Rhoda, an "interior decorator" in the dry goods department of "The Big Bear," a mammoth merchandise and produce market in industrial Elizabeth, wears falsies (this information by way of my older brother) and sheer frilly blouses, and family lore has it that she spends hours in the bathroom every day applying powders and sweeping her stiffish hair up into a dramatic pile on her head; but despite all this dash and display, she is, in my father's words, "still afraid of the facts of life." He, however, is undaunted, and administers therapy regularly and gratis: "Let 'em squeeze ya, Rhoda—it *feels* good!" I am his flesh and blood, I can reconcile myself to such scandalous talk in our kitchen—*but what will Dr. Kafka think?* Oh, but it's too late to do anything now. The massive machinery of matchmaking has been set in motion by my undiscourageable father, and the smooth engines of my proud homemaking mother's hospitality are already purring away. To throw my body into the works in an attempt to bring it all to a halt—well, I might as well try to bring down the New Jersey Bell Telephone Company by leaving our receiver off the hook. Only Dr. Kafka can save me now. But to my muttered invitation, he replies, with a formal bow that turns me scarlet—who has ever seen a person do such a thing outside of a movie house?—he replies that he would be *honored* to be my family's dinner guest. "My aunt," I rush to tell him, "will be there too." It appears that I have just said something mildly humorous; odd to see Dr. Kafka smile. Sighing, he says, "I will be delighted to meet her." Meet her? He's supposed to *marry* her. How do I warn him? And how do I warn Aunt Rhoda (a very great admirer of me and my marks) about his sour breath, his roomer's pallor, his Old World ways, so at odds with her up-to-dateness? My face feels as if it will ignite of its own—and spark the fire that will engulf the synagogue, Torah and all—when I see Dr. Kafka scrawl our address in his notebook, and beneath it, some words *in German*. "Good night, Dr. Kafka!" "Good night, and thank you, thank you." I turn to run, I go, but not fast enough: out on the street I hear Schlossman—that fiend!—announcing to my classmates who are punching one another under the lamplight down from the synagogue steps (where a card game is also in progress, organized by the Bar Mitzvah boys): "Roth invited Kishka to his *house!* To *eat!*"

Does my father do a job on Kafka! Does he make a sales pitch for familial bliss! What it means to a man to have two fine boys and a wonderful wife! Can Dr. Kafka imagine what that's like? The thrill? The satisfaction? The pride? He tells our visitor of the network of relatives on his mother's side that are joined in a "family association" of over two hundred and fifty people located in seven states, including the state of Washington! Yes, relatives even in the Far West: here are their photographs, Dr. Kafka; this is a beautiful book we published entirely on our own for five dollars a copy, pictures of every member of the family, including infants, and a family history by "Uncle" Lichtblau, the eighty-five-year-old patriarch of the clan. This is our family newsletter that is published twice a year and distributed nationwide to all the relatives. This, in the frame, is the menu from the banquet of the family association, held last year in a ballroom of the "Y" in Newark, in honor of my father's mother on her seventy-fifth birthday. My mother, Dr. Kafka learns, has served *six consecutive years* as the secretary-treasurer of the family association. My father has served a two-year term as president, as have each of his three brothers. We now have fourteen boys in the family in uniform. Philip writes a letter on V-mail stationery to five of his cousins in the Army every single month. "Religiously," my mother puts in, smoothing my hair. "I firmly believe," says my father, "that the family is the cornerstone of everything." Dr. Kafka, who has listened with close attention to my father's *spiel,* handling the various documents that have been passed to him with great delicacy and poring over them with a kind of rapt absorption that reminds me of myself over the watermarks of my stamps, now for the first time expresses himself on the subject of family; softly he says, "I agree," and inspects again the pages of our family book. "Alone," says my father, in conclusion, "alone, Dr. Kafka, is a stone." Dr. Kafka, setting the book gently upon my mother's gleaming coffee table, allows with a nod how that is so. My mother's fingers are now turning in the curls behind my ears; not that I even know it at the time, or that she does. Being stroked is my life; stroking me, my father, and my brother is hers.

My brother goes off to a Boy Scout "council" meeting, but only after my father has him stand in his neckerchief before Dr. Kafka and describe to him the skills he has mastered to earn each of his badges. I am invited to bring my stamp album into the living room and show Dr. Kafka my set of triangular stamps from Zanzibar. "Zanzibar!" says my father rapturously, as though I, not even ten, have already been there and back. My father accompanies Dr. Kafka and myself into the "sun parlor," where my tropical fish swim in the aerated, heated, and hygienic paradise I have made for them with my weekly allowance and my Hanukah *gelt.* I am encouraged to tell Dr. Kafka what I know about the temperament of the angelfish, the function of the catfish, and the family life of the black molly. I know quite a bit. "All on his own he does that," my father says to Kafka. "He gives me a lecture on one of those fish, it's seventh heaven, Dr. Kafka." "I can imagine," Kafka replies.

Back in the living room my Aunt Rhoda suddenly launches into a rather recondite monologue on "scotch plaids," designed, it would appear, only for the edification of my mother. At least she looks fixedly at my mother while she delivers it. I have not yet seen her look directly at Dr. Kafka; she did not even turn his way at dinner when he asked how many employees there were at "The Big Bear." "How would I know?" she replies, and continues conversing with my mother, something about a grocer or a butcher who would take care of her "under the counter" if she could find him nylons for his wife. It never occurs to me that she will not look at Dr. Kafka because she is shy—nobody that dolled up could, in my estimation, be shy—I can only think that she is outraged. *It's his breath. It's his accent. It's his age.* I'm wrong—it turns out to be what Aunt Rhoda calls his "superiority complex." "Sitting there, sneering at us like that," says my aunt, somewhat superior now herself. "Sneering?" repeats my father, incredulous. "Sneering and laughing, yes!" says Aunt Rhoda. My mother shrugs: "*I* didn't think he was laughing." "Oh, don't worry, by himself there he was having a very good time—*at our expense.* I know the European-type man. Underneath they think they're all lords of the manor," Rhoda says. "You know something, Rhoda?" says my father, tilting his head and pointing a finger, "I think you fell in love." "With *him?* Are you *crazy?*" "He's too quiet for Rhoda," my mother says, "I think maybe he's a little bit of a wallflower. Rhoda is a lively person, she needs lively people around her." "Wallflower? He's not a wallflower! He's a gentleman, that's all. And he's lonely," my father says assertively, glaring at my mother for coming in over his head like this *against* Kafka. My Aunt Rhoda is forty years old—it is not exactly a shipment of brand-new goods that he is trying to move. "He's a gentleman, he's an educated man, and I'll tell you something, he'd give his eye teeth to have a nice home and a wife." "Well," says my Aunt Rhoda, "let him find one then, if he's so educated. Somebody who's his equal, who he doesn't have to look down his nose at with his big sad refugee eyes!" "Yep, she's in love," my father announces, squeezing Rhoda's knee in triumph. "With him?" she cries, jumping to her feet, taffeta crackling around her like a bonfire. "With *Kafka?*" she snorts, "I wouldn't give an old man like him the time of day!"

Dr. Kafka calls and takes my Aunt Rhoda to a movie. I am astonished, both that he calls and that she goes; it seems there is more desperation in life than I have come across yet in my fish tank. Dr. Kafka takes my Aunt Rhoda to a play performed at the "Y." Dr. Kafka eats Sunday dinner with my grandmother and my Aunt Rhoda, and at the end of the afternoon, accepts with that formal bow of his the Mason jar of barley soup that my grandmother presses him to carry back to his room with him on the No. 8 bus. Apparently he was very taken with my grandmother's jungle of potted plants—and she,

as a result, with him. Together they spoke in Yiddish about gardening. One Wednesday morning, only an hour after the store has
opened for the day, Dr. Kafka shows up at the dry goods department
of "The Big Bear"; he tells Aunt Rhoda that he just wanted to see
where she worked. That night he writes in his diary, "With the
customers she is forthright and cheery, and so managerial about
'taste' that when I hear her explain to a chubby young bride why
green and blue do not 'go,' I am myself ready to believe that Nature
is in error and R. is correct."

One night, at ten, Dr. Kafka and Aunt Rhoda come by unexpectedly, and a small impromptu party is held in the kitchen—coffee
and cake, even a thimbleful of whiskey all around, to celebrate the
resumption of Aunt Rhoda's career on the stage. I have only heard
tell of my aunt's theatrical ambitions. My brother says that when I
was small she used to come to entertain the two of us on Sundays
with her puppets—she was at that time employed by the W.P.A. to
travel around New Jersey and put on puppet shows in schools and
even in churches; Aunt Rhoda did all the voices, male and female,
and with the help of another young girl, manipulated the manikins
on their strings. Simultaneously she had been a member of the
"Newark Collective Theater," a troupe organized primarily to go
around to strike groups to perform *Waiting for Lefty;* everybody in
Newark (as I understood it) had had high hopes that Rhoda Pilchik
would go on to Broadway—everybody except my grandmother. To
me this period of history is as difficult to believe in as the era of the
lake-dwellers that I am studying in school; of course, people say it
was once so, so I believe them, but nonetheless it is hard to grant
such stories the status of the real, given the life I see around me.

Yet my father, a very avid realist, is in the kitchen, *schnapps* glass
in hand, toasting Aunt Rhoda's success. She has been awarded one of
the starring roles in the Russian masterpiece, *The Three Sisters,* to
be performed six weeks hence by the amateur group at the Newark
"Y." Everything, announces Aunt Rhoda, everything she owes to
Franz, and his encouragement. One conversation—"One!" she cries
gaily—and Dr. Kafka had apparently talked my grandmother out of
her lifelong belief that actors are not serious human beings. And
what an actor *he* is, in his own right, says Aunt Rhoda. How he had
opened her eyes to the meaning of things, by reading her the famous
Chekhov plays—yes, read it to her from the opening line to the final
curtain, all the parts, and actually left her in tears. Here Aunt
Rhoda says, "Listen, listen—this is the first line of the play—it's the
key to everything. Listen—I just think about what it was like that
night Pop passed away, how I thought and thought what would
happen, what would we all do—and, and, listen—"

"We're listening," laughs my father.

Pause; she must have walked to the center of the kitchen linoleum. She says, sounding a little surprised, " 'It's just a year ago today that father died.' "

"Shhh," warns my mother, "you'll give the little one nightmares."

I am not alone in finding my aunt "a changed person" during the ensuing weeks of rehearsal. My mother says this is just what she was like as a little girl. "Red cheeks, always those hot, red cheeks—and everything exciting, even taking a bath." "She'll calm down, don't worry," says my father, "and then he'll pop the question." "Knock on wood," says my mother. "Come on," says my father, "he knows what side his bread is buttered on—he sets foot in this house, he sees what a family is all about, and believe me, he's licking his chops. Just look at him when he sits in that club chair. This is his dream come true." "Rhoda says that in Berlin, before Hitler, he had a young girlfriend, years and years it went on, and then she left him. For somebody else. She got tired of waiting." "Don't worry," says my father, "when the time comes I'll give him a little nudge. He ain't going to live forever, either, and he knows it."

Then one weekend, as a respite from the "strain" of nightly rehearsals—which Dr. Kafka regularly visits, watching in his hat and coat from a seat at the back of the auditorium until it is time to accompany Aunt Rhoda home—they take a trip to Atlantic City. Ever since he arrived on these shores Dr. Kafka has wanted to see the famous boardwalk and the horse that dives from the high board. But in Atlantic City something happens that I am not allowed to know about; any discussion of the subject conducted in my presence is in Yiddish. Dr. Kafka sends Aunt Rhoda four letters in three days. She comes to us for dinner and sits till midnight crying in our kitchen; she calls the "Y" on our phone to tell them (weeping) that her mother is still ill and she cannot come to rehearsal again—she may even have to drop out of the play—no, she can't, she can't, her mother is too ill, she herself is too upset! Good-bye! Then back to the kitchen table to cry; she wears no pink powder and no red lipstick, and her stiff brown hair, down, is thick and spiky as a new broom.

My brother and I listen from our bedroom, through the door that silently he has pushed ajar.

"Have you ever?" says Aunt Rhoda, weeping. "Have you *ever*?"

"Poor soul," says my mother.

"*Who?*" I whisper to my brother. "Aunt Rhoda or—"

"Shhhh!" he says. "Shut *up!*"

In the kitchen my father grunts. "Hmm. Hmm." I hear him getting up and walking around and sitting down again—and then grunting. I am listening so hard that I can hear the letters being

folded and unfolded, stuck back into their envelopes and then removed to be puzzled over one more time.

"Well?" demands Aunt Rhoda. *"Well?"*

"Well what?" answers my father.

"Well what do you want to say now?"

"He's *meshugeh,*" admits my father. "Something is wrong with him
all right."

"But," sobs Aunt Rhoda, "no one would believe me when *I* said
it!"

"Rhody, Rhody," croons my mother in that voice I know from
those times that I have had to have stitches taken, or when I awaken
in tears, somehow on the floor beside my bed. "Rhody, don't be
hysterical, darling. It's over, kitten, it's all over."

I reach across to my brother's "twin" bed and tug on the blanket. I
don't think I've ever been so confused in my life, not even by death.
The speed of things! Everything good undone in a moment! By
what? *"What?"* I whisper. *"What is it?"*

My brother, the Boy Scout, smiles leeringly and with a fierce hiss
that is no answer and enough answer, addresses my bewilderment:
"Sex!"

Years later, a junior at college, I receive an envelope from home
containing Dr. Kafka's obituary, clipped from the *Jewish News,* the
tabloid of Jewish affairs that is mailed each week to the homes of the
Jews of Essex County. It is summer, the semester is over, but I have
stayed on at school, alone in my room in the town, trying to write
short stories; I am fed by a young English professor and his wife in
exchange for babysitting; I tell the sympathetic couple, who are also
loaning me the money for my rent, why it is I can't go home. My
tearful fights with my father are all I can talk about at their dinner
table. "Keep him away from me!" I scream at my mother. "But,
darling," she asks me, "what is going on? What is this all about?"—
the very same question with which I used to plague my older brother,
asked of me now out of the same bewilderment and innocence. "He
loves you," she explains. But that, of all things, seems to me to be
precisely what is blocking my way. Others are crushed by paternal
criticism—I find myself oppressed by his high opinion of me! Can it
possibly be true (and can I possibly admit) that I am coming to hate
him for loving me so? praising me so? But that makes no sense—the
ingratitude! the stupidity! the contrariness! Being loved is so obviously a blessing, *the* blessing, praise such a rare bequest; only listen
late at night to my closest friends on the literary magazine and in the
drama society—they tell horror stories of family life to rival *The Way
of All Flesh,* they return shell-shocked from vacations, drift back to

school as though from the wars. What they would give to be in my golden slippers! "What's going on?" my mother begs me to tell her; but how can I, when I can neither fully believe that this is happening to us, nor that I am the one who is making it happen. That they, who together cleared all obstructions from my path, should seem now to be my final obstruction! No wonder my rage must filter through a child's tears of shame, confusion, and loss. All that we have constructed together over the course of two century-long decades, and look how I must bring it down—in the name of this tyrannical need that I call my "independence"! Born, I am told, with the umbilical cord around my neck, it seems I will always come close to strangulation trying to deliver myself from my past into my future. . . . My mother, keeping the lines of communication open, sends a note to me at school: "We miss you"—and encloses the very brief obituary notice. Across the margin at the bottom of the clipping, she has written (in the same hand that she wrote notes to my teachers and signed my report cards, in the very same handwriting that once eased my way in the world), "Remember poor Kafka, Aunt Rhoda's beau?"

"Dr. Franz Kafka," the notice reads, "a Hebrew teacher at the Talmud Torah of the Schley Street Synagogue from 1939 to 1948, died on June 3 in the Deborah Tuberculosis Sanitorium in Browns Mills, New Jersey. Dr. Kafka had been a patient there since 1950. He was 70 years old. Dr. Kafka was born in Prague, Czechoslovakia, and was a refugee from the Nazis. He leaves no survivors."

He also leaves no books: no *Trial*, no *Castle*, no "Diaries." The dead man's papers are claimed by no one, and disappear—all except those four *"meshugeneh"* letters that are, to this day as far as I know, still somewhere in amongst the memorabilia accumulated in her dresser drawers by my spinster aunt, along with a collection of Broadway "Playbills," sales citations from "The Big Bear," and transatlantic steamship stickers.

Thus all trace of Dr. Kafka disappears. Destiny being destiny, how could it be otherwise? Does the Land Surveyor reach the Castle? Does K. escape the judgment of the Court, or Georg Bendemann the judgment of his father? " 'Well, clear this out now!' said the overseer, and they buried the hunger artist, straw and all." No, it simply is not in the cards for Kafka ever to become *the* Kafka—why, that would be stranger even than a man turning into an insect. No one would believe it, Kafka least of all.

KEITH FORT

(1933—)

Fort was born in Tennessee in 1933; he got his B.A. at the University of the South, his Ph.D. in comparative literature from the University of Minnesota. He has worked as a journalist and, since 1962, has taught literature at Georgetown. Fort writes short fiction and has completed a novel. He is fascinated by the process of fiction and the relation between fictional form and perception; he believes that "to experiment with form is to deal with the way we perceive and order experience—a radical intrusion into the most basic foundation of ours, or any, culture." But "The Coal Shoveller" is more than an experiment; it is a sensitive examination of the relation between personal need, cultural image, and fictional form, of the play of self-deception through which we experience what we call the *world*.

The Coal Shoveller

KEITH FORT

"The clock is ticking."

That's a poor beginning for my short story. The trouble with "clock" is that it symbolizes time, and I don't want to introduce any big ideas into my story. Besides, I actually have an electric clock which whirrs.

It is a snowy day in midwinter. Out of my second-story window I see the street. The snow is so deep that all traffic has stopped. The last vehicle to come by was a truck which dumped five or six tons of coal on the sidewalk beside the red brick Victorian building across the street. It was once a fine mansion, or so my mother told me during her visit. She had lived in Washington in the early 1900's when her father was a senator. She said that a school for young ladies was there, and the "best people" sent their daughters to it. Now the building is divided into small, cheap apartments for government workers. When I walk by, I sometimes see rats in the yard. The land is quite valuable, and in time the grey cupolas, the bay windows, and the portico will come down to be replaced by a new glass and steel office building in the style of the Holiday Inn which is just behind it. On top of the inn is a lattice fence which, I assume, shields some kind of sun porch. At night they turn pink floodlights on the lattice.

A Negro man is shovelling the coal into the basement. I am separated from him by Massachusetts Avenue. The task I have set myself is not a very difficult one. The scene is visually appealing to me. I would like to write a simple short story describing the scene and, perhaps, giving some idea of the rather interesting neighborhood in which I live. I have no theme to draw out of the scene. The thing itself is enough. So it seems that the best style for me would be something on the order of the new novels.

The northeast wind blows the snow almost horizontally down Seventeenth Street. It slaps against the coal shoveller's face, sticks to him briefly, melts and falls. He is wearing a faded green army jacket. A black strip over his left breast has the words "U.S. Army" printed on it in gold letters. The Negro's face is partially muffled by a grey hat with ear flaps and a red scarf wrapped high around his neck. His eyes are turned onto the coal pile in front of him. The lumps are of various sizes, the smaller pieces on the bottom. The head of the coal scoop runs along the snow and enters the coal. The handle is brown with a faded red stripe where it meets the scoop. The shovel comes out. He swings around to the south. The blue flag on the Australian embassy. The white house next to it. The tops of parked cars. The whiteness of Seventeenth Street. The elaborate concrete curves of the B'nai Brith building. The blue fence around the Holiday Inn swimming pool. The red brick building. The black hole into the cellar. The coal clatters down into the chute. Black dust flecks the snow. He continues his movement, turning north into the wind. The apartment building across Massachusetts Avenue. The window on the second floor. Up Seventeenth Street. The flashing red sign "The Bacchus." The coal pile. The shovel goes in. The wood is brown, surrounded by a red stripe where the handle meets the black scoop. A grey glove with a hole in it. The skin beneath the hole is black.

I can't go on like that. Words have a powerful integrity of their own which no amount of authorial intention can eliminate. I could write a hundred essays on how objective I am going to be, but the connotations of "white," "snow," and "black" would still be there. All that I wanted was to describe the scene, but who could fail to see in my story a comment on the white noose that is strangling our black inner-city?

You might argue that my objections to continuing my story as I started it are based solely on the assumption of a faulty reader reaction, and that I should be skillful enough to remake the consciousness of my audience as I write. Can someone like Robbe-Grillet actually believe that he is reshaping the mind of man as he writes? I don't have the arrogance to deny reality in the name of an idea of reality.

Nor am I convinced that fiction *should* try to approximate painting (or the films). Prose has been headed in this direction for some time, but like most movements in art this one was begun on ill-defined premises and succeeding writers merely spun out a potential. We have come to a point now where the weaknesses inherent in the original assumptions prevent us from going further. To ask words to make fiction into photographic realism is to demand a performance which they are totally incapable of giving.

Since I cannot escape words and since words are necessarily symbols, I might as well write a more traditional story in which I admit that every time I use a word I am interpreting reality. The only ideas I can draw out of the scene are my own because they are obviously the only ones I know. I have no concept of the way in which the coal shoveller sees the world.

Amelia, who was six, had exhausted every possibility for entertainment she could find in the house. She had played with her dolls, colored the book she had been given at the school Christmas party the day before, and had made two entirely different houses out of the sofa pillows. An unusual inclination to help her mother had resulted in her being ushered out of the kitchen when she had spilled a cup of milk that was to be used for the Christmas cookies. On most holidays she would have gone to visit one of her friends, but the private school she went to was in the suburbs where most of the pupils lived, and her mother wasn't willing to risk driving through the snow. If she were at someone else's house they could at least watch television, but her father allowed only two programs a week and she had squandered her time for two solid hours on Sunday. Amelia had finally settled by the window where she watched the snow and the old colored man across the street who was shovelling the coal. She wanted to go outside and play, but it wasn't allowed because of the traffic.

In desperation she went back to the kitchen and asked her mother to take her out, but "There is too much to be done, darling," was all she got.

"There's not any cars in the street."

"It's still dangerous. Maybe your father will take you out when he's through working."

Amelia went back into the living room and tried to color another picture, but the tiger she was working on didn't interest her. She closed the book and looked at the door which led into her father's study. The rule that "Daddy is not to be bothered when he's working" was, she knew, an absolute one.

Under most circumstances this suited her well enough because she was actually frightened by the room. The study had been built on the side of the house the summer before when her father had published a book and had been given a big raise. To help him in his work the room had no windows and a special control which kept the room at the same temperature all the time. The darkness and the quietness bothered her, but she had reached her limit.

She walked to the door as quietly as she could, turned the knob, and had started in when her mother heard her.

"Don't bother daddy."

Her mother came running from the kitchen and pulled her away. The door was open a crack. She saw her father in the dark room with the bright light over his typewriter making his face look all black and white.

"I'm sorry, Michael," her mother said as she closed the door. "It's snowing and she wanted to go out."

"That's all right," Michael said through the closed door. "I'll take her out in a few minutes. My train of thought is broken now anyway." He had been married for ten years and the way his wife said "snowin'" still bothered him. It was embarrassing for a sociologist, active in the Civil Rights movement, to have a Southern wife.

Michael turned back to his desk. Actually he was pleased with the interruption. He was almost through with the article he had been working on about the problems of urban Negroes in Washington. He had attacked the question from various angles, poking at it first with the intellect then with the emotions. The piece now had about the right amount of feeling and thought to make it acceptable to one of the slick magazines. It would be good to let the manuscript sit overnight. One more polishing tomorrow, and it would be finished. He took the last page out of the typewriter, laid it neatly with the others, leaned back in his chair, and surveyed with satisfaction the day's production.

The bright lights in the living room hurt his eyes. His wife was making more than the usual amount of noise in the kitchen. Out of the window he saw the curtain of snow that was falling over the street. In the distance the old Negro man was shovelling coal.

"Let's go, daddy," Amelia said. "There's lots of snow."

She was dressed in a bright red snow suit.

"Where are your galoshes?" he asked.

"Margaret," he called into the kitchen, "are you trying to make the child sick by letting her go out without her galoshes?"

His wife came out of the kitchen. "Amelia. I told you to put them on."

"I don't want to go out," Amelia said sullenly.

"Now that I've stopped work," her father said, "we are going out into the snow."

Amelia went to the closet, and with her mother's help laboriously pulled on the galoshes. Michael got on his own overshoes and coat.

"I wish I could go with you," his wife said. "The snow is beautiful."

"When I was a boy in Wisconsin, we wouldn't have called this anything but a flurry," he said with a smile.

"I've never seen so much," Amelia said.

From there on the story writes itself. Michael goes into the snow. He gradually discovers the reality of his wife's life and that he has never understood the Negroes at all. Finally, he arrives at some understanding of the emotional sterility of his own life, which is sentimentally compared to his childhood back in Wisconsin.

Sound familiar? Joyce's "The Dead." I didn't deliberately set out to imitate the story, but it was there waiting for me like a trap. I couldn't avoid imitation.

In addition to my feeling that this has been done already better than I could do it, there are other reasons why I don't like my story. The focus is on the main character's movement towards self-understanding. It posits that intellectual and emotional development is all that counts. The reality of the Negro coal shoveller, even the realness of the snow and the house, is not considered important beside the ideas which I have extracted (or perhaps created) from them. My story would end by suggesting the subordination of thing to idea. I am inclined to agree with those who say that literature (no matter how negative the themes) which reinforces the habit of extracting ideas from reality panders to the self-interest of the middle class. You can be sure that both you and I would prefer a few hours of anguish trying to understand the validity of various attitudes that one could take toward the Negro shovelling coal to five minutes of real or fictional exposure to the reality of that man's life and his work.

Not only am I blocked philosophically from writing a Joycean story—I am also incompatible with its style. I lack the necessary innocence. When the symbolic technique was devised, writers must have been able to allow their symbols to emerge "naturally." I have studied fiction too long. Take the "study" in my story. Is that too heavy-handed? How subtle should a symbol be? I honestly don't know. I rather imagine that a good symbol is one that takes an English teacher about two minutes to decipher and one of his students ten. Talk of "organic symbols" that grow out of reality is absolute garbage at this point in the evolution of fictional techniques.

If I use symbols I also depend heavily on my readers' being willing to accept my symbolism for what I intend. For example, I said in my story that Michael laid the last page "neatly" on the others. "Neatly" is a symbol for certain aspects of his character. But what is actually wrong with being neat? If there weren't a general, if ill-defined, prejudice of modern readers in favor of emotional spontaneity, that word might be honorific. If you say that *in the context* the symbol is made meaningful, I reply that my story is nothing but a pastiche of such symbols.

Underlying all of them is a series of romantic values epitomized by the noble Negro coal shoveller, the goodness of nature (represented by the snow), and the joys of childhood. When I draw these values out of my story, as I am doing now, they are subject to attack. But one of the advantages that comes to the fictionalist is that he doesn't have to defend his assumptions. The critics tell us that he doesn't have to defend his assumptions. The critics tell us that we should examine literature from within. This idea has been forced on them by the "creative" writers. Who can blame an author like Henry James for wanting his value assumptions considered "out of bounds"?

Then there is the rather obvious point that I have completely distorted reality in my story. I live in a small apartment. A house on Massachusetts Avenue would cost a fortune. I am the one from the South, not my wife.

Since I am aware of the ideas behind my symbols, why not write an essay instead of a short story? I reject that at once. My first inclination is to explain this rejection by saying something about the "mystery of art." Many writers talk of this mystery, and it seems to me that they do so primarily to convince themselves that they are somehow "special" and belong to a cult of super souls who have powers (and, more importantly, privileges) that ordinary mortals can't understand. The real reason that I prefer fiction is that it gives me a feeling of righteousness which is denied to me in essays. In fiction I redefine reality by style. When I survey the new world I have created in my story I can say, "Yes, by God, since the world is like that I am completely justified in feeling what I feel." I am quick to admit that I need this kind of self-justification and that I want to use the devices of fiction to make others second my righteousness.

In the fragment of my story on Michael, I disguised, under the illusion of objectivity, my own need to use fiction to justify myself and gain approval of readers. But now that I admit this need, I might as well try an autobiographical story in which I reveal myself more directly and, consequently, make a more overt appeal for approval. I will use the time (mentioned earlier) when my mother came to visit me here.

The woman stands in the small, cramped apartment. She looks down on the oblivious snow in the avenue—not knowing that she or he existed. The woman in front of him—a mother, but not a mother because mothers are associated with home, and here is not home. She, vaguely ashamed to be here—not of him because it is not his fault that he lives here with a Yankee wife, but of herself, of her dead husband, and her dead father and the long line of failures that have reduced the family to the point of living in a small apartment.

He puts her bag on the floor and waits awkwardly for her to do something. She asks for a glass of sherry. It is almost twilight. The snow is falling harder outside—the blanket is making all men equal in cold and misery and accentuating the memory of warm Southern summers with the smell of purple wisteria twisting through honeysuckle when the bright colors differentiated people: blacks from whites and whites from poor whites. And it is all over for her now because there is no more home to live in and no more wooded yards lined with flowers, and she and the son and the Negro servants have all fled north to Washington, where they are equal under the snow but hating that equality—the Negro because the equalness is not real, the son because he is poor, and the Mother because she knows that she is better. She sips sherry in the twilight and the son straight whiskey—waiting.

He has put out on the table a book of family history because it will please her to know that he cares. She looks at it, and the book, like a trigger, explodes the blocks against history, and between sips of sherry there pours out the talk that he has heard so often, but that still can make him desire again to be a child in a world where he could maintain the illusion of a baronial grandeur bequeathed to him by the past—but for him so long away that the memory he had received is like the deformed last of the litter. A tiny final effort from the exhausted womb of the old South. Too twisted and confused to do more than make him wish he had been closer to the source of the myth.

"Do you see that house?" she says as she walks to the window.

"Yes."

"I went to school there when your grandfather was a senator. He was a great man. I drove up every morning to that building in a carriage. All the great people sent their children there. At least I think that's the building. So much has changed."

As she talks, he thinks:

He was a child. It was summer at his grandmother's. The large rambling house with its rows of bedrooms and the porch that ran all around the house high up in the foothills of the Georgia Blue Ridge. "On a clear day," his grandmother said, "you can see to the sea." But even then he knew that was not true. It had been a summer place, but now a few of the downstairs rooms had been insulated so that she could live there—not in isolation but still fighting with the ferocious anger that her mother before her had used to hold the family together after the War, but which had not been able to cope with Yankee businessmen, boll weevils, and resentful Negro workers in South Georgia. Now she lived on the hill surrounded by thick underbrush which kept from her the knowledge of the encroaching townspeople whose squat, white houses lapped at the hill. All that was left outside of the underbrush of what had once been a great estate was the Episcopal church at the foot of the hill which his great-grandfather had built just after the War for the use of the family and the other summer people.

Then the summer when he was seven he came and his grandmother told him that he could no longer play in the church because it had been sold. She said "sold" with an icy pride which made him afraid. On the first Sunday when he was there his grandmother was sitting on the porch reading Sir Walter Scott to him—he not understanding, but made peaceful by the words which flowed in and out of the mimosa trees and the humming of bees. She stopped. "Did you understand that?"

"What, ma'am?"

"What I read to you."

"Not exactly."

"Listen. 'My foot is on my native heath, and my name is MacGregor!' Does that mean anything to you?"

"Yes, ma'am," he lied. But it did. A thousand times since he had said it. When he came home from college and the heath was a quarter-acre yard with an old Ford in it. And even now when he walked into the little apartment on Massachusetts Avenue he said it with bitterness.

Before she started reading again, the church bell sounded from outside of the underbrush. He heard singing coming out of a loud-speaker—cracked twangy accents of country people. He felt his grandmother stiffen.

"Angela," she said.

"Yes'm." The fat old Negro woman came out onto the porch drying her hands on her apron. The enormous kindness of the woman became a natural part of the warm summer morning.

"What is that noise?"

"There's more folks want to go to the church than it'll hold. They put up speakers for those who's outside."

"Thank you, Angela."

Angela went back to fix Sunday dinner.

"I want you to remember," his grandmother said to him, "that Sunday morning is God's gift of Peace. For one as old as I, Peace is sacred."

"Yes, ma'am," he said.

That night as he lay in his bed and watched the moon lie on the state of Georgia he saw a frail woman carrying a big can move like a black shadow away from the house and into the underbrush. He was afraid, too afraid to think, and he waited until the orange light had taken away the silver moonlight, and he slept.

When the vacation was over and he was home he asked his mother and father why it had happened. They pretended not to understand but answered anyway. "Your grandmother is a fine, strong woman," his father said with pride. But he could not understand this because when his father's boss would call on Sunday morning his father would grumble but go to work. "We have to eat," he would say. And his father worked for a Baptist although the boss became an Episcopalian like him later on.

And he could not understand how Sunday mornings could both be sacred and not sacred and he saw that his father loved the strength of his grandmother but also wanted to get a raise from the Baptist. Being a child he could not stand uncertainty and found a third way which he believed could eventually fuse the opposition into one-ness—intelligence, which he now knew was the weakest weapon he could have chosen because it compounded, not resolved, the opposition. The more clearly his mind failed to understand why Sundays were sacred the more he longed to share in his grandmother's pride. But unlike his father for whom the beliefs were closer and more real and who lost his life trying to work for the Baptist and live by his grandmother's sureness, the dream of the peace of Sunday mornings was so far removed from him that he was almost denied the pleasure of having it as a dream; and yet at times like this, when his mother was talking, he could almost reach out to the voice of his grandmother ("MY foot is on my native heath") that created in him, for however short a time, the innocence of dreaming, when he could free himself of knowing the inconsistencies, the injustices, the contradictions that were housed in his grandmother's impoverished Eden.

Perhaps, he thought, if there is another generation the dream will be taken away and we can function in the Baptists' world (although he did not understand the legitimacy of the Baptist as symbol any more) and the sins of the fathers will be gone. But in the small apartment with its books and its typewriter the disease was all the peace and beauty which he had ever known and the cure seemed worse than the illness. And he watched the coal shoveller—a man without hope, for whom jail and the welfare line are the legacies of a belief in the sanctity of Sunday morning, and the mother's voice, now crumbled into mumbling quests after the ability of words to rebuild a belief in the present reality of the dream, is also the legacy. And he knows that the dream has produced evil, but knowing is, as it always had been for him, a false god.

His mother says: "That old colored man—I suppose you say 'Negro' now—reminds me of old Dick the footman who used to open the carriage door for us when we came to school. Your grandfather sent him money every year. . . ."

I wish that I could honestly see the fall of the Old South as tragic in the way that Faulkner did. Only occasionally do I even care about the fact that I don't care. The story gives a completely false impression of what I actually feel on the subject. I blame the misrepresentation on the style which was so intoxicating that it carried me where I didn't want to go.

And where was I going? Deeper and deeper into my mind or at least into the pseudo-mind which the words were creating as they went along. By the time thinking has become words it has ceased to be self.

Style dominates the piece and focuses the reader's attention on my way of seeing the world. Like most middle-class writers I have a decided anti-middle-class bias, and I don't believe the "I" is worth a sustained story. (Someday I would like to study the strong streak of masochism which runs through or even dominates modern fiction. Middle-class writers take great pleasure in writing about the "emotional bankruptcy" of middle-class writers. And certainly there is no better way to be popular with the general public than to tell them how horrible they are. The way in which this masochism works is obvious in my own story of Michael the sociologist. I have some of my hero's characteristics, and in the story I objectified my own sins and controlled things in such a way that Michael is punished. Having paid for my errors by sticking pins in my image, I can continue to muddle along as usual without feeling the need to take any real action.) I am also interested in the extent to which certain kinds of beliefs control ideas. Does my Faulknerian story depend on my putting myself into a frame of mind where I can believe in the reality of the myth of the Old South? And did the symbolic technique in my first story depend on the romantic values which formed the assumptions on which the story was based? I think the answer to both questions is yes.

At this point I accuse myself of not being able to finish any of these stories because I am a nihilist. But I immediately recognize that nothing is further from the truth. I believe in a great many things—so many in fact that the beliefs tend to cancel each other out. Good writers are successful because they can eliminate (at least in a given work) all but one possible way of seeing the world. They develop styles and structures because they are following through with this single vision. Robbe-Grillet's novels, for example, are the product of one particular way of looking at the world. As he was writing, he was able to block from his mind the knowledge that during most of his life he sees the world in many different ways. If he looked at reality in his daily life as he does in his novels, he would never be able to do a single practical thing like catching a train or showing up for a speaking engagement on time. Is arrogant, spiritual narrowmindedness the essence of the writer?

The scene is still there. The janitor is still shovelling coal. Because the street is quiet, I can hear the shovel as it scrapes into the coal. Do you believe that? You might. But it is cold and the window is closed. Massachusetts Avenue is a big street. I hear nothing. Why did I add the sound to my description? Writers are supposed to "render" and not "report." Writing classes do more harm than good.

That's neither here nor there. Since I am beginning to understand the extent to which masochism is a dominant motivation in all of my stories, perhaps I should try to be more honest and objectify my "anti-self" into an active romantic. I must have bottled up in myself an enormous amount of anti-intellectual, anti-establishment hostility. As I have said before, I know nothing of what the coal shoveller actually thinks, but I can easily make him into whatever I want. I'll make him the rogue hero that I might like to be.

My anti-hero's name is to be Reginald Cowpersmith. He is twenty-eight, married, and unemployed. He finds himself on this particular snowy day walking by the pile of coal, where he sees an angry building superintendent starting to shovel the coal. Reginald, who is broke, asks for the job.

"The boy who is supposed to look after this sort of thing didn't show up," the superintendent said. He was winded from the one or two shovelfuls he had tossed down the chute.

"It's hard to know who to trust these days," Reginald said.

"That's very true. I'm lucky you happened to be passing by."

"I could certainly use the work," Reginald said in his most serious tone.

"I'm surprised a nice-looking young man like yourself has to go around looking for odd jobs."

"I'm at the University, sir," Reginald said. "It's very expensive. I also have a family to support. I try to supplement my income in whatever way I can."

"I wish other people in this city had your ambition."

"*They* need our sympathy, sir."

"Quite right. I know I can trust you. Here's five dollars. Shovel the coal into the cellar. I want to get home while I can." The superintendent shuffled toward Rhode Island Avenue and the bus home.

"Cheerio," Reginald called after him as he waved good-by. "And," he added, when he saw the superintendent was out of earshot, "do me the pleasure of applying thy rosy lips to the gentle curvature of my buttocks."

Reginald imagined the superintendent at home in some place like Hyattsville sitting in front of a fire telling his wife, children, and sad-eyed cocker spaniel how lucky he was to find "this white boy" to shovel his coal instead of "that no-good nigger."

"Cowpersmith," Reginald asked himself, "what would you like for Christmas out of this five dollars?"

"Perhaps, a gift for a needy family," Reginald replied.

"Not likely."

"A bottle of whiskey?"

"It's on the list," Cowpersmith said.

"A fuck in a neighborhood brothel?"

"Agreed."

Reginald stuck the shovel into the pile of coal and retired into the apartment house to contemplate the laws of economics which prevented a five-dollar bill from buying both presents.

He lit a cigarette and leaned against the radiator. Beside him was a row of old mailboxes. He reached into the nearest one and came up with a handful of letters. A hand-addressed one from Des Moines. The writing suggested aged parents. A circular from Catholic Charities, Inc. A request for funds from CORE. An announcement of the January offerings of the Apollo film club and a letter from the Civil Service Commission advertising "New Benefits for Government Employees."

"The poor creature must be lonely," Reginald said.

"It's hard to be away from home at Christmas time," Cowpersmith agreed.

"We might as well give ourselves one of our presents free."

"In what apartment does the lonely young lady live?" Cowpersmith asked.

"In No. three. After you, Mr. Cowpersmith."

"Thank you, Reggie."

Reginald walked up the stairs.

The hall smelled of rotten gentility. Reginald pictured the time when liveried Uncle Toms served great ladies in these halls. He had a fleeting image of himself as a Southern Senator walking down these stairs before the big rooms had been divided up into apartments. "Good evening, Senator Cowpersmith, the ladies are waiting in the drawing room."

He knocked on apartment number three.

The girl who opened the door had four immediately observable characteristics. Two large tits and two wide, frightened eyes.

"Excuse me, ma-am," he said. "I'm the substitute janitor and the superintendent asked me to look at your radiator."

"I didn't know anything was wrong with it."

"It'll only take a second."

"All right."

He went in. The apartment was warm and homey. The living room–bedroom was neat. The convertible couch in the corner, for which he had future plans, seemed adequate to support the two of them, and he was sure that the sheets would be clean, a detail which he had come to insist on since he had been married and had come to appreciate some of the refinements that go with domestic bliss. On the desk in one corner were three pictures. Two were of "mom" and "dad." A third tinted photograph showed an insipid-looking young man in a uniform.

As he fiddled with the radiator he talked to her. "It is certainly a cold day. But then Christmas without snow is like a day without wine, as the French say."

She nodded suspiciously. The use of "French" and "wine" had been a mistake.

"Christmas brings out the best in us," he said, taking a new approach. "Love, charity, the simple virtues that seem so far removed from city life."

"You're an educated man," she said. "It's funny but I've lived in Washington now for almost a year and I haven't really talked to anybody during that time."

"I guess the city isn't what you expected," he said. "It must be very lonely for you."

"Yes."

Any "yes" is a good sign, Reginald thought. Affirm one idea and you will tend to affirm everything.

"How does it happen that you are working as a janitor?" she asked.

"I'm a writer."

"Really?"

"Yes. I have a novel I'm working on. I need the money from odd jobs, but I also want to find out the kind of life the poor people live here, particularly the Negroes."

"I've thought of the same thing," she said excitedly.

"They have a hard time." He stopped fiddling with the radiator and stood up.

"I'll bet you do too," she said.

"Adversity is the trifling burden which man must bear if he is to fulfill the kingdom of God on earth. I do what I can." He was a little anxious about the last statement. It might have been too extreme, but he recognized as he watched her that by adopting the "writer" tag he had adequately prepared her for exaggerated language.

"Would you like some coffee?"

"Thank you, but I have to get back outside to finish shovelling the coal. I think your radiator will be all right now."

"You have time for just a cup."

"I guess so."

She went into the tiny kitchen. Her ass, a fifth characteristic which he had not previously had the opportunity to observe, waved in a friendly way. He followed her. As she put the pot on the stove he moved in on her . . .

God, but I hate bastards who write stories like that. They think that cruelty is cute and justified in the name of their own super souls. Kerouac, Donleavy, Miller, the whole lot of them. Dividing up the world into two parts—themselves and the squares. They condemn with a thoughtless pride grounded in a morality of immorality which is more rigid than the Calvinist code which they profess to hate. Being "right," they are justified in doing anything to the enemy. How many people could Reginald Cowpersmith hurt in the course of one short story? Four or five probably. Maybe two dozen in a novel. When I read *The Catcher in the Rye* my sympathies are with Mr. and Mrs. Caulfield and "old Spencer." I care more about Miss Frost in *The Gingerman* than about the Gingerman.

Does that sound too moral? I would personally be happy with a situation where writers had no effect at all on the immediate existence of readers. But fictionalists have for so long thought of themselves as prophets that they have talked a gullible, freedom-escaping world into believing that they are. Given the function of art in our time, I agree with Bellow when he says that we must have writers who think.

What would happen if the neo-romantics did think? They would find among other things that they are paranoid. They write fiction in which Society tries to destroy them, a theme which serves no other purpose than to inflate their egos. Actually Society cares very little about them. The rôle of the rebel is a self-serving one.

And, furthermore, the rebellion of these anti-heroes is usually much tamer than it seems on the surface because they don't challenge the basic value systems of society. I also feel that my own story (like most of those in the genre) would have ended sentimentally with Reginald showing that at heart he was a swell fellow and that my readers should love him. Behind every romantic hero is a maudlin child.

What is left to me? I seem to lack the necessary emotional commitment to follow through with any of the styles I have tried. Of all writers, the satirist is the closest to being beyond innocence. He accepts, as a given, the futility of self-assertion. Ultimately, of course, no one who bothers to write can be completely un-innocent, but by writing satire I can approach this condition.

I have a perfect scene for my story. There is a little bar around the corner called "The Bacchus." I go there occasionally. It is *the* place for Washington hipsters, so I can ridicule my romantic enemies who hang out there. These habitués are also vaguely associated with the arts, and there is nothing more delightful to one in my position than to attack those who still are committed to the muses.

I need a norm by which the objects of my satire are to be measured. The coal shoveller will do. He is a man who has a job to do and a family to support—a practical, realistic person.

The man was sitting alone in a booth near the bar, drinking beer and watching the scene in front of him. The young hipsters and their older gurus milled around. The door opened. The man turned around. An old Negro was shuffling through the room toward the bar. He wore a "surplus" green jacket. Over his left pocket was a black strip with "U.S. Army" stitched on it in gold. The man in the booth felt suddenly excited. He tried to call to the coal shoveller, but he had already taken a seat at the bar. The man watched and listened.

The coal shoveller spoke to the bartender. "I'll have a beer," he said. The bartender gave him a large draft. "I been shovelling coal so long," the coal shoveller said. "I was mighty cold. The boss gone home."

"A cold day," the bartender agreed.

"I wasn't sure about coming in here. Some places still don't like the colored customers."

"It's okay in here," the bartender laughed.

"I knew it'd be okay. I seen that sign over the door. About Bacchus and all. He's the place kicker for the Cardinals ain't he? Man he sure is a fat fellow. Can you think of gettin' all the money he does without having to stay in shape."

The bartender, who was waiting on another customer, nodded automatically.

"I knew it was okay to come in a place where football fans come. I know a good bit about football. I seen Bacchus kick four field goals on TV against the Browns just last Sunday."

He drank some of his beer. "Lots of Redskin fans in here. But you can carry that football business too far. Letting your hair grow long just for a football team."

The bartender wasn't listening to him, so he spoke to the man beside him.

"I think Jerry Smith's a good tight end."

"Really?" said the man. "I don't know him, but I'd like to."

A pretty white girl sat down on the other side of him. "Do you use consciousness expansion drugs?" she asked.

"No, ma'am. I'm a janitor."

"You're cute," she said.

The coal shoveller was embarrassed. Several others were now standing around him. "Do you play an instrument?" one of them asked.

He pulled a harmonica out of his pocket.

"Give us a tune," they said. A crowd had gathered. He began to play "Ole Black Joe."

The man in the booth looked on with disgust at the hipsters.

God, but I hate bastards like that, the man thought. In their arrogant moral sureness. Dividing the world up into two parts— themselves and the squares—and condemning with a thoughtless pride grounded in a morality of immorality which is more rigid than the Calvinist code which they profess to hate. They know nothing of the coal shoveller and they don't care. Poor bastard caught in that stupid conversation.

The coal shoveller had finished his tune.

The crowd standing around him joined in a chorus of praise.

—It's *it*.

—The real thing.

—No Joan Baez crap here.

—Authentic.

—Close to Leadbelly.

—Real Delta Blues.

"Thank you," the shoveller said.

"You must come and give us a concert," the blonde girl said.

"I'll try to," the coal shoveller said. "Right now, I've got to get back to my shovelling."

He got up from the bar stool and shuffled toward the door.

The man in the booth impulsively grabbed his arm as he passed. "Have a beer with me," he said.

"Thank you," the coal shoveller replied, "but I got to get back to my shovelling."

"Please."

The urgency of the request startled the coal shoveller. He sat down. The man ordered two beers. "Those people are all phony," he said. "They don't understand you. They are using you as a symbol."

"I was glad to have a chance to play my harmonica," the coal shoveller said. "My wife don't let me play at home."

"I've been watching you shovel the coal. I live on the second floor of the building across the street."

"Is that a fact."

"I don't come in here often."

"What kind of business you in?"

"I'm a writer," the man said, "but I try to avoid attributing an essence to myself in view of the cultist associations with *the Artist* in our time. I prefer to say, 'I write.' "

"What you write? I like stories on sports."

"That's why it's so important that I talk to you. Right now I'm trying to write a story about you shovelling coal."

"Is that a fact?" the coal shoveller said. He smiled broadly. "Where can I read it?"

"I don't know who'll take it. It's an experimental story."

"Oh." He looked disappointed. "What you experimenting about?"

"With the problems of language," the man said, growing excited. "I am trying to show that literary language is a shifting kaleidoscope of lights and shadows, full at once of absences and replenishments. A word is a door that opens onto the hypocritical and inexact world of idea. The very fact that I must attempt such a story shows that Western tradition has run its course. Art has been dehumanized so that no man can honestly write on anything but the problem of writing. The word as means has become the word as end. But I say to myself, so what? Let's not avoid the reality of this problem, but face it as I am in my story. We can reduce the long history of ideological and bourgeois domination of the arts in which reality has been subordinated by idea . . ." He punctuated his last statement with a violent wave of his arm. He knocked over the bowl of pretzels on the table. The coal shoveller began carefully to replace them.

"You see," the man continued, looking urgently at the shoveller, "words are symbols. Perceiving is not done with words. So when I try to describe you shovelling coal, my story takes on connotations and implications which I don't want and which inevitably reflect my own mind. But if I can help to make both readers and writers question the assumptions on which they work, we will begin to level Western society. The hunger for the word, the nutritive value of idea will be burned out of the literate middle class. And from the courage to criticize the assumptions which have thus far guided our civilization we will reach the zero degree of culture. Of course, I am no fool. I know that the absolute is an abstraction which will never be reached, because you cannot use language to destroy language . . ."

"You're right," the shoveller interrupted. "Zero is a little low. I was listening to WOOK a while back and they said it'd be about 15 tonight. Could I have a cigarette?"

"Sure," the man said. He gave a cigarette to the coal shoveller and took one for himself. "Got a light?"

The coal shoveller lit the cigarettes.

"Nor do I think," the man continued, "that destruction of this cultural edifice we have raised would be any great loss. Art has become only another profession. Words are used by people to get ahead in their jobs, to gain prestige. It is not like it must have been with the grand amateurism of my grandfather. But all of these minds working on art with the tools of science eventually will see the emptiness as the center of art. Now literature is a worthless commodity in the market place where it is bartered for money . . ."

"Having money troubles?" the coal shoveller asked sympathetically. "Christmas is a hard time."

"It's not a question of money," the man said irritably. "You see in my business it's publish or . . ." He checked himself. "After all my short story has enormous social overtones as well. You and the other poor people of the world have been hoodwinked by ideas for so long. You will be the ones ultimately benefited by writers' willingness to examine their assumptions."

The man clapped the coal shoveller on the back with such force that he bumped against the table and spilled the pretzels again. "It is for you that I am writing this story."

"I certainly appreciate that," the coal shoveller said as he started replacing the pretzels. "Not many white people think about us colored people. Have a pretzel."

But, good Lord, what has any of this got to do with the original aim of my short story?

Little has changed. It is darker now. The snow is still falling heavily. The streets are still empty. The streetlights are on. The coal shoveller is slowly and steadily shovelling. I don't want to turn on the light because it would prevent me from seeing clearly out the window, but it is too dark for me to continue writing.

QUESTIONS

1. Fort tries out a passage "on the order of the new novels." He is referring primarily to the fiction of a group of French novelists of the 1960's, whose chief theoretician is Alain Robbe-Grillet. Trying to give us back the world as-it-is, without trappings of "humanism," Robbe-Grillet rejects any description by which the author imposes human interpretation on a scene:

a *desolate* hillside, a *gay* party. What is Fort's objection to Robbe-Grillet's way of getting at reality?

2. In the narrator's second "try," why does he place the father in a sealed room? What does Fort mean, "I couldn't avoid imitation"? What is wrong with this version? It is dramatic and thematically unified. Why is the narrator dissatisfied?

3. As in the stories by Barth and Woolf, self-consciousness seems here to be destroying the very possibility of fiction. Discuss.

4. The narrator tells us that the beautiful passage on his mother and grandmother was emotionally false: he doesn't feel the tragedy of the fall of the Old South. Why then did he write as he did? Imagine writing a piece about a relative you weren't close to who has died. What false voices might you find yourself employing?

5. If the writer imposes an interpretation on the world, a "single vision," then, asks Fort, "is arrogant, spiritual narrowmindedness the essence of the writer?" What do you think?

6. In the satire toward the end of the story, Fort gives us a character, a writer, who says to the coal shoveller much of what Fort's narrator has been saying throughout the story. What is the effect of this talk? Is Fort making fun of his own ideas? What's wrong with his speech to the coal shoveller?

7. What does Fort imply by the choices in the final sentence?

8. Is such self-examination useful? Is it fiction? Is it an expression of self-disgust? Analyze it, keeping in mind Ambrose's need for self-consciousness in "Lost in the Funhouse."

RICHARD BRAUTIGAN

(1935—)

Brautigan, a San Francisco writer, became well known in the mid-1960's for a series of short "novels," *Trout Fishing in America, A Confederate General in Big Sur,* and *In Watermelon Sugar;* and volumes of poetry, *The Pill Versus the Springhill Mine Disaster* and *Rommel Drives on Deep into Egypt.* More recently he has published *A Hawkline Monster, Loading Mercury with a Pitchfork,* and *Sombrero Fallout.*

The strange titles give some sense of the flavor of Brautigan's work: magical, maverick, surreal, comic. They don't give a hint of the sadness, the loneliness and desolation that the magic must defeat. The sadness and the magic are both there in "Sea, Sea Rider," a selection from *Trout Fishing in America.*

Sea, Sea Rider

RICHARD BRAUTIGAN

The man who owned the bookstore was not magic. He was not a three-legged crow on the dandelion side of the mountain.

He was, of course, a Jew, a retired merchant seaman who had been torpedoed in the North Atlantic and floated there day after day until death did not want him. He had a young wife, a heart attack, a Volkswagen and a home in Marin County. He liked the works of George Orwell, Richard Aldington and Edmund Wilson.

He learned about life at sixteen, first from Dostoevsky and then from the whores of New Orleans.

The bookstore was a parking lot for used graveyards. Thousands of graveyards were parked in rows like cars. Most of the books were out of print, and no one wanted to read them any more and the people who had read the books had died or forgotten about them, but through the organic process of music the books had become virgins again. They wore their ancient copyrights like new maidenheads.

I went to the bookstore in the afternoons after I got off work, during that terrible year of 1959.

He had a kitchen in the back of the store and he brewed cups of thick Turkish coffee in a copper pan. I drank coffee and read old books and waited for the year to end. He had a small room above the kitchen.

It looked down on the bookstore and had Chinese screens in front of it. The room contained a couch, a glass cabinet with Chinese things in it and a table and three chairs. There was a tiny bathroom fastened like a watch fob to the room.

I was sitting on a stool in the bookstore one afternoon reading a book that was in the shape of a chalice. The book had clear pages like gin, and the first page in the book read:

BILLY

THE KID

BORN

NOVEMBER 23,

1859

IN

NEW YORK

CITY

The owner of the bookstore came up to me, and put his arm on my
shoulder and said, "Would you like to get laid?" His voice was very
kind.

"No," I said.

"You're wrong," he said, and then without saying anything else, he
went out in front of the bookstore, and stopped a pair of total
strangers, a man and a woman. He talked to them for a few moments.
I couldn't hear what he was saying. He pointed at me in the bookstore. The woman nodded her head and then the man nodded his
head.

They came into the bookstore.

I was embarrassed. I could not leave the bookstore because they
were entering by the only door, so I decided to go upstairs and go to
the toilet. I got up abruptly and walked to the back of the bookstore
and went upstairs to the bathroom, and they followed after me.

I could hear them on the stairs.

I waited for a long time in the bathroom and they waited an
equally long time in the other room. They never spoke. When I came
out of the bathroom, the woman was lying naked on the couch, and
the man was sitting in a chair with his hat on his lap.

"Don't worry about him," the girl said. "These things make no
difference to him. He's rich. He has 3,859 Rolls Royces." The girl was
very pretty and her body was like a clear mountain river of skin and
muscle flowing over rocks of bone and hidden nerves.

"Come to me," she said. "And come inside me for we are Aquarius
and I love you."

I looked at the man sitting in the chair. He was not smiling and he
did not look sad.

I took off my shoes and all my clothes. The man did not say a
word.

The girl's body moved ever so slightly from side to side.

There was nothing else I could do for my body was like birds
sitting on a telephone wire strung out down the world, clouds tossing
the wires carefully.

I laid the girl.

It was like the eternal 59th second when it becomes a minute and then looks kind of sheepish.

"Good," the girl said, and kissed me on the face.

The man sat there without speaking or moving or sending out any emotion into the room. I guess he *was* rich and owned 3,859 Rolls Royces.

Afterwards the girl got dressed and she and the man left. They walked down the stairs and on their way out, I heard him say his first words.

"Would you like to go to Ernie's for dinner?"

"I don't know," the girl said. "It's a little early to think about dinner."

Then I heard the door close and they were gone. I got dressed and went downstairs. The flesh about my body felt soft and relaxed like an experiment in functional background music.

The owner of the bookstore was sitting at his desk behind the counter. "I'll tell you what happened up there," he said, in a beautiful anti-three-legged-crow voice, in an anti-dandelion side of the mountain voice.

"What?" I said.

"You fought in the Spanish Civil War. You were a young Communist from Cleveland, Ohio. She was a painter. A New York Jew who was sightseeing in the Spanish Civil War as if it were the Mardi Gras in New Orleans being acted out by Greek statues.

"She was drawing a picture of a dead anarchist when you met her. She asked you to stand beside the anarchist and act as if you had killed him. You slapped her across the face and said something that would be embarrassing for me to repeat.

"You both fell very much in love.

"Once while you were at the front she read *Anatomy of Melancholy* and did 349 drawings of a lemon.

"Your love for each other was mostly spiritual. Neither one of you performed like millionaires in bed.

"When Barcelona fell, you and she flew to England, and then took a ship back to New York. Your love for each other remained in Spain. It was only a war love. You loved only yourselves, loving each other in Spain during the war. On the Atlantic you were different toward each other and became every day more and more like people lost from each other.

"Every wave on the Atlantic was like a dead seagull dragging its driftwood artillery from horizon to horizon.

"When the ship bumped up against America, you departed without saying anything and never saw each other again. The last I heard of you, you were still living in Philadelphia."

"That's what you think happened up there?" I said.

"Partly," he said. "Yes, that's part of it."

He took out his pipe and filled it with tobacco and lit it.

"Do you want me to tell you what else happened up there?" he said.

"Go ahead."

"You crossed the border into Mexico," he said. "You rode your horse into a small town. The people knew who you were and they were afraid of you. They knew you had killed many men with that gun you wore at your side. The town itself was so small that it didn't have a priest.

"When the rurales saw you, they left the town. Tough as they were, they did not want to have anything to do with you. The rurales left.

"You became the most powerful man in town.

"You were seduced by a thirteen-year-old girl, and you and she lived together in an adobe hut, and practically all you did was make love.

"She was slender and had long dark hair. You made love standing, sitting, lying on the dirt floor with pigs and chickens around you. The walls, the floor and even the roof of the hut were coated with your sperm and her come.

"You slept on the floor at night and used your sperm for a pillow and her come for a blanket.

"The people in the town were so afraid of you that they could do nothing.

"After a while she started going around town without any clothes on, and the people of the town said that it was not a good thing, and when you started going around without any clothes, and when both of you began making love on the back of your horse in the middle of the zocalo, the people of the town became so afraid that they abandoned the town. It's been abandoned ever since.

"People won't live there.

"Neither of you lived to be twenty-one. It was not necessary.

"See, I do know what happened upstairs," he said. He smiled at me kindly. His eyes were like the shoelaces of a harpsichord.

I thought about what happened upstairs.

"You know what I say is the truth," he said. "For you saw it with your own eyes and traveled it with your own body. Finish the book you were reading before you were interrupted. I'm glad you got laid."

Once resumed, the pages of the book began to speed up and turn faster and faster until they were spinning like wheels in the sea.

QUESTIONS

1. What do we know about the young man at the start of the story? How has he changed by the end?
2. What is the power of books, according to the story?
3. Examine the style of the story. How is it illogical and irrational? What effect has the style on your spirit? What model of experience does the style propose? (See Preface, pp. 1–5 and 27–28.)
4. The date is 1959; the young man is waiting for the year to end. The rich man has 3,859 Rolls Royces. The sex was like the eternal 59th second when it became a minute. Discuss the contrast between these numbers and the pages of the book which "began to speed up and turn faster and faster until they were spinning like wheels in the sea."
5. The bookstore owner may not be magic, but he is a kind of guru. He *knows*. After offering him the sexual encounter, he tells the young man two stories built on literary clichés. What is he teaching the young man?

JOYCE CAROL OATES

(1938—)

One of the most prolific and energetic of contemporary writers, Oates, who lives and teaches in Toronto, has published a large number of novels and short stories, including *Do With Me What You Will, Edge of Impossibility, Expensive People, A Garden of Earthly Delights, Marriage and Infidelities, Them, The Wheel of Love, With Shuddering Fall,* and *Wonderland.* Like Barth's "Lost in the Funhouse," "How I Contemplated . . ." is told by a narrator struggling to make sense out of her life and to organize and communicate her experience. In contrast to a traditional short story, we do not hear the result of her struggle but are in on the process itself; we see someone telling the truth, deceiving herself, telling multiple versions of the truth. But here again, as in "Lost in the Funhouse," Oates's story is not a mere technical experiment in angle of vision and organization; it is a moving piece of fiction about an adolescent, about identity, about growth.

How I Contemplated the World from the Detroit House of Correction and Began My Life Over Again

Notes for an essay for an English class at Baldwin Country Day School; poking around in debris; disgust and curiosity; a revelation of the meaning of life; a happy ending . . .

JOYCE CAROL OATES

I *Events*

1. The girl (myself) is walking through Branden's, that excellent store. Suburb of a large famous city that is a symbol for large famous American cities. The event sneaks up on the girl, who believes she is herding it along with a small fixed smile, a girl of fifteen, innocently experienced. She dawdles in a certain style by a counter of costume jewelry. Rings, earrings, necklaces. Prices from $5 to $50, all within reach. All ugly. She eases over to the glove counter, where everything is ugly too. In her close-fitted coat with its black fur collar she contemplates the luxury of Branden's, which she has known for many years: its many mild pale lights, easy on the eye and the soul, its elaborate tinkly decorations, its women shoppers with their excellent shoes and coats and hairdos, all dawdling gracefully, in no hurry.

Who was ever in a hurry here?

2. The girl seated at home. A small library, paneled walls of oak. Someone is talking to me. An earnest, husky, female voice drives itself against my ears, nervous, frightened, groping around my heart, saying, "If you wanted gloves, why didn't you say so? Why didn't you ask for them?" That store, Branden's, is owned by Raymond Forrest who lives on Du Maurier Drive. We live on Sioux Drive. Raymond Forrest. A handsome man? An ugly man? A man of fifty or sixty, with gray hair, or a man of forty with earnest, courteous eyes, a good golf game; who is Raymond Forrest, this man who is my salvation? Father has been talking to him. Father is not his physician; Dr. Berg is his physician. Father and Dr. Berg refer patients to each other. There is a connection. Mother plays bridge with . . . On Mondays and

Wednesdays our maid Billie works at . . . The strings draw together in a cat's cradle, making a net to save you when you fall . . .

3. *Harriet Arnold's.* A small shop, better than Branden's. Mother in her black coat, I in my close-fitted blue coat. Shopping. Now look at this, isn't this cute, do you want this, why don't you want this, try this on, take this with you to the fitting room, take this also, what's wrong with you, what can I do for you, why are you so strange . . . ? "I wanted to steal but not to buy," I don't tell her. The girl droops along in her coat and gloves and leather boots, her eyes scan the horizon, which is pastel pink and decorated like Branden's, tasteful walls and modern ceilings with graceful glimmering lights.

4. Weeks later, the girl at a bus stop. Two o'clock in the afternoon, a Tuesday; obviously she has walked out of school.

5. The girl stepping down from a bus. Afternoon, weather changing to colder. Detroit. Pavement and closed-up stores; grillwork over the windows of a pawnshop. What is a pawnshop, exactly?

II *Characters*

1. The girl stands five feet five inches tall. An ordinary height. Baldwin Country Day School draws them up to that height. She dreams along the corridors and presses her face against the Thermoplex glass. No frost or steam can ever form on that glass. A smudge of grease from her forehead . . . could she be boiled down to grease? She wears her hair loose and long and straight in suburban teen-age style, 1968. Eyes smudged with pencil, dark brown. Brown hair. Vague green eyes. A pretty girl? An ugly girl? She sings to herself under her breath, idling in the corridor, thinking of her many secrets (the thirty dollars she once took from the purse of a friend's mother, just for fun, the basement window she smashed in her own house just for fun) and thinking of her brother who is at Susquehanna Boys' Academy, an excellent preparatory school in Maine, remembering him unclearly . . . he has long manic hair and a squeaking voice and he looks like one of the popular teen-age singers of 1968, one of those in a group, *The Certain Forces, The Way Out, The Maniacs Responsible.* The girl in her turn looks like one of those fieldsful of girls who listen to the boys' singing, dreaming and mooning restlessly, breaking into high sullen laughter, innocently experienced.

2. The mother. A Midwestern woman of Detroit and suburbs. Belongs to the Detroit Athletic Club. Also the Detroit Golf Club. Also the Bloomfield Hills Country Club. The Village Women's Club

at which lectures are given each winter on Genet and Sartre and James Baldwin, by the Director of the Adult Education Program at Wayne State University. . . . The Bloomfield Art Association. Also the Founders Society of the Detroit Institute of Arts. Also . . . Oh, she is in perpetual motion, this lady, hair like blown-up gold and finer than gold, hair and fingers and body of inestimable grace. Heavy weighs the gold on the back of her hairbrush and hand mirror. Heavy heavy the candlesticks in the dining room. Very heavy is the big car, a Lincoln, long and black, that on one cool autumn day split a squirrel's body in two unequal parts.

3. The father. Dr.   . He belongs to the same clubs as #2. A player of squash and golf; he has a golfer's umbrella of stripes. Candy stripes. In his mouth nothing turns to sugar, however; saliva works no miracles here. His doctoring is of the slightly sick. The sick are sent elsewhere (to Dr. Berg?), the deathly sick are sent back for more tests and their bills are sent to their homes, the unsick are sent to Dr. Coronet (Isabel, a lady), an excellent psychiatrist for unsick people who angrily believe they are sick and want to do something about it. If they demand a male psychiatrist, the unsick are sent by Dr.
(my father) to Dr. Lowenstein, a male psychiatrist, excellent and expensive, with a limited practice.

4. Clarita. She is twenty, twenty-five, she is thirty or more? Pretty, ugly, what? She is a woman lounging by the side of a road, in jeans and a sweater, hitchhiking, or she is slouched on a stool at a counter in some roadside diner. A hard line of jaw. Curious eyes. Amused eyes. Behind her eyes processions move, funeral pageants, cartoons. She says, "I never can figure out why girls like you bum around down here. What are you looking for anyway?" An odor of tobacco about her. Unwashed underclothes, or no underclothes, unwashed skin, gritty toes, hair long and falling into strands, not recently washed.

5. Simon. In this city the weather changes abruptly, so Simon's weather changes abruptly. He sleeps through the afternoon. He sleeps through the morning. Rising, he gropes around for something to get him going, for a cigarette or a pill to drive him out to the street, where the temperature is hovering around 35°. Why doesn't it drop? Why, why doesn't the cold clean air come down from Canada; will he have to go up into Canada to get it? will he have to leave the Country of his Birth and sink into Canada's frosty fields . . . ? Will the F.B.I. (which he dreams about constantly) chase him over the Canadian border on foot, hounded out in a blizzard of broken glass and horns . . . ?

"Once I was Huckleberry Finn," Simon says, "but now I am

Roderick Usher." Beset by frenzies and fears, this man who makes my
spine go cold, he takes green pills, yellow pills, pills of white and
capsules of dark blue and green . . . he takes other things I may not
mention, for what if Simon seeks me out and climbs into my girl's
bedroom here in Bloomfield Hills and strangles me, what then . . . ?
(As I write this I begin to shiver. Why do I shiver? I am now sixteen
and sixteen is not an age for shivering.) It comes from Simon, who is
always cold.

III   *World Events*

Nothing.

IV   *People & Circumstances Contributing to This Delinquency*

Nothing.

V   *Sioux Drive*

George, Clyde G. 240 Sioux. A manufacturer's representative; children, a dog, a wife. Georgian with the usual columns. You think of
the White House, then of Thomas Jefferson, then your mind goes
blank on the white pillars and you think of nothing. Norris, Ralph
W. 246 Sioux. Public relations. Colonial. Bay window, brick, stone,
concrete, wood, green shutters, sidewalk, lantern, grass, trees, blacktop drive, two children, one of them my classmate Esther (Esther
Norris) at Baldwin. Wife, cars. Ramsey, Michael D. 250 Sioux.
Colonial. Big living room, thirty by twenty-five, fireplaces in living
room, library, recreation room, paneled walls wet bar five bathrooms
five bedrooms two lavatories central air conditioning automatic
sprinkler automatic garage door three children one wife two cars a
breakfast room a patio a larged fenced lot fourteen trees a front door
with a brass knocker never knocked. Next is our house. Classic
contemporary. Traditional modern. Attached garage, attached
Florida room, attached patio, attached pool and cabana, attached
roof. A front door mail slot through which pour *Time Magazine,
Fortune, Life, Business Week,* the *Wall Street Journal,* the *New York
Times,* the *New Yorker,* the *Saturday Review, M.D., Modern Medicine, Disease of the Month* . . . and also. . . . And in addition to
all this, a quiet sealed letter from Baldwin saying: *Your daughter is
not doing work compatible with her performance on the Stanford-
Binet.* . . . And your son is not doing well, not well at all, very sad.
Where is your son anyway? Once he stole trick-and-treat candy from

some six-year-old kids, he himself being a robust ten. The beginning. Now your daughter steals. In the Village Pharmacy she made off with, yes she did, don't deny it, she made off with a copy of *Pageant Magazine* for no reason, she swiped a roll of Life Savers in a green wrapper and was in no need of saving her life or even in need of sucking candy; when she was no more than eight years old she stole, don't blush, she stole a package of Tums only because it was out on the counter and available, and the nice lady behind the counter (now dead) said nothing. . . . Sioux Drive. Maples, oaks, elms. Diseased elms cut down. Sioux Drive runs into Roosevelt Drive. Slow, turning lanes, not streets, all drives and lanes and ways and passes. A private police force. Quiet private police, in unmarked cars. Cruising on Saturday evenings with paternal smiles for the residents who are streaming in and out of houses, going to and from parties, a thousand parties, slightly staggering, the women in their furs alighting from automobiles bought of Ford and General Motors and Chrysler, very heavy automobiles. No foreign cars. Detroit. In 275 Sioux, down the block in that magnificent French-Normandy mansion, lives   himself, who has the C   account itself, imagine that! Look at where he lives and look at the enormous trees and chimneys, imagine his many fireplaces, imagine his wife and children, imagine his wife's hair, imagine her fingernails, imagine her bathtub of smooth clean glowing pink, imagine their embraces, his trouser pockets filled with odd coins and keys and dust and peanuts, imagine their ecstasy on Sioux Drive, imagine their income tax returns, imagine their little boy's pride in his experimental car, a scaled-down C   as he roars around the neighborhood on the sidewalks frightening dogs and Negro maids, oh imagine all these things, imagine everything, let your mind roar out all over Sioux Drive and Du Maurier Drive and Roosevelt Drive and Ticonderoga Pass and Burning Bush Way and Lincolnshire Pass and Lois Lane.

When spring comes, its winds blow nothing to Sioux Drive, no odors of hollyhocks or forsythia, nothing Sioux Drive doesn't already possess, everything is planted and performing. The weather vanes, had they weather vanes, don't have to turn with the wind, don't have to contend with the weather. There is no weather.

VI *Detroit*

There is always weather in Detroit. Detroit's temperature is always 32°. Fast-falling temperatures. Slow-rising temperatures. Wind from the north-northeast four to forty miles an hour, small-craft warnings, partly cloudy today and Wednesday changing to partly sunny through Thursday . . . small warnings of frost, soot warnings, traffic warnings, hazardous lake conditions for small craft and swimmers, restless Negro gangs, restless cloud formations, restless temperatures aching to fall out the very bottom of the thermometer or shoot up over the top and boil everything over in red mercury.

Detroit's temperature is 32°. Fast-falling temperatures. Slow-rising temperatures. Wind from the north-northeast four to forty miles an hour. . . .

VII *Events*

1. The girl's heart is pounding. In her pocket is a pair of gloves! In a plastic bag! Airproof breathproof plastic bag, gloves selling for twenty-five dollars on Branden's counter! In her pocket! Shoplifted! . . . In her purse is a blue comb, not very clean. In her purse is a leather billfold (a birthday present from her grandmother in Philadelphia) with snapshots of the family in clean plastic windows, in the billfold are bills, she doesn't know how many bills. . . . In her purse is an ominous note from her friend Tykie *What's this about Joe H. and the kids hanging around at Louise's Sat. night? You heard anything?* . . . passed in French class. In her purse is a lot of dirty yellow Kleenex, her mother's heart would break to see such very dirty Kleenex, and at the bottom of her purse are brown hairpins and safety pins and a broken pencil and a ballpoint pen (blue) stolen from somewhere forgotten and a purse-size compact of Cover Girl Make-Up, Ivory Rose. . . . Her lipstick is Broken Heart, a corrupt pink; her fingers are trembling like crazy; her teeth are beginning to chatter; her insides are alive; her eyes glow in her head; she is saying to her mother's astonished face *I want to steal but not to buy.*

2. At Clarita's. Day or night? What room is this? A bed, a regular bed, and a mattress on the floor nearby. Wallpaper hanging in strips. Clarita says she tore it like that with her teeth. She was fighting a barbaric tribe that night, high from some pills; she was battling for her life with men wearing helmets of heavy iron and their faces no more than Christian crosses to breathe through, every one of those bastards looking like her lover Simon, who seems to breathe with great difficulty through the slits of mouth and nostrils in his face. Clarita has never heard of Sioux Drive. Raymond Forrest cuts no ice with her, nor does the C⎯⎯⎯ account and its millions; Harvard Business School could be at the corner of Vernor and 12th Street for all she cares, and Vietnam might have sunk by now into the Dead Sea under its tons of debris, for all the amazement she could show . . . her face is overworked, overwrought, at the age of twenty

(thirty?) it is already exhausted but fanciful and ready for a laugh. Clarita says mournfully to me *Honey somebody is going to turn you out let me give you warning.* In a movie shown on late television Clarita is not a mess like this but a nurse, with short neat hair and a dedicated look, in love with her doctor and her doctor's patients and their diseases, enamored of needles and sponges and rubbing alcohol. . . . Or no: she is a private secretary. Robert Cummings is her boss. She helps him with fantastic plots, the canned audience laughs, no, the audience doesn't laugh because nothing is funny, instead her boss is Robert Taylor and they are not boss and secretary but husband and wife, she is threatened by a young starlet, she is grim, handsome, wifely, a good companion for a good man. . . . She is Claudette Colbert. Her sister too is Claudette Colbert. They are twins, identical. Her husband Charles Boyer is a very rich handsome man and her sister, Claudette Colbert, is plotting her death in order to take her place as the rich man's wife, no one will know because they are *twins.* . . . All these marvelous lives Clarita might have lived, but she fell out the bottom at the age of thirteen. At the age when I was packing my overnight case for a slumber party at Toni Deshield's she was tearing filthy sheets off a bed and scratching up a rash on her arms. . . . Thirteen is uncommonly young for a white girl in Detroit, Miss Brock of the Detroit House of Correction said in a sad newspaper interview for the *Detroit News;* fifteen and sixteen are more likely. Eleven, twelve, thirteen are not surprising in colored . . . they are more precocious. What can we do? Taxes are rising and the tax base is falling. The temperature rises slowly but falls rapidly. Everything is falling out the bottom, Woodward Avenue is filthy, Livernois Avenue is filthy! Scraps of paper flutter in the air like pigeons, dirt flies up and hits you right in the eye, oh Detroit is breaking up into dangerous bits of newspaper and dirt, watch out. . . .

Clarita's apartment is over a restaurant. Simon her lover emerges from the cracks at dark. Mrs. Olesko, a neighbor of Clarita's, an aged white wisp of a woman, doesn't complain but sniffs with contentment at Clarita's noisy life and doesn't tell the cops, hating cops, when the cops arrive. I should give more fake names, more blanks, instead of telling all these secrets. I myself am a secret; I am a minor.

3. My father reads a paper at a medical convention in Los Angeles. There he is, on the edge of the North American continent, when the unmarked detective put his hand so gently on my arm in the aisle of Branden's and said, "Miss, would you like to step over here for a minute?"

And where was he when Clarita put her hand on my arm, that wintry dark sulphurous aching day in Detroit, in the company of closed-down barber shops, closed-down diners, closed-down movie houses, homes, windows, basements, faces . . . she put her hand on my arm and said, "Honey, are you looking for somebody down here?"

And was he home worrying about me, gone for two weeks solid, when they carried me off . . . ? It took three of them to get me in the police cruiser, so they said, and they put more than their hands on my arm.

4. I work on this lesson. My English teacher is Mr. Forest, who is from Michigan State. Not handsome, Mr. Forest, and his name is plain, unlike Raymond Forrest's, but he is sweet and rodentlike, he has conferred with the principal and my parents, and everything is fixed . . . treat her as if nothing has happened, a new start, begin again, only sixteen years old, what a shame, how did it happen?— nothing happened, nothing could have happened, a slight physiological modification known only to a gynecologist or to Dr. Coronet. I work on my lesson. I sit in my pink room. I look around the room with my sad pink eyes. I sigh, I dawdle, I pause, I eat up time, I am limp and happy to be home, I am sixteen years old suddenly, my head hangs heavy as a pumpkin on my shoulders, and my hair has just been cut by Mr. Faye at the Crystal Salon and is said to be very becoming.

(Simon too put his hand on my arm and said, "Honey, you have got to come with me," and in his six-by-six room we got to know each other. Would I go back to Simon again? Would I lie down with him in all that filth and craziness? Over and over again.

                                        a Clarita is being betrayed as in front of a Cunningham Drug Store she is nervously eying a colored man who may or may not have money, or a nervous white boy of twenty with sideburns and an Appalachian look, who may or may not have a knife hidden in his jacket pocket, or a husky red-faced man of friendly countenance who may or may not be a member of the Vice Squad out for an early twilight walk.)

I work on my lesson for Mr. Forest. I have filled up eleven pages. Words pour out of me and won't stop. I want to tell everything . . . what was the song Simon was always humming, and who was Simon's friend in a very new trench coat with an old high school graduation ring on his finger . . . ? Simon's bearded friend? When I was down too low for him, Simon kicked me out and gave me to him for three days, I think, on Fourteenth Street in Detroit, an airy room of cold cruel drafts with newspapers on the floor. . . . Do I really remember that or am I piecing it together from what they told me? Did they tell the truth? Did they know much of the truth?

VIII *Characters*

1. Wednesdays after school, at four; Saturday mornings at ten. Mother drives me to Dr. Coronet. Ferns in the office, plastic or real, they look the same. Dr. Coronet is queenly, an elegant nicotine-stained lady who would have studied with Freud had circumstances not prevented it, a bit of a Catholic, ready to offer you some mystery if your teeth will ache too much without it. Highly recommended by Father! Forty dollars an hour, Father's forty dollars! Progress! Looking up! Looking better! That new haircut is so becoming, says Dr. Coronet herself, showing how normal she is for a woman with an I.Q. of 180 and many advanced degrees.

2. Mother. A lady in a brown suede coat. Boots of shiny black material, black gloves, a black fur hat. She would be humiliated could she know that of all the people in the world it is my ex-lover Simon who walks most like her . . . self-conscious and unreal, listening to distant music, a little bowlegged with craftiness. . . .

3. Father. Tying a necktie. In a hurry. On my first evening home he put his hand on my arm and said, "Honey, we're going to forget all about this."

4. Simon. Outside, a plane is crossing the sky, in here we're in a hurry. Morning. It must be morning. The girl is half out of her mind, whimpering and vague; Simon her dear friend is wretched this morning . . . he is wretched with morning itself . . . he forces her to give him an injection with that needle she knows is filthy, she has a dread of needles and surgical instruments and the odor of things that are to be sent into the blood, thinking somehow of her father. . . . This is a bad morning, Simon says that his mind is being twisted out of shape, and so he submits to the needle that he usually scorns and bites his lip with his yellowish teeth, his face going very pale. *Ah baby!* he says in his soft mocking voice, which with all women is a mockery of love, *do it like this—Slowly—*And the girl, terrified, almost drops the precious needle but manages to turn it up to the light from the window . . . is it an extension of herself then? She can give him this gift then? *I wish you wouldn't do this to me,* she says, wise in her terror, because it seems to her that Simon's danger—in a few minutes he may be dead—is a way of pressing her

against him that is more powerful than any other embrace. She has to work over his arm, the knotted corded veins of his arm, her forehead wet with perspiration as she pushes and releases the needle, staring at that mixture of liquid now stained with Simon's bright blood. . . . When the drug hits him she can feel it herself, she feels that magic that is more than any woman can give him, striking the back of his head and making his face stretch as if with the impact of a terrible sun. . . . She tries to embrace him but he pushes her aside and stumbles to his feet. *Jesus Christ,* he says. . . .

5. Princess, a Negro girl of eighteen. What is her charge? She is closed-mouthed about it, shrewd and silent, you know that no one had to wrestle her to the sidewalk to get her in here; she came with dignity. In the recreation room she sits reading *Nancy Drew and the Jewel Box Mystery,* which inspires in her face tiny wrinkles of alarm and interest: what a face! Light brown skin, heavy shaded eyes, heavy eyelashes, a serious sinister dark brow, graceful fingers, graceful wrist-bones, graceful legs, lips, tongue, a sugar-sweet voice, a leggy stride more masculine than Simon's and my mother's, decked out in a dirty white blouse and dirty white slacks; vaguely nautical is Princess' style. . . . At breakfast she is in charge of clearing the table and leans over me, saying, *Honey you sure you ate enough?*

6. The girl lies sleepless, wondering. Why here, why not there? Why Bloomfield Hills and not jail? Why jail and not her pink room? Why downtown Detroit and not Sioux Drive? What is the difference? Is Simon all the difference? The girl's head is a parade of wonders. She is nearly sixteen, her breath is marvelous with wonders, not long ago she was coloring with crayons and now she is smearing the landscape with paints that won't come off and won't come off her fingers either. She says to the matron *I am not talking about anything,* not because everyone has warned her not to talk but because, because she will not talk; because she won't say anything about Simon, who is her secret. And she says to the matron, *I won't go home,* up until that night in the lavatory when everything was changed. . . . "No, I won't go home I want to stay here," she says, listening to her own words with amazement, thinking that weeds might climb everywhere over that marvelous $180,000 house and dinosaurs might return to muddy the beige carpeting, but never never will she reconcile four o'clock in the morning in Detroit with eight o'clock breakfasts in Bloomfield Hills. . . . oh, she aches still for Simon's hands and his caressing breath, though he gave her little pleasure, he took everything from her (five-dollar bills, ten-dollar bills, passed into her numb hands by men and taken out of her hands by Simon) until she herself was passed into the hands of other men,

police, when Simon evidently got tired of her and her hysteria. . . .
No, I won't go home, I don't want to be bailed out. The girl thinks
as a *Stubborn and Wayward Child* (one of several charges lodged
against her), and the matron understands her crazy white-rimmed
eyes that are seeking out some new violence that will keep her in jail,
should someone threaten to let her out. Such children try to strangle
the matrons, the attendants, or one another . . . they want the locks
locked forever, the doors nailed shut . . . and this girl is no different
up until that night her mind is changed for her. . . .

IX *That Night*

Princess and Dolly, a little white girl of maybe fifteen, hardy
however as a sergeant and in the House of Correction for armed
robbery, corner her in the lavatory at the farthest sink and the other
girls look away and file out to bed, leaving her. God, how she is
beaten up! Why is she beaten up? Why do they pound her, why such
hatred? Princess vents all the hatred of a thousand silent Detroit
winters on her body, this girl whose body belongs to me, fiercely she
rides across the Midwestern plains on this girl's tender bruised body
. . . revenge on the oppressed minorities of America! revenge on
the slaughtered Indians! revenge on the female sex, on the male sex,
revenge on Bloomfield Hills, revenge revenge. . . .

X *Detroit*

In Detroit, weather weighs heavily upon everyone. The sky looms
large. The horizon shimmers in smoke. Downtown the buildings are
imprecise in the haze. Perpetual haze. Perpetual motion inside the
haze. Across the choppy river is the city of Windsor, in Canada. Part
of the continent has bunched up here and is bulging outward, at the
tip of Detroit; a cold hard rain is forever falling on the expressways.
. . . Shoppers shop grimly, their cars are not parked in safe places,
their windshields may be smashed and graceful ebony hands may
drag them out through their shatterproof smashed windshields, crying, *Revenge for the Indians!* Ah, they all fear leaving Hudson's and
being dragged to the very tip of the city and thrown off the parking
roof of Cobo Hall, that expensive tomb, into the river. . . .

XI *Characters We Are*
Forever Entwined With

1. Simon drew me into his tender rotting arms and breathed
gravity into me. Then I came to earth, weighed down. He said, *You
are such a little girl,* and he weighed me down with his delight. In

the palms of his hands were teeth marks from his previous life experiences. He was thirty-five, they said. Imagine Simon in this room, in my pink room: he is about six feet tall and stoops slightly, in a feline cautious way, always thinking, always on guard, with his scuffed light suede shoes and his clothes that are anyone's clothes, slightly rumpled ordinary clothes that ordinary men might wear to not-bad jobs. Simon has fair long hair, curly hair, spent languid curls that are like . . . exactly like the curls of wood shavings to the touch, I am trying to be exact . . . and he smells of unheated mornings and coffee and too many pills coating his tongue with a faint green-white scum. . . . Dear Simon, who would be panicked in this room and in this house (right now Billie is vacuuming next door in my parents' room; a vacuum cleaner's roar is a sign of all good things), Simon who is said to have come from a home not much different from this, years ago, fleeing all the carpeting and the polished banisters . . . Simon has a deathly face, only desperate people fall in love with it. His face is bony and cautious, the bones of his cheeks prominent as if with the rigidity of his ceaseless thinking, plotting, for he has to make money out of girls to whom money means nothing, they're so far gone they can hardly count it, and in a sense money means nothing to him either except as a way of keeping on with his life. *Each Day's Proud Struggle,* the title of a novel we could read at jail. . . . Each day he needs a certain amount of money. He devours it. It wasn't love he uncoiled in me with his hollowed-out eyes and his courteous smile, that remnant of a prosperous past, but a dark terror that needed to press itself flat against him, or against another man . . . but he was the first, he came over to me and took my arm, a claim. We struggled on the stairs and I said, *Let me loose, you're hurting my neck, my face,* it was such a surprise that my skin hurt where he rubbed it, and afterward we lay face to face and he breathed everything into me. In the end I think he turned me in.

2. Raymond Forrest. I just read this morning that Raymond Forrest's father, the chairman of the board at   , died of a heart attack on a plane bound for London. I would like to write Raymond Forrest a note of sympathy. I would like to thank him for not pressing charges against me one hundred years ago, saving me, being so generous . . . well, men like Raymond Forrest are generous men, not like Simon. I would like to write him a letter telling of my love, or of some other emotion that is positive and healthy. Not like Simon and his poetry, which he scrawled down when he was high and never changed a word . . . but when I try to think of something to say, it is Simon's language that comes back to me, caught in my head like a bad song, it is always Simon's language:

There is no reality only dreams
Your neck may get snapped when you wake
My love is drawn to some violent end
She keeps wanting to get away
My love is heading downward
And I am heading upward
She is going to crash on the sidewalk
And I am going to dissolve into the clouds

XII *Events*

1. Out of the hospital, bruised and saddened and converted, with Princess' grunts still tangled in my hair . . . and Father in his overcoat looking like a prince himself, come to carry me off. Up the expressway and out north to home. Jesus Christ, but the air is thinner and cleaner here. Monumental houses. Heartbreaking sidewalks, so clean.

2. Weeping in the living room. The ceiling is two stories high and two chandeliers hang from it. Weeping, weeping, though Billie the maid is *probably listening*. I will never leave home again. Never. Never leave home. Never leave this home again, never.

3. Sugar doughnuts for breakfast. The toaster is very shiny and my face is distorted in it. Is that my face?

4. The car is turning in the driveway. Father brings me home. Mother embraces me. Sunlight breaks in movieland patches on the roof of our traditional-contemporary home, which was designed for the famous automotive stylist whose identity, if I told you the name of the famous car he designed, you would all know, so I can't tell you because my teeth chatter at the thought of being sued . . . or having someone climb into my bedroom window with a rope to strangle me. . . . The car turns up the blacktop drive. The house opens to me like a doll's house, so lovely in the sunlight, the big living room beckons to me with its walls falling away in a delirium of joy at my return, Billie the maid is *no doubt* listening from the kitchen as I burst into tears and the hysteria Simon got so sick of. Convulsed in Father's arms, I say I will never leave again, never, why did I leave, where did I go, what happened, my mind is gone wrong, my body is one big bruise, my backbone was sucked dry, it wasn't the men who hurt me and Simon never hurt me but only those girls . . . my God, how they hurt me . . . I will never leave home again. . . . The car is perpetually turning up the drive and I am perpetually breaking down in the living room and we are perpetually taking the right exit from the expressway (Lahser Road) and the wall of the rest room is

perpetually banging against my head and perpetually are Simon's hands moving across my body and adding everything up and so too are Father's hands on my shaking bruised back, far from the surface of my skin on the surface of my good blue cashmere coat (dry-cleaned for my release) . . . . I weep for all the money here, for God in gold and beige carpeting, for the beauty of chandeliers and the miracle of a clean polished gleaming toaster and faucets that run both hot and cold water, and I tell them, *I will never leave home, this is my home, I love everything here, I am in love with everything here.* . . .

I am home.